D1423832

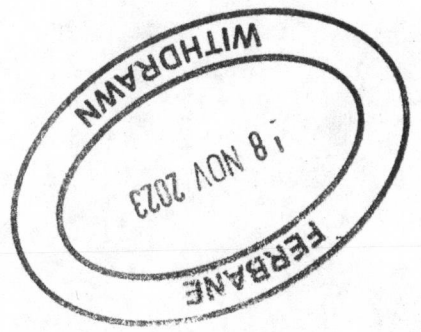

ONE MAN'S ISLAND

BOOK ONE AND BOOK TWO

THOMAS J WOLFENDEN

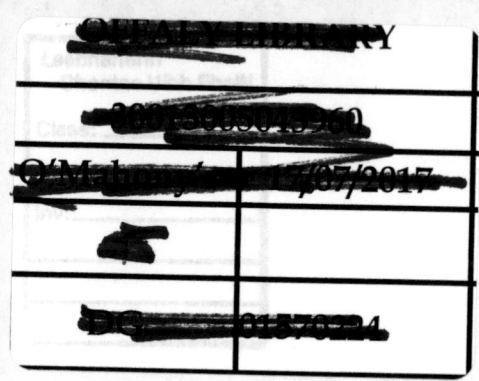

PERMUTED PRESS

Permuted Press, LLC
permutedpress.com

Published in the United States of America

Other books by Thomas J. Wolfenden:

Full Moon Fishtown
Coconut Republic

ONE MAN'S ISLAND

Author's Note

Dear Reader,

A lot of research went into writing this novel, and I took great pains to get everything as accurate as I could. That being said, I did take some literary license in some aspects, sometimes great leaps, especially the naval aspects, in order to make the story work the way I desired. That being said, I hope you'll forgive me these discrepancies, sit back in a nice comfortable place and enjoy the journey.

I would also like to take the time to thank all of my friends and family for your support in the writing of this novel. I'd especially like to thank my best and worst critic, my partner, Catherine. Without your love and support, I'd never have been able to complete this work. You truly are my Soul Mate! I'd also like to thank Ed McDonald and Trevor Emmitt, whom without both, I'd never have been able to finish this work. Thanks guys! You're the greatest!

This is also a work of fiction, and any similarities to places, events and characters, to any persons, living or dead, is purely coincidence.

Newcastle, NSW Australia, August, 2012
Sigatoka, Republic of Fiji, November, 2012

PROLOGUE

It has been said in various scientific circles throughout the years, that 99% of all species that have ever lived on planet Earth, are now extinct.

When we look up at the night sky, we are looking far into the past. What we see isn't the stars as they are now, only images of what they once were, so vast are the distances. In a far corner of our Milky Way Galaxy, 100,000 light years from Earth, almost that many years ago, a huge star exploded into a Supernova. A star's death, is the stuff of life itself, but in that power of life, is also death. It will take many millennia for the light of that huge event, to get to us.

No one saw it coming.

It also will take that much time for another little gift this cosmic event is sending us...

After all the theories, speculation and research, in the end the scientists were wrong. And the most ironic thing about it was that no one was left to know what had actually happened.

Almost no one.

"The past is but the beginning of a beginning, and all that is and has been is but the twilight of the dawn."

~H G Wells

PART ONE

PART ONE

CHAPTER 1:
THE NOTHING MAN

It was a cold and damp November morning when Sergeant Major Timothy Flannery stepped off the jet way at the Philadelphia International Airport. He headed for the baggage claim tiredly, hoping this would be the last time for a while. This last tour was the hardest. Not because of combat, it was being away from his wife and family that was finally getting to him. All of his adult life he'd been in uniform. He'd enlisted right out of high school and spent eight years in the regular Army, then came home and joined the police department. While on the job he enlisted in the Pennsylvania National Guard.

This was okay for a while, until the first Gulf War. That deployment wasn't so bad because he was still young and single, but he had met and married Connie shortly after returning home from the Persian Gulf. After the attacks on the World Trade Center in 2001, things got tense in the Flannery household. Arguing and fighting started and the first deployment came as a relief to him. He came home after that tour and things were back to normal for a while, then the nightmares came and the fights started again. To be sent off on the second deployment, again, was a relief. The letters and emails tapered off, and then stopped altogether.

Between the last time and this, things were absolutely frigid in the Flannery home. The slamming of the door when the taxi came to take him to the airport the last time was like the sound of a casket closing. However, after several emails, phone calls and promises these last eighteen months, Tim and Connie had both decided to try to work on things and patch things up.

That's why he wondered why Connie wasn't answering her damn phone. He'd sent her an email three days ago letting her know when he was coming home. He did think about just surprising her, but he was getting a little old for that bullshit, and just wanted to get home.

Answer the phone, Connie!

Still going right to her voicemail… He closed his phone and dropped it back into his pocket as he arrived at the baggage carousel. The luggage was just coming down the chute and he had to wait for a while until he saw his battered old duffle bag. He quickly shouldered it, placed his ACU cap on his head, and left to see if she was waiting for him at arrivals.

He walked outside to the pavement, and through the exhaust of the courtesy shuttles and taxis, he groped in another pocket and retrieved a battered pack of Winstons and a crumpled book of MRE matches. The security assholes at the airport in Germany had taken his old Zippo, and he had only four matches left. He cupped the flame and lit the smoke, inhaling deeply, savoring the taste. He looked around again and didn't see the blue Chevy Connie had driven for years.

Where the hell could she be?

He leaned back against a concrete pole and closed his eyes.

"Hey pal, can't you read?" someone said sharply. He opened his eyes and saw a cop heading towards him.

The cop pointed at the sign right above Tim's head that plainly read "No Smoking".

Looking at the young officer's face, Tim couldn't resist. "Does your daddy know you're out playing cop?" he said snidely.

"What are you, some kind of smartass?" the officer growled, and reached for his back pocket.

"You might want to rethink getting that sap out; it'll look mightily funny sticking out of your ass."

"That's it! Soldier or no soldier I'm gonna—"

Sensing he had gone too far, Tim said, "Hey, I'm a three-six-nine. Cool off, Troop!" using the Philadelphia Police code for a cop. He reached for his wallet and flashed his badge and ID card.

"Listen, I've just spent twenty-seven hours on planes and this is my first smoke in twelve hours. Cut me a fucking break! When did they do this shit?" he asked, pointing at the sign.

"The city did it a while ago. Listen, Sar' Major, you just get back from the sandbox?" the exasperated cop asked. "This is my first gig out of the academy and my lieutenant is riding my ass."

"Yeah... I know how that goes."

"Anyway, welcome home. Finish the butt before my LT sees you, okay?"

"You've been over there?"

"Two tours," the cop replied, "Marines."

"I had a favorite uncle in The Crotch. Welcome home yourself."

With that the beat cop nodded and walked away. Tim finished his smoke and hailed a cab. He tossed his duffle bag into the trunk the driver had popped for him and climbed into the back seat.

"Eighty-two hundred block of Leon Street," he said.

The driver nodded, turned on his meter, and plugged the address into a dash-mounted GPS.

The drive from the airport was quiet, thankfully. He really didn't feel much like talking and he really hated talkative cabbies. The temperature was even now starting to fall, and the solid, slate gray sky threatened snow. He stared out the window, watching the city pass by from Interstate 95. A lot had happened these last few years, and he thought this time would be the last. Tomorrow he'd go up to the Armory and put his papers in. He had enough time in service to retire. He owed it to himself. He owed it to Connie. All the time away... He'd been in uniform since he was seventeen and now he was on the near side of fifty and he wasn't getting any younger. It's not that he wasn't proud of his service, but it was a long time to be away from his wife. Thank God they'd not had any kids. Being away from his wife was hard enough, but to be away from kids would have been even worse.

The taxi took the correct exit off of the highway and headed west on Cottman Avenue. It was all the same, but different too. It looked dirtier, like no one cared anymore. He remembered as a kid how everyone in his neighborhood had taken pride in their homes. By the looks of it now, no one gave a shit anymore. A thin patina of filth covered everything, even a small dog being walked by a man in a grimy overcoat.

The cab driver made a right hand turn against the light at the intersection of Cottman and Frankford Avenues and he looked to his left to see the shell of the old Mayfair Theater. As a kid, he'd walked there with his friends to watch *Star Wars* and *Jaws* on Saturday afternoons in the summer. It was now a Rite-Aid pharmacy. A lot of the shops were still there, just different names now, hawking junk made in China. It used to be a nice place to live. He wondered what had happened to it.

Apathy, that's what had happened.

No one was willing to work at keeping things nice anymore. It was a goddamn shame. His dad had come home from World War II into a bright, shiny new world filled with hope. And like the millions just like him, they strived to give their kids everything they didn't have, and in doing that, they bred a generation of mostly ungrateful bastards. The world owed them everything. Not his parents.

Tim and his brother were both instilled with a strong work-ethic. When his friends in high school turned sixteen, one by one, all had been given new or almost new cars. The day of his sixteenth, his dad had driven him down to the used car lot on Torresdale Avenue where young Timmy paid cash for a 1969 Dodge Challenger. He'd saved the money after three years of mowing lawns in the summer, and shoveling driveways and sidewalks in winter.

It wasn't the best car in the world. It was in bad need of a ring job and shocks, and there was rust in the floor pans, but by God it was *his* car, and he took care of it. He'd had that car for several years, driving it to Georgia to his first duty station in the Army, and only sold it when he got orders to ship out to Panama. Not one of his friends had kept their cars as long, and one kid, after getting blind drunk at a party, wrapped his brand-new Corvette around an oak tree on Holme Avenue three days after he got it.

"This is fine right here," Tim said as the driver turned onto his block. He looked for Connie's car and didn't see it, but he did see the big "FORCLOSURE" sign on his tiny, overgrown, postage stamp sized front yard.

"What the fuck is this?" he said aloud to no one. He gave the cabbie a $50 bill for a $40 fare. "Keep it," he mumbled, he lifted his duffle onto his left shoulder, and bounded up the small flight of steps to his front door. Standing on his porch he fumbled in his pockets for his key ring. Finding the right one, he inserted it into the lock, but the key wouldn't work.

"Jesus jumping Christ almighty!" he said a little too loudly, the anger beginning to boil up in him now.

"Hey, Tim! Eh, I didn't expect you back..." the words trailed off from the open door of the row home next to his. It was Phil, his longtime neighbor who'd lived in the house longer than Tim had had this one.

"Yeah, well... I'm back," he said with growing frustration. "Can you tell me what this is all about?" He thumbed back at the foreclosure sign.

"Well, Connie moved out about three weeks ago, and then a day later, some guys from the bank came and changed the locks, and put that sign up."

"*Moved out?* Did she say where she was going?"

"No Tim... She didn't. Tim, I really hate to tell you this, but..."

"But what?"

"Tim, she said you were dead... that you got yourself killed over in Afghanistan."

"Well I'm not dead!"

"Tim, I can see that. Don't get pissed off at me. Ah fuck, I'm sorry, man..." he let it trail off. "Look, it's a little early, but you want a beer?"

"Yeah, I think I could use one."

Tim took out his crumpled pack of Winston cigarettes, and lit one as he leaned against the porch railing to contemplate his situation. What the fuck was he going to do now? He let the thought go for the moment when Phil returned with an opened bottle of Miller for both of them. Tim downed half the bottle in one pull and looked over at Phil. "Thanks," he said, lifting his bottle up in a toast. "I have a feeling this is only the first of many today."

"Yeah, man... this just sucks. She told me about three months ago you'd been blown up, one of those IAD things I hear about on the news. Nothing left to send back. She said it like she was discussing the weather. Kinda' gave me the creeps. Like, Oh, Timmy got blown up the other day, you think it'll rain this weekend, Phil?"

"Well, we'd been having problems, but I didn't think it was that bad..." he said, then a long draw off his cigarette. *So much for quitting these things now*, he thought. "So you said she moved out? Anyone help her?" he inquired, sounding very much like the cop he was.

"Ah shit, Tim. She had a big moving van. Mayflower Movers, I think. They had six guys in and out in about four hours."

"No one else? Her sister or dad or anyone?"

"There was a guy. Always wore a cowboy hat. Big 4x4 pickup with Wyoming tags... started comin' round' about three months after you left."

"Wyoming? That's odd." Tim finished off his beer. "Thanks for the cold one, Phil. Looks like it might snow tonight," he said, looking up at the sky and taking off his cap.

"Yeah, that's what Accuweather says, maybe six inches overnight."

"Of course."

"Are you going to be okay, Tim?"

"Yeah, I'll be okay. Just a little pissed off right now."

"I can sure dig that, man. Hey, what are you doing!?"

Tim put his fist into his patrol cap and punched out one of the small panes of glass in the front door.

"I'm just using my universal key to get into my house, Phil," he said, matter-of-factly, reaching into the hole and unlocking the deadbolt.

"You ain't going to go off and do something, are ya', Tim?"

"Nah, I'm good. Just tired and want to get some sleep and try to figure this out. Thanks again for the beer."

"Sure, no problem…" Phil mumbled, watching Tim's back as he walked in the dark house, and the door shut with a click.

"Oh, this is not going to be good," Phil said to himself, and turned to walk into his own home.

Tim's boot crunched on the broken glass when he walked into his living room. The anger was starting to well up. He looked around at a completely bare room and dropped his duffle bag. His footsteps echoed eerily in the empty house as he walked from room to room, to find nothing but some forgotten packing foam, and discarded newspaper pages.

Upstairs, he found three empty bedrooms, even the drapes, closets and bathroom were stripped. She'd even taken the goddamn shower curtain. "That bitch," he said in a small whisper.

He went back down stairs and into the kitchen, looking into all the cupboards and drawers. Not even a coffee cup or a spoon. He tried a light switch, and found that the electricity had been turned off. He went to the kitchen sink and tried the taps. No water either.

"That fucking bitch!" he screamed. He wanted to throw something, but she didn't even leave anything to throw. Then he thought about money. He pulled out his cell phone, and dialed his bank. After a few minutes he got connected with the bank manager, a man who he'd grown up with and considered a good friend. After several minutes of explaining, he'd found out that Connie had cleaned out the account a month ago, but left it active. His US Army pay did go direct-deposit a week ago, so he had a little money, maybe enough for a few weeks, but not enough to save the house. He put a stop on all her credit cards, and blocked her access to the account from that point. It was a little unusual, but the manager being a friend had expedited everything right over the phone. He'd have to come into the office later that day or tomorrow to sign some papers to make it official, though. Tim thanked him and thumbed off his phone.

"Now what the fuck am I going to do?" he said aloud, looking around the empty kitchen, the anger slowly beginning to be replaced by sadness. He looked at the door leading down to the basement. "The guns!"

He opened the door to inky blackness then remembered there was no power. He went back to the living room to his duffle bag, unlocked it, and unceremoniously dumped the contents on the floor. He dug through the uniforms and dirty underwear and found his Maglite.

He went back through the kitchen, turned on the flashlight and was rewarded by a bright beam of light. He went down the steps two at a time until he was standing at the bottom. He shined the beam around to see an equally empty rec room. The bar he'd built himself was still over on the far wall, but all the booze and stools were missing. In the corner was the six foot tall Mosler gun safe he'd had installed several years ago at Connie's insistence. She had hated the guns in the house, and wanted nothing to do with them. The safe was bolted firmly into the concrete floor of the basement, and weighed over seven hundred pounds; no one was going to be carrying that thing out of here. He went over to it, and noticed the door was standing ajar. Knowing already, he had to look anyway. The door swung open silently to expose an empty space.

All the guns were gone. Even his police issue Glock.

Well, maybe not… He went over to another corner of the room and looked up at the acoustic tile drop ceiling. He examined the tiles, and they looked undisturbed. Holding the flashlight with his left hand, he reached up with his right and pushed up the corner of the tile. It moved easily and he pushed it up and out of the way. Reaching up, he was rewarded by the feel of old cotton webbing. It was the handle of a WWII era satchel. He pulled it down, elated by the heft. She hadn't found these! He freed his hidden treasure from its hiding place.

Walking back up the stairs to the relative light of the kitchen, he placed the bag on the counter and unzipped it. A sigh escaped his lips when he saw that everything was still there. He reached in and pulled out his booty. First was a WWII Era Colt .45 1911A1, then a German Luger. He placed both next to the bag and pulled out a M3 "Grease Gun", also of .45 ACP caliber along with six 30 round magazines. The last things he pulled out of the bag were 300 rounds of newer, boxed .45 caliber ammunition and an Army issue cleaning kit. These little toys he'd had for several years. No one knew about them at all, not the Police Department, FBI, or the ATF. These were what were called "Unregistered" and no one at all knew they existed. The pistols he'd probably be able to bullshit his owning, but the M3 was a fully-automatic submachine gun. He'd get a lot of years in Leavenworth for just having it, and he'd done all he could to not let anyone know. Well, almost everyone. His brother knew about them. Even the whole story on how he'd acquired them. Too bad he couldn't tell that story. It was a hoot.

He lit another Winston and busied himself with breaking down each weapon, cleaning each as only an Army Sergeant Major could. Satisfied that all were as clean as he could get them, and properly oiled, he checked the action of each. He then loaded the magazine of the Colt, sliding the action to feed a round to the chamber, and placing the safety on "Condition One", round in the chamber, hammer cocked, safe on. Only very experienced people carried them like that, and he was well trained.

He put the pistol in the small of his back between his pants and t-shirt, then went on loading the magazines for the M3, which took some time.

He looked a little forlornly at the Luger wishing he had some 9mm ammo for that. The M3 he didn't load, just left it laying on the counter with the loaded magazines.

After he was finished with this chore, he was contemplating what to do. Should he hunt Connie down and kill her? No, no matter how much of a bitch she was, she wasn't worth losing what was left of his life to a prison cell. He heard the front door open and looked up.

"Hey, Tim, are you here? It's me, Sean!"

Six years older, his brother Sean was a cop too. A homicide detective, one of the best there was. How the hell had he found out Tim was home so soon? Phil must have called him.

"Yeah, I'm in here," Tim said loudly enough to be heard. The sounds of his brother's footfalls echoed through the empty house and came closer to the kitchen. He looked at the machine gun on the kitchen counter, his heart beginning to pound in his chest. Too late to hide the guns, but Sean already knew about them anyway, so Tim just shrugged and waited.

"I brought some coffee." Sean said, coming into the kitchen and eyeing the guns. "You ain't plannin' on going out on a hunting expedition, are you?"

"No. She isn't worth it."

"Good. I'd hate to be the one to have to lock you up," he said as he handed over a paper cup from Dunkin' Donuts.

"How are you doing?"

"I could be better."

"Yeah, no shit. Look, do you need anything?" Sean said in an even voice, looking at Tim over the rim of his own paper cup.

"I could use a ride to the Armory in a bit. Are you working?" Tim asked, knowing the answer. Sean was in his best Brook's Brothers suit and overcoat. Not a hair out of place, Smiling Jack mustache perfectly trimmed. He was working. He looked like a recruiting poster for Supercops, Inc.

"Fucking bitch took everything, Sean, even my service piece."

"No shit? All of the guns?"

"She took every last one of them. Well, not these, she didn't know about them, or where I hid them. She'd have shit Tiffany cufflinks if she knew about the machine gun," he laughed, not really feeling all that humorous.

"Well, I can make a report on that at least, theft of the guns and the police issue one will be a huge fuckup on her part. That'll get the ATF and FBI involved. Do you have any idea where she went?"

"Phil next door said she had some peckerhead from Wyoming hanging around."

"You want me to pass this off to Northeast Detectives, or do you want me to handle it?"

"You do it, Sean."

"Alright. I'll take care of it this afternoon. Where are you going to stay?"

"Right here. This is my home."

"Do you have power, gas and water turned on?"

"No, I'll get them back tomorrow. I just need to get some stuff from the Armory for the next few nights. I'll be okay."

"Are you sure? You can stay at my place until things settle," Sean offered, sipping at his coffee.

"No, I'll stay here," Tim replied, looking away. Just the thought of staying at his brother's house, with his four bratty kids and snooty wife was making him nauseous.

"You ready to go?"

"Yeah, let me bag this shit up and we'll go." Tim threw the guns into the satchel and re-zipped it. "Okay, I'm ready," he said, shouldering the satchel and picking up his coffee.

They walked through the living room and out the front door. "I'll have to take care of that lock and window later."

"Good idea, Timmy. Neighborhood isn't what it used to be."

"You don't say?" Tim said with a grunt.

He shut the door and followed his brother to the unmarked cop car and got in the passenger side. His brother started the car, and pulled out.

They went along silently for a while, until they turned off Holme Avenue onto northbound Roosevelt Boulevard. The Colt was digging into his spine, and he decided he'd have to get some sort of pancake holster or something to make carrying it more comfortable.

"I'm really not all that surprised at this," Sean said, breaking the silence.

Here it comes, Tim thought. He was wondering when The Pontification would start.

"What did you expect to happen with you running off playing soldier?" Sean remarked. "You should have been at home."

"I wasn't 'playing soldier', I was doing my job!" Tim retorted.

"You *have* a fucking job, Tim. It's called being a police officer."

"More like garbage collector."

"Is that what you think? Our job is very important!"

"Yeah, okay, it's important," Tim said, his words dripping with sarcasm.

"Why did you even become a cop in the first place if you hate it so much?"

"That's what was expected of me, goddamn it! Do you really think I had a choice in it at all? No, it was all decided by you, Dad, and the whole family, that that's what I'd do after I came home from Central America. I had no fucking choice!"

"Yes you did!"

"No I didn't. If I went against what the family thought, can you imagine the guilt that would have been laid on me?

"That's bullshit. You had a choice!"

"No, I did *not*. You and Dad would have made my life insufferable. You weren't there the day I came home from school and told Dad I was enlisting. I thought he was going to have a stroke right there. I almost caved at that point, but I stood my ground. Then when I came home after being away for so long, I thought maybe I'd do it his way for a bit… maybe I could do a good job."

"And you do, Timmy. You're a good cop."

"I'm a shell. The job has sucked all the life out of me. Fuck, *life* itself has done a pretty good job of it too!"

"Then why the hell did you stick with it?"

"The naïve belief that I could actually make a difference…" He trailed off and looked out the window.

"You *can* make a difference. Every time you head out you could stop a crime, save a life, make a difference in someone's life." Now Sean *sounded* like the recruiter for Supercops, Inc. and Tim rolled his eyes.

"You know what, Sean? I never told you this. On my first night out on the job fresh out of the Academy, I was partnered up with this old cop. Mooney was his name. He was so fat the steering wheel rubbed his stomach. He had this stub of a cigar that smelled like burning shit. He pointed at one windshield pillar and then the next, and said; 'If it don't happen between here and there, it don't fucking happen!' then he asked why I became a cop. I told him I wanted to help people."

"And?" Sean asked, popping a piece of chewing gum into his mouth.

"He said 'They don't want your fucking help, kid!' And do you know what? He was fucking right. They don't want our fucking help, Sean. They never want it. You and I are just marking time doing a thankless job that no one cares about anymore,"

Tim said. "We're dinosaurs, Sean. People don't think like we do anymore. And like dinosaurs, pretty soon we'll be extinct."

"Christ, how'd you get so goddamn jaded?"

"How the fuck can you *not* get jaded?" Tim shouted, anger welling up inside of him again. His brother, while meaning well, would never get it. You couldn't see things he'd seen and do things he'd done and not look at the world through jaded eyes. The years spent in Central America, doing things that he couldn't even think about, let alone talk about. How do you tell a man, who's never been outside of the city save for a yearly trip to Wildwood, New Jersey with the wife and kids, what it's like to see real poor people, in a real Third World shithole? What it's like to have your best friend bleed to death in your arms, not being able to do anything about it? Someone who's never fired a shot in anger? Or never had the experience of real terror, to make you feel totally alive. This… this whole life he talked of was just bullshit. How could one person really make a difference? They couldn't, that's how. You try and the world gobbles you up.

"Here we are," Sean said, pulling into the National Guard Armory. "Hey, maybe you should go and see Father McGranahan."

"Let's not go down that path, okay?" Tim said. He unlatched his seatbelt and opened the door. Fat chance he'd see a priest. Why would he go to see a man who had never been married, and have him counseling him about marriage, and faith? He'd quit the Catholics years ago, and the last person he'd be talking to was a priest.

"Why don't you come over for dinner on Friday? The kids and Mary would love to see you."

"I'll think about it. Thanks for the lift."

"See you soon, and I'll work on that report this afternoon."

"Okay bye, Sean," and he shut the door, walking away towards the front doors of the building.

Tim went through the front door and walked tiredly up the stairs to the second floor, where his Brigade's Headquarters were, and his office. He walked into the orderly room to see Sgt. Patterson busy playing FreeCell on his desktop computer.

"It's so nice to see you hard at work, Patterson!" he said as he blew by the soldier.

"Oh shit, Sar' Major! I didn't expect you back until next Monday!"

"Surprise, I'm back early. I need the keys to the M880," he barked.

"Right away, Sar' Major!" Patterson said to a closed door.

Tim looked around at his office. All the usual things were still there, just as he had left them eighteen months ago. He looked at a framed photo sitting on his desk. He picked up the gilt frame and looked at it briefly. He and Connie smiled back at him, drinks hoisted in mock salute. It had been taken on a vacation to Belize several years ago, and was now a distant memory. He looked at the photo one more moment, and with all his strength, he heaved it at the far gray-painted cinderblock wall.

His office door opened and a head peered in. "You alright, Sar' Major?"

"Yeah, John, it's been a long flight. I'm just tired," Tim lied.

"Here are the keys to the 880."

"Just put them on my desk. I need a list of all the equipment that didn't ship over to Afghanistan."

"Do you want that now?"

"No, next fucking week. Yes now!"

"You got it, Sar' Major!" Patterson squeaked.

Tim hated getting 'Sergeant Major' on Patterson, but sometimes he wondered if the Brigade Clerk was really that stupid sometimes. He pulled open the bottom drawer of his desk and removed a half-full bottle of Jameson's Irish Whiskey and a glass, pouring himself four fingers before putting the bottle back and taking a long pull from the glass. Fuck it. No officers around to bitch. Besides, he really ran the Brigade. The door opened again.

"Here's the list, Sar' Major. Anything else I can do for you?"

"No. If you don't have anything else to do today, why don't you take an early quit. I've got a few things to do here and I'll lock up when I go. I've got the NCO's fitreps to do this month, and I'll be in tomorrow to start on them."

"Okay, Sar' Major. It's good to see you back. I'll see you tomorrow!"

Tim looked down at the list without responding, scanning it for what he'd hoped would be there, and he heard the orderly room door shut. *Fucker didn't waste time getting out of here*, he thought. He went through the list and highlighted the things he'd need at the house. It was against regulations, but he'd have everything back before the Brigade got back from Afghanistan. Generators, that was first. He'd have his pick. There was a huge towed one, a 10KW diesel, but that was far too big. It'd power a whole neighborhood and it was loud enough to piss off and keep everyone within four blocks awake.

One of the small 1KW gas gennies would do. It was just enough power to run a refrigerator and a microwave, maybe a small TV. A couple of Jerry cans for gasoline, maybe two for kerosene, also. A folding cot, a few blankets and pillows, kerosene heaters, and a few lanterns. Some dishes, pots and pans, and coffee cups, along with a propane camp stove from the mess, and some MRE's. A few cases, maybe. He'd gotten sick of eating them in Afghanistan.

Meals, Ready to Eat? More like Meals Refused by Ethiopians, he mused.

He'd stop off at the Pathmark down from his house to get some real food and coffee. He remembered to add a coffee pot, and checked that off his list. He pocketed the list and the keys to the truck, then headed out to the motor pool where he found the ancient M880. It was actually a diesel powered Dodge Powerwagon 4x4 pickup truck, built in 1979, and painted camouflage. Not many left in the Army, but the Brigade had held on to this one because it was a good gofer truck.

Tim unlocked the door, and climbed in the cab. After securing his satchel of firepower under the seat, he depressed the clutch, waited until the glow plug light went out, and cranked over the engine. It fired right up on the second turn. The pricks at the motor pool were good for something at least. He drove around to the back of the building to the loading dock. Once there, he expertly backed the tailgate up in one go. He made quick work of opening the door and locating everything on his list. It took about an hour to gather everything and load it onto the truck. He then made a quick hop around the front again, where he dutifully locked up everything, and turned out the lights.

He toyed briefly with going into the arms room, and getting some of the better toys, but thought better of it. The stuff he had gotten right now was easily explained, but it would be an entirely different matter with a few M4 carbines or an M16. He already had way more firepower than he needed anyway, with the grease gun still in its satchel bag, stuffed under the seat. Besides, contrary to Hollywood and TV, it was against regulations to have even one round of ammo in the Armory, so it'd be of no use to have a rifle without any ammo.

The liquor store was right next to the grocery, so that was only one stop there. First stop was a gas station for the gas and kerosene. That he found right away on his dive south on Roosevelt Blvd. He topped the Jerry cans off with unleaded gas and diesel (which would burn just as good in kerosene heaters and lanterns as kerosene) and a carton of Winstons. Next stop was the liquor store, then the grocery store. The Pathmark was on Frankford Avenue, just a few blocks north of his house. He pulled into the parking lot and looked around. He noted there were a lot of cars in the lot. They must be having a sale or something.

He first walked over to the liquor store or "State Store", because the State of Pennsylvania still had a monopoly on the booze business. He bought a half gallon of Ruskova vodka, and another bottle of Jamesons. He locked his purchases in the truck and headed into the grocery store. Getting a cart, he wandered around the aisles, making the mistake of going into a food store on an empty stomach. He tossed in a slew of ramen noodles and canned soups. He then went to the bread aisle, and noticed almost all of it was gone. *Oh I get it,* he thought. *They're calling for snow, which means a run on bread, milk and eggs.* There must be some regressive gene somewhere in everybody that makes them all crave French toast during a snowstorm. He got the last loaf of bread, next to the last gallon of milk, a dozen eggs, and wandered around some more. He was running on fumes at this time, and was surprised himself that as tired as he was, he was still functioning. After getting coffee, a salt and pepper set like the little cardboard-tubed camping ones, and some sugar, he grabbed some mayonnaise, pickle relish and a few boxes of different kinds of pastas. He headed for the canned meats aisle for some tuna. He'd thought about getting some steaks and pork chops, but decided against it. There was nothing to cook them on anyway. He'd not checked the garage, but the bitch had probably taken the BBQ grill too.

He made his way down the aisle and selected a few cans of the store brand tuna when he heard a "tsk" from behind him. He turned to look, and saw a morbidly obese woman, whose age he was unable to determine. He thought to himself with a laugh that she had more chins than a Chinese phonebook. She was sitting in— more like oozing out of— one of those electric buggies the store reserved for the handicapped, looking at him disdainfully.

"You're not going to buy that tuna, are you?" she spat.

"Yeah, I was. What's wrong with it?"

"It's not dolphin friendly tuna!" she said in a tone that reminded him of Sister Mary Magdalene from grade school. She was a bitch too.

"Dolphin friendly, what the hell is that?" he asked, knowing even before he finished he'd get a lecture all about it.

"Well, the dolphins get caught in the tuna nets and die. Dolphin friendly tuna is tuna they catch without nets, saving the dolphins!" she said in a superior tone that was really starting to get on his nerves.

He stood, looking at her deadpan for few moments, crossed his arms, and then finally spoke.

"So let me get this straight. It's okay to kill the tuna, but not okay to kill the dolphins?"

"Well, I didn't say—"

"Yes you did. I guess it's okay to kill the tuna, because a tuna never had its own TV show back in the 60's right? Or is it because tuna aren't cute, like baby seals and otters and shit? Well fuck them, I'm hungry. I'd kill Flipper for a tuna sandwich!" he was shouting now, and he took an arm, scooped several more cans of the non-dolphin friendly tuna into his cart and walked off, not giving her a chance to reply.

I swear to God, he thought. *I've got to have some kind of magnet somewhere that I attract these fuckwits.*

He made his way to the checkout, and of course the person in front of him had a problem with their personal check. Several times the checkout girl tried to run it through, and it just kept rejecting it.

"What else can fuck up today?" he muttered, which the checkout chick heard. She looked at him apologetically, though it wasn't her fault. Finally, after the fourth time the girl tried to run the check through Tim had finally had had enough and asked, "How much it the bill?"

"Thirty seven fifty," she said. He pulled two twenties from his wallet and paid for the man's groceries. It wasn't because he was feeling all that generous; he was at the point where his head would implode if he had to endure one more fuckup today.

The man thanked him, and Tim replied "Merry fucking Christmas, a month early."

The man quickly took his few bags and quickly left, saying, "Thank you, sir! God bless the troops!"

The girl grinned at him, and he just nodded. He was tired, but nowhere near being done for the day. He paid for his groceries and made his way out of the store to the truck. He loaded it quickly and headed off to his house, finally.

He pulled the truck into the alleyway behind the row of homes, and backed into his small driveway, so the tailgate was almost against the garage door. He broke into the back door, the same way he had done with the front door earlier. Gaining entry, he opened the inside door, walked into a small hallway to the inside door to the garage. This he opened, letting in some light. He was delighted for the first time today, when he saw the four cords of hardwood he'd cut, split, and stacked before the last deployment.

Guess Connie forgot about that. It would come in handy in the wood stove he'd had installed in the living room several years ago. He quickly unloaded all his wares to the house, and put it all away. Now, to get the generator up and running. He set it up outside the house, filled the fuel tank with gas, primed the carburetor and quickly pulled the recoil starter. It fired up in one pull. He had to hand it to the Brigade. Maintenance was good. He ran the extension cord through the garage and the rec room, up the stairs to the refrigerator, plugging it in. Next he went back down to the garage, bringing up the lanterns, heaters, and a Jerry can of diesel, shutting both the garage door and the basement door in the kitchen.

He went about setting up the camp stove on the kitchen counter, the heaters, one in the kitchen, the other in the living room, and put a pot of water on to boil. He'd decided on the drive home, he'd just live in the kitchen/living room/dining room level of the house for now. There was a small bathroom off the kitchen he could use for now. He'd bought ten gallons of water at the grocery store, and this he could use to wash up and use the toilet. If he couldn't get the water turned back on tomorrow, he'd have to get more.

He set the cot up in the living room and got a fire going in the wood stove to take the chill off. It was as cold as a morgue in the house, and the temperature was falling fast. He then tacked up a few blankets in front of the open doorway to the upper level of the house. No sense heating a part of the house he'd not be using.

Busying himself by tidying up his clothes and preparing where he was going to sleep took enough time to let the water he'd put on the stove heat up enough to wash and shave. He took his toiletries kit into the kitchen and stripped to the waist. With some soap and a brown Army issue washcloth Tim went about washing his upper torso and armpits. A really nice long hot shower would have been better, but this would have to suffice for now. Next, he took a small metal mirror out and propped it up next to the pot to shave the day-old stubble from his face. It was the first time Tim had really had a look his reflection, and he didn't like what he saw. Who was this old guy staring back at him?

The eyes still looked the same, but there were crow's feet at the corners, and his face took on a weathered, slightly leathery look, from too many years of too much sun. His close cropped hair was salt and pepper now, long gone was the light brown of his youth.

A dinosaur.

Finishing up, he looked out the window noticing the growing twilight, and looked at his wristwatch. Five PM. It'd be dark soon. With that thought crossed, his stomach reminded him that the last meal he'd had was about ten hours ago, somewhere over the Atlantic Ocean. He'd have to eat something soon. He looked around the kitchen, and even though he'd made a big purchase of food, he didn't feel like cooking anything. So that decision made, he redressed back into his uniform, because he had no civilian clothes.

He had no clue what Connie had done with them, and he just couldn't walk around in a half-assed uniform. He was that kind of soldier. Do it right or don't do it at all. He'd sort out some civilian clothes later, but for now he'd just wear his uniform. Even in these new ugly desert ACU's he did look good he thought.

He decided to walk the three blocks down to Garvin's Pub, on the corner of Solly and Frankford Avenues for something to eat and a few beers. He would do that, come back to get a good night's sleep, and figure out the next step tomorrow. He walked the three blocks easily, and just as he arrived at the front door of the bar, it began to snow. He pulled open the door and stepped into the dim light. It was a typical Irish corner bar for the area; several TV's turned to the local ABC affiliate for the local news, sports memorabilia from the Phillies, Flyers and Eagles on the walls, with neon beer signs between. There were a few patrons sitting at the bar, which had a huge full length mirror behind it, with several glass shelves containing hundreds of bottles of all different kinds of booze. He saw a familiar face behind the bar and smiled. He walked up and tossed a fifty dollar bill on the bar, sat down on one of the padded stools and held his right hand out which was immediately taken with a firm grip.

"Hey, Mickey, it's good to see you!"

"Timmy! It's been a long time! How've you been?"

"I could be better."

"Yeah, I heard. Your brother was in earlier. Anything I can do?"

"Yeah, tell my brother next time you see him to shut the fuck up," he said jokingly. He'd always liked Mickey and he considered him a good friend.

"That'll be the day your brother shuts up!" he said. He took a frosted mug from the cooler and poured Tim a beer from the tap, placing it in front of him on a paper coaster.

"It was kind of a rotten thing to do, eh?" Mick asked.

"Yeah, pretty low," Tim agreed, taking a pull of the beer, noticing Mick made no move to touch the fifty on the bar. "Where are all the ashtrays?"

"You can't smoke in here anymore, Tim. It's new city regulations."

"Those fucking smoke Nazis!"

"You said it," he said shaking his head.

"Is the kitchen open?" Mick nodded. "Okay, I'll have a cheesesteak and some fries."

"You got it, Timmy," Mick said and walked off to the back kitchen.

Tim looked around and didn't recognize any of the other patrons, so he took another pull from his beer and looked up at the TV. A commercial for a local furniture company had just completed and the news was back on.

A perfectly coiffed anchorman said that the President was flying back from a visit to Malaysia tonight, and was expected back in Washington tomorrow morning.

"Big fucking deal," Tim said aloud. "He should stop by Afghanistan."

That wouldn't happen he knew. Then the anchor switched over to the sports scores. Eagles were doing great, and the Flyers were in the running for the Stanley Cup again this year. Even though it was November, they both were doing well early in the season. He looked forward to baseball season. Maybe this summer he'd actually get to a few games. Tim sipped at his beer, and watched the weather report, which confirmed what Phil had told him earlier, six inches of snow tonight, and the first bands of the storm were crossing the city line now.

Mick came back and refilled Tim's beer. "It'll be a few more minutes, Tim."

"No problem, not like I have anything else to do."

"Hey, Timmy, you remember the last time they said that?"

"What's that?"

"We'd get a slight dusting to six inches of snow," he said, pointing at the TV over the bar.

"Oh yeah, winter of 96'. I woke up with almost three feet of the shit. It took me a week to dig out my car."

Mick went to the kitchen when he heard the little 'ding' from the short order cook's bell, letting him know Tim's order was ready. He came back carrying one of those red plastic mesh bowls with a wax paper lining, heaped with French fries and a cheesesteak sandwich on top. The steam was rising from the food, and Tim's mouth watered at the smell. Mick left Tim to eat, and went to wash the glassware.

Tim attacked the food with gusto and ate like he'd been starving. When he finished, he pushed the bowl aside, wiped his mouth with a paper towel, and finished off his beer. All in all, Garvin's was a good place to be left alone, which is what he really wanted.

Over the next few hours and several beers, Tim was starting to feel a pretty good buzz coming on. Patrons came and went as the night progressed, and from time to time, Mick stopped by the end of the bar where Tim was sitting to make small talk.

The last few people had left an hour or so before, and Tim basically had the place to himself. Mickey was in the back getting some beer to fill the coolers, when the front door opened, and two kids spilled in from the growing snowstorm.

From the brief time the door was open, he could see that at least six inches of snow had already fallen, and it didn't look like it was going to stop any time soon. The two walked up to the bar, and Tim got his first good look at them. Both were white, about twenty-two or so years of age, covered in tattoos, and had all kinds of metal studs in their faces. Mick went over to them, and they ordered a few beers. They were laughing and joking with each other a great deal, a little too loudly for such an empty place. Tim really wanted to tell them to pull their fucking pants up, but decided to keep to himself.

God, they are becoming annoying, he thought. They were now playing darts at the far end of the bar.

"Hey, Joe!" one of them yelled. Tim ignored it at first, but realized they were talking to him. He turned his head and the mouthier one said again, "Yo, GI Joe! Yeah you! Play darts with us!"

"Nah, I'm ok," Tim said and went back to the TV.

"What's the matter, don't you know how?" he said and it came out like, *'Whatsamatter, doncha knowhow?'*

"Yeah, I don't know how," Tim said. Mick saw the look in Tim's eyes and thought he'd better do something.

"Hey! You guys settle down. I don't want any trouble here," Mickey said.

"There ain't going to be any trouble bro, just askin' GI Joe here to play some darts with us."

"Well he doesn't want to play."

The taller of the two walked over to Tim and looked him over.

"Hey man, aren't you a little old to be playin' soldier? And what's this? Ranger? You some kinda park ranger or somethin'?" Loudmouth said, looking at the Ranger tab on Tim's left shoulder.

"Yeah, that's it, a park ranger," Tim said, smiling in a way that any one of his soldiers would have recognized right away as his *'I am about to unleash so much hurt on you it's going to put your mother in the hospital'* smile.

"Hey, Lenny, he's a park ranger! Protects all the deer and shit! Betcha' he even hugs them trees and all!"

"C'mon, man! Play some darts wit' us!" the other one pleaded.

"I told you, I don't know how to play," Tim said evenly, his voice icy. Tim did know how to play. He was even on a few dart leagues. His photo with a huge trophy for All City was right next to the dartboard, if either of these two morons cared to look closely.

"Alls ya' hafta do is shoot the bull, man!"

"All I have to do is shoot the bull's-eye?" Tim asked with an evil grin. He heard Mickey say, "Oh shit," behind him.

"Yeah, shoot the bull!"

"Alright," Tim said, and in one fluid motion stood, reached behind him, grabbed the butt of the .45, pulled it out and one-handed, thumbed off the safety. With a loud *BAM*, he let one round off, completely obliterating the center cork of the dartboard from fifteen feet away.

"There. I shot the bull," Tim said matter-of-factly, turning the pistol to the face of the nearest loudmouth. The only sound in the bar now was the expended .45 casing rolling on the floor.

The kid's eyes were like saucers and his mouth was like a huge 'O' as he looked, dumbfounded, through the cloud of cordite smoke.

"I think it's time for you two jerkoffs to take your sorry asses out of my area, okay?"

"Whatever you say, man! Just don't shoot us!"

"Get the fuck out of here right fucking now assholes!" Tim bellowed. "And pull your goddamn pants up!" he added at them as they stumbled out the door. He safed the pistol, and put it back into his waistband, concealing it once again.

"Fucking retards," he said, and looked over at Mickey, who was laughing so hard he was crying.

"Sorry about the dartboard, Mick. I'll buy you a new one."

"Ah shit, Timmy! That was classic, and worth the cost of a new one. It'll be great story to tell everyone!"

"I wouldn't be going around spreading that war story, Mick."

"Yeah, I guess you're right… but fuck, that was funny! I think the short one pissed his pants when you pulled out that cannon!"

"I'd better be going, Mick. Again, sorry about the mess."

"Don't worry about it, Timmy."

"What do I owe you?" Tim asked, reaching into his pocket.

"You don't owe me anything. Glad you're home. You're a hero to all of us here, Tim."

Tim winced inwardly at this. He certainly didn't feel like any hero. "Mick, I'm no hero. I'm a nothing man."

"Ah fuck, Timmy. Get the fuck outta here before I call a cop!" "See you later, Mick." Tim downed the last of his beer, got his Gortex jacket, and left through the same door as the two loudmouths.

He stood outside in the snow for a moment looking around, but the snow was getting heavier and their footprints were already being obscured. Tim turned to slog the two blocks back to his house, wondering why people wouldn't leave him alone. That's all he really wanted right now, to be left alone.

He wanted to be alone to think.

He got to his porch and looked around at a silent street. Not many lights on. He looked at his wristwatch and saw that it was nearly 12:30 AM. He had one hell of a buzz going now, made worse by his exhaustion from being awake so long.

One last look up the block, and then without really thinking, he let a bellow out as loud as he could: "Just leave me the fuck alone!"

And with that, he turned the doorknob and entered his house. It had finally warmed up some from the fire in the woodstove. He tossed two more logs onto the fire, closed the glass door on the front of the stove, plopped down on the cot, and had enough energy to take his boots off before collapsing on the bed and falling into a deep sleep.

CHAPTER 2: CAREFUL WHAT YOU WISH FOR

As Tim slept a deep but troubled sleep, a gift from the cosmos had reached Earth. When a star explodes in a massive supernova, it shoots out thin rays from both its poles, of gamma radiation. These bands, only one degree of arc in width, grow wider as they travel out from their source, like the taper of an ice cream cone, but far less savory. If the Earth was in its direct path, it would have been far worse. But worse is a relative term. If it had been a direct hit, the atmosphere itself would have been set alight, burning everything on the surface to a cinder and boiling away the oceans.

As it was, it was only a glancing blow, and the east coasts of both North and South America had it the easiest, only because of the time of day. The effects were the same all over the planet, for gamma rays went straight through the globe in a matter of milliseconds, blocked by nothing, on their unending journey across time and space.

If anyone was awake when they'd hit, the first thing they would have noticed was that the Aurora Borealis— or Northern Lights— were extremely vivid, and it was the best light show they'd ever produced. With the gamma radiation another phenomenon came along, an electromagnetic pulse, or EMP. That lasted a nanosecond, and when it hit, every single electronic circuit board and microchip, if it wasn't hardened specifically for EMP, was fried, sending the Earth back over a hundred years technology-wise in an instant.

All over the world, everything run by computers just shut down. Planes lost power, cars, trucks, buses, trains all shut off. Computers that managed electric generating stations, power grids, nuclear reactors all over the world shut down. It wasn't pretty. Even though countless vehicles had shut down, they didn't stop moving, but careened on uncontrolled until slamming into one another on highways, streets and lanes all over the world. In most of the Americas, the majority of the population was home in bed asleep, but travelling west, on the far side of the Pacific Ocean, most cities were still in daylight.

In Tokyo, where millions commuted in trains and millions of cars every day, there were scenes of the biggest pileups and train wrecks in history. The same was true for Hong Kong, Beijing, Taipei, Jakarta, Brisbane and Sydney. Fires were started all over the world by these wrecks, some of which would burn for days and even weeks.

Planes fell out of the sky when engines stopped and autopilots quit working, starting more fires. For a while, the Earth was completely dark, as it had been thousands of years ago, until the fires grew large enough to be seen from space. These fires would burn uncontrolled until all the fuel was expended.

Some things remained untouched by the EMP. Military aircraft all over the world flew on sans the controls of experienced pilots, all military aircraft and equipment was hardened against EMP. The gamma rays left the bodies, but killed almost everyone on the planet instantly. These planes flew on their set auto pilot settings until they finally ran out of jet fuel and fell to the Earth. A KC 135 air tanker was flying in a racetrack pattern over the central Pacific Ocean, where it was scheduled to rendezvous with Air Force One returning from Indonesia. They passed each other right on time, within two nautical miles of one another, but both kept on their merry way. The KC 135 would fly in circles for another three days before falling into the sea, but Air Force One had only enough fuel left to reach central Colorado on its present course, where its fuel tanks and emergency reserves would finally run dry.

All over the world the Reign of Man ended and the Earth itself went on turning. And just as soon as it did, nature began its slow reclamation of man's works to control her. The electrical grids were now powerless, the pumps that had kept the Netherlands free of water shut off, and slowly but surely the waters started rising. The same happened in New York City, where miles of the underground subway that sat below sea level filled with water.

No more would there be armies of workers to repair valves, paint bridges, repair washouts and ice heaves, clean up damage left by storms and avalanches, and maintain the countless computers which took care of such things. Every city in every nation of the world became a huge Necropolis. The monuments man had made to himself would eventually and assuredly be returned to the Earth.

Some things did keep working, things that had no electronic circuit boards, like the small gasoline powered generator that Tim had set up outside his house. That was still running, along with the refrigerator plugged into it. Tim heard the generator as he slowly stirred from a troubled sleep. The slight hum of the motor reassured him that the gennie was still working.

He slowly sat up, and in the dim early morning light he looked at his watch, an old Timex wind up he'd had for years. 6:20 AM. His head pounded with the worst headache he'd ever had. It seemed like his skin was on fire, and every joint in his body was screaming. He felt like he'd been beaten with a baseball bat. *This is the worst hangover I've ever had*, he thought as a wave of nausea swept over him. He barely made it to the bathroom toilet, when the contents of his stomach came up. He knelt at the porcelain bowl for several minutes, dry heaving after his stomach was empty.

He fell back, and sat on the floor for several more minutes, taking stock of himself. His skin really did feel like it was burning. As if he'd fallen asleep on the beach for a whole day.

He slowly got up and hobbled out to the kitchen, where he lit one of the Army lanterns, and had a good look at himself. He saw his hands first. They were bright red, exactly like bad sunburn. His arms were the same.

A look into the small metal mirror, confirmed his face and neck were in the same condition. He carefully stripped, then realized his whole body was burned. He immediately discounted carbon monoxide poisoning, because the bright pink actually hurt like sunburn. The wood stove was properly vented.

Sunburn?

How the fuck did he get sunburned in his own home on a snowy November night? He went back to the kitchen and took two Tylenol and put the coffee pot on to boil. He looked out the small kitchen window at the snow covering the alleyway. The snow had stopped overnight, and it looked like about a foot of the white stuff had fallen. The sky was clear and starting to grow light in the east. He then noticed there were no footprints at all in the newly fallen snow.

It wasn't that odd, he decided. It was still pretty early, and most people would still be in bed. He lit a Winston and contemplated what he'd do today. On another burner of the camp stove, he put a pot of water on to heat for washing up. When the coffee was done, he poured himself a cup, went to his clothes, and picked out underwear, socks and a clean t-shirt. The sunburn was bugging him, not only physically, but mentally. How did one get burned sleeping fully clothed indoors at night?

With that on his mind, he busied himself with bathing and brushing his teeth. Once he was dressed, he made himself a bowl of instant oatmeal, and ate that with a second cup of coffee. The nausea came back for a minute, but he managed to keep the food down. He hoped he hadn't caught anything. The Tylenol had taken the edge off his pounding head and the sting from the 'burn', but they both were still there nagging him. He looked at his watch again, and saw it was almost 7:30. He'd try and call his brother.

Picking up his cell phone, he flipped it open. The screen was dark. He knew he had a full charge last night, and it was a new phone, but here it was, dead as anything.

What else can go wrong? he thought. He finished getting dressed, then went out the back and checked the generator. At least that was still working. He checked the fuel and topped off the small tank, and started the Dodge truck to warm up. He still hadn't figured out what was happening, but the M880 was hardened for EMP, as were all military vehicles, this one being built at the height of the Cold War. While it was warming up at idle, he locked both front hubs for 4x4 drive, and went back inside to get the .45.

Retrieving that from his cot, he popped out the magazine and replaced the one round he'd fired last night at the two boneheads. He chuckled at that. *What dumbasses.* Putting it into a pocket of his Gor-Tex jacket, he headed back out to the truck. He'd drive back to the Armory this morning, call his brother from there, and then later he'd go to the bank and hardware store to get replacement panes for the two windows he'd broken, and locks for the door.

Backing out into the driveway, the truck made an easy path in four wheel drive. Stopping and looking left to make sure no traffic was coming, he turned onto the side street and headed towards Frankford Avenue. He then noticed that no plows had been through the area at all. That was odd. Frankford Avenue was a major street, and was one of the first plowed. City services must be really going down the sewer. He downshifted up the small hill, north of the Pennypack Creek Bridge.

He drove for a few blocks, and realized that none of the traffic lights were working. He stopped dead in the middle of the intersection and looked around. Not a soul in sight. It was eight in the morning on a Wednesday. There should be at least *someone* around. What the fuck was going on here? He got out of the truck and took a look around, struck by the quiet.

With the exception of a few birds chirping, there was no sound at all. Well, no sounds he thought of as normal. No traffic sounds, no aircraft sounds, nothing at all. He looked up at the sky and noticed no contrails. There should at least be a few planes flying around. The storm wasn't *that* bad. Only about eight inches, he guessed. Not enough to shut down the airports. A chill went over him now, all the way from his feet. The last time the sky was this quiet was right after 9/11, when they closed down all commercial flights.

What the fuck had happened?

He looked around again, and saw two bumps in the snow near a bus stop that was back dropped by Saint Dominic's Roman Catholic Church and cemetery. He took out the .45 on instinct, and made his way through the drifting snow in the street to the bus stop. The bumps were the outline of two bodies.

He crouched down and brushed the snow off the head of one. The face of one of the two jokers from last night was staring back at him lifelessly, a look of shock permanently etched on his face.

Due to his years in the military and on the police force, he was used to seeing dead bodies, but he still recoiled at the sight. He staggered back, falling on his rump, and backpedalling all the way to the truck. He climbed back into the cab and slammed the door.

The heater going full blast was like fire on his burned face, but it reassured him. *The face!* It was burned just like his! Whatever happened had killed both of them out there. Where was everyone else? He tried to get his breathing under control. He looked out of the windshield, and gripped the wheel tightly as his mind raced.

He put the truck back into gear and made his way rapidly towards the Armory. He spotted the first snowplow on Academy Road. It was actually a garbage truck, from the Department of Streets, with a plow on the front. It was askew on the sidewalk where it had crashed, taking out a light pole. He slowed going around it, looking into the cab. He saw the driver slumped over the wheel, but he didn't stop to check on him. Further on, at the intersection of Grant Avenue, he saw a police cruiser, in the same situation as the plow truck. This time he did stop. A cop was a cop, and you always stopped to help a fellow officer.

He made his way through a snow bank to the driver's side door of the police car and opened it. The windshield was starred from the officer's head, but there was no blood, which told Tim all he needed to know. The cop was dead before the impact. The airbag hadn't deployed, even though it looked like a fairly good crash, maybe 35 MPH or so. He reached over the body and retrieved the officer's handheld radio. He turned in on, but got nothing. Not even static. Dead as dogshit, just like his phone.

No, it couldn't be...

Was it a neutron bomb? He didn't think anyone had those. It was just an idea back in the 80's. Even if it was a neutron bomb, it couldn't have killed everyone that fast, could it? And if it was, why was he still alive? Why was the M880 still running? He couldn't answer the first half, but he knew immediately why the truck was still running, it was hardened from EMP.

His mind was racing a mile a minute when he got back into the truck. He headed off to the Armory once again, passing a crashed car here and there. He pulled into the Armory's parking lot and got out, walking towards the front door he'd locked himself not twelve hours previously. He stopped and looked around, and noticed the fresh footprints of a rabbit in the snow. And he did hear birds. How could that be?

He unlocked the front door to the Armory, and as he bounded the stairs, he recalled what he did know about neutron bombs, which wasn't much. They were supposed to replace regular H-bombs. Dropped on a city or area, they were supposed to release huge amounts of short-lived radiation, killing everything organic, like people and animals, but leaving the buildings and infrastructure unscathed. After about a week, when the radiation got down to an acceptable level, an Army could march in unopposed and occupy the area, without firing a single shot.

He quickly made his way to the orderly room and his office.

Opening the door, he went to a file cabinet, and opened the bottom drawer. He pulled out a yellow Geiger counter, with a small blue triangle stamped with "CD", for 'Civil Defense', also a holdover from the Cold War.

He checked to see if the batteries were good and turned it on, making sure the selector was on the correct setting. He breathed a sigh of relief when it showed only normal background radiation. He went to the window that faced east and opened the blinds, letting in the morning light. He checked it again, and saw just a slightly higher reading, most likely from the sunlight. Good. He was okay in that respect. He peered out the window. It looked like it was going to be a clear day, not a cloud in the sky. He noticed several black plumes of smoke, off in the distance. They were pretty big fires, by the looks of it.

They had to be crashed aircraft.

His skin crawled. Not one to be easily intimidated, he was truly frightened now. He sat for a few minutes at his desk, pondering his options. He thought of the bottle of Jameson's in his desk drawer, but decided against it. He'd need a clear and sober head. The power was on here, he noticed. The emergency generator must be running. The Armory was built back in 1972, and since it was slated as a Civil Defense center, had to have been hardened for EMP, so the generator would run as long as the fuel lasted.

He then went down to the basement, where the arms room and communications rooms were. He walked past the arms room for now, right to the communications section.

Most of the equipment was over in Afghanistan with the Brigade, but some of it still remained. He looked through the shelves of outdated radios and field telephones, and found what he was looking for— a digital secure satellite radio, and a hardened laptop computer. He put fresh batteries in both, and turned them on to test them. Both came on in an instant, letting him know they were in working order. Taking these, and several hand held radios as well, he carried them out, along with a large folded satellite antenna, and placed them in the bed of the truck, covering them with a green tarp.

Going back inside, he returned to the basement and the arms room. The door looked like a huge vault one would find in a bank, which was exactly what it was, made by the same company who made bank safes and vaults. The combination dial turned freely, and he quickly spun the right five digits. The tumblers fell into place and he turned the handle, swinging the door open with a light pull. Inside he saw what he'd expected, not much in the way of weapons, only a few spares and older rifles. He went to one rifle rack in the back of the large room, where there was a full twenty, older M16A1's from the 80's.

Why they'd kept them was beyond him, but all the same, he unlocked the rack from the key on his personal key ring and selected one. He relocked the rack, and went forward to another one, and did the same for a rack of M4 Carbines.

He took one of these also, and in heading out, grabbed about 30 empty thirty-round magazines, shutting and locking the vault door behind him. These he put into the cab of the truck, and pondered his next move. His mind was flying a mile a minute now. Should he just stay here at the Armory? No, that was no good. Even though there was power, it wouldn't last for long. Secondly, it'd be a target if it was an attack and an unknown enemy was on its way to occupy the City of Brotherly Love. He'd be better off back at his house, where he could at least hide out for a while.

Locking the front door to the Armory again, he headed back out to the truck, climbed in and headed back south. As he drove back down Roosevelt Blvd. he thought he'd better get some medical supplies. Pulling into Nazareth Hospital's emergency room ambulance bay, he left the truck running and cautiously entered the building. The power was out here, and he guessed that the hospital's emergency generator wasn't protected. When he forced open the dead automatic doors, he was hit with the sickly-sweet smell of death already permeating the building, even with the sub-freezing temperatures. There were several bodies lying about, patients, doctors and nurses. Trying his best to ignore them, he quickly retrieved several packages of antibiotics, pain medications, bandages and suture kits. Hopefully he'd not need any of it, but it never hurt to have it. Stepping over the bodies yet again, he headed back to the truck. Climbing back in the cab after stowing everything, he looked at the doors. He could see one scrubs-clad body lying prone. *They really ought to be buried,* he thought. But he couldn't bury them all, could he?

Then he thought of his brother and his nieces and nephews. He really needed to go over to the house and check on them. Maybe they were okay. He'd get the stuff home, and then he'd head over there. He'd have to scare up some 5.56mm ammo too. There was a gun shop a few blocks from his brother's house. After making his way back to Leon Street, he parked in his tiny driveway, and made short work of storing everything away.

He set the satellite radio up on a folding card table he'd taken from the Armory, and ran the long coaxial cable up the stairs, into the second floor bathroom. This was a full bathroom, with a skylight to the flat roof of the row home. He opened this easily and pulled himself up through the open window to the roof, pulling up the cable and antenna behind him. Setting up the one foot diameter "X" shaped antenna expertly on its folding metal tripod in the snow on the roof, he aimed it by guessing the proper angle with a handheld compass he always carried. Climbing back down through the skylight was trickier, and he almost fell on his head.

Heading back to the kitchen, he turned on the radio and let it do its self-diagnostics check, and when it was through, heard the satisfying beep of the inboard computer synchronizing itself with the orbiting military satellite's carrier signal. Good. He wouldn't have to climb through that damn skylight again to realign the antenna. Checking the date/frequency time stamp in the codebook he'd pocketed, he selected the proper channel on the radio. He then looked up the Brigade's call sign for that day, took the handset and put it to his head. Depressing the push to talk button and waiting a second, he said: "Whiskey six, this is Whiskey Two Six, over."

He released the button and waited. He got nothing but dead air. He should have gotten a reply. He tried again: "Whiskey Six, this is Whiskey Two Six, over."

He rechecked the time, date and scheduled radio frequency. Yep, all correct, but no answer. Unless…

No, that couldn't have happened. Not all over the goddamn world! Not *everywhere!*

Okay, that was the Brigade frequency. Now he'd try the company level. He spent an hour and a half going through every known radio frequency for the Brigade, even the day before, and the next day's listed frequency, and got nothing but dead air. At least he knew the DoD military communications satellite was up and running. Next he went back to his gear and retrieved his Army GPS unit. After the screen was lit, it also synchronized with the military geosynchronous satellites. They were built for the military in the first place.

Shutting down all his electronic gear, he went to the wood stove to make sure the fire was properly banked, and donned his jacket again. Picking up the M3, he took four of the loaded magazines, slamming one home into the machine gun's magazine well, and placed the sling over his shoulder. Heading to the truck, he quickly hopped in, started it and headed out. Even with the snow covering the streets the 4x4 made easy going, and it didn't take him long to reach his brother's house, off of Bustleton Avenue.

It was one PM when he pulled into his brother's driveway. He looked around and didn't see any movement or tracks in the snow, save for some rabbit and other animal tracks. He didn't hear any dogs barking either, nor did he see any cats. Looking at the front door he figured he'd have to break in here too.

Trying the knob anyway, he found it locked, so he took the M3 and, using it as a hammer, broke out the front door glass. It shattered loudly in the quiet, and he looked around sheepishly to see if anyone heard him.

Chiding himself for his silliness, he reached in and unlocked the door. It opened noiselessly, and he slowly made his way into the house. A chill ran up his spine when he found the house was as quiet as a morgue. He quickly searched the main floor, through the kitchen, living room, and den, and found nothing amiss. The house was cold from not having any power, and he could see his breath as he went to the bottom of the stairs.

He stopped. He really didn't want to go up there. He knew what he'd find. He steeled himself for a minute, and slowly took the stairs one at a time. When he reached the top, he looked left, saw the master bedroom's door ajar, and looked inside.

His heart fell when he saw the two forms of his brother and sister-in-law, lying next to each other as if they were still asleep. But he knew differently when he saw their faces in the dim light. The same redness, as if they had bad sunburn. And they definitely weren't breathing. He backed away from the bed, not realizing he'd gotten that close, and went back into the hall.

Next he went to what he found was the twins' room. Ten years old, both boys, they were in bunk beds, in the same condition as their parents. He shut the door and went to the other two bedrooms, and found the other two kids just as dead. His brother had started a family late, as the twins were fourteen and the other two were sixteen and seventeen. Seeing all he needed to see, he went back down stars to the kitchen to figure out what to do. Tim had been raised Catholic, but had given up on Catholicism years ago. His brother and family were still practicing, and very religious.

He really ought to give them a proper burial, but with the weather and temperatures, the ground was frozen solid.

He looked into the refrigerator and spied a six pack of Miller and grabbed it, heading back out to the truck. He leaned on the front fender, cracked open a can of beer, and lit a cigarette.

He remembered a conversation he'd had with Sean many years ago on a hunting trip up to Potter County. They were sitting around a campfire in the sub-zero weather, drinking beer and swapping cop stories, when his brother said; "You know what, Timmy? I want a Viking funeral when I die." Tim smiled when he thought of that time. With that thought, he backed the truck out into the street and went back to the house carrying a five gallon jerry can of diesel fuel. He went through the front door again and stood in the middle of the living room. Uncapping the can, he poured the contents all over the furniture and floor, making a big loop in the room, until the can was empty. He recapped it and placed it by the front door.

Taking out another book of matches, he lit one and placed it on the fuel soaked couch. Diesel wouldn't flash like gasoline, but it'd burn just as well, with the velour sofa acting as a giant wick.

The couch caught quickly, and he rapidly walked to the door, picking up the jerry can on the way. He walked down the driveway to the truck, lit another cigarette, and opened another beer.

He toasted his brother and family, holding the can of beer up in salute. It took twenty-five minutes for the house to be fully engulfed. He stood for over two hours watching the house burn, windows breaking with a loud pop one by one. He could feel the heat from the fire, even though he was thirty yards away. All the snow melted around the house for a good six or seven yards, and the perfect green lawn his brother had taken so much pride in, was exposed. He half expected the Philadelphia Fire Department to come screaming up in their gleaming American Le France fire trucks and extinguish the blaze, but they never came.

It was after five PM, and the sun was low on the western horizon when through teary eyes, he saw the last roof timbers fall into the blaze, leaving only the brick fireplace and chimney standing. He finished off the last beer and slowly got back into the truck, wiped his eyes, and drove back down the empty street. It was like he was in the middle of a nightmare, and he was hoping that he'd somehow wake up. But no, this wasn't a dream, and he really did just burn down his older brother's house with six bodies inside.

Well, that sucked, he thought as he drove to the gun shop. He hated leaving like that, but what else could he do? He was still alive, and he wanted to keep it that way. Looking back, setting the house on fire wasn't the smartest thing he'd ever done, what if someone had seen it? There were still plenty of fires around, but they looked like they were burning themselves out. He pulled up to Jay's Gun Emporium, got out and walked to the front door. A large metal cage was drawn down in front of the window and door. He'd have to breach that barrier before getting the ammo he'd need.

He backed the truck up so the rear bumper was in line with the door then retrieved a thick nylon web tow strap from the bed of the truck. Hooking one end to the cage and door and the other to the pintle hook, he got back into the cab and put the transfer case to 4WD low. He gunned the engine, and the cage held. He gave the engine more fuel, and the cage and front door ripped out of the anchors like they were made of paste.

"Very subtle," Tim said aloud with a giggle.

He hopped back out, unhooked the tow strap, and entered the darkened store. He looked around briefly and saw that all the gun racks were empty. He figured they probably had put everything into a safe in the back somewhere. He went over to a counter where the ammunition was conveniently stacked by caliber. Civilian .223 caliber was the same as 5.56mm military ammo, and he found several cases of it stacked on one end of the counter. He grabbed all the ammo that was there in that caliber and carried it to the bed of the truck, finishing well after dark.

Taking one last look around, he spied a stack of 9mm Parabellum ammo and grabbed two boxes. Might as well get some rounds for the Luger. He hopped back into the truck, and headed back to his house.

On the drive back, he went over what he currently knew. All the power was out for the entire area, that much was obvious. Everyone, apparently except himself, had died overnight, and by the conditions of the bodies he'd seen, almost instantly. Civilian electronics were fried, but not the military ones, and it was the same for the satellites. There were no dogs or cats either, but rabbits and other small animals were still around. He'd not seen any yet, but he saw plenty of fresh tracks in the snow. Maybe whatever happened had killed all the large animals? Was it a zombie apocalypse? He laughed aloud at that thought. He sure hadn't seen any zombies.

Whatever it was, whatever had happened, it had killed off almost four and a half million people in the city of Philadelphia in the blink of an eye. It was all too much for him to fathom right now. He wasn't a stupid man by any means, but this was beyond him. He pulled into his driveway and quickly unloaded all his ammo into the house.

After unloading, he went back to the truck to secure it for the night, and to top off the generator's fuel. When he was done, he took a moment and looked up at the night sky.

The sight took his breath away. Never before had he seen so many stars. On this moonless night, you could almost read a newspaper by the starlight. He could even see his faint shadow in the snow. He'd never seen a sky so clear. Even in the jungles of Central America or the deserts of the Middle East, far from any manmade city lights, he'd not seen this sight. He looked east and easily found Orion, the Sky Hunter, and one star near the constellation shone brighter than any star he'd ever seen. It was brighter than any of the planets he'd seen. Tim was an expert in land navigation, especially at night, and he'd never seen this particular star before. Maybe it was a key to what had happened.

He entered the house and climbed the stairs wearily. Welcomed by the warmth of the wood stove, he walked over to it, took his jacket and shirt off and laid them on his bed. He tossed another log into the stove and returned to the kitchen to make something for supper. He decided on some chicken noodle soup and a grilled cheese sandwich. It was a good night for it.

He'd have to go back to the grocery store tomorrow and stock up for a longer period, but tonight he was just going to stay at home. He lit some lanterns, then opened a can of soup and put it in a small pot on the camp stove to heat.

He let his mind go blank until after he was finished eating and had everything cleaned up. He took a canteen cup, poured a liberal amount of vodka into it, and went to the refrigerator for orange juice. He tipped the bottle of OJ into the cup for a second, giving the four fingers of vodka an orange tint. After he replaced the bottle, he lit a cigarette, and went to his cot in the living room, extinguishing the lantern in the kitchen as he left.

Sitting down on the cot, he took a big pull from the cup and sat it on the floor. He bent down and unlaced his boots, placing them neatly under his cot. He decided to shave in the morning. He was too tired to do anything more than finish his drink and fall asleep. Opening the stove door again, he tossed the finished cigarette into the coals, and added another log to the fire. He turned down the blankets, took his .45 and placed it under his pillow, downed the last of the vodka, and placed the M3 on the floor by his head.

He was asleep in an instant, but the sleep wasn't an easy one. The dreams came next, and they were unusually vivid. Someone asked him once if he'd believed in ghosts, and he had replied that he saw armies of them every night. The person who asked him didn't get it, and never would. But now, once again, the phantom army marched into his dreams...

He was on the tarmac of Port Salinas airport, lying prone with the butt of a M60 machine gun firmly tucked into his shoulder. A Cuban soldier jumped up right in front of him, and he let go a burst, hitting him at waist level, effectively cutting the man in half. As the body fell, the eyes bore into him...

The next was Johnny, still in his jungle fatigues, holding an AK74. He had a huge, bloody hole in his stomach, intestines spilling out from the wound. He loomed out of a steamy jungle somewhere in Guatemala and looked right at Tim with dead eyes...

The mist cleared and he was on Lehigh Avenue. It was a rainy night, and he looked right at the small black child lying in a filthy gutter with a single bullet wound to his chest. The child gripped his hand, and plead with his eyes, "Save Me!" as the life left him, the siren of the Fire & Rescue rig growing louder but already too late...

Then he was in the deserts of Saudi Arabia, going through the wreckage of a gymnasium, finding bodies of the Pennsylvania National Guards men and women, who'd been caught in their sleep by a falling Iraqi Scud missile. They all seemed to be looking right at him with the same hollow, dead eyes...

All seemed to be accusing him of something...

They were accusing him of cheating death.

They were silently asking 'why, oh why are we dead, and you are still alive? What makes you so special? What gave you the right to live?"

Tim woke with a startled shriek, bathed in sweat in the pre-dawn light. He looked at the luminous dial of his watch and saw it was barely five AM. With a shaking hand, he fumbled for his cigarettes and lit one, scratching his face. He stood and walked to the kitchen and put the coffee pot on.

He used the toilet and flushed with a gallon jug of water, tossing the finished butt in the bowl. Back out in the living room, he pulled back the Army blanket he'd tacked up, looked out the front window. No footprints in the snow. He was still trying to make sense of it all, but so far had had no luck.

The coffee was just about ready. Tim poured himself a cup, lit another smoke, and decided on eggs and bacon for breakfast. Maybe some food would get his mind working.

After breakfast, and what would become his normal morning routine, he dressed and sat down on his cot to strip and clean the M4. When that was finished to his satisfaction, he did the same with the M16. Then he loaded each of the thirty round magazines with 5.56mm ammo. . He left the M16 leaning against the faux stone mantel next to the wood stove, but locked and loaded a magazine into the M4. He grabbed his jacket, picked up the M3 and M4 slinging them both over his shoulder, and headed out.

Tim jumped into the cab of the truck and fired it up, smoking another cigarette while he let it warm up for a bit. It was still well below freezing, and even though it looked like it was going to be another clear day, there were no signs of it warming up. He thought of a line in a song from his youth: *'Don't want to spend another fall in Philadelphia'*. Well, that's what he was doing, like it or not.

When the truck warmed up, he put it in gear and drove off with no clear idea of what he'd do. He did need to stock up on more food, but he decided to just do a little exploring. Go out for a little recon, so to speak. For hours he drove around the city, making it all the way to the Old City section, where Independence Hall and the Liberty Bell were located. The further he drove, the creepier he felt. The day old snow that blanketed the city gave no signs of anyone else stirring. There *had* to be other people alive, damn it! Each building he passed seemed to gaze back at him with the same dead eyes as the phantom army in his dreams.

He broke into a hardware store the same way he'd broken into the gun shop and got some hand tools and a garden hose. He then stopped next to the Streets Department garbage truck after he had looked down at his fuel gauge and noticed he was almost empty. Using a section of the hose he skillfully siphoned diesel out of the truck and into his. When the tank was filled, he refilled the other two jerry cans. He took a circuitous route back to his neighborhood, still not seeing any signs of life.

He pulled right up to the fire lane in front of the Pathmark store by his house, and went up to the automatic doors. He knew they would be unlocked because the store was open 24 hours, but he had to force them open on their tracks.

Thankfully there were few bodies in view. The checkout girl who had served him the other day was nowhere to be seen, but a skinny teenager was in her place, slumped over the register. He gave a wide berth to the body, and quickly filled two shopping carts with all the canned foods he could, along with powdered milk, coffee and more eggs. He loaded these into the truck and headed back in to the meat department where he loaded up on as much pork, beef, packaged bacon and frozen fish that he could. His freezer wasn't all that big, but if the temperature stayed below freezing, he could use his garage as one big freezer for the time being.

Once he arrived back home, he unloaded his 'take' for the day. After he had everything put away in a neat and orderly military fashion, he set about fixing the broken panes of glass in both doors and changing the locks. Now he was really secure. He felt drained, and really didn't feel like doing much else. He poured himself a stiff vodka like he'd had the night before, lit a smoke, and thought about his day's exploration.

There had been absolutely no signs of life. But the weather was bad, and if anyone else was still alive, he supposed they'd be holed up in their homes. There were still some things he needed to get, like a barbeque grill, several propane bottles, and more gasoline for the generator. That would wait until tomorrow. It had been a long day. He'd gotten enough food for a few months he reckoned, and plenty of ammo. He was beginning to think in the long term now. What would happen after winter? Right now, every house and building was a deep freezer, as good as the ones at the city morgue, but what would happen next summer? Just the thought of millions of putrefying bodies gave him the chills. It would really start to smell. He looked at the wall of the living room, and thought of his neighbor Phil and his wife, lying on the other side of the wall, deader than dog shit.

"Yeah," he said aloud to the empty room, "it's really going to stink to the high heavens come summer."

He'd have to go somewhere else. He wouldn't be able to stay here, that was for sure. For now, though, he'd just stay put, hole up for the winter. He just wished it wasn't so quiet. He already missed music. He'd used to listen to classical music to relax. Some Brahms or Beethoven would be really nice right now. Or hell, even a little AC/DC or Led Zeppelin!

He'd have to figure out some way to play CDs. Even Charlton Heston, who played in that movie from the 70's, *Omega Man*, where he was the sole survivor of some terrible biological war, had music to listen to to keep from going completely mad in his penthouse bunker. Well, at least he didn't have some zombie brethren, run by creepy Anthony Zerbe, trying to kill him.

With that thought, he took his drink and went to the window, half expecting some robe-clad army with a huge catapult massed in front, ready to lob fireballs at his house.

He pulled the blanket covering the window aside, and even though no mass of torch carrying freaks were there, what was outside startled him all the same. Five whitetail deer were ambling up his street nice as you please, and one stopped at his neighbor's house to nibble on the hydrangea bush. He watched them for over ten minutes until they made their way out of sight, up the street in the growing darkness.

He went back to his cot and sat down, looking into the fire through the wood stove's glass door. So the deer were unaffected... Pennypack Park was a block over to the north, and there was a huge deer herd living there. Sometimes they'd stray out of the park and get hit by a car on Frankford Avenue, but they basically kept to themselves, hidden from people. Now they were wandering around the neighborhood. He finished his drink and smoke, and fell onto the cot, immediately falling asleep.

After another night of dreams, he awoke around the same time the next morning. He got up, washed, and made himself some coffee. Taking that out to the living room where he'd set up the card table, he lit a smoke and said aloud: "It's not a card table, Sar' Major! It's a 'desk, command, wooden-folding, one each! Get the proper nomenclature correct, soldier, or I'll have to write you a bad fitness report!"

Even though he was Army through and through, he was still amused by the way the military described things. Earlier in his Army career, when he was still low enough in rank to have friends (Sergeant Majors didn't have any friends), they'd joke around about the horrid horn-rimmed glasses the Army had issued its soldiers whose eyesight wasn't perfect. "Repellent, chick, one each." He smiled at the thought but it quickly faded when he thought of his situation at present.

What to do today? Another exploratory drive around, maybe?

Yes, that sounded like a plan to him. After that decision was made, he finished his morning routine, got dressed, and left the house. Heading out into the lifeless city with no rhyme or reason, he drove around aimlessly, mostly looking for signs of other people. He thought about the deer last night, and realized that nature was coming back rapidly. More rapidly than he would have thought. He was driving down State Road, saw the sign for the Tacony-Palmyra Bridge, and decided to see what New Jersey looked like.

Halfway up the span, he noticed the bridge was raised for ship traffic on the Delaware River and he stopped the truck and got out. Walking over to the railing, he looked down at the water, where he saw what must have been the reason for the bridge raising. A medium sized cargo ship had slammed into the Pennsylvania side bridge footing, tearing a huge gash in its side. It was now blocking the whole channel, its deck awash where it sank in the shipping channel.

"So much for going to New Jersey," he said. He could have gone a bit further south and crossed over the newer Betsy Ross Bridge, but he decided to head home. After he got home, he sat in the truck for a while, looking at his front door, not sure of what to do next. It frustrated him that he didn't know what to do. He'd always been one to make quick decisions in the past. It was how he'd made the rank of Brigade Sergeant Major, and the one thing he couldn't stand was indecision.

He shut off the truck and stepped out, took his grease gun, and walked down the street towards Garvin's Pub. He really didn't have a plan at this moment, but he walked on anyway. He noticed the deer were really making a highway of the area, and he made a mental note; he'd run out of fresh meat before the end of winter. He got to the front door of the bar, grabbed the knob and pulled. It opened easily, letting him know that whatever happened the other night had happened from between the time he'd left and fell asleep, but before 2 AM, legal closing time for the bar. Mickey would still be here. With that thought in his head, he pulled open the door all the way, and entered the dark room.

Looking around, he didn't see much until his eyes grew accustomed to the dimness. He noticed a patron that must have come in after he'd left sitting propped up in a booth at the far end, his head slightly askew, but still clutching a half-full mug of flat beer. Tim wasn't sure he was losing his mind just yet, but nodded to the corpse in acknowledgment before going over to the bar and sitting in the same stool he'd used the other night. He noticed the fifty dollar bill he'd left was gone. He tossed the M3 unceremoniously onto the wood bar and said loudly, "Barkeep! I'll have a beer, and give another one of whatever my friend is having," motioning with his hand to the dead guy in the corner.

He sat for a moment or two staring at his reflection in the mirror behind the bar.

"Well I guess Mickey is in the shitter, or dead as shit. It's self-serve night guys!"

He got up off the stool and went behind the bar, where he saw Mickey lying on the floor in the doorway to the small kitchen.

"Don't get up, Mick. I know you're probably dead tired. I'll get it myself!" Grabbing a mug, he went to the tap, pouring himself a beer. At least that still worked. No power needed for a good old fashioned beer tap.

He placed the mug on the bar next to the machine gun and spied an ashtray hidden under the bar. He took it and put it next to his beer, and then grabbed a bottle of Jack Daniels from the glass shelf behind the bar. This too, he sat next to his beer, and walked back around to his barstool.

Sitting back down, he took a huge pull from the mug and wiped his mouth with the back of his hand. "So, what do you think the Phillies will do this year?" he asked the dead guy in the booth. "You think they'll get the pennant and go all the way to the series?"

The dead guy with the beer just looked back at him, with sunken, dead eyes.

"Yeah, I agree. Their bullpen isn't worth a fuck." He lit a cigarette. "Hey guys! The city repealed that smoking in bars ban as of three days ago! Smoke em' if you got em'!"

Tim poured a shot of Jack into the shot glass and downed it in one gulp. "Everybody has to believe in something. I believe I'll have another shot!" he said, pouring another, and downing that one just as quickly.

He leaned back into the padded back of the stool, looked up at the ceiling and took a long drag of his smoke. He stubbed it out and looked around. "Yeah, I know the things will kill me. I know I should quit. But fuck! It's the end of the world! We should celebrate!"

After he finished his beer, he went behind the bar to pour another one. He looked around at some of the photos behind the bar of times past, happier times. He was even in some of them, along with his wife Connie. He pulled down one and looked at it. It was a New Year's Eve party from a few years ago. He had on one of those silly bopper hats, with the bouncy antenna. He was holding a drink, and his arm was around Connie. He was smiling, but her gaze was looking to the side, to someone or something out of the frame.

Was she looking at Mr. Montana? he wondered, and crumpled the photo into a ball, tossing it aside. He grabbed a bag of Lay's potato chips, and walked back to his seat. He sat back down, munched his chips, sipped at his beer, and poured another shot of Jack.

"Hey, Mick, got any jokes? Here's one. Two blondes walk into a bar. You'd have thought one of them had seen it! Badda dum dum!"

Tim slammed his beer down on the bar, laughing uncontrollably for a minute. He'd not eaten anything at all that day, except for a light breakfast early in the morning, and the beer and liquor was hitting him hard. The bag of chips would do him no good at this point. He stood again uneasily, and taking his beer, he walked over to the dead guy in the booth.

"Mind if I sit down, buddy?" he asked. Sliding himself into the booth, he got a better look at the man. He was wearing a Tastykake bakery uniform, the name 'Chick' embroidered over the right pocket. He must have gotten off the late shift around 11 PM, and come in for a few cold ones before heading home, wherever that was. He didn't look familiar to Tim, but he'd been gone a while, and there were a lot of new people in the neighborhood.

"Are you new to the area? I haven't seen you around here before," Tim asked the dead man, pulling a chip from the small sack and popping it into his mouth. "Me? Oh, I just got back from Afghanistan. It's a fucked up place far away from here. It's been all over the news for the last ten years or so."

Taking a long pull of beer he pointed at the guy and said, "I've been there on six deployments, *six* of them. Not a goddamn scratch. Oh, I've been injured before. I got one in the groin in Grenada. What's Grenada you ask? It's a little island in the south Caribbean. Ah, forget about it. No one remembers that anyway. People tend to forget shit like that. I've been shot at a lot of times. Honduras, El Salvador, Guatemala, Panama, Iraq. Only the one Purple Heart though. I call it my Cuban Marksmanship Medal. He got one up on me, the fucker. But it's okay, I put a bullet in his left eye so he won't be shooting any more Army Rangers..." Tim trailed off, ate a few more chips and looked at his mug. "Yeah, buddy. I've been all over the world. Join the Army they said. Travel to exotic, faraway places. Meet new and exciting people, and kill them!

"Hey, you want another one? It's on the house!" he asked the dead man, pointing to him. Getting up, Tim crumpled the now empty potato chip bag, tossed it into the corner, and went back to refill his mug. He saw the dartboard with the bull's eye missing, saw the empty .45 casing still on the ground and chuckled, kicking it aside.

"Hey, Bud. You better be careful. The neighborhood isn't what it used to be, me and Mickey had two jokers in here the other night. Wanted to pick a fight with me, they did. I got rid of them. Scared them so bad they'll never come back in here. Right now they're lying dead as dog shit two blocks north of here at a Route 66 bus stop." Tim looked over at the body in the booth as he poured another beer into his mug. Walking back around the bar with the bottle of Jack Daniels, he sat back down in the booth opposite the dead man. "Nope, they aren't going anywhere. They missed that last bus home. And there's never going to be another one. Septa is now permanently out of the bus business. When it thaws in the spring they'll rot away, but first the scavengers will come out. Buzzards and rats, maggots, ants and blowflies will eat all the soft flesh. It's really not a pretty sight, or smell, really. Kind of like the way you're starting to smell my friend..."

Tim downed the beer and poured another shot of whiskey.

"Yeah, this whole town is going to be pretty ripe in a few months." He got up from the booth, walked back over to his stool and sat back down there.

"Yeppers, kiddies. It isn't going to be pretty. The rats and mice will have a field day munching on humanity. You probably won't be able to get within twenty miles because of the stench. The world ended two days ago, and the funny thing is, nobody except me in this whole godforsaken fucking city is here to see it. That's a goddamn hoot, I'm here to tell you!" he said to an empty room, save for the dead guy in the booth.

Pouring another shot of Jack, he downed it at once, then threw the empty shot glass at the bottles and mirror behind the bar. The glass shattered loudly, and cracks ran out from the hole like a huge spider web. He looked at his reflection in the shattered glass, and it gave him a funhouse appearance that made him laugh. Pushing himself back from the bar, the stool's feet made an awful screech. He picked up the M3, flipped open the ejection port cover/safety and cocked the weapon. Holding it mid-chest high, he aimed it at the mirror and all the hundreds of booze bottles lined up on the glass shelves. He pulled the trigger, and at once, the gun began to belch lead with a deafening rattle. A huge muzzle flash extended for about two feet in front of the gun as Tim hosed the barrel left and right.

The gun chugged out a staccato sound, shattering bottles left and right. The bolt slammed home on an empty magazine and Tim quickly and expertly changed magazines, slapping a fresh one home in the gun's well, cocking it and continuing to fire. This he did two more times until all but one bottle remained. Tim looked through a thick haze of cordite smoke, at the bottle precariously perched on a sliver of glass, that had once been a 90 year-old handmade glass and mahogany bar back. His shoulders went slack as all the stress of the last few days was drained from him. He let the weapon hang loose from his hand, and finally, as if it decided to finally give up the ghost, the bottle of unopened imported brandy tipped over and smashed to the floor behind the bar.

"Sorry about the mess, Mickey. Put it on my tab." Tim took a book of matches out of his pocket, and folding back the cover, lit the whole pack and with a flick of his wrist, tossed it behind the bar. Instantly the alcohol erupted in a fireball and a loud *whumph*. He left, not looking back, and staggered in the freezing cold all the way to his house, singing an old Vera Lynn song from World War II. By the time he reached his house, he could see the glow of the fire over the rooftops. He unlocked the door and entered the house on uneasy feet. He peeled off his jacket and top, and in a very un-military way, tossed them on the floor in the center of the room. Without even checking the wood stove, he fell back on the cot, falling into a deep sleep.

Tim's bad day was finally over.

***

Halfway around the world, in the Indian Ocean, and about a hundred nautical miles from the Horn of Africa, another military man was just getting a handle on a very bad day indeed.

A dirty and disheveled man headed to the squawk box on a stanchion and picked up the phone handset. "Yeah?"

A disembodied voice came through the other side on the line. "Mr. Johnson! I don't care what happened; we're still in the goddamned US Navy! Answer the call professionally!"

"Yes, Skipper. Engine room!"

"Good. This is the bridge. Are you about done down there? Can we make revolutions to get underway?"

"Aye sir, just finished. But only one turbine will work, so only one screw. I should be able to get the other three turbines on line in another day."

"Very well. Secure down there and get back topside. There are still a lot of bodies that need to go over the side."

Johnson winced. They really should give them all a proper burial at sea. They were sailors, damn it! They should be wrapped in canvas and weighted down, not just thrown overboard like garbage, where the sharks could get to them. The last batch had been messy, and the sharks were in a virtual feeding frenzy. The seas had turned red a few hours ago. At least now they could get underway and get the hell out of there.

The "Skipper" on the bridge was Lieutenant Commander Winthorpe Wright. He came from old New England money, fourth generation Navy, where his grandfather had distinguished himself at the Battle of Leyte Gulf during WWII, retiring as a Rear Admiral. Where the former was the top of his class at the US Naval Academy, Annapolis, Maryland, his progeny graduated dead last. The Weapons Officer on the Arleigh Burke class Aegis Destroyer *USS Hughes*, DDG-193, or "WEPS", he was now skipper for the mere fact that he was the highest ranking officer left in the Wardroom. He knew now for certain he'd never see Flag Rank. Seeing the small anti-piracy Task Force go to shit three days ago told him that much. It was just by sheer luck they'd missed being rammed by another US Navy ship, and seeing the other ships collide and sink one by one had shocked him to the core.

Besides him, he had Ensign Johnson from the engine room still alive, which was fortuitous, and two enlisted men still alive, to run his ship. They had been foundering on heavy seas for two days when, although hardened against EMP, the ship's electrical systems had been overloaded and they lost power.

Now he finally had his Command, and he didn't know how yet, or exactly what had happened, but he knew he was going to Take Charge and Make His Mark…if it was the last thing he did.

He sat back in the captain's chair on the bridge, his back to his new skipper, and smiled. If the young helmsman could have seen it, he'd have jumped overboard and taken his chances with the sharks.

"Come right to 060!" he barked, savoring the feeling of absolute power.

"Coming right to zero six zero, aye, sir!" the helmsman said smartly, and did as his commander wished.

No, not absolute power yet, he thought. *Not yet…*

And he grinned again.

CHAPTER 3: BOOZE, BOOKS AND BULLETS

Tim woke the next morning with the mother of all hangovers. He felt ashamed at his behavior the night before, or what he could remember of it. At that moment, he decided that he wasn't going to fool around anymore, and needed to get his proverbial shit all in one sack. No more getting blind drunk, having conversations with dead people, and certainly not burning places to the ground for no reason.

Throughout November and December, he started to really get to work. Tacking a large map of Philadelphia and the surrounding counties to the wall in the dining area of the house, he started marking off areas he'd already checked for signs of life. This he found in abundance, though no people as of yet. There were plenty of deer, rabbits and squirrels. And rats, lots of rats. Even though it was the middle of winter, he saw a lot of rats. Crows too, and buzzards were even now starting to come in from the suburbs and countryside. Pickings were good.

On his daily explorations, he'd gone to the police department's mounted unit's stables, but found no live horses. The bodies of the dead horses were already being devoured by predation and scavengers. It was a shame. Horses were one of nature's beauties. He did see a fox one day, and before he could really get a good look, it scampered back into the woods by Holme Avenue. His supply of fresh meat had run out a few weeks after The Event, as he started calling what had happened. He shot a nice sized doe from his front yard with the M16, keeping himself in protein for the rest of the winter.

On his daily excursions, he collected things he thought he'd need, not only for the winter, but for his planned exodus out of the city once the weather warmed. He knew for certain he'd have to leave, because even though the cold temperatures kept the decomposition down, everywhere he went now smelled of death. He could even smell Phil and his wife next door through the wall now, and it was starting to bother him. He'd made several more trips to the Armory, and had gotten an IVIS tablet, actually a hardened IBM laptop made for the military, on which he could not only write a daily log of his activities, but he could connect with the US Army's central computer network through the satellite radio. It also showed him the exact position on a GPS map where every vehicle in his Brigade was located, and showed any movement, which sadly, he noted, hadn't moved a hair since his first look.

It really was global, The Event. Inexplicably, he was alone.

Tim started to think like Robinson Crusoe. On every trip out, he felt like Crusoe heading out on his raft to the stricken ship, retrieving what he could to survive, only instead of a tropical island, he was in a sea of rotting corpses. He headed out every day and brought back a bounty of things: tools, food, more ammunition. He'd hit every gun shop in a forty mile radius of the city, and now had enough ammo to fight off a small army, although such an army, as he had feared invading the city, never materialized.

One day he drove by a branch of the Free Library, and stopped. He broke into it easily, and thankfully, since The Event had happened at night, found it free of bodies. He went from aisle to aisle with a little trolley cart, getting books he thought he might like to read. He took some great classics, along with some popular novels and how-to books, like general carpentry, plumbing, electrical, and one on growing a small vegetable garden. He was thankful for these, because at the end of January came the worst blizzard he'd ever seen. It snowed for three days and left a fresh blanket of snow near three feet deep all over the area, and he couldn't even get out of the house for three weeks.

Tim spent that time reading and making plans, scouring over maps to decide where to go when spring arrived. He decided against going north, too cold. In the end he decided on no place in particular, he'd just gather his things and head west, let the place pick him.

He also kept a calendar, marking off each day as it passed, and had a routine for every day. Monday through Friday was reserved for exploration and gathering. Saturday was "Range Day", where he'd fire five hundred or so rounds through all of his weapons at garbage cans he'd set up at the end of the block. Saturday night was Barbecue Night, when he'd get quietly drunk and cook whatever he'd shot or trapped. He was starting to like rabbit a lot, and since they were so abundant, he experimented with different ways to cook them.

He was, in fact, getting bored. He'd almost wished it was a zombie apocalypse, and maybe things would get a little exciting. But none of the bodies he saw were going anywhere. And honestly, really didn't need any more excitement in his life, he'd had more than his fair share of it earlier in life. On one of his exploration trips, he decided to play soldier, and used a whole city block as his own personal "Hogan's Alley". Going from one end of the block to the other, using parked cars for cover, he burned up over two hundred rounds of 5.56mm ammo, shooting out almost every window. When he reached the far end he was winded. He looked back at the destruction and shook his head.

"Well, Timmy boy, you're most definitely not going to see any people now— if there's even any left— if you continue to go around shooting up the place," he said aloud, deciding to leave the GI Joe shit at the door. No sense running around like a nut, shooting everything that moved, and plenty that didn't.

One Saturday evening in mid-February, while cooking a venison steak on the gas grill that he kept on his front porch, he looked up and surveyed his little kingdom. Despite the harsh winter, he really wasn't that bad off. He'd gotten almost everything he needed to survive, but he still lacked that one thing that was slowly draining him subconsciously. He really needed some human contact, someone to talk to. All of the years of insulating himself from people, shutting off his feelings, hadn't really done him any good. Sure, it made him a good cop and a good soldier, but it sure as shit destroyed his marriage. Maybe once he headed out in the spring he'd find someone to talk to, if only just for a few fleeting moments. He finished cooking his steak, went inside, ate and got drunk, then passed out before eight PM.

By the middle of March, the days were warmer, and beginning to stay lighter longer. He didn't expect any more snow, but several cold rains impacted his trips out and about. He'd worried about his mental stability a time or two, for he'd experience huge swings in his mood. One minute he'd be elated, floating on cloud nine, and the next minute he'd sink into a deep depression, weeping uncontrollably. He really had to keep himself busy. That's what Crusoe did to keep from going mad.

On one of his trips out, his one big dilemma was resolved. He'd been wondering what he was going to do when travelling. Would he use a tent, crash in abandoned houses he'd find along his journey? No, neither would do. He'd had enough of sleeping on the ground while in the Army, and the thought of going into silent homes and finding more bodies, was even less palatable. He located an RV dealership outside of Philadelphia, and had a good look around. Some were virtual palaces on wheels, and way out of his budget normally. Now, however, he didn't have to worry about haggling, and there was no annoying salesman following him around. He eventually decided on a small two-axle tow behind twenty-four footer. He'd briefly thought about a slide-in, but he'd need the bed of the M880 for extra gear. The camper was a nice one, mid-grade. It had a three burner range, a small oven, and a two way refrigerator, meaning it would run on electric or propane. There was also a toilet and shower and a queen sized bed in the back. Over the small dining area, with a table that would also fold down into a bed, was another berth. Best thing of all, it had plenty of cabinet space and hidden storage under the seats and beds. It also had a roof mounted heater/air conditioner he'd have to check out. He wasn't sure about the EMP doing any damage to it.

After pulling the Dodge around and backing it up to the camper, he was dismayed to find that the military pintle didn't match up with the civilian standard ball hitch on the camper. He'd have to fix that right away. He searched through the camping supplies section in the showroom until he found what he needed, a new receiver hitch for the truck, which he threw into the bed. He drove with a newfound determination to the Armory, spending the better part of the day and evening using the tools in the motor pool, drilling out the holes for the bolts in the truck's frame, attached and properly secured the trailer. By the time that was done it was well after dark, and he went outside the garage for a smoke.

The bright star he'd noticed the first week after The Event wasn't there anymore, or was too dim to see. He did look at the sky for a long time, amazed at the wonder of it. Every time he looked, he was awed at the magnitude and the sheer majesty of the night sky. He figured that no one else had seen a sight like this since before the Industrial Revolution. He went back inside, tidied up after himself, and shut down the generator he'd used to power the lights and tools.

After he got back to the warmth of the wood stove in his home, he washed up and made some supper. Several weeks before, he'd found that the IVIS tablet had a CD drive, and was elated that it actually played music CDs. He'd gathered hundreds of CDs one day at a music store on Frankford, and now he could eat and relax to the sounds of music again. Beethoven serenaded him as he enjoyed his meal of homemade rabbit stew in solitude. After washing the dishes and pots, he began another nightly ritual: cleaning every weapon he had, whether he'd fired it, or not.

Upon finishing, he went back into the kitchen and poured himself a strong vodka and orange juice. Back at the window in the living room, he pulled back the blanket covering it and looked out to see the deer were back. One looked right at him from his postage stamp-sized yard with a blank look. It seemed to almost be saying to him,

"What are you doing here? You're not supposed to be here! This is our place now!" The deer went back to grazing, and he let the blanket fall back into place, covering the window, walked over and sat down on his cot to finish his drink.

He sighed. The world's population had been somewhere near seven billion people. Math not being his strongest subject, he attempted the problem anyway. Even if 99.9% of the population died the night of The Event, there had to be at least a few million people left. Maybe he wasn't alone. The thought elated him for a moment, until he thought about the other side of it. If .01% were still alive, they'd be spread all over the world, in ones and twos. It'd be like finding a needle in a haystack.

His best bet to find other people would be a double edged sword. Most people would be in built up areas, the very places he really wanted to avoid. He'd just have to leave it to chance if he met up with other survivors. He wanted to avoid those places like the plague, not only because of the smell, but because of the diseases that would be rife there.

Right now, the world was one big petri dish, and who knew what kind of shit was brewing out there? He chuckled to himself at the thought. Wouldn't that be fucking great, eh? To survive all of this only to be knocked dead by some microscopic little bug?

He also knew that it wasn't just the cities and towns, but farms as well. He'd gone out into the western parts of Montgomery County, and found whole herds of dairy cattle lying dead in the fields.

It was definitely a Catch 22. The towns and cities were places he'd need to go to replenish his supplies, but were also places full of rotting bodies and disease. If he had to go through a town, he'd make his stay very brief indeed. On that thought, he finished his last cigarette of the day and drifted off to sleep.

All the eggs and bacon were long gone, and the next morning he settled for a bowl of stale corn flakes and powdered milk. After he finished his meal, he got dressed and looked at the condition of his uniforms. He was still wearing his Army clothes, and they were getting a little worn. He'd figured out a way of washing them by hand in the wash basin in the basement, then hang them to dry on a cord he'd strung in the living room in front of the wood stove. He'd have to sort out some clothes soon.

After he finished up in the house, he went out and fired up the truck, then drove straight to the RV dealership. He backed up to the camper he'd chosen the day before, and in one reverse move, had it hitched up to the new receiver. The camper was not sitting level. The back bumper on the truck was a good six inches higher than the level of the camper's tongue, leaving the camper leaning backwards, its rear bumper almost dragging the ground. Another hurdle to overcome. *Adapt and overcome.* He laughed, remembering the words told to him so many years ago in Ranger School at Ft. Benning, Georgia.

He went back into the showroom once again, and after a few minutes found what he was looking for— a lift kit for RVs. Shackle bolts and nylon bushings fit between the camper's axles and leaf springs, making it sit higher and ride level with 4x4 pickups and SUVs. These he tossed onto the passenger side seat in the cab, and headed back to the Armory's motor pool. After arriving and setting everything up, he jacked the trailer up with a large hydraulic jack meant to lift up armored vehicles, secured the trailer with its own leveling jacks, and proceeded to remove all the bolts. After installing the lift kit on one side, he moved over to the next and began taking those bolts off. He was lying on his back while doing this, and when he took the last bolt off, his hand slipped on the axle and the whole assembly crashed to the ground, missing his head by an inch. Tim jumped up and scampered away, a cold sweat breaking out on his brow.

That could have killed me!

He sat with his back to the motor pool's outer wall and looked at the axle and wheel hanging down, almost mocking him. *See?* it seemed to say. *I could kill you anytime I want, and there's not a goddamn thing you can do about it!* He lit a cigarette with shaking hands, and thought for a while. After the shakes stopped, he tossed the smoke, got up, brushed himself off, and went back to work. He finished in another hour, tidying up after he was done. Now, with the camper sitting level with the truck, he could breathe easier. He could take it places along with truck, because not only was it level, but it also had the added ground clearance. This had taken most of the day and he drove tiredly back home. On entering his house, he lit a fire in the stove and put on some music. He was hungry, but didn't feel much like eating. What to read tonight? He'd finished *The Great Gatsby* the other day.

He went through the stacks of books he'd gotten from the library. "How about some Hemingway? Way too depressing. Ah, here we go, Tom Clancy. I haven't read this in a while!" he said out loud and sat down with a drink he'd poured. He briefly thought he'd better stop talking to himself or he'd really go mad. He read until about ten PM when his eyes grew heavy. He put the book down, carefully marking his page with a $100 bill he'd found in the street a while back. He put out the lantern and drifted off to sleep.

The next day, while he was on one of his exploratory patrols, he stopped along the banks of the Delaware River in Bucks County near the town of New Hope. This was in the country, and the trees in a small park went all the way to the edge of the river. Just a few miles south was Washington State Park, where it was thought that George Washington had his men sail across the Delaware River to Trenton, New Jersey to catch the Hessians with their pants down. It really was a lovely area, and he decided to enjoy the early spring day. It was warm enough now in the daytime that he wouldn't need a jacket. He took the M4, a MRE and walked down to the riverbank where he sat under a tree and looked out over the water. He took a six pack of beer and tied it by a cord on one end to the truck's front bumper then tossed it into the river. It would chill nicely; the river was still running quite cold from all the snowmelt upriver. He watched a pair of ducks swim along the bank of the river, and ate his meal quietly.

It was a nice day, temperatures in the low 60's, and a few clouds to obscure the sunlight and vivid blue sky.

After digging a small hole with a folding tool, he buried his refuse and cigarette butts. He thought he saw movement to his left, and looked in that direction. About fifty yards away, he spotted a tall, thin figure with a bucket at the bank of the river retrieving water.

Another person! his mind shrieked.

"Hey!" he shouted, but the lone figure looked at him in fear, dropped his bucket, and ran away, back towards the town.

"No! Please! Don't run!" he shouted, and started off after the man, who was scrambling away, blindly running through bushes and briars in a panic, and even though Tim was out of shape, he was steadily gaining on him.

About two hundred yards away from the river, they broke out of a copse of trees onto a road. The man ran blindly up the road, right on the double yellow stripe painted down the center. Tim was gaining ground at every step, but his breathing was becoming labored. The man veered off to the shoulder of the road, and Tim decided he'd had enough running. He launched himself into the legs of the running man, tackling him as if he was sacking the quarterback making a pass. They fell in a heap, and the man kicked wildly at Tim trying to get away.

With what breath Tim had left after the long sprint, he screamed at the man, "Calm down! I'm not going to hurt you! I just want to talk!"

With that, the man deflated. It was like someone had unplugged his power cord. He lay back on the ground, panting and gasping for breath, fear still in his eyes. "You…you're not with them?"

"Them? I'm alone. You're the first person I've seen in months!"

"Oh thank God!" the man said, and Tim watched the relief sweep over him.

"I'm Tim, and you?" he asked, holding out his hand. The man took it after a brief moment. "Paul. I'm Paul Williams."

Tim cocked back his patrol cap and scratched at his growing beard. He'd given up shaving two months prior, and had let it grow out into what he called his "tactical beard", which would make any Special Forces trooper proud.

"Well, Paul, I'm sure glad to meet you! I thought I was the only one left."

"So did I…until *they* came along, that is."

"Who're 'they'?" Tim asked, lighting a cigarette, offering the man one also.

"Thanks. I gave it up several years ago, might as well start again," he said. After accepting the light offered, he coughed a few times and said, "There's three of them. They came into town about a month ago, and started breaking into every store on Main, shattering windows and smashing beer bottles. They took all of the good stuff away. They hang out in the town square at night, getting drunk and smashing things."

"They know you're here?"

"Oh yes. They chased me into the woods once, trying to kill me. They walk around town yelling for me, taunting me to come out. I've been hiding from them ever since."

"Three men you say? What do they want, I wonder? They've got everything they could ever imagine."

"I think they want to… they… want to do bad things to me. Keep on making lewd taunts when they get close enough that I can hear them."

"The world ends and there's still assholes," Tim said to no one in particular.

"Yes. Like you said, they have everything but still want more!"

"You should get yourself a gun, Paul."

"Gosh no, I'm afraid of guns!" he said, eyeing up Tim's M4 carbine slung over his shoulder.

"Don't you worry, I know what I'm doing."

"Are you in the Army?" Paul asked.

"The National Guard, and I am a cop in Philly. Well, *was* a cop. You're safe with me. Have you eaten?" he asked, standing up.

"No. Not today. I'm running low on food, and I've been too afraid to come out. I was just trying to get some fresh water when you saw me."

"Well, come with me. I've got some food in my truck. We'll get you fed, and figure out what we're going to do," Tim said, smiling and standing up.

They walked silently back to where Tim had parked his truck, his instincts from Ranger School kicking in. Now, instead of the carbine slung over his back casually, he held it in the safe-ready position of a patrolling soldier, eyes constantly scanning ahead for threats. When they reached the truck, Tim retrieved an MRE packet and tossed it to Paul. He tore open the pack, and while he ate greedily, Tim looked him over. He was about 5'6", and Tim towered over him at 6' 2". Paul was slight of build, with thick glasses. He was about thirty-five years old or so, bookish. He looked like he was probably a Mama's boy, and most definitely scared out of his mind.

"So, what do you do, Paul? Or should I ask, what *did* you do?"

"I was a professor at Princeton, Applied Physics. I lived here with my mother. She died that night."

Yep. Mama's boy, Tim thought. He seemed like an okay guy anyway. At least he could maybe learn a few things from him, have an intelligent conversation. Couldn't be all bad, he considered, mentally noting that Paul had been teaching at the same school at which Einstein had taught.

"What do you think happened?" he posed. It had been nagging at him for months, what exactly had happened, and the question just popped out.

"I'm almost positive it was a gamma ray burst," Paul said, brushing back a lock of greasy hair from his eyes. "A gamma ray burst from where? I thought it was a neutron bomb at first, but the radiation levels were normal when I checked a day later."

"A neutron bomb was a good guess, but they never made any. It was a star, a supernova, thousands of light years away. Did you see the bright star that was near Orion's belt for weeks afterwards? I think that was it."

"Yeah, I saw it, and thought that maybe that had something to do with it, but wasn't sure."

"I'm almost positive, that's what it was," Paul said assuredly, now discussing something that was comfortable to him. "But I can see what you mean about a neutron bomb."

Rays from outer space sounded like something from a B-movie from the sixties. "Why didn't it kill everything?"

"I think it might have been just a glancing blow. If it had been a direct hit, the Earth would be a smoking cinder right now," Paul said, and it sent chills down Tim's spine.

He went to the front of the truck and pulled on the cord strung out to the river. Out popped the six pack of beer he'd tossed into the cold water earlier.

"Want a beer?" he asked, popping the top on a cold can of Miller and smiling.

"Sure!" Paul took the offered can.

"There's nothing like a cold beer on a nice afternoon," Tim said, saluting his new friend with his own can.

After a long draught from the can, Paul asked, "So where have you been living?"

"At my house in Philly, got it pretty well stocked. I've just been out exploring, gathering things I'll need."

They talked for a few hours, drinking the beer, just small talk really. When they finished their last beer, Tim explained his plans for departing the city, and heading west. Paul agreed that that would be a good idea, as the bodies would really start decomposing in earnest soon. As the thought passed his lips, the slight breeze changed direction, and they could smell it already. Yes, they'd both have to leave the area soon.

"When did you plan on leaving?"

"In a few weeks, I've still got a few preparations to make. I figure about the middle of April or so. You're more than welcome to come along, in fact, I insist!"

A grin split Paul's face, showing off perfect teeth. "I'd love to go with you!"

"Good, it's settled. You can stay at my place until we go."

They got into the truck, and Paul directed him to where he'd been staying, a small "A" frame house off on a side street in the center of New Hope. Tim pulled up in front of the place, and Paul got out.

"Get what you need, and we'll head to my place."

"Right now?" Paul asked. He looked a little frightened.

"Yeah, now. Grab what you want and we'll head out."

"I… I really ought to say goodbye. My mother, she's buried out back…" He trailed off.

"Do you really want to do that? What about those guys you told me about?"

"They only really come out at night. I've been able to hide from them so far. One more night shouldn't hurt. Can you come back for me tomorrow?"

"I really don't think that's a good idea, Paul. If you want to stay the night, why don't I stay here with you?"

Paul shook his head. "No, I think I should be okay for one night. I just want a little privacy for a while, to say goodbye, and gather up some things. You go, and I'll see you tomorrow."

"I really don't like this. We really should stick together," Tim said, thinking he really needed to protect this guy. But if that's what he wanted, he couldn't force him, could he? And he had survived this long by himself. What was one more night?

"Well, I don't want to argue with you. If you really feel like you'll be okay for the night, I'll come back tomorrow. You sure you don't want a gun? I can give you mine."

"No, Tim. I'll be okay," he said. "I really have something to live for now! I'll hide really well tonight."

"I'll be back first thing in the morning," Tim said, and Paul waved, turned, and bounded into the house.

Tim shook his head, not liking it one little bit, but put the truck into gear and pulled away. He really should have insisted on staying with him, but he did respect the guy's desire for a little privacy. He drove back to Philadelphia, his mind in conflict. He really should just turn around and head back. But Paul had insisted, wouldn't take no for an answer, and so he continued on home.

Tim stopped at a camping store, got another folding cot and a nice sleeping bag for Paul. When he got to his house, he set the cot up opposite his near the wood stove, and lit a fire. It was still getting chilly at night, and the wood was almost gone. He could go and get more, but they'd be leaving in a few weeks, so it would be a wasted effort. Making supper, he scratched his face again. He was getting pretty shaggy. His hair was far too long for his liking, and the beard was starting to annoy him. After supper was eaten and the mess cleaned up, he stripped to the waist, washed and shaved. He felt almost human, but he'd have to do something with his hair.

With that thought in mind, he sat on his cot, took off his boots and dropped off to sleep thinking about his newfound friend, hoping he was alright. It was the first time since The Event that he'd fallen asleep without the help of John Barleycorn, and he drifted off to a dreamless slumber, the sounds of an approaching early thunderstorm echoing off empty buildings.

Tim awoke before the sun the next day, and almost felt giddy, like a child on Christmas morning. He got dressed hurriedly, eschewing breakfast. He'd make a late brunch for Paul and himself when they got back, he reckoned. Grabbing the M4, he went out to the truck and looked up at the sky. There was a steady drizzle of warm rain, and he heard the distant rumble of thunder, but didn't see any lightning. The streets were pooled with water, and he figured drainage was going to start being a problem soon without the Department of Streets cleaning the debris from the storm grates.

Leaving the city behind in the growing daylight, he meandered up River Road, along the Delaware River. The storm that had come through last night must have been a pretty good one, he thought. The river was up over its bank and was running fast, churning with brown mud. Quite a bit different than the serene blue flow of yesterday. He rounded one bend in the road and slammed on his brakes. A huge tree had been downed overnight by the storm, leaving it lying across the road, completely blocking his passage.

He turned the truck around, thinking about putting a chainsaw in the truck, for this very purpose. That'd be on the list of things to get, later on in the day. He had to backtrack all the way to Yardley and over through Buckingham to get back on River Road, and it took him far more time than he wanted to take.

It was almost ten AM when he pulled into New Hope, and the town being as small as it was, it was easy to remember where Paul's house was. A cold chill went down his spine when he pulled up and saw that the front door was hanging wide open and every pane of glass in the front of the house was shattered.

"Oh shit," he whispered.

M4 in hand, he was looking at the house when a mountain of a man came out holding a pump-action shotgun in one hand and a half empty bottle of Jack Daniel's in the other. They saw each other at the same time and the man dropped the bottle, saying something Tim didn't hear, bringing the shotgun to bear.

Tim dropped below sight, taking cover behind the truck bed as the man let off a blast, which went wide and hit the far side of the truck. Instincts taking over, Tim popped up from his side of the truck, flipping the safety on the carbine to three-round burst. Seeing the big man rack the slide of the gun, loading another round, Tim squeezed the trigger easily when the man's center of mass entered his sight picture. The carbine rattled off three rounds rapidly, and the *tat-tat-tat* of the 5.56mm rounds gave out a higher pitched bark than that of the louder shotgun.

All three rounds hit the big man right where Tim wanted them— center of his barrel chest. The guy's legs gave way and he fell backwards, dropping the shotgun. Tim rounded the truck in a flash, aiming the carbine at the still body on the ground. It had been an easy shot, only about ten yards or so. Kicking the shotgun away from the dead man's hand, he bounded the five steps up the front porch and took cover behind the doorjamb. Peering around the frame, he didn't see anyone, and he took a second to think about his next action. He peered slowly around the doorjamb into the house. He could see an empty living room, decorated in what looked like, early 20th Century American Matron. There was an explosion of handmade lace and fussy, uncomfortable furniture.

"Hey, Dwayne, what are you shooting at? You okay?" a voice called down from the upper floor.

No, Dwayne is not okay, Tim thought. *He's laying out in the front yard, with a ventilated chest.* The decision was made for him when he saw a pair of feet in grungy work boots start down the stairs. He brought his M4 up to the ready as the second man descended. When his knees were visible, Tim took aim and let out another three round burst, hitting the man twice in the legs. He tumbled face first down the rest of the stairs with a loud yell, dropping a handgun in the process.

Tim rushed in, pointing the carbine at the face down figure, who was screaming in pain. Kicking the gun away from where it lay on the floor near the second man's hand, Tim stepped over him, and bounded up the stairs two at a time, the muzzle of the M4 leading the way. On reaching the top landing, he caught movement on his right. A medium-sized man stood in the doorway to a bedroom with his trousers around his ankles, holding a large knife.

"Who the fuck are you?" the man demanded angrily.

"The Angel of Death," Tim replied in an ice-cold voice, and squeezed the trigger. The muzzle was so close to the man's face that the flash engulfed it, and the three-round burst hit, turning his head into a crimson mist of bone and brain matter that sprayed out behind him in a red fountain. The body fell backwards through the doorway and landed with a thump. He was dead before his body hit the ground, the big bowie knife rattling on the floor. Tim stepped over it, entered the room, and immediately wished he hadn't.

Paul had been stripped naked and tied face down on a bed. It looked like he'd been sodomized repeatedly. Burn marks from cigarettes were all over his back and buttocks. So much blood… he saw. The lower part of the bed was drenched in it. There were several empty liquor bottles lying around. They'd probably raped him with those too. His anger boiled over as he went to the head of the bed. A small groan erupted from the still form. *He's still alive!* his mind screamed.

"Paul, can you hear me? It's me, Tim." He came closer to the bed and sat on the edge of the mattress.

"I… I knew… you'd come… back for me…"

"Ah fuck, Paul! I'm so sorry!"

"It's okay now, Tim. You're here now."

Tim took out a pocket knife to cut away the cords that bound Paul to the bed.

"Paul, they're gone now. They won't hurt you anymore," he said, tears welling up in his eyes. He knew Paul wouldn't survive. There was too much blood lost. Sure, maybe if there had been a doctor, and a good hospital to get him to… but that wasn't going to happen, not now.

"We'll get you out of here. We'll go away together."

"Island…" Paul whispered.

"What was that, buddy, an island?"

"Go to an island, far away. Be safe…"

"Sure! That's it! We'll go to an island and be safe!" Tim said. He sat back down on the bed and pulled Paul up into his lap, brushing his shaggy hair out of his eyes. He'd seen the look before, his life was slipping away. Tim's frustration grew, as he knew there wasn't a thing he could do about it.

"I knew you'd come back for me…" Paul said quietly.

Tim saw that he'd bitten through his tongue at some point during his assault. "Those fucking animals…." He looked down at Paul and saw something in his eyes. Hope… but that was a lost cause, he knew.

"You're going to be okay, buddy."

"Do you promise?"

"Yeah, I promise."

"We'll go to an island?" Paul said, his eyes drifting away.

Tim followed his gaze to an old 1950's framed travel poster on the far wall. It was a travel advertisement for the South Pacific featuring snow-white beaches, and coconut palms. The water was an unbelievable shade of turquoise.

"You got it, Paul. We'll go to the island. I promise." Tim took Paul's hand and looked back down at him. Paul was smiling back at him. "I'd love to take you to that island, Paul. We'll leave today, in fact." Paul smiled, one more time, and Tim could see the last vestiges of life drain from him. With one last deep gasp, Paul died in his arms. Tim sobbed uncontrollably for a while. When he regained his composure, he closed Paul's lifeless eyes, gently laying the lifeless form back onto the bed.

Tim picked up his rifle, and headed back down stairs, where he found mutt number two still lying on the floor at the foot of the steps, bleeding all over a handmade Persian rug and whimpering like a baby. He stepped over him and looked down. His eyes were feral and pleading.

"Man! You gotta help me! It fucking hurts so bad, man! Please!"

"Help *you*? You've got to be fucking kidding," Tim said.

"Help meeeeeeee! My leg don't work, man!"

"You just killed my friend, what makes you think I would help you?"

"You gotta help me! I got rights!"

"Rights? You don't have any fucking rights!" Tim sneered.

"You're in the Army right? You have me as your prisoner, so you gotta help me! Geneva Convention and all that shit man! You gotta!"

"Tell you what, pal. I don't have to do anything," Tim said. He reached down and grabbed the scruff of the mutt's collar, dragging him unceremoniously out the door and down the porch steps, his bad leg bouncing with an accompanying shriek on every step. Tim dragged him over to the lifeless form of his former partner and dumped him, his face inches away from mutt number one.

"You gotta help me, man!" he yelled when he saw his friend's lifeless eyes staring back at him.

"I don't know if you've realized yet in your tiny little mind that there *is* no Geneva Convention, no Constitution, no due process and no Bill of Rights anymore."

"You gotta help me man! Please!" he moaned.

"What there is now is Tim's Law." He'd known pieces of shit like this all his life, they were nothing more than bullies.

Whether it was in a classroom, on a playground or more formally, like terrorists and brutal regimes, no matter what you called it, it was bullying. Subjugating the weak for gain, pleasure, or both. Tim held them in total contempt. The husband who beat his wife and kids after coming home drunk from the bar was no different than a dictator who held power over a nation by fear. They took what they wanted, and left in ruins everything they touched, even people.

"What the fuck is Tim's Law?"

Tim smiled broadly. "That's where I am judge, jury and executioner. It's pretty simple, really, and there are no lawyers to fuck it up."

"What the fuck is that supposed to mean?"

"It means I can do this," Tim said, matter-of-factly. He pulled out his .45 auto, thumbed off the safety, and pointed the muzzle right at the mutt's face.

The man held up his hands in defense and wailed, "Noooooooooo! You can't kill me! I got rights!"

"You know something? You're right, I'm not going to kill you!" And with that he lowered the muzzle down to the mutt's stomach and squeezed the trigger. The pistol barked once, and the mutt let out an *Ooof* and screamed in agony.

"Hurts, doesn't it?" Tim asked, squatting down to be closer to the mutt's face. "Yep, learned a long time ago stomach wounds are really painful. And it takes a long time to die. It's a very slow, agonizing death. I've heard stories about how during the Civil War, soldiers on both sides would lay awake at night, unable to sleep because of the sounds of the shrieks and moans of the gut shot soldiers lying in the battlefield. They'd last for days, writhing in pain." Tim stood up, still looking down at the piece of garbage at his feet.

Screaming now, clutching his stomach, the man screeched, "Help meeeeeeee! Oh God it fucking hurts!"

"In Vietnam, the Viet Cong would take a prisoner, a village chief or someone that they wanted to make an example of. They'd string them up in the center of the hamlet and slice them open from their groin, to their solar plexus, letting their intestines and other guts fall out. Then, while they were still alive, they would let the pigs eat the guts. Yeppers, pal. Not a real pretty way to go." Tim looked up, and saw a few turkey vultures circling. "Yeah…you ain't going to go quick."

"You gotta help me! Puleeeeeze!!!!!!"

Tim turned, and walked back in the house, ignoring the man's pleas. Now he'd have to do something with Paul. Going through the house and into the backyard, he spied where Paul must have buried his mother. A small mound with a homemade cross was near the back fence, under a large oak tree. It looked as if Paul had planted some flowers on the grave but they hadn't yet bloomed in the early spring weather. He went back out to his truck, ignoring the screaming man, and retrieved his entrenching tool. Going back through the house, he reentered the backyard and began to dig. He should have made the Mutt do it, he thought after a while. In an hour or so, he had a decent sized hole dug next to Paul's mother.

He went back into the house, back up to the bedroom where Paul's lifeless body lay, and wrapped him in the bloody sheets. Carrying the body over his shoulder, he made his way down and back into the backyard, where he laid the body as gently as he could into the shallow grave. He then took the entrenching tool and covered the body over the best he could. Standing upright, he thought that maybe he should say something, but not being religious, thought that that would have been a little hypocritical on his part, so he just said, "Sorry, buddy. I'm so fucking sorry. I hope you find your island."

Tim went around the front of the house, and when he walked by the still shrieking man, looked down to him again.

"You know the first thing buzzards eat? They dig out the eyes," he said flatly, devoid of all emotion. Walking around to the driver's side door, he opened it, changed magazines in the M4, and tossed it up on the dashboard. He could hear the mutt begging him not to leave him alone as he drove away. He looked up and saw that the clouds were building up to another storm, so he pushed the truck a little harder to get home before the rains started. He chain-smoked almost a whole pack of cigarettes on the drive home, going over in his mind what he should have done differently.

He came to the conclusion that there was nothing he could have done differently. He couldn't do a damn thing, and really there was no point going over it. It was the past. He couldn't change it; he'd just have to live with it. Another ghost had just joined his phantom Army. Why was that tree blocking his way, making him take the long way around? Why couldn't Paul have just come with him yesterday? No way he could have forced him, but he was really worried about those men. Well, they wouldn't be hurting anyone else, at least.

He got home and quickly ran to his door as the rain was starting. Huge drops that made a heavy plop on the pavement. He quickly shut the door and bolted it. Paranoia was starting to set in. What if there were more bands of assholes like that roaming around? He tossed the carbine on his cot and then looked over to the other cot that would never be used, and his heart sank. He wept some more, wishing he could somehow change the clock back twenty-four hours, and drag Paul back here by the scruff, kicking and screaming. But no, he couldn't do that.

He got up, poured himself a stiff drink, and sat at the table. He tossed his pack of Winston's on the table, along with a butane lighter. Thunder rolled like a walking artillery barrage, and the hail crashed loudly onto the roof while he drank and smoked. He knew he had to leave soon. Phil was getting a little ripe, and the smell was worsening through the thick firewall which separated their houses.

He looked around at what he had, which wasn't much. Booze, books and bullets. It was plenty enough to last a while. He'd raided almost every State store in the area for the booze, and every gun shop within forty miles for the ammo. He'd spend one last night in the house, pack up everything in the morning, and head to the Armory for the last few days. There, he could make some final preparations and head west at the end of the week. The entrance to the Pennsylvania Turnpike was only a few miles north of the Armory.

He thought about the three guys he had killed at Paul's place. Over his years on the police department he'd seen hundreds like them, mini-terrorists in their own right. They were quick to beat up children, women, and old people, just for the sheer joy of it, thinking the law was for other people, not them. They could do whatever they liked as long as it suited them. As soon as they were called out on it, they placed blame on everyone else but themselves, never willing to admit culpability. Then, at the first drop, they were just as quick to scream about their rights, and wanted help or protection.

The jitbag he'd drilled in the stomach had a little time to scream his goddamn head off for help, just like poor Paul probably did when those three were sodomizing him with broken bottles. He'd scream until he finally bled out internally, and then the buzzards, crows and rats would feed off of him. He could have gone back into the house, retrieved the asshole's pistol, unloaded it save for one round, and given it to him to let him take the easy way out. He'd decided against that. It was against Tim's Law. That was too easy. Let him suffer.

He didn't get any pleasure out of it, but some people just needed to suffer the way they'd made others suffer. There were far too few folks left to go on some avenging angel kick. He just wanted to find a place to lay low and live out the rest of his life quietly. Maybe meet a few other nice people, a woman maybe? He hadn't thought of that in a while. No, no need to think of that, but where to go? An island maybe? Like what Paul had wanted?

Tim remembered the poster in Paul's bedroom that looked like it had been his since he was a child. Paul was an actual professor of applied physics, and yet was living at home with his mother. He probably didn't have a mean bone in his body. The poster was probably a fantasy of his. In the short time they'd talked, he never said one word of it. Maybe he had lain awake at night, picturing himself lying on the beach surrounded by bikini-clad cuties feeding him drinks in coconut shells.

He chuckled at the thought, and raised his glass in a toast to Paul. The mini Irish wake was over, and he got down to some serious drinking as the thunderstorm raged. He cleaned and reloaded all of his weapons. He'd only used ten rounds in the lopsided firefight. Well, there was nothing fair in a gunfight, he remembered. Nine rounds from the M4, and one round from the .45. They had been armed, a shotgun, a handgun and a knife, three against one, one Army Ranger. Yep. As fair as fair could be.

"When it positively, absolutely has to be destroyed overnight!" he said aloud, making a joke with the 75th Ranger Regiment's unofficial motto, which was actually a pun on an old FedEx commercial from the 80's. He'd actually not served in the Rangers since the late 1980's, but he did go to Ranger School and had the coveted "Ranger" tab on his left shoulder to prove it. Once a Ranger, always a Ranger.

"I'm absolute badass," he said to the empty room. "Yes sir, it was a fair fight! Odds were three to one. We handed them their asses on a silver platter!"

After cleaning his weapons, Tim briefly thought about food, but wasn't hungry at all. He poured himself some vodka, went to the front window and looked out. It had stopped hailing, but the rain was still coming down in buckets and lightning was splitting the sky every few seconds. He'd never seen a storm this nasty. It had rolled in from the southwest, and he wondered if it was strong enough to spawn a tornado.

Philadelphia, being far from the Storm Belt, still wasn't immune to having tornadoes touch down in the area. In the flashes of blinding lightning, Tim saw that his street looked like a river, with the water rushing downhill from the south and making a quick dogleg to the right, headed east onto Solly Avenue.

He went back to his IVIS laptop and selected some fitting music for the evening's light show. Toccata and Fugue in D Minor… all he needed now was Bela Lugosi to pop in dressed as the Phantom of the Opera to play the organ. He laughed at the thought. He sat down on his cot, and was immediately overwhelmed by exhaustion. Finishing off his drink, he didn't even bother to take his boots off, just laid back and was asleep as soon as his head hit the pillow.

Then the dreams came again. And there was Paul, marching along with the rest of the ghastly phantom army, dead eyes silently accusing him…

CHAPTER 4:
CONFLAGRATION & EXODUS

Tim woke the next morning feeling like hell. The booze the night before hadn't washed the ghost army from his dreams, and he hadn't slept well at all. He was still deeply troubled by what had happened to Paul, and felt even worse knowing he couldn't have done anything differently to change the outcome. He just had to swallow it and live with the memories, like all the rest.

The storms from the previous night had passed through, and now the skies were clear. There was a lot of debris in the curbs though, probably a bunch more in other places. The grates over the storm drains were probably clogged solid. Tim put on the coffee and sat in his underwear at the folding table to ponder his next move. He'd already decided yesterday to head to the Armory. He needed to leave soon; the smell was getting pretty bad. He remembered one time as a rookie cop he'd received a "welfare check" call. It was late August, and the temperatures had been hovering around the 100 degree mark for over two weeks, with the humidity level around the same.

Apparently, some distant cousin or aunt or sister in Gofuckyerself, Arkansas, hadn't heard from good old Auntie Mabel in a while, and now she wasn't answering her phone. Could the nice police officers go over to her house and make sure she's alright?

Tim did as he was told, and when he pulled up in front of the house, even before he got out of his sector car he knew it was going to be bad. The windows in the front of the house were completely covered with blowflies— on the inside. His skin crawled as he walked up to the door and knocked, knowing full well there wasn't going to be an answer. He looked at the ground and saw the mail piled up at the front door. Good old government employees for you, never noticing the mail piling up, considering that something could be wrong, so just keep on doing your mediocre job and not say a word. He walked over to the window, and peering through a break in the flies, he could see the blackened, bloated body, lying prone on the floor in front of an easy chair. It had been there quite a while, and he could smell it now, even through the closed window.

When the fire department arrived, Tim was right next to the firefighter with the axe who finally got the door opened, and the smell hit them both. Even the veteran firefighter gagged, but Tim lost his lunch right there on the front steps. To this day Tim had never forgotten that smell. And it was the same smell starting to permeate the entire city coming though the very walls of his home. He needed to get out soon.

The thought was in his mind when as a single fly landed on his hand, and a chill went through his body. Yeah, the flies were going to be pretty bad this year too.

He took most of the morning going through his belongings and loading them out in the camper. When he had everything he thought he'd need, he took one final look around, knowing he'd never see this place again. Getting into the cab of the

M880, he drove away, northward to the Armory. He pulled into the motor pool area in the rear of the building and stopped when he was through the gates. He got out and padlocked the gate behind him. The chain-link fence was eight feet high, topped with razor wire. No shitheads like the ones who attacked Paul would get to him here. They could try, but he'd know it before they got in.

Running the power cable from the generator, he plugged in the camper and entered his new home. Everything was still secure, and on reflection, he actually would be more comfortable in the camper. He'd have a queen size bed to stretch out in, a shower and toilet, both with running water, as long as he remembered to keep the freshwater tank filled. He'd have to go over the Brigade's supplies again to see if there was a water purification device available.

He'd stay here for a few more days to double check everything, and head out at the end of the week. He was finding it harder and harder to keep track of the days of the week, and was really grateful for the IVIS computer tablet for helping him to do so, besides helping him keep a journal of everything. He powered that up and plugged it into the camper's built in speakers for a test. He put a CD of The Who in the tablet, hit 'play' and was rewarded by the sounds of Pete Townsend's guitar. He let it play while he took a shower in the tiny bathroom of the camper. The hot water felt good. He'd have to remember to be quick, as the camper's water heater was a small one, only five gallons.

Stepping out, he toweled off and got dressed in some new clothes he'd gotten from the local Walmart. He looked at his reflection in the mirror and smiled. He actually looked human. Wrangler blue jeans, new Redwing boots, a clean t-shirt and a brand new ball cap. He looked like a civilian puke.. He made some lunch for himself, and ate, wondering if he'd be able to somehow pipe the music into the cab of the truck. Tim hated driving without music.

He stepped out of the camper and had a look around. The sky was an unbelievable blue, not a cloud in sight. He looked at the horizon to the south, smudged with a black stain of smoke, coming from two separate fires it looked like. Grabbing his M3 (he had decided to not go anywhere without a firearm now), he walked over to the Armory's main building and went up to the roof. At three stories high, it was the tallest building in the area, and the rooftop gave him a good look around for several miles. He could see Center City's skyline way off to the south, and two growing smoke plumes to the southwest. Not much else could be seen from the rooftop, but at least he couldn't smell the decaying flesh of all the bodies. The Armory was in an industrial area of Northeast Philadelphia, and not many homes were nearby.

He made his way back down to the camper and stretched out on the bed, drifting off to sleep at the sounds of The Who singing about a magic bus. When he woke, it was late afternoon. He stepped outside, and noticed the smoke clouds getting bigger. Grabbing two six packs of beer, his smokes, and a folding camp chair, Tim made his way back to the roof. *Might as well enjoy the show*, he thought, and set his chair up near the south parapet of the roof. He lit a smoke, and cracked open a beer and leaned back.

The smoke was thicker and heading higher into the sky. It almost looked as if the two fires had formed into one. He thought about the thunderstorm the previous night, and figured the fire was likely touched off by a lightning strike. Had it happened before The Event, the Philadelphia Fire Department would have been on scene and would have had both fires under control by morning, but there were no fire alarms to sound, and no firefighters to respond. A few more buildings would burn to the ground tonight in the City of Brotherly Love.

Tim smoked his cigarettes and drank his beer, watching the sun dip below the horizon. The weather was quite warm now for a late March evening, probably in the high 70's. A slight breeze picked up from the north. It seemed the fires were burning longer, no sign of them burning out. He could see actual flames in the smoke now, and the large smoke cloud looked like a huge mushroom, flattening out on the top at over twenty-five thousand feet. This was going to be a big one. Bigger than the Arco Refinery fire that had happened when he was still a child. He could see that from his house, he remembered.

Tim was correct that it would be a big fire, but he had no idea how big it would become. He was also correct about the lightning touching off the blaze. The old row homes, many built well over a hundred years before, were like kindling. The two lightning strikes, only about a mile apart from each other, touched off exposed roof beams, where each smoldered for hours before flames licked out from them. The flames spread, igniting the lathing in the ceilings, which in turn spread out over the oil-based tar roofs. From house to house, the fires spread, getting hotter, and they danced across the rooftops to the trees lining the streets, which burst into flame, and then the cars parked along the curbs, igniting their fuel tanks.

The fires spread larger, and as the cars burnt along the sides of the road, the very streets, which had stood as firebreaks in earlier times, caught fire. They had originally been paved with concrete, but now were paved over with cheaper asphalt which, being oil based, were very flammable. The flames spread across city blocks, igniting more cars, which in turn ignited more houses, and the fire grew even larger. All the while, the flames grew higher and higher. The gentle breeze that Tim felt on his back was actually the beginnings of what would become gale-force winds. These winds would feed the raging inferno, encompassing the entire city of Philadelphia. In the next forty-eight hours, it would become a firestorm, rivaling the one that had consumed Dresden in WWII, if not for its death toll, (because there was no one left to kill), for its sheer size.

By ten PM, Tim had a pretty good buzz happening up on the roof, with a good show to entertain him. The fire was indeed growing, and he could see sparks and flames several thousand feet up in the smoke, which was getting its own weather, it looked like. Several bolts of lightning spread forth throughout the clouds of smoke, caused by the sheer volume of ash in the smoke rubbing together and creating static electricity. Volcanoes did the same thing, he remembered. Tim finished his last beer, gathered his belongings, and carried them down the stairs and over to the camper. Stowing away the chair, he stripped to the waist, crawled into bed, and fell asleep. Outside, the wind was gathering speed, whistling though the razor wire.

When Tim awoke the next morning, the first thing he noticed was the rocking of the camper. The wind had picked up overnight, and was tossing the little trailer around like it was an empty beer can. The second thing he noticed was how dark it was. Stepping out of the camper, he looked up at a completely black sky, the sun utterly blacked out from the smoke. Lightning flashed in the smoke, and he could actually *hear* the fire now.

Rushing back onto the roof, he stood in fear and awe when he saw the fire was vast. It seemed like it was right at the bank of the Delaware River in the east, all the way to the Schuylkill River in the west, and was marching steadily northward, right towards him. The leaves of the trees in Pennypack Park had yet to sprout, and the fire looked like it was nearing the southern edge of the tree line. From his vantage point on the roof, it looked like the very gates of Hell marching steadily towards him. If he didn't leave soon, the fire would surely engulf the city, even here in the industrial section.

He scrambled down the stairs, ran to the camper, and unhooked the power cable, shut down the generator and tossed it unceremoniously into the bed of the truck. He made sure he had enough diesel fuel in the Jerry cans, unlocked the gate, and drove his rig out onto the street. He didn't look back again until he was at the entrance to the Pennsylvania Turnpike where, for the first time in his life, he drove right through the gate, not stopping to take a ticket.

The wind was fierce, and it took all of his driving skills to keep him and the camper, upright and on the road. He did have to weave around crashed vehicles from time to time, but they were growing fewer, as he headed west, and the wind subsided a little more with each mile he traveled. A few miles west, the sky cleared as the prevailing winds blew the huge smoke cloud east, but he could still see it in the rearview mirror. The winds finally subsided about ten miles west. He was frustrated that it couldn't have waited another few days, but he knew he'd had to leave anyway, and even though it looked as if the fires started somewhere in North Philadelphia, it most assuredly had consumed his Mayfair neighborhood by now.

By the time he passed the King of Prussia interchange, the road had completely cleared of all crashed or stalled vehicles, and he put his foot down to gain some speed. From time to time, he would see gatherings of buzzards over dairy farms, but no signs of people. It took him several hours to drive the hundred or so miles to the bridge that spanned the Susquehanna River before the exit for Harrisburg. He stopped for a piss break on the shoulder of the road by the edge of the bridge and looked eastward. He could see the huge plume of thick, black smoke, flames dancing through it even from here. The mushroom cloud gave him chills, and he thought of his fears during the Cold War, which he'd actually missed. He mused aloud once to a group of soldiers who had been born after it had ended and had no idea what it was, that at least during the Cold War you knew who the enemy was.

Wasn't that the truth, he thought now as he sped along the Turnpike at greater than the posted speed limit. Then, you knew who the enemy was. Who was it now? It could be anyone. The three he'd killed the other day were Americans just like him, but far different than him, on so many levels. Sometimes, you had to destroy in order to rebuild.

Why did I just think of that? he asked himself silently. Well, it was the way of nature. *Just look at what's happening behind you. The fire is going to erase everything from your hometown, and in time, nature will cover it up, so that in a hundred years or so no one will even be able to tell it was ever there.*

Hell, nature was coming back pretty good, he supposed. Even though it was early spring, every expansion joint and crack in the pavement in the road he was driving on was already sprouting with weeds. He could feel the thump of the tires on them. In about ten years, he reckoned, the road itself would be covered with weeds and grass. Even faster down south, where the kudzu grew like wildfire. Every crack in every sidewalk, every loose chunk of mortar between bricks, would fill with water, freeze and thaw, expanding. And with the widening of these fissures, weeds, then plants, and roots of trees, would take hold. Vines would scale buildings.

Yeah, Tim thought, the breeze from the open window ruffling his growing hair, *Nature will take over soon. Clean up the mess we made, and move on.*

He wondered what the world would look like in a hundred years. He thought of this along with his choices of roads to take. He could take Interstates 81 or 83 headed south, or keep on I-76 west. He decided to stay on the turnpike, or I-76, because he reckoned it would be the most free of heavy trucks, and therefore no pileups or wrecks to block his passage, at least to the Ohio border. The semi-trucks that travelled the nation's interstate highways would stay clear of a toll road like the Pennsylvania Turnpike and stick with the freeways, like I-40 to the south, and I-80 to the north.

About twenty miles west of Harrisburg, he came to several tunnels cut through the Appalachian Mountains, the first being Blue Mountain tunnel, followed by Kittatinny Tunnel. He turned on his headlights, slowing almost to a crawl to drive through these, because without power, there would be no lights, and he didn't want to drive up on a huge pileup of wrecked cars at seventy miles an hour. He relaxed a little as he went through each tunnel and saw daylight at the other end. He made it all the way to Bedford, Pennsylvania before he came upon a huge pileup at the interchange, blocking any westward travel from that point.

He checked his watch, then his road atlas, and decided to take US Rt. 220 south. He'd have enough daylight left to make it to Cumberland, Maryland, where he'd stop for the night, and decide where to head from there. At least, he was far enough westward now that he couldn't see the smoke plume from Philadelphia. The thought saddened him, that there was so much history there. It really had been a great place to grow up. The thought of it all gone now made his heart sink. He had wanted to go to the cemetery, to say his farewells to his mother and father, but never got the chance. The fire had stopped him from doing that, and he understood Paul a little bit more at that moment.

He stopped for the night at an empty rest stop, and in the morning after coffee and a shower, he headed south again on US 220, crossing into West Virginia at a little town called Keyser. There he stopped, and topped off his diesel fuel by siphoning out the tanks of a stalled Peterbuilt. His tank and Jerry cans again full, he decided to take US Rt. 50 west from there. Twenty miles or so west of Keyser, he passed into Maryland for a few miles, and then back into West Virginia. The roads were smaller than the interstates, but thankfully they were free of any major blockages. At one point, right before Grafton, he'd had to find a way around a huge dump truck lying on its side, its load of coal spilled across all the lanes of travel.

He really needed to get back on an Interstate, and by looking at his map he saw that he could pick up I-79 a few more miles away in Bridgeport. With a few small detours made around stalled vehicles he made it to Bridgeport around noon. Driving past the cars and trucks, he made special effort not to look at what was behind the wheels. He didn't need to see that, not now.

He stopped on the middle of a bridge, right before the green and white signs telling him to keep left for I-79 south, keep right for I-79 north. He took a can of potted meat and a package of stale crackers, and sat on the hood, eating in silence, mentally tossing a coin to decide with way to head. When he finished eating, he looked past the sign for the highway and saw a church with an overgrown lawn. Someone had spray painted *Where is your god now?'* in blood red paint on the front door.

Absolutely, he thought, *some God*. He gathered his garbage, tossed it into the bed of the truck, then he hopped in the cab and headed for the southbound on-ramp without looking back. While he drove, he thought about God, or the lack of one. If God was so forgiving and loving, why the fuck did He kill everyone? Oh, that's right, he'd done that before with the great flood. *Worship me or I'll kill you all. Seems legit*. He continued south, taking in the landscape. He'd never been through West Virginia before, and was sorry that he'd missed the chance before now. It was really quite beautiful.

By late afternoon he'd reached Sutton, and decided to stop for the night. It was still daylight, but it would be dark in less than an hour. Finding a truck stop off of the highway, he pulled around to the rear so as not to be seen from the highway. Setting up camp on the far end of the parking lot near some trees, he took the M3 grease gun and decided to do a little exploring. There was a small diner attached to the fueling center, and also a convenience store. He searched both, and found them picked clean of supplies. That left him with mixed emotions. Should he seek out whoever had cleaned the place out, or avoid them?

He really did desire to find other people, but what if they were like the three who'd done Paul in? Firepower or not, there was only one of him, and if they were like that, chances are they'd get the better of him. What had happened in New Hope was actually a fluke. He'd surprised them, and had the upper hand. No, he didn't like the law of averages, and made his way as stealthily as he could back to the camper. When he got to it, he looked at how obvious it was. The M880 was painted camouflage, but the camper was a bright, glossy white that stuck out like a neon sign. He'd have to do something about that.

Entering the camper, he shut the blinds to hide the light, and made himself a supper of canned chili and beans. After dinner he cleaned up, and with the .45 automatic and M3 by his side, he extinguished the lights and stretched out on the bed. Sleep, didn't come easy that night.

Thoughts of roving bands of assholes and thugs kept interfering. Try as he may, he couldn't get to sleep and the frustration built. His subconscious had him worked up into a pretty good lather by 2AM, when he sat upright and screamed, "Fuck I just want to sleep!"

He poured himself four fingers of vodka and downed it in one gulp. Falling back into bed, he was immediately asleep, but it wasn't a restful slumber, as the phantom army began its nocturnal march, robbing him of the rest that he desperately needed.

The next morning, Tim woke feeling not a bit rested, like he'd been run through the wringer. He dragged himself out of bed and made a pot of coffee.

When the drink was ready, he poured himself a cup, and thought of his next step. First thing, he'd really have to do was stop being so damn paranoid. It wasn't helping him one little bit. But there were other people about; he'd seen the signs yesterday. What to do? He hated being this way. He generally loathed indecisive people. In his line of work, indecisiveness got people killed. Now here he was, second guessing himself and unsure about everything. Securing the camper for travel, he got into the truck cab with the grease gun on the seat next to him, and placed the M4 on the dashboard.

He drove around to the front of the truck stop again to see if there was any fuel to be had. Taking an empty Jerry can and the hose, he went from truck to truck, checking their fuel tanks. When he found one that wasn't completely empty, he quickly filled the fuel can. There definitely had been some people through here. All the trucks in the lot were just about drained dry of diesel. He'd have to check the underground tanks anyplace else he'd stop at, and then figure a way to get the fuel out without power to the pumps.

He drove out, heading west, saw the signs for US Rt. 19 south, and decided to head that way. As before, it was a smaller road than the interstate, but as he'd seen on the map last night, he would be avoiding the bigger city of Charleston, and this way he could pick up I-77 in Beckley. Going through the town of Summersville, he barely slowed down, and kept heading south. By 1 PM, he had reached Beckley and stopped at a rest area off of the Interstate to eat some lunch. When he finished, he gathered his garbage up, walked over to a dumpster, and tossed it in. "Keep America Beautiful!" he said aloud, closing the lid on the dumpster. When he was walking back to the truck he saw several pigs cross the road, heading away from him and figured they must be domestic pigs gone feral. He began to salivate. The Event hadn't killed them off, and he'd love some roast pork.

He took the M4 off the dashboard, and stalked the pigs, seeing how close he could get. They were busy rooting through the underbrush along the shoulder of the road, completely oblivious to Tim, who got within twenty yards. He squatted down, placed the carbine's selector on semi-auto, took aim at a nice fat pig, and squeezed off a round.

The shot pig squealed loudly and spun around in circles as his friends all abandoned him, scattering to the four winds. Tim walked over to the pig and put another round into its head, and it dropped stone-dead on the spot. Gutting and cleaning it quickly with his K-bar knife, he dragged it back to the camper. Now how to cook the damn thing? He really should have thought of that before he shot the goddamn beast. It was almost one hundred pounds cleaned out, far too much for him to eat all by himself.

He busied himself with gathering wood to make a decent sized fire, and after several trips, he had a goodly sized pile. He made a fire near the camper, and with some rebar he had scavenged, used it to make a spit to put the pig on. He really ought to have dug a pit and cooked it that way, but this would have to do. As the sun went down, the fire lit up the surrounding area near where Tim, had staked out for the evening. He pulled out a folding camp chair and sat watching the pig cook. He figured he'd just slice off pieces, and eat it that way.

Once or twice, he got a weird feeling like someone was watching him, but it quickly faded each time. He reached in with a plate and knife, sawing off chunks of pork. Sitting back down, and throwing out his manners, he chewed on the large chunks, swallowing greedily. He moaned and closed his eyes. It tasted delicious! How could anyone not love pork or bacon? It was just so damn *good!* He stuffed himself with the delicious meat and drank several beers. He let the fire burn down enough and went to his camper where he quickly stripped, showered and climbed into bed. His last thought before falling to sleep was that it was a shame to waste all of that pork.

The next morning when he woke, he felt a lot better. He put the coffee on, lit a cigarette, looked out the window, and his heart dropped. The pig was gone! Not knocked down by a bear or something, the spit and everything was gone! He grabbed the M3 and ran outside in his underwear, looking around frantically. It was still early enough in the morning to have dew on the grass, and he saw several wet footprints near and around the still smoldering fire. By the looks of it there were four people, two adults and two kids. He *was* being watched last night! He looked around some more, and saw something fluttering on the bottom step of the camper, that he'd stepped over on his rush to get outside. It was a crumpled bit of paper weighted down with a rock. Tim reached down and picked it up, unfolding it to read a note written in what looked like blue crayon, in a child's handwriting:

> *"Thank you sir for the nice pig.*
> *It bin a wile since we all had good cooked supper.*
> *God bless U!"*

There really had been someone watching him last night! He went back to the fire and spun around.

"Hey, you guys! Please come back!" he yelled. He screamed for over an hour and still no one came back in reply. Whoever they had been, they stayed far away from him, and left as stealthily as they had come. Finally, after yelling himself hoarse, he collapsed in a ball in the middle of the overgrown parking lot and wept.

After he regained his composure, he quickly packed up his things and headed south along a smaller road that paralleled the highway. Traveling this road was slower, but free of stalled cars and was away from larger towns. He stopped at two places— a convenience store and a small grocery— and was able to restock most of his canned goods and fuel. Going through Athens, he spied a small hardware store and decided to stop. He broke into the building easily, finding several five gallon pails of flat matte paints to camouflage his camper. Backtracking several miles to a state park he'd passed earlier, he drove in and after an hour of searching, found a nice secluded spot in the woods to camp out for a few days.

Setting up the camper and leveling it, he took a large carpenter's pencil and drew the outline of the camouflage pattern from the M880 onto the outside of the camper. After that was done, he took the paint brushes and started to paint the camper, starting at the roof and working his way down, coloring in each spot like a giant paint-by-number. After several hours he was finally finished, and had every spot of the white camper completely covered. The flat exterior latex would cure overnight, and would be completely dry in about two days. It wasn't pretty, but the matte colors would hide the brush strokes. It was effective, if not aesthetically pleasing. He'd have to scare up some cammo netting too. Any Reserve Center or National Guard Armory would have that.

He glanced around at his surroundings and figured it was pretty much hidden from the road, so he felt confident he wouldn't be seen by passers-by on the road. Just no campfires, and no bright lights on after dark. He'd have to follow strict light discipline. He cleaned up, got himself some supper of beef stew, and ate listening to the breeze through the trees. It was not a bad place really, and he thought he might just stay here for a few weeks. At least he was far enough away from anyplace where there would be bodies lying about. So he was free from the smell, and there wasn't a really bad fly problem.

The weather was getting warmer by the day, and he sat outside as the sun fell in the west. He watched the stars appear one by one, still amazed at the night sky he was treated to every evening. He smoked his cigarettes, drank his beer, and looked up, wishing for some answer but knew he wouldn't get one.

Using the park as his base camp, he spent his time exploring the area, driving a little further every day. He found an Army surplus store, and acquired a 20'x20' cammo net, along with some other things, including several cases of MREs and enough canned goods to last him several months.. He was staying well away from larger grocery stores now because the smell from the rotting meat was every bit as bad as the smell of rotting humans, and for the most part, everything in them had been picked through by rats, mice and cockroaches now anyway. He was really surprised at how fast everything was starting to let go. Mother Nature was taking back everything very quickly. It had only been five months, but the weeds and grasses were taking over everywhere, and even though the leaves weren't fully out on the trees yet, he spied a small sapling poking its branches through the boards of a porch of an empty house the other day.

Animals were all over the place too. Still no dogs or cats to be seen, but he did hear a coyote one night. Deer were literally bumping into each other. That will probably go on for another two years or so, until there will be so many of them around that they'd eat all the vegetation, then they'd begin to die off from starvation. The same thing would probably happen with the rats and mice too. They were having a feast on all the cookies, crackers, bread and rice lying around, but when that was all gone in another few months, they'd start to die off too. Another animal that was literally multiplying daily, it seemed, was rabbits. There were thousands of them all over the place, and with the lack of cats to keep their numbers down, he was almost stepping on them. On one of his exploratory trips, he broke into another gun shop and got himself two .22 Rugers, a 10-22 rifle and an MkIII target pistol. He figured that would be better for shooting rabbits, and a lot quieter than the M4 or M16. He was pretty well hidden in this part of the park and he wanted to keep it that way.

He had several rabbit furs hung out to tan, and several rabbits in the camper's tiny freezer. He was experimenting all the time with different ways to cook it. Today he decided on breading and frying it, like one would chicken. He hummed along with Mick Jagger as he cooked dinner in the camper's tiny galley type kitchen. The weather turned a bit cooler and the skies threatened a storm later on in the evening, so he thought he'd just cook up some supper, listen to the Rolling Stones, eat, and get to bed early.

The three burners on the small range were close together, and he had to juggle for space. He had just enough room for the frying pan and one small saucepan, which he had on one of the back burners, filled with canned creamed corn.

If he stayed here for a bit, maybe he'd plant some fresh veggies, some corn and tomatoes, something easy that wouldn't require a lot of attention. He was a soldier, not a farmer. He was turning into a fairly good cook though, and the frying rabbit smelled wonderful.

Taking each piece out of the pan, he blotted the extra grease off with paper towels, and stirred the corn a bit, making sure it was hot enough. He thought about the pig, and the note. He really wished whoever it was had stopped and taken the chance in talking to him. Then again, they might have run into the same kind of people Paul had run into, and were giving everyone a wide berth. That made more sense.

He ate in silence by the light of a kerosene lantern. He decided to not run the generator every day, not only to conserve fuel, but to keep some sort of noise discipline. The camper did have 12 volt deep-cell batteries for lighting, but the lantern light was nice and saved the batteries for other things. The refrigerator ran just as well on propane as it did electric, so that used hardly any power at all. He'd just use the generator to recharge his IVIS tablet and the camper's batteries every few days. As he finished the last of his dinner, he heard the distant rumble of thunder. Lighting a cigarette, he sipped on a beer and thought about his lot. With the exception of almost everyone being dead, he really didn't have it much worse than when he was still in his house. Better actually, if you counted the fact that he could take a hot shower and use a toilet that actually flushed. He stubbed out his smoke and went to check the voltmeter on the batteries; it still held almost a full charge. He'd toyed with the idea of running the generator during the storm to hide the sound, but that would entail him going outside and getting soaked. If there was one thing an infantryman hated, it was getting wet for no reason. The batteries were good, so he stayed dry.

Another good thing was having the queen sized bed that he could stretch out in, unlike the tiny Army cot. He showered and shaved, brushed his teeth, and after extinguishing the lantern, crawled into bed between clean sheets. That he was able to do that was just by sheer luck. On one of his explorations into Athens, he'd driven by a Laundromat. With a little bit of tinkering, he got one of the washers and one of the dryers working. With the help of the generator and several long garden hoses leading down to a creek far behind the building, he was able to do his washing. So about once a week he'd head down the road a few miles to Athens to clean his clothes. Tim had it pretty good. He had a roof over his head, hot food in his belly, clean sheets, and a soft bed to lie down on.

He lay there, for what seemed like hours, as the storm came through, passed and diminished, finally being overcome by sleep in the early hours.

That night he dreamed of Iraq. He was a First Sergeant then, back when they'd invaded after 9/11, and in his dream he was riding in the command cupola of an M2

Bradley fighting vehicle. The gunner on the 30mm chain gun was a nineteen year-old PFC just out of Advanced Training. They were approaching a small village on the road to Baghdad, and the gunner was boasting on how he was going to kill all the ragheads.

"Kid?" Tim had asked. "How long you been in the Army?"

"About six months, Top," he said with a toothy grin.

Tim had to admire the kid's confidence. "Kid, my dick has been in pussy longer than you've been in the Army. Stay alert, there are bad guys out there, and they have guns too!"

"Okay, Top," the kid said, and went back to his gun sight.

Tim looked up and saw a flash, accompanied by a streak of smoke off to his left. "RPG! Button up!" he yelled, dropping down into the vehicle as the rocket propelled grenade hit squarely on the turret ring, blasting a molten hot stream of steel outwards, catching the gunner squarely in the face and killing him instantly. The vehicle lurched to a halt, and he heard an ear splitting scream from the driver's compartment. The uninjured infantrymen in the rear spilled out of the now burning vehicle and scrambled to safety. Tim groped in the smoke for the driver. Grabbing a handful of uniform sleeve, he pulled the driver out behind him. The soldier was screaming his head off, and as Tim got him clear of the now fully engulfed burning Bradley, he saw why. Half his face had been burned away, and his whole upper torso was charred black.

Another Bradley came up and stopped near and the gunner of that vehicle found its target four hundred meters away and engaged it with his chain gun. The rapid *crack crack crack!* of the gun was loud, but the nearest foot soldier to Tim heard him call for the radio. The soldier and another sergeant from the platoon came over in a crouch in the cover of the second Bradley, and Tim reached for the radio's handset.

"You!" he yelled, pointing at the sergeant. "Take care of him while I call for a MEDEVAC!" The soldier wordlessly complied, pouring a canteen's worth of water over the driver's burns, and giving him a morphine injection.

As Tim held the radio handset to his ear, a helicopter flew low overhead. Looking up, he saw it was a British Lynx chopper, probably supporting the Brit armored brigade off to his battalion's left. He reached over the Sp4's head, turned the radio to the Air Guard frequency, and depressed the push to talk button.

"POP A GODDAMN SMOKE!" Tim yelled over the cacophony of the now raging firefight. Small arms fire was sounding all around him, and he could barely hear. He saw yellow smoke billowing off to his right and called on the radio. "British helo flying over my yellow smoke, we need a dustoff for WIA! Please land immediately to my rear!" When no reply was forthcoming, he repeated his request a little more forcefully. The squelch broke on the radio, and he heard a distinctive female voice with a Scottish accent, "Sorry, Army, we cannot comply, we're taking heavy fire!"

Tim keyed the microphone. "Listen here, you fucking pompous British fuck! I've got wounded down here, and I'm under heavy fire too, goddamnit! If you don't land that fucking piece of shit right fucking now, I will fucking shoot you down myself!"

He didn't get a reply to that, but the helicopter circled around and began its descent, flaring out fifty meters behind his burning Bradley. He and the sergeant grabbed the driver, placed him in a poncho liner, and carried the wounded soldier to the waiting chopper. The pilot's hand was on the throttle, a collective, ready to launch back into the air as soon as the wounded man was on board. The whole time, the soldier never stopped screaming. Screaming for his mother, his father, someone named Judy. They slid him in onto the floor of the helicopter and the soldier at the door slammed it shut. As soon as Tim and the other sergeant were clear of the fuselage, he saw the pilot yank back on the collective, and the helo shot into the air, throwing sand and grit into their eyes. The last look he had of the pilot was of an ashen face drawn tight, lips a severe red gash, and a wisp of red hair licking out of the corner of the helmet. As they both ran back to the cover of the second Bradley the younger sergeant looked over at Tim.

"You really wouldn't have shot them down, would ya', Top?"

Tim gave the sergeant an evil grin. "The fuck I wouldn't have!"

"Fuck, Top. I'll follow you anywhere!" the sergeant said with a big grin, and then left in a scramble to find out what was going on. Someone higher up had also been on the radio, and an Apache attack helicopter came into view, and with rockets and chain gun of its own, turned the building the Iraqi gunmen were using for cover into rubble.

Someone else was yelling, "Cease fire! Cease fire!" as Tim stood cautiously, slinging his M16 and lighting a cigarette. He scratched his bare head, and heard a familiar voice from behind him.

"Those things are going to kill you, First Sergeant."

Tim tuned to see his company commander. "Oh, hey, Cap'n. These?" he held up the smoke. "The last thing I'm worried about right now is a little lung cancer." He took a drag, wondering where his helmet had gotten to. "Listen, Cap'n, you might get a call later requesting a court martial."

The captain raised his eyebrows in surprise. "Oh really, Top?"

"Yeah," Tim said ruefully, then gave him a complete SITREP (Situation Report) on what had transpired, right down to him threatening an Allied Army Officer with shooting down a friendly aircraft. The captain had a good laugh over that, and when he was done, looked at him and grinned.

"You did good, getting him out of here that quick, you might have saved his life. If anything is said, I'll squash it the best I can." What Tim didn't say was, *yeah, I might have saved his life, but what kind of life is that kid going to have now, with half a face, if he even survives those burns?*

"You're a good man to have around in a tight spot, Top. Keep up the good work!"

Tim woke with a start, bathed in sweat in spite of the cool breeze blowing in through the open window. He lay there in the dark listening to distant thunder roll through the hills, which sounded like artillery. He looked at his watch, and saw that it was almost 5 AM. He sat up and coughed then lit a smoke. He stood and put the coffee on. Might as well start the day. He was beginning to like this area. The forest suited him, and he liked the quiet and the animals. Plenty of game to keep him fed, but he'd have to venture out some the next few weeks, to restock on the canned goods. It was only the beginning of summer, but he thought it was never a bad time to stock up, especially when the weather was good. He knew the winters here would be fairly cold, and probably a lot of snow, judging by the surrounding mountains and the elevation of his encampment.

He thought about the dream as he drank his coffee in the pre-dawn stillness. The storm had completely passed, and the forest was quiet. Unlike the other dreams he had, this one was quite vivid. He'd not even thought about that incident in years. He'd later learned that the driver had died of his injuries in a hospital in Germany. The gunner and driver, both kids really, were dead. He thought of them as *his* kids. He remembered when the unit had gotten its activation and shipping orders, and he'd personally assured his gunner's mother, a single parent, that he'd take care of her little boy. It was the main reason he'd assigned him to his own Bradley crew. Kids, too many kids, died in that game. Besides those two killed, three others had suffered injuries, but he'd not gotten a scratch. It had always bothered him as to why.

He was supposed to protect his soldiers and bring them all home, but he'd failed, on so many levels. That and broken promises. There were so many broken promises. Maybe he was meant to be alone. Maybe it was the reason he never let anyone get too close to him anymore. Every time someone got close, they wound up getting hurt. Friends he'd had in the past, the little boy who got a stray bullet in the chest, whose only transgression was being in the wrong place at the wrong time, his failed marriage; it seemed like everything was a culmination to this very point in his life. Even Paul, that gentle man who had probably never hurt a soul, had died a horrible death because of a failed promise. Maybe if there really was a God, he was being punished for his failures. He'd tried so hard to do the right thing, but he'd always fallen short of his own expectations.

His brother had been wrong. One man can't change the world. Of all the things he'd done, the main ones he'd failed miserably, and now he was left alone to wallow in the waste of what had become of his life. He was on the near side of fifty years old, over half of his life was over, and he'd not made one ounce of difference. His life was for nothing. If he had been a less cerebral person, he might have turned to a religion for solace, but he used too much reason. He had given up on the thoughts of God or any other deity a long time ago. His reasoning was that there was too much evil in the world to allow for the existence of an all-loving God. Even if there was a God and a Devil, like he'd learned so many years ago from the Sisters of the Blessed Bleeding Heart of the Storm Troopers, God wouldn't let even the devil do all the terrible things that happen to Man. It was inconceivable so therefore, he reasoned, there was no God.

Now he was far from home, in a place that he'd never dreamed of going, living the life of a modern day Robinson Crusoe, with no hope of even finding his Friday. With that thought in his head, he made himself breakfast in silence. After another cup of coffee, he got dressed, grabbed the M4, and headed out to the truck thinking he would take a little drive to scrounge and to clear his head. As he drove away from his camp, he stopped and looked back. He noted that he couldn't see his camp at all, even from as close as a hundred meters. At least he could do something right. Heading south, he went through Athens and on to Princeton, where he took Rt. 460 to Bluefield. There he found an undisturbed grocery store where he picked up three cartloads of canned soups, stews, vegetables and fruits. He was pleased to also find several boxes of rice and pasta that hadn't been spoiled by rats or mice. Loading this up in the truck, he broke into a service station's caged propane tank area and filled up the bed of the truck with as many tanks as he dared. After filling his tank up with diesel from a semi parked in the lot, he headed out again, and on a whim headed west on Rt. 52 towards the town of Welch, and the West Virginia/Virginia/Kentucky border, right smack-dab in the center of Hatfield & McCoy territory. He knew a little of that history, and found it interesting. Maybe he'd stop at a library and find a book or two on the subject, something to keep him busy over the next winter. He was also in a big coal mining area, he saw as he passed several coal mines right up alongside the road in what would be called 'hollers', in the area. It was deep in the mountains too, and the road was very twisty, and filled with plenty of blind curves, so he kept his speed to a minimum, as from time to time, he'd come upon crashed or stalled dump trucks, mostly filled with coal.

After a few miles of clear road, his confidence picked up and he sped up a bit. Right before he got to the spot on his map that said it was Keystone, he crossed over a small bridge then topped the crest of a hill at forty miles an hour to see a small, waiflike figure standing in the middle of the road.

"Oh shit!" he said, and slammed both feet on the brake pedal by instinct, forgetting to depress the clutch, and the truck stalled, screeching loudly to a stop mere feet from the motionless figure.

CHAPTER 5:
FRIDAY

Tim sat behind the wheel and stared out at the figure. When he regained his breath, he slowly opened the door to the truck with a shaky hand, never taking his eyes off what appeared to be a small child, facing away from him. He then noticed the shoulders shaking, as if it was crying. Getting out, he walked around to the front of the truck to the sobbing child.

"Hey there, are you okay?"

No reply. He walked to where he was facing the child, and put a hand on its shoulder, which flinched slightly. He noticed it was a girl, in filthy jeans and an equally dirty t-shirt, skinny as a rail, with a fright wig of dirty and matted hair.

"Hey, you shouldn't stand in the middle of the road like that. I could have killed you!"

"Geoffrey! Geoffrey got hurt!" she said, looking up at him with a dirty, tear stained face.

"Who's Geoffrey?"

"My friend, we was playin' and I was chasin' him through the woods, and he fell down a hole and he's hurt!"

"Where was that?" Tim asked.

"Over there," she said, pointing to the woods, and began to cry again.

"Okay, take me there. Maybe I can help."

"Really?" she said, her eyes brightening hopefully.

"Yeah, really," he said, smiling to reassure her. He went back to the cab of the truck and retrieved his M4.

"What's that for?"

"I never leave home without it. Show me where Geoffrey is."

"This way!" she said, and ran off into the woods. Tim hesitated a moment before following, glad he'd brought the carbine. Maybe he was being just a bit paranoid, but the Taliban had used kids to lure GIs into ambushes before, and he wasn't taking any chances. They both ran for several hundred yards through the thick brush to a small clearing where she stopped and pointed to the ground. At first he didn't see anything but some thigh high grass and vines, until he took a second look to where she was pointing. There was a small hole in the ground, about three feet in diameter, with a few old, rotted and broken boards lying near.

"I was gainin' on him, and he just disappeared! He fell down that hole and hurt hisself!"

"Okay, let me have a look." Tim knelt down by the edge, set his carbine by his side and peered into the hole.

"Hello?" he called out, and got nothing in response. Turning to the girl, he asked, "How long has he been down there?"

"A while. Two sleeps maybe," she said, with a sniffle. "He could talk a bit at first, but he just stopped talkin' a while ago."

Tim shook his head. "You wait here. I'll be right back with some stuff, okay?"

"You really gonna come back?"

"Yes, I'll be right back."

Tim headed back to the truck, wondering what he'd gotten himself into. What the hell did 'two sleeps' mean? Two days? If that was the case, the kid was already dead... No, he had to at least try. He retrieved a coil of rope, and dug through the cab until he found a headlamp, like the kind that spelunkers use. He'd found at a camping supply store on one of his foraging trips and thought it might be useful. With the rope and headlamp, along with a pair of leather gloves, he headed back to the clearing. The girl thankfully stayed out of his way while he tied one end of the rope around a nearby tree stump, and tossed the free end down the hole. Putting the headlamp on and checking to see if it worked, he looked over at the girl.

"I'm going to lower myself down, and see if he's okay. I can't promise you anything, but I'm going to try."

"Please help him, mister, he's all I gots left!"

"I'll do my best."

He sat on the edge of the hole, figuring he could shimmy his way down with his back against one side, and then use the rope to climb back up. If this kid was hurt down here, he'd have to figure out some way of bringing him up without doing more damage. About ten feet down he looked up to see a round hole of sunlight broken by the outline of a small head and fright wig. How deep was this hole? Was it an old well or an air shaft to a coal mine? If it was the latter, it could be hundreds of feet deep, and the rope was only about forty feet long. He got another ten feet down and stopped there, looking down between his legs. About five more feet below him a shape of a body was lying in an unnatural position.

"Hey, Geoffrey, are you okay?" he called out with no reply. Scrambling the rest of the way, he was at the bottom of what was now clearly an old well.

He saw right away that Geoffrey was definitely not okay at all. On leg was folded completely under the body and he could see the femur bone sticking out of a gash in his pant leg, which was black with dried blood. Lifeless eyes looked back at him, through half open eyelids. Geoffrey was dead, probably bled to death from the fracture.

"Shit," he said under his breath and stood to look up at the figure so far above him. This was the part he hated. Taking a deep breath in the cold dampness of the well, he took hold of the rope and started climbing his way out. When he reached the mouth of the hole, wide, red-rimmed, hopeful eyes were staring at him. His eyes and expression belied him, and he could see the bottom lip start to tremble and the eyes welled up with tears.

"I'm sorry. I don't know how else to say it. Your friend Geoffrey is dead, honey."

The sobs became a steady wail, and the child threw herself to the ground. Tim let her go for a bit while he recoiled his rope and took his headlamp off. Going over to the girl, he helped her get up.

"He was all I had!"

He pulled her to him and she latched on tightly, sobbing into his torso. After several minutes she calmed a bit, but still wouldn't let go.

"Come back to the truck and we'll get something to eat."

"'Kay..." she said, and sniffled again. They walked silently back to the road together. When they got to the truck, Tim tossed his gear into the bed and got some canned fruit cocktail out. Kids loved fruit cocktail. He opened a can of soda for each of them, and they ate with plastic spoons silently. Finishing her food, the girl belched loudly.

"Scuse' me," she said, and giggled. "I kinda' knew he was dead, but I was really hopin', you know? Then you came and I *really* got to hopin'."

"It's okay. I did try. My name is Tim. What's yours?"

"Robyn, with a 'y'."

"Well, Robyn with a 'y', it's really nice to meet you!" Tim said, and held out his hand to shake.

"You're not from 'round here, are ya?" she said in an accent dripping West Virginia.

"No, I'm not," Tim said. "I'm from up north a bit. Philadelphia. I came down after the winter to see if I could find anyone else."

"Did ya?"

"Well, I found you, didn't I?" he said, not really wanting to bring up Paul and the others he'd had the misfortune of running into. The last thing this kid needed was something like that to worry about.

"I reckon you did!" she grinned.

He laughed at that. He then looked at the girl, and wondered what to do.

"Where do you live, Robyn?"

"Just over there," she pointed down the road.

"Well, let's get you there, and we'll figure out what to do. Sound like a plan?"

"Okay," she said agreeably, and he helped her into the truck. He started it and put it in gear, then he asked, "How old are you?"

"I'm thirteen."

"*Really?*" he asked with a raised eyebrow. She looked more like ten. Skin and bones really, probably suffering from borderline malnutrition that went back before The Event, he supposed. She couldn't have been any taller than four foot ten, and maybe eighty pounds soaking wet.

"Really! A lot of folks think I'm just a little kid!"

"I believe you," he said with a smile. He followed her directions, and it only took a few minutes to get to an overgrown and run down trailer park, and he stopped in front of a shabby singlewide, garbage strewn all around a tiny, rickety porch.

"Is this home?"

"Yep. Mama was savin' for a new doublewide with her tip money from the diner."

"Is there anyone else here besides you and Geoffrey?"

"Nope, just us was all."

Tim could immediately smell the slow decomposition of the bodies in the trailers all around him. He couldn't let her stay here. They walked through the front door, and another smell immediately hit him.

Flies were all through the trailer, and the stench of human waste assaulted his senses. Apparently, they hadn't thought to use water in buckets or something to flush the toilets, or bathe for that matter. He looked around the living room of the small trailer and saw two mattresses on the floor next to a wood stove, the floor almost covered, with empty potato chip bags, soda cans and canned soups and stews. A roach crawled across his foot, and he was reminded of some tenement hovels he'd been in Philadelphia.

"Okay, Robyn, here's what we're going to do," he said finally. "I want you to get things of yours, whatever you want to take, and you'll come and stay with me. My place is tiny, but it's clean and comfy. You okay with that?"

"Well, I guess. Where's your place?"

"I'm over near Athens, in Pipestem State Park. I've got a little camper with running water and a shower and everything," he said, hoping to get out of this depressing dump as soon as he could.

"I've been there before! We went on a class trip there once."

"Alright then, get what you want to take, and let's go."

"Wait. My Mama always said not to talk to strangers. How do I know you ain't gonna hurt me or anything?"

"Robyn, hurting you is the last thing I'd do."

"Okay," she said, after a moment's contemplation. She looked around, and dug through some blankets on one of the mattresses, pulling out a very soiled stuffed teddy bear that looked like it had seen better days.

"Okay, I'm ready."

"That's all you want to take?"

"Yeah, Mama gave it to me when I was little. He's Bad Bear. Got nothing else I really want."

"Bad Bear? He's not going to cause any trouble, is he?"

"Nah, he's not bad anymore!"

Poor kid, he thought. As they piled into the truck and headed back east, his mind was reeling. *What the hell am I going to do with a thirteen year old? I don't know what to do with a goddamn kid!* They drove on, and he thought he'd better get her some new clothes. He remembered seeing a Walmart just off of I-77 and Rt. 460 in Princeton. They'd stop there and get her a whole new wardrobe. He pulled into the parking lot and her eyes widened.

"Are we going to Walmart?"

"Yep, we're going to get you some new clothes to wear. We can't have you running around in those old things."

"Wow! Walmart! Mama always said it was a fancy place she'd take me to one day when she got enough money! Can I get anything I want?"

"Yes, but within reason, only stuff that is functional, okay? That means jeans, sturdy shoes, underwear and warm jackets for winter."

"Oh, okay," she said, a little crestfallen, but still excited. He parked where he usually parked, in the fire lane. They got out and walked to the doors. Tim used his shoulder, easily pushing the automatic doors open, and they walked into the unlit store. Every time he did this, he got the creeps. He didn't know why, he just did. He could smell the bodies lying somewhere unseen, and hoped they didn't bump into one. Using flashlights, they wound their way to the children's clothing, and started picking things she'd like. He had her go to the dressing rooms, checking for bodies first, and had her try on several pairs of jeans until she found some that fit her. He had her get them slightly larger than what would normally be her size, in the hopes he could put a little weight on her with some proper food. They loaded up a cart with her booty— ten pairs of jeans, several shirts, girls' underwear and thermal underwear for winter, flannel shirts, a down jacket, wool socks and two pairs of sturdy hiking boots, along with some shorts, tank tops, sneakers and flip-flops for the summer. She walked by the bras and briefly looked, a dark cloud crossing over her face for a moment, and then quickly passing. Tim got himself some more t-shirts, underwear and socks while he was there. He also went to the personal hygiene aisle and got some girly shampoo, some toothpaste and two new toothbrushes. As they were heading out of the store, they both passed the checkout lanes.

"Typical Walmart, I've got a full cart, and no one at the registers!" he laughed, but Robyn didn't get the joke.

"Tim, is this stealin'?"

"Well, not really, honey. Things have sort of changed."

"Yeah, they sure did."

They loaded their swag into the now overloaded truck and headed for the park. They rode in silence, and Tim was furiously thinking about his lot. He had no clue how to raise a child, especially a girl. Now what was he going to do? He'd have *some* idea if it was a boy…

They pulled into the park and wound their way along the road until he came to the hidden turnoff he'd carved out of the woods to lead him up behind his camper. He parked and got out.

"Help me unload the truck, and then we'll get you cleaned up."

"Why you got all this stuff hanging over it?" she asked when she took in the camper.

"What stuff? Oh, you mean the cammo netting? So no one can see it," he replied, grabbing a handful of stuff out of the bed of the truck.

"Why wouldn't you want anyone to see it?"

"I'll tell you later, after supper, okay?" he said, skillfully avoiding the question. They unloaded all their booty into the trailer, and then Tim unloaded all the propane tanks he'd acquired and stacked them up with the rest of the filled ones outside, covering them up with a green Army tarp.

He double checked the pump and hose he had run up from the creek and fired up the generator. After rearranging things in the cramped quarters of the camper, he made up the girl's bed in the front berth that was over the little dinette table. He looked around and decided it was going to be really cramped, but they'd make do. He handed Robyn a fresh towel, soap, shampoo and a toothbrush, and pointed her in the direction of the shower.

"You need a bath, young lady!" he said, and she hung her head and marched off to the tiny bathroom. "The water heater is small, so you won't have a lot of hot water." In a few minutes he heard the water turn on, and he busied himself with what to have for supper. He decided on some spaghetti, and used the untainted pasta he'd found earlier that day, and opened a jar of pre-made sauce to heat on the range.

In about ten minutes Robyn came out wrapped in a towel, looking like a drowned rat. Her hair was soaked, but looked a lot cleaner, however he could still see dirt behind her ears. He decided to leave it at that, and went outside in the evening air to let her dry off and get dressed in privacy. It wasn't too bad now, but it was going to be really hard to keep one's modesty in the winter. He sat on a folding camp chair and smoked a cigarette, looking at the sky. Storm clouds were brewing, and it would probably rain later on. He heard the door of the camper open, and turned to see Robyn come out wearing a pair of shorts and a tank top, but still barefoot. Her hair was still wet, and he tossed her a brush he'd forgotten to give her before.

"Thank you," she said, sitting down in another chair next to him, and began to brush through the tangles. The dirt still behind her ears bothered him, but he didn't say anything. He'd get her to take another shower later before bed. They sat silently for a while, and Tim finished his smoke, and expertly field-stripped it in Army fashion.

"My Uncle Jake used to do that."

"What?"

"With his cigarette butts; he used to do that."

"Oh, old habit from the Army." he said, pocketing the refuse.

"Are you in the Army?" she said, brightening.

"Yeah, something like that."

"I want to join the Army when I'm older!"

"Oh, you do, eh?"

"Yeah, Mama said it'd be the only way I could get money for school, and get out of the Holler."

"Well, you don't have to worry about that anymore. You like spaghetti?" he asked, changing the subject.

Her eyes widened and her head bobbed rapidly. "I love spaghetti!"

"Okay, spaghetti is what we'll have! Come on, you can help me."

The pot he'd left to heat was going at a good rolling boil now, and he took an amount of pasta he'd reckoned was enough for both of them, out of the box, broke it in half, and put in in the boiling water. He then stirred the sauce. He got two plates out of the cupboard and some forks from the flatware drawer, and handed them to Robyn.

"Here, you can set the table."

When the pasta was about ready, he tipped the pot into a colander in the sink and let it drain, then brought it over to the table and split the steaming noodles evenly between the two plates. He then returned with the sauce, and did the same, making a big flourish with the spoon, which earned him a laugh. He grabbed a can of Coke for her, and a beer for himself out of the tiny refrigerator sat down opposite her.

"Dig in!"

"Aren't you gonna say grace?"

"Eh, you don't have to if you don't want to, Robyn," he said.

"You say it!" she said. He was really uneasy. It had been years since he'd said grace at the supper table.

"Okay, here it goes..," He bowed his head. "Rubba-dub-dub, thanks for the grub! Yayyyy, God! Now let's eat before it gets cold."

Robyn laughed heartily and dug into the food. She ate ravenously, and was done in a few minutes. She wiped her mouth daintily with her paper towel and belched loudly.

"I'll take that as a compliment to the chef," Tim said jovially. "Do you want more?"

"No sir. Thank you. That was really good. Ain't had a nice supper like that in a while!"

"I'm glad you liked it," he said, standing and picking up both plates. "I'll wash, you dry, okay?"

"Okay!" she said, He handed her a dishrag, filled the tiny sink with water and some dish detergent, and began scrubbing away, handing off each vessel to her, which she dutifully dried and put on the rack. After they were done, he put all the dishes away, checked the battery charge level, and saw that it was fully charged. He went outside and shut down the generator then went to his laptop, putting in a CD of The Who, and took the M4 to the dinette table.

"You got a computer?" she asked excitedly. "We can get on the interwebs!"

"Sorry, honey, no interwebs. That's all gone now too. Just some music is all we can do with it now."

"Oh," she said crestfallen. "Mama always said you can contact anyone on the interwebs. What happened, what killed everyone back in the holler…that happened everywhere? Like even in Charleston?"

"Yeah, I'm sorry to say, everywhere, like the whole world."

"Everybody?"

"Well, I guess not *everyone*, but most," he said, looking her right in the eye. He didn't know how to explain what had happened to a thirteen year old. Hell, he didn't know it all himself either, like why it seemed only domesticated animals were killed, at least those that didn't adapt readily to returning to the wild. Pigs could apparently, but not cows or sheep.

"Is that why you have that?" she asked, pointing at his carbine.

"Yeah, honey. I didn't want to scare you earlier, but a while back, I had a run-in with some really bad people. So that's why I stay hidden and I have this," he said, and began to break the weapon down for cleaning.

"Why are you doing that?"

"Well, a good soldier takes care of his weapon, and I like to believe I'm a good soldier."

"Oh, okay," she said, watching him intently.

Noticing her curiosity, he explained what each part was, what it did and how to clean it. She paid rapt attention to him, but he really wasn't sure that everything he said was sinking in. Probably not, he figured, but hell, it was conversation. That's what he really craved. He finished cleaning the rifle and reassembled it, putting it away next to his bed.

"Okay, Robyn. Some ground rules that if you want to stay here, you can't break. The number one rule is, don't ever touch any of the guns without asking me, okay? I'll teach you to shoot if you want. I've got a little .22 rifle you can use, but you mustn't ever, ever touch them without asking. That's one rule I'm very strict with. No ifs, ands or buts."

"Yessir!" she said, saluting him.

"I mean it. This isn't a toy."

"I understand. My Papaw was the same with his at his house. He didn't have really cool ones like that though. You really gonna teach me to shoot?"

"Sure, maybe tomorrow. First thing now though, you need another shower. You left some dirt behind your ears, and there's still crud under your fingernails. Go and shower again," he said with mock sternness. "Now get going!"

He went back outside and lit a smoke, wondering where this would take him. The last few hours weren't so bad, but did he really know what he was doing with a kid in tow? The last of the daylight had passed, and he watched lightning in thunderheads, miles away. The thunder rolled as he smoked and drank another beer. Finishing that, he went back inside where he saw Robyn standing with one of his t-shirts on.

The sleeves went all the way to her elbows and the bottom hung clear below her knees. She was scrubbed pink this time, and he saw that she'd washed her hair again.

"I saw it on your bed, and thought I needed something for PJ's. It's okay I hope?"

"Yes, it's okay. I didn't think of that at Walmart today, you're welcome to it."

"Cool! Thanks!" she said with a squeal, and gave him a big hug. He hugged back slightly, feeling a bit uncomfortable.

"Come on, let's get you tucked into bed." He helped her climb into the bunk and get under the covers.

"Comfy?" he asked, as he tucked her in.

"Yep, thank you, Tim. Good night."

"Oh, almost forget. Here's your bear," he said, handing her the soiled stuffed toy, which she took from him and hugged tight.

"Good night, honey. I'll see you in the morning," he said, brushing a lock of flaxen hair from her eyes. He didn't know her hair was that light, it now looked almost the color of corn silk, it had been that dirty.

With that said, he turned around and walked to his bed and turned off all the lights. He sat down on the bed, took off his boots, stripped to his underwear, and got under the sheets. When he was comfortably situated, he lay there a while listening to the thunder, interspersed with Robyn's steady breathing. That night, he drifted off to a dreamless sleep, lulled by gently falling rain on the tin roof of the trailer.

He woke early in the morning to sunlight coming through the slits in the blinds. He sat up, coughed and scratched his head.

"You snore," he heard from the far side of the camper, and he looked up, seeing a small nose and two pairs of eyes looking at him, one a deep blue the other set hard and plastic.

"Well, there's nothing I can do about that," he mumbled.

"Sounded like the last coal train over Cheat Mountain!" Robyn giggled.

"Thanks," he said and made his way to the tiny bathroom. When he was done, he donned a pair of jeans, put on a pot of coffee, and lit a cigarette.

"Those are bad for you," Robyn said.

"So is bugging me about them."

"Just sayin'..."

"Alright, let me get some coffee," he said sternly, letting her know he really wasn't a morning person.

"Can I have some?"

"Aren't you a little young for coffee?"

"No, I used to drink a cup with my Mama before school every morning."

"Really? How do you like it?"

"Black," she said, sitting up, letting her feet dangle off the bed over the dinette table.

"Okay, black coffee for the young lady, it is," he said, getting a second cup from the cabinet and putting sugar and non-dairy creamer into his cup. He could never drink coffee black. When the pot was ready, he poured two cups and set one down on the table across from his, where he sat to finish his smoke and sip his brew. Robyn hopped down off the bunk, bounded to the bathroom, and shut the door noisily. He stubbed out the smoke in an ashtray and shook his head. He heard the toilet flush, and she came out and sat down across from him.

"Good morning!" she beamed cheerily.

"It's morning alright," he grumbled.

She took a sip of the coffee. "This is really good!"

"I'm glad you approve."

"It's not as good as Mama's, but good anyway," she said, looking down, as a dark cloud crossed her face.

"You miss your mom, huh?"

"Yeah…" She looked out of the window, avoiding his gaze. "Why did she hafta die? She never hurt nobody."

"I don't know, Robyn. I lost people I loved too. I guess we'll never know."

She sat for a minute and sipped her coffee, and Tim didn't push her to talk. She'd tell him what was on her mind if she wanted to.

"You know what I think?"

"What's that, sweetheart?"

"There is no God," she said flatly, in a voice that belied her age.

It sounded like it was coming from a middle-aged, jaded cynic and he was taken aback. Not that he disagreed with her, he was in total agreement, but it was just the way she said it.

"I mean, if there really was a God, and he really loves us all like they said in Sunday School, why kill good people like my Mama, and leave people like you and me alone to just get by?"

"And you're thirteen?" he asked, raising an eyebrow. If she thought that, he wondered why she wanted to say grace last night. Probably out of habit, he figured.

"Yeah," she nodded, and sipped her coffee.

Tim didn't know how to respond to that. He drank more of his drink, and then put the cup down. "So tell me, Robyn. How did you and Geoffrey survive all winter?"

"Oh, Geoffrey was really good at finding things. He got us food, and water, and wood for the stove," she exclaimed, growing animated. She sat up and drew her legs under her bottom so she was sitting almost eye to eye with Tim. "Only thing he couldn't figure out was the toilet. It got all clogged, and we didn't know what to do about poopin' and stuff."

He laughed at that. "Well, I'm good at fixing things like that. No worries about the toilet here."

"No, and that's really nice."

"I can identify," he said. "So you and Geoffrey just holed up at your trailer for the winter?"

"Yeah. Geoffrey buried Mama out the back, and then he buried his folks before the ground got too cold. He found lots of stuff, beanie-weenies and Vienna sausages, chips and soda and stuff," she said, Vienna coming out as 'Vy-Anner'.

"Well, from now on, we'll be eating as much real food as we can."

"Like spaghetti?" she asked hopefully.

"Yes ma'am, and rabbit and pig if I can shoot one. Not much fresh veggies, so we'll have to rely on the canned stuff for those."

She wrinkled her nose a bit at the mention of vegetables, but he said nothing at this point. He was the same when he was that age, and there was no need to push the issue.

"Would you like some breakfast?" he asked, and her face lit up. "Eggs and hash browns sound good?"

"You have *eggs*?" she asked, wide eyed.

"Well, they're powdered, same with the potatoes. You can have the eggs anyway you like them as long as it's scrambled!" he said, getting up and taking the two steps to the galley kitchen. Breaking out everything he'd need, he took a gallon jug of water out of the refrigerator, using it to mix up the fixings for the eggs and reconstitute the freeze-dried potatoes.

"Can I help?" Robyn asked.

"Nah, I got this. You want more coffee?"

"Can I?"

He nodded in reply, and came over to warm up her cup, with the still hot coffee pot.

"Sorry, I don't have any bacon."

"That's okay. Eggs and hashies sound great!"

He busied himself with cooking breakfast, and was getting quite adept at juggling the pans on the tiny three burner stove.

"I never knew men could cook!"

"Well, one has to do what one has to do. I learned how to cook for myself a long time ago. If I didn't do it myself, it didn't get done. So instead of going hungry, I learned to cook!"

He took a spatula and scooped out some scrambled eggs and hash browns onto a plate, placing it in front of the girl. He then got two forks out and placed them on the table with a few paper towels. After making a plate for himself, he sat down opposite, took the salt and pepper, and sprinkled some over the lot. He then added some Tabasco sauce to spice it up a bit. He handed over the condiments to Robyn, who used the salt, but eschewed the pepper or hot sauce. They ate in silence, and even Tim had to agree that the powdered eggs weren't really all that bad. When Robyn was finished, she looked up at the makeshift bookshelf Tim had made over the window.

"Did you read all of those?"

"Yeah I did, most of them anyway. I like to read. It keeps my mind occupied."

"Me too. Sometimes when I'm reading a really good story it's like I got this little TV screen in my head and I can picture it all there," she said, looking away and turning red, like she was telling him a secret she shouldn't have.

"I'm the same way. It's like a little movie in my head."

"Really, you do that too?"

"Yep, really. Feel free to read anything you want up there. I pinched them from the library," Tim said, winking conspiratorially.

"Mama couldn't afford to buy me the books I wanted, so I'd go to the library and read all day. I love to read!"

"It's really good that you read. To me, every book is like an adventure, taking you places you might never get to see yourself." He reached up on the shelf and took down a book, handing it to her. "Here's one of my all-time favorites."

She looked at the cover, and read aloud, "*Robinson Crusoe*. What's it about?"

"It's about a man who gets marooned on a desert isle, and how he survives by himself until he meets a native he named Friday. I won't spoil the story for you. I loved it when I was your age."

"He named him Friday, huh?" she said curiously. "That's *my* name!"

"What?" Tim said, sitting up abruptly.

"Well, it's 'Freitag'. It's German…"

"For Friday," he finished for her.

"Yeah, how did you know?"

"I spent a little time in Germany a long time ago, and remember some words and phrases."

Now what do you say to that! He thought in amazement. He'd met his 'Friday'. Wasn't that a hoot? Things were getting curiouser and curiouser…

"Well, my last name isn't Crusoe," he said, "it's Flannery."

"Can I really read it?"

"Sure thing, but first, help me clean up this mess from breakfast, then we'll go for a walk and maybe find some fresh mushrooms."

They busied themselves with the washing up, and it amazed him that it hadn't even been twenty-four hours since they met, and there wasn't really any problem. She was an extremely bright and polite young girl, which he was immensely thankful for. As they were washing up, he remembered some flour and other baking things he'd acquired, and thought maybe tonight he would look up a bread recipe in one of the cookbooks he had gotten. He really craved some fresh bread, and the camper did have a small oven. After the chores were done and they were both dressed, Tim took his M4 and the .22 rifle, and they walked outside to a rather beautiful late spring morning. With only a hint of a breeze, the temperature was somewhere in the mid 70's, with not a cloud in the sky. That might change later, but for now it was a really nice morning. Looking at his watch, Tim saw that it was just 10:30 AM, reassured that his watch still worked. It was his one OCD trait, he was completely lost if he didn't know what time it was or couldn't look to see. Slinging the M4 over his shoulder, he carried the .22 in his right hand, and he and Robyn walked away from the camper into the woods. No stranger to the outdoors himself, he was nevertheless impressed with

Robyn's knowledge of the local flora and fauna. Well, she *was* a down-home country girl, from West Virginia, he remembered.

"So, are you going to teach me to shoot?" she said, looking up at him.

"I guess." He looked around for something to use as a target. After a few moments, he found an old rusted can, set it up on a fallen tree, and stepped back about twenty-five yards. He loaded the rifle and handed it to her, explaining how to properly hold it, and how to use the sights. She pulled the stock into her bony shoulder and peered down the sights.

"Let her rip!" Tim said.

POP POP POP POP POP!

Five rounds let loose rapidly, and the rifle never jerked in her hands. The tin can teetered for a moment and fell. She let the rifle hang loose, looked at him and grinned.

"Like that?"

"Yeah, just like that!" He walked over to the where the can had fallen and picked it up. He whistled and looked back at the still smiling girl.

"Never shot a rifle before, eh?"

"Just my granddad's BB gun once. It's about the same, really, only louder."

Through the can were five tightly grouped .22 holes, about a half-inch in diameter.

"Well I'll be dipped in dogshit. You just keep shooting like that Miss Oakley!"

"Who?"

"Never mind, it seems like you're a natural. It took me a while to be able to do that. Looks like you're going to shoot us some supper tonight, that is, if you want to."

"Sure!" she beamed. "Like what, a squirrel?"

"Nah, I was thinking more like a big fat rabbit"

"I like rabbit. Ain't had it in a while though. You reckon there's any 'round here?"

"Oh, they're plenty about. There's a clearing over that way a bit, and they're usually around that way some."

"Okay, let's go!"

They headed off towards the clearing where they sat with their backs against a huge oak tree and waited silently. They sat like that for maybe twenty minutes when all of a sudden, Robyn stiffened, grabbing his leg to let him know she'd seen something. Smiling inwardly, he thought she really did have the instincts for this. He followed her gaze to a spot about sixty yards away, where a fat cottontail was munching on some clover. He leaned over to her and whispered, "Try for a head shot. It's a bit far, but see if you can."

She nodded slowly and raised the rifle up to her shoulder, thumbing off the safety. Her cheek was against the stock, and she let out a breath, squeezing the trigger.

POP!

The rabbit looked like it did a backflip, and fell on its back. They got up and walked over to the lifeless form. It was a perfect shot, right behind the left eye. *One rabbit dinner, coming up*, Tim thought.

"Nice shot!"

He knelt down, taking a pocket knife out of his jeans, and quickly gutted and skinned it. He looked up to see Robyn a little pale, but still smiling.

"Not everything is real pretty, Robyn. But at least we'll eat well tonight!"

They walked back to the camper together and sat outside. Tim looked over at her thoughtfully. The waif was surprising him. They sat and drank cans of soda from the fridge, and watched the clouds build up in the afternoon heat.

"Probably more storms tonight," he said aloud.

"Good! I like them. The sound of the rain on the roof is really cool."

"Yeah, I like them too. Sometimes, though, they can wreak a lot of havoc." Tim went on to tell her of the storm in Philadelphia, and the firestorm that ensued from it, and why he'd left and come to West Virginia.

"Maybe you were 'spose to find me?"

"Hmm. Maybe," he grunted. He really didn't want to think of that, because it raised the whole 'God' question again. He got a plate from the camper and cut up the rabbit into pieces, easy enough to fry. He took a quick look at the cookbook for the bread recipe, and decided to forgo that for the night. It looked a little involved and he didn't have any yeast. He'd have to go back to a grocery store and get that.

They went into the trailer and Tim put on some music. They made small talk while Tim poured some olive oil into the large frying pan and heated it. While he floured and breaded the pieces of rabbit and placed them into the hot oil, he asked, "So tell me about your mom, Robyn."

"She was really pretty. Daddy got kilt in the mine a long time ago so it was just me and Mama. She worked in the diner. She said she never finished school, so she was always after me to study real hard, an' stay in school. Sometimes Uncle Jake would come over and help around the house with things, fixin' a window that got busted or somethin'."

"So he was her boyfriend?"

"No! He was Mama's brother!"

"Oh, okay. And he was in the Army?"

"Yeah, he'd come home on leave and stay for a visit, help around the house some. Then, a while back, Mama said he went to someplace, Berserkastan I think, and then she told me he wasn't comin' home anymore. That night she cried and cried. I didn't know what to do, so I just hugged her real tight like."

"Berserkastan, yeah, that's a good name for it. I've been there myself. Not really pretty."

"Maybe you knew him?" she asked with a hopeful smile.

"I really doubt that, sweetie. There were a lot of soldiers over there."

"Oh, okay."

"Here, help me with this and we'll eat."

They went about setting the small table and Tim portioned out the fried rabbit and creamed corn, which he figured was a safe bet on a vegetable with a probably finicky kid. They each ate ravenously, and he was correct about the corn; she ate it greedily, and that made him happy.

After they were done eating, Tim got up, and without being asked, Robyn helped him with the dishes, which again made him really happy. It was still light out, but the sun was falling rapidly in the west, he saw when he went outside, sat down with a beer, and lit a cigarette. She called to him from the door, and he turned to see her standing with the book in her hand.

"Tim, is it okay if I just read for a while?"

"Sure. I think there's a little light over the bunk."

"I found it! Thanks!" she said, and turned, letting the screen door shut behind her. He sat in his chair, and drank his beer, the carbine across his lap. He watched the storm grow until way past full dark, and in the process drank an entire twelve-pack. He got up unsteadily and made his way to the camper. When he got inside, he looked at the girl in her bunk. She was sound asleep with the book opened in her lap. He took the book from her hands and saw that she was already on page ninety three. Finding a piece of paper to use as a bookmark, he marked her page and set the book aside. He pulled the covers over her and turned off the small, built-in reading lamp. Double checking the battery's charge, he figured it could wait until tomorrow before he charged it up again. He then made his way drunkenly to the tiny bathroom. Looking in the mirror, he stared at his reflection. He didn't recognize the old guy staring back at him. Although clean-shaven, his hair was way longer than he'd ever had it in his adult life, and it was then he realized just how gray he was getting. He'd have to cut it at some point. Brushing his teeth and shaving, he finished and stumbled to his bunk. He fell back onto it and stared at the ceiling.

"Well, Timmy boy, you've got your Friday..." he said to himself as a rumble of thunder rolled across the valley. "Let's see if you can keep from fucking this up!"

CHAPTER 6:
REPLENISHING HANDS

The *USS Hughes* sat at anchor five hundred yards out from the small Sri Lankan port, and the skipper, watched from the wing bridge as the whaleboat overloaded with fuel drums came alongside. The destroyer had seen better days, and the lack of crew evidenced itself with the lack of preventative maintenance. The paint was chipped and rust showed through, the chains and handrails were rusty, and there were several dents and a huge gash in the hull feet above the waterline. Right now, Lt. Cmd. Wright had a handful of conscripts welding metal plate over the gash. Over the last several months, they had hopscotched up the Horn of Africa, stopping at every small port to gather what supplies they needed. What the skipper really needed was a full crew, and he was well on his way to achieving that. In every port, they had shanghaied every able-bodied person they had found, and now had a complement of around thirty men, women and children. Language was a bit of a problem, but discipline turned out to be easier than he'd thought.

"What seems to be the problem, Mr. Johnson?" he called down over to the whaleboat over a bullhorn.

"Rasheed says he doesn't want to work anymore. He's tired."

"Oh really, is he now? Bring him up here to the bridge!"

Ensign Johnson grabbed the thin Somali man by the shoulder, pushing him up the ladder, while ordering the other men in the boat to start transferring the bunker fuel up using a hand pump.

The skipper sat back in the captain's chair on the empty bridge and lit his pipe. He could smell the food the Indian women were cooking in the galley from here, and even though he really wasn't fond of curry, he had to admit they were pretty good at making a decent meal out of water buffalo and rice, but the goddamned curry was stinking up the wardroom.

Ensign Johnson came onto the bridge with Rasheed in tow. The bony black man stood shirtless and shoeless, glossy with sweat. His yellow eyes showed fear, but also exhaustion.

"Mr. Johnson here tells me you won't work anymore, is that correct?"

"Yessir! I am tired and need a rest. I been working for two day straight now."

The skipper put down his pipe and looked at his hands for a moment.

"Come with me." He got up from the chair and walked out to the wing bridge. "Haven't I been very generous with food?"

"Oh yes sir!" the man beamed with perfect white teeth.

"And haven't I provided you with a nice bed to sleep in?"

"Oh yes sir!" he said again, nodding his head vigorously.

"All I ask is for you do a little work for me in return for my generosity."

"Oh, but it too much work! From way before sunup, to way past sundown, we work seven days!"

Commander Winthorpe Wright started to get a little tic under his right eye, but smiled in a friendly way and put his arm around the skinny Somali. They walked over to the railing and looked over the water.

"So, you think I work you too hard, is that it?"

"Oh yessir! Just asking for a rest is all."

"Well, that's that then. You want a rest, I'll give you a rest." He pulled a Beretta M9 9mm automatic pistol from his holster and in one fluid motion, put the muzzle to the man's head, pulling the trigger. A muffled 'pop' was heard all the way down to the whaleboat, where the other workers looked up at the sound. The skipper holstered the pistol and motioned for Ensign Johnson to toss the limp body hanging over the railing into the harbor. The body hit the water with a loud splash. Grabbing the loudhailer, he brought it to his mouth and pointed it down to his 'crew'.

"Now hear this. You will work until I say it is time to stop working. Is that FUCKING CLEAR?"

The others in the boat all scrambled back to work, pumping the fuel into the ship's bunkers as rapidly as the pump would allow, not daring to look back at their captain but eyeing the floating body drifting slowly away from the ship.

"And get someone in here to clean up this mess on my deck!" he said to Johnson, and walked back to the dimness of the bridge.

He sat alone for several minutes, closing his eyes, and he again saw the carnage on the day when everything when to shit. The replenishment ship alongside the cruiser cutting into the hull of the warship, the fuel lines breaking and igniting... F/A 18s flying into the rear deck of the carrier like Kamikazes from another era, bursting into flames... That ship turning to port wildly at thirty knots, cutting another destroyer in half before grounding itself on a shoal several miles away where it burned for days. It was all too much for the man, and he opened his eyes to see Ensign Johnson return with a sari-clad East Indian woman carrying a mop and bucket. The ensign pointed to the blood and brains on the deck, and then went over to the captain.

"Make it quick!" he snapped at the woman, who may or may not have understood him, but did make it her business to be quick about it. Just being around the captain scared her.

"Sir, we should have the bunkers topped off by 2100 hours tonight. It'd be nice if we could get an oiler fired up and brought alongside, but there's nothing seaworthy at the docks. Looks like a pretty good typhoon came through a while back and tore everything to shit."

"What else?"

"Well, sir, me and Nakamura got the engine room pretty ship-shape. He was a blessing, and he's been a great help getting everything in engineering automated. By the time we're about to weigh anchor, we should be able to run everything from the bridge."

"Nakamura?"

"Yes sir. He's that Japanese guy we pulled off the fishing trawler north of the Seychelles about a month ago. He's really happy to be working, and he's been a big help down there."

"Good. When we set sail, let him have the pick of the women for a few nights," the captain said with a wink.

"Aye sir," Johnson nodded, with an inward wince. He hated this.

"How are our weapon stores?"

"We've got all of the 20mm ammo for the Phalanx and 30mm for the Bushmasters, all of our Mk 46 and 50 torpedoes, plenty of small arms ammo for the 16s and shotguns, all of our Tomahawks, Mk 41's and RIM 66 missiles. The only thing really we're low on is ammo for the forward five inch gun. We used up a lot of that sinking those last two tankers off of the Maldives before we got here, sir."

"And our Tomahawks? Are you certain we don't have any 109As?"

"That I'm sure of. I double checked myself. Everything we have is B, C or D."

"Damn! Very well, son. See to the refueling, and we'll weigh anchor at first light. High tide will be at 0700."

Ensign Johnson was about to take his leave when the captain asked one final question. "Do you think there's any BGM-109As at Diego Garcia?"

"Sir, that would be an Air Force issue, or the Brits. They were supposed to be getting the 109s starting in '09, but I don't know if they have any As and it is a British base."

"So you don't think it would be worth heading back south then?"

"It'd be a long shot sir, and we'd waste fuel on a…a wild goose chase." He almost said, *'fool's errand'*, but caught himself in time.

"Very well, carry on, Johnson."

"Aye, sir."

Johnson made his way aft and below, and as he made his way through the passageways to the weather deck he was seriously wondering about old 'Winnie's' mental health. He smiled at the name. 'Winnie the Pooh' was tacked onto the skipper in plebe year at Canoe U, and he hated it. Once he overheard an enlisted man mumble it, and he thought the man was going to be drawn and quartered. And why was he so gung ho on getting the As? He couldn't arm them without the codes.

The thought of crazy old Winnie with nukes made his bowels turn fluid. The BGM-109A, was a nuclear armed Tomahawk cruise missile, that had a W80 thermonuclear warhead, with a yield of about 20 kilotons.

Thank fuck we don't have any of those.

The only real smart thing the captain was doing was sinking all derelict vessels they spotted. They were definitely a hazard to navigation, but it was using up a shitload of the 5" shells in the process. Maybe he could talk the skipper into using up some of the Mk 46 torpedoes next go around. If anything, it was a morale booster to shoot the shit out of some hulk and send it to the bottom. His 'crew' loved the show, and it showed off the captain's prowess. But the way he was collecting the crew made him sick too. It harkened back to the way the British Navy did it back in the 1700s— pull into a port and announce the presence of the ship. Any survivors would come scampering out and jump at the offer of a clean bed and food, were welcomed aboard, and then were shanghaied and forced into becoming a member of the crew. He had witnessed just a few minutes earlier how discipline was enforced. Anytime now, he figured, they would reintroduce keel-hauling.

Shaking his head, he came out onto the weather deck to see the hoses trailing up to the fuel bunker fill caps. He looked down and saw several Kenyans and Somalis taking turns with the hand crank. Sure was a shitty way to refuel.

If the asshole would just grow a pair of balls and come alongside the pier for once, they might make the job go a little bit shorter than seven goddamn days. Alas, the skipper, for all his bluster, was really lacking in the boat handling department; the gash in the portside that another crew was repairing was testimony to that. Another shudder ran through him. When he was on the bridge earlier he'd snuck a quick look at the chart table. A red line was drawn on the acetate cover of the chart in grease pencil from Sri Lanka due east to the Strait of Malacca between Sumatra and Malaysia. It looked like the skipper's next port of call was going to be Singapore. If they could just get there without running aground or worse, *sinking*, he'd be a very happy man. He leaned on the railing, and looked down at his work party. They were pumping away, singing some song he'd never heard, but the rhythm was going with the cranks and he guessed it was helping them work.

"Excuse me, Mr. Johnson?" he heard from behind him. He straightened up and turned to see Petty Officer Suplee standing at the hatch.

"Yes, what is it?"

"We should be pretty well topped off in about two thousand more gallons, sir."

He did the mental arithmetic and figured four more trips in the whaleboat. "Okay, we'll be at this for a while yet. Rig up some lighting over the side for when it gets dark, and tell those fuckwits that the smoking lamp is definitely not lit until we secure from refueling!"

"Aye, sir."

"I'm not real happy about the other crew over the side welding at the same time, but the skipper wants to sail at first light."

"Ah, sir! We won't even have time to put a coat of primer over the patch!"

"I know that, Suplee. I'm not happy about any of this shit."

"You said it, sir. What's Winnie's next move?"

"I'll forget you called him that right now," he grunted. "I'm really not sure he'd take kindly with you calling him that. You saw what happened earlier, didn't you?"

"Yes, sir. Just between you and me, sir, if I can speak frankly?"

"Go ahead."

"I think Old Lead-Bottom has lost both oars."

"Suplee, you have been watching too many reruns of *McHale's Navy*."

"No shit, sir. I mean, look at what he's been doing." His voice dropped to a whisper. "Hijacking all these people, then when they get outta line, he puts a bullet in their melon. It just ain't cool, sir!"

"I don't like it either, but really what choice do we have?"

"Dunno, sir. Just sayin' is all."

"I do know one thing. With all these people we're getting, it's going to be an interesting dynamic."

"What do you mean, sir?" Suplee asked, scratching his head.

"Look at it this way. We're gathering a group of people from all over this part of the Indian Ocean— Hindus, Muslims, Christians, Pagans; Kenyans, Somalis, Indians, Pakistanis, Sri Lankans. Next we'll probably get some Indonesians, and once we're out in the Pacific, we'll probably pick up Samoans, Maoris, Tongans, Fijians, all peoples who traditionally hate each other. The captain thinks the discipline is hard now? Yes, it's going to be very interesting indeed."

"I never thought of it like that. It's like having a crew of Israelis and Palestinians. Nothing good will come of that."

"Exactly, and to answer your first question, bets are pretty even odds that our next port of call will be Singapore."

"Okay, sir. I'll get on those lights right away."

"And Suplee, belay anymore of that other bilge, alright?"

"Aye, sir!" he said and vanished into the darkness of the passageway.

Ensign Johnson decided to take a quick tour of the ship, and made his way aft to the hangar deck near the fantail where the one helicopter they had, a MH-60 Seahawk, was secured. There he found Petty Officer Stevens talking to two of the Sri Lankan 'draftees' that were brought aboard last night.

"Afternoon, Mr. Johnson!" he said with a smile. The sailor was enjoying this just a little too much for Johnson's taste, but he had to stifle his feelings.

"Stevens," he said, nodding. "The smoking lamp is still out," he added, pointing to the cigarette the sailor was smoking.

Stevens quickly tossed it over the side. "Hey, Mr. Johnson, one of these Sri Lankan guys says he's a helicopter pilot! I was just showing him the Seahawk."

"Is that so?" he asked, and the taller of the two dark skinned men came over and offered his hand.

"I am Major Vishdi Paleen, Sri Lankan Air Force, at your service." After a brief handshake, the man saluted.

"I'm Ensign Johnson, US Navy. And it is I who should be saluting you. Welcome aboard."

"It is a pleasure, I'm sure," he said, and Ensign Johnson's expression belied his thought: *Oh I don't think so, Major…*

"I'm sure the captain will be pleased to hear you're an experienced pilot. He has been waiting to commence air operations for a while. What aircraft are you familiar with?"

"I am greatly familiar with the MI8 and the UH1, nothing as technical as this fine aircraft I'm sure," he said, gesturing to the MH-60.

"But you do think you can fly it?"

"I am sure, sir."

"Very well, the captain will be most anxious to meet you, Major," Johnson said, again turning to the seaman. "Make sure you direct the Major to the Wardroom at 1800. Make sure our newest crewman is berthed, and make sure the Major gets a bunk in Officers' Country."

"Aye, sir!" the seaman said. "I'll see you for supper in the wardroom, Major. I've got to complete my rounds now," he said, turning to walk forward and look up at the mainmast. A tattered American flag flew, and it had seen far better days.

"Seaman Stevens?"

"Yes, sir?"

See if you can scare up another Stars and Stripes. That one has seen better days."

"Aye, sir, but wouldn't a Jolly Roger be more apt?" he said with a grin.

"Just do it, Stevens!"

"Aye, aye, sir!" Stevens said to the Ensign's back.

Ensign Johnson agreed with the seaman, but kept his feelings in check.

At exactly 1800 hours, or 6 PM local time, Ensign Johnson entered the Wardroom, followed by Major Paleen. The skipper was already seated at the head of the table meant for about twenty people; the destroyer's officer complement should have been around thirty. The Ensign made the introductions and was shown to a chair. A bottle of Scotch was presented, and the Ensign had the honors of pouring the drinks.

"For years, it was the tradition in the US Navy that no alcohol was permitted on ships. I'd like to keep that tradition alive for the enlisted ranks, but I'm lifting the rule for us officers," the captain said, raising his glass for a toast.

They all sipped their drinks, and the captain spoke again. "Mr. Johnson here tells me you're a helo pilot."

"That is true, sir. Twenty years in the Sri Lankan air force. About four thousand hours in the MI8 and UH1."

"And you think you can fly our bird?"

"Yes, sir! Let me have some time to familiarize myself with the controls, and I am certain I can fly her."

"Major, that makes me very happy." Two sari-clad Indian women came in and began serving the evening meal. "I'm not sure what this is, curried goat brains I think."

Major Paleen winced inwardly at the comment, but said nothing. This was far better than what he'd eaten over the last several months, and he was truly grateful for it.

Between bites of food, the captain went on. "We've got about thirty or so people on board now, and we're doing our best to shape them into sailors. I know it won't be easy, but we've had some good luck so far. As long as they want to work they'll be well taken care of."

"But of course," the major agreed.

"I believe in discipline, Major."

"As do I, sir."

"Good. We plan on setting sail tomorrow morning with the high tide. We're going to Singapore next, but my ultimate goal is to get back to Pearl Harbor. Our fuel capacity is such that we can't make the journey directly, so we'll have to stop at various places to replenish our stores and gather any other things we might need."

"That sounds like a splendid plan, sir. I will be honored to accompany you."

Commander Wright nodded his pleasure and turned to Ensign Johnson. "How is the rest of the provisioning going?"

"As well as can be expected, Skipper. We should be secured from refueling around 2100, and our freshwater tanks are full. Nakamura got the desalinization plant fixed, so that shouldn't be a problem. Plenty of fresh fruit and meat, although some of our Muslim crew aren't really happy about the pigs we brought aboard."

"Well, they'll just have to get over that. I think they should realize by now that after everything that has happened, there is no god, or Allah, or Buddha or whatever," the captain said dismissively.

"Yes, sir. Anyway, sir, we should be able to get underway in the morning like you planned. I would like a little more time to get a few coats of paint over the patch in the hull, but I guess that can wait until we get to Singapore."

"Very well, Mr. Johnson," he said, and then turned to the Major again. "So, what do you think happened, Major?"

"Do you mean all the deaths? I am not fully sure, maybe something cosmic?"

"I thought it was a nuclear detonation in the atmosphere at first, Major. Thought it was localized. But then I realized it was global in scale, and began to wonder…" He trailed off, looking at a spot on the far wall with a faraway look in his eyes. "Yes, truly cosmic. And Divine Providence I think. It gave me a golden opportunity to show the world what I can achieve!"

Ensign Johnson sat back silently. He'd heard this speech far too many times, and not wanting to correct the man for contradicting himself, he held his tongue. For if had truly had been 'Divine Providence', that would mean there really *was* a God. Suplee was right. He really didn't have both oars in the water.

The major nodded with a smile that didn't let on what was really on his mind.

"Anyone care for coffee?" the captain asked.

"I'll pass, sir. I have a few more things I have to do to get everything ready for when we set sail in the morning," Johnson said.

"Very well, you are excused."

Ensign Johnson got up from his chair, left the captain and the Major to their coffee and discussion that he really didn't want any part of, and made his way aft to the engine room, where he found Nakamura reading an X-Rated Hentai comic book.

"Is everything ready for the morning?" he asked.

"Hai! Everything ready! Fine turbines! They will work fine!"

"Good. Any problems, you let me know, okay?"

"Hai!" he said with a bow.

"Oh, and the skipper said you can have your pick of the girls tonight," he said distastefully.

"I alright, Johnson-San. Maybe we find Japanese girl next time?"

"I don't know about that, Nakamura. We're going to Singapore next. Maybe there'll be a nice Asian girl for you there." *Maybe one with tentacles,* he thought with a cringe, eyeing the Hentai comic book. Jap porn was some sick shit.

"Ah! That would be nice!"

"Any problems, you come and get me."

"Sure thing, Johnson-San. I come if problem, but no problem come up! I fix everything good!"

"Okay. Good night. We're sailing early, so lay off the sake and be ready to fire the turbines up."

"Hai!"

With that, Ensign Johnson left the compartment, wishing he was anywhere but there.

The next morning Cmd. Wright and Major Paleen were on the bridge with Suplee at the helm. The four General Electric LM 2500-30 turbines fired up just like Nakamura promised, and they could feel the vibration through the deck. Wright leaned out onto the wing bridge with his bullhorn and called down to weigh the anchor. It had barely broken the surface and wasn't completely in its anchor well when he barked out, "Right full rudder, give bells for one third power!"

"Right, full rudder, one third power, aye!" came the reply from the helmsman, who smartly turned the wheel and plugged in the command for power to the automatic controls in the engine room. The deck vibrated more noticeably, and the ship heeled over to starboard with the rudder.

"Helm, when we clear the outer harbor marker, make for twenty knots and steer a course for zero seven five degrees!" he said again, sat down in the high-backed captain's chair and lit his pipe.

"Aye, sir, twenty knots at zero seven five!"

Turning to the Major, who was duly impressed, he said, "I love this shit, Major. A man and his mistress, the sea!"

"Yes, Captain. Truly it is exciting!"

The bow rose and fell with the waves coming through the breakwater, and the helmsman applied power when they cleared. At almost five hundred and ten feet long, with a beam of sixty-six feet, the ship, although big, was still tossed around some by the waves.

As they cleared the outer marker letting them know they were now back into deep water, the helmsman turned the wheel again and applied power.

"Captain, my rudder is amidships and steering for one zero five. Making turns for twenty knots nominal!"

"Very well." The captain picked up the phone handset next to the chair and pushed a button to ring the radar space. After a moment it was answered by the other seaman, Stevens, who was manning the radar with one of the Kenyans, to whom he was teaching the system.

"Radar room!"

"Radar, this is the bridge. Anything on the scope?"

"Negative, sir. We're clear for at least one hundred miles."

"Very well. Keep a sharp eye out for hazards to navigation."

"Aye, sir!" Stevens said into a dead handset.

The next person the captain called was Johnson in the engine room.

"Is everything running smoothly, Mr. Johnson?"

"Yes, sir. Everything's nominal."

"Good. Let that Jap be in charge for a while, and come up here and relieve me on the bridge."

"Aye, sir," he said, also into a dead receiver. *What a fucking asshole!* he thought, grabbing his hat and giving Nakamura a few instructions before heading forward. On his way, he passed several of the newly conscripted crew sitting on the deck with their feet dangling over the side, laughing and joking. They smiled at him as he passed. He thought they must all be having a pretty good time. This was one big adventure to them, and it was probably the best existence any of them had had in their entire lives. He made his way onto the bridge, and reported.

"Okay, Mister Johnson. You have the conn. I'm going to give the major here a tour of the ship."

"Aye, sir. I have the conn," he confirmed, sitting in the now vacated captain's chair.

As they departed through a rear compartment hatch, the helmsman called out, "Mr. Johnson has the conn!"

He sat for a moment looking out of the forward windscreens as the ship sliced easily through the gentle two foot seas.

"Hey, Mr. Johnson, has the skipper gone aft?"

"Yeah."

"Are we going to do the same thing in Singapore?"

"Probably."

"Is the scuttlebutt true, that the skipper is looking to get nukes?

That made Johnson rise up a bit, and turn, looking behind him.

"Where'd you hear that?" That was the last thing he needed, for that to start spreading around.

"I overheard you and the skipper talking about the 109As yesterday. I know they're nukes. We had them when I was on the Kennedy a few years ago, and I know they don't have them on tin cans."

"Yeah, he's after them alright. Just don't spread it around." The thought of nukes was making him physically ill.

"Don't you have to have an order from the President or something to shoot them?"

"Yeah. You need the launch codes from the National Command Authority."

"If we don't have the codes, sir, what good are they?"

"Maybe he thinks he'll find the codes once we get back to Pearl."

"We headed to Pearl?"

"Eventually. I have no idea what's going on in his head, and he hasn't let on to me. Frankly, it's scaring me." He cut himself short at that. He'd said too much already. "What's our course?"

"Sir, I'm steering for zero seven five at twenty knots."

Johnson got up and went over to the plotting board. They had hundreds of miles of ocean before they got to the Nicobar Islands, before the Strait of Malacca. They'd just have to keep an eye out for 'hazards to navigation', of which he was sure there were plenty.

"Keep at that heading," he instructed. He got up from the chair and went out to the wing bridge, letting the air hit his face. It was shaping up to be a warm one, probably rain squalls, later in the day. He'd have to get some of the new crew members trained as lookouts. There should be more busy work too; the condition of the ship was getting to be dreadful. Everything was starting to rust, and it was really beginning to bug him. Maybe he didn't go to Annapolis like the skipper, but goddamn it he was a sailor and an officer, and this wasn't how you ran a ship. You didn't let things rust. You didn't leave things lying around in the passageways. You had to keep things ship-shape!

He shook his head in disgust. What could he do? He was as trapped as the rest of them.

By noon the wind had picked up and clouds were starting to build up in the east. A slight chop formed on what had been a smooth sea, and the bow of the destroyer started to rise and fall with the growing waves. The growler phone rang, and Johnson picked it up.

"Bridge!"

"Bridge, this is radar. I've got a contact bearing zero zero one, twelve thousand yards. Looks like a big one."

"Do you think it's another crude carrier?"

"It looks that way, sir. Whatever it is it's not moving much."

"Okay, keep me informed." He hung up the phone. "Helm, steer a course for zero zero one"

"Zero zero one, aye, sir!" The helmsman steered his course for almost due north. Johnson took a pair of big Zeiss binoculars out of a rack by the chair, and went out to the wing bridge. Twelve thousand yards was almost six nautical miles. If it was one of those big crude carriers, he should see it in a few minutes. He thought that radar should have caught it more quickly, but he let that slide. It only took a few minutes until he found it on the horizon. It was one of those Extra Large Crude Carriers, or ELCC's. As they approached it, he could see that it was listing badly, maybe a thirty degree starboard list, and the handrails were almost awash. It looked like it was empty, and he thanked God for that. The last one they'd shelled was fully loaded, and the third shell had ignited two compartments of the black mess, and burned for over three days, sending a vast black plume of toxic smoke skyward before it finally slipped below the waves.

Johnson walked back into the bridge just as the captain and Major Paleen reentered.

"I was just about to call you, sir. Radar has a sighting at twelve thousand yards, and I've steered a course to make contact. I've also verified the contact visually as an ELCC, directly due north. We should be in range of the five inch gun in about twenty minutes."

"Very good Mr. Johnson," Cmd. Wright said, as he took his seat in the captain's chair. "I now have the conn!"

"Captain has the conn!" the helmsman said.

Turning to Major Paleen, he said, "This is one of the major things we've been doing. Every time we see a ship floundering like this one we put several shells from our five inch gun forward into her, hopefully sinking her, and in the process removing a hazard to navigation, and avoiding a future environmental disaster if the ship were to run aground somewhere."

"Ah, I see! That is very smart of you!" the Major replied.

Ensign Johnson stood back and shook his head. *Avoiding a future environmental disaster.* That was a joke. What about all the oil slicks, flotsam and jetsam floating around after they put one of these hulks on the bottom? Or even worse, if the cargo didn't burn, the hulk would lay on the sea floor leaking oil into the waters for years afterwards. He walked out on the wind bridge with the binoculars and studied the target more closely. It appeared to have been adrift for a while, probably broken loose from its mooring lines while it was being loaded. He could see several of the hatches were open and there seemed to be no life at all on board.

"Mr. Johnson! Sound General Quarters!" the skipper barked.

"Aye, sir!" He hit a button on the rear bulkhead and the alarm went throughout the ship. That was another joke, him sounding General Quarters. What that meant now was that instead of a highly disciplined, well trained crew scrambling to their battle stations, a handful of the conscripts would stand out on the weather decks and watch the show, cheering as each shell hit the target. It was like a big party.

When they got to within three thousand yards, the captain ordered the battle klaxon sounded and an earsplitting *Whoop! Whoop! Whoop!* sounded across the distance, hopefully alerting anyone still alive on board. Taking one look at this battered hulk was enough to ensure that there was no one left alive, but he thought he'd do it anyway, just in case.

Picking up the phone, the captain called radar and instructed the sailor manning the scope to go to CIC— Combat Information Center— and man the computer controls for the automatic five inch cannon in a turret on the bow of the ship.

It was the last vestiges of the old Navy, but no longer were the guns manned by gunner's mates, and everything was automated. The turret slued around rapidly and the muzzle of the gun was pointed directly at the battered hulk, now only one thousand yards away. The skipper picked up the phone again and called the sailor in the CIC.

"Okay son, just like last time. Walk your rounds from bow to stern at the waterline. It looks like the deck facing us is almost awash so take your time! You may fire at will!"

"Fire at will, aye, sir!"

A high pitched *crack* sounded from the gun, which recoiled and spat out an expended brass shell onto the foredeck just like a huge semi-auto pistol. One of the Somalis ran over and grabbed it, and even though it was still hot to the touch, cheered as he held it over his head. The shell hit several seconds later, about fifty feet flat of the bow, exploding on contact, with a bright flash and a huge cloud of black smoke. A cheer went up from the crew on deck as the gunner shifted his aim slightly and let another round fly. Again, that round hit about a hundred feet aft of the first, with the same results. Through his binoculars, Ensign Johnson could see seawater pouring into the huge holes made by the exploding shells when the smoke cleared for each explosion. He had to admit, it was pretty exciting.

Things were going to get a little bit more exciting, unbeknownst to the crew of the Hughes. The USS *Hughes* drifted closer to the foundering hulk, and when the first shell left the forward gun they were now only seven hundred yards away.

The sixth shell pierced the hull, but didn't explode on contact. About two seconds after it had travelled through the ship's hull and punched its way into a half-filled compartment of crude oil, was when it went off. The fumes of the crude in the confined space had been building over several months and with no crew to vent the compartment, had built up to a dangerous level. This was right about amidships, and the hulk virtually lifted into the air almost thirty feet, splitting in two, and the resounding fireball and shockwave that followed was almost the size of a small nuke when it detonated. The USS *Hughes* heeled over almost twenty degrees, and paint blistered on the side of the ship that was nearest to the now rapidly disappearing hulk. Within minutes, the only thing left was a burning oil slick a hundred yards wide and a few bits of foam and fiberglass. The blast had knocked everyone on the bridge off their feet, and when they regained their footing they looked around at each other in amazement.

"Damage report!" the captain bellowed, and Ensign Johnson went to assess the condition of the ship.

"That was one hell of a blast. I think from now on we'll stay a bit further off when we engage the crude carriers!" the captain said with an evil grin. "That could have put us on the bottom!"

"Wow! Did you see that fucker?" the helmsman said, stunned.

"Yes I did, son. If everything is okay with Mr. Johnson's report in a few minutes, we'll return to our original course."

"Aye, sir!"

Just then Stevens, the sailor who'd been firing the gun, came into the bridge from the CIC. "Sir, can I have a word with you?"

"It wasn't your fault sailor. We'll just lay off a bit next go around."

"Aye, sir. But that's not really wanted to talk to you about."

"Oh?"

"Yes sir. Last night I went into the comms shack and started playing around with the radios. When I was a kid, I was an amateur ham radio operator. Had all kinds of shit and would talk to people all over the worl—"

"Your point is?" the captain cut in impatiently.

"Morse Code, sir. It's one of the reasons I joined the Navy. Anyway, sir, around midnight I was dicki— I mean playing with the radios, and I picked up something on the three meter band. Was really faint, but it was definitely Morse Code on the ham band."

"Really now?" The captain perked up. He sat up straighter on the chair and lit his pipe. "Tell me more."

"Not much else to tell you, sir. I only made out a few words, and it kept fading in and out. If I could, with your permission, sir, I'd like to see if I could find it again and find out where it's coming from."

"Permission granted. Take all the time you need. Are those two Pakistani men trained up on the radar?"

"They're about as well trained as they're going to be, sir."

"Good. You are now relieved at the radar. Tell those men that they have to work twelve hour shifts on the scope from now on. I want you in comms indefinitely until you can pinpoint that signal!"

"Aye, sir!" he said with a grin and departed.

"Well, isn't that interesting?" he asked aloud to no one. Just then the growler phone rang and the captain picked it up. "Bridge!"

"Bridge, this is Ensign Johnson. Damage report is negative. We lucked out on this one. Some of the hull plating is bent inwards on the port side and paint is blistered, but everything is seaworthy. There were a few minor injuries on the crew on the weather decks, but nothing serious."

"Very well then. Make your way back up here and we'll get underway."

"Aye, sir!" he said, and the captain hung up.

"Helm! Make turns for twenty knots, and steer for zero seven five!"

"Zero seven five at twenty knots aye, sir!"

The turbines came back to life, vibrating the deck under their feet reassuringly. The ship turned onto the new course, the bow rising with the swells, brass shells rolling forgotten on the foredeck under the turret.

The captain leaned back in his chair, puffing on his pipe. He started to grin.

CHAPTER 7:
ANOTHER WINTER

All throughout the summer, Tim and Robyn had made strides in improving their little camp in the woods of West Virginia. Tim had solved a problem with the toilet waste by making a French drain behind the camper, and it actually worked like a small septic system. He had also gotten a small metal shed kit at a local home improvement store, and they now had it stocked with canned goods and other things they'd need to get by in case they were snowed in. They had made several trips to the library and had a huge collection of books in the increasingly cramped trailer. Every evening after supper they would both read, and Robyn proved to be a virtual sponge for information. Tim had never had any children of his own, and really had no clue on how to raise one, so he just went with the flow and taught the young girl everything he knew. He spoke to her as an adult, which wasn't really the way all the books said to do it, but it was the only way he knew how.

Over the past several months, she not only put on weight and was no longer the skinny kid he first met in the beginning of the summer, but she had almost lost her thick West Virginia accent, and spoke in a manner that belied her age. When they talked of things, she didn't just dismiss topics because they were 'stupid' like most kids, she really wanted to learn about history, science and mathematics. She'd ask 'why' if she wanted to know about something, and then listened and retained the information. She also proved to be an excellent shot, and would disappear into the woods with the .22 rifle, most times returning with a rabbit or two, or a few squirrels.

The days were growing shorter, and in the twilight of the day they sat with an American History book open, and were having a discussion on the Spanish-American War. They had started a few months prior with the trips of Christopher Columbus and the discovery of the New World, and had progressed through the American Revolution. It had started innocently enough, by Robyn's question to an offhand comment he'd made, and ended with them both going to the library and getting as many history and geography books as they could carry. Now they were huddled in their trailer with the textbook and a world atlas, because he always thought that history and geography went hand in hand. Every time they'd get to a passage where it would mention a location, Tim would flip open the atlas, and show her where it was on the map. She was a voracious learner and Tim was amazed at her intelligence. Despite her lack of a proper education, she showed a remarkable ability and desire to learn almost everything.

"So you're saying that we went to war with Spain because of a mistake?"

"Well, people were paranoid. The *USS Maine* exploded in Havana harbor and everyone thought it was Spanish terrorists. It wasn't until years and years later that a few researchers theorized that the explosions were probably caused by coal dust combusting in one of the coal bunkers."

"I know about coal dust explosions. One happened in the mine a few years ago."

"Yes, and people just jumped to conclusions and we went to war with Spain. But in the process we gained a bunch of new territories and became a world Power. We had a pretty big Navy at the time, and the Great White Fleet would sail around the world, letting everyone know that the US wasn't going to take shit off of anyone."

"The Great White Fleet, what's that?"

"All the ships were painted a really bright white, unlike the ships of today's Navy, so everyone began calling it 'The Great White Fleet'."

"Isn't that a little arrogant?" Robyn asked.

Tim had to smile. It was like he was talking to a thirty year old sometimes. Her vocabulary was far greater than his when he was that age. He took a sip of beer and nodded his head solemnly. "Yeah, it was. People and countries tend to get that way, unfortunately. They forget where they all started."

"Can I have a beer?"

"No you may not!" Tim exclaimed.. "Maybe when you're older, but not now and that's my final word on it."

Robyn screwed her face into a tight little knot for a second and then laughed. "It was worth a shot."

He laughed hard at that. "How old are you again?"

"I'm thirteen."

"More like thirty!" he said.

"Okay, enough history for one night, it's time for bed."

"Okay," Robyn said agreeably, carefully marking her pages and packing up the books. After her shower was taken and teeth were brushed, Tim helped her into her bunk. Her covers were pulled up tight, and Bad Bear was securely in her arms, tucked under her chin. She looked at him seriously.

"Tim?"

"Yes?"

"Thank you."

"I'm just doing what I can," he said.

"I know. I'm not scared anymore. Like I was when everyone died. I feel safe with you."

He was starting to feel uncomfortable, and he really didn't know what to say, so he just said, "Like I said, I'm doing what I can, Robyn."

"You won't let anything happen to me, will you?"

"I'll do my best to protect you."

"Do you promise?"

He winced, hoping she didn't notice. After a second or two he replied, "I promise, baby. Now get to sleep," and without thinking, he leaned forward and kissed her on the forehead.

"Good night, Tim."

"Good night, Robyn."

Tim made his way to his bed, turning off the lights as he went. He sat down on his bunk and looked back at the already sleeping child, and thought about making promises. He lay down on his bed, staring up at the ceiling. So many promises in the past he'd broken. Now here was one he had to keep, no matter what. With that unsettling thought he drifted off to a troubled sleep.

September made way for October. The leaves changed and fell from the trees. A cold, wet rain heralded in mid-November, and now the daytime temperatures barely rose above 40 Fahrenheit, and the rain threatened to turn to sleet. Tim dragged a nice sized whitetail buck he'd shot earlier up to the camper. Robyn bounded out of the trailer and ran up to him, admiring the deer.

"Nice one, Tim!"

"Yeah, and he's heavy too. I thought I was going to have a heart attack dragging it back."

"I hope not. Are you okay?" she asked seriously, a terrified look sweeping over her face.

"I'm fine, Robyn, I was just making a joke."

"It wasn't funny," she said flatly, screwing her face into a knot.

"I'm sorry. I didn't mean to upset you."

"You can't die! If you die I'll be all alone again!" she said, her tears flowing.

"Honey, I'm not going to die anytime soon, okay? I can't die. I've got to stick around a while longer anyway."

He went over to her and held her close until the tears diminished to a few sobs. "I promise. I'm not going to die, okay? Besides, my brother told me a while ago I had to make a difference, whatever that might mean, and I haven't made a difference. So I can't go yet!"

"Made a difference?"

"Yeah, something my brother said to me a long time ago." It was only a year ago, but Tim thought it seemed like a lifetime already.

"C'mon, want to help me butcher it?"

"I'll get the knives!" Robyn said, her mood changing instantly. She bounded back into the camper, returning with the proper cutting tools. He had already gutted the animal where he'd shot it, so they made quick work of skinning and cutting the meat up into manageable sizes. They wrapped most of it and put it in the storage shed, securing it tightly. This time of year he really wasn't concerned with the possibility of a bear raiding their food because they should be hibernating by now, but it never hurt to be doubly sure. The shed would act as a natural freezer since the temperature was already noticeably colder. He had saved two big steaks and put them on a plate, showing them off to Robyn theatrically.

"Dinner, Madam!"

"Yum!" she said, clapping happily.

"I'll take these in and marinate them a little with some salt and pepper, and I'll fire up the grill and cook them properly."

"It's going to snow," she said. "You're crazy!"

"It wouldn't be the first time I've barbequed in the snow, young lady. And you are most probably correct in your assumption that I am crazy."

Robyn laughed again and they went into the camper. She sat down at the dinette table, while he took out the spices and sprinkled both sides of the freshly cut steaks liberally with them. Watching intently, she said, "What are you going to do with the skin?"

"I don't know. I was thinking that maybe we could try to dry it out and tan it somehow, like the Indians did, and then make a few deerskin vests or something." He had done it a few times with the rabbit pelts, and made them both winter hats out of them. They weren't pretty, but they would keep their heads warm, so he figured he'd do the same with the deerskin.

"That's why I asked. I was thinking the same thing!"

She had a habit of doing that. It was almost like she could read his mind sometimes.

"Then it's settled. We'll tan it and make vests."

"Cool!"

He grabbed a beer out of the fridge and picked up the plate of meat. "Get the door for me please?"

She jumped up and opened the door for him, and stood there as he walked past.

"Can I have a beer?"

"No!" he laughed.

"I had to try," she giggled.

"Want to help?"

"Sure!"

"Get a can of whatever veggies you want with dinner and heat them on the stove for me."

Robyn bounded off to the back of the trailer where the shed was. She came back a few minutes later with two cans. "How about creamed corn and asparagus?"

"That sounds good to me," he said, and she went into the trailer where he could hear the pots being banged around. He had to laugh. At that age he'd hated asparagus, and this kid loved it. She liked all kinds of vegetables. In fact, after the first few days with him, she had completely lost all aversion to them. With little urging from him, she was eating very healthily now, compared to the cookies and potato chips she had been eating. Her only straying from that was that she loved the sweet tea powder drinks and the occasional can of Coke. He was trying to set a good example by cutting down enormously on his beer and alcohol consumption, and had weaned himself down to only about three or four cigarettes a day. He'd eventually have to quit those altogether, because it was getting harder and harder to find any that weren't stale or gnawed through by mice or rats.

He lit up a Winston and turned on the gas to the grill he'd acquired, lighting two burners with a click of the built in igniter. It was a nice one. The price tag on it read 'Marked Down! Now Only $1,200!!!!' He'd have never have been able to afford something this nice, even on a cop's salary. Now he was living high on the hog, so to speak. Anything he wanted he'd just go and get. He figured that's what being rich was like, never having to worry about the price of something.

He sipped his beer and let the grill get hot. He looked around at their little homestead, and thought they had it pretty well here. He'd have to flip the cammo netting around to the brown side in the next day or two, because what was perfectly hidden in the summer now stuck out like a sore thumb. He called out to Robyn to let him know when the veggies were ready, and she did in a few minutes. He placed the thick steaks on the grill, and they sizzled satisfactorily. After a few minutes on one side, he flipped them with a pair of tongs. Something he'd remembered from years ago, never, ever use a fork to turn meat. It lets the juices escape, drying out your steaks, and venison was lean enough to begin with, so he didn't want these beautiful pieces of meat to wind up like old shoe leather. After a few minutes on the other side, he decided they were done to their liking, so he shut off the burners and closed the valve on the propane tank. Getting the dish, he used the tongs to load them up, and he carried them back into the trailer. He saw that Robyn had set the table already, and there were two steaming bowls of veggies along with all the condiments, including a bottle of A1 Steak Sauce. When he'd been that age, he would have had to be dragged away from whatever he was doing by an ear to get him to do anything to help around the house. Now here was this thirteen year old girl who did it without even being asked.

"Did you wash up?"

"Yes sir," she said, holding up her hands. "Not even crud under my nails!"

"Very good, but don't call me sir. I work for a living."

"What should I call you then?"

"Sergeant Major!" he said with mock severity. "Only officers are called sir!"

He set the plate down on the table and went to the small sink to washing his own hands. He came over and sat down at the table, portioning out the veggies and steaks onto each of their plates.

"So is that what you are in the Army, a Sergeant Major?"

"Yes ma'am. Best job in the Army."

"Is that pretty high up?"

"About as far as you can go, enlisted wise," he said, cutting a piece of steak and popping it into his mouth. "Mmmmmmmm!" When he'd chewed and swallowed, he looked over to Robyn who smiled back at him, mouth full of food and gave him a thumb's up sign.

"Well, I'm glad you approve of my culinary expertise!"

They ate in silence and Tim looked up at a calendar he'd pinned up on the far wall behind Robyn. He noticed the date with a start. It was a year ago today The Event had happened. He'd completely forgotten his wedding anniversary, and that really didn't matter anymore, but this one was important. He decided not to say anything to Robyn about it and continued eating. He thought about everything that had happened, and was really thankful for a lot of things. He then looked back at the calendar and saw that Thanksgiving was only a few weeks away. He'd have to do something for that. There was plenty of wild turkey around in the woods; he'd shoot one and whip up a whole Thanksgiving spread. Then he thought about how he'd cook a big bird like that. His oven was far too small. He figured he'd use the barbeque. It was large enough to put a roasting pan on one side, and use offset heat to cook it like a huge roaster. Throughout dinner he made his plans, hoping to surprise Robyn later.

After they were finished eating, they busied themselves with the washing up and Tim noticed the light sleet had turned to snow, so he went back outside and covered the barbeque grill with a tarp. Reentering, he saw Robyn already curled up with a book at the table. He decided to grab one he'd been reading, a Melville classic, and sat down opposite her. After only about a minute or so, she began to laugh. He peered over the edge of the book with a raised eyebrow.

"And what is so funny?"

"*Moby Dick!*" she snickered.

He laughed heartily. "It doesn't mean that!"

"What's it about then?"

"It's about a sea captain of a whaling ship back in the 1800's. He goes crazy chasing after this huge white whale all over the seven seas, taking everything with him as he slips into madness."

"Is it good?"

"It's very good. You can read it when I'm done."

"Cool."

"What are you reading?"

"I'm reading *Treasure Island*. It's really good too."

"I loved that when I was a kid. How did you like *Robinson Crusoe*?"

"I loved it. I really like this one too. Are there really places like those islands?"

"Yes, there are thousands of islands like that all over the world."

"I'd like to go to them some day."

"Well, we'd better find someone who knows how to sail a big boat then, sweetheart. I know a lot about a bunch of things, but I'm no sailor." He thought about Paul again, Paul and his island. It kept coming back to him, and he didn't know why.

He thought again about her reaction to the name of his book. *Moby Dick* had been banned in several libraries many years ago, just because some uptight prig was offended by the name. He always thought a really good library should have enough books to offend just about everyone. His way of thinking was this: *You were offended? Don't read the goddamn book. Don't force your views on anyone else.* Again he snickered to himself. Another thing he'd always said was that the world would be a much better place without all the people. *Well,* he thought, *I was right about that idea.*

They read silently for a few more hours until Tim heard Robyn yawn. He put his book down and looked over at her.

"Are you ready for bed?"

"Yeah, I'm getting tired."

"I'm about ready too," he said, looking at his watch, seeing it was already ten thirty PM. "Better go and brush your teeth."

Robyn closed her book, carefully marking her page. She grabbed an old faded t-shirt of Tim's and headed to the tiny bathroom. He continued to read for a few more minutes with increasingly heavy eyes. He heard the shower turn on, so he figured he'd read a few more pages while she did her thing. After several minutes she came out, her hair wet and shiny. She was toweling it off and had on his t-shirt. She had put on some weight, although it looked as if she'd not yet grown an inch. His t-shirt almost swallowed her up, covering her from way below the knees and halfway down her arms.

"Did you leave me any hot water?"

"Yes I did," Robyn said. "I took a submarine shower like always, just like you said we should do."

"Just checking."

She came over to him, bent down and kissed him on his cheek. "Good night, Sergeant Major," she said, and launched herself easily into her bunk. He turned out the light over the dinette, dimming the interior of the camper significantly. He pulled the blankets up to her chin, and said goodnight then went to the rear of the camper and repeated what she had done. Drawing a privacy curtain, he stripped, and took a short 'submarine' shower himself, (turning the water on just long enough to get wet, then turning it off, soaping up and washing, then turning the water on again to rinse.) It conserved a shitload of water. He did that, shaved and brushed his teeth. By the time he was done, he was bone tired. Drying off, he got into a pair of long johns and made sure the camper's propane heater was working properly. It was bound to get even colder overnight, and he didn't want anything to freeze up.

When he went to his berth he saw the uncleaned M16 laying there. "Shit!" he whispered. He'd forgotten about that. He pulled out the rifle cleaning kit and broke down the rifle to clean it. He was slipping. Only fired one round, but he needed to make sure the weapon was clean before he went to bed. As he busied himself with that mindless chore, his mind was running over the last year. The one thing that kept coming back to him was the whole island thing. There seemed to be a recurring theme to it, but he never believed in coincidence. He'd been a cop and soldier far too long. There had to be something to it. And why did he bring up his brother's conversation from last year? He still didn't know how one man could make a difference. Change the world.

Save it.

Just the mere thought that he, an almost fifty year old broke-dicked cop and soldier, was going to save the world. Him, the Messiah? Now there was a joke that was almost insane. He had his hands full enough just trying to keep Robyn and himself alive through another winter. He most definitely did not need the weight of the world on his shoulders. He reassembled the M16 and put it up beside the M4 carbine and the grease gun. He looked at that old relic from a different era. He'd have to get Robyn out to shoot that. She'd have a blast. He turned out his light and crawled into bed, pulling the covers up snugly. The wind was picking up and he was thankful for the heater. He slipped quickly into a deep, dreamless sleep.

As usual, Robyn was awake before Tim, and he heard her puttering around in the galley as he stirred from his sleep. He dragged himself out of bed and made his way out to greet the day. Tim was still not, and would probably never be, a 'morning person,' but Robyn was up and full of life, cheery as could be.

"Good morning, Sergeant Major!" she said brightly as Tim stepped out from the privacy curtain.

"It's morning alright," he grunted. Seeing she was already making the pot of coffee, he went to the dinette and sat down. Although he wasn't a morning person, he did really miss reading the newspaper with his morning coffee, especially the crossword puzzle. Maybe they could take a trip into town and see if there were any puzzle books at the local book store.

"Coffee is almost ready," Robyn said. She was still dressed in his t-shirt, but had brushed out her hair and tied it back into a ponytail.

"Good. I need some," he grumbled.

"That's what I love about you, Tim, your cheery disposition in the morning!"

He had to laugh; a thirteen year old with the ability to understand the nuances of sarcasm, and the ability to wield it. She was turning into a carbon copy of him, and he didn't know whether to be proud or frightened. He sat and watched her silently as she measured out the correct spoons of sugar and canned milk for his coffee, and poured a black coffee for herself. She brought them both over to the table, setting his down in front of him.

"Thank you," he said, taking a sip of the hot beverage.

She took a sip of hers, and looked behind her at the calendar. He sat up a little when he saw a dark cloud sweep over her face. In a tiny voice, almost too low to hear, she said, "It's been a year."

"What's that?"

"It's been a whole year since everyone died."

"Yeah, I know. I noticed yesterday but didn't want to say anything to upset you."

"I'm not upset, just sad."

"We both lost people we cared a lot about, honey. But the main thing is we're still alive, and they would want us to keep on surviving."

"I know. It's just sad, so many people gone."

They sat for a while, drinking their coffee quietly, and Tim peered out the slats of the blinds to see about six inches of fresh snow on the ground. It had stopped sometime overnight. He turned back to Robyn and when he was facing her again she asked, "Do you think that's what happened to the dinosaurs?"

"I don't know. I know that the scientists weren't completely sure about it. Some thought it was a comet or meteorite."

"Do you think we're going to be extinct?"

"Well, I hope not. You and I are still alive and kicking, and I'm going to do my best to make sure you and I don't go extinct."

"Good! So no one really knows what happened to the dinosaurs?"

"Not a hundred percent. I do know there's a thin layer of soil called the 'K-T' Boundary that spans the entire globe. I'm not sure of the exact age, but it was a long time ago. Above it there are no dinosaur fossils at all, like they all dropped at once."

"Like last year..."

"Yeah, but look at it this way. Sharks have been around for millions of years. They were around in the time of dinosaurs, and they're still around today. And several years ago, fishermen caught a coelacanth, a fish thought to have been extinct for millions of years."

"So I shouldn't worry?"

"No, you shouldn't. My final word on worrying: can you do anything about it?"

"No," she replied.

"Then don't worry about it."

Robyn giggled and finished her coffee. "Do you want another cup, Sergeant Major?"

"Yes, please," he said, handing over his cup. "And just say 'Sar' Major'. You'll sound like a real soldier then."

"Okay, Sar' Major!"

As he watched her make their second cups of coffee, one thought did cross his mind that he thought he should just keep to himself. Tim knew that over ninety percent of all species that had ever lived on the planet were now extinct. Was Man's reign on Earth really over? He hoped not. He let that thought slip as Robyn came back with two fresh steaming mugs and sat down.

"Tell me about the Army," she said.

"Not much to tell you. It's a good life, but hard too. Can be really dangerous and you're away from home a lot."

"Have you been in a war?"

"Yeah, honey, a few of them. But I really don't like talking about it."

"Have you been many places?"

"That's one of the really great things about being in the Army. You get to travel a lot. I've been to a lot of places," he said, reaching up to the bookshelf, and retrieving the world atlas. He began to show her all the places he'd been, all the countries in Central America, the places in Europe and the Middle East. He told her he'd even been all the way down to Australia, two times.

"Wow! This is the farthest I've ever been out of the holler! Do you think I'll ever get to see some of those places?"

"Well, maybe someday. We're kind of stuck here on this continent unless we meet up with someone who knows how to sail."

"Yeah, you said that before," she said with a frown.

"Tell you what," he said, changing the subject. "After we finish our coffee, let's get dressed and head into town."

"Anything special we're looking for?"

"Yes," he said, and told her about his idea of putting on a big spread for Thanksgiving. She was all for it, and they quickly finished the coffee. Tim gave her some privacy to get dressed, and got dressed himself. He went outside into the crisp, morning air and walked to the truck to start it. It hitched a few times before turning over, and he thought he'd better start it daily now, just to keep the battery charged up. Last winter he'd used it almost daily, so he'd never had to worry about it, but here it sat for days at a time without moving. Going back inside the trailer, he left the truck to idle and warm up. He retrieved the M4 carbine and a few magazines that he put in the pockets of his Gortex ACU jacket. They piled into the cab of the truck, Tim tossed the M4 onto the dashboard, and they headed out. The going was fine, with the truck's front axle locked into four wheel drive, and they made good time in spite of the snow.

As they made their way off Rt. 20 and onto Rt. 460, Tim stopped suddenly on the crest of the bridge that crossed over Interstate 77. Tim got out and walked through the snow to the railing of the bridge, and looked down on the interstate highway. There, he could plainly see two sets of fresh tire tracks in the snow in the southbound lanes. Whoever it was, they had continued south, deciding to pass Princeton on their journey. When he climbed back into the truck, Robyn asked what had happened, and he told her of the tire tracks. An excited but worried look crossed her face, and he explained it looked like they hadn't stopped.

"Are we ever going to try to find more people?"

"Yeah, I think we should. But we've got to be really careful."

"I know. Bad people are out there."

"I think they'll never go away," he said. He put the truck back into gear and continued on. They pulled into the lot of the local Food Lion grocery store, and Tim looked around. No tire tracks here. They got out, and quickly entered the darkened store. This one had been gone through before, and not just by them; it looked like other people had been through too. The shelves were practically empty. They went up and down the aisles, getting the things they thought they'd need: canned cranberries, candied yams, some stuffing mix that looked as though it hadn't been gnawed through, and one single Betty Crocker pre-made pie shell. It was probably stale, but you couldn't have a Thanksgiving spread without pumpkin pie! He got that, and found several cans of pumpkin pie filling. When they were done, Tim asked Robyn, "Anything else you think we might need? This may be the last chance to get into town this winter."

"Maybe some Coke, if there's any left."

"Let's go look," he said, and turned the shopping cart around to look for it. There were still several cases left, so they took a few, and Tim thought he should get some more beer, and they went to that aisle. It was a refrigerated aisle close to the meat department. It had been over a year, but the lingering smell of rot permeated this section of the store. All the good beer was gone. The only thing left was a few cases of Pabst Blue Ribbon.

"I guess the Sar' Major will have to get by with PBR," he said, grabbing the last two cases.

They headed outside, loaded up their goodies, and made their way back to the camper. When they arrived, they quickly unloaded their stuff and stored it away. Then Tim had another thought.

"Robyn?"

"Yeah?"

"Would you be okay here by yourself for a bit? I just want to make a quick run back into Athens for something I forgot."

"Yeah, I guess..." she said worriedly.

"I'll only be about a half hour, I promise."

She ran up to him and hugged him tight. "You just hurry home, okay?"

He nodded and smiled at her, turned and got back in the truck. As he pulled away, he looked in the rear-view mirror to see her still standing there, watching him leave, and his heart dropped. It wasn't the first time he'd left her to her own devices. She had also at times gone off by herself into the woods, but this made him a tiny bit nervous. He shook the thought off as he pulled back out onto Rt.20, heading back south the few miles to Athens. There, he pulled up to an old True Value hardware store. He had been here on several occasions, but never for this reason. The door of the store, had already been broken open by him several months ago, but he still took a pair of bolt cutters that he kept behind the seat. He walked in, and straight to the back of the store, where there was a place that they had sold guns too, just like a hundred years ago. There was a glass counter with a long rack behind it. Several rifles and shotguns were in it, with a long steel cable through the trigger guards, and padlocked at the end. Using the bolt cutters, he quickly dispensed of the heavy Yale padlock, and pulled the cable out. He walked down the line of firearms and found what he was looking for, a Remington 12 Gauge shotgun with a 28" barrel. *Can't hunt turkey without a shotgun.* He pulled it down, also grabbing a few boxes of 3" magnum shells for it. Something caught his attention from the corner of his eye. He walked to the end, and what he saw he didn't believe. He hadn't seen one of these in years, a World War II M1 carbine paratrooper model, the kind with the side folding metal stock. He pulled it down, and for laughs looked at the price tag. $1,500! He remembered when you could get a decent M1 carbine for a hundred bucks! He put that down next to the shotgun. Robyn was ready to graduate to something a little bigger than the .22, and this fit the bill nicely. Weighing only five pounds, the little .30 caliber cartridge it fired had a lot more power than a .22, but had almost no recoil. He scrounged around and found four fifteen-round magazines for it, as well as several boxes of ammo. He took all this back out to his truck, wrapping the carbine, magazines and ammo, in a wool Army blanket. He hid it behind the seat of the truck, placing the bolt cutters on top. He put the shotgun on the front seat, along with the boxes of shells, and lit a cigarette.

Down the street, he saw the old Rexall drug store sign. He'd been through this one too, getting all the pharmaceuticals he thought they'd need, but he did remember they had all kinds of stationery and the like also.

Walking down the block a short way, he entered the drug store, quickly finding what he was after. A few rolls of Christmas wrapping paper and bows and a roll of scotch tape. He strolled back to the truck with his take, and placed that behind the seat also, then quickly headed home. When he pulled up to the camper Robyn came out to meet him.

"What did you get?" she asked.

He held up the shotgun. "Can't shoot a turkey for Thanksgiving without a shotgun!"

They walked back into the camper, and Robyn presented a tuna sandwich on the bread he'd finally figured out how to bake. He took the offered plate, setting the shotgun against the wall next to the door, and then sat down at the dinette.

"Kill Flipper, did we?"

"Huh?"

"It's a joke. You had to have been there," he said, and began to devour the food.

"Want a beer?"

"Not right now, maybe a Coke?"

"Can I have a beer?"

"You don't give up, do you?"

She just smiled and handed him a can of Coke from the fridge. Sitting down opposite of him, she said, "I mixed up the tuna, mayo and relish while you were gone. I already had a sandwich. There's plenty more if you want some."

"No, this is fine right now, honey."

"So why didn't you want me to come with you back into town?" she asked with a sideways glance of suspicion.

"There was no reason at all, really. Just remembered about the shotgun and thought I'd just run back and get it."

This kid was intuitive as hell. It was hard getting anything past her, and now the hard part, hiding the carbine from her until Christmas.

"Why are you smiling?"

"No reason."

"I bet," she said, and kicked him under the table.

"Ow! That hurt!"

"Teach you to hide things from me!"

"I'm not!"

"Sure you aren't!" and she stuck out her tongue.

"Okay, I admit it! I had a hot date with a hair stylist!"

"Speaking of hair, you're getting shaggy again. Want me to cut it for you today?"

"Yeah, might as well. It might be a long time before we can do much of anything outside again."

"Okay. Finish your sandwich and I'll get the clippers."

His hair was easy to cut. Although he still had a full head of hair, the military style was easy, so easy in fact, he could do it himself. But it was nice to have Robyn do it for him. He finished his lunch and headed outside where she had already set up a folding chair for him to sit on and had a towel to drape over his shoulders. Right before she clicked on the clippers, he noticed the generator was running a little ragged, and said something about it.

"Yeah, it was running like that last night when I went out to shut it down, and I forgot to tell you."

"It's probably stale gas."

"What's stale gas?" she asked, and began to shear off Tim's salt and pepper locks.

"Gasoline has a finite shelf-life, and it gets stale, turns to turpentine really, and it's not much use after that."

"So none of the gas is going to be any good?"

"Pretty much. In a few more years, it'll be good for cleaning paintbrushes and starting fires, but won't be worth a shit in engines."

"So what are we going to do?"

"We'll use diesel fuel. It'll last for a long, long time. Might gel up some in the winter, but it'll be good for years. We'll just have to find a bigger diesel generator is all."

"So it'll be okay?"

"Yeah, we'll be fine. There's plenty of propane and diesel around. We'll get by."

"You had me worried there for a minute," she said with relief. She shut the clippers off and removed the towel with a flourish. Tim stood and ran his hand over the close-cropped stubble. "Nice! It's another perfect job, Vince!"

"*Vince?* My name isn't Vince!" she said incredulously, hand on her hip.

He laughed. "Every barber I ever knew in Philadelphia, was named Vince. And none of them was anywhere near as pretty as you are!"

"I thought maybe you had slipped a track," Robyn said, snapping the towel to get the hair off of it. He shook his head and smiled. She was even picking up the Army slang he used.

"Let's get inside, it's getting cold out here."

They both went inside, and just as they reached the camper door, it started to sleet again. They sat down opposite each other, and Tim thought about his present. How the hell was he going to keep that hidden for over a month? He'd figure something out. That he'd actually thought of it that far ahead, surprised him. For years he'd forgotten birthdays, Christmas and anniversaries until the last minute, rushing out to buy a gift the day before, and usually his choice in presents showed his haste. Maybe he needed this kid as much as she needed him.

He stood up. "How about some hot cocoa?"

"That sounds great!" she almost squealed.

He went to the cabinet over the stove, pulled out a box of instant cocoa bags, selected two, and replaced the box. He then filled the teapot with water, and put in on the range to boil. While he waited, he emptied each bag into a coffee cup.

"Oh, these got the little marshmallows!"

"Yum!"

The kettle whistled and he swiftly poured the boiling water into the two cups, stirring the mix, until each was blended perfectly. He brought both back over and sat down, sipping the hot concoction. They each savored their drinks in silence, listening to the sleet pelt the trailer. It was getting worse, and he was glad they had gotten all the errands done today. This might turn out to be one nasty ice storm before it was over with.

"I think it's a perfect night for grilled cheese sandwiches and soup."

"That sounds great to me."

He again went to the cabinets, opening the door. "We've got cream of mushroom, tomato, cream of broccoli…" he looked at her with a wrinkled nose and she laughed. "Chicken noodle, chicken with stars, and a few alphabets, your choice."

"Let's have chicken noodle."

"That is an excellent choice, madam!" Tim got two cans out and set them aside. The bread he'd made was actually quite nice, better than any store brand he'd ever had, and after he figured out the yeast and the altitude combination, it was fairly easy to make. The problem now was finding flour that wasn't spoiled by rodents. The cheese for the sandwiches wasn't a problem either. He didn't know what they did with it, but he thought the packaged American cheese slices they had plenty of would last until the next Ice Age. He looked at his watch, and saw that it was just about 4PM.He sat back down, finishing his cocoa, and looked out the window to see a thin film of ice already forming over everything that was exposed to the weather. Yes, it was going to be a nasty one tonight.

They read their books in silence for a while until it was time to cook supper. They ate in silence, and of that he was glad. Sometimes there was no need for words; just the person's company was all that was needed. Something Connie had never figured out. That woman would never shut up, and it drove him mad sometimes. The thought of Connie just then saddened him, and it showed.

"What's wrong, Tim?"

"Ah, just thinking about someone in my past is all."

"How you could have changed it?" she asked.

"And you're thirteen?"

"Yes. But like you said before, you can't change the past. And like, worrying over stuff you have no control over, it has no use," she said. If he'd been on the phone with her, and never knew her right at that point, he'd have put her at around thirty-five.

Well, I guess that's what the world ending does to you.

"True. I wasn't worrying or anything. Just thought of someone and got sad for a minute. I'm fine now."

After they were finished with supper, he took a moment to tuck her into bed and kissed her forehead.

"Goodnight, Robyn," he whispered, turning out her light.

"Goodnight, Tim," she said back sleepily.

He yawned and turned up the heater a bit, then went to bed, quickly climbing under the sheets. His last thought that night was where he was going to get that prize turkey for Thanksgiving.

CHAPTER 8:
HOLIDAYS PASSED

Tim need not have worried. The wild turkey, like most big game animals in West Virginia, had grown used to the lack of man in the woods over the past year, and the big Tom that Tim bagged that day was close enough that he could have almost reached out and grabbed it. His heart was pounding when he pulled the trigger. In all of his years of hunting in the woods in Pennsylvania, never had a turkey gotten this close. His idea about using the barbeque worked like a charm, and the big Tom turned out perfectly. Even all the trimmings were fantastic: cranberries and marshmallows, the candied yams, even the pumpkin pie with the stale crust was delicious.

Tim and Robyn sat at the dinette until late in the evening, swapping stories of Thanksgivings past, and laughed and cried. Tim told the same dubious story of the first Thanksgiving that his father had told every Thanksgiving, which made Robyn laugh until she cried, and at the end of the day, they were truly thankful for one another. Tim even relented a tiny bit, and let her have a half glass of wine with dinner, which she turned up her nose at after the first sip. That night they left the cleaning up until the next morning, and went to bed with really full bellies and satisfied hearts. Even though winter was settling in with a heavy, cold fist, they were snug and content in the tiny homestead.

November gave way to December, and winter had finally set in for good as they made final preparations for their imminent confinement. They moved as much of the canned and jarred goods as possible from the shed to the trailer, and every nook and cranny was crammed to the bursting point with food. Last winter, he really didn't have to worry much about it, he'd been in his house, and he was alone. Now, there were two people in an increasingly tiny space, and they were rapidly running out of room. They had discussed earlier the pros and cons of moving into one of the houses in town, but had ultimately decided that removing the rotting corpses— and the lingering smell that would always remain— was something they couldn't live with. Therefore, they decided on staying in the tiny camper for the winter. He thought that maybe they'd find a larger one in the spring. Maybe a fifth-wheel type, that the M880 could handle, and move it to a better location. The tiny gasoline generator was running even rougher than before, and was beginning to worry him. They used it less and less for electricity, relying on kerosene lanterns for light. But the pump that brought the water from the creek needed electricity. If it didn't snow, he thought he'd drive back up to Beckley and raid the National Guard Armory there for a bigger diesel generator.

One thing they did have plenty of was propane. They'd amassed a huge stockpile of the thirty-pound bottles over the last few months, and now had enough to last all winter, even running the heater full-blast all the time. Tim wondered also how well the camper was insulated. Probably not real well, because most people who used them, only used them in the summer months. These trailers were not designed to be used in the way that he and Robyn had been using this one, permanently living in it. It was going to be a big test, of a lot of things, including their ability to still like each other, and not want to kill each other by spring. A few days before Christmas, the weather looked like it was going to hold for a bit, so on a crisp morning, they bundled up and headed up I-77 towards Beckley to find the Armory. Following a map he'd found, they made their way off the Harper Road exit, and wound their way through town, finally locating the Armory. Making quick work of the chain and padlock on the gate that accessed the rear of the building, they drove to the back and found the motor pool. After alighting from the truck, they wandered around looking for things they'd need. Tim found a 100kw towed generator right away, and backed the M880 up to it, hitching it easily with the military pintle. It was far too large for what they really needed, but it was diesel, and if he could find enough cable in the workshop, he might be able to set it up far enough away from the camper as not to be a nuisance with the noise. The only downside of that was, if he set it up far enough away to not be heard from their camp, they'd have to walk that far in bad weather just to refuel it. They needed the power, though, so he'd thought he'd just take the chance.

He broke into the workshop next, and found the cables and a junction box he could run several extension cords from. Dragging them back out to the truck, he loaded them into the bed with Robyn's help. After they were done, they walked back into the building, heading deeper into the darkness using a police Maglite to light their way. Finding the supply room, Tim cut the padlock off that door. He found racks and racks of ACU uniforms, and quickly located several new sets in his size, including a few new pairs of boots. He stopped suddenly, looking at Robyn. He put his clothes down on a table by the wall, and smiled.

"What?" she asked.

"Just come with me," he said. He walked back into the racks, and started to pull out a few ACU tops, trousers and hats in the smallest size he could find, then did the same thing with a few pairs in sizes a little bigger, then the same with boots. A confused look washed over Robyn's face when they finally made it back to the table where Tim had left his uniforms. He pointed at the table, and she plopped everything down with a grunt. He pulled a duffle bag off the nearby shelf and tossed it to her.

"Put everything I just gave you into the bag," he said.

She did as she was told, cramming everything, not bothering to fold anything. When she was done she looked up at him.

"Here's the deal. When you can fit into those uniforms, I'll swear you in to the US Army and you'll be a soldier."

Her eyes widened in excitement. "Really, Tim?"

"Yes, really, and it's Sar' Major!" he said. "I know it's what you want, so consider the time from now until you can fit into those uniforms your basic training. We won't be doing all the forced marches and hours of PT, but we won't get fat and lazy either," he said, knowing his own aversion to PT. His knees were destroyed from years of abuse, and when he'd gotten back from Afghanistan last year, he knew he was going to fail his yearly Physical Fitness Assessment, and was resigned to the fact that he'd be forced to retire.

"This is so great!"

"Good. I'm glad you approve. I hope you won't disappoint me."

"Oh, I won't!"

"Good. Now grab your shit, and come with me," he said, picking up his clothes, and walking out of the storeroom. He looked back, saw her dragging the duffle bag behind her, and stifled a grin. The bag was almost as big as she was, but she didn't complain a bit, and even though she was having difficulty, she was beaming from ear to ear. They reached the truck, and he helped her toss the duffle into the bed. Walking around to the driver's side, he opened the door, and stopped. He hadn't been feeling quite right all morning, and just got a little dizzy. He shook it off, and climbed into the truck.

"Are you okay, Tim? You didn't look so hot just then," Robyn asked worriedly.

"Yeah, I'm fine. Just a little tired I guess. We've been really running around the last week or so," he said, starting the truck and putting it in gear.

"Are you sure? You look a little pale."

"I'm okay, sweetheart. I'll get to bed early tonight. I just need some rest."

"If you say so…" she said, clearly still worried.

They made their way back to the highway and headed south, commenting on how pretty the area really was. Most of the farm animals that had died had long since been picked clean by buzzards and other scavengers, and a shudder ran through Tim thinking of those two kids at the bus stop back in Philadelphia. He knew their fate was the same as every other person caught outside when The Event happened. Then it occurred to him that maybe that might have been a better fate than dying inside and festering away in some building for years. At least with the scavengers it was quicker and nothing was left except for some bones strewn around.

They pulled into Athens, and stopped at the drugstore to get some Christmas decorations.

"You can't have Christmas without garland and lights!" Tim told Robyn.

When they finally got back to the camp, Tim found a good spot for the generator about two hundred yards away from the camp and set it up there, running the cables back and hooking everything up. He then went back to the generator to start it but it wouldn't turn over. He cursed the National Guard Unit's shoddy preventative maintenance program, and finally got it started by using jumper cables from the M880's battery.

"Shit wouldn't have been this sloppy in my goddamn brigade," he remarked. He needn't have worried about the noise. It was a huge generator, capable of running a whole hospital unit, but this one was running at just a hair above idle and was producing enough power to run the whole camper and the water pump, yet could hardly be heard twenty yards away. After insuring the seventy-five gallon fuel tank was full, he added the proper amount of diesel stabilizer to the mix.

"What's that for?" Robyn asked.

"It keeps the diesel from gelling up in winter. I put it in the fuel tank of the truck too. "What happens if you don't?"

"If you don't use it, the fuel will get thick and not be able to get through the injectors, and the engine will stop running."

They got back in the truck and drove the two hundred yards to the camp, where they were both pleased at the sound— or lack thereof—from the generator. If it had been running full-bore it would be different, but this would suit them nicely. They made a light lunch of canned tuna and got to work decorating their little homestead. He thought the Christmas lights defeated the whole purpose of the camouflage, but it *was* Christmas. He'd take them down right after. Robyn stowed her new gear at the foot of her bunk, and they busied themselves with hanging the garland and stringing the lights, listening to a CD of Christmas favorites. When they were done, they inspected their handiwork.

"It looks quite festive!" Tim said, putting his arm around Robyn. She hugged him back tightly.

"Yes, it is, isn't it?"

Shortly after sundown they retired early. Tim woke the next morning, feeling like he'd gone fifteen rounds with Joe Louis. Every bone in his body ached, and his knees screamed in protest as he made his way to the galley, where he found a cheery Robyn already making the coffee. He sat down at the dinette, and looked out the window to see a fresh blanket of snow, about six inches, covering everything.

"Good morning, Tim," she said, setting a steaming cup of coffee down on the table in front of him.

"It's morning alright, and it looks like we got more snow overnight."

"Yeah, I saw that. It's really pretty."

"That it is. Good thing we got everything we'll need. The sky still looks like more is coming," he grumbled. "At least we'll have a white Christmas."

Robyn came and sat down opposite Tim with her own cup of coffee. "Are we going to have a tree?"

Tim looked around the tiny trailer and grunted. "I really don't see where we could put one, Robyn. It's cramped enough in here."

"Pleeeeaaase?"

The look she gave him melted the very last vestiges of ice, and he couldn't refuse her smile. He always was a sucker for pretty blondes.

"Okay, okay," he said in defeat. "We'll go looking this morning for a *tiny* tree."

Even though Tim was really starting to feel run down, he didn't let it show to Robyn. He thought maybe another night's rest would do him good, so he kept it to himself. Tim retired to his space in the back to get dressed. When he came out, Robyn was already standing at the door, clad in a down coat and her rabbit skin hat.

"Nice brain bucket. Where on Earth did you get that?"

"A really weird guy from Philadelphia made it for me," she said with a snicker.

Grabbing his own rabbit fur hat, he reached under the dinette and pulled out a toolbox he kept there, pulled out a bow saw and stood.

"Let's go!"

"Aren't you forgetting something?"

"Not that I know of," he said, looking back quizzically.

"You forgot your American Express card!" Robyn said, rolling her eyes.

He slapped his forehead theatrically and went back to his bed, returning with the M4, slapping a thirty round magazine home. "Okay, now I'm ready," he said, slinging the carbine over his shoulder and leading the way out of the camper. It was cold outside. At least there was no wind right now, but it was crisp, and well below freezing. The fresh powder crunched under their feet as they made their way deeper into the woods. They could see their breath, and white wisps of steam curled around their heads on their march through the woods searching for the perfect Christmas tree. They walked for several hours, and Tim finally stopped to rest near a small copse of fir trees.

"I don't know, honey. They all look too big."

"I know, right? There's got to be something around here," she said. Tim looked up at the leaden sky, and saw that it was growing darker. He looked at his watch and saw that it was already almost 3:30 PM. "Well, we've got to find something soon, or it'll be too dark, and we'll be stuck out here all night!"

"Oh we will not. You're a Ranger, you'll get us home."

"Yep, I'm one of those alright," he said, nodding gravely. "Hey! I just got an idea!" he exclaimed, handing her the saw, walking over to the nearest tree. It was a nice full one, stood about six feet tall, and Tim was just tall enough to see over the top of it.

"What are you thinking?" she asked.

He reached into the tree and with all his might bent it down and held it there under one of his armpits.

"Now you go and saw off about a foot of the top, and we've got an instant mini-tree!"

She did as she was told, lopping off the very top of the fir in a few short strokes of the saw. She picked it up from where it had fallen on the snow, and shook the snow off.

"Perfect! It really does look like a mini-tree," she said.

"Okay, let's get back home before it gets dark on us," he said.

He figured he could have probably sawed the top off himself, but wanted Robyn to feel like she was helping, since she came all this way in the freezing cold, without a whimper of complaint. He felt her tiny hand find his, and her fingers interlaced his and held tight. He looked down to see her admiring face beaming back at him. They walked together in the silence of the woods back to their tiny homestead. Tim sawed a thin slice off the stump to make it even, then used a cordless drill to drill a small, square piece of plywood to the bottom, giving the tiny tree a firm base.

"Fantastic!" Robyn said when he held it up for her inspection. She took it from him and immediately placed it on the dinette table near the window.

"Just where I reckoned it would look nice too!"

Tim put the tools away and removed his jacket, then sat down at the table. He unbuttoned several of the buttons on his checked shirt. He was soaked with sweat, and felt very warm.

"Are you hot?" he asked.

"No. Is anything wrong?" Robyn asked.

"No, I'm just a little warm. Why don't you use the rest of the tinsel and garland to decorate our Hanukkah bush and I'll start to get supper ready," he said.

She laughed at him calling their little tree that, but busied herself with the decorations. He put on some Christmas music again, and pulled a whole rabbit out of the fridge, where he'd put it to thaw the day before. If there was one thing they had plenty of, it was rabbit. It was just the right size for the camper's tiny oven, so he got the small roasting pan out and started to prepare the meal. When Robyn was done she called to him and presented her handiwork.

"That looks great! I've never had a nicer tree."

"Thank you," she said with a tiny curtsy.

"Why don't you head off into the shower now, and get washed up. This will be a few hours yet."

"Okay," she said, and bounded past him carrying a towel, and a pair of flannel PJ's he'd found on one of his forays. As soon as he heard the door to the bathroom shut and the water turn on, he quickly leapt out the front door and over to the truck. As fast as he could, he grabbed the carbine, the magazines, the ammo, the tape and the wrapping paper. He got it all back into his bed and under his blankets before Robyn exited the shower. He sat down with a hot cup of cocoa at the dinette, pretty proud of himself for being able to do that quickly enough. He'd wrap everything up after she went to sleep. Just then the shower door opened, and he looked up. Her wet head appeared in the door and he smiled.

"Did you go outside?"

"No," he said, with what he hoped was an innocent look on his face.

"I thought I heard the door open."

"Nah, just me making some cocoa is all."

"Hmmmph!" she grunted, and shut the door. He had to laugh. He really couldn't get anything by her. When she came out again, she was dried off and dressed in her PJ's. She curled up at the dinette opposite, and Tim made her a fresh mug of cocoa. When he was again seated, he looked right at her, and very seriously said, "You know we'll have to go to bed really early tonight, so Santa Louse can come."

"Don't you mean Santa Claus?" she giggled.

"Oh no, Santa Claus is old hat. He's for little kids. Santa Louse is another guy. He wears an old Army paratrooper suit from World War II, has a five o'clock shadow, and smokes Cuban cigars. He flies all over the world on Christmas Eve, giving presents to all the good boy and girl soldiers!"

"C'mon! I *am* thirteen! I don't believe in that stuff anymore!"

"It's true! I shit you not!"

"You're making this up!"

"He flies around the whole world in a tricked-out M2 Bradley, pulled by eight Army mules. And besides giving out goodies, he provides covering and defilade fire to any dogfaces that need it. It really is a sight to behold, I'm here to tell you!"

"You're full of shit, Sar' Major!"

"Oh! Where did you ever learn such language, young lady?"

"I learned it from you!"

"Fair enough!" he said with a wink. He then got serious. "Robyn. I know we're okay here, but it's getting kind of cramped, and I was thinking over the last few days, about going someplace else, maybe finding a bigger camper too, so we'd have more space. What do you think of that?"

"Do you mean right now?"

"No, not now, in the spring when the weather clears up."

"We can go someplace warmer, maybe?" she asked with a shy smile.

"Anyplace you'd like, as long as we can drive there. I'll let you think it over during the winter, and then I'll let you decide where when the time comes."

"Okay," she said, looking down at her cup, deep in thought. They sat like that for a while, not saying anything, and Tim stared out the window at the gathering dusk. He saw a few snowflakes, and he thought of Christmases past. As far back as he could remember, none were all that great. He'd have to really dredge the depths of his memories to find a really pleasant one, and they were all when he was younger than Robyn. He got up and rinsed his cup in the sink, then opened the oven to check the roast. A wonderful aroma escaped, and made him smile. He looked over at Robyn, who was beaming from ear to ear. He'd thought about a Christmas goose, but by the time the thought crossed his mind, all the Canada geese had flown south for the winter. He'd have to plan better next year.

"Dinner will probably be in another half hour or so. You decide the sides."

Robyn scrambled out of her seat, going to the cupboard. "How about powdered mashed potatoes, creamed corn and carrots?"

"Sounds like a plan to me," he said, basting the rabbit with the juices in the pan. He stood, feeling slightly dizzy again, and had to steady himself on the refrigerator. When he regained his equilibrium, he quickly glanced over to Robyn. She hadn't seen it.

"Do you want a beer, Tim?"

"Nah, I'm okay."

"Can I?"

"No!"

"You can't blame a girl for trying!" she giggled.

"How old are you again?"

"I'll be fourteen tomorrow!" she said proudly.

"You're a Christmas baby? Why didn't you tell me? I'd have baked a cake and hired a band and all that good shit."

"I never really tell anyone when my birthday is, or used to tell them, anyway," she said, her face growing dark.

"Why's that?"

She sat down at the dinette and looked down at her hands. "Every time someone would find out when my birthday was, the first thing they'd start off on was how I must get spoiled. How I must get double presents."

Tim stopped what he was doing and sat down opposite her.

"But the thing was, me and Mama was so poor, some Christmases she wouldn't have enough money for presents at all, and I could hear her at night, crying over it. I really began to hate Christmas because of it."

"Robyn, you don't have to worry about that anymore," Tim said, reaching out and taking her hand.

"Mama always said I was the best Christmas present she ever got." And then the tears that had begun to flow turned into huge sobs. Tim stood up and pulled her to him, hugging her tightly.

"Your mama was right. And now you're *my* best Christmas present ever too!"

Her face was buried in his chest, and the sobs faded to sniffles, but she still held him tight. He realized she had grown probably two inches in the last few months, and had put on about ten pounds. He was glad they had got some bigger sized clothes at Walmart, as she was now growing like a weed. She was still built like a girl much younger, and he put down her lack of physical maturity and arrested development to a life of abject poverty in Appalachia. She hadn't once asked about feminine hygiene products, but she would soon, and that scared the hell out of him. He knew the mechanics, but absolutely dreaded the time when she might need to talk about anything in that department. He knew such a time should be coming around soon. He hoped her mother had at least filled her in on the basics.

"Listen, you and I are the richest people in the world now, because we've got each other, and nothing is going to change that. We can't change the past, only remember and learn from our mistakes. The only thing we have control over is the future. It's why your mama wanted you to go into the Army and get an education. She wanted a better life for you. I know this isn't exactly what she had in mind, but I'm sure she's very happy, knowing you're safe and eating well. I don't know what the future holds for us, baby, but what I do know is, I'm going to do everything I can to make sure we both have a good life."

"It's not fair," Robyn said into his chest.

"I know. Life is never fair. We just have to take what we can get out of it, and try to make every day just a little bit better."

"I'll try," she said.

"Good. That's all I ask is to just try. Now let's eat!" he said, pulling away from her and sitting down at the dinette. They piled their plates up with mashed potatoes, veggies and rabbit, and ate like it was going out of style. When Tim was finished, he pushed his plate away and let out a huge belch, which made Robyn laugh.

"Excuse yourself!" she said with mock disgust.

"Why? It was a compliment to the chef!" he winked.

He looked over at Robyn and smiled. She really was turning into a beautiful young lady, a far cry from the dirty, malnourished, skinny waif he'd met several months ago. He still had no idea how to raise a child, especially a girl, but he thought he was doing an okay job. He was so used to the kids in his Army unit that even though he still thought of them as his kids, he could abuse the shit out of them with streams of expletives that would make a sailor blush. He curbed his language as much as possible around Robyn, but still things would come out from time to time. She just picked up on them and would use them also, much to his chagrin. One time several weeks back after making a most improbable shot at a squirrel, he asked her how she did it, and she replied, matter-of-factly *'oh it was easy. I just held off a red cunthair…'* and that made him laugh.

After supper, he looked at his watch and noted the time.

"Well, it's almost twenty hundred hours. Time for bed or Santa Louse won't come!"

"Yeah, I bet!"

"Honest! Get to bed or he won't come."

Robyn sighed deeply, rolled her eyes theatrically and got ready for bed. She climbed under the covers, and through sleepy eyes, looked at Tim, Bad Bear clutched tightly under her chin.

"Good night, darlin'," he said, leaning forward to kiss her forehead. "Sleep tight."

"Good night, Tim," she said with a yawn. He turned her light off, and went to turn away when she called to him. "Tim?" she said in a soft voice.

"Yeah, baby?"

"Aren't you going to turn off the Christmas lights?"

"Nah, you got to leave them on all night tonight, or Santa Louse won't be able to find our AO!"

"Ay Oh?"

"Area of Operations. This is our 'AO'. Although he's one tough fucker, Santa Louse never went to Ranger School, so he can't find folks' AOs really well. That's the reason why we've got to leave the lights on for him."

He walked to the galley, where he poured himself a glass of water and took two extra-strength Tylenol. His body aches were getting worse, and he could feel a headache coming on. He listened for Robyn's breathing to even out. Once he knew she was asleep, he ducked into his sleeping area in the rear and pulled the privacy curtain. Gathering up all his goodies, he made quick work of wrapping everything up, trying to be as quiet as possible, even though the kid slept like a rock most nights and probably wouldn't wake up through a mortar barrage. When he was done, he peered around the curtain conspiratorially, looking to see if she was awake. In the dim light of the outside red and green lights coming through the windows, he could see her still lying in the same position, and could hear her tiny little snores. Feeling safe to do so, he gathered up the festively wrapped gifts and tiptoed out, placing them on her side of the dinette bench seat. Giving her one final glance, he grabbed his coat and went outside to have a final smoke for the night. Standing there in the snow, he looked around. It was still snowing, and big fluffy flakes were wafting down at a great rate. There was absolutely no wind, and he always was amazed by how quiet everything was when it snowed. In the distance, he could barely make out the sound, but did hear the new generator chugging away satisfactorily. He lit a cigarette, and thought about the last year. Before The Event, he'd just been marking time throughout his life, going through the motions; going to picnics and barbeques, weekends at the Jersey Shore, a vacation away someplace a time or two. None of it meant anything. *This* was real. *This* was tangible. *This* was *important*. Before he'd stumbled upon Robyn, his life didn't mean anything. Now that sweet kid sleeping not ten feet away from where he stood meant the world to him. He had an obligation to help her along, and shape her into someone. Someone that maybe someday could make a difference. Maybe that's what his brother meant so many months ago. He finished his smoke, and chinked out the ember, pocketing the butt. He coughed once, then twice, a little harder the last time, and brought up some phlegm, which he spat out onto the freshly fallen snow. Even in the dim light of the string of Christmas lights, he could see it didn't look right. It had a yellowish tint.

That isn't good, he thought.

Going back inside, he checked on Robyn again, and satisfied she was still soundly asleep, he went to the tiny bathroom to brush his teeth. He coughed again, brought up more phlegm, and he spit in into the basin. It had a dark yellow tint that was definitely un-good. He'd better start taking a vitamin C supplement or something. He couldn't afford to get sick. Maybe a good night's sleep was all he needed. They had been working pretty hard getting prepared for winter, and maybe he was just run down. A few days of lounging in bed would probably do him a world of good. Besides, he'd be forty-eight this year, and he wasn't getting any younger. There was no sense trying to run around like he was still a twenty year old. He crawled into bed, and sleep came immediately.

When he was stirred from his sleep the next morning by a happy and cheerful Robyn, it felt as though he hadn't slept at all.

"Wake up, Tim! It's Christmas! Merry Christmas!"

"Okay, okay," he groaned. "Let me get up and get some coffee."

"I already have it made."

"Good. I need some," he said, as he sat up in his bed, and groaned again. He felt like he'd been placed into a steel drum and rolled down a boulder-strewn hillside. Every bone in his body ached. As quickly as the pain would allow, he got dressed and stepped out to see a beaming Robyn standing there still wearing his t-shirt. She was holding a steaming mug of coffee out to him. He took it, and noticed a box about ten inches square and beautifully wrapped in red paper sitting on his seat at the dinette table.

"I see Santa Louse has been here. Stealthy fucker, isn't he?"

She just giggled and said, "Sit down, Tim. There's a present there for you!"

"I see that," he said. He took a seat, and glanced out the window. It was snowing even harder now, and he could barely see halfway across the meadow. Looking back at the box, he picked it up, surprised at the weight of it. He looked over at Robyn curiously.

"Go ahead! Open it!"

"Why don't you open your presents first."

"I can wait. I hope you like it, Tim."

Tim relented, tearing off the red paper and bow, and placed in on the seat next to him. That revealed a plain cardboard box, which he opened. Reaching in, he pulled out a quart mason jar of clear liquid and held it up. The box contained three more exactly like it.

"Now where did you find these?"

"Remember that day about a month ago when I went hunting by myself?"

"Yeah, you went to shoot a rabbit or two. As I recall you came back empty-handed."

"Well, I walked through the woods and came out on this road about two miles from here. There was this little general store, and I broke in the way you taught me. There wasn't much in there. Most of the stuff was gnawed through by mice already, but I found a whole bunch of that in the back. I thought you might like a little with supper once in a while."

Great, he thought, *I'm teaching her how to be a B&E artist.* But he did have to smile. Never in his life had he been given a whole gallon of 100% pure West Virginia corn liquor moonshine by a thirteen year old. *Fourteen today,* he quickly corrected himself.

"I love it, baby. Thank you," he said, putting the jar back in the box and placing it on his seat. "Now you open yours and see what Santa Louse brought you!"

She quickly tore into the paper and held up the carbine.

"Oh wow! This is so cool!"

"It's a World War II era M1carbine paratrooper model. I figured you were ready to graduate to something a little bigger than the .22!"

"Tim, it's perfect! I love it!" she exclaimed excitedly, and went on to unwrap her other gifts, the ammo and magazines. It was a far cry from a Barbie Doll, and a shitload more practical, considering their situation. He then went on to teach her how to break it down for cleaning and reassemble it. That was fairly easy, because there were few moving parts. It really was a rather simple rifle to use and maintain. They made toast with margarine and strawberry preserves for breakfast and as they ate, Tim thought of the stollen his father would bring home from the German bakery on his way back from Christmas morning mass. He could still smell the fluffy pastry and wondered if he'd eat anything as delicious as that ever again. When they were done, Robyn got up and went to Tim, hugged him and gave him a big kiss.

"This has been the best Christmas ever."

"I agree, sweetheart. Now I'm going to go and top off the generator before it gets too bad out there. I'll be back in a few minutes."

"Keep warm; it looks bad out there already this morning." she said. "I'm just going to sit here and read for a bit," she said, picking up her latest book.

Hemingway. She was reading some pretty heavy shit now. Grabbing his coat, Tim headed outside and grabbed two jerry cans of diesel, already pre-mixed with fuel stabilizer. Carrying them the two hundred yards to the generator through the now foot-deep snow was hard going, and he was glad he had decided to do it now. It would only get worse later, and he wanted to make sure it was completely filled with fuel. Using a funnel, he topped off the tank of the purring motor.

He was pleasantly surprised, that it had used hardly any fuel so far and it only took half of one jerry can to fill it. He stowed both under the generator and started to make his way back to camper. He couldn't see it from where he was, but he could still see his footprints in the snow from his trek out. When he got within ten yards of the trailer, he started to get dizzy again. He felt like he was burning up, and could feel the sweat running down his back. His vision dimmed, and his peripheral vision began to fail until all he could see was a tiny circle of light right out in front of him. Then everything went black and the aches and pains went away.

Robyn was curled up, reading her book. After a while, she wondered what was taking Tim so long to get back. Surely he should be back by now. She got up and opened the door to the camper. Immediately, all the blood drained from her face and turned to ice. A huge knot appeared in her stomach, and her knees went weak.

"Tim! Oh God! *Tim!*" she screamed, and ran out barefoot in the snow. She fell down to her knees in the deep snow next to the face down form lying at her feet. She grabbed hold of Tim's jacket with both hands and shook with all her might, wailing, "Wake up! Oh, *please* get up!"

One last dreadful wail escaped her lips, and threatened to tear the very breath from her lungs. "Daaaaaadddddddyyyy! Noooooooooooooooooooo!"

CHAPTER 9:
PORTS OF CALL

The USS *Hughes* sat tied up smartly alongside the pier at Subic Bay in the Philippines. The area had once been a sprawling US Navy base, but was returned to the Philippine government back in the 90's. The ship itself was now a shell of its former glory, and showed the increasing lack of maintenance. Huge streaks of rust scarred the gray paint, and the brass work fittings were green with tarnish. Watertight hatches no longer swung easily for lack of lubrication, and also didn't seal properly anymore. Anchor chains were crusted with mud, and uncoiled ropes lay about on the decks. Sailing into Singapore, they had experienced a harrowing journey through the Strait of Malacca, pummeled by a huge gale that blew up, and they almost ran aground. The winds and waves had tossed the ship like a Coke bottle, and they had lost the top half of their antenna mast. The only antennas they had remaining were the navigation radar and high gain. PO Stevens quickly built and installed a dipole antenna for the ham bands, but all other communications were out, not that they had anyone to contact. In Singapore, they were also able to 'recruit' seven more survivors, one of which was a lieutenant in the Malaysian Navy. Lt. Cmd. Wright was very pleased to be filling up his wardroom, but all in all, the ship was a mess.

They had departed Singapore and headed out into the Pacific Ocean, making stops at New Caledonia, Vanuatu, Fiji, then the Solomon Islands before turning northward into the Marshall Islands, then west again to the Philippines. All along the way, picking up a survivor here and there, food and provisions, and topping off their fuel bunkers when they could. Now they sat tied up to the pier at the former US Navy base, and the captain watched the landing party bring aboard five new 'crewmembers'. He didn't even try to hide it anymore. As soon as they came ashore, they fanned out, armed to the teeth, and brought back whoever they found, kicking and screaming. Anyone who resisted, even a little, was summarily shot in front of anyone else present.

"Johnson, you were never at Subic back in the old days, were you?" the captain asked, looking down at the gaggle coming up the gangway.

"No, sir. This is my first cruise," he replied, knowing damn right well the skipper knew that. Why was he asking?

"Oh that's right. You didn't go to the Academy, right? University of Wisconsin, wasn't it?"

"Minnesota, sir."

"ROTC. Well, you're a good officer anyway, Johnson," he said, smiling that sick smile of his.

"Thank you, sir," Johnson replied, inwardly seething. *No, I didn't go to Canoe U, but I'm a far better officer and sailor than you'll ever be!*

"Always was good liberty here. You could get anything you wanted. I mean *anything*. The locals were always so accommodating! 'Little brown fuck machines' I believe the enlisted called them."

"Yes, sir, I've heard the sea stories."

Grabbing the loudhailer, the captain called down to the shore party that was just reaching the weather deck.

"Petty Officer Stevens! Bring that one, the one in the rear, up to the bridge immediately!"

Stevens waved in acknowledgment, grabbed a small girl's arm roughly, and pulled her aside, disappearing through a hatch. The others were herded through another one farther down, into the bowels of the ship. The captain turned to Ensign Johnson. "Yes, the Philippines were always a good port of call. I think we'll sail tomorrow after the provisioning is completed and head for Midway, then straight to Pearl after that."

"That sounds good to me, sir. The sooner we get to Pearl the sooner we can make the necessary repairs to the ship. That patch we put on in Sri Lanka is barely holding on, and leaking like a sieve. The pumps are just keeping up with it now, and I'm not sure it'll hold up to another gale like the one we had in the strait."

"And we'll be able to get parts for the broken equipment too, Mr. Johnson. I'm well aware of the state of the ship, and I will correct any defects when we get to Pearl."

Petty Officer Stevens came into the bridge with a terrified young girl. She looked like she was around ten or eleven years old, with long dark hair and tear filled almond shaped eyes. Cmd. Wright walked over to the child, who was still being held tightly by the arm by Stevens. He smiled, brushing her hair from her tear streaked face, and cupped her chin.

"She will do quite nicely, Stevens. Good find. I'll make sure you get a nice bottle of Johnny Walker for this. Clean her up, she stinks. And when you're done, bring her to my cabin."

"Aye, sir!" Stevens said with an evil grin.

"And, Stevens? Don't lay a hand on her!"

"Aye, sir!" he replied, looking crestfallen. Ensign Johnson felt nauseous. Now more than ever, he truly hated his captain. The sailor dragged the now crying young girl off the bridge, and the captain looked back at him.

"Yes, just like the old days, Mr. Johnson." He smiled that creepy smile that never failed to make the hairs on the back of Johnson's neck stand up. Johnson involuntarily shuddered.

"Mr. Johnson, you have the mid-watch. I'm going to…*relax* in my cabin for a while. I'll see you in the wardroom for supper?"

"I'll try to be there, sir. I've got a lot of work to do after I get off watch, if we're going to be sailing tomorrow."

"Very well, call me if anything arises." He swiftly turned and exited, without another word.

Ensign Johnson shut the hatch leading to the wing bridge, looked around the empty bridge and sighed. He sat up in the captain's chair, contemplating his situation. He soaked up the cool air coming from the air conditioning vents, thankful that was still working. It was well over a hundred degrees today, and extremely humid. If that had failed, it would be absolutely unbearable below decks. As usual when he was left alone, his mind reeled with options. He could go overboard here, but they'd probably send out a search party to find him. Plus the thought of being on the receiving end of the skipper's 'discipline' was not something he looked forward to. Between Singapore and here, they'd had three lashings and a hanging, just for good measure. The sight of the East Indian guy swinging from a rope off the antenna mast sent a bolt of fear through the rest of the crew, and no signs of dissent were seen after that. No, he was stuck here. Maybe he'd think of something when they got to Pearl. At least it was a fairly big island, and it was part of the US, anyone he'd encounter would speak English. Maybe he could find a sailboat and sail back to the States. His thoughts were interrupted by the sound of the hatch opening. He turned in the chair, to see Petty Officer Suplee peering around the edge of the steel hatch.

"Yes, Suplee?"

"Is the skipper around?"

"No, he's 'retired' to his cabin for a while. If you need him, I would suggest waiting a while unless the ship is sinking."

"Actually I was looking for you. Stevens said you had the mid-watch."

"What can I do for you?"

"Sir, this shit is really beginning to bother me."

"Come in, and close that hatch!"

"Sorry, sir," Suplee said sheepishly, closing the hatch behind him. "Sir, this is crazy. The ship is starting to turn into a floating whorehouse."

"As I recall, you have partaken in that pleasure a time or two."

"Yes, sir, at first. Then it really started to bother me. Here we are, bouncing all over the Pacific, basically kidnapping all these folks, and forcing them to work. The way you and Nakamura have the boat wired up now, it only takes a few people to sail her. And that new officer we got in Singapore, man can he conn a ship!"

That was true. The Malaysian Navy Lieutenant was a true sailor. The way they had docked here was evidence enough. They had come into port, swung the bow around, and kissed the pier like it was a newborn. They didn't even need bumpers. The captain was impressed, but you could tell he was extremely jealous, and kept a close eye on the man while also giving him the shittiest watches.

"What we should be doing is *helping* these people we find. Not kidnapping them! At least try to find a doctor or something. That's what we really need, not some helicopter pilot, and a bunch of sex slaves."

Again, the sailor was right. Last month they had a man fall ill and before anything could be done, the man's appendix burst, killing him. They really needed to find a doctor somewhere.

"So what do you propose we do?"

"Ah shit, sir. I don't know. I just needed to vent a little, and you're the only one I can talk to."

It was true. They both had on several occasions sought each other out for a venting session, albeit a covert one.

"I guess you still can't talk to Stevens?"

"He'd be the last one on board I'd talk to. He's enjoying this way too much. And where did he get that bullwhip he always carries? He scares me almost as bad as the skipper does."

"I know. He is a little disturbing." He had to agree. Stevens was showing a sadistic side that was becoming rather worrying.

"Sir, I'll do anything you say. After your watch, we can say we're going to take a little walk and explore some, and just never come back."

"I already thought of that. All they would do is send out a search party and bring us back or shoot us. Maybe we'll try when we get to Pearl."

"Like I said before, I'll do anything you want, just say the word, sir."

At twenty-five, Ensign Johnson was only two years older than Suplee, but being an officer, he had to take a fatherly approach sometimes.

"Where are you from, Suplee?"

"Iowa, sir. Carson, Iowa. It's just a little bit east of Council Bluffs."

"You're a far cry from Iowa."

"No shit, sir."

"Why did you join the Navy?"

"I never wanted to see another stalk of corn again."

"I left Minnesota for almost the same reason. I never wanted to see another snowfall."

"So where does that leave us, sir?"

"I'm not sure. I'm still not sure what the skipper has in mind. He's keeping that very close indeed. I do know he's still looking for nukes and the codes. From Pearl I'd imagine. But from there I haven't a clue."

"I feel like I'm in the middle of a nightmare and can't wake up."

"I know exactly how you feel."

"You know, sir, most places we'd sail into, the people would be happy to see a US Navy warship. Not shit-scared like they are now."

"It's almost like word is getting out somehow," Johnson commented.

"I think it's those ham radio guys Stevens is trying to locate. But he tells me most of it isn't in English, so he can't make a lot of it out."

"Or figure out where any of them are."

"Yeah, he says he's gotten at least seven different stations operating now, but can't triangulate where any of them are."

"That's what I'm thinking. We're coming into a place, tearing it up, stealing all the good stuff and leaving. Whoever is left in hiding is getting the word out to not trust us. The last few places we've been to, especially the Marshalls and Marianas, there was no one to be found."

"Here's another thing that's been bugging me, sir. When we left Singapore, why didn't we just sail a little further south to Australia? At least there we'd meet up with some people who speak English."

"That's an easy one to answer, Suplee. If we had sailed into Darwin, Cairns, Brisbane or Sydney, any Aussies we'd find there would have told the good captain to get fucked!" Johnson said, and Suplee got a good laugh over that one.

"That's very true, sir!"

It was highly unusual for an enlisted man and officer to speak so familiarly with one another, but these were very unusual times, and they only did it in private.

"There is one good thing the skipper is doing now."

"Oh, and that is?" Johnson asked.

"Well, at least we're not coming in and firing broadsides like John Paul Jones at any tankers we find, anymore. I think that last one scared the hell out of him!"

"True. He figured out we've got torpedoes and the ASROC missiles, and can stand off a few miles."

"And even over the horizon with the ASROC."

"Yeah, I'm glad I could talk him into that. Had we been a hundred yards closer, I am sure we would have been on the bottom."

A chill ran through them both, and it had nothing to do with the air conditioning.

Every sailor, all over the world, wants to keep their feet under the keel. The food chain is a little different in the sea, and most sailors liked being on the top of it.

"Would you like some coffee, sir?"

"Yes, please. And pour yourself one too."

Suplee went to the small coffee service built into the aft bulkhead on the bridge, and poured two mugs of the black concoction the Navy called coffee into wide-bottomed mugs, and presented one to Ensign Johnson. Taking a sip, he thanked the sailor.

"Who's relieving you on watch this afternoon, sir?" Suplee asked.

Johnson had set down his mug, taken out the big pair of Zeiss binoculars, and was looking at the thunderheads build up over the jungle. They'd probably get some rain tonight with the humidity this high.

"What was that?" he asked, dropping the binoculars from his eyes and turning back to face the sailor.

"I was just wondering who your relief was going to be tonight."

"The Malaysian officer, I believe."

"Lieutenant Alphabits," Suplee said.

"Lieutenant who?" he asked, almost spilling his coffee.

"Alphabits. Stevens and I can't pronounce his name, so we call him Alphabits."

"Not to his face I hope?"

"No, sir. We just smile and nod our heads, and say 'aye, aye' a lot."

"But he is a member of our wardroom now, show him the due respect," he said, just a little too forcefully.

"Sir, he may be an officer, but last I figured this was still a US flagged warship, and he's not an American."

"That might be true, Suplee, but he is an officer, and should be offered all the respect his rank holds."

"Will the skipper be holding high court tonight as usual?" Suplee said.

"Yes, he probably will," Johnson replied. "Always does in port, he loves all the drama and protocol. I'm glad I'm missing it tonight."

"I know sir. I acted as a steward the first night into Subic. It was a huge love-fest. 'I love me!' And let's all now form a circle-jerk!'"

"That's about right," Johnson said, nodding and sipping his coffee.

"And that Major Paleen, I think he's all bullshit, sir. He's not once flown the bird, and only has had it out of the hangar deck once. To tell you the truth, I think he's afraid of it."

"I've had those same thoughts myself."

"Well, sir. Thanks for letting me vent and have some of the skipper's coffee too. The coffee we get down in the mess is shit, now that we've got those curry-munchers running the show."

"No problem, Suplee. Oh, and I spoke to the captain about you and Stevens. We're going to have you both frocked as chiefs. We need a couple of chiefs, and you two are already set up down in the goat locker anyway and doing the job of chiefs, so we figured we'd make it official."

"Gee, sir, what'll I do with the big pay raise?" Suplee said with a grin.

He laughed loudly. "Okay, sailor. Don't you have something to do?"

"Yes, sir. I do need to take a walk around the ship, tidy things up a bit."

"Good. Go do it and leave me to my misery."

"Aye, sir!" Suplee said, exiting through the same hatch as he'd entered.

Ensign Johnson finished his coffee, put the mug up, and sat back. He thought again of their skipper. Over the last few months he, Suplee and Stevens had begun to always carry a holstered Berretta 9mm pistol on a web pistol belt at all times, taking the captain's lead, for no other reason other than to protect themselves from their 'crew'. It was insane. He shouldn't have to walk armed throughout the ship because he was afraid of the crew, but the mere methods they'd employed to acquire the crew in the first place demanded it. He'd heard stories about 'the bad old days' back in the 60s and 70s, where officers were taking their lives into their own hands just walking through some sections of Navy ships, but in this day and age it was just crazy. This being the case, there were many times he'd had the chance of un-holstering the pistol, walking up and putting the muzzle to the skipper's head, and pulling the trigger. There. Problem solved.

But he just couldn't bring himself to do it for some reason. The main problem was that in every port they visited, things got more and more out of hand. The Somalis they had first gotten were especially brutal. In one place in the Marshalls, when they didn't find anyone around, they took everything that wasn't nailed down and burned the village to the ground. They came back to the ship with armfuls of TVs, VCRs and stereos. When they were told that none of the things would work, they just threw them overboard into the harbor. Something had to be done.

He didn't know what he could do, but he had to do *something*. The skipper was definitely losing his mind. And if he actually did get his hands on nukes, and then got the codes for them in some weird twist of fate, what would he do with them? That was the thought that kept Johnson awake at night.

What were the skipper's plans? Surely it couldn't only be piracy or robbery . Things that once were valuable were virtually worthless now, including gold, silver and money. They were all equally worthless, because there was hardly anyone left to covet those things. You couldn't hold nations hostage, because there were no nations left. The very few people that were left were barely surviving as it was. It was all too much for him to contemplate, and even though he was an educated man, it boggled his mind. His thoughts drifted back to Pearl Harbor, to a more pleasant time.

He had met Mary at a small nightclub in Honolulu shortly after he'd reported for duty at Pearl Harbor. They danced and he bought her a few drinks. Into the night they talked, and at the end of the night, they exchanged phone numbers. He had then walked her to the bus stop, and waited there with her like the gentleman he was.

When she was safely on the bus home, he walked back to base on a cloud. Several days passed before he decided to call her so as to not look too desperate. It was a short call, and he was sure she was blowing him off. She had said she was at work, and would call him when she was done.

He was pleasantly surprised when in a few hours his cell phone rang and it was her. They chatted for a bit and made plans for dinner the next Friday night. They met at a little seafood restaurant with a view of Waikiki Beach. He was drowned by her beauty, which resulted from a mixed lineage— Pacific Islander, Japanese and European— giving her an unreal glow and a face that was radiant when she smiled. She had unbelievably long hair, dark brown with streaks of gold through it, most probably from being in the sun. He longed to run his fingers through it… or have it splayed out across his bare chest.

They talked about each other; she was twenty-one, worked as a teller at a local bank, and was going to school at night to be a journalist. He told her he wasn't sure about his career in the Navy, but felt confident that with his engineering degree he could find work just about anywhere on the planet if he decided to leave the Navy. After dinner, they decided to forgo the dancing and instead took a long walk on the beach. After a while, they found a secluded spot far from the hotels and people. They talked some more and watched the moon rise over the water. He decided to make his move. He leaned closer to her and gently kissed her lips. She kissed back, gently at first, then more passionately. They lay back in the white sand and explored each other's bodies. He slowly disrobed her, and then she had told him that he was to be her first. He didn't believe her but had held his tongue (smartly, he thought in retrospect), for a few minutes later he realized she was telling the truth when he entered her. They made love silently to the sounds of the breakers crashing over the reef and were lit only by the moon. When it was all over, he lay back looking at the stars. She had her head on his chest and her fingers were playing with one of his nipples. His hands found her hair and he ran his hands over it, and so it began, again…

She had never dated a sailor before, but said she was prepared for the long months of separation. Every chance they could, they would get together, even at odd times, for he being a new junior officer had the worst watches imaginable. They only had a short six weeks to get to know each other, but they made the best of the time they had. On the day the USS *Hughes* set sail, she was there in her finest dress to watch her lover sail away, hoping to see him again someday. He could see her weeping as he stood on the rail in his best set of dress whites, and wished he could have leapt over the railing and back into her arms.

Not into the nightmare this cruise has become.

"Mr. Johnson, you're not asleep on watch, are you?"

He jumped in his seat and turned to see the skipper standing there in his starched dress uniform. He had trimmed his beard, and he looked even more cartoonish now than when he first started letting it grow a few months ago. He stood and came to attention.

"No, sir, I wasn't asleep. I just had my mind somewhere else."

"Good. My wardroom is small enough without a captain's mast removing one qualified conn officer," he said flatly.

"No, sir," Johnson gulped. Despite the coolness of the air conditioner, he broke out into a sweat. He had been a starting lineman on the University of Minnesota's football team and was no pussy when it came to facing people, but this man truly frightened him.

"Lieutenant Whatshisname will be relieving you at 2300. Until then, we'll be in the wardroom if you need us."

"Yes, sir."

The captain turned and walked aft towards the wardroom, slamming the hatch shut behind him. A wave of nausea swept over Johnson and he rushed out the seaward side wing bridge, leaned over the rail, and vomited until his stomach was empty, then dry-heaved for several minutes after that. When he regained his composure, he straightened out his uniform and reentered the bridge, where he went to the coffee pot and poured himself a cup of coffee. He noticed his hand was shaking violently, and he had to put the pot down. He went back to the captain's chair, and sat down. His heart felt like it would leap from his chest. After a few minutes he calmed down, angry with himself still for letting that prick scare him like that. But he knew from experience the skipper's threats weren't idle, and he could almost imagine himself being tied shirtless to the hangar deck hatch, a smiling Petty Officer Stevens at the ready with his bullwhip.

I'm going to have to watch that bastard like a hawk. He shook his head and wondered what God out there had this sick sense of humor. He heard the hatch open again and jumped at the sound. Turning, he saw one of the East Indian woman from the galley come in holding a plate.

"Ensign Johnson? Captain says I bring you sammiches."

"Thank you. You can put them by the coffee service."

She did, and left quietly. He went over to the dish and saw there were several tuna salad sandwiches on freshly baked bread. Well, that was a pleasant surprise. He was expecting curried goat brains, or goat vindaloo, or something equally disgusting. Now that he felt better he was ravenous, and he ate two of the sandwiches standing by the coffee pot. He then took a third, and sat back down.

He looked at the sandwich and wondered if it was dolphin friendly tuna. He'd always heard the horror stories about the way the Japanese caught the tuna and slaughtered the dolphins in the process. The thought quickly passed, and he took a bite of his third sandwich, shrugging.

Meanwhile, down in the goat locker, what the Navy affectionately called the Chief's quarters on a ship, PO Suplee was lying in his bunk reading a Hentai comic book that he'd gotten off of Nakamura. It was all in Japanese, but he didn't care; he just looked at the photos. The story was easy to figure out: Girl gets abducted by aliens, after which, girl gets sexually violated by said aliens. It was always the same story, different book.

"What is up with this Jap porn?" he asked no one.

"What up, dogg?" It was PO Stevens.

"Oh nothing, I was just looking at one of those Jap comics from Nakamura. All the tentacles…"

"Dat's just wrong man. Get yourself some fine readin' material like this!" He held up the latest and last *Playboy* to ever be published. "Now dat's fine!"

"Yeah, she's hot alright," Suplee agreed.

"She okay for a white girl. Me, I prefer the sistas."

Suplee shook his head. Stevens was as white as he was, but came from some shithole town in Detroit and fancied himself to be the next Slim Shady.

"Yeah, dogg! I had dis one sista back in San Diego. She had dem big ol' titties and a big ol' ghetto butt! She suck yo' dick so hard, your balls would shrink to da' size a peas, when you nutted!"

Suplee hated when Stevens talked like that. He could speak normally in public, but turned on this ghetto rap when he was with Suplee and the other crewmen. It annoyed the shit out of him, and Stevens knew it. Stevens lit a cigarette and pulled up a chair, sitting on it backwards.

"So what did you and Ensign Johnson talk about today?" he asked with a sly grin.

"Nothing, just college football mostly. He used to play for Minnesota," Suplee replied in the prearranged cover story they'd both came up with in case anyone got nosy.

"You two talking' football, huh?"

"Yeah, we were talking football."

"Wouldn't be talking anything stupid, like jumping ship, would you?"

"Fuck no. Where the fuck would I go?"

"You got that right. Listen, this is the best gig I ever had. All the booze I want, all the herb, and all the pussy I want. I just go and take it. It's all okay by the skipper because he knows I'm the man to go to. I'm da' one who keeps shit in line on this scow."

"It's like I said before. Where the fuck would I go, Stevens? I'm just trying to get along, do my job, and take one day at a time."

"You just keep it like dat. You be cool and when we get back to Pearl and get the nukes the skipper's been after, we're going to be kings!"

"How do you figure that?"

"He'll be in charge, man. No one will fuck with him. He'll tell them to give up whatever he wants, and if they don't, we tell them they'll get nuked. It's as simple as that. He'll rule the whole fucking world, and we'll be his number one *compadres!*"

"I'll believe that when I see it."

"Oh, it'll happen, man. He knows where the nukes are stored in Pearl. It's all up to us to break into COMPAC and get the codes from his office. He's probably dead like the rest of them anyway!"

Suplee then thought about his mother back in Iowa, and his little brother running the farm, and his stomach turned. Maybe they really were all dead. If they weren't, they'd have heard something by now. He was all alone in the world. Alone that is, except for Ensign Johnson in this floating madhouse. Maybe they were the only two sane people left.

"But why take the nukes?" he asked. "Nothing's worth anything anymore, not money, not gold or silver, not anything. What could be worth more than that?"

"I'll tell you why, my main man!"

He was getting a huge headache, wishing Stevens would just go away somewhere for a while and leave him alone.

"Power."

"Power?"

"Yeah, dogg. Power. The old man will have all the power and he'll be king!" With that Stevens dropped the butt on the deck, crushing it with his deck shoe. He stood and pointed at Suplee. "He'll have absolute fucking power," he stated, and walked out of the goat locker.

Suplee was gob smacked. Was it really as simple as that? And had Stevens ever heard the term *'Power corrupts, and absolute power corrupts absolutely.'*?

He probably hadn't. The thought made Suplee nauseous. This occurred at almost the exact time that Ensign Johnson was spewing up the contents of his stomach over the seaward wing bridge. He had to tell him, but not now. He'd wait until tomorrow after they'd set sail. He'd get some sleep tonight and have a fresh outlook tomorrow. That was, if he could sleep at all. He turned off the light over his bunk and put the magazine away. He lay there in his bunk for a long time, bathed in the red lights that lit the interior of the ship after sundown, and wondered what he'd tell Ensign Johnson.

Somewhere off in the distance through the heating and cooling ducts, he thought he heard a girl scream, and he curled into a fetal position, shuddering uncontrollably.

CHAPTER 10:
INTESTINAL FORTITUDE

Robyn knelt beside Tim's still form in the snow, wailing for almost a half hour until she couldn't cry anymore. She looked up at the sky into the falling snow, which was getting heavier by the minute. Already, a thin blanket covered Tim's back, and her bare feet were numb. Never in her life had she been more frightened. She brushed the snow off Tim's back and hitched a few sobs back. She reached under the still body, and with all the might she could muster, rolled him onto his back. She put her hand on his face and realized he was hot, *really* hot. She bent down close to his face; he was still breathing— short, ragged gasps were escaping from his mouth. He wasn't dead. He was just sick, very sick, and now she had to try to get him into the camper. But how? Her numb hands and feet forgotten, she stood up at Tim's head, grabbed hold of the collar of his jacket, and began to pull him backwards towards the trailer. It was slow going; it took all she had to drag his dead weight of over two hundred pounds to the trailer. She stopped for a minute, breathless. After she regained her breath, she again grabbed hold of his collar and slowly dragged him inch by inch up the two steps and into the camper. She had half of him inside now, and he groaned. Now for the really hard part. She had to turn him forty-five degrees, drag him down the narrow passageway through the tiny galley, past the bathroom, and up two feet onto his bed.

This she did with great difficulty, taking almost an hour, and using up all of her strength. She sat on the edge of Tim's bed and looked at him. He was white as a ghost, and his breath was ragged. She felt his head again, and he was still burning up. Her feet and hands were starting to warm up in the heat of the camper, and little pins and needles attacked her skin from her feet all the way to her knees. She had to get warm herself, or she'd be no use to Tim. She stood on unsteady feet and walked back to shut the door to the trailer, pulled off her t-shirt, and tossed it aside. Grabbing some warm clothes, she quickly got dressed. When she was done, she looked around, and her eyes caught a small wooden plaque Tim had hung on the wall. He'd told her he had taken it from his office when he left Philadelphia. It was the Ranger Creed, carved into the wood, and she had laughed at one part where it spoke of having the 'intestinal fortitude' to carry on the Ranger Mission, until Tim had explained what that meant. It meant having the guts to keep on going, even though things looked hopeless.

Well, things couldn't be more hopeless than this, she thought. It was time to Ranger Up, just like Tim would say.

Robyn knew she had to get his fever down, but at the moment she was unsure as how to do it. She stripped him to the waist with difficulty, and when that was done, she grabbed a few of the small plastic bags from the cupboard, the type you'd get from the grocery store. They had been using them as garbage bags, and had plenty. She went back outside and filled up several bags with snow, bringing them back inside. Going over to Tim, she placed one bag under each armpit, and others along both sides of his head and neck. She had seen this once on some medical drama on TV, and hoped it worked. She then went to the makeshift bookshelf and pulled down a copy of the American Red Cross' *Home First Aid* book, and riffled through it. It said to give the patient plenty of fluids. Now how was she going to do that with him out like that? Taking mental notes from the book, she grabbed one of the mason jars and a washcloth and walked back to the edge of the bed. Un- capping the jar, she took the washcloth and soaked up some alcohol and rubbed it all over Tim's chest.

"Please, Tim. Please get better!" she said to the still form. "I don't know what I'll do without you!"

She continued to give him alcohol rubs for several minutes, humming a song she and Tim liked. "Sorry about using up your Christmas present like this, Daddy, but I gotta get your temperature down. You're burning up!"

It surprised her that she'd called him that, and she remembered saying it earlier too. But that's the way she had started to think of him. He own father had died when she was too young to remember, and she had never really had another father figure in her life. Her mother had rarely dated, and Uncle Jake wasn't there all the time. Besides, Tim treated her just like a daddy would treat their daughter, she supposed, and she really did love him. He was gruff and grumpy at times, especially in the mornings, but that was one of the things she really liked. He didn't hide what he was feeling and made sure you knew he was happy with you, or angry with you. He wasn't phony like a lot of folks she knew from before. He was a great teacher too, patient in a firm way until you got it right, and then he was full of praise. But he let you know right away if you'd done something wrong, and then told you why.

"There, Daddy. That should fix you up some for a while," she said, placing the lid back on the jar and putting it on the shelf at Tim's head. She took another washcloth, soaked it with cold water and wrung it out, then folded it, and placed it on his forehead. "You get some rest, Daddy. I'll just be out at the table if you need anything," she said lovingly, and bent down and kissed him. She walked back into the main area of the camper but left the privacy curtain open so she could keep an eye on him. She sat at the table for a while, listening to his breathing, and when she was satisfied he was sleeping, she took her new carbine out and loaded three of the magazines the way he'd shown her that morning. The rifle had something else she thought was pretty neat; on the metal folding stock there was a small canvas web pouch for two spare magazines. This she filled with the two other magazines she'd loaded earlier. She stood it up on the counter next to the door so she could get to it in a hurry. She put on the teakettle, made herself a cup of cocoa, and was finally able to relax and get back to her book. She looked out of the window to see the snow being whipped around by wind, which had picked up in the last hour or so. It showed no signs of stopping at the moment, and she couldn't even see her footprints in the snow. It looked like almost another foot had fallen since she'd first found Tim. She shuddered at the thought of going back out in that, but she knew she would have to soon to get more bags of snow. She shoved that thought to the back of her mind and opened her book, keeping an eye on Tim at the same time.

About five PM, Robyn got up and went to check on Tim. Finding the snow almost completely melted, she decided to go out and get some more. The bags had leaked too, and now the top of the bed was soaked but she couldn't do anything about that right now. Donning her jacket, she took fresh bags and opened the door to the camper. Her breath was immediately taken away by the wind and the bitter cold. She was almost blinded by the snow, and filled the bags by feel. When she had finished that chore, she turned to head back but couldn't find the camper. *Where is it?* her mind screamed. *I only took two steps out of the door! Where is it?* Panic was starting to set in when she saw for a brief moment the red and green Christmas lights Tim had strung up. Fumbling blindly towards them, her hand finally found the trailer and she fumbled alongside until her hand felt the latch to the door. She virtually launched herself inside, slamming the door behind her.

Robyn stood there breathless until the panic had subsided. She pulled off her coat and took the bags of snow over to Tim. Sitting down on the edge of the bed again, she placed the snow filled bags under his armpits and along his head, and then took the damp rag off of his forehead.

"Daddy, I just had a bad scare, but I'm okay now. I'm going take care of you until you're better," she said, taking the moonshine and rubbing him down with it again. She'd love to be able to give him some medicine, but she didn't know what to give him or how to administer it to him in his unresponsive state. She would have to just do what she was doing and hope for the best. He was still burning up and the fever showed no signs of breaking, so she just did the best she could. Tim was sweating profusely; she wiped him down and tried to make him comfortable. By this time it was well after dark, and Robyn could hear the wind whistling through the awning rails. She had an alarming thought as she turned off the outside Christmas lights: *What if the generator runs out of fuel? I'm going to have to go out there and fill it back up! In that weather! I may get lost and never find my way back!* She pushed the bad thoughts to the back of her mind and shut off the rest of the lights in the camper. The snow outside made it bright enough inside to be able to see everything, so she stripped and put on Tim's t-shirt, and then climbed tiredly into bed. Sleep didn't come easy even though she was bone tired. She lay there, watching Tim's dark outline, and could hear his ragged breathing. She watched his chest fall and rise for well over an hour before sleep finally took her.

That sleep didn't last long. It was well after midnight when she was awakened by a terrible scream. Tim was thrashing around in his bed and talking loudly. She quickly jumped out of bed and ran to his side. Turning on the light, she saw his skin was a bright pink color and he was bathed in sweat. His eyes were open, but she could tell he couldn't see her. It seemed to her like every bad dream from every person who had ever lived had been bottled up and planted inside Tim's brain, being released at this exact point in time. The look on his face was one of absolute terror. He flailed around on the bed violently and it was all Robyn could do to keep his arms by his side and keep him from hurting himself. Her mama called them 'night terrors', and that's exactly what it looked like. Tim spat out streams of expletives in a tirade of abuse directed at some unseen enemy in his nightmares, and even though Robyn had heard them all before, she still blushed. This went on for a half hour or so until Tim finally collapsed in a heap on the wet sheets. He was so soaked that it looked as if he'd just gotten out of a swimming pool.

She removed the now empty snow bags, got the damp rag and wiped away the sweat on his brow, then his chest. His breathing was a little more regular now, and when she felt his forehead, she realized that whatever had transpired in his dreams— the night terrors, his delirium— the fever had reached its pinnacle and had burned itself out. Taking the moonshine again, she gave him another alcohol bath to calm him. An unpleasant smell hit her nose and she realized with a groan that Tim had soiled himself. She got another washcloth, soap and a bucket. Putting on the teakettle for some hot water, she returned to Tim's bed and unceremoniously stripped off the rest of his clothes without a hint of shyness. There wasn't time for that now. Holding the offending clothes at arm's length, she walked out to the door of the camper, opened it, and tossed the whole mess out into the still falling snow.

The teapot was just about to boil. Turning off the burner on the range, she poured a good amount of the boiling water into the bucket, then added cold water to it until it was just the right temperature. She tossed the rag and soap into the bucket, and carried the whole lot back in to Tim, where she quickly washed him up and cleaned as much off the bed as possible. She wasn't shy about it at all. She figured the mattress was ruined at this point, but couldn't do a thing about it. She just knew she couldn't let Tim lay in his own filth. After she was finished, she rolled him over and got a towel underneath his bottom. That done, she rolled him back and pulled the sheet up to cover him then sat down on the edge of the bed and took his hand. It felt cool and dry now, and that comforted her.

"Daddy," she said in a whisper, "you get some sleep now. I've got you all cleaned up and your fever broke. So just rest up and get better, okay?" She leaned down and kissed him again, turned off the light, and went back to the dinette table. She opened the blinds and saw that it was growing light, and that the snow had stopped. She made a pot of coffee, contemplated her situation, and recalled that she'd never been so scared in her life. Even when The Event happened and her mama died she wasn't as scared, and that shamed her a little bit. When the coffee was done, she poured herself a cup and sat back down, looking at the newly fallen snow. She thought about the generator again, and knew she'd have to go out there and check on it at some point. At least now it wasn't a blinding blizzard.

When it was full light, she got dressed in her warmest clothes and sturdy boots, tied her hair back into a ponytail, and donned her rabbit fur hat. She looked in on Tim, and he was sleeping peacefully, his breathing steady and rhythmic. She went to step outside, then stopped at the open door.

"I can't forget my American Express Card!" She picked up her carbine, slung it over her shoulder, and headed outside. When she got a few feet from the door, she saw Tim's soiled clothing lying in the snow. She went over to them and checked his pockets to find his wallet that he still carried around with him. She pocketed it, wondering why he still carried it, and took the soiled clothing, putting it all into a barrel Tim had set up to burn the paper trash. She looked in the direction of the generator. In the quiet of the newly fallen snow, she could hear it chugging away. She slogged her way to where they stored the diesel fuel and picked up a five gallon jerry can, then started her way towards the generator.

Almost two feet had fallen overnight, and that, on top of the six inches that had fallen the previous day, made for hard going. The snow was almost up to Robyn's waist, and she could hardly pull the fuel can through it. Then she got the idea of tossing it a few feet in front of her, then trudging her way to it, and do a sort of leapfrog all the way to the generator. It was hard work, and it took almost an hour to make it the two hundred yards to the generator. When she got there, she was drenched in sweat and took a moment to cool off by removing her hat and unbuttoning her coat. She looked to see that Tim had already taken two fuel cans out, and one of them was still completely full. He probably did that yesterday when he came out to check on it, and she mentally kicked herself for dragging another can out. But she really hadn't known, and it would have been worse if she hadn't brought fuel out with her only to find there was none there when she got to the generator, making for a double trip instead of one.

She took the funnel Tim had left and emptied the remainder of the half full can into the generator's tank, and that topped it off. She saw how much fuel it had burned, and she figured it would run like this for probably seven to ten days. Good! No slogging around in the snow! It was cold enough as it was, she didn't need to be out in it any more than absolutely necessary. Besides, she had to take care of Tim. She replaced the fuel cap and put all the fuel cans underneath the generator, then turned to make her way back to the camper. An unfamiliar sound caught her attention. She turned slowly and froze. A coyote was standing in the snow not ten feet from her. It was covered in mange, and was missing one ear. As soon as she was facing it, it bared its teeth and snarled. Tim had told her to stay away from what was normally a nocturnal animal, like raccoons or coyotes, if you saw them during the day because that usually meant rabies. Get bitten by one, and it was not a really pleasant way to die.

"What the fuck else can go wrong?" she asked aloud. She slowly and carefully reached behind her, picked up the carbine and pulled it up to her chest, snapping open the folding stock.

"Nice doggie, nice, nice doggie!" she said, and it took one step towards her in the deep snow. She cocked the gun, slamming a round home in the chamber, which made the rabid animal jump. It was definitely rabid. She could see the foam dripping from its maw. It was growling at her as she slowly brought the rifle up to her shoulder, and when she had acquired a good sight picture just like Tim had shown her, she squeezed the trigger rapidly three times.

Crack! Crack! Crack! The carbine barked, jumping minutely in her hands.

The coyote spun like it was a top. It yelped loudly and fell into the snow. She lowered the rifle and took stock of the still form lying only a few feet from her. It was the first time she'd fired it, and she was quite happy. There was little recoil, and it was easy to regain the sight picture after each shot; almost as easy as the .22. It was just as Tim had promised, and had made short work of this little bastard. Walking over to it, she saw that it was still alive, so she brought the rifle up, putting one final round into its head, and after the report of the last round, the only sound she heard was that of her rapidly beating heart, and the sizzle of the expended brass shell cooling in the deep snow.

"That'll teach you to fuck around with girls in this neck of the woods!" Robyn said. She folded the stock back, and placed the weapon on safe, slogged her way through the deep snow back to the camper. On returning, she ejected the round in the chamber, reloaded it into the magazine, and propped the rifle up next to the door. She shucked her jacket and hat and looked in on Tim. He was still sleeping soundly. She sat tiredly at the dinette table, and with a deep sigh, looked at the little tree they had gotten for Christmas. Surely this would be a Christmas she'd never forget. Over the next four days, she busied herself around the camper, and read her book in between taking care of Tim. She had to clean him up several times, and did it robotically, but with great care. He was starting to get dehydrated though, and she tried unsuccessfully several times to get some fluids into him, and she was beginning to worry.

On the morning of the fifth day, she was just getting up and making some coffee when she heard stirring from Tim's bed. She looked over and saw him sitting up on the edge of the bed with the sheet pulled up to cover his lap.

"I feel like fifteen miles of bad road," he said, scratching his head. "And I think a bobcat snuck in here and took a shit in my mouth."

"DADDY!" Robyn screamed, and ran to him, throwing her arms around his neck.

"Whoa! Calm down. Not so loud, my head's pounding!"

"That's because you've been really sick," she said. She got a huge glass of water and two Tylenol, handing them to him. He took the glass and the pills and downed them both in a few quick gulps. She took the empty glass and refilled it from the tap, and brought it back to him. "Drink it up. You're dehydrated."

"Yes ma'am!" he said. "How'd I get undressed?" he asked, giving her a sideways glance.

"I undressed you. You'd messed yourself and I had to clean you up," she said, looking away.

He felt the mattress, and felt it was still wet. "You cleaned me up?"

"Yeah, several times, you were a mess."

"Several times? How long was I out?"

"Five days."

"Five *days*? Holy shit on a stick!"

"You had me shit scared. When I found you lying out there in the snow I thought you were dead."

"Last thing I remember was walking back from the generator..."

"Yeah, and I almost peed my pants when I found you. Dragged you all the way in here and got you in bed."

"You did?" he asked in disbelief. "Oh, baby. Come here," he said, holding out his arms. Robyn came to him and they hugged tightly.

"Don't ever scare me like that again, alright?"

"I won't," Tim said, still holding her tightly.

"I'm not joking, Daddy. Tell me next time you're not feeling well."

"I'll tell you. I promise!"

"You'd better!" she said, stepping away from him. "Want to try some coffee?"

"Maybe in a minute, I'd like to get a shower and get dressed."

Robyn turned to leave and pulled the privacy curtain closed. Tim shook his head and smiled. *I was out for five days?* he thought. *Jesus. I must have been really sick.* He still wasn't feeling a hundred percent, but he was alive, and that was good. He headed to the tiny bathroom with his shaving kit, and was shocked at what looked back at him in the mirror. He was pale and gaunt, and must have lost fifteen pounds. His skin had a gray tint that reminded him of a dead fish. The five days' growth on his chin made him look even worse. He got into the shower, not bothering with a submarine shower, and let the hot water cascade off of him until it ran cold. He shut the tap off and dried himself, brushed his teeth, and lathered up to shave. He scraped the whiskers off his face, and went back into his sleeping area to survey the mattress. Maybe he could just flip it and get by until winter was over. Once he was dressed, he went back out to the dinette where Robyn had some margarine, toast and a cup of coffee waiting for him.

"Thank you, baby," he said, sitting down and taking a bite of the toast. As soon as he bit into it, his stomach growled, letting him know it was empty and needed refilling. He literally inhaled the toast, and Robyn got up and made him some more.

"Here's some more," she said, "but that's it. You need to take it slow for a few days. I'll make you some soup for lunch if you want."

He nodded and thanked her, taking a sip of his coffee. He really was amazed at the change in the girl since he first encountered her. Not only had her backwoods accent almost completely disappeared, her vocabulary had grown in leaps and bounds, and she had matured emotionally so much it was kind of scary. She was soaking up information like a sponge.

"So, I guess it was a little scary for you, huh?" he asked.

"I was shit-scared, but I remembered what you told me about intestinal fortitude so I Rangered up and did what I had to do," she said, looking him dead in the eye. She then went on to tell him how she had dragged him all the way into the trailer, how she'd packed snow in bags around him to get the fever down, and how she rubbed him down with the moonshine.

"Sorry about that, Daddy. I reckoned you wouldn't mind."

"No, I don't mind at all. And what's with this 'daddy' stuff?"

"Well, I figured since you and me are together like this, and how you've taught me all kinds of things, and the way you treat me, it must be like how a daddy is. And since I don't have one… well… now you're my daddy and that's that!" she said.

"I guess that's settled then, huh?"

"Yep, and you can't get out of it now."

"I suppose not. I've got the job whether I want it or not. I've been volunteered!"

"Drafted!"

"And here I was thinking all along we now had an all-volunteer Army."

"Stuck like glue!" she giggled.

She went on to tell him of her trip out to the generator and her encounter with the rabid coyote, and he was really impressed. He thought back to his nieces and nephews, and how they might have reacted if they were in this position. They'd probably be dead by now. Looking back on how they were, he thought sadly that they would have just curled up and died because they had no one to do anything for them. His brother and sister-in-law gave them everything they wanted, and the never had to earn anything. He recalled one Christmas he was home, and he and Connie had spent it with his brother's family. His brother had gotten one nephew some toy, he couldn't remember what it was, but it had cost him over $400. Apparently it wasn't the 'right' one, and the seven year old boy threw a fit and smashed it on the wall, and his brother said nothing. Looking back, he wished he could have taken those four little brats to some of the Third World shitholes he'd been to, and shown them real poverty, but he thought that that lesson would have been a waste of time.

"So I take it the carbine works fine?"

"Oh yeah, it's sweet!"

"Did you clean it?" he asked, reaching behind him and getting the rifle. He opened the bolt halfway and saw that there was no round in the chamber, just like he'd instructed, and he was satisfied that all he could smell was Hoppe's No. 9.

"Yes I did. Right after I got back and took care of you. It was the last thing I did before going to bed that night."

"I can see that," Tim said, putting the weapon back where she had stored it.

"I do need a .30 caliber bore brush though. I only ran patches though it, but it cleaned up nice."

"We'll get one once the weather clears up some and I can get back on the road."

He looked again at the calendar, and did the mental math. "Hey, it's New Year's Eve!"

"It is?"

"Yeah, we'll have to have a New Year's Eve party!" he said.

"Are you feeling up to it? I mean, you're probably not still completely better," Robyn said with a worried look.

"Ah, I should be alright. Besides, history will most probably repeat itself, and I'll be sound asleep well before midnight anyway!" Tim drained off the last of his coffee, which Robyn quickly refilled. He really wasn't feeling a hundred percent, and he thought better of a party. "Well, if you'd rather not, we can forget about it. It really doesn't matter to me anyway. Back before The Event, I used to call it 'amateur night'."

"Why did you call it that?"

"Because all the people who thought they could handle their booze would go out on that night and drink and party like there was no tomorrow. They were amateurs. Me on the other hand, I am a professional drunk. I stayed home those nights mostly. I hate being in the company of amateurs!"

"So you're saying you're an alcoholic?" Robyn asked.

"No, I'm a drunk. Alcoholics go to meetings," Tim said, giving her a big wink. He still did feel a little drained, and decided to lie down for a nap. He retired to his bed, and Robyn busied herself around the camper, cleaning up, and reading her book. He woke around sundown, and he and Robyn played Scrabble until late. Again, he was amazed at her growing vocabulary, and had to check the dictionary several times. At the end of the game, she took a pencil and marked down the score on a small notepad.

"Okay, you now owe me $379,500!"

"I think I've been sandbagged," he grumbled. "Okay, sweetheart, time to hit the fartsack."

"Oh, alright," she said, getting up and putting the game away. She went and got ready for bed, and when she was in the shower, Tim took a last sip of the moonshine for the night. "Nice!" he said to himself. The stuff sure was smooth. He screwed the lid firmly onto the mason jar.

When Robyn came out wearing one of his t-shirts again, she came up to him and gave him a kiss. "Good night, Daddy!" she said.

He turned to her and tucked her in. "Good night, sweetheart. Sweet dreams!"

She would sleep well that night, he knew, and it would probably be the best night's sleep she'd had in the last few days of taking care of him.

He went to the rear of the camper, showered again, and when he was finished, crawled into bed. When he was comfortable, he lay there in the dark listening to the wind blowing through the trees outside, and thought about his lot. It could be a lot worse. He could still be alone. If that had been the case, he'd have probably died out there in the cold like one of Hemingway's protagonists. He had one opportunity to make it right, with whatever demons he had in his subconscious, and he couldn't fuck it up. Just by sheer tenacity… intestinal fortitude, he reminded himself, she'd saved his life. He had to do right by Robyn, and in the process try to raise her up properly. He silently thanked her mother, who most definitely did a fine job raising her so far with what limited resources she had. The kid did have mettle, that was for sure. He thought of her saying she 'Rangered Up' and smiled. Shit, she had more balls than some soldiers he'd known. Dragging him like that in the middle of a blizzard, stripping him and cleaning up his shit and piss. That took balls. He knew he'd do the same for her, but looked back on others he had known in the past, and wondered who really would have done the same. Not many he thought, bitterly. Surely not Connie, she'd have been too worried about breaking a nail or something. No, he had to do right by Robyn, which was for certain. The 'Daddy' thing made him happy too. He'd never had any kids, but he was sure in his heart that he was doing it right. He was actually enjoying it, more than he'd ever enjoyed anything else.

He woke the next morning feeling a lot better than he had the day before, got up and tossed some pants on. He checked the thermostat to the heater and turned it down some. No sense wasting gas, and it felt warm enough in the tiny camper already. He'd go out later and check the gas bottle, and make sure it was full or change it out if it wasn't. He looked over at Robyn sleeping peacefully in her bunk. She was still out like a light, which was unusual for her. She was almost always awake before him, and would have the coffee ready for when he stirred. She must be completely wiped out from the last few days. He decided to just let her sleep. As quietly as he could, he made the coffee, put the pot on to boil, and sat down at the dinette, looking out at the winter wonderland that lay before them. Everything was still blanketed in a thick covering of snow, and a quick glance at the outside thermometer he'd put up told him it wasn't going to be going anywhere soon. -5 F. It was a good thing they'd gotten everything stocked up. They'd be stuck there for several weeks. He looked out over the snow and watched the sun come up over the denuded trees. When the coffee was done, he got up and fixed himself a cup, and went back to his seat watching for any wildlife, but he knew that with it being this cold, most critters would be bedded down and not moving around a lot. He heard stirring from over his head, and then Robyn's head popped into view, hanging upside down with blond hair hanging far below her, wearing a sleepy smile.

"Good morning, Sar' Major!"

"What, no Daddy this morning?"

"Oh, you're still Daddy, but you're also 'Sar' Major!" she giggled, and hopped down from the overhead bunk, landing heavily on the carpeted floor. "I gotta pee!" she announced, and ran to the bathroom.

When she was finished in the bathroom, she came out and poured herself a cup of coffee, kissed Tim on the forehead, and sat down across from him.

"Did you sleep well?" she asked.

"I slept like a log, and I feel shitloads better too," he said, taking a sip of coffee.

"I slept really well too. I don't even remember you turning off the lights."

"You were probably exhausted from all the shit you had to do the last few days."

"And all the shit I had to clean up too!" she reminded him.

"Well, thank you for that. Not a lot of people would have done that."

"I know, but I figured it had to be done, so I just did it. Besides, you stank!"

"Gee, thanks."

"So, do you want to try some oatmeal this morning?"

"Okay, but you finish your coffee first. Relax a little bit," he said firmly.

She sighed, sipping her coffee and looking out the window. "Sure is pretty out there."

"That it is, but I wouldn't want to be out there in my underwear for too long," he said, and she laughed hard, and almost spit out her coffee.

"Now there's a sight I'd like to see!"

"Not on your life!"

Robyn got up and put the teakettle on to boil and asked, "Do you think we'll ever meet up with other people?"

"I don't know. We probably will, considering the odds."

"What do you mean?"

"Well, before The Event, the population of the US was somewhere around three hundred and fifty to four hundred million people, not including Canada or Mexico."

"And?"

"It's like this. Even if ninety-nine point nine percent of the people died in The Event, that would still leave several hundred *thousand* people that are survivors. It's just a matter of statistics."

"Oh, wow. So we'll meet up with others someday?"

"The odds are for it," he said with a frown.

"You don't seem too happy about that," Robyn remarked.

"I'm not really. It all depends on what those people are like. We'll just have to wait and see."

"But they could be good people like us," she insisted.

"Yeah, but they could be bad ones too. That's why we will be very, very careful when we do encounter anyone else." He thought of the tire tracks he'd seen in the snow earlier in the year, heading south. What sort of people were they? And the four who took his pig, up in Beckley. Apparently they were somewhat polite, leaving him that note and all. But he was still nervous about it. The three animals he'd dealt with who killed Paul were still fresh in his mind.

"Maybe someday everyone who survived will get together and build up society again," Robyn stated.

"Could be, but that would take years for everyone to find one another. And they'd have to do it right this time."

"They could just follow the Constitution."

"That they could, if they were smart. That little document that's only seventeen pages long can make a difference, but they can't let it get away from them like they did before."

"You're smart. *You* could do it!"

He laughed. "Honey, I may be smart, but I'm not that smart. Those men who wrote that up over two hundred years ago were far smarter than me."

"Don't sell yourself short, Sar Major," she said, pouring hot water from the teakettle into the two bowls with instant oatmeal and stirring them. Bringing the bowls over, she placed one in front of Tim and sat down with her own.

"You are the smartest man I ever knew. You could do it, I know you could," she affirmed.

"Maybe I could, but I really don't have too much faith in people, haven't for a while."

"You're a ....what's the word?" she said, looking up at the ceiling. "Cynic? Yeah, you're a cynic."

"No, I'm a realist. I've seen people fuck over one another for far too long for trivial things, just to get a leg up. I don't want to be part of any society that condones that."

"Then you could be king."

"No, absolutely not, the US got rid of one king a long time ago. That would be too much, and I don't have the ego to be king!"

"King George III, right?"

"Yes, ma'am you win the pop-quiz. No, you see, that kind of power is corrupting. It even makes good men turn bad. And absolute power corrupts absolutely. So, no thank you. I'd rather live free and in peace and be left to my own devices."

"Yeah, I guess you're right."

"Yep," he said, taking another spoonful. "Remember what I told you about the American Revolution?"

"Yes," she nodded.

"King George had all this power over in England and didn't give a rat's ass about the colonists. He just saw them as a tax base and a place to get cheap wood to build his fleet, and he was bleeding them dry. So when the colonists had finally had enough, they took up arms knowing that if they lost the war, they'd all be tried for treason and hanged. So they had a lot riding on one little gamble."

"Scary thought," Robyn said gravely.

"Those men knew it too. They had huge brass balls to do that. Anyway, what they started out to do, somewhere along the way got corrupted and the people in power forgot who they were working for, and they loved all that power. So no, I do not want to be part of any society that will let that happen again."

"Why did it happen?"

"Because people got lazy. They expected the government to do everything for them. They forgot that *'The Pursuit of Happiness'* wasn't a right, just that you had the right to *pursue* it. The government didn't hold the keys to happiness, you had to go out and find it on your own. That's where it all got muddled. We forgot that little key point, and that's where it all turned to shit."

"Like when I played softball. We never kept score and at the end of the season we all got trophies even though some of us sucked?"

"Exactly right, sweetheart! See, when you let people fail, they strive to achieve better for themselves. It's a natural human trait. When you give people a safety net, they give up trying."

"So that's where everything went wrong?"

"Well, it's a little deeper than that, but yes, in a nutshell, that's what did it. I don't know when it started, it sort of crept up on us, but that's what happened."

"So that's why you don't trust people?"

"Yeah, that's why."

"So we won't look for anyone?" she said sadly.

"I didn't say that, honey. I just said that when we do travel out from here, we'll just have to be really careful with who we meet up with. There's probably some madman out there somewhere who thinks this is some grand opportunity to rule the world."

Robyn said after a moment's contemplation, "I hope we never meet up with someone like that!"

"I hope so too, baby."

"So where will we go?"

"In the spring?" he asked, getting up and pouring himself another coffee.

""Yes, that's what I meant. In the spring, where will we go?"

"Well, I think most of the smart people have already moved south to where it's warmer by now. Not stuck around where it's cold, like us dummies."

"Speak for yourself!"

"I'm only joking. I haven't really given it a whole lot of thought except that we'd better do the same thing— go where the weather is a little bit nicer. We do have a whole continent to choose from. I think those who have survived and were able to move as far south as they could. Florida, Texas, California… probably all the way down into Mexico. Southern Mexico along the ocean is actually rather nice."

"I'd like that," Robyn said, looking out at the snow and shivering involuntarily.

"Do you have any ideas?"

"Not really. I know you said it was my choice, but I don't know enough about anyplace else to really have a good idea."

"Well, how about this, we head west in the spring, and then south. We'll let the place pick us, not we pick the place. Sound like a plan?"

"Sounds fun, actually!"

"Like I said, we'll still be very careful, but that's what we'll do. We'll find a bigger camper also. I think there's a Camping World in Bluefield we can check out."

"Sounds like a plan, Sar' Major!" she said, smiling. At least now they had a goal to shoot for. Not long term, but it'd get them moving.

Later that night, Tim lay awake for quite some time, thinking about what they had talked about earlier in the day, and one thought kept coming back to him. Could there really be some new Adolph Hitler or Joseph Stalin out there with his eyes set on ruling the world? A chill ran through him at the very idea. If that were the case, it was very bad indeed. And it really wouldn't end well. In the past, throughout history, it had always been left up to people like him, soldiers, to straighten out other people's fuckups. But he was alone now, well almost alone, and he surely couldn't save the world from some madman, could he? It took millions of men like him to save Europe and the Pacific years ago in the last great epic struggle. His very own father and two uncles were part of that great crusade, but he was just one man.

He couldn't do that, could he? Did he have the intestinal fortitude? He'd overcome many obstacles in his life, adapted and overcome barriers, and bested enemies, but save the world? That couldn't have been what his brother was talking about. It was all too much for him to contemplate, and he drifted off to a troubled sleep.

CHAPTER 11: GO WEST YOUNG MAN

The winter seemed like it would never end, and each cold, blustery day made way for the next in the tiny camper in West Virginia. Tim and Robyn made the best of it though, spending their time reading and playing board games, and Robyn continued with her daily lessons. Tim taught her to play cards also: Blackjack, Five Card Draw, Stud and Texas Hold Em.' She even learned to deal from the bottom of the deck so well that even Tim watching carefully couldn't pick it up. He taught her some phrases in German and Spanish he'd learned during his time spent in Central America and Germany in the Army, and again, she picked it up so fast he was stunned. But the winter was brutal, and Tim couldn't remember a colder one. He wasn't sure if The Event had anything to do with it, or it was just a particularly bad winter. It snowed on top of snow, barely warming up in between enough to melt the last snowfall. In between the reading and the lessons, they made preparations for their migration, as Tim began calling it. They would definitely have to find a new camper, as things were beginning to break and wear out at a continuous rate that Tim could mend, but he was having a hard time keeping up. The camper's designers never imagined it would be used in this way, for full time living. The continuous use was taking a heavy toll. Roof vents leaked, taps on the sinks broke, and now the roof leaked in several places. Tim secretly worried about the roof collapsing at some point.

As the days eventually grew longer, the snows finally started melting, and the little creek behind their camp turned from a gently babbling brook into a raging river overnight. They became increasingly restless with each warmer day until one bright sunny day towards the end of April they decided it was time to move. They packed up everything they thought they would need into the bed of the truck. Tim expertly hitched the tiny trailer to the M880 and pulled it from its resting spot, where it had sat for over a year. The tires had sunk into the mud some, but the big diesel engine in the old M880 made it an easy job.

When they were ready, Robyn hopped into the passenger side of the truck and placed her carbine on the dashboard alongside Tim's M4. They headed out south on RT 20. Passing through Athens, they were both a little sad. The little town had sustained them for over a year, and all in all, as little towns go, this really wasn't a bad one. Tim noticed a ragged American flag flying from the flagpole at the local volunteer fire department across from the convenience store and Laundromat, and decided to rectify the problem. He pulled over, reached behind the seat of the truck, and retrieved a brand new flag, still in the box. He had several he'd gotten at the Walmart on a whim. Walking over, he lowered the tattered rag that was flying and raised the new one. When it was fully raised, he tied off the cords on the cleat, stepped back, and saluted smartly. Robyn followed suit.

When they got back into the truck, Robyn asked, "Why did you do that?"

"Well, I figure this little town has done a lot for us, just by being here. I thought it'd be a nice gesture in return."

"But no one will see it."

"You and I know it's here, flying proudly. That's all that matters. It's a sign of respect to the men and women who once served their community from this building."

Tim put the truck back into gear and Robyn rolled down her window, making a wing with her hand and floating it on the passing breeze. They reached the intersection of RT 460 and headed west, passing through Princeton and into Bluefield, where they easily found the Camping World dealership. They parked and got out to look around. They could see that nature was coming back in a big way, with every crack in the asphalt lot sprouting weeds, and even a few sumac trees. The roof of the building looked like it had a lawn growing on it, and peering through the dirty window he could see that part of the roof had collapsed at some point during the last winter. It looked like a tree was growing up through a shattered display case.

They walked around the lot looking at each camper, finding some fault with each one they looked at. At least there were no pushy salesmen rushing out to pester them and they could browse at their leisure. After a half hour of searching, Tim found the one they were looking for. A full thirty feet long, it had everything they'd need— a full kitchen with a large refrigerator, and a full sized range top and stove, a good sized bathroom that even had a bathtub, several 'slide-outs' that would make it even larger when parked, a large couch, and even a gas fireplace. He was also very happy to see that it had a washing machine and a dryer! There was a queen-sized bed at one end with plenty of storage underneath, and another berth type bed in the front over the dinette table, which would also fold out into a bed if they were expecting company, which they weren't. The thing that really sold him on it was the full bank of photovoltaic solar panels on the roof, and the brochure said that it was a full fifty-amp service.

This camper was built a lot sturdier than their old one, as this one was built for full-time RVers in mind. It was also a tow-behind, and that was the kind Tim preferred. He had eschewed the idea of a fifth-wheel camper, because he'd lose a lot of storage in the bed of the truck. He busied preparing it to move, and when he was ready to back up the truck to hitch it, Robyn stopped him, a concerned look painted across her face.

"Daddy?" she said softly.

"Yes, Pumpkin?" he said, looking up from the hitch.

"We're never going to be back here, are we?"

"Chances are, probably not, baby."

"Okay," she said, and looked away.

"What's the matter?" he said, walking over to her.

"Well, I was wondering if we could… well, I'd like to say goodbye to my mama."

Tim thought for a minute. It wasn't that far from here, if his memory served him correctly. It couldn't hurt, he thought.

"Okay, hop in. We'll take a drive over right now."

"Really?"

"Yeppers! Lets' go!"

They hopped into the truck, and Tim had to admit it was easier driving it without the trailer behind them. They got onto Rt. 52, and headed for Welch. Here the road was discernibly narrower, as the weeds were rapidly overtaking the road, and the tires thumped over each crack in the weed-choked macadam. Pretty soon it would look like a long, narrow meadow, and you'd never know there was a road here once. At two places, kudzu had already crept all the way across the road and up the power poles on the other side. Yes, nature was coming back in a big way, and in a few years you'd never know there were people ever there. Rounding a bend in the road on a blind curve, Tim slammed on the brakes, skidding to a dusty stop.

"Shit that was close!" he said, looking out the windshield.

Robyn looked out, and said "Oh wow! That was close!"

A mere ten feet in front of them the road just disappeared. It was almost the exact spot where he'd encountered Robyn for the first time last year, and looking around, he was really glad they'd left the trailer back in Bluefield. There was absolutely no place to turn around the road was so narrow, and Tim would have to back up several times to turn even with just the truck. They got out, walked to the edge of the pavement, and looked down. There had been a bridge here until recently, and with the heavy snows came an extremely heavy melt off that had turned this little creek ten feet below them into another raging river. It was now a little stream again, but what it had done was tear out the bridge, leaving a thirty foot gap in the road and steep ten foot banks of loose dirt on either side.

"Well, somebody better call West Virginia Department of Transportation!" Tim said.

"You know what is white with a blue and gold stripe, and sleeps four comfortably?" Robyn asked.

"No, what?"

"A Double-U Vee Dot truck!" she laughed, and he caught the joke and laughed heartily too.

"That's a good one!"

"My mama used to say it all the time."

"Your mama must have been a funny lady, Pumpkin!"

"She was," Robyn said, looking down. "I guess this means we won't be saying goodbye now, huh?"

"Never say never, because this is just an obstacle, and we can get over it," Tim countered.

"But how?" she asked. "It's so wide and deep!"

"Oh, don't you worry," he said with a wink. He went to the bed of the truck and pulled out a large coil of rope and a small rucksack. He walked over to a huge oak tree that was growing alongside of the road and tied one end of the rope to it, then walked to the edge and tossed the rope across the thirty foot gap, where it landed on the other side.

"You wait here. This is the hard part."

"Okay," she said nervously, as she watched Tim go to the edge and sit, then push off and slide on his bottom down the embankment, stopping at the creek's edge. He waded through the stream, and it was only a few inches deep where he stood, until he got to the far bank. *I am getting too old for this shit.* This is where a dumb, eighteen year old private came in handy. They were the ones you sent to climb over this stuff like a monkey. He slowly climbed up the bank, slipping back several times, which made Robyn catch her breath, until he finally got to the edge of the asphalt on the far side and pulled himself over the top He lay there out of breath for a moment or two.

"Are you okay, Tim?" she yelled across. Tim just held up his hand with a thumb's up gesture. He lay there for a few more minutes, then stood and picked up the coil of rope. Walking over to an equally large oak tree on the far side, he tied that end of the rope so it was taut all the way, and suspended about six feet off the ground. He then opened his pack and removed a short section of rope about twelve feet long and a snap-link carabiner. He used the rope to tie a 'Swiss seat' around his waist and legs, then snapped the link to the seat, right where his belt buckle was. Hoisting himself up onto the rope, he snapped the link onto it, and quickly shimmied himself back across to the other side, unhooking himself, and dropping at Robyn's feet.

"There, easy as taking a dump," he said.

"But how am I going to get across?" she asked.

"I'll show you. Grab your piece," he said, and she went and got her carbine. "Grab mine too!"

She did as she was told, walking back over to him and handing over his weapon, which he slung across his chest.

"Sling yours like I just did and hop on my back."

She did, wrapped her arms around his neck, and he hitched her legs around his waist.

"Now close your eyes, and whatever you do, don't look down."

"Okay," Robyn said, holding on as tightly as she could. He reached up, quickly reattached himself to the rope, and shimmed his way easily across to other side, thinking she didn't weigh much more than a rucksack. He planted his feet on the ground and unhooked himself. You can let go now."

Robyn dropped off and looked at him, smiling.

"See, told you it was easy!" he winked. "C'mon, let's get to walking."

They walked the few hundred yards to the old run-down trailer that Robyn had once called home. The winter hadn't been kind to it, and the heavy snow had totally collapsed the roof, bowing out the outer walls. The waist high grass was heavily overgrown by weeds. Kudzu vines were rapidly overtaking the whole area here with a vengeance, and it wouldn't be long before nature swallowed up the whole trailer park. They walked hand in hand to the back of the trailer and found the spot where Geoffrey had buried Robyn's mother. The makeshift wooden cross Geoffrey had made was still there but leaning haphazardly to one side like a drunken sailor. He stopped a few feet short and let her go by herself to the grave, where she sat down right by the cross. She tried to right it, but it just leaned back where she had found it, so she gave up.

"Hi, Mama, I came back to say goodbye. This is Tim, and he's been taking care of me since you've gone. I won't ever be back this way, Mama, so you rest easy. I'll be okay with Tim. You'd have really liked him. He's taught me all kinds of things, and he'll protect me, so don't you worry. Well, I guess this is it," she said, standing and brushing off the grass and hitchhikers from her pants.

Walking back over to Tim and taking hold of his hand, she turned one last time and said, "Goodbye, Mama. I love you and will never forget you!" She stood there for a minute more, and then looked up at Tim. "We can go now."

They made their way back to the truck, crossing the chasm as easily as before. When Tim had the truck started and turned around, she looked over at him and said, "Can we get out of here quick? It really is depressing around here."

"Sure thing, baby, we'll beat feet!" He put the truck in gear, spinning wheels to leave. They left the rope where it was, as it would have been too much trouble to retrieve it, and they could always get more along the way. They made their way back to Bluefield silently, and quickly found the camper dealership. Once there, they transferred all of their belongings to the new camper, and hitched it to the truck. Tim took one final look at the little camouflaged trailer they were leaving behind. It really had served them well, and in a way, he'd miss it.

Making sure they had enough fuel, they headed back east on Rt. 460 until they came to I-77.. They turned onto the highway heading south, the same way that the others that had left the tracks in the snow those many months ago had gone. Only a few miles south of that exit they crossed from West Virginia into Virginia, and that part of the Interstate was very steep. Tim was thankful for the electric brakes on the camper. As they made their way, Tim laughed at a road sign that read "Bland, Virginia."

"Glad we didn't stop there, it's far too bland for my taste!" he said, and Robyn laughed. Shortly after that, they passed through two tunnels slowly, and a few miles later met up with the junction of Interstate 81, which ran west to where it would eventually meet up with I-40 near Jefferson City, Tennessee. There they headed west in the late afternoon sun, Robyn's feet dangling out of the passenger side window, and Tim smoking a cigarette. They crossed into Tennessee, into a city called Bristol, and seeing the billboard signs, Tim remembered it was famous for its NASCAR races. They made it all the way to an overgrown rest area on the highway near a town called Bailyton, where they stopped for the night. After setting up their new home, they made a light supper, and Tim took two folding camp chairs and set them up outside. Propping his carbine up next to him, he cracked open a beer. Robyn came out wearing shorts and a t-shirt, holding a can of Coke, and sat down next to him. The sun had set an hour ago, but the evening air was still warm enough to sit out in shirtsleeves, and they both looked up at the night sky in silence for a long time.

"Sure are a lot of stars," she said, finally breaking the silence.

"That there are. Never would see a night sky like this in Philadelphia."

"It's amazing," she said. "Just think, what we're seeing happened millions of years ago. Some of those stars might be long gone by now. We're just looking into the past."

He would never cease to be amazed at what fell out of her mouth. "How old are you again?"

"Fourteen."

"More like thirty!" he said. "And you're exactly right. What we're looking at is ancient history."

"What's that?" she asked. "Is that a plane?" she added excitedly, and he looked to where she was pointing.

"No, that's a satellite. There are thousands of them still up there, orbiting the Earth. Probably will for thousands of years to come."

"And they still work?"

"Maybe. At least the military ones would. That IVIS pad we listen to the music on?"

"Yeah?" she said, nodding her head.

"Well, I can contact the military satellite with it, with that special antenna I have. All the military computer networks are still up and running. They're probably powered off solar or something."

"Really?" she asked in amazement. "Then if someone else is out there with one, you could contact them?"

"In theory, but the several times I've tried I never got any response, except a prompt from whatever computer I was synced with, that everything on the network was nominal."

They watched the satellite travel across the night sky until it passed into the Earth's shadow, hiding it until its next pass.

"Oh, okay then."

"Honey, don't rush it. We'll eventually meet up with other people," he said, finishing his beer and crushing the can.

"Want another one?" she asked.

"Yeah, one more maybe, then it's time for the fartsack," he said.

"Can I have one?"

"You never give up, do you?" Tim chuckled.

"Nope," she said, hopping back into the camper. Tim sat and looked up at the stars some more. The moon had not yet risen, and he had a clear view of the sky. It always made him feel really insignificant, like a single grain of sand on a beach. She came back out and offered a cold can of beer to him, and the coolness and the sweat on the can felt good in his hands. He popped the tab, took a sip, and sat back to watch the sky. As soon as he was comfortable, a huge meteor slashed across the sky, leaving a bright red and green tail behind it that lasted for several seconds.

"Wow! Did you see that?" she squealed.

"I sure did.

"Did you make a wish, Daddy? You've got to make a wish on a falling star!"

"Baby, I have everything I need right here. No need to wish for anything else," he said, taking her hand. Robyn didn't say anything more, but didn't let go of his hand. They sat like that until Tim was finished his beer, and they packed up and headed inside for the night. Just as Tim was closing the door, he heard an owl hoot, and figured they were getting their fill of mice and other rodents. They both took showers and climbed into their new beds, luxuriating in the fresh sheets. They were asleep in minutes.

The next day, they woke before sunrise, and after a quick breakfast, were back out on the road. They made good time, only having to cross the overgrown median twice, to go around pileups. The huge piles of twisted and burned metal in each instance looked like it had been there a thousand years. They made it all the way west through Knoxville and Nashville, where they were finally forced to take I-24 northwest due to a massive pileup blocking all the lanes. It was almost dark when they crossed into Kentucky at Clarkesville, and Tim reminisced about a time long ago when he saw signs for Fort Campbell, where he'd gone to Air Assault School. They then headed north on the Edward T. Breathitt-Pennyrile Parkway, and Robyn laughed at the name. It was well past ten PM, when they pulled into another overgrown rest area near Crofton, for the night. Tim decided to wait until morning to check all the parked trucks for fuel, hoping to top off all of their jerry cans, and fuel tank. When they finally bedded down for the night, Tim lay there, and thanked himself for making the move when he had. If they'd waited one more year, the roads would be even less passable, as nature was taking back what man had tried to conquer faster than he'd thought possible. Everywhere they passed, houses and buildings were already in bad condition, and the roads were getting worse. At least they hadn't come across anymore washouts.

In the morning, they sat and had their coffee some toast. It was the last of the bread for a while, and they decided to finish it. After Robyn finished her last slice, she brushed the crumbs from her fingers.

"So where to today?"

"Let's take a look at the map," Tim said, pulling out his road atlas. "We're here in Kentucky. I think we'll keep heading north and cross over the Ohio River here, and into Indiana at Evansville."

"Then are we going to pick up I-64 here?" she asked, pointing to a spot on the map just a little north.

"I don't know. Maybe we'll head a little further north on this Rt. 41, and then head west into Illinois at Vincennes."

"Why there? I mean, the highway is right here, and we can head west right there?" Again she pointed at the map and looked at him questioningly.

"I don't know. Something is telling me we might be better off going this way." She rolled her eyes. "You're the boss!"

He didn't know why, but something in the back of his mind was telling him to go that way. He couldn't explain it. Whenever he felt like this in the past, even if it went against common sense, he did it, and it usually was the right decision. Tim went out with his siphon hose and jerry cans, and in no time he had enough diesel fuel to fill up the truck's tank and all his jerry cans for spares. After that they packed up and headed out north, and this time Tim took the IVIS pad into the cab with them so they'd have music to listen to along the way. Tim was in an 80s mood, and played all the CDs from the post-modern era he was fond of: Pet Shop Boys, Tears for Fears, The Fixx, Madness, Ice House, Men at Work, and a bunch of others. Robyn loved the mix. The travelling wasn't as easy that day, and they had to cross over the median on several occasions to go around wrecks. They stopped for lunch at another rest stop, and Robyn was able to shoot two rabbits with the .22, which she expertly skinned and gutted, just like Tim had shown her.

"You're turning into a great hunter, Robyn."

"Thanks! I learned it all from you," she said, wrapping them up with butcher paper, and putting them in the freezer. "So, how much farther is it to Indiana?" "Oh, I reckon it's about another fifty miles or so. We should be there before nightfall."

"I was just wondering," she said, putting away the .22 rifle, washing her hands, and then opening a can of Coke. "I like the music, it makes the travelling go by easier."

"Yeah, I always loved to listen to music while I drive. One time when I was still in school, I hopped in my car one night, popped in a Ted Nugent tape, and headed out. Before I knew it, I was in Altoona, Pennsylvania, well over a hundred miles from home," he laughed. "My dad was so pissed at me!"

Robyn laughed, trying to imagine Tim at that age and couldn't. "What happened?"

"Well, I had no money, and because I was only sixteen, I couldn't check into a motel. So I had to sleep in my car that night, and call my parents in the morning to Western Union me some money so I could get home."

"And?" she asked, loving the story.

"Well, I got home late the next day, and my parents grounded me. A lot of good that did, though. I just stayed in my room and read my books!"

"So you were a rebel?" Robyn asked.

"Let's just put it this way. I wasn't the most well behaved kid on the block, and if I hadn't gone into the Army when I did, I'd probably have wound up dead or in jail," he said with sincerity.

"*Really?*" she gasped.

"The Army was the best thing that ever happened to me. Before that, I was sort of a disappointment to my dad."

"That's kind of sad. I hope I'm never a disappointment to you," Robyn said, taking his hand across the table.

"Don't worry about that, baby," he smiled. "I don't think you'll ever be a disappointment to me."

They both got up and headed out to the truck. They had gone several miles when they started seeing the signs for Evansville, so they knew they were getting close to the Ohio River. They had seen several more wrecks along the way, passing them without even a second glance, until they came upon a single car sitting on the shoulder of the road in the southbound lane. It looked like an older car, and the trunk was open. Finding it curious, Tim pulled over to investigate. He grabbed his carbine out of habit, and Robyn did the same with hers, and they walked across the overgrown grass median to where the car sat. Tim saw right away that it was an older, rusted out Plymouth Valiant, probably around a 1971 or '72 model. As he got closer he began to get nervous, and he heard the unmistakable sound of blowflies buzzing around. He stopped and unslung the M4, pulling on the charging handle to load a round into the chamber and held the weapon at the ready position.

"What is it?" Robyn asked quietly.

"Shush." He walked slowly and cautiously towards the parked vehicle. He noticed the passenger side door was hanging open, and there was a form in the driver's seat. He got within a few feet and cringed, seeing what looked like a shotgun blast pattern of holes, in the windshield on the driver's side. He peered in the window, and there sat the driver's headless body, still sitting upright in the seat. Blood and brains were sprayed out behind him, covering the back seat and windows with a dried brown film. The flies covered this, along with the stump where the head used to be. He stifled a gag at the smell, and he reckoned it had only been a few days. He looked over at the passenger's side, and saw a pair of women's flat shoes on the floorboards. He stepped back and looked around.

"Dad, what is it?" Robyn hissed, sounding very scared. She unslung her rifle too, and racked a round into the chamber.

"Just stay back, okay?"

Tim looked at the ground where the car sat, and saw the skid marks of this vehicle and another one, very fresh in the asphalt. He didn't know exactly what had happened, but he had a pretty good idea what went down. They had to get out of here, and fast.

"Robyn? When I turn around, I want you to run as fast as you can back to the truck, okay?"

"Eh… okay."

"Just do it!" he hissed. He turned, and then they both bolted back to the truck, throwing their rifles in and slamming the doors. Tim put the truck into gear and peeled out, hauling the big trailer behind them. Faster and faster Tim drove until the speedometer was pegged at 85 MPH. They crossed over the Ohio River thirty- five miles later and never even slowed to look. They sped their way through Evansville and headed northward, only slowing when they were miles north, and well into farmland. It was not until then that a still ashen Robyn spoke.

"Dad, what happened back there?"

"I'm not a hundred percent sure, but it looked like two people— a man and a woman— were heading south, and were run off the road by someone. They shot and killed the man, and took the woman, along with all their shit."

"Was it, like, recently?"

"Yeah, I figure only a day or two ago, the way the blood was dried," Tim said, lighting a cigarette.

"Oh shit!" Robyn gasped.

"Yeah, oh shit. It's why I want to be very careful if we're going to meet up with people in the future. You have no idea who the fuck is out there. We could run into Mother fucking Teresa, or Charles fucking Manson."

"Okay, Dad. I trust you," Robyn said, reaching out and grabbing hold of his arm. She could feel the tension there, and it worried her. They drove on for a few more hours, pulling into a truck stop in Patoka, Indiana, way after dark. Tim pulled their rig out behind the building, where it couldn't be seen from the highway, before he could let himself relax some. They got out of the truck, locking it up, and took their rifles with them to the camper. They went inside and closed all the blinds before switching on any lights. Tim double locked the door, and very unlike him, he left the M4 carbine on 'safe' with a round in the chamber, and set it by the easy chair where he sat down. He lit another cigarette, and rubbed his forehead.

"Do you want a beer?" Robyn asked.

"Nah, sweetie. Not tonight," he sighed.

"Want some supper?"

"Maybe after a while, I need to think right now."

"Okay," she said, opening the fridge and pulling out a soda. She sat on the sofa and looked at her feet. After a while, her stomach started rumbling, so she got up and started to heat up some beef stew. While she was stirring the stew in a saucepan on the range, she looked over at Tim. She'd never seen him so troubled.

"Daddy, are you sure you're okay?"

"Yeah, I'm fine. Just didn't expect to see that here. I knew it could happen, but I just didn't think it would again," he said. Then he told her about meeting Paul, and the three men who'd hurt him. He left out the gory details, but told her enough to let her know they weren't very nice people at all, and he'd 'taken care of them'.

"So you killed them." It wasn't a question.

"Yeah, I did."

"Good. People like that shouldn't be allowed to live."

"Well, we'll just do our part and try to avoid those kinds of people, baby," he said, as he stubbed out his smoke in an empty beer can.

"Have you done it many times before?"

"What? Killed people?" he asked with a raised eyebrow.

"Yeah."

"Too many times to count," he said. "It's not like the movies or some video game, sweetheart. Once you squeeze the trigger, you can't bring the bullet back or hit 'reset'. It's final."

"But you had to do it right? To protect yourself and the other soldiers around you? So it's okay then. And those guys who attacked your friend, well, I think they got what they deserved, and not only that, they won't be hurting any more nice people."

"Yeah, honey. But I don't have to like it. Sometimes you have to do things you'd rather not, bad things, in order to get by and survive. A soldier trains his whole life in the fine art of bringing death and destruction to his fellow man, but hopes he never, ever, has to use those skills. Sometimes, you have no choice."

"But you do have those skills, and you use them for good, like protecting me and yourself," she said, turning off the flame under the pot, and ladling the stew out into two bowls, bringing it over to the dinette table. "C'mon, let's eat."

Tim walked over to the table and sat down. The stew smelled wonderful, and as soon as he got a whiff, his stomach let him know to feed it. He began to relax, and by the time he was done eating, he was finally back to his old self. He realized that whoever had attacked those people were probably far south of them now. Probably just local punks that didn't stray far from their home turf, and he and Robyn were miles and miles north of there now.

"Do you want a beer now?" she asked.

"Sure, why not?" He looked at the wall of the pullout section across from the easy chair and sofa at the nice sized flat-screen TV and DVD player, and was saddened by the thought of it not working. He plugged in the IVIS laptop and put on some after dinner music.

Robyn handed him the beer. "Can I have one?"

"You never give up, do you?"

"Nope, I'm a Ranger in training, and won't ever give up!"

"Is that so?"

"Absolutely. Does that mean I can have a beer?"

"Absolutely not!" he said. It felt good to laugh after the scene on the highway today.

"Can't blame a girl for trying," she said, winking at him. "Dad, do you think we could stay here just one day so we can bake some more bread?"

"Sure, I don't see why not. We've made damn good time getting this far, all things considering. I could use a day to rest up from driving, anyway."

"Good. I'll make the dough and let it rise overnight. How many loaves do you think?

"Only two. I hate to see them go bad before we get a chance to eat them. How much flour do we have left?" he asked. She went to the cupboard and checked. "Looks to me like about ten pounds or so."

"Alright then, go ahead and make the dough tonight. I'm not sure of the altitude here, so keep that in mind. We're probably a lot closer to sea level here than back in West Virginia."

"Okeydokey!"

Tim sat and watched her, busy in the galley. She was turning out to be a very beautiful young lady, and she was a pure pleasure to be around.

"Where'd you learn all of this stuff in the kitchen?" he asked.

"From my mama, she was a great cook."

"I'm sure she was, Pumpkin."

"She'd have really liked you, even though you're a Yankee," Robyn said, turning to smile at him, and he could see a smudge of flour on her nose.

"Oh, is that so?"

"Yeah, it's a shame that you guys couldn't have met before all this happened. She'd have probably taken a shine to you. Then you guys could have gotten married, and we all could have lived together."

"That's a really nice thought, Robyn. But I already had a wife."

"True, but you could have left her and come and lived with us."

She was maturing in so many ways, but this thought was a throwback to wishful thinking. Yeah, he probably could have left Connie. He knew now for certain he didn't love her anymore. Hell, he didn't even like her anymore. He kind of knew that before his last deployment to Afghanistan, but he was in denial, just going through the motions. Whatever Connie had done before he came back was inevitable, just like the rising of the sun.

"I'm sure your mom was a beautiful woman, and I would have loved to have met her," he said.

"Oh, she *was* beautiful. Here, look," she said, pulling out the silver chain that she always wore around her neck. There was a heart shaped locket attached to it, and Tim had always wanted to ask her about it, but thought it was maybe something private and never had. With flour-covered fingers, she opened the locket to reveal a small photo of a mirror image of what she herself would someday look like, a stunning blonde with deep blue smiling eyes.

"I agree. Your mom was beautiful, and I can imagine you'll be that beautiful one day too," he said, looking into her eyes to see if there was any sadness there.

"Nah, I'll never be that pretty," she said, and closed the locket, dropping it back into her t-shirt. She went back to kneading the dough.

Tim sat back and closed his eyes, thinking about Connie and whatever had possessed him to marry her in the first place. In retrospect, even on their wedding night, he'd not even liked her. He thought of all the other women in his past that he should have married and shook his head. He got up and walked to the fridge, and got himself another beer.

"That's too many bridges burned," he said to no one.

"What was that?"

"Nothing, I was just talking to myself."

"You know what they say about people who talk to themselves, don't you?"

"Yeah, they're having the only intelligent conversation they could have," he said.

Robyn poked her tongue out at him and went back to her dough. Tim went back to his easy chair and looked around. From the outside, it looked like a very normal existence for both of them. But how normal was the end of the world, and their crossing of the country, paranoid and armed to the teeth? About as normal as could be, he guessed.

When Robyn was done, she cleaned up the galley, got a can of Coke out of the refrigerator, and sat down at the dinette table.

"What did you mean earlier about burning bridges?"

"It's just an old saying; it's like once you cross this bridge, you burn it, and you can never go back. Like when you leave a job on bad terms. You know you'll never be able to go back there. It's the same with friends or family. You have an argument, and it lasts forever, and you can never change it."

"So have you done that?"

"There are plenty of bridges in my past that are burnt to a crisp."

"Like why you left Philadelphia?"

"Sort of, but that was a real fire I was escaping from."

"Yeah, we have seen a lot of places burned down, haven't we?"

"Yes, that's true. Probably lightning strikes or something like that. Sometimes barns filled with hay will spontaneously combust."

Robyn just nodded her head and drank the rest of her Coke. Tim finished his beer and tossed the can into the waste bin.

***

Tim smoked a final cigarette of the night and shooed Robyn off to bed.

"Good night, Daddy," she said, reaching up and kissing him on the cheek.

"Good night, Robyn," he said, helping her up into her bunk, and turning off the lights, making sure Bad Bear was snug in her grasp. She was sound asleep in a flash, and Tim headed off to bed himself. He made sure there was still a round in the chamber of his M4 and the safety was still on, before propping the rifle up by his bed. He still had the old .45 auto under his pillow because it never hurt to be sure. He lay in bed for a while, listening for any sound, but all was quiet except for the screech of a barn owl somewhere off in the distance. He was soon fast asleep, and dreamt of a girl he knew in high school. He couldn't remember her name but he could remember her kisses, and in his dream, he thought that maybe she was the one he should have married.

The next morning, when he was woken by Robyn's screams, it felt as though he had only just fallen asleep.

"Daddy, Daddy! Come quick and look at this!"

He quickly sat upright to the early morning light was streaming in between the cracks in the blinds. He looked at his watch and saw that it was 6 AM.

"Alright, alright, hold your horses!" he shouted.

"Daddy, please come quick!" she shouted again, and it sounded like it was coming from outside. He quickly donned some flip flops and a t-shirt, and grabbed the carbine, because he had no idea what the girl was shouting about, but she was sure excited over something. Walking out to the common area of the camper, he saw no sign of Robyn but the door was hanging wide open. He rushed outside to find her standing about ten feet from the camper.

When he saw what she was so excited about, he lowered the rifle.

"Daddy, would you look at that!" she almost screamed.

"I see it. That's just incredible!" he said, just as amazed as she was.

He walked over to her, and looked up. Only about a hundred feet from where they'd parked behind the truck stop was what looked like an overgrown soybean field. Right up to the edge of the barbed wire fence that separated the field from the truck stop parking lot was the nose of a huge Boeing 747. Driving in at night like they had, they completely missed it. There it was though. Split into what looked like four sections was the fuselage of the big plane. Looking back towards the rear, you could see the wings and engines off in the distance where they'd sheared off during the crash. The bright white and blue paint was still as shiny as it had been the last time it took off from Indonesia, almost two years ago. Tim knew exactly what plane this was, because he could still see the Presidential Seal of the United States on the nose.

"What is it, Dad?"

"Air Force One," Tim said, shouldering the carbine.

"But what's it doing here?"

"Looks like it crashed, honey. C'mon. Let's get back inside and get dressed, and we can have a look around," he said, turning to go back inside. After he got dressed, he grabbed his carbine again and went outside where found Robyn already halfway across the parking lot. She tuned when he called to her, and she waited until he was by her side.

"Is this really the President's plane?" "Sure is. The night before The Event, I was at a bar at home, watching the news." He didn't add *getting drunk and feeling sorry for myself*. "The President was on his way home from Asia. Anyway, it's a military plane, so it had all its electronics hardened, I guess. When everyone died, it must have missed its air refueling plane, and kept flying until it ran out of fuel, then glided all the way here before crashing. I guess that's why it didn't burst into flames and burn up."

"How far can they glide?"

"I don't know. It must be pretty far to end up in a soybean field in Indiana," Tim said, helping her through the barbed wire fence. They walked around and found bits of cloth and bones strewn all over. The bodies were most probably thrown clear and then taken care of through predation. He found a rusty automatic pistol and reckoned it was from a Secret Service agent. A large ceramic ashtray was the next find, and it was completely intact, with gold trim and the Presidential seal on it. He pocketed it. Apparently smoking wasn't a fire hazard on Air Force One like on commercial jets. For over an hour, they walked through the wreckage, finding bits of clothing, a microphone, a smashed TV, camcorder, loose paper and other bits and pieces of metal. They found a set of seats sitting upright and Tim sat down on one.

"Nicer than the coach seats I'm used to," he said aloud. All finely handcrafted leather and even sitting out in the weather for as long as it had been, it was still comfy. Robyn tested it out too, and showed her pleasure.

"Too bad we can't take these back to the camper to lounge out it," she laughed. Tim got up walked around some more, and found a $50,000 Rolex watch lying in the dirt. He held it up to his ear and found that it had stopped. He tossed it aside like so much other junk that they found. After about another hour of wandering around the wreckage, Tim had seen enough.

"Come on, Pumpkin, it's time to head home."

"Alright," she said, taking his hand and walking back to the trailer with him. They had almost made it back to the barbed wire fence when something caught Tim's eye.

"Wait a minute," he said, letting go of her hand and walking over to another pile of junk. He crouched down, and from under another set of seats, he spied the corner of a worn leather case. He lifted the seats up some, and was temporarily startled by a garter snake, which slithered away harmlessly. Pulling out the case, he examined it. It wasn't the typical executive brief case. This one was bigger, fatter, and opened at the top scissor like. It had a leather clasp closing the top, and thick leather handles. Then it dawned on him what it was. He'd seen this same case held by a uniformed Army Warrant Officer who followed the President everywhere he went.

He went slack jawed, and just stared at it in his hands, which were shaking. He couldn't believe it, but there it was, right in his hot little hands.

"C'mon, let's go!" he said, grabbing her hand and helping her back through the barbed wire.

"What is it, Dad?"

"It's very, very important, baby!"

He was stunned. He couldn't believe he'd almost missed it. One question, the one that would keep him awake for nights, formed in his head: *What the fuck am I going to do with it, now that I've got it?*

CHAPTER 12:
RUDE RECEPTION

Lieutenant Commander Wright was beside himself. None of the other crew had ever seen him so angry. After a thirty minute tirade of abuse to everyone on the bridge, he went to the captain's chair and sat down, face still beet-red and a noticeable tic in his eye. A vein in his forehead beat rapidly, and his hands were clenched onto the armrests, as if to hold back from throttling anyone nearby. When his breathing slowed down to a somewhat normal rate he turned to Petty Officer Stevens.

"So, tell me again what happened?" he said through clenched teeth.

"Well, sir… we, uh, when we got to the main gate someone started shooting at us."

"Someone who?" he asked with a tremor in his voice.

"We don't know, sir. They wouldn't let us get out of the main gate. Killed one of the Pakis, and wounded one of the Somali guys."

"And you don't know how many there were?"

"No, sir. They were pretty well hidden. They didn't have any machine guns, but whoever it was could shoot."

"So you didn't go after them?"

"Sir, like I said before. We're not soldiers, and there was too much fire on us. It was almost like they didn't want us to leave the base. That's what it seemed like they were trying to do," PO Stevens said in a shaky voice.

"But you did get all the As stowed below?"

"Aye, sir. hey didn't seem to want to follow us, they just didn't want us to leave the base at all, is what it seemed like to me."

"So we've got everything we came for?"

"Yes, sir. Fuel bunkers are topped off, we've got plenty of canned goods from the ship's store, more 5-inch shells and ten BMG-109As."

"Good. Did you find the codes?"

It was the question that Stevens was dreading. He wished he were anywhere else at this point.

"No, sir," he said. "Looked like all of the buildings at Headquarters burned to the ground a while ago."

"Now let me ask you this, sailor. How am I supposed to *USE* the goddamn things WITHOUT THE FUCKING *CODES*?" he screamed, spittle flying from his mouth.

"I… I don't know sir," Stevens said, looking at the deck.

"Well, you do this, Stevens. You go and find that little Nip Nakamura, who seems to be our resident electrical genius, and have him take a look at them. Maybe he can figure a way to arm the warheads without the codes!"

"Aye, sir!"

"Oh, and one more thing. Once you've done that, I want you to go into your radio shack, and find every last goddamn one of those ham transmitters in the Pacific. I don't care how long it takes, you *find* them and *triangulate* them!"

"Yes, sir!"

"Now get the fuck out of my sight."

Stevens almost fell over himself getting off the bridge.

"Nothing on Midway, and now I have people shooting at us at Pearl," Wright said aloud to no one. "Mr. Johnson?" he asked, and Ensign Johnson, who had been standing off to the rear, trying to stay out of sight, came forward.

"Yes sir?"

Lt. Cmd. Wright wrote something down on a slip of paper and handed it to him. "I want you to target these areas with four 109Ds right away. When you have them targeted, fire at will."

Ensign Johnson took the slip of paper and glanced at it briefly. "Aye, sir."

"That will teach these bastards who is boss in this ocean!" he said. "How fucking *dare* they!"

"Yes, sir. That will teach them, sir," he said, restraining to hold back a growing rage.

"Once Stevens has found the other broadcasting stations, we'll give them a little bit of the same medicine," Wright said smugly. "Now get to it! What are you doing standing there still looking at me?"

Ensign Johnson quickly turned and headed for the CIC. The ship was now ten nautical miles south of Oahu, on a course to get them back to Midway. Ensign Johnson sat down at the targeting computer, and opened up the program in the dim red lights of the CIC. He then looked at the paper the skipper had given him, and his stomach did a flip. He wanted two cruise missiles targeted for Honolulu, one for Pearl City, one for the USS *Missouri* and the other for USS *Arizona* monument. Sweat broke out on Johnson's brow, and he turned to see if anyone else was in the room. His mind was spinning. He thought of Mary, and the slim possibility that she was still alive back in Honolulu. He couldn't fire these missiles there! He had to think quickly, or the skipper would know something was wrong. But what was he to do? After another moment of thought, he began typing coordinates into the targeting computer, which fed the information down to the missile's guidance system. He programmed two of them to target the Ko'Olau Range, twelve miles north of Pearl, one for the center of Hickam Air Force Base, and one for an unpopulated area just north of Schofield Barracks. At least the skipper would see the launches , and if he was looking at the island through the binoculars, he'd see the smoke from the explosions at Hickam and be satisfied. Johnson was not going to drop bombs on fellow Americans, destroy the '*Mighty Mo*', or desecrate the *Arizona*.

He finished keying in the proper information, picked up the growler phone and called the bridge. When he heard the captain answer on the other end, he said, "Bridge, CIC, missiles targeted and ready to fire."

"Very well, Mr. Johnson, fire when ready."

Ensign Johnson heard the general quarters alarm go through the ship as a warning that the missiles would be firing. He thumbed the button and felt the ship shudder once, then a few seconds later a second shudder, then a third, then finally the last one. He got up and walked back to the bridge where the thick white smoke of the missile's booster rockets was still blanketing the ship. Slowly the smoke cleared, and walking with the captain out onto the wing bridge, he could see the streaks of the smoke trails heading up to altitude where they'd stop and jettison the cruise missiles, falling back to Earth, and firing up their ramjet engines; flying guided by GPS at one hundred feet all the way to their programmed targets. They stood at the rail looking north and after a few moments saw a dark black cloud reach up over the horizon.

"That will teach them!" the skipper said, lowering the binoculars. The BGM-109D cruise missile was a ground attack version which had hundreds of softball sized bomblets, and was primarily used against troop formations and armored columns. Once over the designated target, they split open and spread mayhem over a large area. The three he'd targeted let loose their bomblets over empty jungle, but the one he'd targeted over Hickam laid a swath of destruction over the main runway and into the fuel storage area, causing the huge black plume that they could see now with the naked eye even ten miles away. The skipper would never know about the other three.

Johnson had a deep, sinking feeling settling in the pit of his stomach as he watched the island slowly disappear, and with it the hope of ever finding Mary. He knew it was just a pipe dream to think that she was still alive on the island; the odds were too high for that.

"If that Stevens can locate all these other radio transmitters out there that are spreading the word ahead of us, we'll give them the same. It's *my* ocean now. It's time the bastards learned that."

"Yes, sir," Johnson said, afraid to add anything more.

"We'll head back to Midway and use that as our base."

"Yes, sir, excellent idea."

"Of course it's an excellent idea!" the captain said with an evil grin. "It's *my* idea!"

Ensign Johnson turned away from the growing smoke plume and looked forward, into a stiffening breeze. The waves were forming whitecaps, and the bow was starting to rise up to meet the growing swells.

"Mr. Johnson, you have the conn. I'm going to retire to my cabin for a little relaxation."

"Aye, sir, I have the conn!" he said, trying to blot out the idea of his 'relaxation'. He could still hear the little girl's screams from the last time deep in his mind, and he couldn't get the sound out. Every time he'd look into the young girl's pleading almond eyes, all he could see were Mary's eyes, and it maddened him to the point where he just wanted to cave in the skipper's head, with an axe. The skipper had gone completely mad, there was no doubt about that. He was at a loss as to what to do. He likened himself to Mr. Christian on *The Bounty*, but he had no other person to back him up. Suplee agreed with him, but he was only one other man, and the rest of the new 'crew' were actually happy to be where they were.

Yes, the skipper had certainly lost both oars, yet unfortunately, he couldn't put together a mutiny. Johnson was alone in this increasingly terrifying nightmare, with no signs of it ending. Now that the skipper had the nukes, it was only a matter of time before he figured out how to arm them, and that frightened him more than anything. Even at the height of the Cold War, with thousands of nuclear warheads pointed at each other, no one in the Soviet Union or the US was crazy enough to actually launch them. This bastard would.

The wind picked up even more, and the bow rose and fell in the swells discernibly now, waves beginning to break over the bow, and the sky ahead of them was darkening.

A huge bank of thunderheads that went all the way to the stratosphere from one end of the horizon to the other were in front of them, and he saw a flash of lightning in one of them. He heard the hatch to the bridge open, and turned to see the Malaysian officer, Lt. Alphabits, enter.

"Mr. Johnson. I am your relief!"

"That's good, Lieutenant," he said. "It looks like the weather is taking a downturn, and I should think things will be getting a little nautical later this evening."

"Ah, yes indeed!" he replied. "That is a good euphemism! You Americans love your euphemisms!"

"That we do," Ensign Johnson smiled. This guy wasn't so bad, he was a great sailor, and knew how to drive a ship. Johnson handed over his binoculars, gave him the proper information on course and speed, and said, "The Lieutenant has the conn!" The East Indian helmsman nodded and adjusted his course slightly. "Okay, Lieutenant, she's all yours."

He decided to head down to the galley to get something to eat. Halfway down, the boat began to rock even more, and he almost lost his footing on a ladder. On entering the galley, he saw several of the Indian women cooking something that reeked of curry. His stomach immediately turned sour so he just grabbed a few bananas and a cup of coffee, and headed back to his cabin. He didn't know where Suplee was. He hadn't seen him all morning, and he hoped he had done his usual tour of the ship before they sailed to make sure everything was battened down. Once reaching his cabin, he set his coffee mug on the small desk along the bulkhead. The cabin was his now to have privately, but he'd once shared it with three other junior officers. He was glad for the solitude and sat down to look at the photograph of him and Mary wearing matching Hawaiian shirts, standing on the bow of the USS Missouri. They were both smiling and happy, his arm holding her tightly by her thin waist. He ate his bananas and finished his coffee, then kicked off his shoes and climbed into his bunk.

He lay there and thought of the events of earlier. They had sailed into Pearl Harbor, and with Lt. Alphabits' aid, they easily docked, and the crew fanned out all over the base looking for supplies and the nukes. Those they found in a heavily locked bunker, which was once guarded by Marines armed to the teeth. With the help of cutting torches, they quickly gained entry and loaded up their catch onto trollies, towing them back to the ship, where they used block and tackle to load them. Fueling up and refilling the galley's storerooms with what canned goods they could cram into them, they finally ventured out and tried to leave the base. That's where things turned to shit. As Stevens had said, they were fired upon by several people who were hell bent on not letting them leave the base. Johnson was sure that if they'd had a handful of Marines, they'd have made short work of those people, whoever they were. But in reality, what they had was a handful of bullies with machine guns used to intimidating anyone they came in contact with, but when faced with real resistance ran away like scared little kids. He laughed at that one, and then his mind turned to Mary again. What if she was with those people shooting this morning? What if she was still alive?

No, she couldn't be.

Thinking again of those people this morning that had shot at the shore party, he thought the skipper was right about one thing. They had been forewarned of their arrival, and were ready for them when they got there, with a very rude reception indeed. He laughed, thinking, 'good for them'. Now he was sickened by the thought of the skipper's plans to deal with any resistance. Hadn't there been enough people dead already? Several billion people, he reckoned, all dead in the blink of an eye for no reason he could think of. Certainly it was no Rapture, such as the ones his preacher used to talk about when he was a boy in church. It had to have come from outer space. He was sure that really bright star, the one they'd seen for weeks after, held the key, but it eventually faded from view and took its secrets with it. He closed his eyes and thought of the last time he and Mary were together, the feel of her skin, the silky smoothness of her hair, her perfume that smelled so wonderful. He was almost asleep despite the pitching of the ship when he heard his cabin door open.

"Mr. Johnson, you awake?"

"Not now," he grumbled, sitting up.

"Oh shit, sorry, sir,." It was Suplee.

"No, it's okay. You saved me from a nightmare that was bound to come anyway. Come in, and close the hatch behind you."

"Okay, sir," he said, coming in and taking off his ball cap.

"Have a seat, and tell me what's on your mind," he said, gesturing to the chair at the desk.

Suplee sat down, and immediately noticed the photograph. "She's very beautiful, sir."

"Yeah, she is. Or *was*, I should say."

"Hell of a thing, sir. All this shit."

"What's on your mind, sailor?"

"I already gave my report to Lt. Alphabits, but I figured I'd give it to you too, you being a real officer and all."

Johnson ignored that and sat up a little.

"I walked the ship and have everything battened down for rough weather. I tried to get some of the others to help, but most of them are too busy puking in the heads."

"Very good, anything else to report?" he asked, rubbing his temples.

"The patch in the hull is still leaking. The pumps are keeping up with it, but if one of the hatches gives way and we start taking on any more water, they'll be hard pressed."

"As much as you can tonight, keep a watch on all the hatches. Make sure none of those dumbasses opens one and decides to take a midnight stroll on the promenade deck."

"That I will do, sir. If any one of those bastards goes overboard, I don't think the skipper will turn the boat around to go look for them."

"I wouldn't in his position either. With this weather blowing up, it'd be a fool's errand anyway."

"That's true, sir."

"Is there anything else?"

"Well, sir, I've been thinking…. Why didn't we just stay at Pearl and make the repairs?"

"I don't know. Maybe the skipper was afraid of whoever was shooting at the landing party."

"That was some shit, eh?"

"That it was. I asked the skipper why we were leaving, but he didn't answer me. He just said to plot a course back to Midway."

"Ah shit, sir. There's nothing there but fucking gooneybirds!"

"I know, but that's where he wants to go."

"Sir, I've got to ask about those missiles this morning. Where'd we fire them on?"

"The captain thinks they were on Pearl Harbor and Honolulu. What he doesn't know, won't hurt him, right?" he said, raising his eyebrow.

"Right, sir, he won't hear it from me."

"Good. I targeted them for the jungle north of the city."

"What about the big explosion then?"

"That was Hickam. I had to at least target something that would blow up spectacularly to make it look good."

"Good thinking, sir," Suplee said, looking at the photo. "Do you think she's still alive?"

"I doubt it. Odds are too great to even begin to hope," Johnson said, feeling terribly sad.

"I was going to get married too, sir. Here's a picture of her," he said, pulling out his wallet, and offering up a photo of a skinny girl with stringy, bottle blonde hair, who was very pregnant. He looked at it for a minute, and handed the dog eared photo back. "She's very pretty, Suplee."

"Jolene. She was my high school sweetheart. We've known each other since we were six years old."

"First time daddy?"

"Yes, sir. It came as a surprise to us both," he said smiling broadly, and then the smile quickly faded. "Sir, will everything ever get back to normal?"

"Fuck if I know. I'd like to think so, but I see no end to this and no way to stop *him*," he said, pointing overhead.

"I saw this movie once, an old black and white job from long ago. That dude from *Casablanca* was in it, and played some nutty captain."

"*The Caine Mutiny*," Ensign Johnson said, remembering the movie. "Humphrey Bogart."

"Yeah, that's the one. The skipper reminds me of him. Being all crazy and shit, all he needs is those two little metal balls to play with all the time."

"So what are you thinking?"

"I don't know, sir. I thought you might have a few ideas."

"Well, do you think we could have a mutiny?"

"Ah shit, sir, I don't know…" He trailed off, looking at the deck.

"Don't think I haven't thought of it. Especially after you told me what Stevens told you," Johnson said, as the ship rose and fell violently and a shudder ran down the hull. "It's definitely getting nautical tonight."

"Yes, sir. I'm remembering now why they call these 'tin cans'."

"So let me ask you this, Suplee. Do you really think that just you and I can take over the ship?"

"No," he muttered.

"Half the crew can't speak English, and are quite happy to be going around the ocean spreading mayhem. And the skipper and Stevens have them so scared of anything else now, that they'll follow them blindly. No, we can't mutiny. If we did that, we might as well just go up to the deck and hang ourselves."

Suplee looked like he was about to throw up.

"And why do you think the skipper won't let us on any landing parties?"

"Don't know, sir. I wondered about that myself."

"It's because he doesn't trust us off the ship. We're too valuable to him here on board, but he can't take the chance we'd bolt. That would leave him with two less experienced sailors."

"So we're just prisoners here?"

Johnson nodded. "That's exactly right. He's just giving us the illusion of being free. We're not. We might as well be slaves to him as far as he's concerned."

"That goes against everything I was brought up to believe in, sir. I mean, what the fuck?"

"He's got us screaming across the Pacific now on some vengeful crusade. When Stevens locates all of those transmitters we'll go and he'll obliterate them."

"That's insane!"

"That it is."

"Mind if I smoke, sir?"

"No, and give me one."

Suplee took out a pack of Marlboros and offered Johnson one. "I didn't know you smoked, sir," he said, lighting both smokes with a zippo lighter.

"I quit a few years ago. Now seems like a good time to take it back up." He took a deep drag and coughed a few times.

"Sir, if you want, I can sabotage the radios."

"I thought of that too. They'd figure out at some point that it was one of us. Besides, once we get to Midway, Stevens will probably go over and use the huge transmitter there. You've seen all the antennas?"

"Yes, sir."

"Well there you go. It'd only be a temporary interruption, but in the long run they'll still win."

"Shit, sir, I've never felt so helpless," Suplee said, and the ship took another heavy roll to starboard.

"Nor have I. We just have to go with the flow for now, and take an opportunity when we see it."

"When will that be, sir?"

"I don't know. It could be tomorrow, it could be next week, and it could be a few years."

"Ah fuck, sir. I don't think I could stand this shit that long!"

"Well, we're going to have to. All we have is each other," Johnson said, pointing at Suplee. "Don't go gall squirrelly on me. I need you!"

"Sir, every time I walk by the skipper's cabin I hear that little girl whimpering, and I just want to vomit!"

"I know. I feel the same way. We've just got to put on a face that they'll like and hold it all in. We'll get our chance, I just don't know when."

"Okay, sir, if you say so."

"We have to, it's the only hope we've got."

"The old man has the nukes. That scares me most of all."

"It scares me too," Johnson said, a huge lump forming in his gut. The ship took another roll, this time to port. "I hope to hell that patch holds."

Suplee finished his smoke, looking around for somewhere to put it.

"Here, use this," Johnson said, handing over an empty soda can.

"He still can't use the nukes because he doesn't have the codes, right?"

"For now. He had Stevens get Nakamura working on it."

"Oh shit. Do you think he'll be able to arm them?"

"I don't know. He is an industrious little fuck. He might just do it."

"That scares me even more."

"It does me too."

"So, do you think we'll just stay in the Pacific? Not head back to the States at all?"

"No, I think we'll just stay here. I think the skipper got a little taste of what would await him if he went back to the States or out in the Atlantic. People on that side of the world are less likely to be cowed."

"Africa?"

"Perhaps. No other First World nation though. Just like why we probably didn't sail south to Australia. Anyone who is still alive with half a brain would tell him to get fucked and send him a lot of lead. Besides, sailing all the way to the Atlantic would take too long and use up too much fuel."

"What about the Panama Canal?"

"No, that would probably be out. Even if it isn't clogged with derelict ships, which it probably is, you'd need a whole crew just to run the locks. We'd have to sail around South Africa or South America. Take too long, like I said. We're stuck here by practicality. Besides, east of here there's probably a lot of Asians, and once cowed, they're easy to subjugate, or so the skipper thinks."

"So we'll never see home again?"

"I didn't say that. Just that the skipper will probably want to stay in waters he feels comfortable in."

They felt the bow rise with another heavy swell, and when it slammed back down, they felt the shudder run through the hull, the vibrations of a ringing bell, then the ship heeled over again to port, worse this time.

"Yeah, it's nasty topside. I'll bet no one sleeps a wink tonight."

"There's already enough puke in the heads below. I'd better go and take another walk-through," he said, standing. "Thanks again for the talk, sir."

"Anytime, Suplee, and remember, we bide our time."

"If you say so."

"I do. Do not go off and do anything stupid."

"Yes, sir. I won't. I promise."

"Go on and get out of here. I'm going to try to get some sleep in this shit. You come to me if you find anything wrong, okay?"

"Yes, sir," Suplee said, walking out of the cabin, closing the door behind him. Johnson lay back down on his bunk and stared at the overhead for some time, sleepless, and it wasn't because of the rough weather. Finally giving up after forty-five minutes, he stood and put his shoes back on, grabbed his hat and strapped back on his pistol, then headed out for a walkthrough himself. He made it through half the ship, and found nothing out of order, and he figured he was probably just following up Suplee, who would have made sure everything was secured. He wandered through an empty galley— the Indian women nowhere to be seen. He took another banana and ate as he walked along, grateful that at least they had fresh fruit.

He got down to the crew's berths and could already smell the vomit. He walked by one set of bunks in the red light and as soon as he passed, saw a man's head appear from behind the curtain and vomit on the deck. The man wiped his mouth and went back into the bunk. *Great,* he thought. This place was really going to smell wonderful tomorrow morning. He'd have to get a gang together and swab out the whole place. The smell sickened him already. Heading further aft, he made his way to the hangar deck to where the helicopter was still tied down securely. That would be the last thing he needed, the explosion and tirade from the skipper if that tore from its moorings and was smashed against a bulkhead. He'd come unglued, and Johnson didn't want to be anywhere near him if that happened.

Everything checked alright here. He headed back forward through several passageways on the tossing ship, and heard several loud claps of thunder through the steel. He was passing the missile storage bay and he saw lights on through a half-open hatch that was swinging with the swells. He peered inside at Stevens and Nakamura hovering unsteadily over the access panel on one of the missiles still in its shipping crate. He stepped in and was still unnoticed, until he spoke up.

"Stevens, what the hell do you think you are doing?" he asked, incredulously.

The diminutive Japanese man looked up briefly, and went back to whatever it was he was doing.

"Ensign Park…" he caught himself. "I mean Ensign Johnson. What brings you down here?"

"I'm asking the questions, Stevens. What are you doing?"

"What the skipper ordered, sir. He told me to get Nakamura here working on the warheads to see if he could arm them without the codes."

"In this weather? Are you completely insane? Use your fucking head. The ship's being tossed around like a cork, and you're here playing around with a nuclear weapon!" As if to emphasize his words, the ship crashed through another breaker so strong it threatened to rip the ship in two.

"Sir," Stevens said, patting the nosecone, "I give you the BGM-109A tomahawk. It has a W80 thermonuclear warhead, with a nominal yield of 20 Kilotons, a lot bigger bang than the ones we dropped on Nagasaki and Hiroshima, ain't that right, Nakamura?" He looked down on the Japanese man, who looked up briefly, a dark cloud passing over his face, then he went back to working. He had a manual open in his lap and a screwdriver in his teeth.

"That's not funny, Stevens. And spare me the lecture on the weapon. I know full well what it's capable of," he said flatly, and his skin became cold and clammy looking at the white, smooth body of the missile, wishing he could throw them all overboard right now.

"It won't go off, sir," Stevens said, still smiling.

"Again, that's not what I'm talking about, Stevens. Use that brain you have for once. What would happen if one of these broke loose from its shackles? Do you know how much that thing weighs? You both could be crushed!"

"Oh fuck, sir. I didn't think of that!"

"I can see that. Now secure from this detail until we're out of this weather."

"But the skipper said—"

"I don't care what the skipper said. This is too fucking dangerous. It can wait until we've got better weather. He says anything you tell him I ordered you to stop, and why. Is that clear?"

"Yes, sir, right away, sir!" he said, but a dark look crossed over his face.

"Do it now. Mr. Nakamura, you can get back to this when the weather clears. Head back to engineering so you can oversee things down there."

The little Japanese man looked relieved and gathered his tools, departing silently. Turning back to Stevens, Johnson gave a little sigh. "All I'm asking it to use your head. I know the skipper wants these armed. Fine, do it. I don't care. But do it safely. Remember, we still don't have a corpsman or a doctor. You get hurt bad, and you're fucked."

"I wasn't thinking, sir," he said, and started to put the lid back on the shipping case.

"Here, I'll give you a hand with that."

After they were done, they exited the compartment, and Ensign Johnson secured the watertight hatch. Turning to Stevens, he asked, "Do you have anything else to do?"

"No, sir."

"Head down to the goat locker and try to get some rest. We'll have to get a work party together after the weather clears some and have a field day in the crew's berths. There's puke overflowing the scuppers down there."

Stevens cringed. "Yes, sir. Good night."

"Good night, Stevens," he said, and continued to walk forward. He was only several yards forward on the same deck when he came across an East Indian man wearing a Nehru jacket and eating a sandwich. He was sitting on the deck in the middle of the passageway, eating away with no other sign that he was doing anything, and it struck him as odd.

"Ah, Ensign Johnson, how are you this evening?" the smiling man asked. Johnson thought that he ought to get him trained up as a helmsman or something if this weather didn't bother him. Even Johnson was starting to get a little ill from all the rolling and rocking.

"I'm fine. And you?"

"I am very, very good sir! You tell me, are we going to America soon?" 'Very, very' came out as 'berry, berry'.

"Sure, sometime soon we'll be going to America. But not right now."

"Oh, that is most unfortunate. I look forward to going to America very, very much! You tell me about America?"

"Not right now, maybe some other time. There are plenty of books in the ship's library you can read in the meantime."

"Thank you! I will do that immediately!" the man said, standing up and walking away from him.

Ensign Johnson watched him disappear down the passageway, and shook his head in disbelief. "I'm going crazy. I have to be," he said, shaking his head and walking forward on a crazily pitching deck, he too looking like a drunken sailor…

CHAPTER 13: PASS INTERCEPTION

Tim sat for a long time at the dinette table, the case lying before him. He brushed some dirt off the edges, but otherwise did nothing, just stared at it. Finally, he removed the ceramic ashtray with the Presidential Seal on it from one his bellows pockets on his BDU pants and sat it down on the table in front of him.

"Smoke 'em if you got 'em," he said, pulling out a pack of Winstons, and lighting a cigarette. "Don't mind if I do, Mr. President!" he said. He sat back and scratched his forehead.

"Dad, you've been sitting there for ages! What is it?" Robyn asked, exasperated.

"This, young lady, is The Football," he said, waving his hand over the case theatrically.

"Doesn't look like a football to me. Just looks like an old suitcase or something."

"Oh, but it's not *a* football. It's *The Football*. There is a difference."

"I don't get it," she said.

Tim took a long drag of the cigarette, drummed his fingers on the case, and began to speak.

"This here is what's called The Football. Back in the bad old days of the Cold War, it was decided that only the President could order a nuclear strike. He had a list of codes to launch the strike, and he needed the codes and plans wherever he was. So they came up with a simple plan: An Army Warrant Officer would carry those codes with him, and follow the President everywhere he went. Even after the Cold War ended and the Soviet Union imploded, we still had thousands of nuclear weapons and he still controlled them."

"And?"

"So this Army Warrant Officer had this," he said, tapping on the scratched leather case, "and he went everywhere the President went. I think he even sat outside the Presidential shitter, while the Prez took a presidential dump."

"And you think that's it?" she said.

"That's exactly what I think it is. They called it 'The Football'."

"So why is it so important now?" she asked.

"Well, if someone should get hold of this and have access to a laptop like mine, he could, in theory, launch a few nukes."

"That's bad," she said gravely.

"That's very, very bad." At least she understood the gravity of it. He'd taught her history for a reason.

"Those nukes sitting all over the world now are really quite harmless. But given the proper codes, you can arm them and launch them at anyone you want."

"But wouldn't they not work now after all this time?"

"Some maybe, but they have everything pretty automated now, took the human out of the loop several years ago. There used to be a time when each missile silo in the US was manned by Air Force officers called 'Missileers' and they once did a test to see how many officers given the order would actually launch their missiles. The report's findings were classified, but shortly after the test they pulled all of the Missileers out of the loop and automated things. You can guess what the findings were."

"But don't other countries have them too? Like Russia?"

"So did Pakistan, Great Britain, France and China too. Israel denies they have them, but it is an even-money bet that they do."

"So, if that's the case…" she stopped.

"Someone could destroy a whole city or small country," he finished for her.

"And you're sure this is The Football?"

"No, I'm not sure. It could be the secret Presidential recipe for cupcakes, or notes for his last speech to the Rotary Club in Akron, Ohio, for all I know."

She giggled a little and turned serious again. "And if it is The Football, what are you going to do with it?"

"That I don't know. Get me the toolbox and I'll see if I can get it open."

Robyn went towards one of the cupboards under the sink, coming back with a medium sized Snap-On red toolbox and putting it down on the floor next to him. He leaned down and opened it, retrieving a small hacksaw. He went to cut the hasp, and then stopped. What if it was booby-trapped? It could have some James Bond type secret device to explode in your face if you didn't have the correct secret decoder ring or some shit like that.

"Robyn, do me a favor. Go outside for a minute while I do this, okay?"

"Why?" she asked. "I want to see what's in it."

"Because it might be booby-trapped is why. If it goes boom, I want you far away from it if it does."

"Dad!" she moaned.

"I mean it! Get out and stay well clear until I call you."

"Okaaaayyy," she said, heading out the door.

"Aren't you forgetting something?"

"No, what?"

"You're forgetting your American Express Card, never leave home without it!"

"Oh yeah," she said, picking up her carbine. She stopped at the door and looked at him. "Dad, please be careful and don't blow yourself up."

"I won't. Now get out of here!" He waited until she left and went back to the case. He looked at the latch carefully, and didn't see anything outwardly different from the average clasp lock. He took the hacksaw and slowly sawed at the lock. Within a minute he was all the way through and the latch popped open. He let out a breath he didn't know he was holding and slowly opened the case, peering inside. It couldn't have been that easy, could it? What he found was a large, plain black, government contract Skillcraft ring binder with several pages and a laptop computer, similar to his, made by IBM. In a small pocket was a red card laminated in plastic with one word on it printed in block letters: DESPERADO. He set that aside, and opened the laptop, noticing it had a built-in satellite communication antenna. Other than that, it was no different than the one he had. He tried to boot it up, but apparently the battery was dead. He looked back into the case, and found a normal power cord, only this one had an adapter to fit any electrical outlet on the planet. He found the normal American one, and plugged it into a wall socket next to him. Immediately he saw a little icon pop up, telling him it was plugged in and charging. He remembered Robyn and went to get her. He looked out the door and saw her standing by the end of the truck stop building about fifty yards away. She was crouched over, eyes closed and her fingers in her ears dramatically. He laughed and called her. She looked up in relief and came running.

When they went back into the camper and were both seated again, Robyn asked, "So, is it The Football?"

"Yes, ma'am. I'm just powering up this tablet to see what's on it."

She switched sides so she was sitting next to Tim, where she wouldn't miss a thing. Tim took the now empty case and placed it on the floor to give them more room on the table. They watched the screen run through a self-diagnostics test that read 'SYNCRONIZING WITH SATTELITE'. After a few seconds it changed to 'SATELLITE SYNCRONIZATION SUCCESSFUL', then an image of the Seal of the President of the United States appeared, and under it was a query that read 'PLEASE AUTHENTICATE' with a flashing cursor.

"Well, what now?" Robyn asked.

"I guess I'll authenticate," Tim said. He picked up the red card and looked at it again, then typed 'DESPERADO' and waited. The icon disappeared, and in about thirty seconds, the screen turned green and a new phrase popped up: 'NATIONAL COMMAND AUTHORITY AUTHENTICATED'

"Who's National Command Authority?"

"That's the President."

"So it thinks you're the President?" she asked, wide eyed.

"Apparently so."

The computer went through and started listing Air Force bases that had missile silos, then ships and submarines.

Tim's heart was beating so hard he thought that it might beat right out of his chest. After each Air Force Base, a prompt appeared that read, 'COMMUNICATIONS ENABLED'.

Alongside each ship name, after a few moments, a prompt appeared that read 'UNABLE TO CONTACT ASSUME LOST' and at each submarine 'ELF MESSAGE SENT AWAITING REPLY'.

"Holy dogshit!" Tim said.

"What's 'elf'?"

"It stands for Extra Low Frequency. It's a radio band that is so low that it can actually contact submarines underwater."

"That's cool!"

"Yeah, it is, but it's so low that it takes a long time for the message to print out in the sub. Most of the time it's just a short message, like 'get to the surface or periscope depth, we have a longer message for you' and then the sub goes up, raises another antenna and gets the whole message on another frequency," Tim said, remembering most of it from what he'd read in Tom Clancy novels.

"So there may be submarines still out there?"

"I seriously doubt that. It seems like all the ships are out of the picture too, at least those that had nukes on them. By the names, they were mostly aircraft carriers and a handful of cruisers," he said, running his finger down the screen.

He moved the cursor over Offutt Air Force Base and clicked on it. A small window appeared and listed missiles by silo number. Next to each, a prompt was asking, TARGET? YIELD? LAUNCH CODE? with a little box next to each to type the response.

A cold sweat broke out over Tim's brow and he started to shake. He shut down the laptop and quickly put everything back into the leather case. He'd already looked through the binder and it had all the codes listed. The most amazing thing was everything still worked, and he now held the key.

It frightened him to the core. He took the case, placed it in the compartment under his bed, and went back out to the front of the camper where he sat down with a plop on the easy chair. "Another fine mess you've gotten us into, Ollie!"

"What was that?"

"Nothing. I was just thinking about what to do with it now that I've got it."

"If it's that dangerous, why don't you just throw it away?"

"No, I can't do that," he said after a minute.

"Why can't you?"

"I don't know. Something in the back of my mind is telling me to hold on to it, safeguard it," he sighed.

"It scares me," Robyn said.

"It scares me too, baby, but I've got to safeguard it," he said, still unsure of why he needed to keep it, when every fiber in his body was screaming at him to build a big fire and toss the whole lot into it.

Maybe he wanted that power?

No, no way did he want that power. He could do what his brother had said so long ago right now— change the world. Make the world a safer place by getting rid of it, destroying it. But then who knew what another person out there in Russia, or Pakistan, or China would do if they found the codes for their bombs? The thought was mindboggling. In the end, he decided to sit on it. Maybe somewhere down the line he'd know what to do with it, but right now he was clueless. He lit another stale cigarette and stared at the dead TV.

"Dad, are we still going to stay here for the day? I've got this dough to bake."

"Yeah, we'll stay here for another night. You go and bake the bread, and I'll scrounge around for some more diesel fuel and anything else we might need." He stood and picked up his carbine.

"You be careful and bring back lots of goodies," Robyn said, now smiling, The Football forgotten for the moment.

Tim went out and explored, looking back at the wrecked fuselage from time to time, thinking if they'd just kept driving last night and not stopped there, they'd have never seen it. And he wouldn't be in this position now, either. Then he thought of the whole randomness of what had happened. Him finding Paul by chance, him finding Robyn on a spur of the moment decision to take a side road that really, in retrospect, he had no business going down at all. Everything was by chance, yet it seemed like it was planned. That couldn't be true, though. There was no greater being pulling the strings like a marionette. And his brother's words kept on coming back to him: *One man can make a difference.*

The only thing he knew for certain was that he had to protect Robyn and find them a place where they could be safe. All else was secondary. But now he had this little glitch. It would be so easy to dig a hole and bury the goddamn thing. But again, that little voice in the back of his mind was telling him to hold on to it, that he was going to need it one day.

"And just what the fuck do I need several thousand thermonuclear weapons for?" he asked aloud to no one as he walked into the front door of the truck stop. Being off the beaten path had ensured it was left undisturbed by other survivors, so he had the pick of everything. He walked in and looked around, and saw that most of the potato chips and things like that had been devoured by mice and rats a long time ago. There were, however, plenty of canned goods, sodas and beer. He got a shopping cart and loaded it up with everything he saw, and had to make several trips back and forth to the camper, with his take. Robyn helped each time he came back, storing everything, and after the fourth trip he joked about breaking the springs on the camper with so much weight. He then thought about the truck, and about doing some preventative maintenance. He went back into the garage area of the truck stop and found the correct oil filter, filter wrench and oil, and changed the engine oil, discarding the used oil in a bin at the back of the building. He checked all the radiator hoses and fan belts, and everything looked alright so he shut the hood and washed his hands in the galley sink. Robyn had just taken the loaves of freshly baked bread out of the oven and the aroma filled the camper, making his stomach growl.

"So what's for dinner?" he asked.

"I was thinking fried rabbit."

"Sound good to me. I'm just going to go out and scare up some more fuel and propane, I shouldn't be too long."

She looked at the wall clock. "It's three now. Be back at five, okay?"

"Yes, Mom!"

"Oh! Get out of here!" she said, snapping him with a hand towel.

He unhitching the truck from the camper and drove all around the lot, stopping at several trucks and siphoning out the fuel. When he had the truck's tank full, and also all of the jerry cans, he drove over to the front of the building where there was a metal cage filled with thirty pound propane bottles. He popped the padlock easily with the bolt cutters, filling up the rest of the bed of the M880 with them. That finally done, he looked at his watch, and saw it was just about five.

"Better get home for supper or Mom will be pissed!" he said aloud, hopping back into the truck and driving around the rear of the building where they had parked. He figured he would re-hitch everything tomorrow morning before they left, and pulled up next to the camper. When he walked in, Robyn had everything set up, and was putting the rabbit on the table. She had it in a big bowl lined with paper towels to soak up the excess grease she fried it in, and it smelled wonderful.

"Now you wash up mister, you stink!"

If the men in his battalion could see him now, obeying the orders of a fourteen year old girl like a good little boy, they'd have never have let him live it down. Some Sergeant Major he was. He washed up in the sink, getting most of the grease out from under his fingernails, and dried his hands with a few paper towels. He went over to the dinette and sat down, savoring the aroma.

They really did have it pretty good.

"Dig in!" Robyn said, and he took a few pieces of rabbit and a liberal helping of instant mashed potatoes and canned corn. They ate in silence, and when they were done she brought him a beer.

"What, you're not going to ask for one yourself?"

"Can I have one?"

"No."

"Why did you ask me if I was going to ask for a beer if you were going to say no anyway?"

"Dinner just wouldn't be complete without you asking," he said with a grin.

"One of these days, Sar' Major!"

"You'll what, darling?"

"Oh, I don't know, just one of these days!" "Tell you what, Pumpkin. Remember when I said I'd swear you in as a soldier when you fit into those uniforms?"

"Yeah!" she said, brightening.

"Well, when I do that, you can have a beer. But not before."

"Deal?" she asked, holding out her hand.

"Deal," he said, shaking it.

She went and grabbed a pair of ACU pants and top, along with a patrol cap and disappeared into the bathroom. Several minutes went by, and Tim sipped on his beer and had an after dinner cigarette. When she came out, he laughed so hard beer came out of his nose. Robyn put her hands on her hips and frowned.

"What's so funny?" she asked. The hat fell over her eyes and over her ears, the top was still about two sizes too big for her, and the cuffs hung down a few inches past her hands, with the bottom coming all the way down to her knees. The trousers were baggy, and were about four inches too long in the leg, bunching up comically around her feet. The image was precious and he couldn't stop giggling.

"I think you've still got a while, honey."

She shrugged her shoulders. "Well, you can't blame a girl for trying," she said, going back into the bathroom. She came out dressed in shorts and a tank top, holding the ACU uniform in her hands.

"There, that's much better!"

She went and stowed the uniform in her bunk.

"Don't rush it too much, Robyn. We all grow up too fast as it is."

"I know, I just really want to be older is all."

"I can tell you this from experience, don't rush it. Look at me. Some mornings I wake up, and in my mind I'm still that eighteen year old private, but when I look into the mirror, I freak out and wonder who the fuck that old guy is staring back at me!"

"But—"

"But nothing." he said, cutting her off. "Look, when we met, you were still a little girl. What's happened to the world has made you grow up a lot faster than would be normal. You're doing things now that only people much older would do as it is. Be a kid for a while yet. Have fun, laugh. Because at some point it won't be fun anymore and you'll be faced with decisions, hard decisions that you won't really want to make."

"That's what I have you for," she said, smiling.

"Come here and sit down," he said, pointing at the couch. When she was seated Tim said, "You're not going to like what I've got to say next."

"Oh, come on, Dad."

"No, really. I've got to say it and you've got to listen and let it sink in."

"Okay," she said, fidgeting in the seat.

"There's going to come a point in your life when I'm not going to be around to make those decisions."

"I don't want to think about that, Dad."

"You're going to have to at some point, Robyn. You can't go through life with blinders on. I'm pushing fifty years old. You're still only fourteen. I'm not going to be around forever, and that's just a fact of life."

She started to tear up.

"Hey, listen. I'm still here and I'm not going anywhere just yet. But I want you to be aware that things won't always be so rosy, and it'll be up to you to make the decisions."

"But you can't!" she wailed, full blown sobs coming on strong now.

"Look, I'm your dad now, right?"

She nodded and sniffled.

"And what do dads and moms do? They prepare their kids to go out and face the world. That's what I'm doing for you. Every day is a life lesson I really hope you take to heart."

She got up and came over to him, sitting down on his lap and wrapping her arms around his neck. She buried her face into his neck, and cried and cried. He held her tightly, running his fingers through her hair and let her cry it out, hoping his words sank in.

"But you'll still protect me, right?" she said into his neck.

"Yes, baby, I will do everything in my power to protect you. And during that time, I'll teach you to protect yourself too."

"And I'll be a soldier, like you?"

"Yes, you'll be a soldier then, just like me," he said, patting her back. "Okay, now hop off, I can't feel my feet!"

She got up and looked at him through teary eyes. "I don't like to think about it. But I guess I have too, eh?"

"Yeah, not everything in life is pretty or nice. We've got to face the bad stuff too. We hope it never happens, but we've got to be ready for it if it does happen."

"Like you said before about soldiers training for war, but hoping they never have to go?"

"Exactly," he nodded.

"Did you ever have to make really hard decisions?"

"Absolutely, all the time, comes with the job. You don't have to like them, but you've got to make them. Good, bad or indifferent."

"I'll do my best, Daddy."

"I know you will," he smiled. "Now let's get this dinner mess cleaned up."

While they cleaned up the camper, Tim thought about what he'd said to Robyn. He'd faced his own mortality on several occasions and cheated death, but he still didn't like thinking about it. He hated dumping on Robyn like that, but he figured he'd have to say it at some point. Of course he'd protect her, protect her with his own life if he had to, he knew that for certain. But at some point, he knew he wouldn't be around anymore, and it was his job to teach her everything he knew so she could make it out there on her own. The thought of her alone put a chill over him, and he quickly pushed that thought out of his mind. She was growing up so fast already. He didn't want her to be a cynic at eighteen.

After they were done cleaning up, Tim shooed her into the shower to start get ready for bed. He helped her into her bunk, pulling up the covers and handing her Bad Bear. Seeing her with the old, ragged, stuffed bear tucked under her chin really made her look like a little girl, and he really needed to protect her at all costs. He turned off her light and kissed her forehead.

"Good night, baby."

"Good night, Daddy," she said sleepily.

He went to turn around, and she called out to him. "Tim?" she asked, using his name, which seemed odd now that she had been calling him Daddy.

"Yes, Robyn?"

"Will I ever be a great soldier like you?"

"What do you mean, honey?"

"Well, like you, a hero."

"Honey," he said, "I'm no hero."

"But you are to me."

"I hope you never have to face what I have had to, but if you ever do, I do believe you'll be a hero in someone's book."

"Good night. I love you."

"I love you too, baby. Now get some sleep, we'll have a busy day tomorrow."

He walked to the bathroom and even before he shut the door, he could hear her gentle breathing and knew she was sound asleep. He wished he could sleep like that. He took a shower and washed off the rest of the day's grime, put on a pair of shorts, and set his carbine next to his bed. He crawled under the sheets in the darkness and lay there for a while, his thoughts returning to the computer, the codes and the binder. Just what was he supposed to do with it? He still didn't know, and like everything in his life now, he let the thought slide to the rear of his mind and decided he would make the decision about it when he had to, but not now. Just safeguarding it was pressure enough. He switched his thoughts to the nameless chestnut-haired girl he knew in high school, and with a smile on his face drifted off to a deep sleep.

He was awakened the next morning by the smell of brewing coffee and toasting bread. His stomach growled, and he got up from bed and stumbled towards the aroma where he found Robyn standing at the counter in the galley spreading margarine on toast.

"Good morning, Daddy. Want some toast with your coffee?"

"Does the Pope shit in the woods?"

"Daddy!" Robyn laughed.

"Does a bear wear a funny hat?"

"Sometimes I wonder about you, Sar' Major," she said, sliding a plate of toast, margarine and strawberry preserves in front of him. He took a bite of the toast while she poured his coffee. When she put it in front of him he took a sip and smiled.

"Good stuff!" he said. "You've outdone yourself with the bread too. It's yum!"

"Glad you like it," she said, sipping her own coffee and taking a bit of toast. "Are we going to head out again this morning?" she asked between chews.

"Yes. I just needed a day to rest up from all the driving."

"Where are we headed next?"

"Let's take a look at the map," he said, grabbing the atlas and opening it up to Indiana. "We're here in Patoka, and I figure we'll head north to Vincennes— that's about fifteen or so miles north— and then head west into Illinois on Rt. 50." His mind went back to his spur of the moment decision to keep travelling north on Rt. 41 instead of taking Robyn's suggestion about traveling on I-64 west. That decision left him holding The Football, literally.

Some hell of a pass interception.

"It sounds good to me," Robyn said, finishing her toast, brushing the crumbs from her fingertips onto the plate. They finished their breakfast and got dressed, stowing everything in the camper for travel. When they were finished, Tim re-hitched the truck, and they drove out to the front of the building where he got out and motioned for Robyn to follow him back into the store. They took as many gallon water jugs as they could carry from the shelves out to the trailer, where they took the time to refill their fresh water tank. After that chore was done and all the empty plastic jugs were tossed into a nearby dumpster, they got back onto the highway. It only took them a short while to reach the junction of Rt. 50, and they headed west, crossing over into central time, and Tim took the moment to stop and reset his watch.

Robyn asked why he did that, and he explained to her about the different times zones, and how back in the 1800s the railroads came up with them so everyone would be on the same time. She was duly impressed again by his knowledge, or what he told her was his never ending supply of useless information. She didn't think any of it was useless, and soaked up everything he told her like a sponge. They travelled west most of the day, picking up I-64 in O'Fallon, then going through East St. Louis, crossing over the Mississippi River into St. Louis, Missouri, where they picked up I-70 heading towards Columbia, Missouri. It was growing dark when they reached the outskirts of Columbia and were forced to take Rt. 63 because of a major pileup of several cars and semis blocking all the lanes. They finally stopped outside of Moberly for the night, finding a grocery store parking lot to camp out in. After setting up and getting some supper, they sat in the camp chairs looking out at the night sky.

"Dad, are we ever going to find a place to live?"

"Eventually," he said, shrugging.

"This is just so… boring," she said. "There's nothing out here but overgrown roads, overgrown houses, overgrown fields. It's all so boring!"

"Yeah, that's what I think of the Midwest myself."

"Weeds everywhere, and in a few more years this parking lot will be a meadow."

"Nothing we can do about that," Tim said, but had to agree with her. "You've got to remember, it's nature's way of cleaning up the place."

"I wish it would hurry up," she said with a laugh. "I'm boooored!"

"Don't rush excitement, Robyn."

"I'm going to bed," she announced, and walked into the camper. Tim followed her. She was in the bathroom when he entered, and he waited for her to come out. When she did she was dressed in one of his t-shirts again. She came up to him and on tiptoes kissed him. "I'm sorry. I guess I'm just a little tired is all."

"That's okay, baby. It's alright to get frustrated once in a while. It lets off steam."

"I do feel better now."

"Good, get into the fartsack," he said, slapping her on her butt. She hopped into bed and crawled under the covers. "Good night, Daddy. I love you."

"Love you too, baby. Get some sleep. We got another big day tomorrow."

He washed up, crawling into bed himself.

The next morning they headed out early, only a few cups of coffee in them to start the day. It was really starting to warm up, and the cloudless sky promised a hot day. They drove north through Macon and onto Kirkville, crossing into Iowa late in the day. They turned west onto Rt. 2 west of Bloomfield, Iowa, and headed down the two-lane blacktop towards Centerville, which looked to be about twenty or so miles west. The blacktop road was rapidly being overgrown with weeds from both sides of the shoulder, and a barbed wire fence lined the north side of the road, bordering an overgrown cornfield that was rapidly going fallow. Travelling due west, the sun was in his eyes, and he almost didn't see the vehicle sitting in the middle of the road before it was too late.

"Look out, a car!" Robyn screeched.

Tim hit the brake pedal with both feet, stalling out the truck and almost jackknifing the trailer in the process. When the dust settled, he saw three figures standing there by what looked like an old Chevy Suburban. A lug wrench and jack were lying on the ground next to one of the tires, and it looked to him like whoever it was had just fixed a flat. The hair on the back of his neck started to rise as he slowly opened his door, reaching behind him for his .45 in a pancake holster.

"Stay here and don't move," he hissed to Robyn under his breath. "Hi there, fancy meeting you here!" he said to the people outside. "Need some help?"

He took note of the three unmoving figures and time seemed to crawl. There were two men, big, with long stringy hair and beards, and a gaunt looking woman with equally stringy unwashed hair, all standing by the rear of the Suburban. The two men looked amused, but the woman looked absolutely terrified.

"No thanks, pal, just got her fixed," the one on the right said, looking over at the other one. They were definitely acting squirrelly, so Tim unholstered the pistol behind the cover of his open door and thumbed off the safety.

"Jake, he got a girl!" the one on the left said, giggling.

"Now hold it right there, we don't want any trouble," Tim said in a calm voice at odds with his beating heart. At that very moment, the woman bolted from the two men, running right for Tim.

"Help me *please!*" she screamed, and before Tim could do anything, the man on the left leveled a pump action shotgun that Tim didn't see before and let loose a blast, catching the running woman square in the back from about fifteen feet. A look of astonishment crossed her face as the pellets exited her chest, and she fell flat right in front of him, a huge pool of blood rapidly expanding from under her still body. The man then racked another round into the chamber and Tim fired off a single round from his .45, missing his target in his haste, taking cover behind the door. The pellets from the second blast penetrated the door through and through, catching him on the left shoulder, and a piercing pain went through his head. It felt like someone had hit him with a baseball bat. He flew backwards onto the macadam with a bone crunching thump. From his position looking straight up at the sky, he couldn't move, and his vision was blurring. He heard Robyn screaming out for him.

"Daddy! Help meeeeeeeeeeeeeeeeeeeeeeeeeee!"

He heard a scuffle and more cursing, but couldn't move, as if he was paralyzed.

"I'm going to take the girl, Jake. You take care of him and get his stuff."

"Okeydokey!" Jake said with a high pitched giggle. "I'll get er' done! Ha!"

"Daaaaaaddddddddeeeeeeeee!" he heard Robyn yell again. Then he heard the other man yell out.

"Ouch! You little bitch! That fucking *hurt!*" Tim heard what sounded like a slap to her face, and Robyn screamed out in pain again. "We gonna have some fun tonight fer sure!"

Tim rolled his head to one side, saw blood spreading out on the asphalt, and thought it had to be his. He could see his .45 laying inches away from his hand but he couldn't make it move. His head hurt so badly. He heard car doors open and slam, and could hear Robyn's wails. He heard the other vehicle start and drive away with screeching tires, and looked up at a shadow that crossed his face. He looked up at the face of a really ugly man. The man hauled back one foot, and with lineman's boots, kicked Tim in the head and everything went dark.

CHAPTER 14: Q&A

Tim started to see grays, and then his vision slowly cleared. He didn't know how long he'd been out, but looking up at the sky, it was just turning twilight. Though the sky was still a dark blue, he could make out the first few stars of the evening. He tried to move his arm and though it hurt, he could move it. He began to assess himself lying there, and reaching up to his still pounding head, realized the pellet had to have been a big one, maybe OO buck. Luckily, it had just grazed the left side of his head. Hell of a headache, and would probably leave a nasty scar, but he'd live. He sat up and checked out his left shoulder next. He saw the hole, dried blood caked around his t-shirt. He moved it around some, and although it hurt also, he could move it. It was probably a through and through, not hitting any bone. He looked to where he'd last seen his pistol, but it was gone. Slowly he stood, and listened for any sounds. He looked into the cab of the truck, and saw that his M4 and Robyn's carbine were missing, and then he heard a noise coming from the camper. Whoever it was— that Jake fellow he guessed— was rummaging around. He was now fully standing, and his headache was still there, but tolerable. He guessed it hurt worse because of the boot to the head. Reaching behind the seat as quietly as he could, he found the only weapon he had at the moment, his pair of bolt cutters. He circled around the off-side of the camper, carefully avoiding the windows and rounded the camper to find Jake standing outside, facing away from him. It was a good fifteen feet he had to run, and he crouched down in a sprint, coming up behind him, and clocking him at the base of his neck where the skull met it. There was a dull 'thwack' and Jake crumpled to the ground in a heap. Tim reached into the man's waistband and retrieved his .45 auto, re-holstering it.

Inside the camper he found the place was a shambles, but quickly located the toolbox and took out two plastic zip-ties. Going back outside, he grabbed the man by the collar, and dragged him over to the wooden fence post, where he quickly zip tied his hands behind his back, around the post. Going into an outside compartment, he retrieved a rubber mallet and two tent pegs, that he used to stake down Jake's legs through his jeans to the ground, legs spread as far as he could get them. That done, and knowing Jake wasn't going anywhere anytime soon, he went back into the camper and cleaned his wounds, using the first aid kit he'd made up with the stuff taken from the hospital back in Philadelphia. His head and arm now bandaged, he could take care of more pressing needs: Find out where that other little fuck had taken Robyn.

In his sleeping area, he found the old canvas satchel bag and opened it up to retrieve the Ruger Mk III .22 target pistol and a box of .22 ammunition. These he pocketed, and then filled a large plastic glass with cold water from the tap. Walking back outside, he took a folding chair with him and set it up in front of his unconscious prisoner, then went inside for a lantern, and he sat this down next to the chair, along with the glass of water. He turned the chair around backwards and sat down. Now he was ready.

Taking the glass of water, he tossed it into the man's face, immediately waking him up.

"What the fuck you doing, man!" Jake shouted, spitting and sputtering.

"Now that you're awake, you and I are going to have a little discussion."

"Who the fuck are you? I thought you were dead!" he yelled.

"Well then, if you thought that, you were sadly mistaken."

"Fuck you!"

"Fine, be that way," he said, taking out a pack of Winstons and lighting one.

"Hey! You can't do this! I got rights!"

"Oh, I see I've come across another person that has had the pleasure of the accommodations of the county jail. Or was in the state pen? Ah, it doesn't matter," Tim said in an icy voice, eying Jake with a cold stare through blue tobacco smoke in the rapidly fading evening light.

"Who the fuck are you? Are you a cop? You gotta be cop with a haircut like that!" Jake said with a sneer. "I'm not telling you shit! I got rights!"

"Now here's what's going to happen. We're going to play a little game called 'Q & A'. I'll ask you a question, and you will give me an answer. It's very simple, really," Tim said calmly, despite the rage that was building inside of him.

"What are you going to do, waterboard me?" he said with a little smirk.

"Jake— may I call you Jake?— if you don't answer my questions honestly and rapidly, you will *wish* you were being waterboarded."

"You can't do this! I got fucking rights!"

"Jake, would you like me to call you a lawyer? Oh, sorry. I can't. They're all dead," Tim said, pulling the magazine out of the pistol and loaded it, one round at a time, very slowly. Jake's eyes followed his hands, and Tim smiled inwardly. He knew from experience that ninety-nine percent of torture was the mere thought of pain. But even so, he was willing to inflict a lot of pain to get Robyn back, and that was one thing he knew how to do… inflict pain.

"I'm not telling you shit!"

"Oh, believe me. You *will* give me the answers I want," Tim said. He pulled out the pistol and inserted the magazine, racking the slide to chamber a round. He could see Jake break out in a sweat in the light from the lantern and smiled; the kind of smile that would give little children nightmares.

"I got rights! You can't do this!"

"Okay. No more fucking around, Jake. Where did your friend take my kid?"

"Fuck you!" Jake spat.

In one fluid motion, Tim raised the .22 pistol and pointed it at Jake's foot, only two feet away from the muzzle, and pulled the trigger. Jake let out a bloodcurdling scream.

"Ah fuck! You fucking *shot* me man! You can't do that! I GOT FUCKING RIGHTS! Oh fuck that hurts!"

"Where did your friend take my kid?"

"FUCK YOU!"

Tim raised the pistol again and fired another round, into his ankle this time.

"Ah! Fuck! Jesus fucking Christ! That *hurts* man! You can't *do* this! I got fucking *rights*!"

"You know what, Jake? I can go at this all night. I have over two hundred rounds for this pistol," he said, holding it up so the man could get a better look at it.

"Ah fuck you! This is torture man! I got rights! You can't do this!"

"Where did your friend take my kid?"

This is torture, man! You're not allowed to do this!"

"That was the wrong answer, Jake," Tim said calmly, and shot him in the lower shin.

"Aaaaaaaaahhhhhh fuck!"

"Tell you what, Jake. Way back in the 80s I was in El Salvador. We grabbed this Sandinista one night, right out of his bed. We asked him questions just like this, with a little .22 caliber persuasion. The little fuck took thirty-six rounds before he started to talk, up one leg and down the other. I had a lot of respect for the balls on that guy. But you, I just think you're a piece of shit," Tim said, taking the final drag off of his cigarette, flicking it away mindlessly.

"I GOT FUCKING RIGHTS MAN!"

"I'll ask one more time, Jake. Where'd your friend take my kid?"

"I got rights, man!" he said, beginning to hyperventilate.

"Wrong answer again, Jake." Tim shot him again, this time a little higher up on the shin.

"Ahhhhhh! Fuck! I got rights!" he screeched and started to cry.

"You know what, Jake, you'd better calm down. Your heart gets to racing like that, and you pump more blood, and it looks like you're bleeding pretty well already. Where did your friend take my kid?"

"I got—" Tim didn't even give him a chance to finish and shot him in the kneecap. "Aaahhhhhhhh fuck!" he screamed and wailed like a little baby.

"No you *don't* have any rights. The only thing you have is me not getting really angry."

"Please! Please no more!" Jake begged.

"Are you going to play my game now?"

"Yes! Just don't shoot me anymore!" he pleaded. "I'll tell you anything you want!"

"Where did your friend take my kid?"

"He took her to the farmhouse," Jake said breathlessly.

"Now we're getting somewhere. Where is this farmhouse?"

Jake hesitated, and Tim raised the pistol up, pointing it at his lower thigh. Jake cringed and tried to move away. "No please! Don't shoot me no more! He'll kill me if I tell you!"

"Let me ask you, Jake, is what I'm doing now even less pleasant?"

"No! Oh fuck please!"

"Believe me, Jake, if you don't tell me what I want to know, you will wish you were dead. Tell me, Jake."

"I can't!"

Tim raised the pistol up and fired a round into his lower thigh and Jake screamed to raise the dead.

"I'm losing my patience, Jake," Tim said evenly.

"He took her to our farmhouse, three miles from here! Go west a mile, turn right on the dirt road. Go another mile, and take the left fork. It's right there on the right! Please don't shoot me anymore! PLEASE!"

"There. That wasn't so hard, was it?"

"Oh fuck oh fuck oh fuck!" Jake panted, again starting to hyperventilate.

"Just one more question, Jake. It's an important one."

"I'll tell you anything, just don't shoot me anymore!"

"How many people are there at the farmhouse?"

"It's just David! It was just me and him!"

"And who was the woman, Jake?"

"Joyce I think her name was. David found her in Ottumwa. Please, no more PLEASE!"

"You're not lying to me, Jake, are you?"

"Oh fuck no mister! I swear to fucking GOD I'm not."

"Because you know what will happen, Jake, if I follow your directions, and I don't find any farmhouse? I'm going to come back here. And if I have to come back here, things will definitely start to be unpleasant for you."

"I swear to fucking god!" he bellowed and began to cry again. Tim packed everything up. He went around to the front of the truck, dragged the dead woman off to the side of the road and laid her down, right next to a whimpering Jake. Tim got into the truck and pulled away. He could hear Jake's screams as he drove off into the night, begging him to help him. He ignored the screams, quickly found the dirt road, and made a right-hand turn. He could see fresh tracks in the loose soil. Jake hadn't lied to him after all. Not like he'd lied to Jake about coming back to help him. He was bleeding like a stuck pig.

"Well, Jake. That's the one good thing about bleeding. It stops, *eventually*," Tim said to the windshield, lit a cigarette, and took the left fork when he got to it. The farmhouse was probably once really nice, but now was ramshackle and run down. He could see lantern light through the windows, and the beat up old Suburban was pulled up right in front. He stopped a few hundred yards away and thought about how he was going to do this. After coming to a decision, he went back to the camper, where he saw that Jake had been so thoughtful as to place his M4 and Robyn's carbine on the sofa for safekeeping. He bent to pick up his M4, then changed his mind. He went back to his bedroom and retrieved the M3 grease gun and three magazines. Loading one, he put the other two in his pocket and put it on the seat of the truck. Climbing back in, he put it in gear, and started off again, pulling right into the driveway of the farmhouse with the nose of the truck almost directly onto the front steps. He left the engine running and the headlights on. He sat there for a moment, and saw the front door open, then he smiled. The other man, who he now knew as David, came out holding a bottle of Budweiser.

"Hey, Jake, what took you so long? I was saving the party until you got back. She sure is a pretty one, not like that skank Joyce!" he yelled to the truck, shielding his eyes from the glare of the headlights. Tim opened the door and cocked the gun, pointing it at the man.

"Jake's a little tied up at the moment," Tim said, letting loose a ten round burst that tore up the doorframe and balustrade in a rain of dust and splinters but miraculously missed David, who cartwheeled backwards into the house, bottle of Budwieser smashing on the porch where David dropped it. Tim bounded the steps and took cover behind the doorframe, amazed that he had actually missed the bastard at that close range. He heard a shotgun's slide cock, and then a blast came out at him from inside, taking out a huge chunk of doorframe. Tim leaned in, and let loose another burst from the grease gun, ducking inside the house into a filthy living room, taking cover behind a couch that smelled of urine. He peered around the couch and didn't see anyone, but could hear shuffling somewhere towards the rear of the house.

"David!" he called out. "I just want my daughter."

"Fuck you! Who the fuck are you?" David yelled out from somewhere he couldn't see.

"I'm the man who has come to get his kid, David. You let the kid go, I let you live, simple as that," Tim said, the rage boiling up inside. He was finding it harder and harder to keep his cool.

"Well, I ain't giving her up! She's mine now!"

Tim stood and started to walk slowly through the living room into a narrow hallway. He heard Robyn's muffled cry, "Daddy!"

"I'm here, sweetheart. Don't you worry a bit!" he shouted.

"You just get the fuck outta here man!" he heard David say.

"Like I said before, David. You give me the kid and I'll go."

"How the fuck do you know my name?" he asked, fear in his voice.

"Oh, Jake and I had a little chat."

"You fuck!" David yelled, and Tim saw movement at the end of the hallway.

He dodged sideways into a side room right before David let off another blast from the shotgun. Tim leaned out with the grease gun and let off another burst down the hall, chewing up cabinets in the kitchen and knocking over a lantern, which broke and started a fire along a back wall. Tim quickly changed magazines and holding the weapon out in front of him, stepped back into the hall, moving closer to the sound of David's voice.

He was almost at the kitchen when he saw Robyn, held by the neck by the man, who stood behind her with the shotgun in her back. "Get the fuck outta here or she dies, man!"

"Daddy!" Robyn called to Tim, and her tear streaked face and the fear in her eyes only solidified his resolve. "It's okay, honey, we'll be leaving soon," he said to her, never taking his eyes off of David.

"You think so?" David said, with an evil grin.

"Oh, I don't think so. I *know* so," Tim said, slowly letting the gun drop and hang from his shoulder on its sling. As he did that, he slowly reached around and pulled out the .45, pointing it right at David's astonished face.

"What do you think you're doing asshole? I got the girl. One more step and she's dead!"

The flames behind David in the kitchen were growing bigger, and had reached the high ceiling, lighting up Tim's face wildly, and made his bruised face appear demonic in the yellow, flickering light.

"You take one more step, I'll kill her!" he shouted out again, almost in a panic, and Robyn started to whimper.

"You and I both know you won't do that."

"What makes you so sure? I kilt folks before!" he spat, fidgeting from one foot to the other nervously.

"Oh, I'm sure you have. So have I. You know and I know, she dies, you die."

"Get the fuck outta here!"

"I'm not leaving without the girl," Tim said with an icy calm.

"Fuck you!" David spat. "Drop your gun!"

"This isn't Hollywood, David. I'm not dropping my gun. You let me take my daughter out of here, I let you live."

"Drop your fucking gun!" David yelled again, pushing the barrel of the shotgun harder into Robyn's back, making her cry harder.

"Not happening, David. Give me the girl," Tim said, the pistol in his hand pointed straight at David's head, his arm steady as a rock. Smoke was starting to fill up the hallway as the fire behind David and Robyn grew. "I'll give you to the count of three, David. One…"

"You'll let me go if I do?" David asked hopefully.

"Two…"

"Answer me!" he shouted.

"Yes," Tim said.

"You swear you'll let me go?"

"Yes. I will let you live."

"Okay! Okay!" he said, pushing Robyn towards Tim, lowering the shotgun. She ran towards Tim and wrapped her arms around his waist, burying her face into his chest, sobbing uncontrollably. Tim looked behind David and saw the fire growing bigger, threatening to engulf the whole kitchen. He hadn't lowered his pistol and still had it pointed at David's face.

"Well? You got your kid. You promised. Get the fuck outta here!"

"Yeah, I promised, didn't I?" Tim said, and started to lower his pistol, the smile on his face growing bigger. When he got it halfway down, at about stomach level to David, he squeezed the trigger and the pistol shot was deafening in the narrow hallway. David screamed and dropped the shotgun, doubled over in pain, holding on to his stomach with both hands as if trying to keep his guts from falling out.

He looked up at Tim and with a pained expression. "Why? You fucking *promised!*"

Letting go of Robyn, Tim walked over to him and kicked him in the face, knocking him down and picked up the shotgun. "Oh, I kept my promise. I said I was going to let you live right *then*. I never said anything about when I got my kid back. Now you can just burn."

Tim turned and took Robyn's hand. "Come on, honey. Let's get out of here."

"What about him?" she asked, looking at the man on the floor.

"Fuck him," he said flatly, and they walked out of the house, down the steps, and got into the truck. Tim started the truck and made a wide turn with the trailer over the overgrown lawn. They could hear David's screams as the fire apparently reached him. They ignored it and drove away. By the time they reached the two-lane blacktop they could see the house was fully engulfed with flames, the old dried wood burning rapidly. They sat in the truck for a while watching the fire in the distance until Tim finally put the truck into gear and headed west into the night. They drove in silence for some time, passing through Centerville, finally stopping in Corydon for the night. Setting up the camper, they busied themselves cleaning up the mess inside, stowing everything back where it belonged. When they were done, Tim gave Robyn a look over, and beside a few bruises, she looked fine. He on the other hand, looked a mess, and Robyn let him know.

"You look horrible, Daddy," she said with a sad look.

"I'm fine, baby. It's just a few cuts and bruises."

"You got one hell of a shiner," she said, coming up to him and rubbing his cheek, tearing up again. "I knew you'd come back for me. I just knew it!"

"I promised I'd always protect you, and besides, you never, ever leave a comrade behind," he said.

"Let me clean you up some," Robyn said, looking at his head. "That looks nasty."

Tim pulled off his t-shirt while she got the first aid kit, and when she came back and saw his shoulder wound she gasped. "Daddy, that looks really bad!"

"Eh, it's okay. Went all the way through and didn't hit bone or anything important," he said. Robyn didn't buy into his bravado, and set to cleaning it out with hydrogen peroxide, which made him wince. She took gauze and wrapped his head and shoulder up, and when she was done said, "There, good as new!"

"You're a regular Florence Nightingale," he said. "Here, hand me the kit."

She handed it over to him and he rummaged around until he found what he was looking for. He took out a small vial and a paper wrapped syringe.

"What are you going to do?"

"Give myself a shot of antibiotics, unless you want to do the honors?" he said, offering her the vial and syringe.

"No way!" she laughed. "Are you really going to give yourself a shot?"

"Sure. I've done it a time or two before. No big deal," he said, dropping his trousers enough to expose his upper thigh.

"Doesn't it hurt?"

"It stings a little, a lot less than being shot though." He stuck the needle into the rubber top of the vial and drew off what he supposed was a proper dose. Lifting up the syringe, he pushed the plunger and tapped it to get the air bubbles out, and quickly poked himself in the thigh, injecting the fluid. Pulling it out, he recapped the needle, stood and pulled his pants back up.

"There, all done," he said, buckling his belt.

"What was that for again?"

"It was antibiotics, just in case. Don't want this thing to get infected," he said, pointing to his shoulder.

Robyn shuddered. "I could never give myself a shot like that."

"You might have to someday."

"I don't want to think about that."

"I'm very proud of you, Robyn," Tim said. "What did you do to make that guy scream when they first took you?"

"I saw you lying there bleeding and I sort of panicked. I thought you were dead. He had his arm around me and he smelled like pee, but I bit him as hard as I could anyway. That's when he hit me really hard, and threw me in his truck. I was a little dizzy after that."

"You did the right thing, and I'm proud of you. Always fight back, no matter how high the odds are stacked against you."

"Like a Ranger?"

"Yep, just like a Ranger!"

"He took me to that house and threw me in a closet. It was really dark and stank of pee and poop. I was really scared, and then I heard the truck pull up, and I knew you'd come back for me. I heard your voice, and then the machine gun. Wow! Where did you get that?" she asked, as Tim picked it up and unloaded it.

"That is a long story for another time," he said. "But it's just as old as your carbine."

"What happened to the other guy, the one that stayed with you?"

"I... persuaded him to tell me where he'd taken you."

"How?"

"You don't need to know that. Let's just say his threshold to pain is a lot lower than mine. He won't be hurting anyone else." He thought briefly about Jake still tied to that fencepost, slowly bleeding to death. With any luck, he'd last throughout the night and into tomorrow, where the sun would beat down on him all day, slowly baking him. That was five now. Three back in Pennsylvania, and two here in Iowa. How many more assholes like that were out there? Had the world changed that much? Had simple human decency completely disappeared? Was it now just down to survival of the fittest?

If that was the case, he had to make sure he and Robyn stayed on top of the food chain and never let what happened tonight happen again.

"Okay, sweetie, time for a shower and bed," he said, yawning. He was bone tired, and could feel the adrenaline crash happening. Robyn grabbed a towel and headed for the shower. He heard the water go on, and he finished his beer and stubbed out his smoke in his Presidential ashtray. When she came out wearing one of his t-shirts, he noticed it wasn't as big on her as before. She was growing fast now. He helped her up into the bed, and she yawned widely. He kissed her, and drew her covers up, making sure Bad Bear was firmly in her grasp.

"Good night, sweetheart," he said, turning off the light over the dinette.

"Good night, Daddy. I love you."

"I love you too, baby. Now get some sleep."

"Daddy?"

"Yes?"

"Could you hand me my rifle?"

He took it and handed it to her, and she checked to make sure the magazine was full before tucking it under her blanket. "Thanks, Daddy."

"Good night, Pumpkin."

For a minute he was angry. Sad fucking thing when a fourteen year old girl has to sleep with a loaded rifle. Fucking bastards. He was glad they were dead. He went in and carefully showered, trying his best to keep his bandages dry, and when he stepped out, he had a good look in the mirror. The right side of his face under his eye was swelling up and turning an angry purple, and he could actually see the tread pattern left by Jake's boot. He got angry all over again. *Never again.* Before climbing into bed he did the same thing as Robyn, took his M4 and laid it beside him on his bed. Turning off his light, he quickly fell asleep, but the sleep wasn't an easy one. The dreams had come back, with a vengeance.

The next morning when they awoke, both Tim and Robyn were feeling sore and achy. Robyn put on the coffee. She brought cups of coffee for both of them to the table, where they ate and drank in silence.

"I had bad dreams last night," Robyn said after a while.

Welcome to the club, Tim thought, perhaps a little callously, but held his tongue. The kid was scared enough as it was, and he could sense the subtle change in her from yesterday. She'd never be the same he knew. She'd never be the same laughing kid. She'd hardened a little last night, and that made him really sad.

"Yeah, baby. I had some too," he finally said, sipping his coffee.

"Do they go away?"

"Not really," he told her honestly.

Robyn took a bite of her toast and a sip of coffee. "Where are we going today?"

Tim pulled out the road atlas. He looked at the map for a minute, and then said, "Looks like we'll drive a little further west and pick up I-35 at Decatur City."

"And go north or south?" she asked, looking at the map from across the table.

"North towards Des Moines, then we'll take I-80 and head west. That'll take us all the way to San Francisco and the Pacific Ocean, if we want to go that far."

"Anywhere is fine with me, Daddy. I really don't like Iowa all that much."

"Yeah, I don't like it all that much either," he said. "Let's finish up here and get ready to hit the road."

"Sounds like a plan to me," she said, a big smile crossing her face, and a little bit of the old Robyn showing through.

They quickly cleaned up their breakfast mess and stowed everything for travel. Tim went out and checked the truck out, and took a look at the driver's side door. There was a tight pattern of OO buckshot holes near the top edge of the door, and thankfully the window had been rolled down or he'd have gotten a face full of glass on top of the pellets. But the window rolled down inside the door was still shattered and he could hear the bits of glass rattling around inside of it.

"Well, this door is fucked," he said. "It'll be okay until the next time it rains. We're going to have to look for another vehicle soon," he told her, getting in and starting up the truck. He'd placed his M4 on the dashboard, and Robyn did the same with her carbine. She shut her door, buckled her seatbelt, and put her bare feet up on the dash.

"Well, what are you waiting for?" she asked. "Let's get out of here!"

Tim put the truck into gear. They drove west, picked up I-35, and turned north on the empty highway, making good time to Des Moines. He saw a sign for the National Guard Armory and took the exit. Following the street signs, he easily located the Armory, pulling up in front. The parking lot was filled with cars, and it looked like this unit was preparing to either go overseas, or have a weekend drill. They got out of the truck and walked around to the rear of the building, and found a row of military vehicles loaded up and ready to set out in a convoy. He did notice several uniforms strewn about, and saw bones and a few rusted M16A2s lying around. He then found his first skull, and a shudder came over him involuntarily. It looked like the scavengers had had their fill of these troops.

He spied a Hum-Vee, the vehicle most readily identified by the general public, sitting near the front of the formation. It wasn't the kind with the slant-back; this one had sort of a pickup truck bed with a canvas cover over it. In addition to that, under a rubberized canvas cover in a ring mount on the roof between the driver and passenger seats, was what looked like an M2 Browning .50 caliber machine gun. Tim hopped up and unzipped the cover that had protected it from the weather, and it looked to be in perfect condition. Hopping back down, he looked at Robyn and smiled.

"It looks like we found our new ride!"

"Cool!" she squealed. "Does that big gun work?"

"It probably does if there's any ammo for it. I doubt it though."

"Aw! Looks like fun!"

"That it is," he said. He tried to start the Hum-Vee, but the battery was dead. He checked the fuel tank, and that too was bone dry. Probably sat and idled here after The Event until it ran out of fuel, then the battery got drained. He could easily remedy that. Going back to the truck, he unhitched it and drove it around to where he was side by side with the Hum-Vee, then popped the hood. He took a jerry can of diesel and filled the Hum-Vee's fuel tank with a few gallons of fuel, attaching jumper cables to the battery, letting it charge for a few minutes. When he was satisfied that it would turn over, he switched the ignition on, satisfied when the glow plug light went out, and turned the engine over. It took a minute for the fuel pump to get the fuel up from the tank and finally he had it running. Unhooking the cables, he shut both hoods and filled the Hum-Vee's fuel tank completely. He then transferred everything from the M880 over to it. Robyn was deeply impressed by his mechanical abilities and told him so, but he just shrugged. That finished, he looked over at Robyn, who was looking down the line of vehicles.

"What is it, honey?" he asked.

"Down there. Looks like a pickup just like ours," she said. He looked to where she was pointing and saw an older M880, only this one had a green canvas tarp over the bed, just like the Hum-Vee. Then he saw the orange diamond shaped placards, and smiled. It was an ammo carrier.

"Come on, let's go have a look-see," he said, grabbing his rifle and walking towards the truck. When they got close enough, he saw the placards read what he thought they might.

"It looks like we're in luck, baby!" He flipped open the canvas flap. Case after case of small arms ammunition was there. He dropped the tailgate, and started to look through it all. He already had plenty of ammo for the M4 and M16, but was looking for ammo for the M2, and in the very back he found it. Several hundred rounds in cases, all his for the taking. He grabbed one and heaved it out to the tailgate. He thought better of carrying it all to the Hum-Vee, so he went and drove the Hum-Vee down to it. After breaking open the wooden cases, he started to transfer each one hundred round can to their Hum-Vee, with Robyn's help. When he figured they had about two thousand rounds, he stopped.

"I think that's enough," he said, grabbing one more box and tossing it up on the roof of the Hum-Vee. He climbed through the ring mount from inside the vehicle, and with Robyn watching him from the hood, he cracked open the can and placed it in the holder on the left side of the machine gun. Opening up the cover, he inspected it for any defect, and didn't see any.

"Robyn, go find me some motor oil. Look in the trucks."

She gave thumbs up and taking her carbine, disappeared. He lit a cigarette while he was waiting. He saw a likely target across the parking lot and on the other side of a vacant lot sat a garbage truck. He smiled at the thought, and soon Robyn reappeared with a plastic quart bottle of motor oil.

"Is this ok?"

"Perfect!" he said, taking the bottle and pouring it liberally over the weapon and into its works. He closed the feed cover and cycled the action several times to get the oil through the weapon, then reopened the cover.

"Watch carefully, Robyn. This is how you load this," he said. He took the first round of the big .50 caliber ammo on the feed tray and closed the cover with a snap. He double racked the charging handle with his right hand, thankful he didn't need to use his left arm, which was very stiff and sore and probably would be for a while. "This mound can turn 360 degrees. You move it by pulling out this pin here, like this," he said, pulling out a small detent pin under the gun. He spun it around until it was pointed at the garbage truck about four hundred yards away. "Now hold your ears, this fucker is loud!" he said with a huge grin. He adjusted the traverse and elevation mechanism slightly, looked down the sights, and with both thumbs, pressed the butterfly trigger. The big gun barked out a loud *'chug chug chug chug'* in a four round burst, and immediately big holes appeared and sparks and chunks of metal flew off the cab of the garbage truck.

"Can I try?" Robyn asked enthusiastically.

"But of course!" He climbed out of the mount onto the roof, giving her the room to climb down into it. Once there, he showed her how to hold the spade handles and where to press the trigger, and how to look down the sights.

"Let her rip!" he said, and she didn't need any encouragement. She pressed the triggers and let loose another volley, and after about fifteen more rounds, the cab of the truck was a smoking mass of twisted metal.

"I wish we would have had this yesterday," she said.

"Yeah, so do I," he said, clearing the weapon and covering it with the canvas gun cover. "Okay, let's get this dog and pony show on the road."

They climbed into the cab and he showed her how to get from the front passenger's seat into the ring mount fast, in case they needed it. She gave another thumbs up and settled into her seat, finding a rack made for a M16 was just as good for her carbine. Tim placed his M4 in the rack on the driver's side and drove around to where they'd left the camper. He quickly hitched it up and went into the camper to retrieve his IVIS tablet and placed it in the mount built for it on the wide dashboard that not only held it securely, but also charged it through the vehicle's alternator. He pulled up the GPS feature and set their waypoints, then minimized that and pulled up his music.

"We can't have a road trip without tunes!"

They took I-80, and about ninety miles west, they crossed over the Missouri River into Omaha, Nebraska. Tim saw the signs for Offutt Air Force Base and thought about The Football again.

"At least we're out of Iowa," Robyn said, and Tim agreed with her.

The sooner they put that ordeal behind them, the better. He spotted a stalled train on the railroad tracks running alongside of I-80 and was saddened. He'd always loved trains, and he thought it was a shame that they'd never run again. Every once in a while they'd pass what looked like a normal house, but with a big ten-foot chain link fence around it, and a huge flat concrete slab in front. It was wide open here, and they could see for miles. Robyn asked him about the weird houses.

"Remember when I was telling you about the missile silos?"

"Yeah, all the nuclear missiles are in them."

"Those weird houses with the big fences and the concrete slabs are those silos. That's where all the nukes are."

"Oh, wow. Right there in the open?"

"Yeppers, you can't hide a giant missile too well."

Robyn looked out the window and fell silent. They drove until sundown, stopping several miles west of Lincoln, Nebraska at another truck stop. They set up camp for the night and after a small dinner, they sat in chairs outside. Tim drank a beer, and Robyn a Coke. Right after sundown the moon had set, giving them a wonderful view of the night sky. They made it a game to spot as many satellites as they could, then he stood her up and looked north to show her the Big Dipper, or Ursa Major, the North Star, and told her how to use them to find her way.

"If you just draw a line in your head with the two stars in the bottom of the Big Dipper, it'll draw a line right to the North Star."

"Wow! So the North Star never moves?"

"Nope, it always stays exactly where it is in the sky, true north. If you know where the North Star is, you'll always be able to find your way in the dark."

"What if it's cloudy?"

"Then you're fucked," he said with a big laugh, making her giggle. They went back to their chairs and sat for a while longer.

"I'm always amazed at how many stars there are, Daddy."

"Back a few years ago when the lights still worked and all the people were still alive, you could hardly see any because of the light pollution."

"Light pollution?"

"Yeah, all the lights from cities and towns blotted the stars out for so long, people actually forgot what they looked like. Back, oh I can't remember exactly when, back in the early 90s, there was a big earthquake in Southern California. They called it the Northridge Earthquake. Anyway, all the power went out all over the city of Los Angeles, and hundreds of people started calling the Palomar Observatory to report these strange lights in the sky."

"They were the stars?"

"Yep, no one knew what they were."

"We're lucky to get to see them like this."

"Yes we are, baby. Yes we are," he said, and leaned back on his chair, looking up at the sky.

"How's your head?"

"It's still a little sore, but I've got a hard Irish melon. It's hard to break this noggin," he said, tapping his head. "Arm is still sore too, and probably will be for a while, but it seems to be fine, no sign of infection yet."

"Well, that's good. Do you want another beer?"

"No, I think I'll turn in."

"I call dibs on the shower!" she said, and ran into the camper giggling, leaving him there in the starlight alone. At least she was getting somewhat back to normal. Kids had a way of compartmentalizing things like what had happened to her, and could deal with them better than adults. He looked up and wondered where all this would lead, and couldn't even get an inkling of an idea. He finished his last smoke for the night, and flicked it out onto the weed-covered parking lot then went inside. Robyn had just finished her shower and was climbing up into bed when he closed and locked the door. He tucked her in as usual, kissed her good night, and went and took a shower himself, happy that they had the bigger water tank and water heater. He put on a ragged old pair of shorts, and taking his carbine with him, crawled under the sheets and drifted off to sleep.

He woke the next morning to the smells of toast and coffee, which had become the normal routine, Robyn waking before him and getting everything ready. The sun was just peering over the eastern horizon. He looked out the window next to his bed, and wondered how anyone could deal with all this nothingness. Dropping the ratty shorts, he pulled on a pair of sweatpants and walked out the rear area where he found Robyn doing her usual thing. After coffee and breakfast, they went around and got as much diesel fuel as they could find, filling up their tanks and jerry cans. Tim then went to the area he'd seen the night before when they had pulled in, and drained their gray water tank properly. That done, they circled around to the front and filled the freshwater tank back up with bottled water.

They set out on the road about 10:45 AM. There was still no sign of a cloud in the sky, and it promised to be another hot day. I-80 was flat and straight, and they could see for miles and miles ahead of them. Far ahead, it looked like something black was covering the road, but at this distance they couldn't tell what it was.

"What is it?" Robyn asked.

"I don't know. Let's get a little closer and find out. We might have to turn around and find an alternate route."

"I hope not. It's getting hot already, and the going is slow on the smaller roads."

As they got closer, Tim couldn't believe his eyes. He began slowing, and when he was close enough, came to a complete stop in the middle of the highway.

"Well I'll be dipped in dogshit!"

"What are they, Dad?"

"That, my dear, are what's called buffalo, or more correctly, the North American Bison."

"There's got to be thousands of them!"

"It's probably only a few hundred. They must have knocked down that barbed wire fence over there." He shut off the Hum-Vee and they got out. They were only a few yards away from them, and the buffalo seemed not to notice the vehicle, the camper or the two humans now sitting on the hood of the Hum-Vee watching their slow progress across the highway. They continued munching on the fresh tall grass growing out of the cracks in the asphalt before heading over to the juicier stuff in the overgrown median.

"I guess with no people around anymore, the herds are quickly coming back," he remarked.

"Coming back?"

"Once, a long time ago, before the white people came west, there were millions of them. Then after the Civil War, people moved west and hunted them almost to extinction. It seems like The Event didn't affect these guys at all."

"So now they're coming back, and the herds will be that big again?"

"I hope so. They are a beautiful animal, and tasty too. Too bad we don't have a freezer big enough. These guys taste way better than any T-Bone steak you've ever had!"

"You've eaten buffalo?"

"Robyn, you have no idea what I've eaten," he said.

They sat there and watched the large, clumsy yet graceful animals slowly graze their way south, finally clearing the road, and Tim thought it was a pleasant diversion. They went to hop down off the hood, and he heard Robyn gasp. Looking to where she was looking, his jaw dropped.

"Dad, what is that?"

He just stood there looking and didn't say a thing. About two hundred yards north, in a large field of tall grass, stood a teepee. A teepee just like he'd seen in countless western movies in his youth.

"That, baby, is a teepee."

"Like the Indians?"

"They prefer 'Native Americans'."

"What's it doing there?" "I don't know…" He was unable to move, just stood staring at it. More amazing than the teepee, was what was tied up outside of it. There was not one, but two horses. A chestnut colored one, and what looked to Tim like an Appaloosa. He'd thought they'd all died along with all the other domesticated animals. He hadn't seen a live horse in almost two years and here were two of them, staring him right in the face. He was dumbfounded.

There was smoke drifting lazily up from a fire outside, and then a flap opened and a tall, bare-chested man with long black hair and dark skin emerged and looked at them. They stared at one another for a while, when suddenly the man waved and began walking towards them with an easy, purposeful gait.

CHAPTER 15: RETALIATION

The smoke was just clearing from the ship as it sat twenty miles off Guadalcanal on a glass-calm sea. Lt. Cmd. Wright opened the hatch to the wing bridge and stepped out into the sun, looking west to where the missile flew. It was too far to see, but he knew in a few minutes the cruise missile they'd just fired would spread its bomblets over the area where the last radio transmitter in the South Pacific was located. He raised his binoculars and scanned the horizon. Petty Officer Stevens came out to the wing bridge and coughed, getting the attention of the captain. Turning, he said, "Yes, Stevens?"

"Excuse me, sir. That was the last of them."

"Yes, I know. They won't be a bother to us anymore."

"Yes sir, that too. But I meant that was our last 109D…" he said, looking down at the deck. Even though he was the skipper's fair-haired boy, he was still frightened of him.

"Well, that's fine. It'll make room for the As in the launch racks. We find any more radios, we'll just have to close in and use the five inch."

"Good idea, sir."

"Of course it's a good idea! It's mine!" Wright replied with that evil grin, the one that never ceased to turn everyone's bowels on board to fluid. "Has that Jap had any more luck finding a way to arm them?"

"No, sir. He says every time he gets to a bit of code in the program where he thinks he can do it, it puts up a roadblock. He's getting really frustrated I think, sir."

"Well, he'd better find a way, Stevens. And he better not be bullshitting us. Because if I find out he's just been pulling our chain, his life on board here will take a turn for the worse." He shook his head. "And you're sure that was the last radio station?"

"Yes, sir, pretty sure. The one on Oahu is still chatting away, but he seems really smart and I can't get a fix on him. Doesn't transmit for more than a few minutes at a time, and from his signals seems like he moves around every day, never staying in one spot. He spends most of his time exchanging weather reports with some guy on Honshu in Japan, and some Ruskie in Murmansk. Other than that, the whole Pacific is quiet."

"Good. Then the whole South Pacific is ours!"

"Yes, sir. You weren't thinking of going up to Japan or Russia, were you?"

"No, Stevens. Far too cold up there, and there's nothing there we want right now. I might change my mind though, once we arm the As."

"That's good, sir. I don't like the cold all that much."

"Have you found out anything on that other little matter?"

"You mean Ensign Johnson and Suplee?"

"Yes. Have you found out what those two are up to? I don't trust them. They're not team players."

"No, sir, I haven't. If they're up to something, they're really good at hiding it. Every time I get close, they're talking college football."

"They talk about college football, eh? Alright, but I still want you to keep a close eye on them."

"Aye, sir, but to tell you the truth, they've been right on a lot of the stuff on the ship, and both have worked really hard to repair a lot of it. They may be a little flaky, but I think they're harmless," Stevens said, thinking he may have overstepped his bounds.

"Be that as it may, Stevens, I still don't trust them."

"Aye, sir, I'll keep an eye on them."

"That is all, Stevens," Cmd. Wright said in dismissal, and Stevens departed like a dog with his tail between his legs.

"Fear is the ultimate motivator," Wright said to the empty deck. He saw a dark speck on the horizon and raised his binoculars. It was the growing shape of the ship's helicopter returning from Guadalcanal. At least that Major Paleen had finally figured out how to fly the damn thing, and about fucking time, too. He watched the silhouette grow larger until he could hear the engines of the helicopter and lowered his binoculars. It came closer, circled the ship once, then hovered over the landing deck on the fantail. The aircraft shakily lowered to the deck and finally dropped the last few inches with a thud. He heard the turbines wind down, then called into the bridge to the Filipino helmsman, who was standing around doing nothing at the moment because the ship was not moving.

"You get word to Major Paleen that once he secures the bird, he is to report to me here on the bridge."

"Yes! I do right away!"

The man scrambled rapidly through a hatch, as if he couldn't get away from the skipper fast enough, leaving Cmd. Wright on the bridge alone. He had to come up with something soon; life on board was becoming mundane. After two years at sea, he was hard pressed to find any more 'hazards to navigation', and whatever they hadn't sunk themselves had either sunk on its own, or washed ashore somewhere. They had seen a few container ships broken in two, stuck hopelessly on reefs on a few occasions, but now the seas were free, and without the excitement of a sinking or two once in a while, the natives were getting restless. He sat back in his chair and ran his finger through his growing beard. It was a dark black, and went all the way to the middle of his chest now. Upon reflection, he fancied himself a modern day Blackbeard, scourge of the seas. He laughed aloud at that one, and he'd even removed all pretenses about a month ago when he had Stevens strike down the Stars and Stripes and raise a huge Jolly Roger on the mainmast. Stevens had found it in one of the crewmen's lockers when he was rummaging through them. He wished it didn't have the white lettering below the skull and crossbones reading, 'Show me yer' Booty!', but it would work for now. Maybe he could get one of those East Indian women to fashion one.

He heard the hatch to the bridge open and turned to see Major Paleen enter wearing a green flight suit. The major came to attention and saluted him in the British fashion, palm outward, which always annoyed Cmd. Wright, but he said nothing.

Without rising, he returned his salute and said, "Stand at ease, Major, do you have anything to report?"

"Yes, sir! Your targeting was most proficient. The target was completely destroyed," the major reported. He hadn't actually seen anything destroyed at all, except for a few hundred yards of jungle, but he knew well enough to tell the skipper what he wanted to hear lest he receive a tirade of abuse.

"Very good to hear, Major. We won't be getting any more trouble from them. Now tell me, how is the bird flying?"

"It is a sheer joy to fly! I only wish my Air Force had some of these fine machines!"

"So you feel confident then, and you're up to speed with it?"

"Oh yes, sir! Like it was part of my body I can fly it."

"Good, good. That is all," he said, dismissing the major with a wave.

The major turned to leave, looking relieved.

"And Major?"

The major stopped and turned slowly, as if he was waiting for the other shoe to drop. "Yes sir?"

"You will be in the wardroom for dinner tonight? I missed you the last few nights."

"I apologize. I was not feeling well that last few times and was lying down in my cabin. I will be there tonight, sir."

"Good, be there at 1800, sharp."

"Very good, sir!"

"That is all."

The major scampered off the bridge like his trousers were on fire. The skipper picked up the growler phone and called down to the engine room, where Ensign Johnson, Nakamura and Suplee were working on one of the turbines. He heard the other end pick up, and Johnson's voice answer.

"Mr. Johnson? How long before we can get underway?"

"We can get underway now with limited power, sir. We still have the fuel pump out of number three turbine, and it'll be a while before we can get it all back together, so we have it offline until we can make the repairs."

"Do you think you can fix it?"

"Yes, sir, but we still have to tear it down. Be about two days I think."

"Very well, we'll be getting underway in a few minutes."

"Aye, sir," Johnson said. "Do you mind me asking where we're headed, sir?"

"I haven't decided yet, Mr. Johnson. That is all," he said, hanging up the phone. He stood and walked over to the chart table and looked over the map of the South Pacific for a long time, until his finger stopped on a speck of land. "There. I think there will do nicely. I've never been to Tahiti!" He looked up to see the helmsman had returned and was standing at his post with nothing to do yet again. Cmd. Wright wrote a few notes on a slip of paper and handed it to him. The man took the slip of paper, looked at it and nodded. He put a few entries into a keyboard in front of him, and they both could feel the rumble and vibrations of the turbines below coming to life. He steered the helm to guide the boat to the correct course, and then added power to the twin screws which spun to life, churning up the water at the stern into a huge froth, and the ship heeled over, turning rapidly onto its new heading. The skipper went out to the wing bridge and let the sea breeze hit his face, feeling like he was the King of the Seas.

Down in the Engine room, Ensign Johnson had hung up the phone and walked back over to the workbench when the turbines fired up and spun up to speed. The noise grew to a deafening level, and he shut the hatch to the workshop, where they had the fuel pump sitting on the workbench.

"What did the skipper want?" Suplee asked.

"He just wanted a progress report," he said. "Where'd Nakamura get off to?"

"He said he had to take a dump, so went off to the head, sir," Suplee said. "Sir, this thing is fucked. There's no way he can fix it without parts."

"Well, I told the skipper it'd be two days."

"Oh shit! What now?"

"What now is we'd better find a way to get it fixed," he said firmly.

"Sir, this thing is *fucked*, just like everything else on this tub. That patch we put on the hull is still leaking, and because we never painted it, is rusting like a motherfucker. The pumps keep breaking, and when we get one pump fixed, another one takes a shit. Sir, we need to stop screaming around the ocean, shooting up everything, and stop and make some serious repairs."

"I know, Suplee. We've just got to work with what we've got. I suggested to the skipper on several occasions that we go back to Pearl and get the parts, or even San Diego, but he'd have none of it."

"Fuck. Now where are we headed?"

"I have no idea. I asked the skipper, but he said he didn't know either."

"But Stevens told me this was the last transmitter. And I think we're all out of the 109Ds."

"Yeah, so who knows? He got his retribution and dealt out his punishment. I have no idea what's in his head right now, and frankly, I don't want to know."

"I hear that, sir. And that fucking beard he's got now… all he needs is a goddamn eye patch and a fucking parrot on his shoulder."

Johnson laughed. "Don't give him any ideas!"

"That fucking flag!" Suplee continued, not being deterred from his rant. "I actually cried when they struck the colors."

"Yeah, that really pissed me off too," Johnson said. It more than just pissed him off, it infuriated him to no end. Seeing the flag come down like that, falling to the deck, being trodden on by those fucking Somali assholes while they raised the Jolly Roger, had struck a chord so deep, he didn't ever think he'd get over it. If he didn't hate the skipper then, he surely loathed him now.

"That fuck is probably up on the bridge singing sea shanties…" Suplee trailed off in frustration, and Johnson had to laugh at the mental image of the skipper on the bridge, tri-corner hat, parrot on his shoulder wearing an eye patch singing *'yo ho ho and a bottle of rum!*

"It's not funny, sir!"

"That's not what I was laughing about," he said, and told Suplee of his mental image, and they both had a long and hard laugh over that. When they had calmed down from their fit of laughter, the hatch opened and Nakamura came back in smiling sheepishly. Ensign Johnson turned to him and asked, "Can you fix it?"

"Ah, need new gasket. Maybe I make one, but not sure. I try though."

"All I ask is to try."

"I will do my best for you, Mr. Johnson!"

"How's your other chore coming along?" he asked, and Nakamura drew a blank look. "The missiles you're working on?" "Oh. That. Not so good. Make code very hard to break into. I not sure if I can do it," he said, looking scared and relieved at the same time.

"Well, just between us three— and this goes no further— I don't care if you ever arm them. Actually, I'd rather you didn't, and we could throw them overboard."

"You no want nuclear bombs?" Nakamura asked with wide eyes.

"No, I don't," he said gravely.

"I do not want nuclear bombs too! I see what they do to my country long time ago!"

"And I know myself, Mr. Nakamura. I hope the skipper never gets control of them."

"Good, I slow down!"

"They scare the shit out of me too, Mr. Nakamura," Suplee added for good measure.

While they were having their discussion, something else was happening in the Number 4 engine room. Since they had automated everything, there was really no one to keep an eye on all the myriad gauges and computer screen readouts on engine performance. At the current power they were running on, the main bearing in Number 4 turbine was getting extremely hot because it was worn to the point of breaking. At two-thirds power, it got quickly to the point that a flash fire erupted in the engine and almost immediately the whole engine compartment was engulfed in fire. Fire alarms blared out all over the ship, and Ensign Johnson, Suplee and Nakamura sprang into action. Slamming the hatch closed to the compartment, Johnson hit the emergency fuel cutoff switch, checked the panel to see if the lights showed that the compartment was sealed, and hit the Halon fire suppression system.

When they had everything almost under control, the growler phone rang and Johnson picked up the phone. "Engine room!" he said breathlessly.

"Give me a report! What the hell happened down there?" Cmd. Wright barked on the other end.

"Not entirely sure at the moment, sir, but it appears the number 4 turbine caught fire. We have the compartment sealed, and I activated the Halon system. I'm going to wait a bit then vent it, and see what the damage is."

"Are the other engines okay?"

"Yes, sir, they seem to be fine. I don't know what the problem was. Everything seemed to be fine this morning."

"You need hands down there?" the skipper asked.

"No, sir, I don't think so."

"Good. Keep me apprised of the situation."

"I will, sir. I'd like to recommend reducing power to the other two turbines for the moment, until we can figure all this out."

After a brief moment, where it seemed like the captain was mulling things over, he came back, "Very well. I'll reduce power to half. And be quick about it down there!"

"Aye, sir!" Johnson said into a dead handset. He hung it up in its cradle and swore. "Holy shit, sir!"

"Yeah, that could have been a disaster. Imagine if we hadn't been down here."

The one thing that gave sailors nightmares, second only to sinking, was a fire on the ship. If not contained rapidly, it could spell doom for the vessel. That was why they trained hard and long on fire suppression and damage control. If they hadn't been there to seal the compartment and activate the Halon system, it would have been the end of the *USS Hughes*, and all three of them knew it. After a short while, Ensign Johnson vented the Halon out of the compartment, and when he was sure it was all gone, he un-dogged the hatch, and with a battle lantern, peered into the compartment. It seemed the fire had flashed so hot that it shattered all the lighting. It was still very hot in the room, and it surprised him that it could get that hot so fast. He could feel the heat through the leather soles of his deck shoes, and dared not touch anything in the compartment for fear of getting burned. All the paint was burned off the overhead and bulkheads, and the metal decking was warped from the heat. The turbine was completely burned up, wiring and hoses completely destroyed. In a few minutes, one of General Electric's greatest designs was now reduced to scrap. He dogged the hatch and looked at Suplee and Nakamura, shaking his head. He went over to a computer monitor and after hitting a few keys, brought up the statistics for that turbine.

"Right here," he said, pointing to the screen, the two other men looking over his shoulder. "Seems the temperature on the main bearing skyrocketed right here. It probably was worn. I don't doubt it, everything is long overdue for preventative maintenance and overhaul." He printed out the reading to show the captain. Taking the papers from the printer, he turned to the two men. "I'm going to go and get cleaned up for dinner in the wardroom, and I'll give the skipper my report then. You men try to clean this place up the best you can and seal off that compartment."

"Aye, sir, we'll take care of it," Suplee said, and he and Nakamura got to work, the fuel pump forgotten on the workbench.

At 1800 sharp, Ensign Johnson entered the wardroom to see the captain and Major Paleen already having coffee.

"Good of you to join us, Mr. Johnson. Please, have a seat," the skipper said cordially. He sat down at the table, and an Indian woman appeared out of nowhere and poured him a cup of coffee. He took a sip and looked at the captain, suppressing a smile when he thought about how comical he looked now.

"Do you have a report for me, Mr. Johnson?"

"Yes, sir, I do."

"Then get on with it!" He leaned forward, resting his elbows on the table, fingers interlaced. "I'm curious to find out what happened down there."

Johnson cleared his throat and began his well-rehearsed report. "Sir, about a half hour after we came up to power on the operating turbines, the temperature of the main bearing in Number four spiked, and before we had a chance to react, the whole compartment was engulfed in fire, destroying everything." He held his breath.

"So you're telling me that we're down to only two turbines?"

"Yes, sir. That is what I'm telling you. The entire compartment is destroyed," Johnson said, handing over the printouts, which the skipper set aside, forgotten.

"That is not good news. Not good news at all," he said with an icy stare at Johnson.

Johnson looked away and caught the gaze of Major Paleen, angered at the smug expression he saw. He wanted to reach over the table and punch him in the throat. He was just a goddamn Nabob, and he didn't hide it.

"We did all we could, it just happened so damn fast. It would have been a lot worse if we hadn't been down there."

"Yes, indeed, it was fortuitous that you were there," he said, tilting his head slightly, a small smile growing on his face.

"Sir, if you are insinuating that I had anything to do with this—"

The captain cut him off with a raised hand. "I'm doing nothing of the sort, Mr. Johnson."

"Captain, if I may speak freely?" he asked, coffee completely forgotten in front of him. After a moment, the captain nodded, leaning back in his chair, crossing his arms over his chest.

"Sir…" he caught himself, he almost said 'you', "we've been screaming all over the Pacific now for over eighteen months, and running her pretty hard."

"Yes, I know that, Mr. Johnson."

"Things are starting to break all over the ship, and it's almost like we're a bunch of one-armed paper hangers. One pump breaks, we get that one fixed, another one goes out. The patch we put on the hull in Sri Lanka is barely holding and rusting to hell. The desalinization plant broke again last week, and it took me and Mr. Nakamura three days to fix it."

"Go on," Cmd. Wright said, again leaning forward, playing with his ridiculous beard.

"I checked the PM and refit schedules. We're a year overdue for a complete refit. The last time we were in dry-dock was well before you and I came on board, seven years to be exact. We're slowing down because the bottom is covered with sea growth. It's getting fouled by barnacles, and I'm surprised the water intake scuppers aren't completely clogged. We need to make repairs, and definitely need to dry-dock soon if we want to keep her afloat."

"You've had your say, Mr. Johnson. That will be all," the captain said, dismissing him with a wave.

"But, sir, we need to get back to Pearl, or at least Midway. The USS Phillips was still tied up there last time we were there, and we can cannibalize her for parts at least."

"That is out of the question! You are dismissed, Mr. Johnson!" the captain said, as the sari-clad women appeared again, bringing only two plates of food, he noticed. So this was all planned. It was staged. *That motherfucker!* he thought, rage boiling up inside of him.

When he turned to leave, Cmd. Wright called to him. "Mr. Johnson, try and get yourself some rest. I've made a few changes to the watch roster. You and Petty Officer Suplee will have the overnight watch on the bridge until further notice. Then both of you can talk football all night. That *is* what you talk about, isn't it, Mr. Johnson?"

"Yes, sir," Johnson said, trying hard to hide his rage.

The Cmd. Wright picked up his linen napkin and snapped it open, placing it on his lap. "That will be all, Mr. Johnson."

Johnson walked out of the wardroom and was heading down the passageway to his cabin when he heard them both burst out into laughter. His head was pounding, and he wanted to scream. By the time he was back inside his cabin, his rage had reached the breaking point. He balled his fist and punched the closest locker to him, making a huge dent. He checked his watch, and realized he only had a few hours before he had the watch again. He lay down and tried to sleep, but sleep eluded him. He lay there thinking about Mary for a long time, but then brushed those thoughts out of his mind, they were too painful to contemplate.

CHAPTER 16:
THE ANCIENT ONES

Tim and Robyn stood, watching the man approach, and as he got closer, they could see his features more easily. Bare chested, he wore blue jeans and boots, and a headband of leather kept his long black hair from his eyes. He walked purposefully, and when he reached where the bison had knocked down the barbed wire fence, Tim started towards him.

"Stay here," he said to Robyn, who sat on the hood of the Hum-Vee with her carbine on her lap. They approached one another, and Tim couldn't see that the man was armed and found no indication of others with him, so relaxed a little. They met a few yards from the Hum-Vee, and the man held out his hand, Tim offered his also, and they shook 'Indian' fashion, grasping each other's forearms, instead of shaking hands.

"Hebe!" the man said, and it sounded liked 'heh-beh'.

"Hello, I'm Tim. Tim Flannery," he said, releasing his grip.

"I am Dawn Redeagle. It's a pleasure to meet you!" he said with a grin, showing perfect teeth.

"We were surprised to see you out here," Tim said, waving his hand in a sweeping gesture.

"I am travelling myself. Your caravan was a sight to behold also," Dawn said, his smile broadening. "Come, let us sit by my fire and we will talk!"

"Eh…" Tim hesitated, turning to look at Robyn.

"Ah, the little one with the itchy trigger finger. She will be safe. I mean you no harm, Tim."

"Can I drive my rig over to you?"

"Yes, the buffalo knocked down the fence. Just drive on up next to my tent and I will wait for you there."

Tim returned to Robyn by the Hum-Vee. "He's invited us to sit and talk. He seems okay," he assured her.

"Are you sure, Dad?" she said nervously.

"Yeah, I'm pretty sure. Just keep your rifle handy if you feel nervous. But I'm not getting any vibes off this guy."

"If you say so," she said, still feeling edgy. She silently got into the Hum-Vee and Tim started it back up, putting it in gear and driving it carefully over the fenced area through the high grass, where he parked it a few yards from the huge teepee. They got out, and walked over to where the man was already sitting crossed legged by the fire. It had a small iron triangle over it, with a blue spackle ware coffee pot hanging above the flames. Tim and Robyn sat down across from him, and Tim introduced Robyn.

"Hebe, Robyn. That's a pretty name for a pretty girl."

"I thought it was 'how'," she said, a perplexed look on her face, and Dawn laughed.

"That's only in the movies. I am Arapaho, and we say hello as 'Hebe'. Some other tribes say it differently, but that is the way the Arapaho greet people."

"Dawn, you'll have to forgive us for our nervousness, we haven't had much luck when running into people."

"Yes, I understand. No need to apologize. I have witnessed some terrible things myself in my travels."

"Where did you come from?" Tim asked.

"I came from Chicago. I was a professor of Native American Studies at the university there."

"You rode all the way from Chicago on horseback?"

"No, I walked some. Amazing really, finding these animals," Redeagle said, motioning with an open hand towards the horses, "I found them in a huge fenced meadow, lots of grass to eat, and a big pond for water. They just walked up to me and I was able to get on their backs right away. Apparently they'd been there, just like that, since it happened."

"Amazing is right. I thought they were all dead."

"So did I, Tim. One is a mare, the other is a stallion. I will breed them, and someday there will be plenty of horses roaming around, just like the buffalo." He poured a cup of coffee out of the battered metal pot. "Would you care for a cup?"

"Yes, please," Tim said. "Robyn, go to the camper and get two cups, please," he said. When she was gone, he reiterated in short what had happened to them in Iowa, leaving out most of the details. Then he came back to the horses and to something he'd just thought of.

"If one is a mare, and the other a stallion, wouldn't they have bred by now?"

"Yes, they have on several occasions."

"But no foal yet?"

"Not yet unfortunately," Dawn said.

"What if, you know, The Event has left whoever had survived sterile?"

"That would be very unfortunate indeed, Tim."

"Some sort of weird cosmic joke. 'OK, I'm going to kill you all off, and leave whoever is left unable to reproduce.' That would totally suck."

"That it would, but I'd like to think not. I'd like to think we still have a chance."

"If that was really the case, it would make all our lives totally pointless," he said with a sigh.

Dawn quickly changed the subject back to Tim's travels, trying to avoid the thoughts that had kept him awake nights too. "Yes, it is wise to be cautious, returning to what you said earlier. It seems like when everyone died, it left only the bad, and the few of us who are not bad are left to fight tooth and nail."

"So you have had the same happen to you?"

"No, I was able to avoid that by travelling overland mostly, staying away from the towns and cities. I had no choice though, when crossing the rivers, and witnessed a lady and a man getting kidnapped by a gang of men. I hid in the trees and watched, unable to do anything."

"You have no guns?" Tim asked.

"No, I have my bow, that's it."

Robyn returned with the mugs. Dawn filled them up, Tim drinking it black like Robyn.

"So you made all this yourself?" Robyn asked.

"Yes. The teepee is made from limbs of a tree, and the hide is of buffalo. I transport it all with my horses," he said.

"Wow! That is so cool!" she said, finally beginning to warm up to the stranger.

"I learned a long time ago how to live off the land, and that is how I choose to live now. One day I will meet a Native American woman, and we will make a new Arapaho tribe together," he said with a laugh, not daring to have the thought of being sterile cross his mind again.

"So, is this all traditional Arapaho land?" Tim asked.

"No, Arapaho is further west, and into Colorado. Here it is Pawnee, but I am just travelling through."

"Following the buffalo?" Robyn asked.

"Yes. I will go where the herd goes. It is they who will provide for me in the winter. You are very astute!"

"They sure have come back fast," Tim said. "It was an amazing sight watching the herd cross the highway like that."

"Yes, they have come back a lot faster than I would have thought. The Ancient Ones are smiling down on me I think."

"Who are the Ancient Ones?" Robyn asked.

"My ancestors are the Ancient Ones. It is told that they spoke of this happening." He went on and spoke of the signs, and when he got to the last one, Tim sat dumbfounded. *"You will hear of a dwelling-place in the heavens, above the Earth, that shall fall with a great crash. It will appear as a blue star. Very soon after this, the ceremonies of my people will cease."*

"Blue star…" Tim said.

"Yes, I saw it too, right after the Great Dying. It was in the sky for weeks."

"Me too, I saw that star!" Robyn said excitedly.

Tim told Dawn of Paul, how he thought it was a gamma ray burst, and that star, thousands of light years away, had exploded and died.

"Yes, that is what I believe also. And did you both have the burn? Like sunburn?"

"Yes, both of us, it baffled the hell out of me. I couldn't explain how I'd gotten sunburn in November sleeping in my bed, and one hell of a hangover!"

"It is what The Ancient Ones spoke of."

"But I thought that was a Hopi belief, not Arapaho," Tim said.

"You are correct, but many native peoples have similar beliefs that go back farther than anyone can remember. It also goes on to say that a great destruction is coming. The world shall rock to and fro. A great white man will battle against other people in other lands, with those who possessed the first light of wisdom. There will be many columns of smoke and fire, such as White Feather has seen the white man make in the deserts, not far from here. Only those which come will cause disease and a great dying."

"I think there has been enough dying," Tim said. Thinking about what Dawn had just said, about the columns of smoke and fire that the white man has made, and of The Football hidden under his bed in the camper, he gave an involuntary shudder.

"But after that, there will be a great rebirth and the Earth will begin anew."

"So you're saying this has been foretold?"

"Yes. It has been passed down from generation to generation that this would happen. You see, the Earth is reborn over and over again. It has a cleansing once in a while to sort of straighten things out. Return the balance if you will."

"Like when all the dinosaurs died off?" Robyn asked.

"I do believe that is true, Robyn."

"That's kind of scary."

"That it is, but it is what happened. It has been left to us now, by the Ancient Ones, to do the right thing."

"This battle?" she asked, sounding a lot older than what she was. "Who will make the fire?"

"The man who holds the key will. That will decide who will win. But there is great evil out there, and it has yet to be decided."

"I don't know about all that," Tim said skeptically.

"It is what has been foretold, Tim."

"Daddy, you have the key!" Robyn blurted out, and Tim gave her a look that said *'shut up'!*

"What does she mean, Tim?" Dawn asked.

"Daddy found The Football!"

"Robyn, *please*," Tim said forcefully.

"I'm sorry, Daddy," she said in a very tiny voice.

Tim looked over to Dawn. He didn't know what to say. Dawn nodded, and didn't say anything for a moment, and Tim was so angry with Robyn at this point, he wanted to scream, and she could tell. She began to tear up, and got up and ran to the camper. Tim looked over at Dawn again and excused himself. Getting up, he walked to the camper and inside, where he found Robyn on the couch face down crying her eyes out. Tim knelt down beside her and rubbed her back.

"Honey, I am angry with you, but I'll get over it."

"I'm so sorry! It just came out!"

"I know, that's why I really can't be too angry with you. But from now on, please, please don't tell anyone else we may meet that I have that. It's that important."

Through sobs she nodded. "I won't, Daddy. I promise!"

"Are you going to be alright?"

"Yeah, I just heard his story, and he made it sound like you were the one that was going to be in the battle. *You* were going to be the one who would cleanse the world!"

Tim was dumbfounded. He didn't get that impression at all from Dawn, but this kid was intuitive. How the hell did he fit into some ancient Indian prophecy? He didn't see it at all.

"It's all right. Are you going to come back outside?"

"No. I think I'll stay here for a while."

"Are you sure?"

"Yeah, Daddy, I'm really sorry."

"Just no more talking about the football. It's our secret and it has to stay that way."

"Okay," she said, and sniffled. Tim stood and went to go back outside. "You sure you won't come?"

"No, I'll just stay here for a while. I'll be out in a bit."

"Alright, I'll be right out there if you need me," he said, walking back out and sitting back down with Dawn. "I'm sorry about that, Dawn. You know how kids are."

"I understand. Tell, me…this football. Is it what I'm thinking it is?"

"Yes. I have the codes. Wish I didn't, scares the hell out of me," he said reluctantly, but he might as well, the cat was already out of the bag. He went on to tell him of the truck stop, the overgrown soybean field, the broken fuselage in Indiana, and how he stumbled across the case.

"That is quite a heavy burden to bear."

"It is, Dawn. It is."

"So tell me, Tim. I noticed your shirt. Sergeant Major?"

"Yeah, or at least I was. I was in the Pennsylvania National Guard. But I did some time in the active Army right out of high school."

"So did I, it's how I got the money for college."

"You got to love the GI Bill!"

"True. I was Seventh Calvary. I love the irony," Dawn said and Tim laughed.

"That is ironic!" Tim agreed, and then said, "Gary Owen!"

"Gary Owen!" Dawn replied. They sat and talked for a great while, both exchanging stories of their travels and what they had done to survive, Tim told of how he found Robyn, and how she'd come along so far, and how smart she was.

"Tim, you are no dummy yourself," Dawn said. "From everything you've told me, it lets me know you are a very smart man, brave and resourceful. I am proud to have met you."

"Ah, I'm not all that," Tim said dismissively.

"Will you stay and have supper with me? I have made a buffalo stew, and there's plenty for all of us."

"Well, I think that would be okay," Tim said with a wide smile.

"Good! And you can spend the night here and continue on your travels tomorrow."

"Let me go get Robyn," Tim said, getting up while Dawn fed the fire with more wood. When he returned, Dawn had replaced the coffee pot with a large Dutch oven, and had it sitting right on the coals. He lifted the lid and stirred what was inside, and already the aroma made both their mouths water. Robyn apologized to Dawn without having to be told, and he told her not to worry. When the stew was ready, Dawn ladled out three bowls full and they ate greedily.

"This is wonderful!" Tim said.

Robyn agreed and asked, "So this is buffalo?"

"Yes, quite delicious, isn't it?" Dawn said.

"Oh, yes!" Robyn said, finishing off her bowl, and going for seconds. After she was done with that bowl, she sat back and belched loudly, making everyone laugh.

"I'll take that as a compliment to the chef," Dawn said, which made Robyn laugh more.

"That's what Daddy says!"

They sat and made small talk, and Dawn told them of the Great Plains, and as the sun went down, Tim asked if Dawn would like a beer.

"I'd love one," Dawn said.

Tim asked Robyn to go and fill the cooler up with a six-pack or two, and bring it out. "Can I have one?" she asked, and Tim laughed.

"You know our agreement. No beer before that!" he said, and she smiled and walked off, and he heard her say, "Can't blame a girl for trying!"

She came back shortly with a large cooler and sat it next to Tim. He opened it and retrieved two cans, passing one to Dawn, who opened it and took a sip.

"Ah, it's been a while since I've had a nice cold beer."

"It does go down nice after a great meal. Thank you again."

"You are quite welcome, Tim," Dawn said.

They talked again of their lives before The Event, and Robyn sat silently and listened to them. Most of what Tim talked about she had never heard before, and was quite impressed with what he did in his past. Army stories; things about when he was a police officer; his failed marriage. About an hour after sundown, Robyn yawned and asked to be excused, as she was tired and wanted to go to bed. Tim kissed her good night, and told her he'd be in soon, that he and Dawn were going to talk for a bit longer. When she had gone inside the camper, they both looked out at the setting moon, which was waxing crescent and looked like a huge orange grin low on the horizon.

Dawn pointed at it and said, "A good sign. The Ancient Ones are smiling down on us."

"Looks more like the Cheshire cat to me," Tim said ruefully.

"Ah, yes. Things are getting curiouser and curiouser," Dawn said, as he drained his beer, and Tim handed him a fresh one.

"Never in my life did I ever think I'd be doing this," he said.

"Nor did I, but we have to play the cards that Fate has dealt us, whether we like it or not."

"I know that. I still don't like it is all," Tim said.

"You know, what you said before, about what Robyn thinks?"

"You mean her thinking I'm some sort of hero?"

"Yes, Tim. She may be right. Look back at everything that has happened up until now, even meeting me. I think it's what the Ancients talked about."

"You mean I'm supposed to be the one who saves the world, or at least cleanses it for the next?"

"That is what I mean, Tim."

"I don't buy into that, Dawn. I'm sorry, I just can't."

"But you can't deny the fact that on your way west, you've done things, taken roads that you shouldn't have, and because of that you've found the one thing you don't want, despise it even, but yet you've got it now, and now you must safeguard it with your life. You don't deny any of that, do you?" Dawn asked.

"But I never asked for any of this."

"We never do, Tim. You might not think it now, but one man can really make a difference, maybe even change the world," Dawn said with a sigh.

"That's what my brother said, right before The Event."

"He was right."

"But how can I do that? I'm only one man with a precocious fourteen year old, travelling around the country in a camper."

"Just trust your instincts. They've served you well before, haven't they?"

"Yeah, but fuck… I don't know what to do. I'm just trying to get by, find a place for Robyn and me to live in peace. Not all this other stuff!"

"Just follow your instincts, Tim. You will know what to do when the time comes, but not before that. I have no idea what I'm going to do myself. I just ride the wind like a feather, and will land where I'm supposed to land."

"It can't be that easy, or can it?"

"Perhaps, and I'll tell you this. A little food for thought, you might say. Three days ago I was camped north of here, about two miles away, far from any roads or highways. I woke up and something in the back of my mind told me to break camp and set up here. Something I never, ever do. I never camp near roads, and try to avoid people as much as you do. I believe now that it was because I was meant to meet you."

"So I just go with the flow, and follow my instincts?"

"Yes. Where exactly are you headed, Tim?" Dawn asked, reaching for another beer.

"I told Robyn that we'd let the place pick us."

"So you're looking for a sign?"

Tim laughed. "Not a burning, talking bush or a bolt out of the blue, but yeah, I guess you're right about that one."

"You're seeking someplace safe?"

"Yeah, and a place where we can live in the lifestyle we've become accustomed to," he said, with a huge grin, and Dawn laughed.

"I believe you'll get your sign, Tim."

"I wish it would hurry up then, I'm getting sick of driving!" he replied. "So you're just going to follow the herd, or do you have a specific place in mind?"

"That I'm not sure of. I know I'll stay around here, but I may just follow the buffalo like I said before, watch the herd grow, and live off the land like my ancestors."

"If I followed my ancestors, I'd be back in Ireland farming potatoes."

"Not much fun in that," Dawn said. He yawned. Tim looked at his watch, and saw that it was close to midnight.

"No, potato farming is not my idea of a great future," he said. "I think I might hit the fartsack. Thanks for dinner and the company, Dawn. It's been really nice to talk to another human besides Robyn."

"Yes, I do understand what you mean," he said, standing. "I'm sure she's a wonderful companion, but it is nice to have others to talk to once in a while. It's been over a year since I had a conversation with someone. Thank you again for the beer."

"No problem. If there's one thing there's plenty of, it's booze."

"True! Good night, Tim."

"Good night, Dawn," Tim said, and watched Dawn climb into his teepee.

He walked to the camper, and opened the door to find Robyn, already showered, in bed and fast asleep. He kissed her forehead, and went to the bathroom for his own nightly ritual and climbed into bed. Even though he was feeling a little buzzed from the beer, sleep didn't come easily, and he thought about Dawn's words over and over again. How he sounded so much like his brother. It was too naïve to think that way. He couldn't change the world. No way in the world could he do that.

Finally sleep took him, and he drifted off to a dream filled sleep. He dreamed he was an eagle, soaring above an island, and there were people on that island that he had to protect but he was at a loss on how to do it. He could see a ship sailing towards them, and felt that danger was approaching, but was helpless, so he just soared above them, looking down. Round and round he soared, and he screeched and grew angry, because he didn't know what to do...

Tom woke early to the usual smell of coffee wafting in from the galley. He sat up and held his head; he had a splitting headache and knew from experience it was a hangover. It had been a long time since he'd sat and drank that much beer. These days he usually satisfied himself with one or two with dinner, but he'd polished off an entire twelve pack with Dawn last night. Getting up and tossing on some sweatpants, he walked out to see a smiling Robyn making his cup of coffee. She came over with a steaming cup and sat it down at the table as he folded himself into his seat. She bent down and kissed him on the forehead.

"Good morning, Daddy!"

"Yeah, it's morning alright," he grumbled.

"Do we have a bit of a hangover this morning?"

"Eh. I'll live," he said as he took a sip of coffee. "Why don't you go out and see if Redeagle is awake? Maybe we can return the favor and have him in for toast and coffee."

"Okay!" Robyn said, wiping her hands with a towel and going to the door. When she opened it, she stopped dead. "Um, Dad...?"

"What is it?" he said, turning around to see her frozen in the doorway, staring out. He got up and stood behind her, and his jaw dropped open. There was no sign at all of the teepee, the horses or Dawn Redeagle. It was almost as if he was never there at all. All he could see in the early morning light was miles and miles of tall grass slowly waving in a slight breeze.

I guess this is the amber waves of grain they sing about in the song.

"Things are getting curiouser and curiouser," he whispered.

"He was there, right? I didn't just dream it?" she asked.

Tim moved her aside and walked the few yards to where the teepee had been. The fire had been extinguished at some point, and the coals were damp and cold. He could see where the teepee had been set up; the grass was crushed flat in a huge circle. He looked over to where the horses had been, and could see some fresh manure laying on the ground, but other than that, there was no sign of Dawn Redeagle.

"No, you didn't dream it, he was here. He must have packed up camp early this morning before we both were awake and headed off."

He looked around as far as he could see, and didn't even see the herd of bison. In the tall grass he couldn't even tell which direction Dawn had gone. It was like he vanished into thin air. He looked down towards the highway in both directions, and saw no sign of him there either. He walked back to the camper.

"I don't know where he's gone," he said, shrugging.

"Did he say anything last night?"

"No, we just said our goodnights around midnight and I came to bed."

"Maybe he said everything he needed to say."

"Maybe, Pumpkin, but it's got me baffled."

"Yeah, he was kind of neat. I'd liked to have talked to him more."

"So would have I, baby," Tim said, reentering the camper and sitting down to finish his coffee. They sat in silence for a while until it was time to pack up and get back out on the road. It only took a few minutes, and taking their rifles, they hopped into the Hum-Vee. Tim started it and was about to put it in gear when he looked up through the windshield and saw what he had missed earlier. Folded in half was a piece of paper under the windshield wiper, and he almost dismissed it as one of those fliers for aluminum siding or pet grooming that he'd find on his car after he was in the supermarket. He reached out and got it, sat back down in his seat and opened it up.

"What is it, Dad?" Robyn asked, trying to lean over the wide console that separated them.

"I don't know. I think Dawn must have left it," he said, unfolding the paper. It was a single sheet of loose leaf lined paper, and had a note written on it: *You wanted a sign. Have a safe journey!* written in perfect cursive. Also folded with the paper was what looked like a glossy color tri-fold flier from some housing development or something like that. He looked at it and shook his head.

It read: *Planning for the end? We have everything the modern survivalist would need! From food storage, to deep water wells, solar and wind power, weapons storage, and much, much more! All homes are double walled, and come with complete Faraday Box protection for all of your electronics needs! All in the Gateway to the Grand Canyon, and just outside of beautiful, Williams, Arizona. Adjacent to the Kibab National Forest, and thousands of acres of tall Ponderosa pines, mule deer and elk hunting! Whatever you're preparing for, we have you covered! Come and see us today!*

The brochure also showed several photos, obviously taken for the full advantage and 'wow' factor. The homes looked like huge log cabins, and had full kitchens, washing machines, dryers, TVs, DVD players, and all gaming needs.

"Well I'll be dipped in dogshit," he said.

"Well, what is it, Daddy?" she asked.

"It's a sign, baby."

"What kind of a sign?"

"It's where we are going," he said, handing over the brochure.

She looked at it for a moment or two, closed it and looked over at Tim. "Is this where we need to be?"

"Well, if Dawn Redeagle was only half right, yes. But even if he's wrong, this looks like as good a place as any. We might as well check it out."

"It looks pretty cool!"

"Not only that, we have a destination, no more wandering and wondering!" he said, with a big grin, putting the Hum-Vee into drive and making a big turn to get back out onto the highway. Robyn laughed, put her feet up on the dash, and rolled down her window. They drove on throughout the day listening to the music that Tim had stored on the IVIS. Continuing west on I-80, they took the exit and merged with I-76. They headed into Colorado, stopping at a truck stop in Sterling to scrounge up some more water and diesel fuel. When they had all of the fuel tanks topped off, Tim took out a map of the local area he'd picked up from inside the truck stop.

"What are you looking for?" Robyn asked.

"The library. I need to look something up that's been bugging me since this morning when I read that brochure," he said, not looking up from the map.

"What was bugging you?"

"What a Faraday Box is. I know I've heard it before, but I'm not sure what it is."

That's easy!" she said with a giggle. "It's a steel cage to protect electronics from static electricity and electromagnetic pulse."

He stopped, looked dead ahead and dropped the map. He slowly turned to her. "And just how do you know about that?"

"It was in one of those books we have on the development of the atom bomb and Oppenheimer and all those other guys. In the late 60s they discovered that atomic bombs let off an electromagnetic pulse when they go off high in the atmosphere, and a Faraday Cage can protect delicate electronics," she said matter-of-factly, and with a look that almost said *You didn't know that?*

"How old are you again?" he asked, stowing the map he no longer needed.

"Fourteen!" she said, sticking out her tongue at him.

He rolled his eyes and put the Hum-Vee back into gear, and headed off back onto the highway. "More like forty!" he said as they drove off. He realized they had crossed into Mountain Time, and changed his watch again, figuring it would be the last time in a while. He was happy the old Timex was still working. It had only cost him $25 at the PX over ten years ago and had served him well all this time. He only had to remember to wind it every day, and if he forgot and it stopped, he double checked it with the time on the IVIS, which was always correct. They drove on until the sun was very low on the horizon and decided to stop within sight of a now dark Denver in a town called Keensburg. Pulling off onto another overgrown rest stop with covered picnic areas, he drove the camper up right in front of one and stopped.

"We'll eat alfresco tonight!" he said with a flourish.

They set up camp, Robyn made tuna sandwiches, and they ate at a picnic table in the twilight, sipping cans of Coke. Tim had decided he'd give his liver a break for a few days, and was laying off the beer. They had watched the sun go down over the Rocky Mountains that night, and he told Robyn they'd be crossing them the next day. The moon again was a little bit higher in the sky, but still the same crescent shape, and Tim thought of the Cheshire cat grinning at him.

Things are most certainly getting curiouser and curiouser.

"The moon looks like the Cheshire Cat from *Alice in Wonderland*," Robyn said.

"Can you read my mind?"

"No."

"That's exactly what I was thinking. I said so to Dawn last night about it."

"I wonder where he is," she said, looking at the moon. "I hope he's alright."

"Yeah, me too."

"I think he was right about everything," Robyn said confidently.

"Don't be so sure. A lot of that was pure myth."

"Like bigfoot?"

"No, bigfoot is real!"

"Come on, Dad, there's no Bigfoot," Robyn said playfully, sticking out her tongue.

"Don't be so sure. The Loch Ness Monster is real, so is La Chupacabra!"

"La Chupra-what?"

"La Chupacabra. Everyone knows about that. It means 'goat sucker,' and it roams around Puerto Rico at night, sucking the blood from goats and other critters."

"Oh, puleeze," she said, rolling her eyes. "Those things aren't real."

"Okay, if they aren't real, what makes you think what ol' Mr. Redeagle told us was true?"

"Because I just know it is all," she said with finality, crossing her arms over her chest.

Tim left it at that, because he knew he couldn't shake the idea from her head. They made small talk for a while, and when the last of the light from the sun had faded over the Rockies, they cleaned up their mess from supper and headed inside. Tim was glad now they had a destination. He wasn't getting any younger, and these long miles on increasingly worsening roads were beginning to take their toll on him. Most nights his knees screamed in agony, and his back was so stiff he could barely move. He needed to find a place where they could relax and he could do some exercises to limber up some, but in the back of his mind he knew that was just a waste of time itself. He was going to be fifty years old before much longer, and the years of abuse he'd put his body through were now making themselves quite evident. He had to continually keep telling himself that he wasn't that physically fit eighteen year old private anymore.

They went to bed early, and were both asleep in minutes. They woke early the next day, and started off again. They passed through Denver, and Tim had to admit it was the prettiest he'd ever seen it. He'd been there a few years prior, and there had been a thick cloud of smog hovering over the city. Now, with no cars, trucks or buses, the air was crystal clear, but thin. Staying on I-70, they continued on, and soon after started to climb the Rockies. The Hum-Vee was straining with the heavy weight of the camper it was never designed to haul, and Tim kept a sharp eye on the temperatures of the coolant and the radiator. The engine was working hard, but the Hum-Vee kept chugging away, and soon they had reached Loveland Pass at 11,990 feet above sea level. The view was breathtaking. They crossed over the Continental Divide, and were now on the downhill side of the Rockies, passing over Vail Pass soon after. After every mile, when Tim thought he'd never seen a more beautiful landscape, they'd come around a bend or crest a hill, and their breath would be taken away again.

"It's sure a lot different than Iowa or Nebraska," Robyn remarked.

"You said it," he agreed.

She laughed at the name 'Rifle' for a town, and laughed even harder when they stopped in a town called 'Parachute' for lunch. Tim checked the engine and fluid levels, and topped off all the fuel from trucks abandoned at a rest area before heading out again, crossing into Utah shortly before sundown at a nameless rest area just across the state border. When they parked, Robyn looked over at Tim, and smiled.

"I love you, Tim, and I love this! It's one big adventure!"

"Well, I hope we don't have any more excitement," he said dryly.

"Where's your sense of adventure, Daddy?"

"I left it on the runway at Port Salinas airport in Grenada in 1983," he said, shutting off the Hum-Vee and getting out, taking his rifle with him.

Tim and Robyn had driven west on I-70 and picked up I-15 south, then Rt. 89 south near Zion National Park, entering Arizona the next day near Fredonia. They circled the North Rim of the Grand Canyon, down through the Painted Desert and the Navajo Reservation, and picked up I-40 heading west just east of Flagstaff. They followed that until they saw the signs for Williams, and took the exit. It took some effort, but when they finally found the development that was advertised on the brochure that Dawn Red Eagle had left on their windshield, they both thought they had found heaven.

***

After only a fitful hour of sleep, Ensign Johnson pulled himself out of his bunk, got dressed and made his way from his cabin to the bridge for his first of many mid-watches. He met Suplee on his way there and they greeted one another.

"So the skipper is on to us you think?" Suplee asked.

"No, I don't think so. I think it's just because we're not 'team players', is how he put it once."

"Nice. Now we're stuck on this shitty watch forever!"

Ensign Johnson just nodded in reply. They walked through the hatch into the red-lighted bridge, and everything looked eerie. Lt. Alphabits gave his report on course and speed, weather and the like. He wasn't a bad officer, he was just caught up in the skipper's bullshit. Johnson repeated everything to him, and let him know he was ready to take over, as did PO Suplee.

"I have the conn," Ensign Johnson said.

"Mr. Johnson has the conn," Suplee answered.

At least they were still acting like sailors. Plus, he was getting a lot of experience in conning the ship. Suplee was at the helm, and Johnson walked over to the chart table and let out a whistle.

"What is it, sir? I'm steering a course north by northeast. Where are we headed?"

"You're not going to believe this one, Suplee."

"The suspense is killing me, sir! Are we headed to San Diego maybe?" he said with a wistful smile.

"Nope, guess again," Johnson said, tossing the grease pencil back onto the chart, then walking over and flopping into the captain's chair in disgust.

"Where are we headed, sir? I haven't a clue!"

"Tahiti," he said exasperatedly.

"We're not going to Midway? Oh for fuck sake!" Suplee cried.

"I think the skipper thinks this is some Club-Med cruise, and he's heading for an island paradise."

"How the hell are we going to find the parts and make the repairs we need in fucking Tahiti?"

"You know, I might as well take a little walk back into the CIC and target a Harpoon right back onto us. It'd be a lot quicker, but with the same results."

"That would do it, sir. This is not the adventure I was promised by the recruiter. I think I'll sue him for breach of contract."

"Didn't you know that all recruiters lie their asses off to get you to join?"

"Ain't that the truth!" Suplee agreed. "Shit, sir, at this rate we'll be on the bottom in no time."

"I know, and apparently the skipper either doesn't know, or doesn't care. I'm leaning towards the latter."

"This is no way to run a ship, sir. Just look at this shit. The whole fucking ship is a shambles. Half the crew, if you want to call them that, is stoned out of their minds half the time. Fucking goats and pigs and shit tied up on the decks. There's Hindu shit all over the place, and the hangar deck has become a mosque."

"I know. I know." Johnson rubbed his temples and thought that even as fucked up and unruly as McHale's crew was in that old TV show, when the time came, he still had a squared away and shipshape boat, and his crew could handle things. But this? This was a complete and utter joke.

"This tub is about to fall apart, and we're headed to fucking Tahiti?" Suplee continued on his rant. "And look at this. Since we're down to two turbines, we're only making fourteen knots. It'll take forever! At least back on Midway, that other tin can was tied up, and we could have scrounged her for parts!"

"I told the skipper that. He'd have none of it."

"Has he at least forgotten about the nukes for a while?" Suplee asked, hoping the answer would be yes. One night as he lay in his bunk, he thought about Nakamura down there fucking around with them and one of them accidentally going off. The thought chilled him to the core, but then he thought if that really did happen, it'd be over very quickly indeed, and he'd never know what hit him.

"No, he hasn't forgotten them. He was talking to Nakamura earlier about them."

"Shit. I've always been a good guy, Mr. Johnson. I was even an Eagle Scout. Courteous, thrifty, kind and brave and all that other bullshit, and because I've been a good guy, always tried to treat others, the way I would want to be treated..."

"Yes, go ahead and finish."

"Sir, I keep looking back into my past to see if there was anything that I did that was so terrible to deserve this bullshit."

"Believe me, I've done the same thing on several occasions," he said, getting up to pour himself a cup of coffee. He was going to need it, he could tell. He poured a second cup, and handed it to Suplee.

"Thank you, sir," he said, taking the offered cup. "I think I'm going to need this tonight."

"That makes both of us," Ensign Johnson agreed. "So now we're off to the island paradise of Tahiti."

"That makes no fucking sense."

"I agree."

"Now what are we going to do?" Suplee asked.

"We wait for our opportunity."

"When will that be?"

"I don't know, but I think we'll know when the time comes. For now, we just do as we've been doing, and at least try to act like sailors in the United States Navy."

"I'll try, sir. But it's getting really, really hard."

"That's all I ask, Suplee. Try." Johnson walked out onto the wing bridge, and letting the cool night air hit him. At least at Midway he'd be closer to Hawaii and Pearl. Tahiti might be the far side of the moon for all that it mattered now. He looked for and found the Southern Cross, and wondered if he'd ever see the Big Dipper or the North Star ever again.

PART TWO

CHAPTER 17:
HOME SWEET HOME

It was the spring of the sixth year after The Event, and in the years since they'd moved in, Tim and Robyn had settled quite nicely into their new home. Tim was correct in his assumption that Robyn would grow up to be just as beautiful as her mother, and Robyn had blossomed into a strikingly beautiful young woman and had turned eighteen a few months prior. It was still cool in the mornings, and in some places in the forest where sunlight rarely reached, snow was still on the ground. Although it got cold and sometimes they'd have terrible blizzards, the snow didn't stay around long in sunlit areas.

It was warming up nicely, and it was another beautiful afternoon in northern Arizona. They were in town today, getting fuel at the Grand Canyon Railroad depot, where there was plenty of diesel fuel to be found. There was also an AZDOT depot right off I-80 that they could also get fuel from, so there was no fear of them running out anytime in the near future.

After putting the last jerry can in the back of the Hum-Vee, Tim turned to Robyn and said, "So, what will we do for supper tonight?"

"I don't know. Maybe we'll do up the elk roast."

"And corn on the cob and baked potatoes?"

"Sounds like a plan to me, Sar' Major."

They were both wearing Army ACU's and had M4 carbines slung across their backs. It had been years since they'd seen other people, but they each still followed a very simple rule: always be prepared for anything. They went to get into the Hum-Vee when Robyn stopped and looked up.

"Dad, do you hear that?"

"Hear what?" He looked puzzled. "I don't hear anything."

"There!" she said excitedly.

"Honey, I still don't hear..." he stopped midway. "Oh, now I hear it."

It sounded like a lawn mower, only higher pitched, and it was running very ragged. It was coming from the northeast, and they stood and listened as the noise grew louder. In a few moments, a sight to behold popped over the pine-covered hill they were looking at. It was an Airlite with a wide red nylon delta shaped wing, and it looked like there were two people on it sitting side by side. The engine was sputtering and spitting, and sounded like it would quit at any moment. They stood and stared as it got closer, losing altitude. When it got right over them, both occupants looked down, and it made a wide turn, settling for a landing on the road leading towards the highway and out of town.

"Well I'll be..."

"Dipped in dogshit!" Robyn finished for him.

The Airlite taxied up to them and the engine sputtered and died. The occupants looked rather comical. The one on the right was wearing a green nylon flight suit, a leather helmet and goggles, like they wore in World War II. The passenger was dressed casually in jeans and a denim jacket, but he also had a leather helmet and goggles. They both got off the contraption, and for a moment the four of them just stared at one another. It was Robyn who finally broke the silence.

"Hi! I'm Robyn, and this is my Dad, Tim," she said, walking forward and offering her hand. The one in the green flight suit pulled off her helmet and a mass of dark red hair spilled out, and Tim caught his breath. She smiled, held out her hand and took Robyn's.

"I'm Holly, and this is Izzy," she said in an accent that for the moment Tim couldn't place.

Her companion, who also took off his helmet, was an older, distinguished gentleman probably around seventy years old, with a great shock of snow white hair. He also smiled and held out his hand. Tim walked forward and shook both their hands and smiled.

"Well, I sure am surprised to see you two!" Tim said, still looking at the woman. "Where'd you guys come from?"

"Colorado. We're headed for California," Izzy said.

"Flying to California in this thing?" Tim asked in amazement.

"Aye, we were. But it's not running right at the moment. I don't know what's wrong with it," Holly said.

"It's probably stale gas," Robyn said. "Gas goes stale after a while."

Scotland, Tim thought. *That's where the accent's from.* She looked very familiar too, and he couldn't quite put his finger on it.

"Are you military?" Tim asked the redheaded woman

"Aye. Well I was, that is. I was Royal Air Force. Flight Lieutenant Holly MacFarland," she said, lieutenant coming out as *'leftenant'*.

"You're a long way from the UK, Lieutenant."

"That I am," she said, looking around.

"You'll have to excuse us, we really haven't seen any other people for quite some time," Tim said, not being able to take his eyes off of the new arrival.

"It has been a while for us too. We were beginning to think we were the last ones. I'm pretty surprised to see both of you here," Izzy said.

"It's kind of a shock," Tim said, scratching his head.

"We were just heading back to the house for supper; you guys want to join us?" Robyn said cheerfully.

"Well, I don't know..." Holly said warily.

"I'm sure these people are okay, Holly," the older man named Izzy said cheerfully.

"We've got plenty. It's been a long while since we've had anyone to talk to, so you're more than welcome," Tim said, dropping his guard completely.

Holly mulled it over for a few moments and consented.

"Dinner sounds fine!" Holly said with a smile that would melt an iceberg.

Tim motioned them to the Hum-Vee, mentally assessing the woman as she and Izzy retrieved their things from the Airlite. He figured thirty- eight or thirty-nine years old, but with her milky complexion and stunning green eyes, she looked ten years younger. She was about five-foot-five inches in height, and about one hundred twenty pounds, and that red hair... so much of it...

Holly immediately tied her hair into a bun behind her head when she got into the Hum-Vee.

Robyn saw Tim's face and rolled her eyes. "Dad!"

"What?" he said innocently.

"*You* know!" she said, putting her carbine in the rack, before shutting her door.

"A lot of firepower you two have there," Izzy noted, growing wary, and Robyn turned to face him.

"We've had some… incidents with some not really nice people in the past, so it never hurts to be safe," Robyn told them.

"I see. That makes sense. And the uniforms too, are you in the military?" Izzy asked, visibly relaxing.

Again Robyn answered, and let Tim drive. "Me, technically no, but my dad swore me in about a year ago. He taught me everything he knows," she said, tapping Tim on the shoulder. "Daddy, on the other hand, is a Sergeant Major. He's a real war hero!"

"I'm not a hero, Robyn," Tim said sheepishly, looking at Holly in the rearview mirror. It was still nagging him. There was something very, very familiar about this lady, and he couldn't help but think her beauty was breathtaking.

"Yes, Holly and I have had the same encounters, thankfully it was from a distance and we mostly hid from them."

"Good idea. That's what we tried to do mostly. But one time it was unavoidable," Tim said, turning off the main road and heading south on what was now almost a dirt track, the asphalt deteriorating to the point of becoming weed strewn gravel.

"These guys, they took me, and Daddy here came and got me," Robyn said. "He's *my* hero."

"Yeah, well. Anyway, where in Colorado did you guys come from?" Tim asked, changing the subject.

"Durango. I was an exchange officer at NORAD when it all happened. I met up with Izzy and his wife about a month afterwards."

"Yes, my wife and I both survived, but unfortunately she died a few years ago," Izzy said sadly. "She had cancer. Nothing I could do really."

"I'm sorry to hear that, Izzy," Tim said.

"It was sad, but she passed quietly in her sleep," he said, the pain still evident in his voice. "So tell me, Tim, you two aren't from around here I take it. From the Keystone patch on your uniform, I'm guessing Pennsylvania?"

"Yes, sir, 28th Infantry Division. I'm from Philadelphia. Timothy Flannery of the Philadelphia Flannerys, at your service, sir!" he said, ending it in a passable Irish accent. When he said that, he could see Holly in the rearview mirror sit up a little.

"And I'm from West Virginia," Robyn added.

"But how is that pos—," Izzy went to ask, and Robyn cut him off.

"Oh, Tim's not my real dad. I just adopted him," she said giggling, and went on to tell the story of how they first met.

"Very impressive. So you two have been through a lot, and a lot of travelling too," Izzy said.

"Yes, it's why we were very happy to find this place," Tim said, turning off the small road onto what looked like a wagon trail through a thick stand of Ponderosa Pine. "I think you'll like it!" Tim added as they came out of the copse of trees into a large meadow, and the house appeared. It was an impressive two-story log cabin. There was another Hum-Vee parked in front, and Izzy could see a large barn and what looked like a greenhouse in the back. There was a huge wraparound porch that was stacked almost all the way around with cut and split firewood. A tall flagpole with the Stars and Stripes flying proudly capped off the picture.

The view took both Izzy's and Holly's breaths away.

"And here we are, home sweet home," Tim said, putting the Hum-Vee in park and shutting off the engine. They exited the vehicle, and looked around.

"Tim, I've got to say…" Holly said, looking at him with a perplexed look.

"Go ahead," Tim said.

"I feel that you and I have met before, but I can't place where," she said, looking slightly perplexed.

"I've been thinking the same thing," Tim said.

As he was about to say something more, Robyn came up to Holly and grabbed her hand. "C'mon! I'll show you around!" They both disappeared up the porch steps and into the house.

Tim shrugged and looked at Izzy. "So, I take it you're not originally from Colorado yourself?"

Izzy laughed. "No, I'm originally from Bensonhurst, New York. Isador Ginsberg. My parents were Hassidic. You would have thought the world was coming to an end when my mother found out I was going to Annapolis. I didn't fulfill her wishes to become a doctor until after I left the Navy. I retired to Colorado several years ago."

"I know the feeling," Tim said. "Come on, I'll give you the nickel tour." They walked into the house, and Izzy was blown away. There was a huge fireplace constructed of river rock, with an equally huge elk head with a huge rack over it, a massive flat screen TV and stereo system, even a desktop computer on a desk. There were black leather couches and two easy chairs in the high ceilinged room.

Izzy let out a whistle. "This place is fantastic!"

"Be it ever so humble," Tim said.

"Does all of this work?" Izzy asked incredulously.

"Yeah, everything works. It's completely powered by solar and wind too, with a backup diesel generator in the barn."

"But how is it all the electric things work?"

Tim went on to explain about the Faraday Cage built into the house, and how everything here was ready to use when they found it.

"Just walked in and turned on the light switch," Tim said. They went into the huge kitchen and dining area, and Tim put on the Mr. Coffee machine and made a pot of coffee.

"This is just amazing. So this place was just sitting here?"

"Not only this place. There are forty more homes just like it going back into the forest about three miles. There's a communal well that runs off solar, and it puts out thirty gallons a minute."

"Unbelievable!" Izzy said.

Tim took out two mugs from the cupboard when the coffee was finished, and poured them each a cup.

"Would you like cream and sugar?"

"Yes, please," Izzy said.

Tim went to a huge refrigerator, opened the door and produced a gallon jug of milk.

"Surely that's not…"

"Real milk? Sadly no, it's powdered. I wish I could find a real cow!"

They fixed their coffees, and Tim grabbed a small pouch off the table next to an easy chair in the living room, and they went back out on the porch. Tim took the pouch, pulled a meerschaum pipe out, and filled the bowl with tobacco, tamping it and then lighting it with a wooden match. They sat down on two chairs and looked out over the meadow.

"Every night at dusk, a huge heard of elk come down and graze here," Tim pointed to the far side of the clearing.

"It's very idyllic," Izzy commented.

"It is. Far cry from where we've come from. I was very happy to find this place. Apparently it was designed and built with the survivalist in mind, very rich survivalists. Each home came fully stocked with five years' worth of food for a family of five, fully furnished with all the appliances you could imagine. The place even has a full basement with a fallout shelter, stocked wine cellar, and arms room. The starting price was $8 million a pop," Tim said.

"So you just walked in and made yourselves at home? How nice!" Izzy said, shaking his head.

"To tell you the truth, I'd have never have known it was here if it wasn't for someone we met in Nebraska," Tim said, then proceeded to tell Izzy about the chance encounter they'd had with Dawn Redeagle. He didn't, however, elaborate on the whole conversation of the Hopi prophecies and Robyn's belief that he was somehow some kind of savior.

As they talked, in the back of his mind, he was still wondering where he'd met Holly before. Her beauty was enough to have been seared into his brain years ago, but he still couldn't place it. Then it hit him. He remembered the pursed lips in a red gash across her face, the dark visor of the pilot's helmet, and the wisp of red hair curling out from under it, and he laughed, interrupting what Izzy had been saying.

"What's wrong, Tim?"

"I just realized where I met your companion, and when she finally realizes who I am, she will not want to stick around," he said with a laugh.

"Why's that?" Izzy asked with raised eyebrows.

Tim went on to explain the incident in Iraq, so many years ago, and when he was finished, Izzy let out a big whistle.

"That, young man, is an incredible story. I don't know what I'd have done in your position."

"I heard later she was pressing for a courts martial, but my battalion commander had it squashed. I'm fairly sure that when she figures it out, I'll be persona non grata!"

"Yes, I'd be gearing up for it. I've seen her go off before," Izzy said. "It's the temper of a redhead."

"Oh, I'm expecting it any moment now," Tim said, leaning back, taking a sip of his coffee and puffing on his pipe.

"*NO!* You've *got* to be kidding!" he heard someone screech, looked over at Izzy, and winked.

"Here it comes!" he said, and sat back and waited. He heard a door slam, heavy footsteps on the wooden staircase, then again across the living room. Then the screen door exploded open and Holly came out and stood there staring at Tim. Her feet were firmly planted on the ground, hands on her hips. Her face was as red as a beet, and it looked like she would explode at any moment.

She just looked at him for several seconds, and then through clenched teeth asked, "Well, did he live? The soldier, did he live?"

Tim took the pipe from his mouth and took a deep breath. "No. He died in a burn unit in Germany five days later. I'd promised his mother I'd take care of him."

She looked at him for a few more moments, and her eyes teared up. She took a few ragged breaths then stormed off across the meadow into the tree line on the other side. Tim looked over at Izzy, and shrugged.

"In hindsight, I wish I could have done things a little differently, but at the time, all I was thinking about was my soldiers, and really didn't care about the consequences."

Izzy nodded. "Hindsight is always twenty-twenty."

"That it is," Tim said, as Robyn came out the door and looked at him.

"I swear I didn't say anything. She just got this look on her face all of a sudden and ran down here," she said. "Where'd she go?"

Tim pointed out to the far tree line and she ran off in that direction.

"Hey! Aren't you forgetting something?" he shouted after her.

"Oh yeah!" she said, running back into the house and coming out with an M4 carbine slung over her back.

"That's better," he said, and watched her run off into the trees on the far side of the meadow.

"I hope she's not going to shoot Holly when she finds her," Izzy said, and Tim laughed.

"No, I taught her never to go anywhere without it. Just for protection. It's better to be safe than sorry."

"I hope she's alright," Izzy said.

"I'm sure she will be. Robyn will talk to her. That kid is smart, a lot smarter than me. You saw all those books in there on that huge bookshelf?" Tim said, leaning toward Izzy. "She's read them all, twice. I think if we could give her an IQ test, the results would come back 'one at a time, please'."

"Really, you don't say?" Izzy said, sipping his coffee.

"And you saw all those antennas on the roof? They're hers. She's a ham. We were driving through Utah on the way here and she saw this house with all the antennas, and she wanted to stop and check it out. We found all this old ham equipment. It was all stuff from the fifties and sixties, all vacuum tubes, no printed circuits at all, so it survived the EMP. I told her about it, and she lugged almost everything in the house out to our camper. Only took her a week to figure it all out by reading the manuals, and now she's doing over a hundred words a minute in Morse code. There are about seven people she's contacted all over the world, and has this huge map on her wall pinpointing them all."

"Vacuum tubes, that's interesting. I recall a story I heard while I was at the Academy," Izzy said. "This young Czechoslovakian pilot had become disillusioned by Marxism-Leninism and decided to defect to the West, bringing with him a brand new Mig-17. When the CIA got hold of it, they were laughing at how antiquated everything was, the vacuum tubes and mechanical avionics, until one of them had a flash of insight and remembered a study about EMP, and realized the Soviets did it on purpose."

"Yeah, I've heard the story myself. The CIA were caught with egg on their faces, and had to figure out a way to harden all the electronics."

"But Robyn can now do a hundred words a minute in code?"

"Yes, so fast I can't keep up with her. Morse was never my strong suit."

"That is impressive!"

"Everything she wants to learn about, she does, rapidly, and it sticks with her."

"But she forgets her rifle?"

"She does it all the goddamn time," Tim said with a laugh. "Come on. I'll get dinner ready."

They went back inside and Tim prepared the roast and all the fixings in the gourmet kitchen.

"So, she's found that many survivors?" Izzy asked, seated on a barstool along the kitchen counter.

"Yeah, I was impressed by that too. But there's little communities growing now in Europe, Russia and in Japan."

"I wouldn't have thought that civilization would have bounced back so fast."

"I didn't think so either, but there it is. Driving across the country, we did see signs of other people, but only came into contact with a few, and those I'd have rather gone without meeting," Tim said, sliding the roast into the oven. "I know this is a little soon to be making this offer, but you guys are welcome to stay as long as you want."

"I appreciate the offer, Tim. I'll discuss it with Holly. It would really be up to her, and I think she still may be a bit upset with you. But it is very tempting," Izzy agreed, looking around the spacious kitchen.

"Well, the offer stands. We've got plenty of room and it's been so long since either of us has had anyone to talk to outside of each other. You think it over, okay?"

"We will, Tim. We did have other plans, but they might be able to be put on hold for a while," Izzy said after a moment of contemplation.

"Other plans?"

"I'll let Holly tell you the details. She knows of an island in the South Pacific. That's where we were headed."

"An island did you say?" Tim asked. *There goes that island again.*

"Is anything wrong, Tim? You just got this strange look on your face."

"No, just had a thought is all. Nothing is wrong."

"You look as though you've just seen a ghost."

"I'm fine, Izzy. Dinner is going to be a bit. Do you want to freshen up? I'll show you to the spare bedrooms and get you a towel for a shower if you want."

"I dream of a hot shower!" Izzy said with a huge grin, following Tim up the stairs and to the bedroom. Tim showed him where the guest bathroom was and handed him a fresh towel.

"We've got plenty of hot water. Take as long as you'd like," Tim said, and left him to his shower.

He went back downstairs and out to the porch, picked up his pipe and lit another bowl. He sat there for quite some time, and after a while, two figures came out of the woods hand in hand like they were best friends. When they got to the porch, Holly came over to Tim and leaned on the railing.

Robyn gave Tim a look that said, *you'd better be nice, Daddy!'* and walked into the house.

"Tim... I..." Holly said, and Tim cut her off.

"Holly, I think I need to apologize."

"No, Robyn and I had a really long chat. She told me the story."

"I had no business scaring you like that. It was a spur of the moment thing, I was just—"

"You were protecting your men. I understand," she said. "I was just so scared... I peed myself," she said, and Tim stifled a giggle.

"It's not funny!" she said angrily, but the smile on her face belied her feelings.

"No harm, no foul."

"Friends?" she asked, extending a hand.

"Friends!" he said, taking it and holding on just a little too long, looking into her green eyes. He looked away then and dropped his hand. "Izzy is up taking a shower. Why don't you get Robyn to show you where everything is, and you can get cleaned up before dinner. It should be ready in about an hour."

"Alright then, I'll do that," she said, turning to go. She stopped when she got to the door, and turned back to him. "And thank you for inviting us here. You didn't have to."

"Yes I did," he said, puffing on his pipe. She turned and went into the house, leaving Tim with the image of her emerald eyes, and a feeling came over him, one he'd not felt in a long, long time. He brushed that from his mind, entered the house, and went to the kitchen to work on supper. Robyn was there, shucking the corn, and she smiled as he came in.

"So, I take it you and Holly had a nice little talk?"

"Yeah, she's really nice, Daddy!" Robyn said with a wink.

"I'm sure she is," he said, checking on the roast and putting a pot of water on to boil for the corn. "I should have roasted it. It tastes so much better that way," he added, pointing at the corn.

"Stop changing the topic, Dad. She was really upset. But I told her how you were just taking care of your troops and it wasn't personal at all."

"Well, we made up."

"Did you kiss?" she said, giggling.

"No! Now bring me the corn, young lady!" She brought over four ears of fresh corn and dropped them in the pot of water.

"Did you really call her a 'Pompous British Fuck' over the radio?" she asked, and Tim let out a big laugh.

"Yeah, I did."

"You didn't add that part when you told me the story a few years ago!"

"It was selective editing," he said. "Now go wash up. Dinner's almost ready."

"Yes, sir!" she said, walking away.

"And don't—"

"Call you sir! I know! You work for a living!"

Tim got out the dishes and set the table, then going went down to the basement, returning with two bottles of white wine and put them in the fridge to chill. They were already cool, but he thought it'd be nice to have it really cold for dinner. He wasn't a big wine drinker, but he knew you chilled whites, and red were served at room temperature. The thing that always confused him was whether it was white with red meat and red with fish, or the other way around. After about forty minutes, he pulled the roast— a big one thankfully— from the oven and let it stand while he readied the potatoes and corn. He'd even gone to the greenhouse for some fresh lettuce, tomatoes and carrots, and tossed a salad. When everything was ready, he called out. All three came downstairs together. Robyn had changed out of her ACUs, and was now wearing Wranglers and a tank top that showed off her nice figure. She was a far cry from that skinny little kid he'd met so long ago. Izzy was dressed in jeans also, and a golf shirt, but Holly still had on her flying suit that Tim thought she filled out rather nicely. She had showered, and her long, naturally wavy hair spilled over her shoulders and almost reached her buttocks. He caught his breath as he held her chair for her.

"Thank you," she said, sitting down. "This is unbelievable!"

"Yes," Izzy agreed. "It's like I've died and gone to heaven!"

"I simply loved the shower! I didn't want to get out! I dreamed for so long to wash my hair like that."

"Well, as we say here in America, me casa, es su casa."

"It's like nothing ever happened here," Izzy said, taking huge helpings of everything. When they all had plenty on their plates, they dug in and ate without conversation. Izzy finished a mouthful and swallowed, looking over at Tim. "You'll have to excuse us. We haven't had this kind of meal in a long, long time"

"That's quite alright. There's plenty, so take more if you'd like."

"So this is elk?" Holly asked. "It's delicious!"

"Yes. I've got more of that, some mule deer and some wild pig too," Tim said. "But we won't cook that for you, Izzy, if you don't eat it."

"Oh, that's alright. I'm a JINO."

"JINO?" Tim asked.

"Jew In Name Only. Izzy Ginsberg loves his ham sammiches," he said, and they all laughed.

When they were done eating, Tim poured everyone another glass of wine and sat back down.

"Well, I'll say it again and the offer stands. You two are welcome to stay as long as you want. There's plenty of room, plenty of food, and plenty of wine! At least this place wasn't set up for Mormons, it has a pretty impressive wine cellar."

"Izzy did tell me of your offer, and we will take that into consideration, Tim," Holly said. "We may stay for a bit, but we did have someplace we were headed."

"Izzy told me about the island. You two weren't planning on flying that contraption across the Pacific, were you? "

"No, we were going to California to find a boat."

"Something like a sailboat?"

"Yes. We are going to find a sailboat and find an island in the South Pacific that Holly had visited," Izzy said, and Tim got a weird look on his face again, but it quickly passed.

"An island you say?" Tim asked, sitting up, and setting down his wine glass.

"Yes, it was rather nice. I had to land on it shortly before everything happened. My copilot and I were taking a C-17 from Diego Garcia to Honolulu for an airshow. I was to leave the aircraft there and fly out commercially to Colorado, where I was to be an exchange officer for two years. We had just refueled in flight with a US Air Force KC-135, and about an hour later we had electronics difficulties. Half our avionics went out. We had to land somewhere, and this US Navy EB-3 Hawkeye vectored us into this island that wasn't on any of our charts."

"Where exactly was it?" Tim asked.

"It was east of Micronesia someplace. The Marshall Islands I think. Anyway, when we landed, it was dark and we couldn't see a thing, but this Navy lieutenant met us and told us all about the island, how it was secret and hush-hush," she said, putting down her wine glass. "The place is called Volivoli, and apparently there's a stockpile of food and equipment, medical supplies and everything to last a Marine Division a whole month. We were there three days, and it was so beautiful! It had snow white sandy beaches and palm trees blowing in the breeze," she said, with a faraway look on her face.

"So we figured we'd set sail for it, and live out the rest of our lives there. I figured if there was enough food and medical supplies to last a division of marines a month, we'd be set for life there," Izzy chimed in.

"Wow, Dad! That sounds like one big adventure!" Robyn said, finishing her wine, and getting a little giddy.

"Yeah, it does," he said, thinking about the island again, and why that dream always came back to him. The one where he was the eagle soaring above an island, sensing danger, and not being able to do anything about it.

"Anything wrong, Dad?" Robyn asked.

"No, I'm alright," he said, and then turned to Holly. "Did you ever think about going back home?"

"Back home to Scotland?" she asked, and Tim nodded. "You apparently have never been to Scotland in the winter!" she said, and everyone laughed.

"Well, it snows here, but it doesn't stick around long. It's a really nice climate, and there's plenty of food," Tim said.

"And everything works here, the TV and everything?" Izzy asked.

"Yep, we've got all the old classics on DVD, plus every known documentary from the History Channel and Discovery Channel. We keep ourselves pretty well entertained here."

"That's just so amazing. So the electric, is it enough?"

"It's more than enough. There's two acres of solar panels and three wind turbine generators on the other side of Bill Williams Mountain that feeds the whole subdivision. I've got all the other houses winterized and isolated, so this house is the only one drawing power."

"And all the houses are like this one?" Holly asked.

"Yes, more or less. It was set up to be completely isolated from the rest of the world, and everything still works. I've got enough food in storage right here to last several more years, and enough seeds to last the same. I run out, I just go to the next house and get what I need, but I haven't had to do that yet, and don't figure I'll have to for several more years."

"So it seems you're set then, Tim," Izzy said.

"Yeah, guess so," Tim said, looking away. "So you think you guys will find a good boat after all these years? Good enough to sail a few thousand miles across the Pacific?"

"We think so," Izzy said. "And I can sail. I didn't go to Canoe U for just anything!"

"And my grandfather was a fisherman," Holly said. "He taught me to sail when I was a little girl."

"Well I wish you all the luck in the world! But until then, my offer stands. You're quite welcome to stay here as long as you want. I'm sure Robyn would love having someone else to keep her company besides me," Tim said, winking at Robyn.

"Dad, c'mon!" she said, and then looked at her watch that Tim had found and given her years ago. "Oh! It's almost 2000, time to go!" she said excitedly, and virtually launched herself from the table, bounding up the stairs two at a time.

Tim looked over at his guests sheepishly. "She chats with a boy in Tahiti on the ham radio. He was stuck there when The Event happened, and lives on his parents' boat. Apparently, they were sailing around the world, and both his parents died."

"You couldn't ask for a better place to be stranded," Izzy said.

"Methinks she's smitten with him," Tim said ruefully, getting up to clear the table.

"Let me help you with that, Tim," Holly said, with a warm smile that sent shivers down his back.

They busied themselves with cleaning up, and Holly was shocked to see a working dishwasher. She stacked the dishes in it and made small talk with Tim. Izzy had excused himself, and made his way out to the living room where he was going through the DVDs so they were alone.

"So, you fly the '17?" Tim asked. "I thought you were a helicopter pilot."

"Shortly after Iraq, I phased into fixed-wing aircraft. I have a thousand hours in the C-17, and fifteen hundred in the Hercules," she said proudly.

"I'm impressed with you flying that contraption you flew here, all the way from Colorado!"

"Thank you. I do love flying. I always thought I could fly anything in the world, just let me at her!"

Tim put the last dish in the washer, closed it and turned it on.

When he turned, Holly moved closer to him. "Tim, again, I'm sorry, and thank you for your wonderful hospitality. I never dreamed this could ever happen again," she said, reaching out and touching his arm, and he could feel little electric charges shoot out from where her fingertips touched him.

"Me either," he said, and moved a little closer.

Just then Izzy came in. "Tim do you mind terribly... Oh, I'm sorry, was I interrupting something?" he asked with a sly grin when they moved apart from one another.

"No, Izzy. We were just finishing up the washing. What was it you wanted?" Tim asked. Holly stepped back and brushed her hair from her eyes with a mirthful look on her face.

"I just wanted to know if I could watch some of your DVDs? It's been such a long time."

"Yes it has," Tim said, and Holly giggled. "Go right ahead and watch whatever you want. There's beer out here too, if you want one."

"The wine was enough for me, thank you," Izzy said gleefully, and turned and went out to the living room where they heard the TV turn on.

"Would you like a beer?" he asked Holly.

"Sure, why not? I don't guess I'll be flying tomorrow."

"We'll go back down tomorrow and find out what's up with your contraption."

"It's an Airlite."

"Whatever," he said with a laugh, and handed her a bottle of Miller High Life. "Let's go out on the porch."

They walked through the living room, and Izzy was already engrossed in something about the Titanic, and didn't even notice them walk by. They sat down in the same chairs he and Izzy had sat in hours before. They were quiet for a few minutes, and then Holly broke the silence.

"Odd how chance works."

"Yeah, it is. I'd have never met up with Robyn had I just kept driving and not taken a side road out of curiosity."

"And if the engine on our Airlite hadn't started acting up, we'd have missed you completely."

"True," he said, taking a pull of his beer.

"She really adores you."

"Robyn? I adore her too. She's been a joy to have around. But it hasn't always been easy," Tim said.

"At least she was thirteen when you met her."

"What do you mean?" he asked, not knowing what she was getting at.

"You didn't have to have 'The Talk' with her is what I mean."

"Oh, there is where you are sadly, sadly mistaken," he said with a little smile. "She didn't go through puberty until she was fifteen."

"Oh…" Holly said.

"You're telling me! She was late blooming I guess, because of the years of malnutrition, so I had to explain some things to her. She already knew some things because she was smart, I just wasn't prepared for it psychologically."

"That's funny!" Holly said with a huge laugh.

"I'm glad you find that humorous. It was extremely painful, I'll tell you."

"I'm sure it was!" she said, still laughing. "Karma was at work again."

"What do you mean?" "Consider yourself completely absolved from threatening to shoot me down."

"Okay, you got me there. I'd rather have root canal than to ever have to do that again."

"I can imagine!" she said, giggling.

"I'm so relieved that you don't derive pleasure from another's discomfort," Tim replied wryly.

"Okay, I will stop," she said with a smile.

"So, tell me about Izzy," he said, finally able to change the subject, and her face turned dark.

"We met at the supermarket. We were getting canned goods. His wife was already sick, and I offered to stay with him and help, and he gladly accepted my offer. I think we both just needed the company, really. It was so sad watching her go like that. He adored her," she said sadly.

"Yeah, I can imagine."

"They were together forty years. Imagine that, forty years with the same person," she said.

"I know, I can't. I couldn't stand to be in the same room with the woman I married at the very end, and we were only together fifteen years. Going to Afghanistan for the last time put the final nail in that coffin."

"The war has ended so many relationships," she said with a sigh.

"It's the nature of our jobs. We're soldiers, and sometimes we have to go off and do things we'd rather not," he said. "So you too?"

"Yes. He was a medical student. Couldn't understand why I had to go away so much. In the end it was a very tearful goodbye in Piccadilly."

"Sounds very Hemingwayesque."

"Aye, it was even raining," she said.

"London always depressed me," Tim said, draining his beer. "You want another?"

"Maybe one more, then I have got to get to bed."

"Be right back," he said, standing and going back inside.

Holly sat alone for a few moments and took in the night. It *was* rather beautiful here, she thought.

Tim came back out after a few minutes and handed her an open bottle. "Izzy is engrossed with that documentary on the Titanic. I could sum it up for him, 'They build a big boat, big boat hits iceberg, big boat sinks, a lot of people die.' End of story!"

"You're a typical career soldier, the consummate cynic."

"At least he's enjoying himself. He looked terrified on that contraption today."

"I don't think he was enjoying the flight at all," Holly said.

"Well, I don't think it was the in-flight entertainment. But you know how airline food is," he said, and she laughed.

"I think he needed the distraction, really. He was a doctor for years, taking care of other people, then his own dying wife. He's never really thought about himself much in the last forty or so years."

"Yeah, I guess you're right. So you really think you guys will find that island?"

"I don't see why not. I have the coordinates right up here," she said, tapping her temple. "I wrote them down when we got our avionics back up. I knew I shouldn't have, but the place intrigued me."

"I'll say, enough to make you fly that thing to California, and then sail across the Pacific."

"It is. Let me ask you something, Tim. Have you ever had a dream?"

He wanted to say a whole bunch of them, usually nightmares, but just nodded.

"I'll go one better. Have you ever had a feeling you've had to do something, just *have* to do it?"

"Yes, I've felt like that before," he said, becoming uncomfortable. He wanted to tell her about Paul and his island, the island in his dreams, what Redeagle had said, what Robyn felt, but he let it lie dormant. Even after all this time, he still couldn't wrap his mind around it, and it chilled him to the bone, so he remained silent.

"That's the way I feel about Volivoli. I just have to go back. I don't know why, but I do. So that's why Izzy and I are going."

"From the outside it seems a little crazy, but I think I get where you're coming from," he said, after a pause.

"Aye, I agree. It does sound crazy. But something in the back of my mind is telling me I have to go there."

"I think I understand," he said.

"From the very moment I set foot on that island, something told me it was important that I get back there some day," she said, and they looked out over the meadow, and watched the elk come out to graze in the moonlight.

"They are such magnificent animals. We'd see them in Colorado too."

"You should hear them in the rut," Tim said, thankful that she'd changed the topic.

"The rut?"

"It's what they call it in the fall when they breed. The males bugle. It's something everyone should hear at some point. It's eerie when you hear the sound echoing through the forest at night."

"Really?" "Yeah, I can't even begin to describe the sound. It sends chills up your spine to think that an animal makes that noise."

"Perhaps one day I'll hear it for myself," she said, finishing her beer. "Now, I think it's time for me to go to bed."

"Did Robyn show you where to sleep?"

"Aye, got me all settled in. She really is a sweetheart, you know."

"I know," he said, smiling again.

"Good night, Tim."

"Good night, Holly," Tim said as he watched her enter the house, her long, wavy hair swinging with her steps. He looked out at the elk again, and sighed.

He laughed to himself as he thought that he felt like a fifteen year old boy that just had his first date with the most beautiful girl in school, only to be left at the doorstep without a kiss. He got up after a while, gathered up the empty beer bottles, and went inside. Izzy was now watching something on the Glomar Explorer, a definite nautical theme to his TV watching, Tim noted.

"I'm going to bed, Izzy. You okay down here?"

"Yes, yes! I'm really enjoying your collection. I may stay up for a bit longer and finish this one. Thank you again, Tim."

"No problem, Izzy. Good night."

"Good night, Tim."

Tim went upstairs to the master bedroom suite, went to the bathroom, and looked in the mirror. He cringed. He looked like his Dad. Not that his dad wasn't handsome, he just looked old. It was the crow's feet at the corners of his eyes and the salt and pepper hair that made him really look old. Where was that eighteen year old private? He put his hand on his stomach at the slight paunch he had going, knowing that no matter how many crunches or sit-ups he did, he'd never get rid of it because it was hereditary. What would Holly want with him, this old, broke-dick soldier that was past his prime? He sighed and stripped, taking a long, hot shower, letting the hot water knead the knots in his muscles until they felt better. Getting out, he shaved and brushed his teeth, then donned a ratty old pair of shorts, turned off the lights and crawled into bed. He lay there for some time, and the moonlight lit up the room almost like daylight. He watched the shadows march across the wall for what seemed like forever before falling asleep.

He didn't know how long he was asleep when he felt the bed move, the covers being lifted, then warm soft skin against his. He rolled over and faced Holly, who just smiled at him in the darkness, took his face in her hands and kissed him gently. He was stunned at first, then his body reacted the way it should, and he took her in his arms and kissed her back, slowly at first, then more insistently. When it was all over, he lay back with her head on his chest, his fingers lazily playing with her hair.

She held him tightly for a long time, then she finally spoke. "It has been a long time."

"That it has. I wasn't sure everything would work," he said.

"Oh, I believe everything worked wonderfully!" she said, kissing his chest, working up to his lips, and kissing him there, longingly.

"I'd almost forgotten what it was like," he said.

"It's like riding a bicycle."

"It's a whole lot nicer than riding a bike," he said, kissing her again, his hand travelling down her back.

"I hope you don't think I'm some slag for crawling into your bed like this."

"No, not at all, I was really hoping you would, actually."

"Were you, now?" she asked, playing her hands lower on his body.

"Yes. All evening I felt like a schoolboy," he said.

"I never just hopped into the sack with anyone before tonight. You... well, you're different." She traced a line with her finger up his chest, and then found the dime-sized hole in his left shoulder. "This is a nasty scar."

"Yeah, it was from when the guy took Robyn."

"Shotgun?" she asked. "Lucky it didn't take your bloody head off."

"Yes," he said, pulling her closer.

"You'd take a bullet for her again, wouldn't you?"

"In a New York minute I would," he said, and she put her head back down on his chest, and squeezed him tightly again for a long time.

"Do you still think I'm a pompous British fuck?"

"Well, you certainly aren't pompous," he said, and she smacked him playfully.

"You're so naughty!" she stated, and bit his nipple.

"Yes I am," he said, kissing her again. "And I think I might be able to be naughty again here in a few minutes."

"Really supercharged, are we?"

"Yes," he said, rolling on top of her and showing her...

They fell asleep later, her lying on her right side, Tim behind her with his right arm around her, holding her tightly. It was well after sunup when they were both awakened by the smell of breakfast cooking. He toyed with her buttocks and she slowly stretched, rolling over into his arms.

"Good morning!" she said, with a sleepy smile.

"And a very good morning to you, too," he said and pulled her close.

"I smell something wonderful."

"I think breakfast can wait a little bit, how about you?" he asked with a mischievous grin.

"You are so naughty!" she said and kissed him. Breakfast did wait for them...

CHAPTER 18: FLY THE FRIENDLY SKIES

After that night, by unspoken agreement Holly moved into Tim's room, and she and Izzy decided to stay for a while, at least for the summer. They both settled in quite nicely, and Holly became not so much a surrogate mom, but more like a big sister to Robyn. Izzy was like a grandfather, and she adored them both. Tim had tried to fix the engine on the Airlite, but the carburetor was too gummed up from the bad gasoline to make it work correctly. In the end, they folded the wings and pushed the tiny aircraft into an empty bay of the local fire department's house, Tim not having a clue where the missing fire engine was. They spent most days lazily, but sometimes Tim would go out and cut fresh firewood that he'd stack and let dry to split later with the hydraulic log splitter that was in the barn, preparing for the next winter. They made several trips to Flagstaff to get Izzy and Holly some more clothes, because they had so few belongings they could fit onto the Airlite.

One day, after a conversation about the Grand Canyon, Tim packed up some camping equipment and a picnic lunch, and they all went down to the railway depot. Tim fired up a small machine he said was called a 'Speeder', although he didn't know why, because it would only go about ten miles an hour. It was a little boxy thing with a tiny diesel engine in it, but it seated them all comfortably and they rode the rails in it all the way to the south rim. Tim had been there years ago, but the other three had only seen photos, and were blown away by the sheer magnitude and beauty that lay before them. They camped out that night, and headed back to Williams the next day, completely satisfied with the trip.

One night in late August after dinner, Tim had lit a fire in the huge fireplace. They were sitting in the living room, having drinks by the fire. Robyn had gone off to her bedroom, where she was chatting on the ham radio with her friend in Tahiti, and would be there for hours.

"Tim, Izzy and I really do appreciate your hospitality," Holly said tentatively.

"I knew this was coming," Tim sighed, sitting down on the big leather easy chair. He looked over at both of them, and didn't say a word, face calm and not revealing a thing.

"Tim, it's not easy saying this."

"You're both leaving. I kind of figured it was going to be soon, the way you two have been acting."

"This isn't easy, Tim," Izzy said. "But we all knew we would be leaving at some point."

"No, it isn't easy. When are you going?"

"We'll be leaving at the end of the week," Holly said. "We'd like to take one of your Hum-Vees, if that's ok."

"Yeah, I got three. I can only drive one at a time," he said with a rueful smile.

"Have you told Robyn yet?" Tim looked right into Holly's eyes. "Because I think she'll be devastated. She adores you both."

"No, I was going to do that tonight," Holly replied.

"Well, you'd better do that right now," Tim said, pointing to the stairs. Holly got up and climbed the stairs. When she was out of sight, he turned to Izzy, "I understand why you've got to, Iz, but I don't have to like it."

"We both know that, Tim," he said with a sigh. "We really don't want to go either. It's just, well… we have to."

"And here I just learned how to cook for more than two people," he said, with a sad chuckle, looking away. "You know, it's just not me. I'm thinking of Robyn. She really does adore you two. You're like family to her… you're family to *us*."

"Tim, have you ever been driving, and just decide to turn off somewhere you had no intention of turning, but not know why? You just had to go there?"

"You know the answer to that. It's how I found Robyn. I've told you the story." *It's also how I found The Football,* he didn't add. He hadn't told them of that.

"I know, and that's my point. Holly and I *have* to go there. It's like it's calling us and neither of us can explain it. We really don't *want* to leave here, we *have* to."

"Do you have the GPS coordinates for it?" Tim asked after a pause.

"Yes. Holly told me them. I've tried to find it on maps from the library, but it doesn't show anything there."

"Could I have them, please?" Tim asked, getting a small note pad and pencil. Izzy gave them to him from memory, and Tim wrote them down and stood. "I'll be right back," he said, and walked through the kitchen and down to the basement. He came back up after a short while, and sat back down in the easy chair.

Izzy looked at him with a puzzled expression on his face.

"Just want to check on something," he said, and Izzy knew Tim wasn't going to elaborate, so he left it go.

A tearful Robyn came bounding down the stairs just then, right into Tim's lap, arms around his neck, and buried her face into his shoulder. "Daddy!" she cried, and Tim hugged her tightly.

"I know, baby. I know," he said, sighing and closing his eyes.

Holly came down right behind her and walked over to the easy chair, kneeling down beside it, and putting her arms around both of them. She'd been crying too, it looked like. Izzy became teary eyed as well as he looked at them. They looked like a perfect family, and he was deeply saddened that he and his wife never had children. It wasn't like they hadn't tried, they had. Izzy was sterile, he later found out. Now here was something beautiful, and in a few short days it was going to be gone forever.

"Everybody I ever loved gets taken away!" Robyn wailed. "Uncle Jake, Mama, now Holly and Izzy!" she said, followed by another round of crying.

"Honey, we both knew they would have to leave someday," Tim sad, rocking her gently.

"But I thought they'd change their minds!"

"So did I. But remember a long time ago, I told you that someday you were going to have to make the real hard decisions, the ones you really didn't want to have to make? Well, this is one of those times, baby. We don't have to like it, but we do have to accept it."

"It's so hard!"

"I know. Now come on, let's get you to bed," he said, lifting her up to her feet. He took her hand and led her up the stairs, disappearing onto the second floor. Holly went over and sat next to Izzy, and put her head on his shoulder. He put his arm around her, and she began to cry.

"I know it was hard. But you had to do it," Izzy said.

"I never, ever want to have to do that again, Iz. The look on her face tore my bloody heart out."

"Tim's not showing it, but it's tearing him apart too," Izzy said.

"Typical man," she laughed through the tears. She sat up and wiped her eyes. They sat like that together and watched the fire, which was slowly burning down, forgotten. Tim came back down the stairs, and into the living room after a while.

"I think she'll be okay after a while. She's in shock right now, really. She'll cry herself to sleep tonight and be her old self in the morning."

"I hope so, Tim," Holly said, and stood.

Izzy stood also. "I think I'll retire and leave you two alone. Good night," he said, and wandered up the stairs. Holly looked at Tim through red, teary eyes, then came over and put her arms around him tightly, burying her face in his chest. She didn't say a word, just held on, and he hugged her back. They stood there for a few minutes, then she pulled away, looking up at him. "Let's go to bed, soldier," she said, with a sad smile.

They went to the master bedroom, and Tim brushed his teeth, undressed and climbed into bed, watching Holly through the open door to the bathroom as she pulled her hair from the ponytail she'd had it tied in and brushed it out. She saw him staring at her through the reflection in the mirror and smiled. When she was done, she turned off the light and came into the bedroom, undressing and climbing under the sheets. Tim turned off the bedside lamp, as she cuddled up next to him, her arm around his chest.

"God how I love these sheets," she said.

"Fifteen hundred thread count, pure Egyptian cotton. Survival after the end of the world is easy when money is no object," he said, holding her tightly.

"Aye, tis' true!"

"Would you like to fraternize with me in an unlawful manner, Flight Leftenant MacFarland?"

"Are you trying to seduce me, Sergeant Major?"

"Well, you are an officer, and I a lowly enlisted man, and there are rules you know," he said gravely.

"Aye, but I like breaking the rules," she said, giggling. He rolled over on top of her, and she wrapped her legs around his waist. "I think we'll both get court martials for this," she added, and kissed him deeply.

"And we'll be drummed out of the Corps."

"Drummed out, heads hanging in shame," she said, and gasped as he found the spot…

After it was over, they fell asleep entangled with each other, and woke the next morning to the smell of coffee brewing. They got up sleepily, dressed, and went down to find Izzy at the table eating toast and Robyn in the kitchen making waffles.

"It smells divine," Holly said, and went to Robyn to help her. Tim poured himself a cup of coffee and sat down.

"I'd give anything for some eggs and bacon," he said.

"Daddy, we have plenty of powdered eggs."

"I mean real eggs. And bacon," Tim said.

"We did try those duck eggs once," Robyn said, making a gagging noise, and Tim laughed.

"Yeah, we did. Not going to do that again," Tim said, and turned to Izzy, who had a questioning look on his face. "We found these duck eggs in a nest. Thought, hey we'll try them. Every single last one of them was fertilized."

"Oh, I can see where that would spoil the appetite."

Robyn and Holly brought over the food when they were done, sat it on the table, and sat down.

"Typical men, leave all the cooking to the women," she said, with mock severity.

"Now wait just a minute!" Tim said. "Who cooks dinner and kills the tasty animals we eat?"

"He's got a point, Holly," Robyn said.

"Aye, I'll give you this one," Holly said, and took a bite of waffle smothered in margarine and fake maple syrup. "I had an idea this morning," she said, after chewing.

"Yeah?" Tim asked, eyebrow raised.

"Robyn and I will go to Flagstaff today for a 'girls only' shopping outing."

"Oh, I don't like that at all," Tim said.

"That sounds like fun!" Robyn burst out. "Come on, Daddy! We'll be alright!"

He put down his knife and fork and closed his eyes, knowing he wasn't going to win this argument. Against all his better judgment, he relented. "Okay. You guys go. But take the hand held radio, leave it on and keep it with you at all times. And stay together."

"And I'll take my American Express Card," Robyn giggled.

After they were finished with breakfast, Holly and Robyn went to their rooms, changed into jeans and t-shirts, bringing jackets just in case. Robyn came down with an M4 carbine across her back and a pistol belt with two canteens and a magazine pouch.

"She does know how to accessorize," he said to Izzy, winking. Holly came down a minute later wearing basically the same thing, her hair back in a ponytail. She looked naked without a gun.

"You can't go out like that," he said, disappearing into another room, and coming back holding a small box. It was about the size of a hardback book, and had a red bow tied around it. "Here, I was saving this for Christmas or something. You might as well have it now."

She smiled as she opened the box, then her eyes grew wide. "Where on Earth did you find this?" she finally said, picking up what was inside. It was a Belgian Browning Hi-Power 9mm pistol, exactly like what was issued to the British military.

"I found it in the gun shop in town. Figured since you guys didn't have any firepower, you'd like a little something you were familiar with."

"You bloody Yanks, giving pistols as gifts!"

"Just call it an insurance policy. At least I'll feel better with you having it."

"Thank you," she said, and kissed him. She quickly loaded it and placed it in the waistband of her jeans. Turning to Robyn, she said, "Are you ready to go?"

"Yes. I'll drive, I know the way." She walked out the door with Holly behind her.

"You can drive?" Holly asked.

"Sure. I even drove a tank once," Tim heard Robyn say with a giggle as the screen door closed. Tim rolled his eyes and looked over to Izzy, who was smiling.

"You have let her off on her own before, Tim."

"Yes, but not all the way to Flagstaff. Sure, she's been out all over the place around here by herself, but never this far."

"You sound like a worrying, overprotective dad," Izzy said, ribbing him.

"I sound that way, because that's exactly what I am."

"They will be alright. Let's make ourselves busy and clean up the kitchen, shall we?"

They cleaned up the kitchen, and afterwards Izzy excused himself to read a book, so Tim went to the barn and fired up the diesel engine on the log splitter, then spent the rest of the day splitting the wood he'd cut earlier in the summer, stacking it neatly, and worrying about Robyn and Holly. It was around four PM when he decided to call it quits, his frustrations spent on five cords of wood. He showered and dressed in clean clothes, then went out to sit on the porch, smoke his pipe, and fret some more.

Izzy came outside holding a beer and sat down in the chair next to Tim. The sun was sinking low behind the pine trees to the west, long shadows growing across the meadow, and Tim was sitting there, gazing down the dirt track, open beer sitting forgotten on the table between the chairs next to the radio.

"If you're that worried, why don't you call them on the radio?" Izzy asked.

"If I do that I'd sound even more like a worrywart than I already am."

"Suit yourself," Izzy said, taking a pull of his beer. When he sat the bottle down, they heard sounds of an engine. Tim stood up and walked to the railing to see the Hum-Vee emerge from the trees. It pulled up in front of the house, and both women climbed out, laughing.

"It's about time," Tim said, with mock severity.

"Oh, Daddy, you're such a worrywart!" Robyn giggled. They were both carrying large bags, and laughing conspiratorially. "So what did you guys get?"

"I can't tell you, it's a secret!"

"Aye, and if we told you, then we'd have to kill you," Holly said.

Both girls breezed by him and went inside the house. Tim turned to Izzy and just stared, and Izzy burst out into laughter. "You're a big help," he grumbled, pouring out his warm beer and going inside.

As they ate dinner that night, the two women continued to share glances, and would burst into fits of giggles from time to time, driving Tim absolutely bonkers. After dinner, they disappeared into Robyn's room, leaving Izzy and Tim to fend for themselves. They cleaned up the dishes and the kitchen, and watched a documentary about the War of 1812. When that was over, Tim excused himself and retired to bed, exhausted from a day of log splitting and worrying for nothing. He sat up for a while reading a book, but after the fifth time he'd read the same paragraph, decided to turn off the light and go to sleep. As he put his book down, Holly came into the room.

"I was just turning off the light," he said, smiling.

"Give me a moment and I'll join you," she winked at him, and went into the bathroom. She came out a few minutes later, and smiling, undressed and climbed into bed. Tim turned off the light and held her close. "So, I take it you girls had a nice time today?"

Aye! That we did."

"So how much would this have cost me if we still actually had to use money?"

"You know the saying, the one that goes 'if you have to ask the price, you probably can't afford it'?" she said with an evil grin, and he groaned. She ran her hand down his stomach, and then lower, and he groaned some more.

The next day, Robyn and Holly took off early and went out into the woods, leaving Tim and Izzy alone to fend for themselves again. They busied themselves with the preparation of dinner. Tim wanted it to be a special one, this being Izzy's and Holly's last night with them, and had hauled out a huge turkey from the chest freezer he'd shot earlier in the year and was saving for Thanksgiving. He set it out to thaw early in the morning, hoping it'd be ready in time. He spent the rest of the morning and half the afternoon getting everything ready, and around four PM, the turkey was ready for the oven.

"Iz, I hope you're not too hungry. It' probably won't be ready until around seven thirty or eight o'clock."

"That's quite alright, Tim. Anytime is fine for one of your wonderful meals. Sure beats eating canned soups or beef stew."

"I know what you mean," he agreed, and saw the girls coming up the porch steps. They came inside, said a quick hello, and said they'd be down shortly, rushing upstairs. Tim said he would call them when dinner was ready.

At 7:45 Tim opened the oven, pulled out the turkey, and the aroma wafted through the house. He set it up on a cutting board, carving it perfectly, and getting the sides ready, put them in bowls on the table. He had two bottles of wine chilling in the fridge, and one in an ice bucket on the table. Everything was ready, and Tim looked at his watch.

"Tim, haven't you ever learned that when a man says he'll be five minutes, he means five minutes, and when a woman says five minutes, she means an hour?"

Tim laughed and walked to the bottom of the staircase to yell up to them. A muffled reply was heard, and Tim, grumbling, came back and stood at the table. Izzy was leaning against the kitchen counter sipping a beer. A few moments later they heard a door open, and footsteps coming down the stairs. When Holly and Robyn got down to the bottom, Tim was slack jawed and speechless. Izzy just let out a long whistle.

Robyn was dressed in a black evening gown, hair in a French braid down her back, makeup done perfectly, and wearing matching high heel pumps, in which she stood quite wobbly. Holly had her hair in an up-do, and had on a jade green evening gown that matched her eyes, and her makeup was perfect too. They both looked stunning. They could have been entering a fine restaurant in Paris or a high fashion modeling shoot, they looked that good.

"Doctor Ginsberg," Tim said, not taking his eyes off the two beauties across the table from him. "I do believe we're underdressed for this dinner engagement."

Tim walked around and kissed them both, then held out their chairs for them. When he was close enough to Robyn where she could, she whispered in his ear, "Daddy, she had me shave my *legs!*" with a scrunched look on her face.

When they were both seated, Tim motioned for Izzy to sit down, and poured them all some wine.

Izzy held up his glass, "I propose a toast!"

"I make a toast to the most beautiful girls in the world!" Tim said, his eyes lingering on Holly, whose eyes were sparkling gleefully.

"Here, here!" Izzy said, and took a sip.

Tim started passing the food to the right, and looked over at the women again. "I've got to say, you two look stunning!"

"Thank you, Daddy," Robyn said blushing. "I feel, well... I feel all grown up."

"You are, Pumpkin," he said. He turned to Izzy. "Let the girls out shopping, and they run up the credit cards."

"My boy, I think this time it was well worth it," Izzy replied.

Tim turned to the women again. "Did you guys hit every high-end shop in Flagstaff?" he asked, not even daring to guess how much all of that would have cost. And it looked like they were wearing real diamonds in their ears and around their necks. Holly was wearing a diamond tennis bracelet, which he didn't even want to fathom how much would have cost, pre-Event.

Holly chuckled. "I figure, with the jewelry, around five hundred grand."

Tim nearly choked. He picked up his wineglass and said, "I am *so* glad that money is no object." Everyone laughed. They finished with the meal, and everyone was quite happy. Tim ushered the girls out to the living room and put on some Big Band Era music. He excused himself, and he and Izzy took care of the cleanup as fast as they could, Tim coming back with a bottle of some sort, and four brandy snifters.

"Million dollar babes deserve million dollar booze," he said, opening the bottle and pouring some into each glass.

Holly picked up hers and let it roll a little in the glass, and Robyn watched and followed what she did. She took a sip. "Nice," she cooed.

"One hundred year old Napoleon Brandy, only the best for the ladies," Tim said, picking up his glass. Izzy came over to Robyn and bowed gracefully. "Would the lady care to dance?" he asked.

"Love to, but I don't know how," she replied.

"Don't worry, just follow my lead."

Robyn stood shakily on her high heels, and Izzy showed her where to put her hands. "Now just watch my feet, and do the opposite."

Tim and Holly sat by and watched them. Holly took Tim's hand and squeezed it. "Thank you, Tim, for making me believe in humanity again."

"Thank *you*," he said breathlessly, "for everything." He stood and asked her to dance also. She quickly found her way into his arms, and with her head on his shoulder, he held her tight as they swayed to the music.

A faster song came on next, and Izzy was showing Robyn how to jitterbug, and Tim and Holly stepped out onto the porch into the cool late summer evening. Tim walked over to the porch railing.

"You know what I miss?" he sighed. "I miss lightning bugs."

Holly wrapped both her arms around his, resting her head on his shoulder. "Do you mean 'fireflies'?"

"Yeah, they're the same thing. When we were kids back in Philly, we'd run around and catch them and put them in old mayonnaise jars. They aren't around here though. Last time we saw them was in Kentucky."

"And you miss them?"

"Funny, isn't it? Sometimes it's just the little things from your childhood that you miss and it makes you sad."

Another slow song came on, and Holly leaned into Tim. "I love this one."

"Tommy Dorsey's 'Getting Sentimental Over You'. Shall we dance?"

Holly took his hand. When they were holding each other close again, he bent down and kissed her lips gently. "I'll never forget this night."

"Aye, it's why I did it. I want you and Robyn to always remember us fondly, and not be sad."

"But you know we will. That's going to be the real hard part. Finally meeting you, and now you've got to go."

She placed her hand on the center of his chest. "But I hope I'll always be right here, Tim."

"You will be," he said, not daring to say anymore. The song ended and they rejoined Robyn and Izzy, who were taking a breather. Robyn had kicked off her heels and was rubbing her feet.

"How can someone stay in these for so long? I'd rather have my boots back!" she said, and they all laughed.

The party lasted until the wee hours, and they went up to bed slightly tipsy, the brandy on top of the wine doing a fine job indeed. When Tim and Holly were in their bedroom, she excused herself and closed the door to the bathroom. Tim, feeling a little dizzy, took his clothes off and climbed into bed. A few moments later the door opened, and out walked Holly, wearing a two piece satin lingerie number, the same color green as her gown had been, and leaned against the doorjamb provocatively. Tim let out a whistle. She grinned and went to pull the pins out of her up-do, when Tim stopped her.

"No, no, no! Come here and let me do that," he said, and her grin widened.

She walked slowly over to the bed and climbed in. "I want you to remember this night for the rest of your life, Tim," she said, and bent down and kissed him deeply. Tim decided that tonight he'd leave the lights on.

As happy as the party was the night before, the morning was equally as somber. Tim wordlessly helped Holly and Izzy load their things into the Hum-Vee he'd given them. He handed them a map, and showed them how to use the IVIS computer's GPS.

"Robyn and I will drive off ahead of you and show you where the turnoff is. You'd never see it if I don't show you where it is." Tim climbed into the Hum-Vee, and Robyn was already sitting there silently. She'd had another good cry this morning, and he didn't want to do or say anything to start her off on another jag. They drove off down the dirt track that led to their house, and made a left turn when they reached the road. Travelling south, the road progressively got worse, and after a few miles, the blacktop completely disappeared into gravel and weeds. A few miles further, Tim stopped his Hum-Vee, and Holly stopped hers behind him. They got out, and Tim held up a map.

"We're right here," Tim said, pointing to a spot on the map. "You want to go down this hill, and follow the dirt trail, and then you'll turn west. You'll go about ten miles to here, a place called Drake, which is only a place with an old stone walled roofless building and a railroad junction. You'll come out through a stand of juniper trees onto Rt. 89. Take that south, to Prescott and head east again on Rt. 69 where you'll pick up I-17 at Cordes Lakes, and that will take you to Phoenix. Then you can pick up I-10 to California," he said without emotion, like he was giving instructions to a platoon of soldiers.

"Tim, please don't," Holly said.

"I'm trying really hard not to lose it, Holly," he said. She quickly grabbed him and held him close. She let go after a while, and walked over to kiss Robyn.

"Can't I make you stay?" Robyn said tearfully.

"I'm sorry, but someday I hope you understand, honey."

"I hope so, because right now I don't understand any of it at all," Robyn said to her hands, not wanting to look into Holly's eyes for fear of crying again.

Tim was surprised by a hand on his shoulder, and found Izzy standing there when he turned. They shook hands. "You take good care of her, Izzy," Tim said.

"I will. And you take good care of Robyn, too."

"You can bet your life on it," Tim said. Doing it this way just made it more painful to everyone, so at one point, Holly walked back to the Hum-Vee and got in. Tim stood there and watched them drive off down the hill until they disappeared into the dust. He walked tight jawed back to the Hum-Vee, and started it. Sighing, he put it into drive, and didn't say a word all the way back to their house. He got out and started to walk into the house, when Robyn called to him.

"Daddy?" she said in a very small voice. He turned and looked at her. "You aren't really going to just let them go, are you?"

"What can I do? I couldn't keep them here at gunpoint," he said, a little too forcefully, and she burst out into tears and ran to him. Holding her tightly, he sat down on the porch steps, and began to cry too, not afraid to let the tears flow. They sat like that for hours, not wanting to let go of one another for a long time.

They finally broke their embrace and went into the house to make lunch, which they ate silently. Robyn excused herself and went to her room. Tim wandered around for the rest of the day in a daze, feeling like he'd been hit by a freight train. He opened a beer, and it sat untouched for hours, and he finally poured it out and climbed the stairs wearily. He poked his head into Robyn's room, and saw that she was fast asleep on top of the covers, Bad Bear clasped in a death grip under her chin. He walked in, and bent down and kissed her on the forehead, turning out her light, and closing the door quietly, so he didn't wake her. He then dragged himself to his room, and when he got there the bed was still unmade from the morning. His heart dropped again at the memories of how it got so messy. He went and stripped, and took a long hot shower, trying the get the sick, sad feeling off of him, but it didn't work. He got out and dried himself off, and trod slowly to bed. He lay there unmoving for a long while, and when he went to roll over, he could still smell her on the pillows and he cried some more, holding the pillow for dear life.

Suddenly, he sat bolt upright. He wiped the tears from his eyes, and got dressed in his ACU uniform, grabbed his rucksack, loading it with what he thought he'd need for a week or so. Walking out, he dropped his rucksack at the top of the stairs, and went into Robyn's room, switching on the light.

"Robyn! Get up, now!" he said, loud enough for her to wake. She sat up and looked at him. "What is it, Daddy?"

"It's time to ruck up. Get all your shit, full combat load just the way I showed you. Whatever you'll need for about a week in your ruck, and meet me at the Hum-Vee in twenty minutes!"

She shot out of bed as fast as she could, and went to ask him what they were doing, but he was already gone. She grabbed everything she'd need, and carefully packed it in her 'Alice' rucksack. She dressed in ACUs like Tim, shouldered the pack, and started to walk out, then stopped. She went back and grabbed Bad Bear, a small radio that she'd built, and a small Morse key, and put them both into her ruck. "Got to be able to talk to Jimmy too!" she said to herself as she went down stairs, where she got an M4 from the rack and seven loaded magazines.

Tim was just coming up from the basement with a small case, and was folding a few pieces of paper up and putting them in his pocket. He put the case in his rucksack and grabbed an M4, his grease gun strapped on, his .45 in an older style canvas web pistol belt. He looked at Robyn. "Are you ready?"

"Yes, Sar' Major," Robyn said with a curt nod.

"Then let's get going," he said, and headed out the door. He waited for her to exit, and shut and locked the doors, making sure the lights were all turned off.

The moon gave an eerie glow over them, and Robyn looked at her watch. It was 2 AM! *Where are we going?* she wondered. Tim locked the door, then placed the key carefully under a rock by the porch steps. That task completed, he tossed his ruck in the back of the Hum-Vee and his M4 in the rack in the front, Robyn doing the same. They headed out into the night.

"Daddy, are we going to get them and bring them back?" she said hopefully.

"No, baby. I already said we couldn't hold them here. But we can do the next best thing."

"What's that?"

"We can make sure they get to California in one piece and find their boat."

"So we're going with them?"

"Not exactly, We'll bird-dog them all the way. Be like guardian angels."

"Okay," she said.

"Now fire up that IVIS, and see where they are," he said, and she did it smartly. After about a minute, she had the system up and running, and synchronized with the satellite.

"Okay, got them. It looks like they've stopped for the night right here," she said, pointing at the map on the screen. He glanced at it quickly, and put his eyes back on the road.

"It looks like they've stopped for the night there in Bumblebee. Made it a lot farther today than I thought they would," he said, and drove off into the night. They stopped about a mile from where Holly and Izzy had parked, and Tim shut the Hum-Vee down on the shoulder of I-17. He looked at his watch, and saw that it was almost

6 AM at this point. "Robyn. I'm going to catch a few minutes rest. You slept most of the way here anyway." He looked at her and grinned. "They'll probably be heading out soon, once the sun comes up. Wake me when they do."

"Okay, Dad," she said, giving him thumbs up. She had her patrol cap's brim curved in a perfect 'Ranger Curve' just like his. His eyes were barely closed it seemed when she was waking him. He opened his eyes, and the sun was far up on the eastern horizon.

"They just started out," she said, taking a swig from her canteen.

"I gotta take a piss," he said, and got out to relive himself. He got back in, and finding his pipe, filled the bowl and lit it. "How fast are they going?"

"Says here about eighty kilometers an hour, heading due south on the interstate. Why is everything in metric on this thing?"

"It's because everything in the Army is metric."

They were keeping about a two mile gap between them, so even if Holly looked in her rearview mirror, she wouldn't see her tail. They followed them down the winding mountains, down to the desert below that stretched for miles. They could now see the city of Phoenix ahead of them, but not Izzy and Holly, just the blip on the IVIS screen. When they got nearer to the city, Robyn spoke up.

"Dad, they're headed due west now."

"Just keep an eye on them. They must have taken a loop or something," he said and then saw the signs for the junction for the 101 Loop and I-10 west. He followed the signs, and took the ramp, never slowing down.

"Where are they now?"

"They're still about three kilometers ahead of us," she said. They went a few more miles, and the loop turned south. "Wait, Dad, they've stopped!"

Tim slowed and pulled over to the side of the road. "I wonder what they are doing?"

"I don't know. It looks like they just pulled over for a pit stop or something."

"Okay. We wait," he said, tapping out his pipe on the dashboard and pocketing it.

After about ten minutes, Robyn spoke up. "They're on the move again. Wait! They just started heading due west again!"

"That doesn't make any sense. They're still a few miles from I-10," he said, and put the Hum-Vee into drive and headed out. When they got closer to where they stopped, Tim saw the wet spot on the concrete sidewall of the highway, and laughed. "Yeah, someone had to take a piss!" Then he looked up, and saw the Exit sign for Glendale Ave and Luke Air Force Base. *That must be where they've headed*, he thought, taking the exit and following Glendale Avenue west. They stopped at the crossroads to the main entrance to the base, and he looked at Robyn again. "Well, where to?"

"They're over that way it looks like. They've stopped again," she said.

It was in the base itself. Tim started off again, drove through the gates and said, "Sorry guys. I forgot my ID card!" He waved to the empty guardhouse.

"Now that way!" Robyn said, pointing to her left. He followed her directions onto the apron and hangar area, where weeds and Russian thistle were starting to sprout from the expansion joins in the concrete in a big way. He started to round one corner, slammed on his brakes, and threw the Hum-Vee into reverse, stopping when the vehicle was back behind the hangar he was next to.

"What is it?" she asked.

"I don't know. Something doesn't look right," Tim said, taking his carbine and getting out. Robyn followed him, taking her own carbine. He pulled the charging handle and loaded a round into the chamber, and she did the same.

"Alright, you follow me and don't make a sound, okay?"

Robyn nodded, and Tim took off at a lope around the corner and across the face of the hangar, going towards the next one over. A C-130 was halfway out of it, its front landing gear still attached to a tow bar and a tug used for moving the big planes while on the ground. Holly and Izzy's Hum-Vee was parked in front of it, both doors open, but one of the big four-bladed props was still slowly turning and there wasn't a hint of breeze in the air. He stopped and crouched when he got to the end of the hangar and waited for Robyn to catch up. There was about a thirty yard gap between the two hangars, and he looked around but didn't see anyone.

He turned to Robyn. "Here's what I'm going to do. I'm going to dash over to that side, while you cover me. You remember how to do that, right?" She nodded grimly and put the weapon on semi-auto. He dashed across the few yards, stopping at the far wall, peering around the corner slowly, then pulling his head back fast. He motioned for her to follow, and she sprinted the distance easily. Robyn could now hear voices, and one sounded angry. Tim sat down with his back to the wall. "I'm going to go around the hangar to the other side, and come around the nose of this big airplane. Give me ten minutes. When I'm in position, you'll know. When I am, you just use the corner of this hangar as cover. There's a guy in jarhead cammo holding an M16 on Holly and Izzy, and he seems kind of pissed. Just cover me. He makes any hinkey moves, drill him."

She just nodded with a blank expression.

"Remember, ten minutes, okay?"

"Got it, Sar' Major," Robyn said, and he did something he'd never done before. He kissed her, and took off around the other side of the building. He'd never kissed one of his soldiers before going into possible battle, and he had a smile on his face even though this was now deadly serious. It only took him five minutes to make the dash, and he used a few minutes to spare to catch his breath. *I'm getting too old for this shit*, he thought as he slowly crept up on the other side of the C-130.

When he was at a point where he could bring his rifle up to bear, he did so, and yelled out. He saw Robyn round the corner, react when she heard his voice, and bring hers to her shoulder, aiming at the man standing there.

"Drop the rifle now!" he shouted.

The man jumped almost out of his skin. "Who is that?"

"The question is, who the fuck are you?" Tim said, and Holly and Izzy turned to see him behind the tug with a rifle pointed at the man, and they looked very relieved.

"I'm Lance Corporal Juan Jimenez. United State Marine Corps!"

"Well Lance Corporal, I'm Sergeant Major Flannery, United States Army, and I'm giving you a direct order to lower your weapon right now, or things will end very badly for you."

"How the fuck do I know you're really a Sergeant Major?" he screamed, swinging the rifle from the hip at Holly and Izzy, and that did it for Tim.

He wasn't sure if it was the stress of the last few days or the lack of sleep, but something inside of him just snapped. He lowered his rifle and stood, exposing himself to the Marine. "Because here's why, you little sorry-assed, cum-stained, needle-dicked poor excuse for a fuckstick! If you don't take your booger-hook from that bang-switch, in three fucking seconds, exactly *three fucking seconds*, I will come over there, take it off of you, shove it up your ass, and break it off, and then beat you to death with the butt! Have I made myself perfectly fucking clear on the issue, dimwit?"

Everyone could see the color drain from the Marine's face. He wavered for a second, and then lowered his rifle.

"Yeah, you're a Sergeant Major alright," he said. Tim walked over to him and took the weapon from his hand.

"Sit the fuck down, and put your fucking hands on your head, shit for brains," he ordered. He did what he was told very rapidly, and Robyn came out of cover and walked slowly towards him, never taking her sights from him.

"Cover him, Robyn," he said." He makes a move, ventilate him!"

"Now wait a—"

"Did I say you could speak? No? Shut the fuck up then!"

Izzy looked like he was going to faint, and Holly came up to him. "Tim, how did you find us?"

"I followed a trail of crumbs," he smirked.

Holly looked over at him. "Well at least you didn't call him a pompous British fuck!" She wrapped her arms around him and gave him a big kiss. He savored the kiss for a moment, then broke away.

"So, tell me what went down."

"Iz and I were heading over the loop, and we stopped for a rest. We were there for a few minutes and I heard the engines. We turned off when I saw the signs for the Air Force base, and just followed the engine noise to the hangar. We pulled up, and this man shut the engines down, came out started yelling at us, and pointed the rifle at us. That's when you showed up."

"Are you two okay now?" he asked. They both nodded. Holly got some water from her Hum-Vee, and walked over to Izzy, giving it to him. Tim turned to the very scared Lance Corporal. "Okay, shit for brains. What's your claim to fame?"

"Sar' Major, I'm really sorry. I didn't know who the lady was."

"The 'lady' is a commissioned officer in Her Majesty's Royal Air Force, and will be shown due respect according to her rank, is that understood?"

"Yes, sir!"

"And don't call me fucking sir! I'm not a fucking jarhead, I work for a goddamn living. Get on with your story."

"Ever since, well, everyone just died, I had nothing to do see? So this is my aircraft. I'm an aircraft engine mechanic. But I know the whole airframe, inside and out cuz' I watched the other guys at work, you know?"

"Yeah, yeah get on with it."

"I moved in here, and with nothing to do, I just worked on the plane, keeping her running tip-top."

"You're telling me this plane is ready to fly right now?"

"Fuck yeah, sir! I mean Sar' Major. She's ready. I've even taxied her out and around the apron a few times. She's ready to fly."

"So you're telling me, for the last five and a half years, you've been here, just tinkering around with this airplane?"

He shrugged. "Everyone needs a hobby."

Tim rolled his eyes and turned to Holly. "What do you think, Lieutenant?"

"I don't know, Sergeant Major," she said with a twinkle in her eye. "I'll have to check her out myself."

"Well you do that, ma'am, and we'll wait here for your report if that's fine with the lieutenant." She went off to the rear of the aircraft, and disappeared inside through a hatch in the side, one that Tim was very familiar with, one he'd always left from, but never entered. "Corporal?" he said to Robyn. "Why don't you go with the Lieutenant, and make sure she's okay." Robyn took off in a run to catch up with Holly. When she was out of sight, Tim again turned to the scared Marine.

"Now riddle me this, Batman. If you're a jarhead, why are you at an Air Force base working on Air Force planes?" he asked skeptically, one hand on his hip, the other on the side of the aircraft.

"I'm reserve, Sar' Major. This squadron was down one mechanic, so my unit loaned me to them. I worked over at Sky Harbor for Southwest."

"Well, you look like a fucking mess. You said you've been living here?"

"Yes. I've got a cot set up in the back in the office. It's better than the barrio, eh?"

Tim glared at him and said nothing for a bit. "Do you have uniforms and all your shit?"

"Yes, sir, I mean Sar' Major."

"If I let you go back and get yourself cleaned up and into a proper uniform, you aren't going to try anything hinkey on me, are you?"

"Fuck no! I'm so happy to see you guys!"

"You didn't look too happy a while ago, when you were pointing a loaded rifle at my friends."

"I'm sorry Sar' Major! I didn't know who they were, and that lady with the funny accent and flight suit, I thought they were terrorists or something!"

"You thought they were terrorists?" Tim laughed. "It's a long time past for those. Okay, here's the deal. You go off to your rat hole and get your shit together. Come back to me in thirty minutes looking like a Marine, got that?"

The man nodded. "You got it, Sar' Major!"

"My watch is ticking!" Tim said, and the man took off in a dash. "And do something with that shit on your face!" he called after him. Tim turned around to Izzy, who was leaning against the tug, drinking a bottle of water. It wasn't even noon yet, and it was already hot.

"You sure do have a way with people, Tim," Izzy chuckled.

"Fear is a great motivator for the troops, especially when it's fear of severe bodily injury, caused by a slightly upset Sergeant Major."

"It takes me back to the Academy," Izzy said.

Tim walked over to him and sat down on the tug, tilting his patrol cap back on his head.

"What do you think, Tim?" Izzy asked.

"I think our flight *leftenant* has found your ticket to Volivoli," Tim said, as Holly and Robyn came out of the aircraft and walked over to them.

"Where's that dude?" Robyn asked, lifting her rifle. Tim told her, and she lowered her rifle, but was still a little wary.

"I think it will work," Holly said.

"You can't fly this straight there, can you?"

"No, it doesn't have the range. We can fly to Hickam in Hawaii first, and refuel there. I did the calculations already. It's 2,900 miles from here to Honolulu, roughly. This has a range, empty mind you, of 5,200 miles. Even if we take the vehicle, we will be okay fuel wise."

"Vehicles," he corrected her.

"Both of them?"

"Yeah," he said.

"Dad, if you do that, how will—" and then it dawned on her what he was inferring. "Oh, Daddy!" she exclaimed, and rushed up to hug him.

"So, I take it you're coming with us?" Holly asked.

"In for a penny, in for a pound, as they say. Besides, it looks like you guys need me around for protection anyway."

Izzy shook his hand, and Holly came up and wrapped her arms around him, and kissed him hard. "I had a dream last night that you were following us, coming to find us."

"Well, I must be a glutton for punishment," he said, and she smacked him on the arm playfully. "When are we leaving?"

"We'll have to top off her fuel, a few hours maybe?"

"I was just thinking of something. That would be around two or three this afternoon. How long will it take to fly there?"

"About five or six hours, I think."

"With the time difference and everything, that would put us at Hickam somewhere around midnight local time."

"I see what you mean," she said.

"What, Daddy?" Robyn asked.

"It's be dark there, honey. No runway lights and no air traffic controllers to guide us in."

"So we wait until early tomorrow morning?" Holly said.

"That's what I was thinking," Tim said, wondering what in the hell he was doing. "Robyn, go back, and bring our Hum-Vee up here. We'll stay the night."

"Okay," she said, and trotted off.

Holly turned to him and said, "Tim, you're giving up a lot. You don't have to do this."

"I know. But I figure you can always fly us back once you're settled," he said with a wink. "Besides, I think it's about time I cashed in my Frequent Flyer points on a South Pacific vacation." He then saw Jimenez walking towards them, in a very military manner. He marched up to them, stood at attention, and reported for duty.

"At ease, Lance Corporal, you look very squared away now. What did you do to your hair?" Tim said, noticing that the long locks the man had sported a short while ago were now gone, only bare skin showed from under his 'cover', as the Marines called their caps.

"I gave myself a haircut and a shave like you said, Sar' Major."

"Well, I do believe you're now in regulations. We're taking your plane, Lance Corporal. Do you have a problem with that?"

"No, sir, not at all. I'd love to see her fly!" he said. Tim ignored the 'Sir'.

"I'm so pleased that we have your approval. We'll be staying the night, and leaving first thing in the morning. Can you refuel it?"

"Sure thing, Sar' Major!" he said with a big grin.

"Then do it."

"Yes, Sir!"

"Let's go back to the office and see what's around, shall we?" Tim said to Holly and Izzy as Robyn pulled up with the other Hum-Vee.

She walked over to them, and asked, "Where's that squirrelly guy going?"

"He's going to get some more go-juice for the bird. We were just walking to the back to nose around." They walked to the rear of the hangar, and through a door into a cool air conditioned room with the fluorescent lights on. They could hear a generator humming somewhere. There was a huge counter, and Holly walked over to it and began paging through a large book. Tim went over to a refrigerator, and found it stocked with Dos Equis beer.

"At least the kid has his priorities." Tim took one and cracked it open.

"Tim, this is amazing," Holly said. "He's kept all the maintenance records for the aircraft for over the past five years. According to this, it's one of the best maintained birds I've ever seen."

"Well, everyone needs a hobby," he said, repeating what Jimenez said earlier. There was a couch and a desk, and Tim sat at the desk with his feet up. Izzy and Robyn sat on the couch, and Holly sat on the edge of the desk.

Jimenez came in after a while, sweating. "I've got the bird all fueled up, 8,000 gallons worth."

"Good," Tim said, pulling on his beer. "Where do you sleep?"

"In there," he said, pointing to another door.

"Alright, tonight the ladies will sleep in here, and the rest of us will utilize the fine luxury web seating the US government has provided for our comfort and relaxation on the plane."

They settled in, and later that afternoon ate MRE's and drank more of Jimenez' beer, except for Holly, who was following a strict twelve-hour rule of no booze before flying. Shortly after sundown they turned in for the night, but none of them really slept well. Tim, lying on his side, thought about Holly and wanted to go in and hold her, but there was really no place for privacy. Besides, he wanted her rested if she was actually going to fly this thing tomorrow. They woke before sunup, and Tim and Jimenez made short work of loading the Hum-Vees into the cargo compartment and shackling them down to the deck. Jimenez then towed he aircraft out further away from the hangar, and when everyone was on board, he shut the cargo ramp in the rear. Tim followed Holly up to the cockpit, and she sat in the left seat like she'd been doing it for years, which she had. She took a set of headphones and put them on, and as Tim climbed into the right seat, she motioned for him to do the same. When he had it plugged in, he heard her voice in the speakers.

"These are so we can hear each other talk. You want to talk to me, just press the button on the left side of the yoke."

"Check!" he said, pressing the button.

"Here goes nothing!" she said.

Tim looked over the instrument panel completely lost, and he was glad she knew what she was doing. Each Allison turboprop engine, one by one, whined to life. When all of them were warmed up, and all her gauges looked normal, Holly released the brakes and the plane began to move. She taxied the plane across several taxiways until she found the end of the runway. When the nose of the big plane was dead center, pointed right down the runway, she looked over at Tim, and winked. Tim gave an uneasy smile and a thumb up as she knocked off the brakes and throttled up the engines to full power. They screamed to life, and the plane rolled faster and faster down the runway. Tim got a little nervous when it looked like they were rapidly running out of runway, and looked over at Holly again, who was deep in concentration. In what seemed like the last minute, she pulled back hard on the yoke, and the plane virtually leapt into the air, climbing higher and higher, at what seemed like to Tim an almost 45 degree angle. All he could see ahead of them were a few puffy clouds, and blue early morning sky. She leveled out some a few minutes later, but he could still feel the Hercules climbing higher. He then heard her voice again through the headphones.

"We'll climb out to thirty thousand feet, and level off. I've got the cabin pressurized now, so it should be a decent ride!"

"Speak for yourself. I'm used to being in the back in these things," he said to her.

"Fly the friendly skies!" she said with a wide smile, and Tim smiled back, wondering why he was even doing this.

CHAPTER 19:
ALOHA HAOLE!

They had been in the air for about an hour and were flying along smoothly. Tim looked out and down at the ground so far below. They'd be reaching the coast soon, he thought, and keyed up his mike to talk to Holly.

"So, I take it the kid's PM was pretty good?"

"Aye, he's done a good job. Everything's running fine. I think the climate of Luke helped a lot too," she said.

"Yeah, the desert is good for that. There's a big airplane graveyard down near Tucson where they stored retired aircraft."

"Aye, Davis-Monthan Air Force Base. I always wanted to go and just walk around there." She went to get up, and saw the look on his face, and she smiled mischievously. "Don't worry, I've got the autopilot on!" She unstrapped from her seat and went to the rear, where the latrine was.

Tim just stared at everything, not daring to touch a thing. He felt a hand on his shoulder, and saw Robyn standing there wide-eyed. He pulled the headset off one ear, and she leaned forward. "Are you flying this?"

"No, baby! Holly's just gone to the bathroom. The autopilot is on."

"That's good, because I didn't see any parachutes!"

"Oh, so now you're a comedian?"

"Daddy, it's really loud back there!" she said crossly.

"Go ask that Jimenez joker where the earplugs are. I forgot about the noise. There should be a little box of disposable earplugs somewhere along either side of the cargo hold."

"Okay!" she said, and kissed him, disappearing to the rear. Tim was still looking out the windows, and saw the Pacific Ocean and the California coast dead ahead. He caught movement again, and Holly came back and flopped into the pilot's seat, strapping herself back in.

"Looks like we'll be over water soon," he commented.

"Aye, and you didn't touch anything!"

"Is everybody a smartass this morning?" he asked

He remembered something, and reached into his pocket, bringing out a few folded pieces of paper, handing it over to Holly. She opened the pages for a moment, and shot a look at Tim. "How did you get these?" she asked.

"That is your island, right?"

The papers that Tim gave her, printed out on a LaserJet printer, showed it was her island, an atoll really, with an opening to the sea directly west from a wide lagoon in its center. It was circular, about two miles wide, and the land area was about four hundred yards wide and shaped like the letter "C". The runway of crushed coral, laid down so many years ago by US Navy SeaBees, cut through one end and jutted out into the sea on either end. It looked like it hadn't been used in quite a while, as it was strewn with dead palm fronds from end to end, but she figured she'd still be able to land on it, because the Hercules was designed to take off and land on short, expedient strips like this. There was a coral reef that almost completely surrounded the atoll, with a channel cut into it to let ships enter the lagoon from the gap in the west side. The island was completely covered in coconut palms, save for the runway, but in this photograph she could clearly make out the two concrete structures near one end of the runway that had a long pier running out into the lagoon, another leading out to the reef, and two large fuel storage tanks. She could also see the narrow road that circled the island, only broken by the runway and the gap into the sea, and here and there, she could make out the shadows of all the bunkers, hidden away in the trees. The last thing it showed was a ship, obviously run aground and split in two, on the south side of the island. It showed what looked like its cargo of cars and SUVs spilled out into the sea around the gaping hole where it broke apart.

"It is what you said it was. 'MPPSD, Volivoli. It's not on any other listing, except for one small one on the US Navy Weather Service as a weather station. It seems like everyone at the Pentagon forgot all about this tiny little place."

"MPPSD, what's that?" she asked.

"It stands for Military Pre-Position Supply Depot," he said.

"But, Tim, the date-stamp on this photograph—"

"I know, three days ago. Izzy gave me the latitude and longitude for it, so I looked it up," he said with a grin.

"I really don't understand, Tim. Even if there were still people around, not just anyone can get this information. Look at this resolution! I can almost count the coconuts lying on the beach!"

"I know, amazing, isn't it? If a beautiful and sexy woman was sunning naked on the beach, you'd be able to tell if she was a natural redhead or not!" he said, with a wicked grin, and she slapped him.

"How did you get it?" she asked.

"I looked through a keyhole," Tim said, now toying with her.

"A keyhole?" she asked, perplexed.

"A Keyhole 11, a CIA KH11 satellite," he said. "I tasked it to do a fly-by. I've got the infrared and Doppler images too, in case there was cloud cover, which we didn't need."

"Tim, how in the world did you task a spy satellite?" she asked, now completely exasperated.

"I have access to all the satellites."

"All of them?" she gasped.

"Well, at least the US military ones. Just call me Desperado!" he said, and leaned back into the copilot's seat.

She was sitting there, not saying a word, and looked at the photographs again. She looked back over to him, and keyed her intercom. "Tim, it says here on the bottom 'NCA'. I've seen that before at NORAD."

"National Command Authority, I guess that's me now." Not wanting to tease her anymore, he went on to tell her of the crashed Air Force One, in the overgrown soybean field in Indiana, how he'd found The Football and that he still had it.

"And everything is still on line?"

"Mostly everything, there's no ships or subs, and there's a few air force bases offline, but NORAD and everything, is still up and running, including all the military satellites."

"And you've still got it?"

"Back there in my ruck, in the back seat of my Hum-Vee."

She let out a long whistle, and sat back in her seat. "Tim, you know you can't let anyone else get hold of that, right?"

"I know. That's why I've got it with me. Hadn't thought about it in years until you and Izzy showed up and started talking about your island. So I asked Iz for the coordinates and looked it up."

"Tim, you surprise me at every turn!" she said, smiling finally. "Does Robyn know what it is?"

"Yeah, she was with me when I found it. I couldn't hide it from her. She knows all about it." And then he went on to tell her of prophesies told to them by Dawn Red Eagle and everything else. "You're not upset with me, are you?"

"Oh God no, It's just now this changes everything. Instead of you protecting me, it's *us* who need to protect *you*!"

"I could just depressurize the cabin, lower the ramp and toss it into the sea," he said.

"No, you can't do that," she said, grabbing his arm.

"Why not, it would solve a lot of problems, wouldn't it?"

"Because it's important. Don't ask me why, but something is telling me we still need it."

"I have that same feeling. I don't know what it is, but I need to hold on to it right now for some reason, but it scares me too. All that power," he sighed.

"Maybe that's it," she said. "Just the fact that you have it means that someone else doesn't. And that's the most important part of all." She reached across and took his hand, and held tightly for a few moments. "Tim, I…"

He looked into her deep green eyes for a while, waiting for her to finish, but she didn't. She just smiled, and squeezed his hand.

"I'll tell you what. If you landed a C-17 on that airstrip, in the dark, with no avionics or lights, I'm really impressed with you, lady!"

"Thank you. Just doing what I was trained to do," she said, somewhat abashed.

"And another thing, that ship. Was it there when you were there?" he said, pointing to the wrecked freighter.

"No, must have washed ashore and broken up after everything happened."

"Looks like a car carrier from all those cars spilled out."

"That's exactly what I thought."

He unstrapped himself from his seat and climbed out, leaned over and kissed her, and she kissed him back. "I'm going to the latrine, and check out how everyone is in the back."

"Hurry up. It gets lonely up here!" she said, her eyes twinkling. Finding the small toilet, he availed himself, and when he was done, went to the back, and walked around the tied-down Hum-Vees, found Izzy fast asleep, lying lengthwise on the web seats. He went around the back, rounding his Hum-Vee, and got his pipe and tobacco. He saw Jimenez chatting up Robyn, or at least he was trying to. Robyn was sitting on the web seating with her feet propped up on the Hum-Vee, her left hand toying with the bayonet in its scabbard on her belt. She was eyeing Jimenez skeptically. He was sitting next to her, leaning close, and saying something Tim couldn't hear. When Robyn saw Tim, her eyes lit up, and Jimenez moved away slightly. Tim walked up to both of them, and smiled that old evil smile.

"Jimenez, that is off-limits, period."

"I was just talking to—"

Tim held up his hand. "I'll put it to you this way, Jimenez. I do know how to open these hatches in flight, and it's a long, long way down. Do I have your attention now?"

"Yes, Sar' Major!"

"Good," he said, winking at Robyn, and walked forward, leaving them alone again.

"You heard him!" she said.

"Man! What is up with the Sar' Major? Who stuck a weed up his ass today?"

"He's my Dad," Robyn said with a sweet smile.

"Oh, shit!" he said. "I think I'd better go check on things. Talk to you later, eh?"

Robyn sat back still smiling, and toyed with the hilt of her bayonet. "Yeah, you do that," she said, and when he left, burst out into laughter.

Tim made his way back to the cockpit and climbed into the copilot's seat again. When he was strapped in, and had his headphones on again, Holly keyed up.

"Everything okay back there?"

"Izzy is sound asleep, Robyn is fine, and I had to explain the dangers of deceleration sickness to Jimenez."

"Deceleration sickness?" Holly asked.

"Yeah, it's not the fall that kills you, it's the sudden stop at the end," he said. "He was sidling up to Robyn, trying to lay his Latin charm on her."

"I'll assume that she wasn't buying into it?"

"When I walked up to them, she was toying with her bayonet, and looking at him like she does a rabbit, right before she guts it."

"You've taught her well, Sar' Major!" Holly said, laughing so hard tears came to her eyes. "I really do pity the boy she finally meets!"

"I don't. He'd better have his shit together!"

As he said that, Holly looked behind her, and smiled. Tim turned to see Robyn standing there, looking at the instrument panel. He got up from his seat. "Here you go. Sit here and maybe Holly will let you fly her," he said, taking off his headphones and handing them to Robyn. "I'm going to go back and have a little nap, maybe catch the in-flight movie." He bent over, and kissed them both. "I'll leave my two favorite girls to get us there in one piece."

Holly told her how to use the intercom, and when she was comfortable with it, she asked; "You want to fly her?"

"Can I?" she said excitedly, forgetting to push the button. She fumbled for a second, then found it and pressed down. "Can I?"

"Sure. Just put your hands on the yoke, that's this thing that looks like a half steering wheel, and your feet on the pedals."

"Like this?" she asked, her hands and feet where she'd been told to put them.

"Aye, that's perfect. Now those two dials in the middle? One looks like a blue planet with wings? That's the artificial horizon. The other one that has a plane on it, that's the compass. Just use the yoke and pedals to keep them right where I have them."

"Okay," Robyn said a little bit nervously.

Holly reached over and flipped a switch, turning off the autopilot. "Now you're flying the plane!"

"Wow! This is so cool!"

Tim found Jimenez asleep on the roof of one of the Hum-Vees, and Izzy was still fast asleep too. He grabbed his coat from his Hum-Vee and rolling it up for a pillow, he lay down on the web seat. As soon as his head hit the jacket, he was fast asleep. He awoke later, as the plane was descending. The air pressure change in his inner ear gave a pop to let him know. He sat up and yawned, and put his patrol cap back on. He stood, and began to walk towards the cockpit. The plane hit a few pockets of turbulence, and he entered the flight deck on unsteady feet. He leaned on the unoccupied seat, in between and behind the copilot and pilot's seats, and looked out the windshield. He saw that they were over land, and that Holly was now flying the plane and that Robyn was watching with rapt interest.

"Hi kids!" he said, loud enough for them to hear him.

They both turned and smiled, and Holly said, "Hi sleepy head! We're just crossing over the Big Island now, and getting a little turbulence from the volcano. We should be in Honolulu in about forty minutes." Holly said, and went back to flying.

"Holly let me fly the plane for a long time! It was so cool!"

"That's great, sweetie," he said, and climbed in the middle seat, finding another set of headphones. Locating a place to plug them in took another minute, but when he finally got it all figured out, he keyed up. "Nice ride, Captain!"

"Thank you! I had a most pleasurable copilot with me on this flight."

"So how are we doing on fuel?"

"We've got plenty to spare. I'm going to make a few low passes over the runway to eyeball it before we land."

"Good idea. If I had known all of this beforehand, I would have gotten some pictures of Hickam too."

"Aye, that would have been good. But it's still daylight, and the weather looks clear, so I think a few passes should do it."

"You're the expert!" he said and sat back to enjoyed the show. Soon they were over water again, and passed Maui, Lanai then Molokai on the right, and at about two thousand feet, approached Oahu rapidly. Descending still, Holly approached Hickam, and when they had the aircraft over the runway, travelling at what looked like a ridiculously low altitude and fast speed, she climbed and banked sharply for another pass, circling out over Honolulu, and back over the water.

"There looks to be to be some damage down there. There's a few hangars destroyed for some reason, and it looks like the fuel storage tanks burned up some time ago, but the runway doesn't look like it's in too bad of shape."

She made three more passes like that, and settled into an approach pattern to land. She lowered the landing gear and flaps, the plane slowing noticeably, and as she passed the threshold, pulled the nose up slightly. When they touched down, the wheels just kissed the runway, and Tim let out a whistle. As soon as all the wheels were on the runway, she reversed the pitch on the props and throttled up, pushing the air out in front of them, instead of pulling them through the air, effectively slowing the plane down rapidly.

What Holly didn't see on her three passes was a small, unexploded softball-sized bomblet, which had been sitting on the concrete runway for over five years, and had survived typhoons and several storms. It had remained unexploded there since the cruise missile the USS *Hughes* targeted there had dropped them. Sometimes they all didn't explode, and this was one of them that didn't. They were still rolling out, going about fifty miles an hour, when the right landing gear hit it. It was then that it decided to do what it was designed to do, and exploded spectacularly with a loud bang. The wheels collapsed, the aircraft banked into make a wide right hand turn, and the wing dipped. Holly slammed the throttles to neutral, cut the fuel to the engines, and there was nothing more she could do as everyone held their breath and held on. The plane slid on almost sideways for about another hundred yards with a sickening screech of metal on concrete, until it finally came to rest halfway down the runway. No one said a word for several seconds, just stared out the windscreen, and watched the dust settle. Then Tim heard the intercom click, and Holly's voice.

"I would like to thank all the passengers on behalf of the entire crew for flying MacFarland Airlines today, and we hope you've had a pleasant journey. I must remind all the passengers to remain seated until the aircraft has come to a complete stop at the terminal."

"What the fuck happened?" Tim asked, taking off his headset, and unbuckling his harness.

"I don't know. We hit something on the runway."

"That was exciting," Robyn said, looking over at them both, slack-jawed.

Tim got up. "I'm going back to see if everyone else is okay," then he disappeared to the cargo hold.

"Man that was scary!" Robyn said again.

"Aye, that usually doesn't happen," Holly said. She and Robyn both got up and went to the rear to find the side hatch already open, and no one to be found. They went outside into the afternoon sun, and saw Tim and Izzy looking at the shredded landing gear, and Jimenez already underneath, looking around. He crawled back out from inside the landing gear bay.

"Well?" Tim asked.

"Landing gear is fucked. I don't know what we hit, but it shredded the shit out of all the tires and collapsed the first strut. And all these little holes... no telling what kind of damage is inside. Looks almost like shrapnel or flack damage."

"I didn't see anything on the runway," Holly said.

"I know. It wasn't your fault," Tim said to her, turning to Jimenez. "I'm going to take a walk back down the runway. See if you can get the Hum-Vees out, and then see if there's any more damage."

Tim walked off down the runway while the rest of the group helped lower the ramp to get the Hum-Vees out. Jimenez was back looking through the damage, and Izzy, Holly and Robyn, sat on the front of one of the Hum-Vees. They watched Tim walk around, looking at the ground, kicking things here and there with his boot, all the while puffing on his pipe.

"I don't know what it could have been, Iz," Holly said.

"I don't know either, Holly. But I think Tim knows," he said, pointing down the runway.

"Sounded like a bomb," Robyn said.

"Aye, it did."

"But why would a bomb be on the runway?" Izzy asked, not expecting an answer.

Jimenez walked up to them, wiping his hands on a rag. "Excuse me, ma'am?" he said to Holly. "Besides the landing gear, whatever it was took out three hydraulic lines and an electrical harness."

"Can they be fixed?"

"Yes, ma'am. I can go over to the hangars and see if there's another Herc. Probably is, and I can take the parts I need off of it. Bad news is, it'll probably take me a few days."

"Then go ahead and look."

"Ma'am, do you think it'd be okay if I had my rifle back?" he asked sheepishly.

"I don't know, Lance Corporal. Are you going to be waving it at us again?" she said, with a little grin.

"No, ma'am! I promise."

"Alright," she said, getting up and getting it out of Tim's Hum-Vee. She handed it to him, along with a loaded magazine.

"Be right back!" he said, taking off at a jog towards the nearest hanger.

Tim saw him heading towards the hangars and started walking back to the plane. When he got there he asked, "Where'd he go off to?"

"He went to see if he can find another Hercules to cannibalize parts from," Holly said.

"So he thinks he can fix it?"

"Aye, but he said it will take a few days. Did you find anything down there?"

"Yeah." he said, and handed over a twisted piece of metal that was scorched. "It was a bomblet, probably from a cruise missile. That's what all the other damage is from over that way," he said, pointing to the destroyed fuel tanks and hangars.

"Why would anyone launch a cruise missile at Hawaii?" Izzy asked.

"That I don't know. It wasn't recent, but it would have been after The Event, that's for sure."

"That's just crazy," Robyn said.

"They come off of ships, don't they?" Holly asked.

"Yep, and subs," he said.

"But I thought you said all the ships were offline?"

"The ones with nukes on board are, I haven't a clue about any others," Tim said, shaking his head. Izzy looked perplexed at the conversation, and when Tim gave him a Cliff-Notes version, his eyes grew wide.

"But why launch one here?" Izzy asked again.

"That's one thing we'll probably never know. Let's drive over to see what Don Juan is up to," he said, walking to his Hum-Vee. They all followed, and taking both the vehicles, drove out over the taxiway towards the hangars, Tim in the lead with a sharp eye out for anymore unexploded bomblets. They pulled up in front of the hangar Tim had seen Jimenez walk into, and the huge doors were ajar. They all walked in, and heard metallic clanks coming from a C-130 sitting inside. There were several windows broken, and puddles of water on the floor. They could also hear water dripping from somewhere. Tim walked over to the aircraft and called inside the darkened cargo bay. He saw the light from a flashlight, and then Jimenez appeared at the door, smiling.

"Hey, Sar' Major. I can scrounge all the parts I need off this crate, and get ours fixed up cherry in a few days."

"Good. You need anything?"

"Nah, I got this for now. I will need a hand when I have to change out the landing gear struts and tires though. I'm just getting the hydraulic lines and wiring harness I need right now."

"Okay, you do that. We're going to set up camp right here."

Jimenez nodded, disappearing back into the cargo hold, and Tim walked back and told everyone to get comfortable. Robyn and Izzy said they were going to look around some in the hangars, and Tim told them to be careful. He went back outside, followed by Holly. He sat down on the ground with his back resting on the outside wall of the hangar, and Holly sat down next to him, putting her head on his shoulder.

"I can picture it perfectly, just sitting here."

"Picture what?" she asked.

"I can see where the Japanese planes came, swooping down on that Sunday morning. See it all in my mind," he said, pointing over to Ford Island, where all the battleships were moored so long ago. He could see the USS *Missouri* from where he sat, and he thought she looked pretty sad. Listing to one side, her entire superstructure was now layered with a coating of white bird droppings, her gray sides streaked with rust.

"Sad way for that old girl to go, isn't it?"

"Aye, it is."

"And look at the flag over the USS *Arizona* monument. Before we go, I need to get over there and replace it," he said, pointing out the torn and tattered Stars and Stripes.

"We'll do that, Tim," she said, seeing tears forming in his eyes.

"There are so many dead, here and all over the world, and for what?"

"I don't know, Tim," she said softly, and held him tighter. They sat silently until the sun dropped below the hills to the west, and they got up holding hands. They went back into the hangar, and found Izzy and Robyn.

"We found a room in the back with a bunch of couches we can all sleep on tonight," Izzy said.

"That sounds good. We'll have to settle for MRE's tonight," Tim said.

They walked back to the rear. Jimenez had found a few lanterns, and had them lit inside the room. It looked like a break room of some sort but had a musty, stale smell to it. There was a refrigerator on the far wall, but Tim decided not to open it; no telling what sort of science projects were growing in it. They ate, and bedded down for the night. Tim looked over at Holly on her couch, wishing he could go and hold her, then his mind began to wander, and he thought about the way she filled out that flight suit and drifted off to sleep with that image in is head.

The next day Jimenez got busy with the repairs, and Robyn and Holly offered to help. Tim liked that in Holly. A lot of officers didn't like to get down and dirty with the troops, especially the British ones he found, but there she was with her sleeves rolled up wielding a wrench.

Tim looked over at Izzy. "Want to go for a drive?"

"Sure. Beats sitting around here."

He told the others what they were doing, hopped into the Hum-Vee, and drove off towards the front gate.

"What's your plan today, Tim?" Izzy asked.

"I was thinking of scaring up a flag and trying to find a way over to the Arizona monument to replace the ratty one there."

"That's a nice gesture, Tim."

"They're my brothers, too," he said, and Izzy nodded. "You never talked about your time in the Navy. I guess it wasn't too eventful, eh?"

"Oh, I had more than my fair share of excitement. I was Brown Water Navy, Mekong Delta, 70' and 71'."

"PBRs huh? Yeah, I understand why you don't talk about it then."

"True, but it wasn't all bad. Got out then, and went to medical school, and lived a good life after that. I've been meaning to ask you. That old grease gun you have strapped to your rucksack. I haven't seen one of those in years. Where did you get that?"

"About a year after I got on the police department, I was only about twenty-two or so, I get this call on the radio, see this woman, unknown problem."

"I thought you had found it after everything happened."

"No, I've had it a long time," Tim said. "Anyway, I get to the address, and this older woman answers the door, very happy to see me. She told me that her husband had recently died, and when she was going through his things, found 'this old gun he must have brought back from the war', and didn't know what to do with it. So I said 'let me take a look at it', and she brings out this old satchel and there's the grease gun, extra magazines, a .45 auto and a Luger. I closed the bag and told her not to worry, that I'd take care of them for her!"

Izzy laughed hard. "And you sure took care of them alright! I'm sure you'd have been in big trouble if you'd been found out."

"That I would have, but I knew what would have happened to them if I turned them in. I couldn't let a few pieces of history go to the smelter like that," he said, as they drove through the main gate out onto the street. As he was turning, a loud crack startled them. It sounded like a rock had hit the windshield, and Tim slammed on his brakes as another crack was heard. The corner of the windshield starred, and a small hole appeared. He slammed the Hum-Vee into reverse and backed up all the way to the main gate guardhouse. Grabbing his carbine, he went to get out, and said to Izzy, "Stay here!"

"Don't worry about that, I'll stay right here!" Izzy said fearfully.

Pulling the charging handle to load a round into the chamber, he rounded the Hum-Vee and took cover by the guardhouse. It was then he noticed the walls were pockmarked with bullet holes, and he looked on the ground and saw several empty shell casings lying about. He picked one up. A 7.62x39. *An AK-47*. He dropped the shell, peered around the building, and saw nothing.

"I am getting entirely too fucking old for this shit!" He shook his head in anger.

"Hey!" he yelled out. "Why are you shooting at me?"

He heard nothing for a few seconds, then someone yelled back, "You just stay where you are, and don't come into town, okay?"

"Why the fuck not?" he yelled back.

"Because of what you did the last time you fuckers were here, that's why!"

"Last time?" he called out. "I've never been here before! Who the fuck are you?"

"Staff Sergeant Williams, US Army!" the voice called back. Now Tim was getting really pissed. He stood up and exposed himself, feeling the gun sights on him. "Well I'm Sergeant Major Flannery, US Army and I'm coming out there to talk to you, Goddamn it!"

He started to walk out into the open, into the middle of the street, the M4 hanging limply off his shoulder. He spread out his arms and looked around.

"Okay, asshole. Shoot me or come out here and talk!" He waited a full minute before he saw a man pop up out of the weeds across the street holding an M4 on him. He was a tall black man, about Tim's height, and he was dressed in older green jungle utilities, like the ones Tim had worn in the Ranger Regiment. His face was painted with camouflage paint and his green patrol cap had a perfect 'Ranger Curve' to it also. Tim put his hands on his hips as the man got nearer, and when he reached out to frisk him, Tim spoke up.

"You touch me, and I'll take that rifle and beat you with it. I said we talk, not play grab-ass."

"Well, you sure sound like a Sergeant Major," the man said, straightening.

"Now what's this 'before' shit? We've just flown in from the mainland yesterday. You didn't hear the fucking Hercules fly over?"

"We thought it was the same people who came a few years ago on the ship. We got word of them tearing around the Pacific, kidnapping people, especially the women, and basically spreading mayhem like a bunch of pirates from the seventeenth century."

"Got word on them how?"

"By ham radio. There used to be a bunch of stations all over the place, all along the Pacific Rim. Then he found out about them, and one by one, got rid of them somehow. At least that's what we think, because they'd transmit he was back, then they'd be off the air."

"So, it was like a sailing ship?"

"No, a goddamn US Navy ship is what it was. Aegis class destroyer."

"So when they came here the last time did they by any chance lob a cruise missile at you?" Tim asked. He felt like he was in an episode of *The Twilight Zone*.

"Yeah, they did, few of them, as a matter of fact. Three went into the jungle north of here, but one plastered Hickam pretty good."

"I know. It damaged our plane landing. One of the bomblets didn't go off until we hit it. So you're telling me some rogue captain is sailing the seas, swashbuckling like Errol Flynn?"

"About like that, Sar' Major."

"Well, I'll be dipped in dogshit," he said, pulling out and lighting his pipe. "Come with me, I want to make sure my passenger is alright. He's seventy years old, and you've probably given him a heart attack."

"Sorry, Sar' Major, but we weren't sure."

"We?" Tim asked.

Williams raised his hand in a circular motion and ten more men stood up from the weeds. They had been there the whole time, camouflaged so well, that even Tim didn't make them.

"I'm impressed," Tim said.

"I was a Ranger and instructor at the jungle school here."

"We've got something in common, Sergeant. I was first 'Batt', Sua Sponte," Tim said, holding out his hand, and Williams, now smiling, took it.

"I was Third Batt. Sua Sponte!" Williams said, repeating the Ranger motto in Latin. The men headed off towards town, and Williams followed Tim over to the Hum-Vee, with Tim making the introductions.

"You're a doctor?" Williams asked.

"And I've never been on TV," Izzy said with a smile.

"We could sure use you, Doc. We got one sick kid in town. He's badly infected, and really sick."

"Take us there then," Izzy said, now feeling a lot less like a third wheel. They piled into the Hum-Vee, and Williams gave the directions.

"We've got a few professions around, but no doctor. We had a nurse until two years ago. She decided to go over to the big island with her partner and hasn't been back."

Tim pulled up in front of a small cottage with an overgrown front yard, and they all got out and started to walk towards the front door. An attractive Eurasian woman with long dark hair and a worried look, came to the door to meet them.

"Mary, this is Doctor Ginsberg, and Sar' Major Flannery. They're here to help Billy," Williams said, and you could see the relief on her face. The woman showed them the boy's bedroom, and they found a boy with Asian features but snow-white blonde hair lying on the bed, obviously very sick. Izzy brushed by them all and sat down next to the boy. The other three left him to do his work, and went out to the living room.

"How old is the boy, ma'am?" Tim asked.

"He'll be six this year. I hope he gets better, he's all I have left."

"Izzy will fix him up, ma'am."

Izzy came out and asked for a sheet of paper, which Mary got for him. He wrote down a long list of things and handed it over to Tim. "I need those things. Go to a pharmacy or better yet, the hospital, and get all of those things listed. Some of the equipment you can forgo if you can't find it, but the drugs are a must. He's one very sick boy, indeed. Hopefully, with those drugs and other things, I'll be able to get him better."

Tim handed the paper to Williams. "Take the Hum-Vee and I'll stay here. You know your way around here, I don't."

Izzy told them it was a bad case of tetanus, and he needed some heavy duty antibiotics.

"He was playing in the yard next door and cut himself on a nail or something," Mary said.

"That will do it. I'm going back in with the boy. I'll keep you informed," he said, and went back into the bedroom. Tim sat down on the couch, and Mary sat on a chair across from him. "His father is on that ship."

"You mean when they were here he—"

"No, no! We met before it sailed for the Indian Ocean. We dated for several months. He's an officer, or he was. I don't know if he's dead or not."

"So he doesn't know?"

"No. I didn't know I was pregnant until after they sailed. I thought about emailing him several times, but I lost my nerve," she said, looking at her hands.

"You don't think he's got anything to with what the ship has been doing?"

"No, I don't think that. Bill was a kind, gentle man. He'd never condone what they've been doing."

"And you're sure it's his ship?" Tim asked, and then felt bad, because he thought he was beginning to sound like a cop.

"Yes, it's his ship. The USS *Phillip J. Hughes*. The big '193' on the bow says it all," she said, getting up to make some tea. When she was finished she came out with two cups and handed Tim one. They sat and drank in silence, and Tim looked around the room where he saw a photo of Mary and a bear of a towheaded man. They both were wearing loud Hawaiian shirts, standing arm in arm on the bow of the *Missouri*, and smiling. He guessed that was Bill. They made uncomfortable small talk for about an hour before they heard the Hum-Vee pull up. Tim went outside and helped Williams unload everything and bring it to Izzy. He asked Mary to stay and help him, and Tim pulled Williams outside.

"So tell me the whole story, Williams," Tim said, pulling out his pipe and lighting a bowl.

"Well, the best we can figure is this. Right after everything went to shit, someone took charge of that ship and started going from port to port, taking everything that wasn't nailed down, including people. With each place they stopped, they got more and more brutal. After a while, when people overcame the shock of what happened, ham transmitters started to pop up all over the Pacific. We thought we were alone out here, but apparently we weren't." He paused and looked out over the neighborhood.

"Go on," Tim urged.

"By the time they got here, we had prepared for them, and gave them a little welcoming party when they tried to leave the base. They never got off the base, but they got what they were after here anyway," he said with a grimace.

"And that was?"

"They grabbed the nukes from the base from where they were stored. And now he's after the codes."

Tim let out a long whistle. "And then what?"

"He left here, lobbed a few cruise missiles at us, but they didn't hit anything of importance. He sailed south from here, and one by one, every little transmitter started disappearing."

"You keep on saying 'he'. Who's 'he'?"

"Whoever is now in command of that goddamn ship."

"And you haven't heard from him since?"

"Well, sort of. We know he's in Tahiti, been there for a while. He's been talking to some girl in Arizona, and apparently she's got the codes and everything, or at least her dad has them."

Tim felt like he'd been kicked in the stomach, and sat down on the steps.

"Are you okay, Sar' Major?" Williams said, seeing Tim go pale.

"Yeah, go on."

"Like I was saying, he's in Tahiti and wants those codes, but I don't think he's willing to travel north to the mainland then walk to Arizona for them."

"I need a drink," Tim said, cocking his patrol cap back on his head. "Let me ask you something, Williams. Have you heard this girl talking to them recently?"

"I don't know about last night. All of us were busy and no one was monitoring the radio, but the last time she talked to him was a few nights ago."

"Okay, I really need a drink."

"Some water?"

"No, whiskey, bourbon, vodka, that kind of drink."

"Why? What's wrong?"

Tim told him everything, and it was Williams' turn to pale and sit down. "Oh fuck!"

"Yeah, oh fuck," Tim said, lighting his pipe and puffing away.

"Listen, Sar' Major, I wouldn't be too hard on the kid. The operator he's got down there in Tahiti is a real player. Played her like a violin. At first I think he was just bored and heard it was a girl on the other end of the Morse key, but then one night she let something slip, and he grabbed on and played her, and she walked right into his grasp."

"I know, I'm angry and sad all at the same time, Sergeant," Tim said.

"The name's Jerry," Williams said. "Jerome Williams, but everyone calls me Jerry."

"Tim. Call me Tim, but not in front of the troops, okay?" he smirked. "Now, Jerry, we get to figure this one out all by ourselves with no officers involved."

"Just the way I like it, Tim! I just saw a little flash go off in your eyes. What's on your mind?"

"You said that as far as you know, they still think we're in Arizona, right?"

"As far as we know, that's correct," Jerry said.

"And your men, would they be willing to do a little travelling to take care of some business?" Tim asked, a smile growing on his face.

"Most of the men are islanders, not Haole like us. These fucks on that boat have been going around kidnapping and raping every islander they come across. My men will travel."

"And you've got them pretty well up to speed on most everything?"

"Fuckin' A I do!"

Tim stood and Jerry did the same. "Jerry, what's the one thing we both learned in jungle school?"

"Ambush!" Jerry said, with a broad grin.

"How to set up and then execute a pisser of an ambush. Now let's you and I go back to the base and explain it to my people, and while we're at it I'll explain to a very naïve young girl the real meaning of COMSEC."

"Sar' Major, I have a feeling this is the beginning of a beautiful relationship!"

"So do I, Sergeant. Now let's tell Izzy what we're doing," Tim said, and went into the house. He told Izzy they were headed back to the base, and Izzy said for them to go, he'd be staying here with the sick boy, and would probably stay the night. Tim and Jerry got into the Hum-Vee and drove off in the direction of the base.

"Didn't get a chance to tell you this, and it might help for whatever you got cooking. We've been in contact with a group of Aussies for a few years."

"I thought they could hear your transmitter?"

"The ham bands they can. This is on an old analog single side band military channel from World War II that nobody uses anymore, and we're using a code of Pidgin English and Tagalog. The same as the Coastwatchers used. I doubt seriously they'd figure it out, even if they did hear us."

"Yeah?" Tim said, grip tightening on the wheel.

"The Aussies never had to worry about the Cold War, so most of their shit was never hardened for EMP, what I think zapped all the electronics. Anyway, there's a group of about twenty-five Aussies led by some naval officer down there in Darwin trying to get a warship ready to sail because all their shit was fucked, and they want a piece of this fucker."

"Really, that's interesting. How long before they can sail?" Tim asked.

"I'm not sure, but I think they're almost ready, and it would be nice to work them into the plan."

"Jerry, remember how it was in the Ranger Regiment?"

"I do."

"We'll, it's going to be like that all over again. A bunch of really pissed off eighteen and nineteen year olds, armed to the teeth, and absolutely no adult supervision!" Tim grinned. *But then again*, he thought, *we aren't eighteen and nineteen year olds anymore*. He started to whistle 'Waltzing Matilda' as they drove through the front gate.

CHAPTER 20:
THE ISLAND

Tim and Jerry pulled up in front of the hangar, and went inside to find Robyn, Holly and Jimenez taking a break by the Hercules they were cannibalizing, drinking warm sodas. They were surprised the see Williams, but after Tim made the introductions, they settled down. When he had everyone's attention, he gave them a full briefing on everything Jerry had told him. When he was done, he lit his pipe and puffed away, looking right at Robyn, who had her head down and was looking at her hands.

She looked up, and with tears in her eyes said, "Daddy, I'm so sorry."

"Robyn, I am very angry with you. But it wasn't entirely your fault. Like Sergeant Williams said, this guy played you like a fiddle."

"Tim," Holly said, "if all this is true, we don't have to do this. We can just fly back to Arizona."

"Yeah, I'm all for that!" Jimenez said excitedly.

"No, we're not. I've got a plan, and Robyn?" he said, and she looked at him, about to break out in tears. "You're the key in this."

"Me? How am I the key? I screwed everything up!" she said, trying hard to hold back tears.

"Let me ask you this. Have you talked to this 'Jimmy' fuck since we've left the house?"

"No, I brought my radio so I could, but I haven't had the chance 'cause we've been working on the plane."

"Perfect. Taco, you said the bird will be fixed in a few days?" he said, turning to Jimenez.

"Yeah, Sar' Major. We've already got the hydraulic lines and the wiring harness swapped out. Now I've got to change out these struts and tires. That's the heavy part, and I can't do it alone."

"I can help with that," Jerry said.

"So if you have help, how long?"

"A day, day and a half maybe, and it's Jimenez, Sar' Major."

"It's easier to say Taco than Jimenez so now you're Taco," he said, turning back to Holly. "Here's what I've got planned. Robyn here will tell this Jimmy fuck that we're still in Arizona, but have found a plane, and we're heading to this island for good. She'll tell him we'll be there in, oh I don't know, two, three weeks maybe?" he said, looking at Williams, who nodded.

"And then what?" Holly asked.

"In the meanwhile, we get this bird fixed and with about ten of Sergeant Williams' men, we fly down there as fast as we can, set up an ambush and wait for the Good Ship Lollypop to show up."

"That's crazy!" Jimenez said.

"How do you know he'll show up?" Robyn asked.

"I think he will."

"But won't he see the plane on the runway and know something's wrong?" Holly asked.

"They won't see the Hercules because it won't be there!" Williams said.

"Won't be there?" Holly echoed.

"After you drop us off, you and Robyn will take the plane somewhere else. Our island is directly between the Marshall Islands and Kiribati. Howland and Baker islands are southeast about a thousand miles, and Palmyra Atoll is about fifteen hundred miles due east. You'll refuel at Volivoli, fly to one of those islands, and wait to come back and get us," Tim explained.

"And how will we know when to come back?" Holly asked, with concern on her face.

"We'll let you know by radio."

"Eh, Sar' Major, you said the lieutenant and Robyn fly out. Who's going to help them refuel at those other islands, or fix the bird if she breaks? They need me to go with them," Jimenez said nervously.

"No, they'll be fine. They're big girls and can figure out how the get JP5 into the fuel tanks."

"But I'm just a jet engine mechanic!" Jimenez said. "I should stay with the plane!"

"Taco, what is it that I've been hearing for years and years about you jarheads? Oh, I remember now. It's how every single last swinging dick is a rifleman first, no matter if he's a cook or mechanic. Time to show me how fucking great you jarheads are," he said with a smirk. "Now get back to work fixing this thing."

Jimenez said nothing, but was visibly shaken. Robyn walked up to Tim. "Daddy. I'm really sorry I caused all this mess. But I can't go with Holly. I'm staying with you. I want a chance to get at this Jimmy guy too!"

"That's not happening. You are going with Holly when she takes the plane out, and there's not going to be any arguments over it."

"But I'm just as good as Sergeant Williams' guys! You taught me everything you know!"

"That I did, but this is a little different. I promised you a long time ago that I'd always protect you, and having you far away from this when it starts is the best way I know how."

"But I want to help!"

"And you will be helping, baby. You're going to be the one who sets the trap," he said with a big grin.

"But—"

"End of discussion. I'm not going to change my mind. Now go and help Taco, and if he tries to get cute again, remind him I promoted you to corporal so he didn't outrank you, and if he persists, cut his nuts off."

She grumbled her complaints and stalked off.

"She's got spirit, I'll give her that. Hard to believe that's who was behind that Morse key. The girl is fast!" Williams said.

"You're telling me! Now let's go hash out some details. Holly, do you still have that photograph?"

"It's in my flight bag."

"Good, let's all three of us go into the back and look it over."

They went to the break room in the back of the hangar and sat down at the table. Jerry looked over the photograph, and smiled. "Yeah, this has a lot of potential. There are plenty of spots along here where all the bunkers are."

"What kind of firepower do you have?" Tim asked.

"I can get everything that the 25th Division has."

"Be nice if we could put a Bradley on the bird," Tim sighed. "But they're too heavy. Could you get a few TOWs?" Tim asked, meaning 'Tube launched, Optically sighted, Wire guided' anti-tank missile.

"That'd be about the biggest we could come up with. Everything else is too big to be man-portable. And we could put a nice hole in the ship's hull with it."

"If this place is a Pre-Position Depot, there should be plenty of things already there we can use too," Tim added.

Williams stood up. "Well, I'd better go and talk to the men, then head over to Schofield for a little shopping trip."

"I'll go with you. I'd like to meet them also, and talk to them. I'm the one who'll actually be asking them to risk their lives, and I'd better let Izzy know what we're doing too."

Holly came over to Tim, hugged and kissed him. "You be careful, Tim."

"I will. Be back soon," he said, and he and Jerry walked out to the Hum-Vee. They got in, and drove off towards the main gate again.

"Sar' Major," Jerry said, "I know this may be none of my business, but you were a lot more 'friendly' with the lieutenant than what's normally accepted."

Tim laughed and lit his pipe. "Let us just say, Jerry, the Leftenant and I have been fraternizing in an unlawful manner according to the UCMJ for some time." (The Uniform Code of Military Justice, UCMJ, states unequivocally that enlisted personnel should never, ever, have any kind of personal relations with the officers.)

"She is a looker, I have to say," Jerry said appreciatively.

"That she is, and one hell of a pilot. You saw that little coral strip on the island?" Tim asked.

"Yeah."

"Well she landed a C-17 on it, at night, with no instruments."

"No shit?"

"And the landing we made here, before we hit that bomblet? She kissed the runway so smoothly, that if you were standing in the middle of the cargo hold, holding onto nothing but a gin and tonic, you wouldn't have spilled a drop. That's how good that lady is."

"That's pretty damn smooth."

"And to think, I almost shot her down," he said with an evil grin.

"Oh? How so?" Jerry asked, and Tim told him the story of Iraq, and Jerry almost wet himself laughing.

"Oh, shit that's funny!"

"She didn't think it was all that funny at the time."

"And to figure you guys met up after all this time."

"Yeah, it is. But don't let on you know that story. I think it may still be a sore spot for her," Tim said. "So what's your story?"

"Not much to tell, Tim. I'm originally from New Orleans and enlisted right out of high school. I got orders for Schofield right after my last tour over in the sandbox, and was here for about eighteen months before everything went to shit."

"What then, after that?" Tim asked.

"I thought I was alone for a while, and then I started to meet up with others, one or two at a time. A few others and I started getting things organized, getting the power on and making sure everyone had food. Once we got the transmitter set up, we found others all over the Pacific. That's when we got word on the ship, and what they were doing. I put together a little reception committee for them for when they got here."

"That was pretty effective," Tim said.

"Yeah, but this whole thing puts a new twist onto everything. Do you really think we can pull it off?"

"I hope so, for everyone's sake," Tim said, not sounding all that sure.

They drove on to Mary's house, and went inside. Tim found Izzy drinking a cup of tea with Mary in the living room.

"So how's the boy?" Tim asked when they walked through the door.

"He's still very sick, Tim. I've got him filled with antibiotics right now, and I hope they'll work, having been around so long, way past their expiration date."

"Iz, we're going to be leaving here in a few days for the island. It's going to be a lot more dangerous than we thought. I just wanted to ask you if it's okay, that you just stay here with the boy and make sure he gets better."

"Yes, I figured as much. Mary's told me about the ship. So you are going to take care of him? The captain of that ship that is?"

"Yes. I figure you'd be better off here taking care of the kid, if that's alright with you," Tim said, feeling a little bit uncomfortable.

"Tim, don't worry. I need to be here for at least a week to see to the boy. And it is nice to have a patient again. If I was thirty years younger, I'd be taking your grease gun and coming along with you, because a man like that needs to be taken care of. He's a disgrace to the US Navy," he said, looking at the floor and shaking his head. "But you go and you take care of yourself. Robyn and Holly need you."

"I will, Iz. You take care of yourself, and get this kid better, okay?"

"You got it, Sergeant Major!" Izzy said, shaking Tim's hand. He pulled Tim close and gave him a warm hug. "You bring Holly and Robyn back to me, you hear?"

"I will, Iz."

"Shalom! Now get out of here!"

"Shalom, Iz," Tim said, and walked outside with Jerry. Getting back into the Hum-Vee, they drove a few miles and stopped at another house. There were several men standing around outside. Jerry gathered them all together, introduced Tim, then went on to explain what they were going to do. When he was finished, he asked, "Anybody want out?"

There were no dissenters. One dark skinned man in the back spoke up. "I had a mother and sister in Papua, New Guinea. I hate to think what that fucker's done to them if they're still alive. Fuckin' A, bro! I'm in!"

Tim welcomed them all on board and did a head count, twelve of them. Plus Jerry, himself and Jimenez made fifteen. He hoped it was enough to go against an Aegis destroyer. Williams gave one of them a shopping list, and half departed for Schofield barracks. The others volunteered to go to the base and help with the repairs to the plane. Tim sat down on the lanai and lit his pipe.

"What do you think, Tim?" Jerry asked him.

He laughed. "I'm thinking have I lost my mind?"

"I'm thinking the same thing, Tim. We must be mad to be doing this, but I think it needs to be done."

"Yeah, I feel the same," Tim said.

A man came out of the house and spoke to Jerry for a few minutes, and he turned to Tim to fill him in. "It seems like the Aussies are ready to sail at the end of the week. I sent them the coordinates to the island and they said they'd be there in about seventeen to twenty days."

"That is good news. They know of the plan?"

"Not all of it. I told them I'd message the rest once we got set up on Volivoli," Jerry said.

"Good. I hope they can get there in time."

"Agreed. Why don't you head back to the base? I'll get everything organized and meet you back there, say, around 1830?"

"That sounds good. Thanks for everything, Jerry. You don't have to do this."

"No problem. It feels good to be going out and doing what I was trained to do again. And besides, that bastard needs to be dealt with, and I'm more than happy to be a part of it."

"Let's just hope we can pull this fucked up abortion off," Tim said. He shook Jerry's hand and got into the Hum-Vee, driving back to the base. When he got there and approached the plane, he saw it up on jacks and a whole gang of men working on it. He pulled up, and they ignored him, continuing to work under the direction of Jimenez.

"They came pulling up about an hour ago and frightened the hell out of us," Holly said. "Then they said they came to help, and with Jimenez' direction, got right into it. They should be done in about an hour."

"Outstanding! So much for Taco's two to three day estimate he gave us."

"Aye, I know. We should be able to leave first thing in the morning," Holly said, taking his hand. They walked together to the side of the hanger where they had sat the day before. They sat down with their backs against the wall.

"Tim, I'm really worried about this."

"So am I, but I have to do it."

"Somehow I think this is my entire fault. Once we met you and Robyn, we should have just stayed put at your place. We were all safe there."

"Eh, what do we need with clean sheets, running water and electricity anyway?" Tim said with a wry smile.

"I mean it, Tim. I'm not ready to lose you."

"You were ready to walk away in Arizona," Tim said flatly.

"Aye, but you were ready to let me go."

"I felt like Rick at the end of *Casablanca*," he said and Holly laughed. "It's like this, Holly. I feel this is bigger than you and me. If we pack up and go home, these people here will never be safe. The whole Pacific will never be safe, unless we do something to get rid of this guy. We've done that far too many times in the past, left people who thought we were friends hang out to dry as we pulled up stakes and left. This time we play by our own rules, there won't be any politicians in Washington or London setting the rules that only one side will abide by."

"And what rules will you have?"

"There won't be any rules." He kissed her head and sighed, and looked out over the dead base.

"I just want you to come back to me."

"I will. I'm too goddamn ornery to kill," he said.

Two military trucks were pulling up, M35's, or 'Deuce and a half" trucks. Tim and Holly got up and walked over to see the rest of Williams' men unloading crates and cases.

"And what kind of goodies do you have there, Sergeant?" Tim asked Jerry.

"Oh, shit Sar' Major! I feel like a kid on Christmas morning. We got all kinds of good shit. Ammo for the M4's, got an M60, frags, and claymores. Can't have an ambush without claymores, can we?"

"It would be unheard of, Sergeant. claymores add dignity to what would otherwise be a vulgar brawl! Did you get a TOW?"

"We found a few TOW launchers, but oddly enough, no TOW missiles. That was fucking odd. But we did get a few AT4s," he said, meaning Anti-Tank 4 rocket, a small man-portable rocket launcher that replaced the M72A2 LAW rocket in the late 1980s.

"That will have to do."

"We're ready to go as soon as the lieutenant says the bird is ready," Jerry said, looking at Holly.

"Jimenez says it should be ready in a few hours. It's too late to fly out this afternoon. We'll just get her ready and fueled, and fly out first thing in the morning," Holly said.

"What about the Hum-Vees?" Williams asked.

"I think we just take mine with the Ma Deuce and leave the other one here."

"Okay, Sar' Major, now if you'll excuse me, I'll go see to the preparations and get everything set for tomorrow."

"Roger that, Sergeant. And if you see my wayward child, tell her to come see me," Tim said, and Williams nodded before going off to his men. Tim looked at Holly. "See? I'm in good hands."

"Aye, I'm happy to see you now have adult supervision."

They walked into the hangar and back to the break room, where he found Robyn putting away her radio.

"Did you talk with him?" Tim said, when he came up to her.

"Yeah, he was really excited. Said he was going to get his boat ready, and sail up to meet me."

"Good. You did good, Robyn. Consider yourself absolved," he said, and hugged her.

"I'm still really sorry, Daddy."

"What's done is done. The important part is what you just did now. Now all we have to get down there and lure him into our trap. Do you really think he fell for it?"

"Yeah, Dad, I told him exactly what you told me to tell him. The power on this little radio isn't like my big one at home, so it will look like to him I'm talking from a lot farther away and think that I'm still in Arizona."

"Then that's all we need. Once we get down there tomorrow, I'll still have you talk to him, feeding him lines of bullshit until you guys have to take the plane somewhere else."

"I still want to kill him. I feel like such an idiot for falling for his shit, Dad."

"You just leave that to me. I'll take care of him, don't you worry about that," he said. "Now go see if Taco needs any help out there."

That evening, they sat around swapping stories of The Event, and everyone told almost the same story, waking up with terrible sunburn, feeling like they had a hangover, the coppery taste in their mouths, and the extra-bright star in the sky for weeks afterwards. They discussed how they'd all met up with one another, and finally them hearing of the ship, and their ambush, how Williams had taught them all the basics to resist. Some had been in the military, some hadn't, but all were ready they said, ready and eager. Tim hoped they were.

The entire group slept in and around the plane that night, and in the morning they all helped load the Hum-Vee into the cargo hold, and shackle it down. Then Jimenez had everyone do a 'FOD' walk— Foreign Object Damage— down the runway to pick up everything bigger than a pebble so as not to do any damage to the Hercules when it took off. When everyone was seated in the web seats along each bulkhead, Tim went and shut the cargo ramp while Holly fired up the engines and Jimenez made sure everyone had earplugs.

Tim went up to the cockpit and strapped himself into the middle seat behind the pilot and copilot's seats. Robyn was already seated in the copilot's Holly turned the plane around to face the wind at the end of the runway, and immediately throttled up all four engines and released the brakes. The big plane began its roll, gaining speed, and again, in Tim's mind, at the last minute, Holly pulled back on the yoke, and the plane leapt into the air at a ridiculous angle, clawing for more altitude.

When they had reached the proper altitude, Holly programmed the GPS internal navigation with the coordinates of Volivoli and turned on the autopilot. Tim heard the intercom click, and then heard Holly's voice.

"Good morning, ladies and gentlemen! Thank you for flying MacFarland Airlines. We'll be leveling out at thirty-five thousand feet, and the fasten seatbelt lights have been turned off. The flight crew will be through the cabin shorty to serve light refreshments. Please sit back and enjoy the flight, and we hope you take advantage of the inflight entertainment."

"Does this airline have a frequent flyer program?" Tim asked.

"Aye, but you can only redeem them on the third Wednesday of February, and only if there's a full moon."

"The cheap-assed bastards!"

"Fly with someone else then!"

"How long do you figure?" he asked, becoming serious once again.

"It will take about five hours or so, about the same time from Luke."

"I'm going to go back and see how everyone's doing," he said, taking off his headphones and unstrapping himself from the seat, leaving Holly and Robyn alone.

Holly pressed her intercom button. "Robyn, I've got to go to the loo. You've got the plane!" she said.

When Holly got up, one foot caught the strap slightly to her flight bag that she'd stashed beside the pilot's seat. She didn't notice, but Robyn saw it tip slightly and a few things spilled out. She unstrapped herself, and began picking everything up, stopping when she picked up a narrow white plastic thing. Holding it up, she saw it had a little window in it with a green 'plus' sign. She put the bag back and sat down, holding on to the thing she found. Once she had herself strapped back in, she hid it in her lap. She may have been naïve in a lot of ways, but she knew exactly what this was.

Holly came back after a few minutes and sat back down. "Everything fine with the aircraft?" she asked once she had her headphones back on.

"Yep, everything's fine. But I think you dropped this," Robyn said, handing over what she had found. Holly's eyes got wide, and she looked at Robyn, who now had a small smile on her face.

"Does Daddy know?"

"Oh, Robyn, no, he doesn't know yet."

"When are you going to tell him?"

"I don't know. I don't think now is a very good time for it."

"No, you're right there. But he's got to know at some point."

"Aye, but I don't want him thinking about this now. It's the last thing he needs on his mind."

"Ain't that the truth? So I'm going to be a big sister?"

"Yes, you are," Holly said with a huge grin. "But please, don't say anything to him. I don't want him worrying about this right now."

"I won't. It'll be our secret!" Robyn beamed, thinking how great it would be to actually have a little brother or sister. "Robyn, I've been meaning to ask, and it's a wonder Tim hasn't thought to ask himself. When you and this Jimmy bloke where chatting, how did the topic of the codes ever come up?"

Robyn was silent for a minute, and looked out her window. "I'm really not sure. He didn't come right out and ask. Like Sergeant Williams said, he played me. We were talking one night, and he was going on how his dad was rich and powerful, how he had all this money, and that's how they were able to sail around the world. I guess it pissed me off, and I just came back with 'yeah, but my dad is more powerful than that! He's got this case you see...' And it just went from there," she said with a shrug. "Holly, I'm really sorry!"

"Honey, don't worry about it. What's done is done. But let's keep things to ourselves from now on, like we're supposed to."

"Holly?"

"Aye, what is it?"

"I love you."

"And I love you too."

"Do you love Tim?"

"Yes, I love Tim too. I haven't told him that either, but I will soon."

They flew on like that silently until soon the GPS beeped, and she checked her instruments. She began her descent, and Tim, feeling the difference, came up to the cockpit.

"It's been another great flight, Leftenant. About how long until we get there?"

"About thirty minutes."

Tim strapped himself back into the seat for the last leg of the journey. He noticed Robyn and Holly exchanging glances and giggling, and wondered briefly what that was all about, and then he saw the island from the wide windscreen of the Hercules. A feeling of déjà vu swept over him. A photograph taken from orbit was one thing, to see it for real was another. Here was the island from his dreams, where he was the eagle soaring above, feeling helpless. Holly brought the plane down to a few hundred feet and flew over it several times, never reducing speed, and her banks and turns made some of her passengers sick. Seeing the palm trees fly by the window that fast gave Tim an uneasy feeling, but he knew that Holly could handle the plane. She pulled the plane up and flew out to sea again, and in a wide bank, brought the aircraft in line with the runway, which from his vantage point looked ridiculously tiny. She lowered the flaps and the plane slowed in the air noticeably as it came closer and closer to the tiny airstrip. She had Robyn lower the landing gear, and was satisfied that all the lights were green. It looked like Jimenez' handiwork was good enough. She brought it down for another smooth as silk landing, the plane bumping a few times on the rough strip. As soon as all the wheels were down, she reversed the pitch on the props, and a huge billow of white dust engulfed the plane, and they couldn't see a thing out the windows. The Hercules came to a full stop a few hundred yards later. Using a small wheel in the center of the console, Holly turned the nose wheel and switched the pitch of the props on one side back to their original position, spinning the bird in place one hundred eighty degrees facing back down the runway. She then reversed the pitch on the props again so they were all pulling the aircraft forward, and taxied back down the runway towards the two small concrete buildings and fuel storage tanks.

Tim let out a breath he didn't know he was holding. "Lady, you never cease to amaze me!"

"Nor you either, Timmy," she said, with a twinkle in her eyes that made Tim blush. He quickly pulled off his headphones and made his way to the back, where some men were already unshackling the Hum-Vee from the deck. He squeezed by them and opened the loading ramp, which slowly went down on its hydraulic rams. When it was fully down, he stepped off and planted his feet on the old crushed coral runway. He could see places where the old Marston Mat showed through, and was amazed that it was still here after all these years. He made room for the Hum-Vee to drive down the ramp, and as it came to a stop at the bottom, Jerry Williams looked out the passenger window.

"I'm going to go on a little recon and check out those bunkers. And there was something that looked odd in the photo that I couldn't make out. I want to check out. I'll meet you back here in a bit, Sar' Major."

"You do that. I'm going to take a walk over to those concrete huts, and see what I can see."

He saw some of the other men wandering down, and said, "You men! If you want, find a nice shady spot and relax for a bit."

It was a hot day; it felt like it was over one hundred degrees, and after only a few minutes on the ground, Tim was already sweating. Holly and Robyn were coming down the ramp now, and came over to him.

"Isn't it fabulous, Tim?" Holly said. He looked around, and had to agree, it *was* rather beautiful. It could have been the poster on Paul's bedroom wall. It had snow white beaches, thousands of coconut palms, and a turquoise lagoon that was breathtaking. Paul would have loved it, he thought with a sad smile.

"It's beautiful, Holly," he said. "Is that where the HQ of a sort was?" he asked, pointing to the huts.

"Yes, it was where the lieutenant had a small room, and one for the enlisted man. All the radios and things were in the larger one, like an office. In the back was a small galley."

"I'm going to take a look-see," he said, trying to not think about how she knew of the officer's sleeping arrangements.

"I'll go with you," she said, and then Robyn chimed in that she was going too. They walked over to the big building, about twenty feet by twenty feet. All three walked up to the door, and Tim opened it up. It swung easily on the hinges and a blast of cool air hit him.

"I guess the air still works," he said, and walked inside. He flipped a light switch and the fluorescent lights flickered to life. "And the solar power is still up."

He walked over to a desk, and in front of a dark computer monitor was a full US Navy dress gray uniform, neatly folded on the desk with the hat placed on top. It looked as if it was placed there that morning. Next to the uniform was a large ledger book and he picked it up. Flipping through the pages, he found scrawled a large manifest of writing. From edge to edge, from top to bottom, each page was crammed with writing. He sat down and started reading. Holly and Robyn disappeared into another room, then came out to go outside, leaving Tim to whatever he was doing. Tim continued reading for some time, intrigued. Then he started to get angry. After about an hour, he put the book down and rubbed his temples.

"Fuck I need a drink," he said, aloud to himself. The door opened, and Holly and Robyn returned. Tim stayed seated with his feet up on the desk with a blank look on his face.

"Well, the solar power is running at a hundred percent, the desalinization plant is working, and there's food in the stock house," Holly reported.

"So when you landed here, this Navy lieutenant, he gave you the story about this being some super-secret stockpile to supply a whole Marine Division? Real Secret Squirrel type shit, huh?"

"Well, yes… that's what he told me."

"Last I saw Elba…" Tim said.

"What do you mean, Dad?"

"Elba was the island that they exiled Napoleon to, Robyn," Holly said, a worried look crossing her face.

"And this is your fair lieutenant's Elba. Seems he and another fuckup seaman were exiled here to keep them from fucking up anymore shit. It's a weather station. That's it. If it was a Supply Depot, it's long gone."

"How do you know that?" Holly asked, sitting down in a chair opposite Tim.

"I know that, because he spelled it out in great detail in this here book," he said, lifting it up, and letting it fall back down on the desk theatrically. "Oh, and I might add, you certainly left a big impression on him too. He wrote all about that in great detail too."

"Tim, I just went by what he told me," she said, turning red at what he'd just said. Robyn walked up behind Holly and put her hand on her shoulder.

"And apparently after his enlisted companion died in The Event, he was here alone for several years, slowly going nuts, until about a year ago, when he decided to take a swim and never come back. That's his uniform there." He was about to speak again, when Williams came back in with an armload of things.

"Sar' Major! You're not going to believe this one. Ever since I got to Schofield, I heard rumors about places like this all over the Pacific, but I never thought they were true, let alone me finding one," he said. Tim sat motionless, feet still propped up on the desk, but now one elbow was propped there too, and his hand held the right side of his face. "Look at this!" he said, and began laying things down in front of Tim on the desk. "We only broke into about ten bunkers so far. It was easy, the locks were so rusted, they literally crumbled in our hands. Look at this stuff!"

Tim started picking through it. "Yep, what I sort of expected after reading a little manifesto," Tim said, pawing through what Williams had brought. "Sulfa powder, dried up morphine syrettes, K-Rations." He picked up a dry-rotted bandolier of .30-06 ammo, and put it down. "I bet nothing is dated any later than say, nineteen forty three or four, right?"

"That's about it, Sar' Major."

"Wonderful," he said, looking right at Holly, who began to tear up, and suddenly got up and ran out of the building, Robyn chasing after her. Tim looked at Williams and sighed, and went on to tell him about the missing lieutenant and the manifesto of self-flagellation the long missing Navy lieutenant had written.

"Well, how do you feel about eating almost eighty year old K-Rations, Jerry?"

"Not too excited about it, Tim, but there's plenty of fish out there we can catch, so I know we won't go hungry. But there's something you've got to see."

"What is it?"

"It's better if I show you. Come with me," he said, and they both went out and got into the Hum-Vee. Jerry drove, Tim got in the passenger side, and they headed off. They drove past the parked Hercules and down the runway to where a small road was barely visible through the underbrush. "Tim, this place is amazing! It's like we've stepped back into time, going through this shit."

"I'd heard about places like this too. During the war, factories in the States were cranking out millions of tons of equipment and materiel a day, and when it was over, they had all this shit stacked up everywhere. The places like this, crammed full with the stuff, were forgotten, because it was too expensive to ship back after the war was over. There's supposed to be hundreds of islands all over the Pacific, just like this."

"Look, I can tell you're pissed at your lady friend. Don't saddle all this shit on her, okay? She didn't know," Jerry said.

"Oh, I'm not pissed at her. I'm just pissed that she let some fuckwit sailor con her out of her flight suit, and into her panties, because he was some Guardian of the Realm with all this Secret Squirrel shit. She's far too smart to let that happen."

"And so is your kid. Smart that is. They both fell for a line of bullshit. It happens to the best of us. I barely remember my twenties, and then one day I woke up at Ft. Benning at thirty wondering what the fuck I was doing married."

"I can relate," Tim said ruefully. "So what's so hell-fire important that you couldn't tell me back there?" he asked, as they drove past bunker after bunker, concrete faces aged by water stains and moss, the grass-over dirt long overgrown with palm trees, ferns and weeds.

"Tim, you're just going to have to see it to believe it. And it might just help us out. When I was looking at that photograph, I saw the bunkers hidden in the trees, but there was something in the weeds that didn't look right, and I couldn't make it out. So I came over here, and almost shit myself."

"What was it?" Tim asked, as they passed the last bunker, and stopped almost at the opposite end of the channel, directly across from the concrete huts.

Jerry got out. "This is what I'm talking about," he said, pointing to a large growth of palm trees, high weeds and vines. He walked over to what looked like a vine covered wall, took his M4 and poked through the leaves. A definite metallic clink was heard, and he smiled. Tim stepped back and then he saw it. The vine covered turtle-shaped turret of a Sherman Tank.

"Well I'll be dipped..." he said slack jawed.

"I reckon there's about thirty of them here, along with the same amount of Amtracks over there."

"So what are you thinking, Jerry? I mean, surely they won't run. The engines would need a complete overhaul, and they're probably seized up sitting here all this time."

"No, I figured as much. But the muzzles all have rubber caps on them, as do the exhaust pipes. The things are pretty well sealed up. Inside they're as new as when they rolled off Cadillac's assembly line."

"Okay, I'm following you now. They'd be a sort of pillbox, with a 75mm high velocity anti-tank gun. One problem though. The turrets... wouldn't they need power from the engine to slue?"

"Yeah, but they've got hand cranks too in case they lose power, and the sights were optical, not electric."

"What about ammo for the main gun?"

"I've got some of my men looking in the bunkers for it now, maybe an old Browning M1919 for the coax gun too. That would be a nice touch and a nasty surprise for anything that tries to come through that channel!"

"Jerry, you're a fucking genius!"

"I've still got some problems to work out. The optics might be fogged to hell, and the recoil system seals might be dry rotted. If that's the case, we can't use them. But I'll try. And I've got one of my other guys, used to be a Combat Engineer, looking for anything else in the bunkers, we still might be able to use."

They got back into the Hum-Vee, and Jerry made a wide turn to go back the way they came.

"Shame we couldn't salvage at least one. With that many, we'd surely be able to piece together one running Sherman," Jerry said.

"Maybe after all this shit is over, you and I will do that. I love this stuff."

"Me too, Tim, I was going to school on line for my history degree when everything turned to shit."

"That's too bad," Tim said, looking around at everything. He could almost picture all the sailors smoking their Lucky Strikes, listening to Glenn Miller and The Andrews Sisters, while they stowed everything away.

"Yeah, too bad, but if wishes were horses, beggars would ride. Now it's time, if you don't mind me saying so, Sar' Major, to get back and have a little talk with that lieutenant of yours."

"I was just thinking that, Jerry. That is on the top of my priority list right now."

"Good. She seems like a nice lady."

"That she is.. I'll work things out with her," he said, as they pulled up in front of the huts.

Jerry looked at Tim and said, pointing at him, "You'd better!"

"Go take care of your shit. I'll go find her now." He walked away, and Robyn came running up to him. Before she could say anything Tim asked, "Where's Holly?"

"She's down on the beach, Daddy. She's really upset."

"I'll take care of it. Sergeant Williams is working on something you might get a kick out of. Why don't you go find him, and see if you can help? Tell him I sent you."

"Okay, Dad. She really needs you. Go talk to her."

"I will, now git!" He walked through a stand of coconut palms, over a slight rise and onto the ocean side beach. He saw her sitting there on the sand about two hundred yards down the beach, her arms wrapped around her knees, and head buried between them. He went over to her and stripped down to the waist, folding his ACU blouse, setting it on the sand, and placing his carbine on top. He sat down next to her, put his arm around her shoulder, and pulled her close. She looked at him briefly, then put her face back down.

"What are you doing?" she asked.

"Well, I've always been told that when you go to an island paradise, you work on your tan. So that's what I'm doing, working on my tan."

"You're bloody mad!"

"Maybe so, but I do know I'm mad about you."

"But why would you? I've messed things up for you so horribly."

"Holly, you didn't mess anything up for me."

"Aye, I did. You and Robyn had that wonderful house in Arizona, and you could still be there, safe and sound if it weren't for me."

"But I'm not, and I'm here with who I want to be with. It doesn't make a difference where we are as long as I'm with you," Tim said, reaching out for her chin, and pulling her face towards him. The red rimmed eyes tore his heart out.

"But this place isn't what I thought it was."

"No, it's not. But it still is one of the most beautiful places I've ever been to, and having you here with me makes it even more special," Tim said and kissed her.

"But why did he lie like that?" she asked, and Tim sighed. "Because he was trying to get into your flight suit, that's why. And to be honest, the way you fill that thing out, I don't blame him," he said, trying to lighten his words.

She laughed a little for the first time. "But then I keep on thinking, now you and Robyn are in this mess that I've caused."

"Holly, I think I was meant to be here," he said, thinking about Dawn Red Eagle, and what he had told them so many years ago in Nebraska. "Now we're here, Jerry and I will sort this out. It's the nature of the beast. Williams and I are trained to deal with this sort of thing, you know that. But you and Robyn will be safe and sound on Howland Island, or wherever you decide to go."

"But don't you see? I've put you all in danger. If something happens to you, I'll never be able to forgive myself!" she said, tears beginning to flow again.

"Holly, I'm too ornery to kill."

"But all you have is rifles and a few grenades to go against a ship with cannons and missiles!"

"Ah, but we've got a few surprises for them. Now we've got a tank!"

"A tank? Where did you find a bloody tank?"

"Jerry found it. Them actually. There's about thirty of them one the other side of the channel. We're going to get one to work, at least the main gun, and nothing is going to get through that channel without a bloody nose."

"What if this doesn't work? That's what I'm worried about."

"Baby, worrying about that now is like a private on a landing craft a hundred yards off Omaha beach in Normandy on D-Day, wondering what he's going to do on his first night in Paris," Tim said, pulling her close. "We've got a few weeks to prepare, and like I said, we've got some nasty surprises for our Captain Kangaroo and the Good Ship Lollypop."

"I'm still worried, Tim. I can't help it."

"Holly, this island has plenty of places to defend from. Jerry and I can do it," he said. Then the thought of another island, not far from there, crossed his mind. Tarawa was not even a thousand miles from here, and long ago its Japanese defenders thought the same thing, and it didn't end too well for them. He looked out over the ocean. There was a thunderstorm brewing several miles out to the southwest, and the sun was sitting on the horizon.

"Have you ever seen the green flash?" he asked.

"No, what's that?"

"When the sun is just about to drop below the horizon, when the very top of it slips out of view, there's a millisecond long 'green flash' of light. It's a view to behold."

"I've never seen it," she said.

"Let's just sit here, and watch it then." She put her arms around him. He moved her around so she was sitting in front of him, her back into his chest. He wrapped his arms around her waist, she pulled his hands into her stomach, and they watched the sun slowly go down. He kissed the side of her neck and she sighed. As the sun slipped from view, they saw it, in a little 'pop' of green light.

"That was amazing!"

"Baby, *you're* amazing," he said, and kissed her neck again, pulling out the pin holding her hair in a bun and it spilled out over her shoulders.

"Sergeant Major Flannery, you are incorrigible!"

"That I am. It might just be the location and the company, though," he said, and lingered on her neck with his lips. They watched the thunderstorm far out to sea until it was full dark, lightning bolts dancing through the clouds, too far away to hear any thunder. He lay down and pulled her on top of him, and they kissed more urgently, his hands exploring her body, then the spell was broken.

"Dad, are you out here? Sergeant Williams wants to see you!" he heard Robyn call out.

"Well, I guess we'll have to put that idea on hold," he said wryly.

"Aye, maybe we can come back out here later?" she said mischievously as Tim helped her to her feet.

"I don't think you'll have to twist my arm."

"I didn't think I would," she said, holding on to him as they walked to the sound of Robyn's voice.

Tim had a feeling of dread wash over him then, as the thoughts of the Japanese defenders of Tarawa, flashed to the forefront of his thoughts. Could they do it? The more he thought about it, the more he was unsure.

CHAPTER 21:
THE BATTLE OF VOLIVOLI

They prepared for two weeks, setting up claymore mines, clearing fields of fire in the underbrush, and going through the bunkers of ancient equipment looking for anything that might still be of use. They found several hundred cases of beer in plain green cans that needed what his dad used to call a 'church key' to open them. No brand name, just the word 'beer' printed on them. They all had a good laugh about them, but in the end, no one was brave enough to try any.

After seven attempts, they found one Sherman tank with a recoil system that was still functioning, but its optics were hopelessly fogged. So they found the sights of one that wasn't, and swapped them out. Now they had a pillbox of sorts, with a functioning 75mm high velocity anti-tank gun. The sounds of the men practicing with the rounds echoed with the sharp cracks every day, almost all day, because they'd found an almost unlimited supply of ammunition, that miraculously was still functioning. They'd left most of the vegetation on the tank to camouflage it, cutting just enough away to allow the turret to slue. It was sitting closest to the channel, and would be at almost point-blank range to anything coming into it.

They had found a huge map of the island in one hut and tacked it to the wall. Tim and Jerry went over it again and again, making sure they'd set up everything the way they'd wanted it. In the meantime, Holly, Robyn and Jimenez got the plane ready to depart, making sure it was airworthy and its fuel tanks were topped off from the island's fuel storage tanks. Jerry had brought enough hand held military radios that worked, and issued one to every man in the makeshift squad. They'd found a stockpile of 155mm artillery shells, and with a little help from everyone, they buried several in the lagoon side beach, with C-4 explosive in the fuse wells in the noses, running wires from blasting caps to detonators strategically located by ambush sites.

They were as ready as they ever were going to be, and everyone was tense but alert. Robyn was really on edge the morning before she and Holly were set to take the Hercules to Howland Island. They figured it was the closest, and with Tim's Football, were able to task a KH11 to take photos of it, and the runway looked fine to use.

"Dad, this is really boring," Robyn said to Tim as he looked up in the morning sun to see the Stars and Stripes flying on the flagpole.

"Baby, ninety-nine percent of war is boredom."

"What's the other one percent?"

"It's complete and abject terror," he said deadpan. He walked into the main hut, Robyn following, and found Jerry standing over the map, looking to see if he'd forgotten anything.

"Morning, Tim. I was just going over everything again. Got word from the Aussies, they should be here in about two days."

"That's good. I'll be really happy to see another ship."

"So will I. Never thought I'd say that, but I look forward to the Navy getting here," Jerry said. Robyn was looking at the map, when Holly walked in. She didn't look too well, and Tim let her know, concern in his voice.

" I'm alright. Must have been a bad piece of fish I ate or something." She poured a cup of coffee and came over to the map.

"Are you going to be okay to fly?" Tim asked.

"Aye, I'll be ok."

"When did you plan on leaving?" Jerry asked.

"I think maybe mid-morning. We've got her ready to go, and if you think they'll be here in a few days, I guess it's time for us to leave."

"Yeah, Robyn talked to 'Jimmy' last night, and he said he'd be here in a few days. I just hope that Aussie ship gets here first," Tim said.

"So do I, Tim," Jerry said. "I've got some serious doubts, considering we have no idea what kind of manpower he's able to put ashore, and what weapons he has. He could just lay off shore, and lob a few cruise missiles at us."

"It's kept me awake, too," Tim said. "Do you have any thoughts on that derelict car carrier?"

"No, it's just sitting there. I thought of putting some men on it, but I don't see the use right now."

The door burst open and one of the men came in breathlessly. They all turned and looked at him. "We got trouble, Sergeant."

"Trouble?" Jerry asked.

"Yeah, big trouble, come with me!" He went back out the door, followed by everyone. He walked over to the ocean side of the hut, and pointed out to sea. The man handed Jerry a set of binoculars, which he raised to his eyes. He lowered them, and handed them to Tim, who raised the glasses, looking in the same direction that Jerry had.

"Fuck. It's too late for you to leave now, Lieutenant," Jerry said.

"What do you mean?" Holly asked.

"Here, have a look-see for yourself," Tim replied, handing her the binoculars. "I'm not letting you take off now." She raised them to her eyes, looking where he'd been. On the horizon, steaming towards them, was a gray ship, bow slicing through the waves, and close enough to see the faded white '193' painted on the hull.

"Oh. I see. Maybe I can get her started up and off, before it's too close," she said, lowering the glasses.

"No. It's an Aegis destroyer. They were designed to protect the aircraft carriers. Make a big bubble around a task force, and not let any aircraft near them. They've got all kinds of antiaircraft shit on them, including SAM's. He'd shoot you out of the sky before your landing gear was up," Tim said forcefully.

"Tim, we'd better get going," Jerry said.

"Are all the men ready?"

"Yeah, they've been sleeping at their positions for a few days now."

"Good. You take Holly and head out. I'll meet you at the first set of bunkers."

"You got it, Tim," Jerry said, taking Holly's arm and heading out.

"Jerry, you get Robyn too. And you tell Jimenez to grab his piece and meet me here!"

Williams turned and gave him a thumbs up, and continued towards the bunkers. Tim went back to the hut and grabbed his rucksack and carbine. He jogged over to a dug out foxhole on the ocean side, right inside the tree line. It was connected to a similar one on the lagoon side near the long pier by a deep trench. He dropped down into it and brought the binoculars back to his eyes. The ship was getting closer. He reached into his pocket to make sure he had the small hand held radio, pulled it out and turned it on. He keyed it up, and asked for everyone to check in, and one by one, they all answered. He told the men manning the gun in the tank not to fire until he told them to, and they acknowledged the order. Just then he heard movement to his rear, and turned to look. He saw Jimenez coming over to him through the trench, carrying his M16.

"Glad you could make it, Jimenez. Looks like the party is about to start."

"Oh shit! Should we be getting the plane ready?"

"It's too late. Just stick with me."

"Whatever you say, Sar' Major," he said nervously, and they watched the ship sailing closer. As it neared, Tim took a good look and thought it had seen better days. The once gray sides were now streaked with rust so badly it looked almost a uniform red. The upper superstructure was streaked with bird droppings, and the antenna mast was missing halfway down. It looked like it had been broken off by a giant's hand; what remained was a twisted mess. The numbers were still white, but badly faded, and it looked like there was a rusty rectangle of steel welded and re-welded several times over on the hull almost at the waterline. There were bamboo poles all along the rails, with little red flags flying on them, and it looked as if someone's washing was hanging out on the fantail. And... was that a few goats Tim saw, tied to the railing? Thick black smoke, was billowing from the stack, and topping it all off was a huge Jolly Roger flag flying from atop the bridge.

"What a hunk of shit!" Jimenez said.

"Don't let looks deceive you. It's still got guns and missiles," Tim said as they watched the ship approach. It circled the island, and when it was back to where the channel was steered right for it, doing what Tim thought was around ten knots or so.

"What the fuck is he doing?" Tim said in astonishment. "Can't he see that it's low tide?"

But whoever was conning the ship didn't care, and Tim saw the bow rise, its bulbous sonar dome on the bow covered in barnacles lift up, and they could hear the ship's bottom scrape along the coral. The ship came to a grinding halt, half in the channel. It had once been deep enough, even at low tide, to allow ships to enter the lagoon, but after seventy plus years of shifting sands and no one to dredge it, the coral had reclaimed a lot of it, making the channel impassable to anything larger than a rowboat.

"It's stuck! Whoever it is, he isn't the sharpest tool in the woodshed," Tim said.

"Holy shit, Sar' Major! He's stuck like a dog dick!"

"Yeah, that's good for us. Let's see what he does now. At least we've got twelve hours before high tide. He can't get off of it before then."

"I thought tides were every six hours, Sar' Major."

"This island has a diurnal tide. It's every twelve."

"A urinal tide?" Jimenez asked. Tim looked at him and shook his head.

***

Commander Wright was beside himself with anger, and let forth a tirade of abuse to Lt. Alphabits, who was conning the ship. It was the first major mistake the lieutenant had made, but that didn't make a difference to the captain.

"What exactly were you thinking, Lieutenant?"

"A thousand pardons, Captain! I thought the channel was deep enough. I will get her off, I promise you!"

"Well, you had better! It's low tide. We'll have to wait, and there'd better not be any damage to the hull, or your head will roll!" he screamed. "Mr. Johnson?" he shouted, turning around on the bridge to face the ensign.

"Right here, sir."

"Go take a man and see if there's any damage below."

"Yes sir!" Johnson said, and scrambled as fast as he could from the bridge. The captain sat back in the captain's chair, and toyed with his now very long beard that he'd had one of the girls braid for him, beads and seashells interlaced in it. As angry as he was for having the ship run aground, he was gleeful that he was so close to his goal. He could feel the power course through his veins.

"Stevens!" he shouted out, and the sailor was by his side in a second.

"You take a few men, and go get the codes off this joker on the island."

"Aye, aye, sir, but what if they're armed?"

"Well, you'll arm yourselves, kill them and take the damn thing! It's not rocket science. You've been talking with the girl, you know what she's like. How hard can it be to take a book off a man, a girl and a pilot?"

"Can I have the girl, sir?" he asked, a smile growing on his face, showing rotting teeth.

"Yes, of course you can. Now go and do it!" he said, dismissing him. Stevens disappeared, and the captain sat back, toying with his beard some more.

Below decks, Ensign Johnson was walking through a passageway and bumped into Suplee, who was also checking the hull for damage.

"Mr. Johnson, I think the sonar dome is fucked, but everything else seems watertight."

"That doesn't matter. The sonar hasn't worked in a few years anyway. Just like everything else on this tub," Johnson said with disgust.

"I just wish we could get the air conditioning to work. It's like a goddamn oven in here," Suplee said, taking off his cap and wiping the sweat from his brow.

"It doesn't matter. Remember I said we'll wait for our time?"

"You mean now, sir?" Suplee asked incredulously.

"Yes, now. Follow me. Everyone else will be busy with getting ashore, they won't notice us leaving."

"Sir, that island is tiny. And those people on it are bound to be all killed. Why the fuck would we want to get off here and end up just like them?"

"I don't know, Suplee. But something is telling me, deep down inside, we have to get off this ship right now and take our chances with whoever is on that island. That something is also telling me, they've got a far better chance than the captain thinks."

"This is just crazy, sir. I don't like it one bit."

"Well, I'm leaving this ship. You can stay or come with me, it's up to you," he said in exasperation. Suplee looked like he was thinking for a bit, then said, "Okay, sir. I'm with you. But let me go and find Nakamura, and see if he wants to come too."

"Fine, but if he doesn't want to go, he's got to keep his mouth shut until we're well away from the ship."

"You got it, sir!" Suplee said, and they headed back down the passageway towards the stern of the ship.

***

Tim and Jimenez looked at the ship, now close enough that they could hear voices and yelling, but couldn't see anyone on the decks. He looked at the bow, and saw the turret there, with a large five inch gun, and that worried him. The missiles and other things they had were useless now, they were too close, but that big gun worried him. They waited and watched, and after a while heard the sputtering of a small diesel engine. Tim grabbed Jimenez' arm and pulled him through the trench to the other foxhole, which looked out over the small pier into the lagoon. He picked up his radio, and keyed it up.

"I hear a small engine. You men over on the Sherman see anything?"

The radio crackled, and he got a response right away. "Sar' Major, they've just lowered some kind of boat, and there's five guys in it. It looks like they're coming around the bow towards you."

"Keep an eye out, and let me know if you see anything more," he said and set the radio down. They saw the boat finally, it was one of the ship's whaleboats. There were four men in the front, all holding AK47s, and the man at the rear had a long beard and ponytail, cut off blue jeans, and a sleeveless chambray navy shirt open at the chest. They motored across the lagoon, and pulled up to the pier. Two men got out and tied it up. They were very dark skinned, and he couldn't tell if they were islanders or African. The man in the back shut down the engine, and then the rest hopped out, walking up the pier as if they owned the place.

"What now, Sar' Major?" Jimenez asked in a tense whisper.

"Just sit tight, Taco," Tim said, and sat his M4 on the rim of the foxhole, flicking the safety off. When all five of them got to the end of the pier at the beach, about fifty yards or so, Tim called out to them, "That's far enough, sport!"

They all stopped, and the man with the ponytail came to the front of the pack of men, holding a 9mm Beretta pistol.

"Hey!" he called out. "I'm a friend of Robyn's, and we're just here to say hello!"

"Oh, you must be 'Jimmy'," Tim said. "Spiffy yacht, your rich daddy has."

"Yeah, that's me! Jimmy! We don't want any trouble, we just came to say hello!" he said, and started to take a step forward.

"Don't even think about it, dickhead. Not one more step."

"Hey man! You don't know who you're fucking with!" the man said, all signs of friendliness gone.

Tim leaned over to Jimenez and whispered, "Taco, he takes one more step, see that big fucker in the back, the Samoan looking cocksucker? That Jimmy takes one more step, put a bullet in the black guy's chest."

"But, Sar', I'm just a—"

"You're a fucking rifleman now. Do it!"

"Eh, you got it Sar' Major," he said, and raised his rifle, taking aim at the big man in the rear.

"You and I both know what we came for. You just give it up, we'll leave, and everything will be okay," Jimmy said, and took another step forward. Jimenez' rifle barked, and the big Samoan fell backwards, a small hole appearing in the center of his chest. The ponytailed man fell to the ground, and the other three men let lose a hail of full auto fire from their AKs, spraying the tree line with lead.

Jimenez ducked down, and Tim pulled him up by the collar. "It's all going over our heads. They have no idea where we are. Just sit tight," he said, and he returned to his rifle. When they had expended all of their ammo, and didn't get any return fire, they looked around. 'Jimmy' slowly stood, and did the same.

"Now, Jimmy, if that is your name," Tim called out to them, "you just go back to the Good Ship Lollypop and tell Captain Kangaroo he's not getting it."

"You're making a big mistake, mister!"

"It's Sergeant Major, sailor. And I could have killed all of you just then. Go back to your canoe, and relay my message. He wants it, he going to have to come and take it."

"I don't know who you think you are, but you're making the worst mistake of your life!" Jimmy called out.

"I know who I am. I'm the guy who's going to make your miserable sorry life even more miserable before this day is through. Now go and give him my message before I shoot you too."

Jimmy grumbled a bit, and went to the others, who were busy changing magazines. Tim couldn't hear what was being said, but it looked like they were arguing. Just then, Jimmy leveled his pistol at one of them, and cowed, they all walked back to the boat, started it up, and motored their way back to the beached ship.

Jimenez stood there in the foxhole, and stared at the lifeless form lying on the wood planking of the pier and sighed. "I can't believe I just shot that guy."

"Better him than you, Taco. Now let's go!" Tim said, pulling him out of the foxhole and running towards the Hum-Vee. He jumped in, and started it, Jimenez getting in the other side. They raced passed the Hercules and out onto the runway, heading away from the ship and towards the tree line on the opposite side where the bunkers started. Halfway down the runway, the crushed coral erupted with a large blast that Tim barely avoided.

"They're shooting at us!" Jimenez screamed, looking back to see the turret on the bow of the ship slued around pointing at them. He saw a flash from the muzzle, and heard the shell scream over their heads as they raced towards the end of the runway. It exploded in the trees somewhere, and Tim put the pedal to the floor to try to get out of the open and into cover, as soon as he could. As soon as they pulled into the tree line, out of sight of the ship, Tim stopped and got out, grabbing his rucksack. He hunkered down next to the Hum-Vee and looked across the road at Jerry, who was just inside the tree line next to the first bunker. A shell exploded somewhere in front of them, then it was silent for a moment. Tim ran over to where Jerry was, and sat down, followed by Jimenez.

"You set?"

"I'm all set, Tim. We just wait now?"

"Yeah, let's see what they try next. They're pretty well stuck in the channel, and not going anywhere soon."

They didn't have to wait long. They heard the ship's gun firing again, and the Hercules erupted in flames at the other end of the runway.

"Well that's that. We're not going anywhere now," Tim said.

"Oh we're fucked now!" Jimenez said.

Tim ignored him, and looked back at Jerry. "Where are Holly and Robyn?"

"They're with some of my men, about a hundred yards back."

"Good. Now we need to take care of that gun on the ship," he said, pulling out his radio and keying it up. "Sherman, take out that turret on the ship and then shift your fire to the bridge."

"It's about fucking time!" was the reply he got over the radio. He immediately heard the high pitched crack of the tank gun firing.

Tim looked through the binoculars and saw a huge gout of flame shoot out of the turret on the ship, followed by a black cloud of smoke. The ship's cannon was silenced. He heard the tank fire a few more times, then there was a loud sound like tearing paper, and the tank on the far side of the channel exploded, its turret flying into the air several yards before slamming down onto the ground upside down. Only a plume of black smoke remained, to show where the tank was.

***

"Just like shooting fish in a barrel!" Cmd. Wright said. He turned to the man coming out of CIC, who was frowning.

"Captain! The Phalanx gun has jammed!" the man said.

"That's okay. It did its job. Grab thirty or so men and get them in the other boat, along with Stevens. Ferry them if you have to! It's time we showed this joker who is boss of this ocean!"

"What about the big gun? That is destroyed!"

"Once I get those codes, I won't need it anymore!" he said gleefully. "Now go do as you're told, and get those goddamn codes! He can't be all that powerful!" The man scampered off the bridge like a shot.

"How dare he! Doesn't he know I command these seas?" Wright said to no one, pounding his fist into the armrest. He got up and looked out over the railing to the men now being lowered into the second boat, and to the men scrambling down the rope ladder to Stevens' boat. He leaned over the side and called down to them, "You don't come back until you have the codes, and bring that man's head to me! I'll hoist it up on the mast for all to see!"

Stevens just waved, and took an AK-47 offered to him.

***

"Well, that was short lived. Goddamn Phalanx tore up that Sherman," Jerry said, as he watched the smoke rise from where the tank had been, ammunition cooking off, and exploding at irregular intervals.

"Yeah, and we lost three men just now. At least we knocked out the cannon," Tim sighed.

"What now? We have no ride back," Jimenez said, looking woefully at the burning Hercules.

"We'll just have to hold on until that Aussie ship gets here," Tim said, looking down the runway at the C-130 now reduced to a burning hulk, its wings drooping forlornly from the rapidly melting fuselage. Black smoke and flames were billowing out of the wreckage, obscuring the concrete huts. He got a sinking feeling in his stomach. He lifted the binoculars and saw two boats now, and it looked like they were ferrying men, ten at a time, onto the pier. They were standing around waiting it seemed, to be told what to do. When it looked to be about thirty men on the beach, one of them pointed in the direction of the huts, and several of them disappeared behind the smoke.

Tim smiled. "Good. I left them a little present there when they go inside."

"Yeah, what sort of present?" Jerry asked.

"I put in ten pounds of TNT from the bunkers with a tripwire inside the door. Hope the shit still works." As he finished his sentence, he heard a deep *crump!*. "Well, I guess that answered my question." He looked down towards the huts to see a brown cloud of smoke rising. He saw several of them running around towards the huts, and then come back to the others, who as a group started towards them on the beach.

"Now it's time for my little surprise for them," Jerry said, and picked up a blasting machine. He attached the wires to the two posts, inserted the T handle and waited. When the majority of them were where he wanted, he twisted the handle, and the machine let out a little whir. A second later, the beach erupted in five large plumes of sand and black smoke. A second or two later, Tim and Jerry heard the loud *crump* of the artillery shells that they had buried earlier detonate. "Nice to be giving a little back after so many years of taking shit like that!"

"I agree. But I don't think that took care of them all, unfortunately," Tim said, looking back towards the other end of the runway.

"But it'll teach them not to bunch up like that," Jerry said.

They could see the dust still settling, but several of them were standing up and picking up their rifles, heading back out, a little slower this time. What no one on either side saw were three figures climbing over the railing on the fantail of the ship, dropping into the sea, and swimming away towards the island, out of view of the grounded ship.

Tim grabbed his rucksack and put it on. "Okay, we fall back to the next line of defense, and let them come closer. They want this island? We make them pay for every fucking inch."

"That sounds good to me," Jerry said. "We just hold them off and wait for the cavalry?"

"That's our plan now."

"We just hold out, for now," Jerry replied, "like the Philippines in '41?"

"Well, we don't have a Corregidor to run to, and if my memory serves me correctly, that didn't end too well for the Army, did it?"

"No, you're right there," he said, and went to leave.

"Wait a second. You got a frag?" Tim asked. Jerry stopped and reached into a pocket, pulling out a grenade, and tossing it to him. "Thanks. We'll be along in a few minutes."

He tapped Jimenez on the shoulder, and they both ran hunched over to the Hum-Vee again. Tim sat on the ground next to it with his head by the fuel fill cap.

"Sar' Major, this infantry shit is for the birds!"

"We'll make an infantryman out of you yet, Taco," Tim said.

"Or get me killed!"

"Taco, I've lived a long life, and have seen and done some pretty fucked up shit. But one thing is for certain. I came into this world kicking and screaming, covered in someone else's blood, I'm not afraid to go out that way either!"

"But I didn't sign up for this shit!"

"Nobody here did. Just one thing you have to remember; if you've got to go, take as many of the bastards with you as you can. The jarheads taught you how to use that rifle, now use it and don't let me down."

"What are you doing?" Jimenez asked when he saw Tim pull a roll of electrical tape from his rucksack and wrap some a few times around the safety lever of the grenade, then uncap the fuel cap.

"Taco, did you ever wonder why on all military vehicles and equipment, the fill caps on the fuel tanks are really wide like this one?"

"Yeah, it did always strike me as odd."

"It's so someone like me can do this," he said, pulling the pin on the grenade, and dropping it into the tank, calmly putting the cap back on. "Petroleum doesn't act that great with plastics or glue. If you've ever got to leave vehicles and equipment behind, you do this. At some point, hopefully when the enemy thinks they've got a great new ride, the fuel eats through the glue on the tape, the spoon flies, arms the grenade and boom!"

"That's pretty slick!" Jimenez said, clutching his rifle.

"Yeah, now let's beat feet," Tim said. He ran down the road between the bunkers, heading towards where Williams had the next line of defense set up. They reached the line where Williams was set up and took cover behind one of the bunkers. Williams met them, and gave him a brief.

"I've got two men on the roofs of the bunkers on either side, one with the M60. I got a daisy chain of claymores set up about thirty yards back that way in a perfect kill sack. We let them come into the zone, I trigger the ambush."

"What about the rest of the men?"

"They're over there and there," he said, pointing back down the road. "Nothing is going to get past this point without getting a bloody nose and a hard kick in the nutsack."

"Where are Holly and Robyn?"

"They're behind the next bunker down. That kid of yours is a pistol! She's been itching for a fight all morning. She keeps coming forward with her rifle, ready to drill anything that moves."

Tim smiled. "That's my kid!" He left Jimenez with Williams, heading around to the other bunker, where he found the two women with one of Williams' men. Tim sat down with his back resting on a palm tree. They both ran over to him, and hugged him tightly.

"Tim, the Hercules?" Holly said.

"It's gone."

"What will we do?" Robyn asked.

"Hold them off for as long as we can and wait for that Aussie ship to show up."

"But, Tim, they won't be here for another two days!" Holly said, her face pale.

"Well, there's a lot less of them now than there was a while ago. We've just got to keep thinning them out."

"I guess if you say so," Holly said.

"It'll be like Corregidor. We just have to hold out a little while."

"That's a really bad analogy, Tim. No one ever came to the rescue on Corregidor," Holly said, starting to feel sick.

"The Alamo, maybe?"

"Dad, they lost at the Alamo," Robyn whined.

"Look, we've just got to do what we have to do. We've given them a black eye and they're hurting. We just need to hold them off and keep on thinning them out."

"I'm really happy you're so optimistic," Holly said in exasperation.

"No sense worrying about it now." He heard a whistle from atop the bunker and looked up. The man up there pointed to his eyes, then back down the road. Tim gave a thumbs up to him and picked up his carbine. "You two stay here, and I'll come back for you. See anyone you don't recognize, put a bullet in their melon."

Holly kissed him and rubbed his cheek. "You come back to me, you hear?"

He kissed her back and left, going back to find Williams. Sliding up behind him, he low crawled to his side. "You know, Jerry, I'm getting too old for this shit. What have you got?"

"About twenty of them, be-bopping up the track like it was a walk in the park. Only two of them in front have their weapons ready. It's like taking candy from a baby."

Tim watched them come into sight. Yep, they were clueless. When they got to the middle of the kill sack, they stopped and looked around.

"Easy, easy. Nobody fire until I trip the claymores," Jerry whispered on the radio. Just then, one of them, looked like an African to Tim, bent down and picked up one of the claymores, its bright yellow detcord exposed and trailing off in either direction from the mine in his hands.

"Oh fuck! Would you look at that?" Tim said. The man holding the mine called out to one of his buddies. They were conferring; apparently they didn't know what it was. Tim looked over to Jerry, who was smiling broadly.

"You know that curiosity killed the cat." He snickered. "Gee, can I, dad?" he asked gleefully.

Tim stifled a laugh. "By all means, be my guest!"

Jerry picked up the detonator, slammed the handle three times, and all seven of the mines detonated, sending out several thousand stainless steel balls at several thousand feet per second. The unfortunate man holding one of the mines never knew what hit him, and was completely vaporized by the three pounds of C4 explosive he unwittingly held in his hand. As soon as the mines went off, all hell broke loose as the

M60 began to chatter, and all of the riflemen fired into the mass for over a minute, raking the whole kill zone with lead. Jerry let it go on for about that long, and finally yelled out, "Cease fire! Cease fire!"

The small arms fire rapidly dwindled and fell silent. Now only the moans of the wounded were heard from the carnage. It had always amazed Tim that even after all of that devastation, some people were still alive. He saw several of the men from the ship running as fast as they could back the way they came. One of Williams' men decided to fire a few rounds after them, and Jerry quickly put a stop to it. Tim and Jerry both stood and walked to the center of the road. Tim looked back and saw Holly peering around a moss covered concrete wall before disappearing back behind the cover.

One of the men came out of the weeds and over to Williams. "Everyone is accounted for, no injuries. Shall we go and take care of them out there?"

"Yeah," was all Williams said, with a curt nod to Tim as he watched three more men step out of the weeds and walk to the wounded men from the ship. As they got to each one, they pulled pistols out, and put a bullet in each of their heads.

"I told them no prisoners," Jerry said.

"Good," Tim said. "Now what?"

"We wait, and see what shit they pull next."

***

Cmd. Wright leaned out over the railing and watched Stevens motor up to the ship in the whaleboat. When he was alongside, he called down to him. "What's the story, Stevens? Do you have the codes?"

"No, sir. There's a lot more of them than we thought. They had an ambush set up for us, and were waiting about halfway around the island. I don't know how many we lost, but it was a shitload."

"You wait right there, don't you dare go anywhere!" he screamed down to him. He turned to Major Paleen, who had just walked into the bridge. "You! Grab as many men as you can fit into your helo and fly them across the lagoon to the other side! Have them come in from the beach on the other side, and we'll squeeze these simpletons like a teenager's zit until they pop."

"Yes, sir! Very good, sir!" Paleen said excitedly, and hurried off. Wright then leaned back over the railing, and called down to Stevens. "I'm coming down! I'll bring more men with me. It seems like if you want the job done right, you've got to do it yourself."

***

Tim and Jerry went back to where Holly and Robyn were and sat down, drinking water from their canteens. About an hour passed when suddenly the radio came to life. "There are more of them, coming up the beach!" someone called over the radio.

Tim picked up his handset, and keyed it. "How many do you think?"

"Looks like about twenty-five, maybe thirty."

"Okay, let me know when they start into the trees," he said into the radio, and then set it down. "How many of these fucks does he have?" he asked rhetorically.

"Your guess is as good as mine, Tim. It looks like we'll be busy again here shortly."

"Great." He looked up at the sky. "Do you hear that?"

"What?" Jerry asked.

"Sounds like a Blackhawk," Jimenez said.

"Yeah, now I hear it. That's just fucking wonderful. Now the fuck has a chopper to go around us," he sighed.

"I wish we had a Stinger or two," Tim said.

"I looked right at them at Schofield, and decided we didn't need them," Jerry said.

They could hear the sounds of the engine getting louder, and Tim and Jerry walked through the trees carefully to get a better look out across the lagoon. They could see the helicopter taking off from the rear of the ship, its doors open, and he could see men inside.

"I'm going to ask again. How many people does this fuck *have*?" Tim said angrily.

"I don't know, but I bet you any amount of money he's trying to get some people behind us."

Holly came running up to them at this point, and looked at the aircraft gaining altitude and heading their way.

"It's a Seahawk, your Navy's version of the Blackhawk," she said.

"Does it have rockets or guns?" Jerry asked.

"Not that I know of, just anti-submarine warfare stuff," she said.

They watched it cross the lagoon, and then suddenly burst into flames and white streaks, with a loud bang that made them all jump. It split in two, and then nose-dived down to the lagoon, the still spinning rotors slamming into the turquoise water and disintegrating. It sank in seconds, only leaving a dark smudge on the water and a black cloud of smoke rapidly dissipating in the air.

"Now what do you suppose caused that?" Jerry asked.

"Beats the fuck outta me, but I'm not complaining," Tim said. He heard a loud *crump!* come from down the road and saw a fireball rise up over the palm trees, then heard screams of agony. "Well, I know where they are at now. I left another little surprise for them. Let's get into position. Holly, you go back to Robyn."

They ran back to their positions in the trees between the bunkers and waited. Just then, one of the men came up. "Sarge! We got a present for you!"

"What?" Williams asked, and turned to see one of his men holding three men at gunpoint. Two obviously white men, bare chested and wearing soaked trousers, their feet bloody and raw, obviously from walking over the reef. With them was a similarly clad diminutive Japanese man.

"I thought I told all of you no prisoners!" he said, and the looks on the three men's faces turned from relief to horror.

"Now wait a minute," the tallest of the three said plaintively. "We gave ourselves up. We were getting away from *him!*"

"Who the fuck are you?" Tim asked, standing up and pulling them all behind the bunker into cover.

"I'm Ensign William Johnson, United States Navy."

"And I'm Petty Officer First Class, Harry Suplee, US Navy," the second one said. "This one's Mr. Nakamura. His English isn't so good." The Asian man smiled and bowed.

"Okay, Mr. Johnson. What's your claim to fame?"

"Look, Sergeant, we've all basically been his prisoners since everything happened. We were sick of what he was doing, but couldn't get away for so long. When we got here, we figured it was now or never to jump ship!"

"Was that you with the chopper?" Tim asked.

"Yeah, pretty cool, eh? Mr. Johnson said he saw it in a movie once. Put a white phosphorous grenade in the helo's fuel tank with tape on the lever thing," Suplee said.

"Is that so?" Tim said.

"What about those cruise missiles on Oahu?" Jerry asked with a glare.

"I targeted them into the jungle. I couldn't bring myself to target the city or the *Arizona*, which he wanted destroyed. I did let one go into Hickam, just so he could see some smoke."

"What's his story?"

"The skipper you mean? He's gone mad. Thinks he's the Big Kahuna, and has the nukes to prove it. He got ten BGM109As we got in Pearl, and now he's after you because you have the codes," Ensign Johnson said, hanging his head.

"He's not mad, he's completely batshit fucking crazy is what he is!" Suplee piped up.

"Okay. He's nuts. How many men does he have?"

"About seventy, I think," Johnson said, and Jerry and Tim looked at each other.

There were so many questions Tim wanted to ask, but there was no time. "Take these three back to where Holly and Robyn are, and if they get squirrelly at all, kill them," Tim said to the man who brought them, who moved them to the rear at gunpoint.

"You know, even if we've got a third of them already," Jerry said, "that's still almost a platoon's worth of guns coming at us."

"I know. Listen, we'll do our best and hold them here for as long as we can. When it gets too bad, or looks like we can't hold them any longer, I want you to take everyone to that derelict car carrier on the reef. There's got to be lifeboats or something you can get on from there, and I'll keep them away as long as it takes."

"But wouldn't you need power to lower the lifeboats?" Jerry asked.

"Probably not, they most likely have a manual feature in case the ship is sinking and loses power. Like a safety feature or something."

"What about you?"

"I'll be along right behind you guys. Just do as I say when the time comes. Trust me on this. I'll buy everyone a little time to get away."

"If you say so, Sar' Major," Jerry said, and keyed up his radio. "Listen up people. They're coming at us again. Conserve your ammo. One shot at each target. When you run out, we don't have anymore. When that happens, rally behind the second bunker from my position, and we'll take it from there." He got several 'clicks' in return as acknowledgment.

They sat and watched down the tract, and finally they saw the first man appear, holding an AK47 at the hip and walking cautiously. Tim raised his carbine, squeezed the trigger, and saw the man crumple and fall. It was the impetus of pure bedlam after that. Full automatic fire was heard in the front, and then the M60 started barking. He heard screams and yelling, and every time he saw a man in front of him, he fired a round. Several grenades went off in between the shooting, and the whole area was beginning to be covered in a blue haze of cordite smoke. One by one in front of him, one of his men popped up out of the weeds, and made a hasty retreat past him and Jerry, who was also firing away at targets that Tim couldn't see. Tim's bolt slammed back and locked on an empty magazine, and he reloaded his carbine with his last thirty rounds. He pulled his rucksack around so he could use it as a rest, went down to the prone position, and scanned ahead of him for targets.

Behind Tim at the next bunker, Holly and Robyn were crouched down with the three men from the ship, and two more of William's men. Jimenez was on the other side of the road, using a bunker's concrete wall for cover and firing his rifle down the road. Robyn looked over at him, and as she did, saw two men with AK47's come around the rear of the bunker, and take aim at him.

"Taco, behind you!" she screamed, and raised her M4 to her shoulder, rattling off four three-round bursts, killing both men instantly. Jimenez looked behind him at the two bodies, and then over to Robyn, who was lowering her smoking carbine. She smiled at him, and he shook his head. He fired two more rounds down the road and made a mad dash over to where the others were, sliding to a stop in the dirt next to her.

"Thanks. I owe you one!" he said breathlessly. "And it's Jimenez."

"Whatever, Taco," she said, leaning around the bunker and firing off another burst.

Ahead of them things were getting a little hairy. Williams fired off his last burst, and the bolt slammed back, locking on an empty magazine.

"I'm out!" Jerry said.

"I got your back. Take everybody over to the car carrier now."

"Tim, I can't leave you here!" he screamed over the noise of battle.

"Yes you can, and you will. Do it *now*!" Tim said, never taking his eyes off of his sights, and cranking off another round. "Why aren't you gone already?"

"Okay! Okay! I'm gone. It's been a pleasure, Sar' Major!"

"Buy me a beer next R and R!" Tim said, and pulled off another round at an unseen figure moving through the weeds.

Jerry picked up his ruck and ran back to the second bunker. He did a quick headcount. With the three from the ship, he figured only ten left, not including Tim.

"Where's my Dad?" Robyn screamed.

"He's back there covering us. Now come on, follow me!" Jerry said.

"No! I'm not going anywhere without him!" she screeched, terrified. Holly was a ghostly pale, but took Robyn by the hand. "Come on, love. We've got to go!"

"No! I can't leave him! A Ranger is never supposed to leave a comrade behind!" she shouted over the din.

Jerry got down on one knee so he could be eye to eye with her. "Look Robyn. Tim's covering us so we can get away. He'll be along as soon as we're safe!" he said, hating to lie to her like that. Both he and Holly physically dragged her away, and she was fighting them, still trying to get back to Tim. They made it to the beach and the broken up ship only lay about a hundred yards off the beach. The tide was slowly coming in, but the water was still only waist deep, and they waded single file out to the wreck. Once there, through breaking waves, they all climbed into the cargo hold, careful not to cut themselves on the twisted and jagged metal. Jerry took out an angle-head Army flashlight and lit the way. He had no idea how to get up there until he felt a hand on his shoulder. He turned to see the Japanese man, Nakamura, offering to take the light.

"I know way! I sail on this ship before. It Nissan Maru!"

"By all means," Jerry said, handing over the light, and following Nakamura. They quickly made it all the way up to the rear of the ship where the lifeboats were. The small Japanese man quickly took charge, and in minutes had the boat ready to lower.

"Lifeboats have manual setting so we lower boat with no power."

Everyone piled on board, he and Suplee started the hand cranks, and the boat got closer to the water outside of the reef on the ocean side. They could plainly hear the sounds of the battle raging, by a one man Army at this point, and they were all enraged that they couldn't help.

"That's Daddy's grease gun!" Robyn said in a tiny voice as she heard the distinct sound of it firing out steady staccato bursts over the crack of the AK47s.

Jerry and Holly looked at each other, but said nothing. If Tim was using the old submachine gun, things were getting very up close and personal indeed. When the boat's keel was in the water, Nakamura lifted the cowling of the engine and tinkered for a minute, and to everyone's surprise, the diesel engine belched to life.

He looked up and smiled. "Good Japanese motor!"

Suplee went aft to the helm and took it after he made sure all the lines were off. "Where to, Skipper?" he asked, looking at Jerry.

"We go south. Get as far away from here as possible. There's supposed to be an Aussie ship coming to meet us."

"You're the skipper," Suplee said, and throttled up the engine, turning the helm to head south.

The sun was sinking in the west, and Holly wondered where the day had gone. She looked towards the now shrinking island with a heavy heart. Several plumes of dark, dirty smoke billowed out from the once serene image of the coconut palms, forever destroying her image of the idyllic paradise she had envisioned.

***

Back by the bunker, Tim had fired his last round from the carbine, and was now using the grease gun in short bursts. He had four more magazines for that, but that wouldn't last him too much longer. He was rapidly running out of options. Then a thought crossed his mind. What he'd said to Jimenez earlier: *If you've got to go, take as many of the bastards with you as you can…*

Without hesitation or second thoughts, he grabbed his rucksack and ducked behind the bunker. He pulled out the laptop computer with the odd satellite antenna and opened it up. He then pulled the Skillcraft ring binder out and sat it on the ground next to it. His hands were shaking as if he had palsy, and he had to try to calm himself. He looked at the screen.

SYNCHRONISING WITH SATELLITE…

"Oh, hurry the fuck up already!"

After what seemed like hours, it finally read: SATELLITE SYNCRONIZATION SUCCSESSFUL.

When he was prompted, he typed in DESPERADO and waited. He could hear voices getting closer, and he was sweating profusely. He wiped his eyes, and finally saw the prompt: NATIONAL COMMAND AUTHORITY CONFIRMED

The voices were even closer now, and they sounded more urgent.

"Will you hurry the fuck up?" he said to the computer. Finally, the Air Force bases began to pop up, one by one. He clicked on the first one he saw, Offutt Air Force Base.

TARGET? It queried. He quickly typed in the island's GPS coordinates. He waited again for what seemed like hours, and finally it accepted his input with: TARGET COORDINATES ACCEPTED

A few seconds later it asked: YIELD?

"How the fuck should I know?" he said in exasperation. He typed in '20 kt.'

YIELD INPUT UNACCEPTABLE. YIELD?

"Oh, for fuck sake, I don't know!" What Tim didn't know, was that on the other end of the satellite connection he was inputting to was what they called a 'Dial-A-Yield' W87 thermonuclear device, that ranged from 300 kiloton to 20 megaton and could be preset to a detonation yield, depending on the target. The largest thing he'd ever called in was an artillery barrage on a target, and was way out of his league with this. By just a guess, what they'd call in the Army a 'SWAG', or 'Scientific Wild Assed Guess' he typed in '1 MT' and hit enter. He picked up his grease gun, peered around the corner, and there were two men standing not three feet from him. He brought the weapon to bear and let a long chattering burst go, and watching them crumple and fall, went back to the tablet.

YIELD ACCEPTED. LAUNCH CODE?

Breathlessly, he flipped through the binder, looking desperately for the codes for Offutt Air force base. Finding it, he ran his fingers down the page, stopping on the line. He typed in the code and waited for what seemed like an eternity, as time seemed to slow to a crawl.

INVALID LAUNCH CODE. LAUNCH CODE?

"Jesus jumping Christ Almighty!" he swore. He looked at the code again and realized he'd mistyped it. His hands shaking badly now, he slowly typed each number and letter in one at a time, and then, right before he hit enter, all the things his brother had said, Dawn Red Eagle and his prophesies, his dreams, Robyn's ideas about him, came flooding to the forefront of his mind. Was this really what he was supposed to do? Was he really predestined to be here at this very moment and do this? Could he really make a difference, save the new world by doing this one little thing? Sweat was running in rivulets down his face and stinging his eyes as his finger hovered shakily over the 'enter' key. The thoughts kept crashing through the din of the gunfire, and in one final moment, he took a deep breath and hit 'enter'.

LAUNCH CODE ACCEPTED. TARGETING MISSILE NOW

"Oh hurry the fuck up!" he said, in what was now a very panicky voice.

MISSILE TARGETED. MISSILE LAUNCH IN T-MINUS 10 MINUTES

"It's about goddamn time!" he screamed, and slammed the top closed on the laptop. He stood and peered out from behind the bunker, and saw five more men standing close by. He trained the grease gun on them and let another long burst go, and the bolt locked back on an empty magazine. He turned and ran, changing magazines on the fly. Maybe he could still get away, catch up with the others if they aren't already dead. *Catch up with them and get far enough away before it gets here*, he thought. He turned between two more bunkers and heard a burst from an AK behind him. A sharp pain hit him just above his right hip, and he spun like a top, hitting the ground like a sack of potatoes, knocking the wind from him. He couldn't catch his breath for a moment, but ignoring the pain, got up and fired another burst, ran through the weeds and around coconut trees towards the ocean side beach and what he hoped was safety.

***

Back at the bunker Tim had just vacated, the smoke was clearing and Lt. Cmd. Winthorpe Wright approached a Pakistani man who was smiling and holding up the binder. There were several dead and wounded lying around on the ground, but he ignored them all, eyes on his prize. He was a sight to see, and if Tim had been there, he would have probably burst out laughing. Beard now blowing in the breeze, beads and seashells clattering like a wind chime suspended from his chin, his dress cap filthy but still perched on his head jauntily, dress white tunic with the shoulder boards and front unbuttoned and hanging open, bare chested with more gold chains and baubles than Mr. T ever wore. All he needed was the eye patch and a parrot.

"Keptin!" the Pakistani man screamed with glee. "I have the code you are seeking!"

"Good! Good!" he smiled, stepping heedlessly over a dead man towards the Pakistani holding the now battered ring binder.

"We go after them?" the man asked.

"No, let them go. They'll probably die out there of exposure in a few days anyway. Here, let me see it!" he said, and grabbed the binder, flipping through the pages, giggling with laughter. Another man came up to him then, holding the computer.

"What do you want us to do with this, sir?" he asked.

"Oh, I don't know, does it work?" he asked. The man shrugged and opened it up.

"It is counting down something, sir!" he said and turned it towards their captain.

Wright took one look at it, blanched, and swore. "We must get back to the ship at once!"

"What is wrong, Bwana?" a Kenyan man asked.

"Just get back to the ship now!" he said, and took off in a dead run, beard flapping behind him over his shoulder comically, ring binder clutched under his arm like a schoolboy running to catch the bus.

***

Tim reached the beach, stripped down to the waist, and saw a nice hole in him about where his kidney would be, and coming out on his lower stomach in the front. Blood oozed from the wound, and he could hardly breathe. All the firing had stopped, and he was surprised when they didn't come after him. He waded out into the water, but saw no signs of the others or a lifeboat. He looked to the derelict ship and saw the loose lines swinging in the late afternoon breeze from the empty davit, so he knew they must have gotten away. He waded out into the warm water, and when it got to waist deep, he sucked in a hard breath as the water hit the wound. The salt water burned the wound like no one's business, and he almost passed out from the pain. He brushed it aside, and with all his strength, he started to wade through the water towards the reef. When he reached it, he put the sling for the grease gun around his neck and forced his way through the breakers until he was out into deep water. When he was well clear, he shucked his boots, and began to slowly swim away from the island, trying to make as much distance between it and him as possible. He was several yards out now, and took a break to tread water to catch his breath.

A gray dorsal fin broke the surface of the now calm, almost flat water, outside the reef and his bladder became weak. It wasn't ten yards from him, circling all the way around before disappearing back underwater. He thought about the wound, and all the blood he must be losing, and cursed his luck.

"Wonderful. All this, and I'm going to be eaten by a shark," he said to no one, as he looked around the empty sea.

CHAPTER 22: ROCKETS' RED GLARE

The coded information that Tim had typed into the laptop computer was digitally scrambled, and in a millisecond was transmitted to a geosynchronous satellite, then transmitted back down to Earth to a huge dish on Offutt Air Force Base in Nebraska. From the dish, it was relayed to a bank of computers powered by solar panels, which had sat dormant, hibernating, in a bombproof concrete sub-basement of a nondescript building near post headquarters. That computer came to life, then digested the information it had just received. The necessary information was then transmitted through armored cables buried deep underground to a missile silo twenty-five miles away that sat in the middle of an overgrown corn field. The data was then transferred to a second computer via a slave-cable attached to the missile, which in this case was a Minuteman III ICBM encased in the thick hardened concrete silo to the missile's internal navigation system. This process, from the time Tim hit 'enter', took approximately thirty seconds. When the computer in the silo had received the message back from the missile that it had accepted the targeting information and was now ready, it sent another message to fire the explosive bolts and open the five foot thick steel and concrete cover on the silo. The cover slammed back and exposed the opening, spraying dirt for yards where it stopped.

This is when the missile itself came to life. Sitting all these years in the hermetically sealed silo, it was almost as new as when it was lowered in place in the early 1990s, waiting for this information that its builders had hoped it would never receive. Its long-dead builders would be pleased that everything was performing optimally, and just as they had programmed it to. Seconds after the heavy steel and concrete reinforced cover that was designed to protect the buried missile— and could withstand a direct hit from a thermonuclear weapon—, was slammed aside, another order from the computer gave the launch order in the form of digital code. This order ignited the main engine on the first stage solid fuel booster in a huge fireball that, with nowhere to go, sped up the shiny, burnished aluminum sides of the missile and out the top, causing a huge smoke plume and perfect smoke ring. The rocket motor was so loud it rattled windows in vacant houses several miles away, and a small tremor was felt by the huge bison herd and the myriad prairie dog nests for several miles around, spooking the animals.

The missile, now free of its shackles, slowly rose out of the silo, and in three seconds was clear and gaining speed on its ascent. At four seconds, and at approximately two hundred feet, the missile made a pitch maneuver to aim it at its target to the southwest. It was now trailing a huge white smoke trail, and its tail was burning brightly, lighting up the pre-dawn sky for miles around. At ten seconds, it made its first roll maneuver, tilting forty-five degrees on its longitudinal axis.

***

Ten miles away, the deep, loud rumble and tremors of the missile's launch woke two figures out of a deep sleep. The flap of the bison-skin teepee flipped open, and two people emerged. Dawn Red Eagle helped his pregnant partner, another Native American with the same round features and same long, dark hair. They stared out as the rocket rose and headed west, the noise still loud enough to spook the five horses he had tied to a line.

"What is it?" she asked, grabbing onto his arm with one hand, instinctively holding on to her round belly with the other, as if to protect her unborn child.

"The cleansing, I believe. A new world is about to begin, just like the Ancient Ones said," he said, putting his arm around his partner, and holding her tightly.

"I see, but why?"

"It is the way of the Earth. The decision has been made, and cannot be taken back now."

"But why do it, and who did it?"

"The ones I told you about, The Chosen Ones I met here on the prairie so many years ago. It needed to be done, and the decision has been made, and that is a decision I believe wasn't made lightly," he said. "Tim and Robyn, I truly wish you well."

They stood together, watching the rocket rise until it completely disappeared. Standing on the open prairie, they stayed there motionless, holding hands tightly.

***

At nineteen seconds after clearing the silo, the Minuteman III was already travelling at over one thousand feet per second, was at eight thousand feet in altitude, and still gaining speed. At thirty-nine seconds, it was at Mach 3 and thirty eight thousand feet. Six seconds later, it made its second roll maneuver, and was at fifty thousand feet, still gaining speed. At one minute, two seconds, the first stage rocket booster depleted its solid fuel and burned out, separated, and fell away. It was now eighteen nautical miles downrange from the silo, and at one hundred thousand feet. Eighteen seconds later, the second stage rocket booster ignited, thrusting the missile higher and faster still. The now expended first stage dropped and fell to the Earth, no longer needed.

At two minutes after launch, now free of the Earth's atmosphere, the rocket jettisoned the Reentry Vehicle Shroud at three hundred and fifteen thousand feet. Three seconds later, the second stage booster burned out and separated, and the third stage fired. It was now ninety nautical miles from the silo, and at an altitude of two hundred forty thousand feet.

***

At that exact moment, several thousand miles southwest, Tim was contemplating his fate. He was treading water and losing strength with every sweep of his arms as he watched the gray dorsal fin sink below the surface again. The water around him was turning a deep red from his blood, and he knew it had to be attracting them from all over. He was losing strength rapidly now, and could hardly catch his breath from the pain in his side, and wasn't sure how much longer he could last.

"Is it a reef shark or a tiger shark, Timmy boy?" he said aloud. "It doesn't really make a difference. I'm still chum." He felt something swim by his leg, and he jumped. He gripped the grease gun tightly in one hand, even though the sling was around his neck. Maybe if he nailed one of the sharks, they'd go after it and leave him alone! He went to raise it, when the water broke right in front of him, and the narrow snout of a bottlenose dolphin popped up, looking like it was smiling at him. It squeaked a few times and bobbed its head, then just looked at him.

"You have *got* to be shitting me!" he said and laughed. "I think I'm the wrong Timmy, Flipper! You'd better get well clear of here now, buddy, or you're going to be poached."

***

Five minutes after the Minuteman III left the silo, the third stage booster burned out and separated, leaving only the post-boost flight vehicle and its payload, the reentry vehicle, a single pre-programmed to 1MT W87 thermonuclear weapon, travelling very fast just above the Earth's atmosphere towards its target, the Atoll of Volivoli.

Back in the days of the Cold War, each post-boost vehicle would have had up to six warheads each, targeted for different areas inside the Soviet Union, and was called an MIRV, or Multiple Independently Targeted Reentry Vehicle. More bang for the buck, one might say. Now there was only one, but for its purpose this day, it was more than enough. This flight of the post-boost vehicle would now last only twenty more minutes. Again this, as with everything else since Tim hit enter, worked flawlessly.

***

Back on Volivoli, Lt. Cmd. Wright was met halfway down the runway by Petty Officer Stevens.

"Captain, those two fucks have jumped ship, and they're on the island somewhere!" he said, and his captain ran right past him, trying to get back to the whaleboat and the ship as fast as he could, beard flowing behind him like a great woolen scarf. He was followed by the Pakistani man that had found the codes and the computer, who was struggling to keep up. Stevens stopped him and screamed at him, "What the fuck is going on? Why are you and Skipper running?"

"I do not know! I show him this and he scream run!" he said, breathlessly, handing the computer to Stevens.

He took it from the panting man, and opened it up. His eyes bugged and the blood ran out of his face. He threw the laptop into the lagoon and took off in a sprint towards the captain and the whaleboat. They had to skirt the still burning hulk of the destroyed Hercules, but Stevens caught up to him as he was untying the ropes that held the boat to the pier. The bodies of their dead comrades still littered the beach from where Williams had set off his wired artillery shells, and one stared back at them accusingly.

"Skipper, was that what I think it was?" he asked as he hopped in the boat and started the motor. There were several more men on the beach, running down the wooden pier, not sure why their captain was abandoning them.

"Yes! The damn fool launched something at us! Now we've got to get back on the ship, and get out of here as quickly as possible!" he screamed.

"I hope the fuck Alphabits can get her off the bottom!" Stevens said, still not believing what was going through his mind. "Was it a nuke he launched?"

"Yes! And for both our sakes he'd better get the goddamn ship loose!"

"He couldn't have really done it, Captain. I mean fuck, why launch a nuke at yourself? He's gotta know he wouldn't make it out himself!" Stevens said, as he steered the whaleboat alongside the ship.

"Yes! Only a lunatic would do that!" he said, grabbing onto the rope ladder hanging down over the side and starting to climb up.

The Indonesian officer, who they all called Alphabits, looked down over the wing bridge, and saw the captain's urgency. He ducked inside the bridge, and Stevens, who was halfway up the ladder, could hear the turbines come to life with a large billow of black smoke out of the stack. By the time he got to the weather deck, the screws were turning at full power in reverse, churning up huge amounts of frothy water. When he entered a hatch to head to the bridge, he heard the bottom scrape loudly across the reef, as the ship was now slowly inching its way off of it. Then all the men on the beach started to run into the water, and swim frantically towards the slowly reversing ship. They didn't know why they were leaving, but they surely didn't want to be left marooned on the island.

**

Three miles south of the island, the lifeboat from the Nissan Maru was steadily motoring at ten knots on an almost glass-smooth sea. Robyn was in Holly's arms, not making a sound, as the older woman brushed her hand over her hair and rocked her gently. The others were huddled together, silent and watching the island slowly disappear. They could see the smoke plume from the still burning Hercules and several other fires. Ensign Johnson walked over to Sergeant Williams.

"Thank you for letting us come, you didn't have to."

"Yes I did," Williams said.

"Why's that?"

"It's because there's a little boy in Honolulu that needs his dad," he said, not taking his eyes off the island.

"Any sign of Tim?" one of the men asked.

"No sign at all," Williams said angrily, and he heard Robyn moan.

"What do you mean?" Johnson said.

"You are Ensign William Johnson, from the USS Hughes, right?"

"Yes I am," he asked. "What boy are you talking about?" "Mary made me promise I wouldn't hurt you."

"Mary! She's *alive*?" he asked excitedly, grabbing Williams' arm.

"Yes, she's alive. And you have a little boy named Billy."

Johnson sat down in shock and didn't say another word, just had this odd little smile on his face, before he brought his hands up to his face and began to weep. "It's over! It's finally over!" he said through the tears.

"It isn't over, not by a long shot. It looks like that tub of yours is trying to get off the reef," Williams said, pointing at the now distant island and ship, and they all looked. Billows of black smoke were now pouring out of the stack.

"Oh, no…" Johnson said.

***

About one hundred miles northeast of the island, at an altitude of five hundred thousand feet, the post-boost flight of the warhead ended. The flight from the silo in Nebraska to this spot took approximately twenty-nine minutes. The post-boost vehicle maneuvered to a downward facing angle, at a pre-determined window in space, and released the reentry vehicle. The W87 warhead looked nothing like a conventional bomb; it was cone shaped, similar to a sugar cone for ice cream, but about one meter in length and gunmetal gray. As soon as it had separated from the post-boost vehicle, spin-gas generators on the rear of the device fired and put a clockwise rotation on it to stabilize its reentry. The beauty of the weapon was in its simplicity. The designers, in an attempt to save weight, used the weapon's own fissionable material, in this case Plutonium, for its heat shield. Once separated from the post-boost vehicle and spinning rapidly, the weapon now used gravity to pull in to its intended target with an accuracy of about one hundred meters. Like the old saying goes, close only counts in horseshoes, hand grenades and thermonuclear devices, and one hundred meters was close enough. It fell faster and faster, gaining speed as it got closer to the Earth. As it fell, the air got thicker, and friction with the outer plutonium shell caused it to glow white hot, leaving a streak in the darkening twilight sky, not unlike a meteor. Volivoli had been around for thousands of years, born of a volcano deep on the ocean's floor, now long since dead. And born of fire, would now die of fire.

***

On the bridge of the USS Hughes, the captain walked out onto the wing bridge, and watched the slow progress. The men who had swum out to the ship were now trying desperately to climb up the rope ladder, still dangling over the side. Finally, after what seemed like hours, the ship broke free of the reef, and began backing up into deep water. He let out a sigh of relief and looked up. What he saw removed all relief he might have felt. He saw a glowing, white-hot streak coming directly towards the ship from high up in the atmosphere. He was frozen in place, unable to move when he felt a warm trickle run down his leg as his bladder released.

***

Five miles away on the lifeboat, Robyn finally looked up. "Look! A shooting star! Make a wish, Holly!"

Holly looked to where the girl was pointing, and got a knot in her stomach. She grabbed Robyn, pulling her down and covering her eyes. "Everyone get down! Cover your eyes! Do it quickly!" she screamed. They all hesitated for a moment, then the gravity of her voice told them they'd better do what she said. As soon as they were all down below the gunwales, the darkening sky, just starting to become starlit, turned to day. At exactly one thousand feet above the atoll and the ship, the barometric triggering device gave its order to the device to detonate. A white hot ball of fire spread out directly from over the channel where the warhead had detonated a millisecond ago. Everything within five hundred yards was reduced down to its molecular level. The expanding ball of hot gas, ten times hotter than the surface of the sun, engulfed everything within that radius. Everything on the island further out was instantaneously flattened, then set ablaze by the thermal radiation in a widening circle reaching out to two thousand yards. At that point, the whole atoll was wiped flat. The once soft, snow-white sand was turned to molten glass, and all the ammunition stored in the bunkers detonated, adding to the utter destruction. The shockwave, in the form of compressed air, raced outwards in an ever expanding bubble at the speed of sound, and that wall and the sound of the blast hit the tiny boat at the same time. It was loud, louder than any blast any of them had ever heard, and the shockwave rocked the boat to almost capsizing. It righted itself, as the designers had intended, though they certainly would not have been envisioning these circumstances when designing a self-righting lifeboat. After the shockwave had passed, they all looked up in amazement that they were still alive. The fireball was now rising into the air at a rapid speed, turning into a huge mushroom cloud still alive with fire.

They all stared for what seemed like hours, watching the cloud rise into the stratosphere and widen, and there was still a steady rumble like a thousand freight trains passing at once, that seemed like it would never end. They looked at where the island had once been, but could only see a white hot glow.

"Nothing could have survived that!" Suplee said. "Holy shit!"

"Oh my God, would you look at that!" Ensign Johnson said. "He's gone. He's finally gone."

Holly was speechless as she held Robyn. "Holly, why did he do it?" Robyn said in a tiny, tiny voice. "We should have gone back for him. It's what you're supposed to do. Never leave a fallen comrade..."

"I don't know, honey. Maybe he just wanted us to get free," Holly said, holding onto Robyn, tears flowing freely.

"What about radiation?" one of Williams' men asked. Holly, still holding onto Robyn answered. "We're far enough away now and heading south. The prevailing winds blow east, so that's where the fallout will go."

Watching the glowing mushroom cloud rise into the night sky, no one heard the splash of water and a dolphin's squeak, and nobody saw the hand come up over the gunwales. Another hand appeared, then Tim's head. The clatter of the grease gun hitting the deck made everyone turn.

"*Tim!*" Holly screamed, rushing to pull him into the boat. Williams grabbed an arm, and Nakamura grabbed the other, and they hoisted him into the boat where he plopped on the deck unceremoniously. He looked a mess, and the wound in his side was still oozing blood. He looked up at Holly, and tried to sit up, removing the grease gun from around his neck, and dropping it on the deck.

"Hey, baby," he said drunkenly, looking into her eyes. Robyn came over, and hugged him tightly.

"I thought you were dead!" she said, kissing him.

Everyone on the boat gathered around him, and Williams pushed through the crowd and knelt down next to him. "Tim, you've got balls, man, big giant brass ones. I don't think I'd have been able to do that."

"I had to. It was the only way left. I knew if he got hold of the codes, he would have just come looking for you guys," he said, and then winced in pain.

"Man, you got hit pretty badly," Williams said. "We saw the bomb go off, and we thought you were gone."

"Well, I'm too ornery to die. And I will never, ever eat a tuna sandwich ever again as long as I live," he said, pointing at Jerry, and then passed out in the bottom of the boat.

***

Tim was hovering between sleep and dreams, but could see light through closed eyes that refused to open. He could hear someone talking, but couldn't make out what was being said. He could feel the bed he was lying on and smell the clean sheets. There were other smells. It smelled antiseptic, like a hospital. That was it. He was in a hospital. He tried to remember what had happened, but it was all a jumble. Coming home from Afghanistan... The Event, Paul, Robyn. Red Eagle... Holly and Izzy... the flight to the island... and the craziest thing, him launching the nuke. That was it! He'd been in a car wreck and this was all a dream. It had to have been a dream. He'd been in a coma and everything had all been a terrible nightmare!

But it all seemed so real... Holly... her long, long beautiful hair... He could actually smell her still at this very moment, and longed to feel her again. If it was all a dream, he wanted to go back and find her. He had to go back to sleep and drift off to that place where Holly was. He felt something cool and damp on his forehead. It felt nice, and he didn't want it to stop. He felt a dull pain in his lower abdomen, and it itched. *Yes.* He *could* smell her now. Every woman has a unique scent, and that was definitely what was teasing his olfactory senses now. He forced his eyes to slowly open, and tilted his head a little. The light was bright and cold, sterile. Just like hospital lighting. His eyesight began to clear, and he could see a shadow. That brightened too as his vision cleared, and his heart skipped a beat. That beautiful face! That face of an angel, framed in long red hair was close, and the green eyes were gazing at him hopefully.

"Holly?" he said in a raspy voice.

"I'm right here, Timmy. Don't move. You've been hurt really badly and you've got to stay still," she said, tears of joy filling her green eyes. "Doctor, please come quick! He's awake!"

"Was it all real?"

"Aye, it was real. Now please, lay still, love," she said, kissing his dry lips.

A man wearing horn-rimmed glasses, his hair in a ponytail and wearing a loud Hawaiian shirt walked in and over to the bunk where Tim lay. "Ah good! I see you're awake. You were a very sick bloke when we got you, mate. Luckily for you, your partner here has the same blood type as you!" he said in an Australian accent.

"Where am I?"

"You're on the *HMAS Newcastle*. And we're about a day away from Pearl Harbor."

"How did we get here?" he asked, confused.

"We all did like you told Jerry to do," Holly explained, "we got to the wrecked ship on the reef, and we were able to lower one of the lifeboats and get away. We were about three miles from the island when the bomb went off."

"Yes, and we saw the light show from a thousand kilometers away," the doctor said.

"The Australians picked us up about a day later. Just in time too, you had lost a lot of blood, and we weren't sure you were going to make it," Holly said, tears beginning to well up.

"Everyone got out?"

"Yes, everyone got away. Robyn is up in a cabin asleep. She has been worried sick."

"Good. I was trying to give you all time to get far enough away. I wasn't sure I'd get out in time, but that didn't matter, as long as the rest of you did," he said.

"How did you get to the lifeboat anyway? It was three bloody miles away!"

"You'd never believe it."

"Alright now, he's still not completely well. You've lost one kidney and part of your liver, and you need to get some rest. I don't want any of those sutures ripping out, so please don't move around much for a bit."

"Ah, I've got plenty of liver to go around, and I got two kidneys, I can give up one I guess," Tim said in a weak attempt at a joke.

The doctor showed Holly out.. "Now get some rest, mate," he said to Tim. "I'll let her come back in a bit, but you need your rest."

"You're the doc," Tim said, closing his eyes, and was immediately asleep. The next time he woke, he was feeling a little bit better than before, and could even sit up a little. Robyn and Holly were there at his bedside, and standing behind them was a very nervous Jimenez. He looked around, and saw all the accoutrements of a ship, and could feel the movement. He sipped on some water through a straw offered by Robyn, and thanked her.

"Dad, we were so worried about you. We thought you were gone with the rest of them when the bomb went off," she said, taking his hand gently, careful not to hit the IV that was placed in a vein there.

"I'm okay, baby. It's all over now."

"Was this what Dawn Redeagle told us about? What you had to do?"

"I don't know, baby. I think so. I don't ever want to have to do that ever again. It's over and done with," he said, closing his eyes.

"Yeah, and now we can be one happy family, all four of us!"

"Four of us?" he asked, opening his eyes.

Robyn looked at Holly in surprise. "You didn't tell him?"

"Tell me what?" he asked. "If you hooked up with that Jimenez kid—"

Jimenez quickly stepped back. "No, sir! I swear I didn't do anything! She saved my ass back on the island!"

"No, Dad, not that, although he is kind of cute," she said, giving Jimenez a coy look over her shoulder.

"Now wait just a goddamn minute!" he said, and started to sit up. Holly gently pushed him back down into the bunk and kissed him.

"I'm having a baby, Tim," Holly said with a twinkle in her eyes.

"A-A baby? You're *pregnant*?" Tim said, in shock. He almost said 'how did that happen?' but that would have been a really stupid question.

"Yes. I'm pregnant."

"Now what?"

"Well, I do believe there's a nice house in northern Arizona we can get for cheap, and there are no nosy neighbors," she said.

"Yeah, I do recall mentioning that a time or two," he said, his smile wide.

"I love you, Timothy Xavier Flannery!" Holly said, leaning down to kiss him. "I love you too, babe," he said, kissing her back.

"Where'd 'Xavier' come from? That's funny!" Robyn said, and they all had a good laugh as the Australian ship neared Hawaii...

ONE MAN'S WAR

PROLOGUE

Over a thousand light years ago, a sun, in a far distant part of our Milky Way Galaxy died in a huge Supernova. It took eons for the effects of that stellar blast to reach Earth, in the form of a Gamma Ray burst along with a vast electromagnetic pulse, which killed off almost the entire human population in one fell swoop, along with most of the domesticated animals, leaving only a handful of survivors.

Recently back from what he thought was his last battle, Sergeant Major Timothy Flannery, Pennsylvania Army National Guard and Philadelphia Police Officer, finds himself alone in a decaying necropolis that once was his home.

Struggling to survive and keep his sanity, he first meets a mild-mannered University Professor, Paul. But soon after meeting this other survivor of that terrible night, things go terribly wrong for Paul, who was brutally tortured and murdered. Tim, unable to save Paul, kills his assailants, and makes preparations to leave Philadelphia.

He escapes the city just in time, before a lighting strike in one of the older neighborhoods turns into a huge conflagration, engulfing the historic town in a firestorm.

Traveling westward, he makes it to West Virginia, where he finds a waif of a girl, Robyn. He takes her in, raising her as his own, and after a harrowing winter in the Appalachians, the unlikely pair continue on their trek westward, where they come across more people, hell bent on making life difficult for them.

After Tim rescues Robyn from two kidnappers, they find the wreckage of Air Force One, and sifting through the rubble in an overgrown soybean field, find 'The Football', the codes for the United States nuclear arsenal. This they safeguard, knowing their finding it was somehow important.

In Nebraska, they meet a kindly old Native American, Dawn Redeagle, who, through tales of Native Folklore, they gain new perspective and also find a safe haven. In Williams, Arizona, they set up a nice homestead for themselves, and Robyn grows into a fine young woman.

It was then, years afterward, that they come into contact with two more people, Izzy Ginsberg and Flight Lieutenant Holly MacFarland, RAF. Holly and Tim fall deeply in love with each other, and the four people now travel all the way to the South Pacific, to a tiny Atoll named Volivoli, with the help of another survivor, Lance Corporal Juan Jimenez, USMC.

Before they reach the atoll that was supposed to be their final place, their new home in paradise, they're confronted with a new evil, a rogue US Navy officer, who has been terrorizing the entire Pacific Ocean for several years.

It was on this tiny atoll, with the generous help of another soldier, Sergeant First Class Jerome Williams and his men from Schofield Barracks, Hawaii, they have a final confrontation with evil, and find out what they were meant to do with The Football.

This is their continuing story...

CHAPTER 1:
THE BIG KAHUNA

Tim was waiting on the porch for the taxi he'd called to take him to the airport. He and Connie had just had another blowout fight and now he was sitting there, chain smoking and fuming. How many times had he tried to explain to her that he didn't have a choice, he had to go?

He heard the front door open and he turned to see her head pop out.

"That's right. Just sit out there and wait for your ride. Go ahead and run away from your responsibilities again!" she spat angrily.

"I'm not running away!" he shouted, his anger beginning to boil over. Why she always had to drag these arguments out into the public and broadcast it to the entire neighborhood, he had no clue.

"Yes you are, mister big Army man! Sergeant Major! You do have a choice!"

"How many times do I have to go over this? You knew when you married me this might happen."

"But not six goddamn times! Do you know what it's like to sit at home here, watching the goddamn news every night wondering if you're going to come home in a box?"

He had no answer to that and hung his head.

"That's right! You don't have a clue what it's like!" she finally spat. "You had a choice the last time you reenlisted. You didn't have to do that, did you?"

He was about to explode, and he wished the taxi would show up before he did something stupid.

"It's all honkey-dory when I'm going to weekend drills, right? You love my extra pay from the Guard too. How else would you get your fucking nails and hair done all the time?" he finally said angrily.

"That's not true!"

"Yes it is! You love the extra money and you sure know how to fucking spend it," he spat, standing. "And speaking of hair, what the fuck did you do this time? It looks like you got your head stuck in a blender!"

"I like it," she said.

"I don't. I can't believe you paid good money for that," he said, looking at what once was beautiful long, natural honey-blond hair, that was now cropped severely short and spiky, and was dyed an almost unbelievable purple color that Tim was sure would not be found in nature.

Connie backed up a little in fear, her hand on the doorknob, ready to slam it shut. "I take care of this house when you're away playing soldier, goddamn it! You don't give a goddamn about anything but your goddamn unit!"

"Don't you understand the Brigade needs me?" he said in exasperation.

"They don't need you! You're expendable. Once you're gone, they'll find some other knuckle-dragger to take your place! They don't care about you!"

"They're family."

"Oh! They're fucking family, are they? What about your fucking family right here?" Connie said, her eyes ablaze.

"I have to go!" he shouted, tossing his burned out cigarette onto the postage-stamp sized lawn.

"Well, you go then! See if I care anymore!" she shouted, slamming the door in his face. He looked at the door for a moment and turned to the street, where the bright yellow taxi was pulling up in front of his house. Down Leon Street, peering south, Tim saw a blinding flash of white light, which soon dimmed to reveal an angry black mushroom cloud roiling up into the stratosphere. He stood there next to the taxi, frozen in place, watching the rising cloud, when the shockwave from the blast engulfed him…

Tim woke with a start. He was slightly disoriented, and the dream left him bewildered. He'd not thought about Connie for years, but the nuclear blast was still quite vivid in his mind. An involuntary chill swept over his body, and he was immediately covered in goose bumps.

He wasn't sure if it was the dream, or the temperature in the room. He saw that the window was open, and the early morning sunlight was streaming in, filtered by the fronds of an immature coconut palm outside. Smelling the air wafting in through the open window, he detected the faintest hint of rain on the cool breeze.

It must have rained overnight, he thought. He sat up a little and winced at the now dwindling pain in his side. He looked down and saw the suture scar was almost completely healed, but it was going to be a nasty one, ugly and red, gashed in his lower abdomen like an angry lightning bolt that went all the way to his groin. He reached over to the other side of the bed and through the messy sheets, he could still feel her warmth, and smiled.

"Ah! You're awake I see," Holly said, entering the bedroom wearing only one of Tim's T-Shirts and carrying two mugs of coffee. She walked up to the bed and handed him one of the mugs, which he took with a smile. Holly then walked around the bed and climbed in the other side, careful not to spill her cup. He breathed in the aroma.

"You have to love this Kona coffee," he said.

"Aye, I've never had better! So how are you feeling today?" she said, taking a sip of her coffee.

"Better. Still itches some, but I'm getting my strength back, little by little."

"Oh, I think your strength is coming along just fine, judging by last night's performance," she said with a twinkle in her eye.

He laughed in reply and looked out the window. "Babe, do you think I'm expendable?" Tim asked in an unnaturally soft voice, looking away from her, not daring to look back.

"Where did that come from?" she responded, setting down her mug on the bedside table, pulling her hair over her shoulder and leaning into his arm, pulling him close.

"Eh, just had a thought is all."

"To me you're priceless, Sweetheart. And I'm sure Robyn would say the same thing."

He reached around and pulled her close, leaned in, and kissed the top of her head. "That makes me very happy. You're pretty damn special to me too."

"Another dream?" she asked.

"Yeah, nothing to worry about. It was something from another lifetime."

"Are you sure?" she insisted, knowing how bad some of his dreams were. She'd been awakened by his shouts of terror before, but had never told him so, or pressed him about them. She knew he'd tell her if he thought it would help. I'm sure the last month hadn't been so pleasant, after everything that had happened on Volivoli.

"Yeah, babe, I'm sure. So what's on your agenda today?" he said, deftly changing the subject.

"Our young Mr. Jimenez thinks he may have found our ride home, so I'm going over to Hickam with him."

"Did he find another Hercules?"

"Aye. It will need some work, but he thinks he should be able to get her flying," she said, sipping her coffee and eyeing Tim over the rim.

"How long, do you reckon?" Tim asked.

"I'm not sure. Depends on what Jimenez thinks."

"I don't think the house back in Arizona is going anywhere." Tim sighed.

"Aye, I miss it there. Not that living here in Hawaii is all that bad," Holly said.

"Yeah, it is nice here, but there's something about that place. It's like home. Funny, it's the first place I felt at home, even before the Event."

"I never felt so at home before I met you and Robyn."

Tim reached over and rubbed Holly's belly, feeling the now noticeable bump. He smiled. "So, how's the little trooper doing today?"

"He or she is doing wonderful! Izzy said we're both in fine health."

"That's good news," Tim said, putting his coffee cup on the night table and sitting up. "I think I'll get dressed and get something to eat."

"What would you like for breakfast, Sergeant Major?" Holly asked, pulling the T-shirt over her head, exposing her firm, round breasts.

"You keep on doing that, I may never leave the bedroom!"

"You are naughty! I'm getting dressed, so behave yourself!" Holly stated, sticking her tongue out and tossing the T-shirt at him. She pulled on a pair of jeans and found another shirt to put on. "You get dressed yourself, and come out and I'll make us some breakfast."

"Yes ma'am!" Tim said, standing at attention and giving her his best salute.

He watched her walk out of the bedroom silently. As he got dressed, he couldn't help but wonder about the former residents of this little bungalow. Who were they, and what did they do before the Event? Were they dead and gone, like all the rest?

Jerry had found the place for them, and had purged it completely of the former occupants' personal affects before they'd moved in, for which Tim was enormously grateful. Even after all this time, it still saddened him that so many were dead.

Billions upon billions dead, all over the world, in the blink of an eye. Had it really been almost seven years? He shuddered involuntarily and finished dressing.

Walking out into a narrow hallway, Tim made his way to an equally tiny kitchen with a breakfast nook. Holly poured him another cup of coffee, and he sat silently, looking out the window that overlooked a small beach. He watched the waves break over the sand, while Holly cooked breakfast, and after a short time she brought him a steaming plate of what Tim was elated to see was fresh waffles.

Now, only if there was real butter and maple syrup, he thought silently.

He resigned himself to fake bottled syrup and margarine, laughing a little to himself at the thought of those items lasting until the next Ice Age.

"What's the smile for?" Holly asked, sitting down at the table opposite from Tim.

"Oh, I was thinking about how this syrup will probably last until the next Ice Age."

"That it probably will," she agreed. "It would be nice to have some fresh," she added, pouring a liberal amount on her still steaming waffle. "At least this mix is still good."

Tim sliced up his waffle and ate a few bites, wiping the corner of his mouth with a paper towel. "So tell me more about the Herc."

"Juan has been exploring all over the base, and there's three Hercules in hangars that he thinks he can cannibalize to make one plane airworthy."

"Is Robyn with him?" he asked.

"Aye, he picked her up earlier this morning. He said he'd be around later to pick me up."

"She's been spending a lot of time with him," Tim said flatly.

"Tim, she's a woman now, and he's a nice chap. Give him a chance," she countered, pointing her fork at him, a piece of waffle on the end dripping syrup.

Tim laughed, "Holly, I do like him. I just like breaking his balls. She's a big girl."

"He's frightened of you, Sergeant Major."

"Good!" he stated, forking another piece of waffle into his mouth. He finished chewing, swallowed and then added, "I think it's nice that she likes him. And I know he adores her."

"Then stop being so mean to him," Holly laughed.

"When pigs fly," he said with a wink.

"Speaking of pigs, Jerry said there was a bloke on the other side of the island that had rounded up some wild pigs and is trying to breed them. Hopefully we'll have some fresh bacon soon!"

"That would be nice," Tim agreed. "Jerry said he'd be stopping over today."

"He's nice too. I think everyone here is fab."

"He's been a lifesaver. He's got everything well organized, and now that we don't have to worry about some crazy psychopath terrorizing the whole ocean, I think it won't be too long before he's got the whole island back into some shape of a civilized society," Tim said, mopping up the last of the syrup with the last bite of waffle.

"Do you want more coffee?" Holly asked, finished with her food, and standing with her empty plate.

"I'll get it myself, Babe," he said, standing and taking his plate over to the sink. Holly passed her plate over to him, and he took it from her. "I'll clean up; you go and do what you need to do."

"Thanks," she said with a smile, as the sound of a Hum-Vee pulling up outside made them both turn their heads. "That's probably Juan. I'd better go."

"Tell Taco I said hi," he said, "and I'll be keeping an eye on him!"

"I will do no such thing, Timothy!" Holly said, kissing him on the cheek. "You take care of yourself today, and I'll be back later."

"Is that an order, Flight Leftenant MacFarland?"

"Aye, it is!"

"Okay, wilco, Ma'am!" he said.

Tim busied himself with the washing up, wishing for running water. Jerry said that they were still working on it, but might have it ready by the end of the week. A hot shower would feel wonderful. At least they had the electricity on, and that was a luxury.

He finished washing up the dishes from breakfast, poured himself another cup of coffee, and retrieved his pipe from a table by the front door. He took both and went out the shade of the lanai and sat in a rocking chair.

He filled the bowl with tobacco, tamping it down, and then lighting it with a wooden match. He puffed a few times to get it going, and sat back, looking out over the yard onto the empty street.

Taking another sip of his coffee, he looked to the north and saw a rising plume of smoke several miles away. Out of the corner of his eye, he noticed movement, and turned to look. The figure of a large black man, walking with military precision, had rounded the corner and was heading in his direction.

When the man saw Tim on the lanai, he smiled and picked up his pace. HE came through the gate and up the path to the porch, and bounded up the three steps effortlessly. It was Staff Sergeant Jerome Williams, or Jerry as he liked to be called, a man Tim now considered to be his best friend, or as much as a friend a sergeant major could have.

"I'd have thought there wouldn't be any more bodies to burn," Tim remarked to him.

"Yeah, I thought the same thing, but we keep on finding more here and there. I figure burning them is the easiest thing to do with them," Jerry said, sitting down on a chair next to Tim.

"Probably the best way," Tim agreed, and then noticed Jerry had a canvas satchel with him. "What's in the bag?"

"I keep on forgetting to bring this over to you," Jerry said, handing Tim the bag. Tim took the offered bag, and looked at Jerry skeptically. "Beware of 25th Infantry pukes bearing gifts," Tim said with a grin, and opened the bag. He smiled when he saw what was inside. It was his M3 grease gun, and ten new 30 round magazines. He let out an appreciative whistle. "I thought that was lost forever!"

"I found the magazines in one of the bunkers back on Volivoli, but never got around to giving them to you. They were still wrapped in wax paper, covered in Cosmoline, like they had rolled out of the factory yesterday. The gun was well rusted from your swim in the ocean, but I cleaned it up and oiled it for you."

Tim hefted the gun, opening the bolt to inspect the chamber. "Nice job, Jerry. Thanks."

"That Aussie captain wanted us to toss all of our weapons over the side when he brought us aboard. Damn near had a revolt on his hands. None of my men were going to give up their guns, even though we had no ammo left," Jerry sighed.

"No shit?" Tim said. "Well, thanks for saving this for me, we go way back together."

"He was a real stickler, a real old school sailor. And for being an Aussie, he sounded and acted very British."

"I'm glad he found us when he did."

"Yeah, me too, you were almost dead. I figured another day, well…" Jerry trailed off.

"So they've gone back to Australia?" Tim asked.

"They sailed yesterday. They hung around for a while, getting the ship provisioned, and then yesterday, without as much as a 'thank you ma'am', they were gone."

"That's a shame. I wanted to thank them and the doctor who patched me up," Tim said, puffing at his pipe. He set the satchel on the deck by his chair.

"You can still say thanks to that doctor. He decided to stick around, along with several other Aussies, civilians mostly. I don't think he was all that happy about it, the Aussie skipper that is, but he got some people from here to replace them. I figure it was a fair trade."

"Sorry I haven't been able to get around much except for the last week or so."

"Ah, shit Tim. Don't even worry about that. You needed to heal up."

Tim stood and picked up his now empty coffee mug. "Can I get you a cup of coffee?"

"I'll get it, Tim, you sit here," Jerry said, taking the cup from Tim, and going into the house. Tim watched the smoke from the pyre for a few minutes until Jerry came back out with two coffee cups. He handed one to Tim, and sat back down.

"So what else is going on?" Tim asked, taking the offered mug.

"We should have the water on here in town by Friday. And the power is on now over almost the entire island."

"Any other problems?"

"Last week a kid tried to break into a house a few blocks away. The guy living there decided to beat the dogshit out of the kid. Other than that, no problems," Jerry said, a little disgusted.

"Break in? What the fuck for? I mean, shit. If you want something, you can go and take it from anywhere. Why break into a house where people are living?"

"I'll ask the kid when his jaw heals. Got his jaw broken in the process."

"He's lucky he didn't get shot."

"I know. Now that society is coming back, I guess some of the old problems are coming with it."

"Do you have a plan?" Tim asked.

"Yeah, I already got a few guys I sort of 'deputized', and one of the guys from 25th was an MP, so he's putting together a police patrol of sorts."

"Good idea," Tim agreed with a nod and gazed out towards the funeral pyre.

Jerry sighed. "I wish the end of the world wasn't so damn hard."

"Jerry, the world didn't end. I still don't know what happened, but it didn't end. It will keep on spinning for a few more years, I reckon."

"I guess," Jerry said, then changed the subject. "I understand you guys have decided to go back to the mainland?"

"That we did, Jerry. Holly is over at Hickam right now with Taco and Robyn, checking out another Hercules."

"I'd hate to see you go," Jerry said after a moment.

"We'll be in touch, and we'll probably be back at some point."

"I know, but I could use your help here."

"Jerry, stop selling yourself short. You're doing a hell of a job. We'll get back to Arizona and set up shop there. We'll only be a radio call away."

"Oh, and another thing," Jerry said, "the ensign, and the other sailor from the, oh I don't know, pirate ship? They've got some hare-brained idea of going to San Francisco, and finding some old Liberty Ship that's supposed to be there. They figure on being some new-age merchant marines, setting up a trade route between there and Hawaii."

"No shit, a Liberty Ship?"

"Yeah, they floated the idea past me the other day. I thought I'd better let you in on their plans."

"Why tell me?" Tim asked, perplexed at Jerry's tone.

"Hell, I thought I had to. Everyone here thinks of you as the head of what's left."

"Ah shit, Jerry. I'm just some broke-dick soldier. I'm not the head of anything," Tim said, holding up his hands.

"Anyway, that's their plan." Jerry replied with a shrug, "And one of the Aussie civilians, he thinks he can get the railroads back on the mainland up and running again. He plans on some new trade route in the States leading to 'Frisco, then our fair sailors transporting shit from there to here," Jerry added, sipping on his now tepid coffee.

"Well I'll be dipped in dogshit." Tim let out a sigh and leaned back in the rocker, puffing on the pipe, deep in thought.

"To be honest, Tim, it's not a bad idea at all."

"I agree. There are a lot of variables, too, though. Like actually finding something or someone to trade with, finding anyone at all, really."

"I agree. To get back to what I said earlier, you are the head of this mob. After what you did on Volivoli, word has spread quickly. Everyone here in Hawaii, sees you as our leader."

"I'm no leader. Not anymore. I just want to be left alone, get Holly and Robyn back to our home in Arizona, and bring up my son or daughter in quiet and peace," he said with a little frustration.

"Okay, Tim. I'll leave it be for now," Jerry said with resignation, and finished his coffee.

"I'm sorry, Jerry. I didn't mean to sound like I was jumping down your throat."

"Hey, it's okay. I do understand. I never wanted any of this either. Here I am, though, and people on the island are looking up to me. Looking at me to make things right, to get everything back to the way they were. They're also looking at you. They know what you did, what you've been through."

"Then they should know I want to be left alone," Tim sighed, knowing that his wish wouldn't be granted.

He sat back and puffed on his pipe, looking out at the smoke from the funeral pyre again, his mind wandering back over the last few years; back to that horrible morning, so many years ago. When he found the two bodies in the snow in front of St. Dominic's that first long, lonely winter in Philadelphia, when the realization finally sunk in that he was the only one left.

And then to the time when he'd met Paul, that poor soul, and his horrible fate that he could've prevented... finding Robyn, then Izzy and Holly. Sometimes he'd think it was all a terrible nightmare and he'd soon wake up.

"Let me ask you something, Jerry," he said after a moment. "You said they want to get everything back to the way it was. Do we really want that, things back to the way it was?"

"What do you mean?"

"The wars, the poverty, the crooked politicians? Sure, we all want the power back on. We all want a hot shower and clean clothes, but at what cost? Me, I want to be left alone," Tim said, putting his pipe down and turning to face Jerry.

"I understand. I do. But you've got to understand that people look up to you now, Tim. Not just soldiers. It's everyday people, who see you as a guiding light in all this craziness."

"I don't know about all that," Tim replied with a gruff, dismissive laugh.

"I do know one thing. I'd rather have you, than some nutcase like that crazy captain."

Tim laughed again at that. "Yeah, I see what you mean."

"Let's just hope that there's no one else like him out there," Jerry said. "I know it's a bit much to contemplate right now, but the people will listen to you, even if it's just for advice."

With that said, Jerry stood. "I should be getting back. You think about what I said, Tim. Even if you go back to Arizona, we'll still need your advice."

Tim stood also, and shook Jerry's outstretched hand. "I'll think about it. You're doing a good job here all by yourself though."

"There are little enclaves popping up, all over the place. We talk to them on the Ham radio—Europe, South America, Russia. They've all heard what you did, and ask all the time what you think. I haven't given you all the messages, because I'd need a goddamn dump truck to deliver them."

Tim was dumbstruck. "Listen, Tim. Listen hard, and let it sink in. The world needs you."

"Needs me? Needs me for what?" Tim snapped. He caught himself, and backtracked, calming his voice. "I'm sorry, Jerry. It's a little too much to think about."

"I know you'll be here for a bit longer. Think about what I've said. Talk to Holly about it, she's a smart lady."

"I will," Tim promised, wishing he didn't have to. "Thanks for cleaning up my piece."

"No problem, Sergeant Major," Jerry said with a toothy grin. "I've got to go. I'll talk to you soon."

After Jerry left, Tim picked up both coffee mugs and took them into the kitchen, suddenly feeling like the whole world was resting on his shoulders. And wasn't that exactly what Jerry was talking about?

He decided to take a walk, to think. He walked out the back door and across the yard that led directly to the beach. He sat down under a coconut palm and removed his boots and socks, leaving them by the tree, and set off down the empty beach. He figured that it would have been crowded with tourists in years past; now it was completely empty, and that suited him. He wanted to be alone with his thoughts.

As he made his way down the deserted beach, Tim mulled over what Jerry had told him, and laughed to himself. He thought about that meeting with Dawn Redeagle on the prairies of Nebraska so long ago, and of his Indian prophesies.

It couldn't be that simple, could it? He didn't feel special. Not in the slightest. He felt old and frail. Try as he might, he couldn't imagine himself being anything other than Tim Flannery, formerly of Philadelphia. He'd be hitting the big five-oh this year, he remembered, and he was going to be a dad. He'd brought up Robyn okay, and this child that he and Holly were expecting was going to be the only challenge he wanted.

After an hour of walking, he turned to look back on the way he came. The waves had washed away his footprints. He could barely see the bungalow the three of them shared, and all of a sudden he felt very tired. He sat down on the sand at the high tidemark and looked out towards the empty sea.

The sun was sinking in the west, and he figured he only had a few more hours of sunlight. Where had the day gone? Had he daydreamed the whole afternoon away?

He sat for a long while, looking out at the water, watching the waves tumble over on top of themselves. The weather was pleasant, not too hot, and there was a cool breeze coming off of the ocean that cooled his skin. He leaned back on his elbows and closed his eyes, savoring the feelings, when he was startled by a voice.

"Aloha!"

Tim turned to see a boy with an unruly mop of dark hair standing a few feet from him. The boy was darkly tanned and wore only a pair of cut-off shorts.

"Well aloha to you too," Tim said with a friendly smile. He looked around, but there were no signs of houses anywhere near this part of the beach. "Where did you come from?"

"I came from over there," the boy said with a toothy grin, pointing vaguely in the direction of the trees, then sat down next to Tim in the sand. "Are you waiting for the Big Kahuna?"

Tim gave the boy a once-over and decided he couldn't be any more than five years old, born after the Event, he presumed. He then thought of the ensign's boy, Billy. He was around the same age.

"I'm sitting here and thinking. Who's the Big Kahuna?"

"He's our protector! My mom and dad told me all about him," the boy said, giving Tim a look as if saying 'sheesh, don't you know anything?'

"He's our protector, huh?"

"Yeah, he came from the mainland, from far away. He destroyed the bad men who were attacking us. Now he's here, and is our Great Protector!"

"That's amazing," Tim said.

"Yeah. My mom and dad told me he watches over us all, and will always protect us now," the boy said, digging absently in the sand.

It was all a little too much for Tim to wrap his head around. Could this kid actually be talking about me? He thought. That was a laugh. Now he'd turned into some legend, like some mythical god from Valhalla.

"My mom and dad said the Big Kahuna came from the time before… he must be old."

"How old do you reckon he is?" Tim asked with a barely hidden smile.

"He's really old! Like maybe a hundred years old even!" he exclaimed with wide eyes.

"Wow, a hundred years old, eh? He must be ancient."

"Yeah!" he said, and then his face darkened. "Do you know what it was like in the time before?"

"Yeah, I do. That was a long time ago."

"My mom cries sometimes at night about it. It must have been nice." He tossed some sand away, now digging a trench.

"What's your name?" Tim asked.

"I'm Jimmy. Who are you?"

"I'm Tim. Nice to meet you, Jimmy," Tim said, offering his hand to shake, and the boy took it. "It's getting late, why don't we get you home, okay?"

"Okay," Jimmy said with a grin and stood up, brushing the sand from his hands theatrically.

"Which way is home?" Tim asked when he stood himself.

"That way, c'mon!" Jimmy said, and took Tim's hand, leading him towards his house.

They walked through some bushes onto a narrow path, and soon Tim could see a quaint bungalow not unlike the one he now shared with Robyn and Holly emerge from the tropical flora.

He could see a light in one of the windows, and then he could hear a woman's voice singing a song he'd never heard. It sounded to Tim like a Hawaiian native song, and the woman who was singing had a beautiful voice. Jimmy let go of his hand and went running up to the back door.

"Mom! I found a man on the beach!" he yelled, and Tim laughed.

The woman came to the door and opened it, wiping her hands on a hand towel, her face blanching when she saw Tim. "Jimmy, go inside and wash up for supper."

"Okay, Mom!" Jimmy said, rushing by her into the house and out of sight. The woman relaxed a little and came towards him. Like a lot of native born islanders, she was a mix of Polynesian and what looked like Japanese. In her mid-thirties, long, dark hair, she was very attractive.

"I'm sorry, I didn't want to startle you. I met your boy on the beach, and since it was getting late, I thought I'd better make sure he got home alright," Tim said, offering his hand. "I'm Tim Flannery."

"I know who you are," she said a little abruptly, taking his hand.

"Hey, I'm sorry. I'll go…" Tim said sheepishly.

"No, please, I'm the one who should apologize. I didn't mean it to come out like that. I never thought I'd meet you, is all," the woman gushed, and then smiled.

"Ma'am, it's okay, I understand," Tim said with a smile he hoped would ease the situation.

"Jimmy, he was a blessing. After everyone, died… I had given up hope. Then I met his father, and we met others. Then the pirate ship came, and well, you know the rest."

"I do. What's this story he told me, about the Big Kahuna?"

"Oh my!" she gasped, turning red.

Tim laughed, "I never thought I'd be called the Big Kahuna. A big, well… other things," he said, winking.

"It's just that Jimmy saw we were all worried, and then you came. You took care of the problem… Jimmy kept asking why we were so happy now."

"So I'm kind of like Santa Claus, the Tooth Fairy, and the Easter Bunny rolled into one, huh?" "I'm so embarrassed!" she gushed, turning an even brighter shade of red.

"No, I understand. Kids need to be kids for as long as possible. I've got one on the way myself," Tim said proudly. "Holly is four months along now."

"Congratulations."

"I'm glad I can raise him or her up in a safer world than the one you and I grew up in."

"Yes, thanks to you, and for that we owe you everything."

It looked to Tim that the woman actually had tears in her eyes. He had to get out of here, get back to the house. He needed to talk things over with Holly.

His mind was reeling on his way down to the water's edge, and he started to walk briskly back in the direction he'd come earlier. The whole incident made his skin crawl, the way the woman gushed over him, the story the boy had been told.

He'd been held in awe before, by young soldiers. With them, he'd put the fear of God into them, because to them he was God. A sergeant major staring down a private who'd just monumentally fucked up was God on Earth. This was way different.

Tim peered at the setting sun, wondering where the day had gone. It seemed like only a few minutes ago that Holly had come into the bedroom with a fresh cup of coffee, breakfast, then the conversation with Jerry, his walk on the beach… and then there was this, this bizarre little meeting, first with the boy, then with his mother. It was almost as if…

No! Stop it, Timmy boy! His mind screamed.

He remembered now, after he was well enough to get off the ship, and Jerry had found the little bungalow for them to live in, on the occasions that he'd been out and about, which were few and far between, he'd noticed people would see him, and stop what they were doing, looking at him with… was it awe? He even remembered now that some of the men would take off their hats in his presence.

He finally reached the palm tree where he'd removed his boots earlier. He noticed with some relief that lights were on in the house, and he plodded up to the back door with leaden feet. He could hear the sounds of laughter coming from inside, then he heard Robyn squeal with delight and he smiled.

He left his boots outside next to the door and entered the house, went straight to the kitchen, and retrieved a bottle of beer from the refrigerator. He tossed the cap into the garbage can and followed the sounds of laughter into the living room, where he found Holly, Robyn, and Jimenez. The latter were seated close to one another, holding hands, and when they saw Tim, quickly released their grip and moved apart slightly.

"I hope I'm not disturbing anything," he said with a tired grin, taking a pull off the bottle.

"Oh, Tim, I wondered where you'd gotten to! I was telling Juan how you and I first met," Holly said, coming over to him and giving him a kiss. "You look tired, are you okay?"

"Yeah, I'm alright. The story about how we first met, huh? The very first time?" he said with a sly grin. "Damn near got a general Court Martial for that little escapade," Tim added, collapsing into a lounge chair.

"Shit, Sar' Major, I can believe you would have shot her down," Jimenez said.

"I would have, Taco, believe me," he replied. "I hear you've found our ride out of here."

"That I have, Sar' Major. I've got to swap engines, but I should have it airworthy in a month or so, with a little help," Jimenez said.

"Good, the sooner, the better."

"Dad, what's wrong?" Robyn asked, her voice tense with concern.

Holly had taken a seat on the arm of the chair that Tim was sitting in, and put her hand on the back of his neck.

"Yes, there's something wrong. I can hear it in your voice," Holly said, rubbing at the nape of his neck.

"It's nothing, just tired from the long walk I took. I need to get some supper and get to bed early is all," he said with a sigh, closed his eyes, and leaned back. "Taco, go out and get my pipe from the front porch, would you?"

"Sure thing," Jimenez said, jumping up to comply.

"Really, I'm okay," Tim assured them. "I need to eat something and get to bed, nothing more."

"Alright then, c'mon, Holly, let's make some dinner," Robyn said, getting up and taking Holly by the hand.

"Are you sure you're alright, babe?" Holly asked.

"I'm fine," Tim said, with a hint of irritation.

Okay, lover," she said, bent down, and kissed him on top of his head. "I see how it is. I'm now relegated to the kitchen with the rest of the womenfolk," she called back after him jokingly on her way to the kitchen.

"I heard that!" Tim yelled out. He settled into his chair and Juan came back in, carrying his pipe. Tim filled the bowl up, tamping it with his thumb. He struck a wooden match and lighted the pipe, puffing several times until his head was engulfed in a blue cloud of tobacco smoke.

He looked at Juan with an icy stare that he let go on for what felt like hours to Jimenez, who was sitting warily on the couch across from Tim. Sweat began to bead on his forehead and he fidgeted until Tim finally spoke.

"So what's the story?"

"Sir, I mean Sar' Major, I need to swap out two engines on one bird, then change out some of the avionic—"

"That's not what I was referring to, Lance Corporal," Tim cut in.

"Oh, you mean that," Juan sighed, his bowels loosening and the color draining from his face.

"Yes, I mean that," Tim said with a cold stare that would freeze an Aleut's heart.

"Look, Sar' Major, Robyn and I like each other, and—"

"And what?" Tim snapped, leaning forward with an evil smile crossing his face.

"My intentions are honorable," Juan spat out, about ready to shit himself.

"Relax. I know," Tim said, his voice softening a little, "I have to say this, though, Taco. She's an adult, yes, but she'll always be my little girl, got that?"

"I'm reading you loud and clear, sir," Jimenez said, voice trembling.

"Good, just as long as we have that straight between us, we'll get along splendidly," Tim said with a grin. "If you hurt her, you break her heart? I will fuck you up so badly it'll hair-lip your great grandchildren," Tim promised coldly.

"Aye, Aye, Sar' Major!" Jimenez exclaimed, all color draining from his face.

"Now get the fuck outta my sight, and go help them fix supper," Tim said in a low growl. He leaned back into the easy chair, puffing away at his pipe, glaring evilly through a cloud of blue smoke.

Jimenez all but erupted from his seat on the couch and bolted for the kitchen. When he was gone, Tim laughed silently to himself.

"He's a good kid," he said to no one, and sat back and puffed on his pipe.

Robyn and Holly made a light dinner of soup and spam sandwiches, something that there was no fear of running out of in Hawaii. After they ate, Robyn and Juan washed up while Holly and Tim retired to their bedroom. They undressed and crawled into bed, and Holly laid her head on Tim's chest.

They lay there without a word for several minutes. There was a tap on the door, and then it opened slightly and Robyn stuck her head in. "Dad, I'm going to down to the beach with Juan. I won't be long."

"Okay," Tim said, then as an afterthought, added, "Oh, and Robyn?"

"Yes, Dad?"

"He's a good kid."

"I know. Thanks!" she said with a big grin, shutting the door.

"He's frightened silly of you, do you realize that?" Holly said, playfully slapping Tim on the arm.

"Yeah, I know. I hope it keeps him on his toes, and honest."

"Did you really threaten to hairlip his grandchildren?"

"No. I said I'd fuck him up so badly his great grandchildren would be hairlipped," Tim said, playing with Holly's long, thick, red hair.

Holly giggled. "You are so horrible."

Tim sighed, gathering his thoughts, then proceeded to tell Holly about his conversation with Jerry, his long walk, and his chance meeting with young Jimmy and his mother. When he was done, she lay there silently for a time, going over in her mind what he'd just conveyed to her.

"I knew there was something bothering you," she said eventually.

"I wanted to talk to you about it, alone," he said.

"Aye, now that you mention it, people here do seem a bit queer. And the whole Big Kahuna thing, I can see how it would make you uncomfortable."

"Babe, I don't want to be anyone's leader. It creeps me out that some of these folks are starting to think of me as some divine character. I want to get us back home to Arizona. Raise our child and let us grow old together, nothing more, nothing less," Tim said to the ceiling. "So you're all for us getting out of here?"

"As soon as Jimenez gets the bird fixed up, we'll fly home. Have you asked Jerry to come with us?"

"No, not yet, I've got a feeling he'll stay here."

"Aye, I think so too," Holly said. "Turn out the light would you, love?"

Tim reached over to the bedside lamp and switched it off, blacking out the room. He could feel Holly's hand on his thigh now, inching up.

"And now, Sergeant Major, the only Big Kahuna that's on my mind is this," she said playfully, caressing his inner thigh, reaching higher until she found what she was looking for.

Tim sighed. "You are so naughty, Flight Leftenant…"

CHAPTER 2: HAIL TO THE CHIEF

Over the next several weeks, through his walks on the beach and other exercising, Tim was gradually regaining his strength. Thankfully, he never saw the young boy or his mother again. The meeting that day had left him feeling quite uncomfortable. With the help of Holly, Robyn, and several men from the local area, Jimenez had finally had gotten the C130 Hercules in flying condition.

Tim sat in the shade of a hangar at Hickam Air Force Base, sipping on a warm can of Coke and watching with a bit of trepidation as the large aircraft taxied towards the end of the runway. Holly was at the controls, Jimenez and Robyn her passengers.

He couldn't help but be gravely worried, and kept having visions of it crashing and burning, taking with it the three people in his life he cared most for, not to mention his unborn child.

The sun was bright on this clear morning, not a cloud to be seen. He set the can of soda down next to him and held his breath as the matte gray painted plane stopped and pivoted 180 degrees and then roared up to full power, and began to roll down the runway. It gained speed, and then halfway down, virtually leapt into the air at almost a 45 degree angle, landing gear going up into its stowed position.

It climbed for a thousand or so feet in altitude, leveled off, and banked sharply to the left and made a wide turn, passing out of sight. He let out his breath and leaned back onto the wall of the hangar, a relieved sigh escaping his lips. He sat there for a few more minutes until he could no longer hear the sound of the engines.

Now all he had to do was sit and wait until they get back. He noticed movement out of the corner of his eye and saw a familiar figure walking towards him. Tim didn't bother to stand, and watched the figure approach, sipping his Coke.

"Sergeant Major Flannery?" the man asked when he was within earshot.

"That's me," Tim said.

"Sergeant, you might remember me, I'm Ensign Johnson. I was wondering if I might have a word with you?"

"I remember you, Mr. Johnson. Pardon me if I don't stand, I'm not feeling all that military today, so we'll eschew all the protocol," Tim stated in a tone that let the Ensign know exactly how he felt about officers.

"That's quite alright, eh. Like I said, I want to talk to you for a few minutes," Johnson said a little uncomfortably.

"Pull up a piece of tarmac, Ensign. What can I do for you?" The ensign sat down next to Tim. "First off, I want to thank you for letting us come with you."

"Don't thank me. I was slightly preoccupied with dealing with your Captain Kangaroo the last time we met. Thank Staff Sergeant Williams."

"I already have. I thought I ought to thank you, too. You could have left us on that atoll, and I couldn't have blamed you if you had."

"That was slick, you putting that grenade in the chopper's fuel tank like that," Tim said in muted admiration.

Johnson smiled a little at that remark, and realized it was as close to a compliment as he'd get from the sergeant major. He'd gotten the same treatment from some of the old grizzled Master Chiefs on the ship before the Event.

He nodded. "I saw it in a movie. I wasn't sure if it would work or not, I just thought I should do *something*."

"It was a good move. How's that boy of yours?"

"He's up and around. Your doctor did a great job. I already thanked him. Mary thanks you too."

"I couldn't just let a kid's dad die. Mary was quite convincing, telling me you were an okay guy. I think that's the main reason I didn't put a bullet in your melon when you showed up. You should thank her, too," Tim replied, finishing his Coke, and with one hand, crushed the can.

"She means the world to me," Johnson said, looking away. "They both do."

"I know what you mean," Tim said, looking up at the sky, wishing the Hercules would return. "I'll ask again: what's on your mind? I know you didn't come all the way out here to chitchat about old times."

"I want to come back to the mainland with you. Not only me; Mary and Billy, Petty Officer Suplee, and Mr. Nakamura want to come too."

"Do you now?" Tim asked. He reached into his pocket and retrieved his pipe, filling it with fresh tobacco. "Why's that?"

"The *SS Jeremiah O'Brian*," Johnson stated.

"What might that be?"

"It's a Liberty Ship from World War Two. It's been completely restored, and it's now, or *was*, I should say, an operating museum ship," Johnson said, becoming animated.

"Where is it now?"

"San Francisco."

"So you want us to drop you off in 'Frisco?" Tim asked, a little incredulously.

"No, nothing like that. We'd go to wherever you're going, and make our way to California from there."

Tim fetched a wooden match from another pocket, struck it on the ground and lit his pipe, puffing several times until the bowl was lighted. He blew out the match then looked at Ensign Johnson.

"Okay, we get you to the mainland. Then what's your plan?" he asked, already knowing part of it from what Jerry had told him weeks ago, but he wanted to hear it from the man himself.

"It's supposed to be fully restored to exactly the way it was when it rolled down the ways in 1943. Whatever electromagnetic pulse that fried all of the other electronics shouldn't have harmed anything on it."

"Go on," Tim prodded.

"Me, Suplee, and Nakamura want to fire up the boilers and see if we can sail it."

"And then what?"

"Sergeant Williams is getting civilization started back up here, and I figure you'll probably do the same thing back in the States. I'd provide a trade route of a sort, between there and here, and maybe the rest of the Pacific," he said excitedly.

"It's been over six years. What if it's sitting at the bottom of the bay? Or it broke its moorings at some point and was set adrift, washed up on the rocks of Alcatraz, or wrapped around one of the stanchions of the Bay Bridge? Have you thought about that, and what your options are, if that's the case?" Tim asked, cocking his patrol cap back on his head, and puffing on his pipe.

"I'd still like to take that chance, Sar' Major. Both me and Suplee actually like being sailors, what happened on the *Hughes* notwithstanding, and it would beat sitting around. We'd like to be productive," he stated with resignation.

"What about your woman and kid?"

"I want them to come too. They'll sail everywhere with us. I never want to leave them on shore ever again."

Tim stood, followed by Johnson. He cocked his head slightly when he heard the sounds of the Hercules returning. The turboprop engines grew louder and louder, but try as they might, neither man could locate the plane in the sky.

Then the plane appeared over the hangar at what appeared to be a ridiculously low altitude, going way too fast. The plane headed off, gained a little altitude, and banked in a wide turn, heading right for the end of the runway. Neither could see the landing gear lower, and it looked as though Holly was going to belly-flop in onto the airstrip.

Tim's breath caught in his throat as the Hercules came over the threshold and then leveled off. It then dawned on Tim that Holly was having a bit of fun, and he smiled. The C130 screamed down the runway at full power, barely fifty feet off the deck. At the end of the strip, the Hercules again leapt into the air, and circled the base. They watched Holly finesse the plane until it reached the threshold again, this time the landing gear coming down and locking into place.

With a puff of white smoke, the rear wheels kissed the concrete runway and seconds later the nose wheel did the same. It rolled down the runway, then they heard the engines scream when Holly reversed the pitch on the props, bringing the cargo aircraft to a rapid stop. She spun the fuselage around as if on a pivot, and taxied down to where they were standing.

"That was a perfect landing!" Ensign Johnson said.

"Sir, do you know the definition of a good landing?" Tim asked with a smile.

"What's that, Sar' Major?"

"Any landing you can walk away from is a good landing," Tim said, drawing a big laugh from Johnson.

The plane taxied right up to the hangar, and the engines shut down, props spinning to a stop. The rear side door opened, and then Holly, Jimenez, and Robyn stepped out. All were smiling, and walked over the where Tim and Johnson were standing. Holly came up and wrapped her arms around Tim's neck, giving him a huge kiss.

"Isn't that against regulations, Flight Lieutenant?" Tim asked with a smile.

"Oh blast the regs! Give me another kiss, Sergeant Major!" she exclaimed and kissed him again. Her face split into a grin. "I think our Mr. Jimenez is a miracle worker. It's even better than our first Herc!"

"I'll have to take your word for it, Ma'am," Tim said, then looked at the nose of the aircraft. Hand painted on the side, under the pilot's window, was the word "Bandit" in red paint. "What's the story with that, Taco?"

"It was already there when I found it, Sar' Major," Jimenez said. I thought it was fitting, since we'll be heading back east. You know, like that old Bart Reynolds movie, *Smoky and the Bandit*, 'East bound and down!"

"You mean Burt Reynolds? Yeah, it is apt." Turning back to Holly, Tim said, "Babe, you remember Mr. Johnson, don't you?"

"Yes, I do," Holly said, holding her hand to shake, but Johnson came to attention and saluted Holly smartly. Taken aback, Holly came to attention herself, and saluted back in the British way, palm facing outward. Then she shook his hand with a smile. "It's a pleasure to see you again, Ensign."

"Ensign Johnson here and a few of his people will be flying back with us, at least as far as Phoenix," Tim told her.

"Oh, really?" she asked, then added before Tim could answer, "That's something I wanted to talk to you about. We might not have to go to Phoenix. I might be able to get us close to Williams on the way back."

"Tell me," Tim asked, folding his arms across his chest.

"I was looking at some maps, and saw that there's an airport south of the Grand Canyon, in Tusayan, only a short drive south to home."

"Is it big enough?"

"Aye, its 9,000 feet long, plenty long enough for the Hercules. If you could get a recent overhead off one of your satellites, we can see what condition it's in," she said gleefully.

"That is good news. I'll do it tonight when we get home."

"Good," Holly said. "Ensign Johnson, why are you heading back with us?"

Johnson, now feeling more relaxed, told her of his plans, and of the Liberty Ship. Robyn and Jimenez had disappeared somewhere, and Tim looked around to see where they had gotten off to. Not seeing them, he turned back to Johnson and Holly.

"I think that's a splendid idea," Holly said. "What do you think, Tim?" "I'm okay with it if we have room. There's several people coming back with us, and I'd like to fit at least one Hum-Vee into the hold too. That'd be up to you, you know what the bird will carry."

"I think we should be alright. We'll have the jetstream on our tail, so it shouldn't be too much of a problem."

"There's another guy, one of the Aussies. He wants to come too," Johnson said. "He worked for some Australian railroad for a lot of years, wanted to take a look at that Grand Canyon railroad, and maybe even get a train running between your place and San Francisco. I'll have him talk to you."

"Tim, I'm sure we have enough room," Holly said. "I'll draw up a list of people and things we want to take, and I'll let you know if it'll work. Worst case scenario, I make two trips."

"What about the baby?" Tim asked in concern.

"Timothy, I'm pregnant, not an invalid," she said with a twinkle in her eyes.

His heart always melted when she did that, and being pregnant gave her this glow about her that made her sexy as hell, and he'd never be able to say no to that. "So the Herc is ready for the trip?"

"Aye, it's ready."

"Good. Now where do those two get off to?" he asked, and then saw Jimenez come out of the cargo hold carrying tie-down chains, followed by Robyn, who was dragging rubber chocks, and they busied themselves with tying down and securing the aircraft.

"I'd better be off as well. Mary will be wondering where I got off to," Johnson said. "When do you plan on leaving?"

"I'd say five days, maybe a week, after we get everything together," Holly said.

"Alright then. I'll get home and start making the preparations. I know Billy is really excited about flying."

"I'm sure that the pilot can make arrangements for a cockpit tour," Tim said, holding his hand out for a shake, which Johnson took in a firm grip.

"Thanks again. I'll talk to you both soon," Johnson said, and headed off around the side of the hangar.

Tim turned to Holly and asked, "Are you sure you're up for this?"

"Aye, I'm ready," Holly said.

Jimenez and Robyn came up to them, finished with their work.

"Dad!" Robyn exclaimed. "Holly's teaching me to fly!"

"Is she now?" Tim asked, looking over at Holly with a raised eyebrow.

"She's a natural," Holly said.

"That's fantastic," Tim said, rolling his eyes. "Let's get home, shall we?" He took Holly's hand and walked towards his Hum-Vee parked behind the hangar.

They piled in and made their way towards the bungalow on the beach. When they pulled up outside the cottage, Robyn and Jimenez jumped out, and Robyn called out that they were going for a swim, leaving Holly and Tim alone.

The pair walked into the house, and into the kitchen. When Tim saw it was past noon, he opened the fridge and pulled out a bottle of beer, and another of Coke. He held up the soda bottle and looked at Holly questioningly.

"Aye, I'll have one," she said, sticking out her tongue. "I'd love one of those beers, but I know I can't."

When he had popped the top on both bottles and handed her the soda, he sat down across from her.

"So what's bothering you now?" she asked, taking a long pull of the Coke.

"Nothing," he said flatly.

"Don't give me that. Something's eating at you, I can tell."

"I don't know. Maybe it's all the people."

"What do you mean?"

"For a long time it was just me and Robyn. Then you and Izzy came along. That seemed like enough. Ironic, really. Ever since the Event, I had been hoping to find other people, and now that there's people, I want to be back at our little place in Arizona again, alone. It looks like that's not going to happen now."

Holly set her bottle down in front of her on the table. She was silent for a moment, as if gathering her thoughts, and then reached across and took his hand. She looked into his eyes for a moment, then said, "Timothy, babe, I do understand. But I know, with your brains, and ability to motivate people, your leadership, we can have a nice little settlement back in Arizona."

"That's just it. I don't *want* to lead anymore. The last time I had any leadership, I nuked an island and made several hundred square miles of ocean a radioactive wasteland."

"You did what you thought was necessary, Tim."

"I think I know what Harry Truman felt like in 1945," Tim said, rubbing his temples. "I don't want that kind of responsibility, ever again."

"We're going back to Williams. It'll be the same. The people who want to come with us are just regular people. Some, like us, are starting a family. There are a few farmers, cattle ranchers. Even a geologist wants to come along. Sure, a few of them are soldiers that Jerry trained, and were with us on Volivoli, but it'll be different."

"Until the next joker comes along that wants to rule the world."

"That may never happen. If it does, I know you'll do what you have to do again."

"That's the point. I never want to be put into that position again. Jerry said a few weeks ago that some kid was caught breaking into a house. The old problems we lived with before the Event have never gone away. They'll follow us forever."

"Not if we don't let them. When we get back to Williams, we set down some very basic rules. We use your American Constitution as a guide. People will have to follow the rules if they want to stay there. Make it as simple as that. You always said that the people in charge lost sight of that document years ago, and that we should go back to those principles. Here's your chance to actually make it work," Holly said. She picked up her Coke and took a sip, knowing she had hit a home run with that last statement.

"I'll think about it."

"Don't let what those smart men did a few hundred years ago be in vain," Holly said.

"Okay, you've made your point," Tim said with a laugh.

"Besides, you won't be alone. Izzy is coming back with us, and I think he's pretty intelligent, to use your words, for an officer!"

"Yeah, that's true. He was an officer. Officers, making easy shit hard since 1775."

"We're not all bad," Holly said. "You be careful, Sergeant Major, or I may have to rethink the whole fraternization regulation!"

"Oh, really? I think you enjoy it as much as I do."

"Be that as it may, Sar' Major, I still outrank you."

"That's true, because you have ovaries," Tim agreed playfully. "How is Izzy, anyway? I haven't seen him much since I've been up and around."

"He's keeping himself rather busy. He and that Australian doctor that operated on you on the HMAS Newcastle have set up a clinic in town. They've even got a few nurses working with them. They've had nothing major as yet, a few broken bones and children with the sniffles."

"I think he missed being a doctor, and that kid, Billy, kind of pulled him out of the rut he was in."

"Aye, I agree. He's eager to get back to Arizona with us though. He wants to do the same thing in Williams."

Tim finished his beer, got up from the table, and discarded the empty bottle in the garbage can. He got another from the fridge and sat back down.

"So, how many people are coming back with us?"

"Twenty people now, including Johnson and his mob," Holly told him. "The flight won't be first class, but I'll be able to manage."

"We really will have a little settlement, won't we?"

"Aye, that we will. I've met most of them, and they seem like nice people. A few won't be staying with us, they want to head out and explore, see what they can find and make useful."

"It's a whole new experience, for me. Hell, for everyone," Tim said, looking out the window at Robyn and Jimenez romping playfully in the surf. He turned back to Holly and smiled. "I'll do my best, babe."

"I know you will, Tim," she said, taking his hand. "I almost forgot, Jerry was by the base the other day, and he wants to have a going away party for all of us. He suggested a luau. Cook a pig in the ground and everything."

"That sounds like a great idea!" Tim said. "If he wants, he can do it right here in the backyard and it can spill out onto the beach."

He heard a knock on the door, and went to see who it was. Through the open door, he saw Jerry standing there. He smiled and called out, "We were just talking about you! Come on in, we're in the kitchen!"

Jerry followed Tim into the kitchen, accepted a beer Tim offered, and took a seat next to Holly.

"This hits the spot, Sar' Major." Jerry said appreciatively. "I heard the 130 flying earlier, so I take that as a sign you guys are about set?"

"The plane is ready, and we should be ready to go in about a week or so," Tim confirmed.

"I'm sorry to see you go. I understand, though. I wanted to let you know that the water is on. Run your taps for a few moments before you do anything, to get any sediment out of the pipes."

"Will it be potable?" Tim asked.

"That I'm not sure of. I'd boil it before you drank any of it."

"I'll have to remember to turn on the breaker for the water heater."

"Oh, to have a hot shower!" Holly squealed with delight. "I dream of a hot shower!"

"Ma'am, you'll be able to have one in a few hours," Jerry said, smiling. Holly leaned over and kissed him.

"If I could blush, I would right now," Jerry said in an 'aw shucks' tone.

Tim went to the sink and turned on the water at the tap. For a minute, nothing happened, and then a whoosh of air, a little banging, and a stream of brownish-red muddy water came out. After another minute, it started to clear, then became a steady stream of clean water.

"We'll have to do that to the rest of the taps in the house," he said to Holly, "and it'll be nice not to have to flush the toilet with buckets of seawater."

"Aye, that was getting to be a pain. Like when Izzy and I were at his house in Colorado."

"Thanks to a few of my guys, work is getting done, and everything else is coming along fine, too."

"So tell me," Tim said, "what are your plans here?"

"I did a rough count last week, and I figure between here and the Big Island, there are almost a thousand residents."

Tim let out a whistle. "I didn't think there were that many people!"

"Yeah, kind of threw me for a loop too. I think I told you I've instituted an ad hoc police department. Everyone wants me as some kind of Mayor or something. I said I'd do it, for the time being."

"You're perfect for the job, Jerry," Holly said.

"There is something else I wanted to talk to you about," said Jerry, taking another pull off his bottle of beer, looking at Tim.

"What's that?"

"I don't know how to say it. Do you remember that old Kevin Costner movie, *The Postman?*"

"Yeah, vaguely," Tim answered warily.

"It's supposed to be after some nuclear war. This drifter is walking along and wants to get into some walled off town when he finds a crashed postal truck."

"Okay, I remember it now. He takes the dead guy's uniform and mail bag, and tricks the folks in the town into believing that he's the mailman," Tim said, not knowing where Jerry was going with this. "He has letters for everyone and says he's got a message from the president."

"Yes. I want you to be the 'postman'," Jerry said, quite gravely.

"You want Tim to deliver the mail?" Holly asked.

"Not exactly. Look, Tim. These people have been through a lot. You know that, you've been through a shitstorm yourself. Right after everyone died, anyone who survived was in shock. Hell, we all were. Not knowing what had happened, if anyone was left outside of here, and what they should do, all of it."

"Yeah, I know that. Then that fuckwit of a captain goes tearing across the Pacific, making shit even more difficult for everyone. People want to survive and get on with their lives," Tim said, looking at Jerry across the table. "I'm not following you though."

"They need words of reassurance, Tim, from a *leader.*"

"Jerry, I told you before, and I meant it, I'm done with being anyone's leader. It's bad enough I have a bunch of people coming back with us who expect me to lead them there, too."

"They all want to know that there's more, Tim, that there's someone who will protect them. I want to tell them you're the new president of the United States. That you're going back to the mainland and will be putting the government back together."

Tim looked at Jerry few a few moments in silence, dumbfounded. He started to laugh, but that passed quickly, and a dark cloud passed over his face.

"That's about the craziest idea I've ever heard. What happens when they find out that I'm not the Grand Pooh-Bah, and you've just been bullshitting them?"

"I don't think it'll get as far as that, Tim. If I can get everyone together, more than they are now, with a little glimmer of hope in the future, things will go a lot smoother around here."

"Jerry, come on! This is crazy!" Tim finally said, turning his head and looking out the window. Outside, Robyn and Jimenez were holding each other tightly, Robyn's head buried deep into the man's chest. Tim sighed and turned back to face his friend. "Jerry, you don't need me as some figurehead. You're doing fine without me."

"If we held an election here on the island tomorrow, I'd get a hundred percent turnout, and you'd win by a landslide."

"Remember Nixon won in a landslide in 1972," Tim pointed out ruefully.

"That's not the point. I just want to give the people some hope. And who knows? There might even *be* a government forming, at least somewhere."

"Don't you think we would have heard about that by now, if there actually was?" Tim asked skeptically.

"Tim, I do see his point," Holly said, reaching out and taking his hand across the table.

"Yeah, I do too. In some perverse way, it makes sense, but why me? Why haven't the churches and mosques and synagogues reopened? They've always been good at giving people false hope."

"I think people as a whole have given up on religion," Jerry said. "There was one guy, a Baptist minister; right after the Event, he started preaching from a park. He was talking about the rapture and all, how God was going to come down and rule the Earth. People listened to him for a while, and then his congregation dwindled to nothing after a few months when the messiah never materialized. I found him hanging from a tree not long after. No, people have given up on make-believe friends in the sky."

"I agree with them. Religion has always been a sham, telling people about a fake affliction, in the form of sin, so they can sell them an imaginary cure. I stopped believing in that bullshit years ago," Tim told his friend. "But now you're suggesting I become some make-believe president. Isn't that about the same thing?"

"You've said before, you wanted to see civilization come back, our nation to come back. I'm doing my best to make that happen here in Hawaii. I'm using the Constitution as a guide, but I need a little help and guidance. We'll be in contact through the Ham radio, and I can give people your messages. It'll help me get things going here, and who knows, it might even help on the mainland too," Jerry said.

Tim sat there in deep thought, mulling over in his mind everything Jerry had said. He looked out the window again. He saw Robyn grab Jimenez by the hand, and the pair ran, laughing, back into the surf.

He was frustrated. He agreed with everything his friend was saying, but why did it have to be him? He did want a safe world for Robyn and Holly; a safe world where they could raise their child. But was this the way? He let out a huge sigh.

Jerry smiled. "Even George Washington became president reluctantly."

"Haven't I done enough?" Tim asked with exasperation.

"And now you're even quoting Washington!" his friend beamed.

"Paraphrasing."

"Then you'll do it?"

"Let me sleep on it, Jerry. I'll give you my answer tomorrow," Tim said, but the look on his face let Jerry and Holly know exactly what his answer would be. "As long as I don't have to make any promises to them that I can't keep. There's been far too many of those over the years."

"You got it, Sar' Major. No promises. So you'll think about it and let me know?"

"Yeah."

"Look at it this way, Tim. If the thought of a resurgent America spreads around far enough, an America that won't back down to bullies, stops one wingnut like the late Captain Kangaroo, then it'll all be worth it, to be left alone."

"One that'll nuke them, you mean?" Tim asked. "I never, ever want to have to do that, ever again!"

"You won't have to, Tim."

"Besides, I don't have the codes anymore. They were vaporized when I turned Volivoli into a sheet of glass," Tim lied.

No one knew that shortly after Tim and Robyn had found their home in Williams, Arizona, Tim had painstakingly copied the entire codebook over into a loose-leaf ring binder by hand, in neat block letters, and had secretly squirreled it away in his home's basement, where it still sat today, if it hadn't been gnawed to shreds my mice. No, he really didn't feel bad about telling Jerry that lie.

"I don't think it'll ever get as far as that. I need your help, that's all. At some point, in the far future, we'll have a real election. It's just these baby steps we need to take first," Jerry said, standing. He walked over and tossed his now empty beer bottle in the garbage. "Take a few days to think it over. We'll have a going-away luau for you on Friday, here in your back yard, and you can let me know then."

"Holly and I were discussing having it here right before you came in," Tim said with a little laugh.

"I've got to go and take care of some things. I'll talk to you later. See you later, Ma'am!" Jerry added, nodding to Holly. With that, he departed through the kitchen door, leaving Tim and Holly to their thoughts.

Tim took out another beer, popped the top, and after expertly flipping the cap into the garbage, looked at Holly with a wry grin. "You'd better start learning the tune 'Hail to the Chief', and remember this, you'll be First Lady!"

"Oh, Tim! It's all so unbelievable!"

"And ninety-nine percent of the world's population dying overnight isn't?" he said, draining half the bottle in one pull. He let out a huge belch that made Holly laugh.

"That's not very presidential!"

"Oh shit, babe. What the fuck am I going to do?" he sighed, and sank into the bench across from her.

"To be honest, I think you should do it. Just make a show of it, at the luau, and be done with it. The people will be happy, and it'll give them some hope."

"I still don't know."

"I don't know enough about your laws, if any laws are valid anymore, anyway. Would it be legal, if it was possible?"

"That's the thousand dollar question. I don't know, probably not. I know there's a definite order of succession to the office of president, and I'm pretty goddamn sure that a brigade sergeant major is not on that list."

"Then make a show of it, like that postman in the movie. You did say you wanted the US to come back, and when it did, you hoped that they got back to the principles. Here's your chance to help make that happen."

"I hate the lies. If I do this, I'll be no better than the rest of the politicians before me. I'm no politician."

"Tim, haven't you told a lie before, for the good of the whole? When you were in Iraq? Afghanistan? Told your soldiers one thing, a lie, just to keep morale up?"

"Yeah, but—"

"This is no different," Holly interrupted. "These people need to keep hope alive for something greater than themselves. It's more than simply personal survival now. The stakes are far greater."

Tim stood and walked to the screen door that faced the back yard and the ocean. He stood there for some time without saying a word, his beer in his hand forgotten. He watched Robyn and Jimenez romp on the beach, then, without turning to face Holly, said, "Remember when you told me Taco was frightened of me?"

"Yes."

"This frightens me as bad."

"Tim, do you really mean that?"

"I do. I look back on the last six years and wonder. Six years ago, I was scrounging in abandoned grocery stores, hoping to find something to eat. You were doing the same thing in Colorado with Izzy, just trying to stay alive another day. For what, I still don't know. I told Jerry a while ago the world didn't come to an end. It would keep on turning, in spite of us."

"And you're right," Holly said, toying with her now empty Coke bottle.

"In spite of it all, humanity has come back. I'm not so sure about 'civilization', but man has shown it can come back. I don't know if that's a good thing or a bad thing right now."

Holly went over to Tim, put her arms around his torso and hugged him, resting her head between his shoulder blades. She held onto him tightly, not saying a word.

"I look out at those two kids playing in the water, and thank fuck they're okay. Keeping those two safe, and you and the baby safe, is my number one concern. I'm so sick and tired of making decisions. Let our good ensign start up a merchant fleet, that Aussie guy start up the railroad again, and Jerry can have his little enclave here. I just want to get us all back to Williams and be left alone."

"Are you afraid of the power?" Holly asked into his back.

"Yes. I had that kind of power once, absolute power, and it scared the hell out of me. I never understood what kind of person would actually search out and desire that kind of power."

"It's intoxicating, some people thrive on it."

"I certainly don't. It's corrupting. Turns even the most honest man evil."

"Power tends to corrupt, and absolute power corrupts absolutely. Great men are almost always bad men," Holly said.

"So now you're quoting, who? I remember it was some Brit, wasn't it?" he asked.

"Aye, John Emerich Edward Dalberg Acton, first Baron Acton in a letter to Bishop Mandell Creighton," Holly said with a little smile Tim couldn't see.

"It looks like I'm not the only one in this screwy family that can pull obscure quotes from dead men out of my head."

"Aye, we are that, a family, Timothy. Let's get changed and go for a swim, shall we?"

"Splendid idea, let's!" Tim said in a dramatically effected British accent. "And afterwards, we shall polish the wainscoting!"

"Smashing idea, Sergeant Major!" Holly squealed, and headed off to the bedroom to change into a swimsuit.

Tim watched her leave, admiring her long ponytail swinging from side to side as she sashayed out of sight. He finished off his beer, and with a shrug of his shoulders, followed her.

CHAPTER 3:
ABSOLUTE POWER

At the same time that Tim and Holly were preparing for a swim in the warm waters of the Pacific Ocean, almost five thousand miles and six time zones east, a corpulent, middle-aged man dressed in what had once been an expensive, tailor-made Brooks Brothers suit was sitting behind a massive polished wood desk inside the Oval Office. His gray hair was combed perfectly, and reading glasses were propped studiously atop of his head.

He was sitting in a leather chair, custom made for another man who was no longer the President of the United States. He faced out through the thick, bullet proof windows that looked out onto the now overgrown Rose Garden and vast lawn, that had now become a meadow. The sun had set an hour ago, and in the dim twilight of the cold Washington evening, he saw what was left of the city's skyline silhouetted by a fire somewhere off in the distance. He'd have to find out what was burning, *again*.

When he heard someone come into the room behind him, he spun his chair to face another man, dressed in an US Army officer's uniform. His silver general's stars on his epaulets sparkled in the lantern light. Despite all of their efforts, they could not keep the power on in the city. The few coal powered generating stations near the city had long since burned through their meager supply of the fossil fuel, and no one had yet been able to get any of the nuclear power plants back on line. Most had their computers fried by the electromagnetic pulse of the Event so many years ago, and were now just useless relics of a bygone era.

The officer came smartly to attention and. "You called for me, Mr. President?"

"Yes I did. What's burning this time?"

"I'm not sure, sir. It may be one of the older neighborhoods going up in flames. No one lives there now. Most of the residents are out in the suburbs."

"Are we in any danger here?"

"I don't think so, sir. I'll send someone to find out."

"You do that. How many residents do we have now?" the man asked, picking up a crystal tumbler and filling it with what was once very expensive triple-malt scotch whiskey.

"Our latest census brings the population up to about five thousand, sir, here in the city. They've come from all over the country. There are a few other settlements in the outlying areas, not too far from here."

"Good. Do you care for a drink, General?"

"No thank you sir," the man said, wishing he could sit down, but like a good officer, he stayed standing for his Commander in Chief.

"Suit yourself. I'll have one, I think," he replied. "What else can you tell me?"

"No a whole lot, sir. Some things have been happening out in the Pacific, though I'm not sure what. Just dribs and drabs we've been able to pick up on the Ham bands. It seems like there was some kind of battle a few months ago."

"A battle? A battle between whom?" the fat man asked.

"From what we can pick up, there was a destroyer, one of ours. Its captain had turned rogue and was going around the whole ocean terrorizing whoever was left."

"That's interesting. Is that all?"

"We don't know much more than that. We do know that someone has been accessing some of the satellites," the general said cautiously. He'd learned a long time ago only to give certain information to the new 'president', because he was known to fly off into fits of rage.

"Accessing the satellites? How can they do that?" the man calling himself the president asked, anger starting to boil up.

"We're not sure, sir. It could be someone with access to the DoD computer network. We haven't been able to pinpoint anything. It's almost as if the network is blocking us," he replied uneasily, sweat breaking out under his collar despite the coolness of the room.

"Was your expedition successful?"

"Yes and no, sir. The one and only Blackhawk we had flying crashed, as you know, a year ago, taking the pilot with it. We've found no other pilots in the last census of survivors. We had to mount up a ground survey, and it took them months to find the wreckage of Air Force One."

"Were they able to locate the Package? The Football?" he demanded.

"No, sir. The wreckage was strewn over several acres of land, in what looked like an overgrown soybean field in Iowa. They spent three weeks looking and didn't find a trace of it."

"Damn it!" the president swore, slamming down the tumbler on the desk, carelessly spilling the whiskey. "Do you think someone has it?"

"We don't know, sir. Our guys came back a few days ago, after having been stranded in a blizzard for weeks. They said it didn't look like anyone else had been through the area, but we just don't know anything more," the general said, voice trembling.

"General, I asked you here to tell me what you know, not what you don't know. Do you think whoever is accessing the satellites has it?"

"Sir, with all due respect, we have absolutely no way of knowing for certain."

"With all this technology laying around, and all these survivors coming to us, you still have no way of finding out anything? You have not been able to get one more aircraft in the air?" the president demanded. "Someone *has* to have it! And I want it, do you understand!"

"Yes, sir. I understand completely. We're working on it," the general said.

"So let me get this straight, General. You've found the plane, but haven't found the package. You tell me you're getting 'dribs and drabs' of information about some battle in the Pacific. You know someone has been accessing the satellites, but not who. Tell, me, has our envoy to Europe reported back?"

"No, sir. He sailed in September. We got word he'd landed in the UK, and then was heading for the continent. I don't expect him back here until spring."

"Yes, it is almost like the way it was two hundred years ago, it takes forever to sail there. We need to find a pilot, and we need to find a plane!"

"I concur, Mr. President. However, I think we need to find more food for everyone, and soon. We're running out fast. We don't want another incident like last winter," the general said gravely.

"Yes, the riots were unfortunate. We were able to quell them effectively, as I recall," he said, an odd smile crossing his face, which made the general even more uncomfortable.

"I'll get the major to form up some more supply parties tomorrow morning, sir. Each time, we're having to go further and further out away from the city. We got as far as Philadelphia to the north, and Atlanta, to the south last time."

"Start heading west, then. How about the venison hunts? Aren't they still working?"

"The deer are starting to peter out around here. I'm afraid we've thinned out the herd too much."

"Well, General, aren't you just the bearer of fantastic news this evening? I'm getting rather tired of you telling me what you don't know and what you can't do."

"Sir, we are doing all we can!"

"General, you find out who has been accessing my fucking satellites! You find out if this person has the Football. You send the scavenging parties out for more food. Find out what this hubbub about some goddamned battle was about, and you *will* get these things done, is that understood?" the president said, with barely contained rage.

Even in the lantern light, the general could see the man's face burning red with anger. He had to get out of the room soon.

"Yes, sir, loud and clear, sir!"

"Because, General, I am the goddamn president of the United States, and they are *my* fucking satellites, and *my* fucking codes!"

"Yes, sir!"

"Someone is accessing the satellites and computer networks, and he's using them under *my* name, *my* goddamn authority! That, General, is against the fucking law!" he screamed, and then his voice became barely a whisper, evenly calm. "And when you find him, you *will* bring his head to me."

"Yes, sir, I'll head right back to the Pentagon tonight and start working on that, sir."

"Good, now get out of my sight. You sicken me," the president spat.

The general quickly spun on his heels, exiting the Oval office. He made his way through a darkened White House, which eerily reminded him of a tomb, a monument to a thought and a people who were dead and buried. The thought sickened him, almost as bad as the man he'd just left.

President, indeed! The man calling himself the president was actually the Secretary of Housing and Urban Development, eleventh in line of succession to the office of president, and the general thought it extremely ironic that this person, in his old office, was supposed to improve the lives of his fellow Americans, and now was the head of a decaying city, in a forgotten country.

He exited the building through a side door that once was reserved for servants and staff, which was flanked by two heavily armed guards, who didn't even budge at his passing. He stepped to the curb, pulling on his heavy overcoat to ward off the frigid night air. A Hum-Vee pulled up at the same moment we was fiddling with the buttons, and he jumped in. It was being driven by another officer, this time a Navy Lieutenant Commander. The man put the vehicle in drive and headed off.

"Where to?"

"Back to the Pentagon," the general said quietly.

"How'd it go?" the sailor asked.

"Do you really want to know?"

"That bad, huh?"

"Not as bad as last time, but bad enough. He wasn't happy at all," the general said, involuntarily shuddering even though the Hum-Vee's heater was on full-blast and actually felt like the inside of an oven to him.

"Did you tell him about the launch?"

"Are you crazy? If he finds out someone launched one of *his* nukes, he'll come unglued!" the general told his companion in horror.

"I've got an updated brief for you; I'll wait until we get back to the office."

"That's fine by me. He asked about the fires, too. I told him I didn't know. We'll have to think up some bullshit story to tell him. I, for one, am not going to tell him there was another riot at the food warehouse again."

"Yeah, that would not be good."

"How many killed?" the general asked.

"The Army reckons about twenty-five, and a bunch more wounded. They're mopping up now. It could've been worse."

"Did they declare martial law again?"

"Yeah, and got everyone off the streets. If things don't change soon, if we don't get some food to feed these people, things are going to get a lot worse. We only have a few hundred *'soldiers'*, half of them not even trained, civilians mostly. They are getting scared. No electricity, no water, no heat. They're starting to tear down buildings for the firewood."

"I know, and our *'leader'* is more concerned about getting those codes."

"I'm at a loss," the sailor, said, shaking his head as he drove through an empty, slush-covered street.

They drove silently the rest of the way to the Pentagon, and the Lt. Commander parked the Hum-Vee right in front of the door, completely disregarding the old parking lot. They exited and walked up to a guarded door, where an armed sentry stood at attention and held the door open for the two men. They walked silently down lantern-lined corridors, their footfalls echoing loudly in the empty building.

They reached a conference room in the "D" Ring, or second most outer of the five concentric rings of the building. The Lt. Commander opened the door for the general and the man entered, taking off his overcoat and tossing it on an empty chair. There was another man, dressed in casual civilian clothes, and he made a move to get up and leave when the two officers entered.

"No, John. You can stay," the general told the man, waving absently for him to remain seated, "So, Lt. Commander, talk to me."

The navy man remained standing, fiddling with some papers on the table, cleared his throat and began to speak. "Sir, what we've been able to gather from the still-running DoD network, is that the first time the system was accessed using the National Command Authority codes was approximately six years ago, about eighteen months after The Situation."

"Six years ago?"

"Yes sir. It was accessed once, for about fifteen minutes, then whoever logged on, logged off, and it wasn't accessed again until September, about four months ago. It was at this time they called up, and then tasked a KH11 satellite for a simple visual, radar, and infrared scan of a location somewhere in the middle of the South Pacific."

"Can you tell from where it was accessed? A location, maybe?" the general asked, sitting up in his chair.

"No, sir. Safeguards in the system prevent us from locating the site. If it actually had been the NCA, in the time of war, it would safeguard his location."

"So we have no idea where this person is?"

"That's correct, sir." the Commander said. "Okay, go on. What did he take pictures of?"

"An atoll, named Volivoli. It was a disused military pre-position stockpile location, and a Navy weather station. Other than that, it's been forgotten since 1945."

"No shit. Never heard of it."

"Nor had I, sir. I had to look it up in the archives. Whoever it was accessed the system again, in the middle of November, targeted a single ICBM, and launched it at the same location," the navy man stated, matter-of-factly, and then sat down with a plop into a chair across from the general.

The general sat for a few minutes and let out a long, low whistle. "Are you sure?" he asked, a look of astonishment.

The civilian, who had up until then been silent, spoke up. "With one hundred percent certainty. It was a Minuteman III, from the 319th Missile Command in Offutt, outside of Omaha."

"Holy shit," the general whispered. "So we have no idea who this joker is, or why he did it?"

He looked around the dimly lighted room and swore to himself. The lanterns gave off an eerie glow, and he wished for the cool, hard glow of florescent lights. The Pentagon's emergency generators had long since expended their supply of fuel, and supplies of the precious diesel fuel were becoming rarer and rarer, as the supplies in the surrounding area had been used up by the ever expanding population in the city. They had just enough electricity saved up in banks of deep-cell batteries in the basement to boot up a few computers once or twice a day.

"That's about it," the civilian said.

"Did it have anything to do with this alleged 'battle' out there?"

"We think so. The comms we've been able to intercept are in a code I've never seen before, some language from the islands, and Pidgin English. It's hard to decipher," the Commander said.

"Tell me what you do know, Tom," the general said.

"For a few years right after the Situation, one of our destroyers, the USS *Hughes*, was roaming around the Pacific Rim, and from what we gathered from the plain English transmissions, the captain wasn't on a 'humanitarian' mission. We think someone from Honolulu lured this ship to Volivoli, then when it got there, they nuked it."

"Sort of like using a sledgehammer to kill a fly," the general said.

"That's about it, sir. Crude, but effective," stated the naval officer. "There's been nothing more since the launch a few months ago. Until yesterday, that is."

"Oh?" the general uttered. "What did they do this time?"

"Another satellite tasking."

"Where?" the general demanded.

"Arizona of all places, a speck on the map, smaller than that atoll, the town of Tusayan. Or to be more exact, the airport there."

"What the hell is there? Is there anything of military value there?"

"It's a few kilometers south of the Grand Canyon, nothing there really, except for a gas station, a post office and the airport."

"Another nuke target?"

"I doubt it," the Commander said, wrapping up his briefing. "Are you going to tell the president about this?"

"I'm going to have to at some point. I don't think it would be wise right now."

"Is he that bad?" the civilian asked.

"John, you have no idea. He goes into these rages. Almost like temper tantrums from a three year old. It reminds me of the stories of Hitler, and that scares the begeebus out of me," the general said, shaking his head.

"Cult of personality," John remarked.

"Exactly. He was good at it in the beginning, as you're well aware. However, now that the food is running out and we've stripped all of the fuel from nearby, he's losing his grip. Two years ago, he could go out and make a speech, and everything would be okay. Now? Shit..."

"The natives are getting restless," the Commander opined. "There was still plenty of fuel to keep the lights on two years ago and everyone had a full belly. That's no longer the case." "He *is* the president," the general pointed out in the absent man's defense.

"Maybe so, under the laws from before the Situation," John conceded. "Does it all really matter anymore?"

"It's up to the three of us to try to hold it together. If it takes listening to our president, then so be it," the general stated with little conviction.

The three of them sat silently for some time, contemplating what they should do. All had thoughts, none of which they were comfortable sharing.

"It's a house of cards, and it's about to come crumbling down all around us unless we can find a solution. That's our job, gentlemen. Like it or not, we swore an oath, and now we've got to deliver on that promise. The man over on Pennsylvania Avenue expects our loyalty," the general said.

"To what end?" the Commander asked.

"Is this what we all wanted when he put the government back together?" John asked.

"What *'government'* is that, gentlemen? We have one man who, granted, is by law the president. Then again, we have no laws left to speak of, except a quasi-military state with him at our head," the Commander stated flatly.

"Until we can get the power on, get food to everyone, we've got to do exactly as we have been doing," the general said.

"I suggested a year ago that we should set up farms, start growing our food. You even brought that up to him, General. He shot that idea down in flames," the Commander reminded them.

"Yes, he said that there was plenty of food lying around all over the country, there was no need to start up farms," the general spat.

"That's not the case! You know it, John knows it, *I* know it! The food, what's left that hasn't been spoiled or contaminated by vermin, will soon run out. Cult of Personality is correct, just like Joe Stalin. His empire collapsed, too, when they couldn't feed their people anymore. I fear this will turn ugly, sooner rather than later," the Navy man stated.

"I just know this; he gave me a direct order tonight. We have to find out who's been accessing the satellites. Find him, and get the codes off of him, by whatever means are available," the general said, crossing his arms across his chest.

"So martial law is still in effect, and we'll continue to do summary executions to the people who only want to be fed?"

"That's about it, Commander," the general said with a finality that slammed down like a lead weight.

"What about food?" John asked.

"We'll send out foraging parties again starting tomorrow. Send them west this time," the general said, standing and picking up his coat. "I'll leave that to you, Commander. Get it done."

"Yes, sir," the Commander replied, as the general quickly left the room.

John Thompson, who had been an analyst with the CIA before the Situation, stood also. "I'm going to head home myself, Tom," he said to the Naval officer, who only nodded and dove into a mound of papers he'd spread out before him on the conference table. John grabbed his jacket and headed out through the rabbit warren of corridors, through the doors out to the parking lot, that in years passed would have been packed to all hours of the night with busy little worker bees in the vast military complex. His vehicle, a ten year old Ford, sat alone near the entrance. He'd had it converted to run on propane last year, and it was one of the few non-military vehicles to be seen in the city.

He made his way through the empty city towards Georgetown, where he shared a brownstone with a woman he'd met a few years prior. He was stopped at a roadblock, and his ID was checked by a dirty and disheveled sentry. While he was waiting, he couldn't help but notice a group of several civilians, standing in line, carrying all their worldly possessions, were waiting to be allowed entrance into the city. He shook his head in disbelief. Even now, people were straggling in, looking to find some hope, some help to survive. Didn't they know they stood a better chance out there on their own? He shook his head as the sentry waved him on, and he drove off, leaving the sad scene behind him.

John drove mechanically, his thoughts a jumble, and somehow managed to find his way to the formerly upscale neighborhood. He looked at the façade of his home and smiled ruefully. He'd have never have been able to afford to live in such a place before, not on his meager CIA salary.

He noticed a light in the window and smiled. He exited the car, bounded the steps, and entered the house. Still dressed in shabby scrubs from her shift at the clinic where she and a few other nurses and doctors worked, his girlfriend came up to him and hugged him tightly. Barbra looked tired, and her chestnut hair was a mop, but her eyes still twinkled at the sight of John. He hugged her back, and took in her scent with closed eyes. He felt like crying, though he'd never let it show. He had to be the rock for this lady.

"Did you ask them today?" she asked, taking his hand and leading him into the living room where a fire was burning nicely in the colonial style fireplace.

"I never got the chance, babe," he said dejectedly, flopping into an expensive leather easy chair by the fire. The woman fixed him a drink, three fingers of vodka, neat, in a rocks glass and handed it to him.

"John, we need more medical supplies. We're almost out of everything."

"I know. The president has us on something else."

"John, what could be more important than medicine? Do you we've had almost a hundred people die of influenza this winter?" she said, making herself a drink and sitting on the arm of the chair.

"I know, I'm doing all I can. We're trying to find more food for everyone. The president thinks that's the priority right now," he said, not daring to bring up the real reason. She'd have flipped her lid if she knew the crazy fucker was looking for the codes for a few thousand thermonuclear weapons.

"John, food is going to be the last thing everyone will be worrying about if people start dropping dead of sicknesses that we can easily prevent."

"I know. It's like we've slipped into another Dark Age," he agreed, sipping his vodka, and rubbing her back affectionately, staring into the fire.

"You've got that right. It's damn near medieval the way it's getting out there," she said in a tired voice. "The whole infrastructure, as threadbare and raggedy as it is, is about to collapse, and he's got you out searching for more canned corned beef and beans. If he'd just get the water back on, that would help so much with the sanitary conditions. We got word from another clinic; you know the one over on Baltimore Avenue? They now have three confirmed cases of Bubonic Plague."

"Bubonic Plague, are they sure?" John asked, dumbfounded.

"Yes, they're sure."

"Oh my God, it *is* becoming medieval," he sighed.

"Once it warms up, it'll get even worse," Barbra stated, taking his glass and refilling it with more of the clear liquid. "We can't handle what we've got now."

"I saw more refugees coming into the city tonight on the way home," he said, suddenly feeling very tired. He pinched the bridge of his nose and then rubbed his eyes, trying to ward off a headache he felt coming on.

"That's insane! We can't handle the people we already have!"

"I know. There was another riot earlier at the warehouse."

"I heard the shooting from the clinic," she told him, returning to his chair with his fresh drink.

"I don't know what to do, babe. Everything is telling me to run, get the fuck out of here, but part of me wants to help make it work," John told her, taking the tumbler and putting his arm around her waist.

"Why don't we do that, honey? We can pack up and leave tonight!" she pleaded.

"You know I can't do that. Not right now."

"Then when? We have to get out of here! We can go to Florida, or down to Mexico, anyplace but here!"

"Honey, when I go back to the Pentagon tomorrow, I'll give an order to whoever is in charge of this next expedition to get more medical supplies too. Let's give it some more time, okay?"

"Do you promise?"

"Yes, I promise. I know how important it is."

"Good. And I mean it about getting away from here. This place is rotting away from the inside, and I want to be far, far away when it finally collapses," she said, setting aside her drink and sliding into his lap.

Barbra wrapped her arms around him and buried her face into his neck. He held her tightly and let his thoughts bounce around inside his mind. She was dead-on with her summation that the city was rotting away from within, though hadn't that always been the case? The players changed from time to time, but the game was always the same.

"I promise. Let me work out some things here first, and in the spring, we'll head south," he told her, brushing a few strands of hair away from her eyes, that in the firelight, sparkled like star shine.

She had been looking into the fire, and when she turned her head and faced him, he saw she'd been crying. Her sad blue eyes looked at him pleadingly, and it broke his heart. They'd met shortly after the Situation at a convenience store, and he'd quickly fallen head over heels in love with her.

They'd both lost people who were close to them, and they were now closer to each other than they'd ever been to their former spouses. He took his thumb and gently wiped away her tears from her cheek, and kissed her tenderly.

"I mean it, John. I feel that something terrible is going to happen here," she said after they broke their kiss.

"I feel it too. But I can't leave yet."

"We'll wait, but not much longer," she said. "Because if I have to stay here one more year, I'm afraid I'll go mad."

"I feel the same way."

"Remember when it all first happened? How everyone, even though they were still in shock, was friendly and wanting to help?"

"Yes, I remember," he said, nodding.

"It's not like that anymore. People are angry. They're angry at the government, angry at what they *think* is the government, and it's not, is it, Johnny? It's really a dictatorship now isn't it?" Barbra said, which was what everyone was beginning to realize. "I think you're right, babe," he sighed, not knowing what else to say. The government, the country he'd loved for so long, the country he'd spent the better part of his adult life working for, had dissolved right in front of his eyes, gone without even a whimper, and that thought saddened him to the core.

"Johnny, we had one chance to make things right again, one giant golden opportunity to get back to the principles, and they fucked it up for good."

"Maybe not, maybe there's hope out there still."

"I hope so, I really do," she said, kissing him again. "Are you hungry?"

"Not really. I kind of lost my appetite a few hours ago."

"I'm not hungry either. Let's go to bed, okay?" "That's the best idea I've heard all day," he said with a grin and the both walked out of the room, leaving the fire in the fireplace to burn out.

CHAPTER 4: EAST BOUND AND DOWN

The week went by fast for Tim, and as he sat on a nylon-webbed jump seat in the cargo hold of the C-130, he looked aft to see everyone had settled in as comfortably as they could. They were two hours into the flight east, still somewhere over the Pacific Ocean between Hawaii and California.

He was mentally shaking his head at the craziness of it all. At the luau the other night, the food was delicious, and the alcohol had flowed freely, a little too freely Tim thought, and culminating in the sheer insanity of it all when Jerry, holding a copy of the US Constitution, swore Tim in as president. Tim had insisted they use that, and not a bible, and everyone understood.

Now he sat looking down the cargo hold at a Hum-Vee chained down securely, twenty people, six piglets, four goats, four chickens, and two roosters. He had known about the pigs and goats, and looked forward to the bacon and fresh milk, but was surprised at the chickens. He didn't know any had survived and was elated to see them. Now he looked forward to not only fresh bacon and goat's milk, but fresh eggs and possibly fried chicken at some point. The thought made his mouth water.

He had just come from the cockpit, where Holly and Robyn had full control of their flight, and the sight of Robyn sitting in the copilot's seat made him smile. She was picking it up quickly, like everything else she'd done in her life. He was proud of his little girl, though he reminded himself that she wasn't little anymore. At nineteen years old, she still had the youthful exuberance in life and the sparkle in her blue eyes, but to Tim, she'd always be that little waif he found in the middle of the road somewhere in West Virginia, crying her eyes out.

Tim leaned back and closed his eyes to get a little sleep. He could already smell the pigs and goats, and thought that the aircraft would need to be fumigated when they arrived back in Arizona. He was drifting off to sleep when he sensed someone looking at him. He opened his eyes, and inches from his face, was another round face, that smiled immediately when she saw Tim open his eyes.

"How ya' going, mate?" the face asked, smiling. It came out like, *'Howyagoinmate?'*

"I'm going good, April. How are you?" Tim asked the girl, smiling back at her. April was not much older than Robyn, but mentally, she was somewhere nearer to nine or ten years old. Born with Down's syndrome, she'd come from Australia on the Newcastle, and had been adopted by an Aussie couple who was now coming to Arizona with them, presumably to start a new life. They were the ones with the chickens. They'd left several on the HMAS Newcastle, and several more in Hawaii, and were bringing the remainder with them.

"It's loud in here!" she said, bright eyed.

"I know, April. It won't be long until we're in Arizona," Tim replied with a smile.

"Me and Paula and Ian will be chook farmers!"

"You'll be the most important family in Williams!" Tim told the girl, smiling and remembering 'chook' was the Aussie slang word for chicken. Just then, Ian, the man who'd found April way back when the Event had first happened, came up to them.

"April, you leave Mr. Flannery alone, sweetheart," he said, taking the girl's hand.

"It's alright, Ian. I don't mind at all," Tim told the man.

The girl smiled and headed back aft, and the man sat down beside Tim on the jump seats.

"She's a sweetheart. After everything went to shit, I met Paula, and then we found April. She was almost dead from malnutrition," Ian said. It was loud inside the cargo hold, and the two men had to shout to be heard.

"It was hell for a lot of us. I found Robyn almost in the same condition. I can't imagine how hard it was with a special needs child," Tim told the man.

"She's so trusting of everyone and everything. I'm glad we can come with you, to Arizona, where it'll be safe for us."

Tim inwardly cringed at that. It wasn't going to be easy, and there are no guarantees. He kept his peace. Simply getting everyone back to Williams and settled would be a challenge in itself.

"I think with you and your chickens, you'll be a productive member of our new community, Ian. I'm happy that you're coming along with us."

"I always wanted to go to America, to see the Old West. I'm just as excited as April, to be honest."

"It's still going to be a job. We'll be getting there at the end of winter, so it's going to still be plenty cold," Tim told him.

"In Arizona?"

"It's all elevation. Where we're going, it's over a mile above sea level. Two years ago, we had a blizzard come off the mountains, dumped three feet of snow on us. Robyn and I were stuck inside the house for two weeks."

"I didn't realize that," Ian said, a shocked look crossing his face.

Tim smiled. "It normally doesn't snow that badly, and when it does, it doesn't stick around too long. The summers are rather pleasant. Once we get everyone back to town and we find places for you to live, it should be quite nice for everyone."

"You have an idea where I can set up my chook farm?"

"I have just the place in mind, Ian. We'll have to build some sturdy fencing to keep the coyotes out though. We can keep them in my barn for now."

"That's good. Again, thank you for letting us come with you."

"We still have to be very careful, remember. It's not going to be like on Oahu. I don't know what else is out there outside of the town."

"I've wanted to ask. What's with all the guns?" Ian asked, pointing at the four pallets of ammunition, M4 carbines and an M60 machine gun, not to mention the .50 caliber M2 heavy machine gun on a ring mount on the Hum-Vee, secured in the hold in front of the Hum-Vee. Jerry had happily 'donated' the booty to Tim; he had plenty on the island.

"Insurance," Tim said.

"Insurance?" "Let me ask you something, Ian. Did you have to have automobile insurance in Australia, before the Event that is?"

"Yes, it was required by law."

"Did you ever have to file a claim?"

"No, thankfully."

"Those weapons are our insurance. The world before the Event wasn't safe, not by a long shot; it's even less safe now. I hope we never have to file a claim."

"The real Wild West, eh?"

"Not quite, I don't think, but better safe than sorry. I want everyone to be schooled on their use, and be proficient with them."

"That sounds sensible."

"I'm using Colonial history of the US as a guide. Everyone was required to have a rifle in their home."

"Like Switzerland?"

"Yeah, kind of like that. I'd like to think of it as how the Minutemen were."

"It's all new to me," Ian said, sounding a little uneasy.

"I don't expect any trouble. It never hurts to have a backup plan," Tim said, trying to be reassuring.

"I'll keep that in mind, mate. I'd better get back to Paula," Ian said with a grin.

"We'll be okay, Ian. We just can't let our guard down," Tim said, and the man shook his hand and headed back to his seat further aft.

Tim tried to get some sleep again, but it eluded him. He thought about the logistics of getting everyone back to Williams with only the one Hum-Vee. He mulled that over in his mind for a few moments and came up with a plan. He stood up and made his way to the cockpit, where he saw that it was very crowded. Holly was in the pilot's seat, and Robyn had relinquished her seat to let the ensign's boy, Billy, sit in the co-pilot's seat. Jimenez was seated at the flight engineer's seat, and Tim tapped him on the shoulder. When he saw Tim standing behind him, he removed his headset.

"Do you need something, Sar' Major?"

"Yeah, come with me," Tim said. Jimenez let Holly know where he was going, and followed Tim back into the cargo hold. When they got out of earshot of the cockpit, Jimenez asked, "What's up?"

"When we get on the ground, I'm going to need you to come with me in the Hum-Vee."

"Anything wrong?" he asked in concern.

"Nothing too bad. I was thinking how we're going to get everyone and everything back to Williams. You and I are going to an Army depot outside of Flagstaff when we arrive. A place called Camp Navajo. It's an Army National Guard base in Belmont."

"What for?"

"We'll go there and scare up some larger transportation for everyone and everything we have to transport. I figure a couple of deuce-and-a-halfs will fit the bill nicely," Tim said.

"That's a great idea, Sar' Major."

"Of course it's a good idea. It's mine!" Tim agreed with a grin. "Let the Lieutenant know, will you?"

"Sure thing."

"And tell her the in-flight service and entertainment leaves a lot to be desired on this flight."

Jimenez laughed loudly and gave Tim a thumbs up. "It that all, Sar' Major?"

"Yeah, that's it. Let me know when we're getting close and I'll get everyone ready for the landing back here."

"Wilco, Sar' Major. Oh, and Sar'?"

"Yeah?"

"You have got to be the ugliest flight attendant I've ever seen," Jimenez said, making Tim laugh out loud. The two men parted, Jimenez going back to the cockpit, and Tim finding his seat in the hold. He looked out at the faces of the passengers. Some were asleep, others were talking with each other over the roar of the turboprops, and a few were looking at him, with… hope?

He hoped for everyone's sake he'd be able to pull it off.

He saw Izzy near the end at the upright and secured ramp kibitzing with one of the men from Oahu. He felt bad at not spending more time with his friend, and he thought that maybe he'd make up for lost time once they got back to Williams. He sat down, and was asleep as soon as he closed his eyes.

Tim was shaken awake by Jimenez. The first thing he noticed was that the engines sounded different, quieter. "Anything wrong?" he asked, shaking the cobwebs from his mind.

"No, Sar' Major. The number two and three engines were running a little hot, so the Lieutenant shut 'em down. We're almost to Tusayan. We should be on the ground in about twenty minutes."

"We're only flying on two engines?"

"No problem, Sar' Major. We're in good hands."

"If you say so…"

In Tim's mind, a plane that was designed to run on four engines, had better have all four engines running. But if the kid said it was okay, it was okay. He thanked Jimenez and went about the cargo hold telling everyone to get ready for the landing. After he got everyone ready, he went back up to the cockpit and leaned over the pilot's seat.

"How are you doing, babe?"

Holly looked back over her shoulder and smiled. "I'm doing fine. There's the runway now," she said, pointing out the windscreen. Tim could see the runway off in the distance, and it looked painfully tiny, a single smudge of concrete with a few outbuildings sitting on a high prairie, a few low junipers scattered around.

Tim patted her on the shoulder and looked over at Robyn, who was looking at him with a toothy grin.

"I'll leave it to the professionals, then," Tim said, went back aft, and strapped into the jump seat. He heard the engines power up some and then the whine of the hydraulic motors lower the flaps, then felt the aircraft slow and descend. Next, the sound of the landing gear lowering and locking into place, and what seemed like seconds later, the wheels kissed the runway with a slight jar. When the aircraft slowed and stopped, Tim stood and told everyone that they'd arrived. The aircraft lurched, and the engines powered up, and they all could feel the plane turn and begin to taxi.

When it stopped again and he heard Holly shut down the engines, Tim walked to the rear of the cargo hold and hit the button for the rear ramp, which began to lower with a hydraulic whine. Almost immediately, a cold draft entered the hold, chilling everyone.

Tim checked his watch and did some mental arithmetic, resetting the watch to local time. It was just past 9AM, and a bright, clear morning greeted everyone. When the ramp was locked into place, Tim walked down and flipped over the wheel ramps. Not seeing any movement, he looked back at the passengers, who were staring at him in silence.

He had a moment of panic wash over him, then he chided himself for being so stupid. He was standing there, completely unarmed. The moment passed, but he thought he soon ought to remedy his situation. First things first, though, he put one foot on the ramp. The silence was deafening after the long hours of the engine's whine.

"Welcome to Arizona everyone. We're still not all the way to home; it's about another fifty miles to Williams. Lance Corporal Jimenez and I will be heading out in a few minutes to procure some transportation for us. In the meantime, if you all could give us a hand unloading the aircraft that would be great!" Tim said.

With everyone's help, they unloaded the aircraft and Tim ushered everyone into the airport's tiny terminal building after a quick scan for any bodies left lying about. Finding none, everyone got settled and Tim, Jimenez, and Robyn armed themselves with M4 carbines, and then armed the .50 caliber machine gun on the Hum-Vee that Tim had parked in front of the building.

"How long will you be?" Holly asked.

"I don't know," Tim replied. "A few hours maybe. It depends on the road. I've got a radio with me, so I'll call you when we get there and on our way back. I don't foresee any problems."

"You be careful," Holly said, kissing him.

"Wilco, Ma'am," Tim said, kissing her back. "Get everyone settled here, get them comfortable, and we shouldn't be too long."

Tim and Jimenez climbed into the Hum-Vee, their carbines safely stowed, and headed off with Tim at the wheel. On the road leading out of the airport, Tim noticed several houses that were overgrown with weeds and he shuddered. He still didn't see any signs of life, and there was sure to be bodies in those homes, long dead and mummified in the dry air. He couldn't stop thinking about places like this, all over the world. Homes where families once resided, now turned into crypts of the dead, monuments to a now long-dead society, and it saddened him deeply.

Tim made a left turn onto route 64 and headed south, towards Williams and I-40. "You know, it's funny," Jimenez commented, "I've lived in Arizona my entire life, and I've never once been to the Grand Canyon."

"Yeah, I know what you mean. I was born and raised in Philadelphia, and I haven't seen the Liberty Bell or all those other historical places since I think I was ten or eleven years old."

"Maybe you can get back one day, Sar' Major."

"Nah, that's all gone now," Tim said wistfully, and told Jimenez of the firestorm right before his exodus of the city.

"Wow," Jimenez said with a long whistle. "All that history, gone forever."

"All that's left now are stories in books. It's why I think it's even more important now to keep the history alive, teach our children the importance of it all."

"You said it," Jimenez agreed, nodding slowly.

"Right now we've got to get everyone settled in, and then maybe when babies start to be born, we'll start up a little school," Tim said, lighting his pipe deftly with one hand as he drove down the bumpy road.

"Shit, these roads are in terrible shape," Jimenez remarked.

"Yeah, we'll have to get in touch with the highway department and complain," Tim said, and they both laughed. Jimenez was right; the roads were really starting to fall apart. Every crack in the asphalt had sprouted weeds, which after almost seven years, were starting to spread out, and the wheels on the Hum-Vee thumped over each one noticeably. After several more miles, they finally reached the I-40 interchange at Williams.

Tim didn't see anything different in town from his vantage point on the highway interchange, and thought for a second to take a detour to the house, ultimately deciding against it. It was most probably still in one piece, they'd only been gone a few months; and the chance of anyone finding it over the past winter was slight.

"I figure in about another ten or so years, you'll never even be able to tell there were roads here at all," Tim said sadly.

They headed east on I-40, the road continuing to climb higher in a steady grade. There was a set of railroad tracks, also overgrown with weeds, on the south side of the highway, and Jimenez pointed to a stalled freight train.

"Yeah, Taco. Those Aussies who want to put together a rail route to 'Frisco have their work cut out for them. Even if they get an engine running, they've got several hundred miles of track they need to clear, or switch the tracks around the stalled trains. And they're fucked if they come across a derail."

"What about those squids? Do you think they'll really get that boat to sail?"

"That is yet to be seen, too," Tim told the young Marine.

"I think they're crazy, if you ask me," Jimenez said, looking out the window at the forest passing by.

"The past six or so years haven't been crazy?" Tim asked with a sideways glance.

"You've got a point there, Sar' Major."

"Taco, we will be very lucky if we get through the next few years."

"Isn't that a little... what's the word?"

"Fatalistic? Yeah, it is."

"Why? We've got a nice place here, and you said it's got electricity, running water, plenty of food. We should do alright."

"I'll tell you why, Taco," Tim said, slowing and taking the off-ramp for Belmont and Camp Navajo. "Because somewhere out there, someone will want what we have, and try to take it."

"How can you know that?"

"It's human nature, like that crazy ship captain. I'm sorry to say that there's probably more head-cases out there like that."

"So we just let them?" Jimenez asked.

"No, we don't. We also don't let anyone know where we are either. This place is pretty well hidden, far enough off the highway that passers-by will never find it. The only other person besides us that even knows it exists knows exactly where it is, and that's Staff Sergeant Williams."

"What about the others, the ones who want to travel out?"

"They're going to have to be able to keep their mouths shut," Tim said, looking at Jimenez gravely.

"I hope so, if you're right," Jimenez said as they drove into the post. "What is this place?"

"It's Camp Navajo, or more correctly, Navajo Army Depot. It was built back during World War Two, I think."

"I never knew this place was here."

"There are places like this all over the country. Most were training and maintenance facilities," Tim replied. He steered by the main buildings and headed down another road. "Ah, here we go, the motor pool."

Tim pulled the Hum-Vee up to the front of a building that had huge garage doors, and to the left were rows of the deuce-and-a-half trucks they were after, and two more rows of Hum-Vees. After shutting off their vehicle, both men retrieved their weapons and got out. "Looks deserted," Jimenez remarked.

"I'd think so, Taco. I found this place right after Robyn and I found our place over in Williams. It's got a lot of stuff that we can use stored here," Tim said, pointing over at a row of bunkers, eerily similar to the ones they'd found on Volivoli, grass-covered mounds with a thick concrete façade and steel blast doors in the front. "There are hundreds of bunkers, spread out over a few thousand acres. I've only explored some of them."

"I'd like to go scrounging around and see what I can find," Jimenez said.

"You can, later, when we get settled. This place isn't going anywhere. First things first, let's get a few of these trucks running."

"Sure thing, Sar' Major!" Jimenez said enthusiastically, and they got right to work breaking into the building to find the tools they'd need.

It took the better part of three hours, but the two men were able to get two of the trucks running. They hitched the Hum-Vee to the rear of one of the trucks and headed back out onto the highway, and back to Tusayan.

Tim used the handheld Motorola military radio to call Holly and let her know they were on their way back with the transportation. They made good time getting back to the airport, where they found everyone waiting in the terminal building. Holly came up to Tim when he alighted from the lead truck and she wrapped her arms around him in a great bear hug

"I was beginning to worry," she said.

"I'd have called if there had been a problem, babe."

"I'm just glad you're back. Now what?"

"We get the Hum-Vee unhitched, get everyone and everything loaded, and we head for home!" Tim said, putting his arm around her and walking towards the rear of the truck where Jimenez was already unhooking the tow bar.

Tim went into the terminal to let everyone know they were ready to start loading up. Everyone helped, and even April did her part, helping to put the chicken cages into the back of the rear truck.

When everyone was in the trucks, Jimenez took the wheel of one, one of the Aussie men in the other, and Tim, Robyn, Holly, and Izzy climbed into the Hum-Vee, and they headed back south on Route 64 towards Williams.

The weather was still clear and sunny, but the temperature was only in the upper '50s, and there were some clouds starting to form over the distant, snow-capped peaks of the San Francisco Mountains north of Flagstaff, visible in the distance. Tim wondered if it might snow that evening. If so, they'd have to get everyone into shelter as soon as they arrived, because it would take a few hours to get the power on in all the homes in the survival compound, as Tim had long ago shut off and isolated all the solar panels to feed power to his house alone.

They pulled off of the highway into town, and a feeling of sadness washed over Tim. It did every time he had driven through town. He couldn't help but still think of all the people, long gone, who used to call this place home. He reckoned he'd never stop feeling that way, and shoved the thoughts back into the recesses of his mind.

Driving through town on Main Street, Tim made a right hand turn onto the road that led out of town, heading south, towards Coleman Lake, where the compound was located. They passed a reservoir that was filled to the top with water, and that was a good sign. If it was full, there should still be plenty of water in the aquifer and the communal well that fed all the homes. This part of Arizona was a hit or miss chance when it came to water, and if there was no water to sustain everyone, they'd have to find it someplace else. Just the thought of moving yet again gave him a sinking feeling in the pit of his stomach.

The road continued on and upwards, and through a cut in some ancient basalt, the road curved and then proceeded through a copse of Aspen trees, flattening out to a vast Ponderosa pine forest, broken only occasionally by meadows of tall brown grass, that Tim knew would be filled with vast herds of mule deer and elk grazing come sundown, which elated him. He looked into the rear-view mirror to see if their tiny convoy was still intact, and seeing that it was, slowed and signaled that he was turning left, off the paved road and onto a narrow red dirt road that led through another stand of pine.

They emerged out the other side of the stand of trees where the luxurious log home that Tim and Robyn had called home for so many years was still standing, untouched. There were some patches of snow in the shady areas around the house where sunlight rarely reached this time of year, and the American flag was still flying proudly on the flagpole, albeit slightly tattered, where Tim had left it so many months ago.

Tim pulled the Hum-Vee up to the front of the house and parked. He turned to Holly and smiled. "Honey, we're home!"

Holly beamed. "It's just as we left it!"

Robyn and Izzy got out of the back. Tim looked up a little forlornly and the tattered flag and frowned.

"I'll have to replace that soon," he said. He walked over the short flight of steps up to the porch, bent down and lifted a rock, and was pleased to find the keys still there. He picked them up and handed them to Robyn, who'd bounded up to him.

"Here, go get you guys settled, and I'll handle this with Taco," Tim said, handing her the key ring. He walked over to the first truck to see smiling faces from the back.

"We're here. I hope the ride wasn't too bad," Tim told his passengers.

"It's cold!" a small voice in the back piped up. It was Billy, the young ensign's son.

"Well, young man, it sure isn't Hawaii," Tim said. "It'll warm up soon enough."

"I hope so, I'm freezing!" the boy said, at which everyone laughed.

Tim explained to them what they needed to do, and with everyone's help, they all found a house, and began moving their meager belongings they had brought with them. It took the rest of the day for Tim and Jimenez to get everyone settled, the power turned on, and to make some minor repairs to the solar panel arrays near the settlement. It was well after dark when he finally made it back home. He plodded up the steps onto the porch, and saw that someone had lit a fire in the fireplace, which was nice, because the temperature was dropping rapidly as the sun sunk below the western horizon.

Tim was warmed immediately by the fire as he walked through the front door. He cleared his carbine and placed it by the fireplace. He followed the sounds of noise and a wonderful aroma to the kitchen, where he found Holly, Izzy, Robyn, and Mary fixing supper.

"Ah, Tim, you're back," Izzy said. "The womenfolk are making dinner, why don't we get a drink and sit out on the porch?" He took Tim by the arm and led him out through the dining room into the living room, where he grabbed a bottle of Scotch and poured them both four fingers of the amber liquid in rocks glasses, and handed Tim one.

Tim raised the glass to Izzy. "To being home!"

"Yes, to be at home. Come, let's go outside and enjoy the night air," said Izzy, and went out onto the porch, followed by Tim. They sat on the wooden rocking chairs that were set up on either side of a table, sipping companionably for a few moments before Izzy spoke.

"Is everyone settled?" he asked.

"We've gotten everyone into a house, and the animals are in the barn for now, until we can get some secure pens set up."

"Holly told the young ensign his group could stay with us for a few days," Izzy said, "so they can make preparations to head out."

"That sounds good. We've got plenty of room here."

"I've taken back my old bedroom, the boy is bunking with Robyn, and Bill and Mary have the other spare room. Mr. Suplee and Nakamura said they could sleep on the couches," Izzy informed him.

"I'm glad that's all settled."

"Juan set up a cot in the basement, Tim," Izzy said. "I'm sure he'd much rather be sleeping somewhere else," the old doctor told his friend, watching for a reaction from Tim out of the corner of his eye.

"Taco can stay in the basement, Iz," Tim said with a finality that to Izzy didn't seem all that final.

"I'll be moving out soon myself, Tim," Izzy said.

"Oh?" Tim responded, looking at his friend in the darkness.

"I think I'd like to find a little cottage in town and look for a place to set up a clinic. It will keep me occupied, idle minds, and all that."

"You're more than welcome to continue to live here, Iz. You're family."

"I know that, Tim, but your family is expanding and you'll soon need the room."

"The offer is always open. I'll help you find a place in a few days. I'll get Taco to help run some electricity down to whatever place you find. This whole compound is grossly overpowered, and we'll have plenty."

"I appreciate that, Tim."

"I'm sorry that we haven't had the chance to talk like we used to, Iz. I miss our talks."

"I understand. You've been busy," Izzy said.

"It's funny. You're the closest thing to a father figure I've got. Everyone else is always looking to me for the answers, but who do I have to talk to?" Tim said. He looked at the man sitting next to him, and realized Izzy looked like he was ten years younger, while Tim felt like he was ten years older. He guessed that a few months in Hawaii had done the good doctor a world of good. He'd only wished his South Pacific adventure had been as beneficial to him as it had to Izzy.

"I'm flattered, Tim. And you are like a son to me, also," Izzy replied kindly.

Tim took another swallow of his drink, and in spite of the cold, was feeling quite warmed. The clouds that had been brewing over the mountains to the northeast had spread out to a thick gray blanket just before sundown, and there was a definite crispness in the air. Both men could see their breath, which whipped out into little white puffs with each exhale. Tim looked out onto the meadow in front of his house, lit by the lamps burning brightly though the windows, and saw the first few flakes of snow begin to drift lazily down.

He sighed. "I kind of figured it would snow tonight."

"So did I," said Izzy.

"Good thing we got everyone settled in nicely. No telling how much it will snow."

"It's late in the winter, Tim. It shouldn't snow too much. If it does, it won't stick around too long."

"I think we'll have a good summer, Iz."

"So do I, Tim. So do I," Izzy said and they lapsed into silence for a few moments. After a time, Izzy said, "So tell me Tim, what is troubling you?"

"Nothing, Iz."

"I've known you long enough. I can tell when something is bothering you," Izzy said, leaning over to Tim and whispering conspiratorially, which made Tim smile.

"I don't know, Iz. It's like I'm always waiting for the other shoe to drop, ever since Volivoli."

"It was really bad, I take it?"

"Yes, it was bad. You've been in combat. You understand."

"True. Vietnam was a long time ago, but some things never dim in one's memories."

"And all this *'president'* bullshit, I'm uncomfortable with that," Tim said, his voice dripping with frustration.

Izzy laughed. "I have to agree, it does sound rather insane on the surface, but I think Jerry means well with it."

"Yeah, he does. But I've got a bad feeling that nothing good will come of it."

"Why so?"

"I don't know, I just have a feeling."

"And you always trust your feelings," Izzy asked, but it came out like a statement.

"Yeah, I do."

"I'd suggest going with the flow for right now, Tim."

"That's what I'm going to try to do, Iz," Tim said with a long sigh, setting his almost empty glass on the table. "I'm getting tired of always making the decisions. Ever since the Event, I've been the one having to lead. I want to live out the rest of my life here, with my family, in peace."

"Tim, I know your feelings on God, and I agree with them. However, I do believe some people were born to be leaders, and you are one of them."

"I'm sick of it though," Tim said. "I never wanted any of this."

"I do believe the Army had it right when they kept promoting you. They wouldn't have made you a sergeant major just for laughs," Izzy concluded.

"I have this sinking feeling, like something terrible is going to happen, and quite frankly, I don't want to have any part of it."

"Tim, I trust you'll do what you need to do, as you've always done. You don't have to like it; I don't have to tell you that."

"I don't like it, not one little fucking bit."

"I know you don't. I'll help you as much as I can. I've done some things myself, made decisions, that got people killed so many years ago in Vietnam. I hated it. I live with them, though, Tim, and so will you, because you're a leader."

"Let's just hope everything has calmed down and there's no trouble from now on."

"I hope the same thing," Izzy agreed, and finished off his drink.

The front door opened and the two men turned to see Robyn's head pop out.

"Dad, Izzy, supper is ready," she said.

"Alright, we'll be right in. What did you guys whip up?"

"Rabbit! There was plenty in the freezer in the basement," she said, and disappeared back inside.

Tim looked at Izzy and smiled. "I've always loved rabbit."

"So have I, let's go eat," Izzy said, standing.

"You go ahead, Iz. I'll be in a few minutes," Tim said. Izzy picked up his glass, leaving Tim to his thoughts.

Tim walked to the porch railing and peered out into the night. He could see his shadow from the lamplight in the window, stretching out into the blackness of the night, and looked up into the sky. The snow was falling heavier now, big and fluffy flakes, and they were starting to stick on the ground. An involuntary chill swept over him for a minute, and was thankful there was no wind.

He held his breath for a moment, then exhaled, letting out a cloud of mist that enveloped his head. Off in the distance, he heard a pack of coyotes howl. They always sounded to him like a group of children laughing, and he wondered at that moment if the joke wasn't really on him.

He looked to the sky again and wondered how long the storm would last, and then a darker thought crossed his mind. What other storms were brewing, unseen, out over the horizon? He had a deep, sad feeling this wouldn't be the last one, not by a long shot.

With that thought weighing on his mind, he turned, picked up his glass, downed the last of the warming liquid in one gulp, and with shoulders sagging, he plodded into the house, doing something he'd never done before here: he shut and bolted the door.

CHAPTER 5: A BRAVE NEW WORLD

The snow that fell their first night back in Williams was a heavy, wet snow that lasted longer than Tim would have liked. Two feet of the white stuff had blanketed the entire area, and left everyone marooned in their new homes for several days. With the exception of Tim, Holly, Robyn, and Izzy, all of the residents that had flown over from Hawaii weren't used to the cold. Using a four wheel drive Hum-Vee, Robyn and Jimenez gathered as much winter clothing they could scrounge in the stores and shops along Main Street, and distributed it to everyone in the community.

Tim and Robyn had cut and split over ten cords of shaggy bark juniper the previous summer, before their adventure to the South Pacific, and it was still untouched by their home, so everyone had plenty of firewood to keep warm. Tim made a mental note to get a wood cutting party together as soon as the weather cleared, to ensure they'd have enough cut, split, and dried for the next winter.

Now, two weeks later, the weather was starting to warm noticeably, and the only remaining snow left was in the shadowy places in the forest where the sun's rays didn't reach. It was a balmy morning, and the sun felt pleasantly warm on Tim's back as he walked up the road towards Ian's house. He was going to help them build pens for the goats and pigs, and set up a coop for the chickens.

His thoughts went back to Holly, Robyn, and Jimenez, who at this moment were high above the Sierra Nevada Mountains, flying west towards San Francisco. After a long discussion with Ensign Johnson, Holly had offered to fly them there, over Tim's protests. They figured it would be a few months, not until later in the spring, that they'd be able to drive unhindered across the mountain range that separated Nevada from Northern California, and none of them wanted to wait that long. They had found an old Chevrolet Suburban that Jimenez had converted to run on propane, and they had left earlier that morning, leaving Tim at the house with Izzy.

He'd miss them, and wished them well. The young boy was a joy to have around the house, always amazed at the new sights and sounds. Tim hoped that the baby developing inside of Holly would be just as healthy. Now, as he approached Ian's house, tool box in hand, he saw April dancing around in the meadow, laughing and singing some song that amused her to no end, and it made him smile. Maybe everything was going to be alright.

He stepped up onto the porch of the house that was almost a carbon copy of his, and the front door opened. A smiling Ian came out to greet him.

"G'day, Tim, how ya' going, mate?"

"I'm doing good, Ian. I brought some tools," Tim said, holding up the toolbox, "so we should have this knocked out in no time."

"Then let's get to it then, Mr. President!"

"I wish everyone would stop calling me that."

"Ah, come on, mate. It's all harmless."

I just don't like it, Ian," Tim said, setting down his toolbox and leaning against the porch railing.

"Just think of it like you said on the plane, it's just to help those folks back in Hawaii feel good."

"I do keep on telling myself that. I still don't like it," Tim said, frustration evident in his voice. He looked out at April again, playing in the meadow. She was chasing around an early spring butterfly.

He then noticed another figure, standing in the shadows just inside of the tree line. It was a big bear of a man, and Tim remembered his name was Colin. He'd been one of the men who volunteered to leave the HMAS Newcastle. Like Ian, he'd come from Australia. When the man saw that he'd been seen, he smiled and waved, and walked off towards the house he'd taken over. Something just didn't seem right to Tim.

"What's the story with that guy?" he asked Ian.

"He's kind of a loner, really. Name's Colin something or other. He came up from Victoria when everything turned to shit. He's supposed to be some kind of tradie, electrician or something," Ian said.

"I just wondered what he was doing over there is all. It seemed odd," Tim said, tilting his hat back on his head and scratching the back of his neck.

"Yeah, it does seem odd, him hanging around like that," Ian agreed, now looking at the place in the woods where the man had been standing. "He's gone now, though."

"So he came over on the Newcastle with you? What was he like?"

"A loner, like I said. Always looked busy, but I never saw him do anything, actually, now that you bring it up."

"That's interesting," Tim said, and then shook the dark feeling aside. "Let's get cracking on these pens."

Something didn't seem quite right with the man's behavior, and he wished he'd had more time to get to know everyone who had come over with them a little better. He'd keep his thoughts to himself for right now, so as not to alarm Ian, but decided he'd keep a close eye on this Colin character from now on.

Ian called April back to the house, and the two men went to the rear and started working on the enclosures for the animals. They finished late in the afternoon, and after politely declining an invitation to stay for dinner, Tim packed his tools up and headed back to the house. Halfway back, he stopped and looked up into the clear, cloudless afternoon sky for any signs of the returning Hercules, but only saw a few birds. Upon reaching home, he stored his tools in the barn behind the house, entered the home, and went directly to the military satellite radio set up in the study. He tuned to the agreed upon frequency and called Holly. Robyn's cheerful voice replied right away.

"Hi, Dad! We're okay out here!"

"Are you on your way back?"

"No, we're still in San Francisco. Holly and I agreed to help Ensign Johnson in getting to the ship."

"Did you find it?"

"Yes, sir! We're on it right now. Taco wants to help them get the electricity on, so Holly and I should be back on our way tomorrow," she said, and then added, almost as an afterthought, "That is okay, right?"

Tim laughed a little, then depressed the push to talk button again. "A little late to ask me that, young lady. You just be careful, you hear?"

"Wilco, Sar' Major! I'll keep us at fifty percent tonight and set out an over watch!"

"You do that. Let me know when you'll be heading home tomorrow, okay?"

"Dad, don't worry. I've got everything under control."

"That's what scares me," Tim replied.

"I'll call you on this same frequency at zero nine hundred tomorrow."

"Roger, out," Tim said, and shut the radio off. He sighed loudly, and leaned back into his chair. He looked over at the fireplace and thought of lighting a fire, but decided against it. He fumbled with his pipe, filled the bowl, lit it, and stared off at nothing as he puffed away. He was running out of tobacco and would have to scare up some more from someplace soon.

His mind raced at everything that had happened, and wished he didn't have to make these decisions anymore. He thought about talking to Izzy, but that thought quickly passed since he could hear the older man snoring peacefully in his bedroom. It was getting late, so he placed his pipe in the oversized ashtray on the table next to his chair, rose, and went up to his bedroom, where he stripped and readied the shower. His muscles ached from the work he'd done earlier, and he let the hot water stream over his back. The water loosened the knots and his thoughts melted away with the mist. He shut the water off, toweled dry, and climbed into bed. He fell asleep immediately.

The next morning he was awakened by the smell of freshly brewed coffee. He got up, threw on a pair of sweatpants, and followed the aroma down the stairs and into the kitchen, where he found Izzy pouring a cup of the brew.

"Good morning, Tim, would you like a cup?" Izzy asked with a smile when he saw Tim enter.

"Yes, please, Iz," he said, taking a seat at the breakfast counter. "What have you got planned for today?"

"I was thinking of heading over to Flagstaff. I need to see if I can stock up on medical supplies and drugs. Most of what's left here is woefully out of date, and there's not enough of it."

"Won't everything be out of date?" Tim asked, taking to offered mug from Izzy. "I mean, it's not like anyone is making new stuff."

"Yes, you're correct. At the hospital there may be a good stockpile of things that have been better stored. Beggars can't be choosers."

"I think that time is running out for a lot of things just lying around now. We've had it good for the last few years since the Event, but what's left is really starting to deteriorate."

Izzy sat down on a stool opposite Tim. "Is that's what is on your mind?"

"Look around, Iz. With the exception of these few houses here, everything is starting to fall apart. Without people to do the everyday maintenance, nature is taking everything back. In a few years, even the roads and highways will be swallowed up by vegetation."

"That's why now is the time to amass as much as we can. The houses here that aren't being occupied can be turned into warehouses."

"Yep. We're going to have to start being more self-sufficient, and soon."

"We're well on the way to becoming that, Tim. Ian has the animals, and everyone has started to plant vegetables. Even our power is renewable, with all the solar panels and wind turbines."

"Even those will need cleaning and regular maintenance. I don't want everyone to be complacent. I need for everyone to take a good look around and see what we all can do to help," Tim said, taking another sip of coffee.

"Everyone here is doing just that, Tim. Sometimes I think you worry too much," Izzy said playfully.

"I know, Iz, but…"

"What? What is troubling you?"

Tim thought for a moment, trying to find the right words. "Iz, you're right. We've all got to work on making this work here. I can't help but think that yes, we do have it damn good here. What if someone else out there, who isn't willing or able to work at it, wants to come here and take what we've got?"

"Aren't you just being a wee bit paranoid?"

"How can you not be paranoid after everything we've been through these last few years?" Tim sighed, holding his hands out pleadingly.

"What is your solution?"

"I don't have one, Iz. That's my worry. And now Holly, Robyn, and Taco are off in California."

"You want them back here. Yes, I understand. Are they coming back today?"

"That's what they told me yesterday. Robyn said she'd call on the radio at zero nine hundred," Tim replied, then looked at his watch. "About an hour from now."

"They're all adults, and they can take care of themselves. They'll get back today, and when they do, we can have a meeting and make some plans."

"We'll do that, but it doesn't stop me from worrying," Tim said, and then went on to tell him about what he witnessed at Ian's place the day before, and his feelings about the man Colin.

"You think he was up to no good?"

"I don't know, Iz. It just struck me as odd, the way he was lurking inside the tree line. It certainly didn't look right to me."

"Keep an eye on him. I know what you mean though; something didn't seem quite right with him when I met him in Hawaii."

"That's not helping to ease my mind at all."

"I'm sorry, Tim. I didn't mean to add to your worries. How is everything else going?" Izzy asked, hoping to change the subject.

"As well as can be expected. Our good ensign and his crew are now in San Francisco and have found the ship they were after, so Holly and the rest will be back today, I hope. Ian has gotten everything in order at his place, so we should start getting some fresh eggs soon, and maybe goat's milk, pork and bacon."

"Okay, anything else?"

"Yeah, that other Aussie guy, the railroad dude? He's got a highrail truck running, and he's supposed to be heading out this morning, west I think he said, to start checking the tracks. He said he might be a while."

"Excuse me, highrail?"

"That's what he called it. It's a pickup truck, with these special wheels that fold down so he can drive the thing right on the tracks. He was packing up yesterday morning, taking a few weeks' worth of food and some camping gear. He said he's going to go as far as he can."

"So he's really serious about running a train between here and San Francisco?"

"That's what he plans on doing. It will be interesting if he actually does it."

"Then we'll have a direct overland route to the coast. In the summer only, I guess."

"Yeah, that's what I think. It'll only be a summertime thing," Tim agreed, thinking of the huge snowfalls over the mountain passes in California. "And one more thing. One of the men from Jerry's group, a guy from the 25th Infantry Division, says he wants to try to find my old friend Dawn Redeagle. Apparently he used to be some sort of cowboy in Montana before he enlisted."

"And start another war with the hated redskins?" Izzy asked, wide eyed, and Tim let out a good belly laugh.

"No, he heard me talking about the huge bison herd and his eyes lit up. He's got some notion of finding Dawn, and maybe getting a few of the buffalo to bring back here."

"To do what?" Izzy asked.

"It's really not all that farfetched. I know that Dawn had a few horses, the only ones I've seen since the Event. He thinks he might be able to trade or barter with him for a couple of horses. That is, if Dawn was ever able to get his two to breed, then get a few of the buffalo back here and start up a new herd."

"Domesticate them?"

"He says it can be done. They had them on his ranch where he grew up, so he tells me. I'm all for it, if he can actually find Dawn in the first place. It's been years since Robyn and I met him, he might be long gone by now."

"That's true, if he holds to the nomadic lifestyle of the Native Americans. That is an interesting idea, though. It would add a little more variety to our diet if he can pull it off."

"That's what I thought too, Iz. Not that I don't like venison and rabbit," Tim said with a grin.

"We're down to only a handful of people again," Izzy said, turning grave.

"Now *you* sound worried," Tim said.

"I'm not. But if what you said earlier holds true, there is safety in numbers."

"I just know that there's going to be someone else out there, like our recently late Captain Kangaroo."

"If that's the case, what can we do?" Izzy asked, then rose to get them both another cup of coffee. They sat silently for a few moments, and then Tim spoke up.

"For starters, we can use the terrain as a natural defense."

"How?"

"Like I said before, it won't be long until all the roads are impassable. There are several gorges east and west of here. We can block the passages so the town isn't easy to get to."

"That's a start. How do we get out if we need to?"

"Leave that to me, Iz. I'll go over the topo maps of the area, and once Holly and the crew are back from California, we'll get everyone together and have a meeting. I should have a rough plan together by tomorrow evening."

"I trust you to make the right decision. Now, if you'll excuse me, I'm going to head off to the hospital in Flagstaff. I should be back around time for supper," Izzy said.

"Are you going alone?"

"Yes."

"Want some company?"

"No, I should be fine, Tim. I'll take a rifle with me. I do still remember how to use one. I'll be okay," Izzy stated, politely reminding Tim that prior to him becoming a doctor, he'd served in the 'Brown Water Navy', on PBR's in Vietnam.

"Are you sure?"

"Tim, I'll be fine. I'm going to take one of the Hum-Vees and a carbine, and I'll have a radio with me. I'll be back before sundown."

"Just be careful," Tim said with worry in his voice.

"I'll be fine," Izzy said, placing his used mug in the sink and picking up a backpack that Tim hadn't noticed before. "I'll call if I get into trouble, Sergeant Major!"

Tim laughed and watched him leave. Before the door closed behind him, Izzy called out, "It's a brave new world, Timothy!"

"Yeah, but I'm not sure I'm digging this brave new world all that much," Tim said to the door.

He heard the Hum-Vee parked out front start and pull away, leaving him alone with his thoughts. He looked at his watch and saw that he still had some time before Robyn's promised check in, so he placed the Motorola radio on the counter, and made himself some toast to go along with a third cup of coffee.

When the unevenly sliced homemade bread popped out of the toaster, he spread some strawberry preserves on them and took a bite. Maybe someone would figure out how to make butter with the milk they'd soon be getting from the goats in Ian's pen. His mouth watered at the thought.

He sat back down with his breakfast and coffee, taking mental notes on the things that they would soon run out of. There was still plenty of diesel fuel lying around in storage tanks all over the area, and there was virtually an endless supply of propane, thanks to a stalled unit train of tanker cars filled with it, slowly rusting to the tracks outside of Flagstaff. That would last everyone there indefinitely, or as long as the tanks held up.

There was still plenty of flour in storage in every house, but even though it was stored in plastic containers, it was a finite amount and would have to be replaced at some point if they wanted to continue to have freshly baked bread. Maybe they could make one of the meadows into a wheat field. He wasn't even sure if the climate or elevation would even support it. One more thing to think about.

They could grow corn, which he knew, because he and Robyn had had several crops behind his house in the last few years, and also potatoes, cucumbers, bell peppers and tomatoes, so food wasn't a problem. Even the wildlife around their settlement was plentiful, so they'd have plenty of meat.

He took a final gulp of his now tepid coffee, grimaced, and then the final thought of his short mental list popped up, and made him laugh aloud: toilet paper. They were going to run out of toilet paper at some point, and that, he thought, would be very, very important indeed. He laughed again at the thought of going out in an ever-widening search for asswipe.

He looked at his empty mug, and decided against having another one. He turned from the counter and heard the radio crackle to life. He picked up the handset and replied excitedly, not able to hide his anxiety. "Are you on your way back?"

"Yes, Dad, we're slightly northwest of Las Vegas. We should be back in Tusayan in about an hour," Robyn replied over the encrypted radio in the Hercules.

"Good. I was getting anxious."

"Really, Dad? I couldn't tell," Robyn's voice came out of the speaker with good natured sarcasm and Tim laughed.

"I don't know where you get that mouth, young lady!"

"Dad, I get it from you!"

"Okay, okay," he conceded. "I'll meet you at the airstrip."

"Alright, see you soon! MacFarland Air One, out!"

Tim went back upstairs to the bedroom and got dressed. Going back through the living room, he took an M4 carbine from the rack he'd put there, locked and loaded a magazine and pocketed two more, then headed out the front door.

Hopping into the Hum-Vee parked by the porch, he put the carbine in the rack, and started the engine. Before he pulled away, another thought crossed his mind. He'd better let someone know where he was going. He headed up through the trees along the red dirt road towards Ian's house. He pulled up in front, and Ian, hearing the vehicle pull up, came out to greet him. Tim gave him a radio, told him where he was going and about what time he would be back. Ian reassured him that all was in order. Tim made a U-turn and headed back out onto the road, passed his house, and made a right hand turn onto the deteriorating blacktop road into Williams.

Weeds were sprouting from every crack in the asphalt, and to stress what he was talking to Izzy about earlier that morning, he saw that every house passed as he got nearer to town showed pronounced signs of neglect now, and two he saw had collapsed roofs, one already had trees growing up through it. Yes, nature was taking back what was hers, and it wouldn't be long before it was all swallowed up.

He drove through town, and took a good look around. Cars that were parked along Main Street were now covered in dust thick enough the windows looked opaque, tires were dry rotted and flattened, weeds were sprouting from masonry in desperate need of brick pointing. Several buildings had trees growing on their flat roofs. Curbs, corners, and alleyways were clogged with paper and plastic refuse long forgotten and blown there by winds and storms over the last six years, and it saddened Tim to the core.

He rounded a curve, went under the overpass of I-40, and headed north towards the airport in Tusayan. The right front tire of his Hum-Vee hit a ground heave that he'd failed to notice with a loud bang and jarred the vehicle so badly he had to stop, get out, and check to see if there was any damage. Finding none, he reentered the vehicle and continued on his journey.

"Yeah, things are really starting to go to shit," he said aloud, and continued his drive north. The trees thinned out as he drove northward, and through what looked like ancient lava fields of jagged basalt. Looking at them reminded him of photos he'd seen of the moon, and he remembered NASA had trained its Apollo astronauts at this very place. He remembered then, also, that all the mountains surrounding the south rim of the Grand Canyon, from here in Williams to north of Flagstaff were at one point all active volcanoes.

The morning was cool and pleasant, so he rolled down the window and enjoyed the cool breeze. Nearing the airport in Tusayan, the trees thickened again, and he took notice of the houses surrounding the area. They too were showing signs of neglect, and he added another thing onto his ever expanding list of things to do before the next winter, deciding it might be a very good idea to scour the area, all of the houses, for anything of value now, because whatever was lying around now wouldn't be in very good use for much longer. That was one thing he'd make a priority.

He drove on into the airport grounds, through an open gate onto the apron, then parked in front of the terminal building. Shutting off the engine, he got out, grabbed his carbine, and sat on the sloping front hood of the Hum-Vee. He listened for the sounds of the returning Hercules, but the only thing he heard was a few birds and the rustle of the slight breeze through the overgrown grass surrounding the taxiway and runways. Ever since the Event, the silence had unnerved him, the utter and total nothingness of it all. The only sounds were that of the Earth itself, and that left him feeling terribly alone.

A red-tail hawk screeched off in the distance, and Tim quickly found it circling a grassy area on the other side of the runway. It completely ignored him, circling above a spot that only the hawk could see. Tim watched the raptor with great interest spiraling in the sky, and then, with amazing speed, it dived towards the ground, talons extended. It pounced on something and shot up into the air once again, and Tim could see that it had a fat field mouse in its grasp. Some things would continue on as normal, and there should be plenty of mice for the hawks and owls to eat.

He watched the bird fly off with its dinner, then faintly heard the aircraft's engines. He scanned the skies for the man-made bird and smiled when he spied the dark speck approaching from the south. All looked in order to Tim. The landing lights came on, and the landing gear descended and locked into place. As it passed over the airport's threshold, the nose lifted slightly, and the rear wheels kissed the concrete runway with puffs of white smoke. Soon after, the nose wheel touched down, and then the engines revved to full power, and the air screamed when Holly reversed the pitch of the props, bringing the cargo plane to a rapid stop. Again, the propellers changed pitch, the fuselage turned, and the aluminum beast taxied towards the terminal.

Tim let out a breath he'd not realized he'd been holding and a smile lit up his face. The plane taxied up to where he was sitting, and the right wingtip passed over his head as the props on the starboard side of the wing spun to a stop. The port side engines were shut down next, and the silence was pronounced again after the roar of the turboprop engines' roar. Robyn's face appeared in the copilot's window, wearing aviator sunglasses. She looked down to Tim, a broad grin splitting her face. She gave a thumb up gesture, and doffed her headphones, disappearing from view.

The next sound Tim heard was the electric whine of the hydraulic rams that lowered the rear loading ramp. Tim slid off the hood and shouldered his carbine, walking over to the rear of the plane. When the ramp was all the way down, Tim grabbed the folding wheel ramps and lowered them into place while Holly and Robyn came into view out of the darkness of the hold.

"Another super landing, Flight Lieutenant," Tim said.

"Why thank you, Sergeant Major, but it wasn't me landing the plane!" Holly said playfully.

"What?" Tim gaped, "You don't mean…"

"I landed the plane, Dad!" Robyn squealed, hopping down and hugging him in a tight grip. "Aren't you proud of me?"

"She's a natural, Tim," Holly said.

"I can see that," he said, a little uneasily, and looked at Robyn again. She was wearing a flight suit similar to Holly's, along with a grin that was threatening to split her face in two. He wondered where they had found that for her to wear, deciding to leave that question for later.

"Are you guys ready to head home?" Tim asked, hugging Holly, and noticing her belly was becoming quite pronounced. Pretty soon she wouldn't be able to fit into her own flight suit, and he hoped that this was the last of her flying for a while.

"Taco and I are going to secure the plane, Dad. You and Holly go ahead without us. We've got the other Hum-Vee here, we'll drive home."

He heard the clanging of tie-down chains from inside of the aircraft, and figured Taco was getting the Hum-Vee ready to back out. "Okay, just don't take all day."

"We won't. We'll be about an hour or so," she said, heading back into the fuselage.

Tim turned to Holly and gave her a look.

"Tim, don't start," she chided. "Robyn's a natural. She took off, flew all the way here, and made a beautiful landing. I was right there at the controls too, in case anything went wrong."

"I know, I know. Doesn't mean I can't still be a little worried," he said, taking her hand, and they walked towards Tim's Hum-Vee. "Aren't you supposed to start out flying Piper Cubs or some other tiny plane when you first learn? I mean, I'm pretty sure the RAF didn't just hand you the keys to a C-130 on your first day."

"There are no keys, Tim. And I was right there with her. I wouldn't let her solo yet, not by a long shot, but she's got more natural talent than I'll ever have," Holly said, getting into the Hum-Vee and shutting her door.

Tim thought about that for a moment, and let what she'd said sink in. Tim wasn't stupid, and he trusted Holly's judgment, so he let it slide for the time being as he started the vehicle and put it in gear. When he pulled away, he asked Holly how San Francisco was.

"It was awful. There must have been an earthquake at some point in the last few years. A lot of the city is destroyed. We had to drive all over the city just to get to the wharfs."

"The airport was okay, I assume?"

"No, the main runway has a huge fissure down the middle. We landed on a taxiway," Holly stated.

"What?"

"Tim, relax. It's what the Hercules was designed for. I could have put her down in a field if I had to."

"That doesn't help me sleep at night," Tim sighed. "So 'Frisco was leveled. Was the boat okay?"

"It's a ship," she corrected, "and yes, it was still floating. The whole superstructure is covered in bird poop, but Johnson and Mr. Nakamura say they should have everything ship-shape in a few months."

"That's good, I guess. What's their next move, or didn't he have a plan yet?"

"He figures they'll have to find a different port, maybe head a little further south, San Diego perhaps."

"How come?"

"The port is in shambles. Not a lot left to salvage. It was a miracle that the ship was still afloat. They were going to start scrounging around to find enough oil for the bunkers, but there were a lot of fires, and a lot of the fuel burned up."

"And he's still optimistic?"

"That he is. I think he'll be able to do it, especially with Suplee and Nakamura, though it might take them a while."

"I'll have to get word to our railroad guy and let him know. He left this morning. I'll have him get in touch with our young ensign and coordinate things. No sense running a train to 'Frisco if there's no boat there."

"Aye, that might be a good idea. Do you think he'll do it, the railway chap?"

"Anything is possible. I guess it all depends what the condition of the tracks are, and if he can find a way around any stopped trains or derailments," Tim said, and went on to tell Holly of his thoughts about how everything was really starting to fall apart, and everyone would have to start scrounging for useful items and how they all would have to become more self-sufficient. He left out the part about his fears, and the conversation he'd had with Izzy earlier in the day, figuring he'd talk that over with her later. He'd always had his best brainstorming sessions with her, in bed, right before they went to sleep.

Tim's mind went to the thoughts of San Francisco in ruins, which brought his mind back to his home town, Philadelphia, and his desperate scramble to get out before the firestorm engulfed him along with the rest of the city. It saddened him to the core how everything he remembered was being erased from the face of the Earth. Soon, nothing would look the same.

Holly reached over to Tim and took hold of his hand across the wide space that separated the two front seats. "Tim, I might not tell you often enough, but I do really love you. I don't know where I'd be if Izzy and I hadn't met you and Robyn."

"I love you too, babe. I don't say it enough myself," he said, squeezing her hand tenderly. "I love you so much for everything you've brought to my life, and for the little soldier you've got growing inside you."

"Aye, and he's been quite the active little cheeky monkey the last few days!" she said, rubbing her pronounced belly.

"We'll have to get you another flight suit soon," Tim chuckled.

"I don't think I'll be doing much flying for a while," Holly said, much to Tim's relief. "I told both Robyn and Jimenez to secure the Herc for an extended grounding."

"I can't say I'm saddened by that news," he said, as they drove under the overpass into town.

Holly nodded. "Aye, I can see what you mean. Everything looks like it's ready to fall over."

"It probably won't for several more years, but the heavy snows we get in the winter will definitely take their toll on most of the wood framed buildings sooner or later."

"Maybe we can start going through the houses, gathering up everything that will be useful," she stated, then added with a wince, "and bury what bodies we may find."

"Yeah, I thought of that too, but we might just leave them where they are."

"Won't they be a health hazard?"

"With the dry climate, they'd be mummified after all of these years, so I don't think it'd be a major issue. It's something we can bring up with Izzy."

"Aye," was all Holly said, then she sighed. "Sometimes when we come through town, I can't help but think the ghosts of all of those who've died are staring out at us angrily, wondering why we were spared."

"You think we were the ones spared?"

"I see your point."

Tim slowed and turned onto the dirt road towards their house, driving up through the copse of trees, and up to the front of their house. He placed the Hum-Vee in park and shut the engine off, but didn't make a move to get out. He stared out the windshield, deep in thought. Holly left him to his thoughts for a few moments. When she thought the time was right, she asked, "What's on your mind?"

"I was thinking that if I had launched that missile a little sooner, we wouldn't have to worry about any of this now."

"Timothy, that's a terrible thing to say!" she gasped. "Think of Robyn, and all the rest of us. I know you're still having nightmares about it, but thinking like that isn't going to solve a thing."

"I never want to be put in that situation, ever again."

"We're here now, home. And we're safe."

"For now. Who the fuck knows what will happen next?" Tim spat.

"Tim, we're all in this together. We're safe here now, and we'll just do our best, nothing more, nothing less."

"I wonder what kind of world we'll have for our son," Tim said, laying his forehead on the steering wheel in exasperation.

"Or daughter," Holly said. "We'll raise him or her the same way you raised Robyn. And we'll be safe here."

"I wish you were right," Tim said.

"I *am* right. I'm a woman, remember?" Holly said with a laugh. "What I need right now, Sergeant Major, is a long, hot shower, then some lunch. I'm famished!"

"Okay, okay. Go get your shower, I'll be out here on the porch," Tim said, getting out of the Hum-Vee. He pulled the carbine from its rack in the vehicle, and watched Holly bound up the short flight of steps onto the porch, pulling down the bun she'd tied her long hair into in the subtle, sexy way that always seemed to turn him on, and entered the house through the screen door.

Tim followed her inside, and looked at his watch; seeing it was well past noon, he went to the kitchen and retrieved a cold bottle of Miller High Life, deftly popped the bottle cap, and took a long pull off the bottle. He headed back out to the porch, picking up his pipe and tobacco from the table in the living room where he'd left it the night before.

He sat on one of the rough-hewn timber chairs on the porch, and once his pipe was filled and lit, he sat back and tried to let the rampant thoughts fall into a corner crevice for a few minutes. He sat and sipped on his beer, waiting for Holly to come back down from her shower.

Movement out of the corner of his eye got his attention, and he saw the figures of two men come around the side of his house. When they saw him sitting there, they both smiled. The taller of the two men, in his mid-twenties, Tim reckoned, had a swarthy, Mediterranean complexion with thick, dark hair.

"Sergeant Major?" the tall man said. "I'm Specialist Sam Didinato, and this is John Meadows, we spoke earlier?"

"I remember you Specialist," Tim said. "It's not like I have a whole brigade to look after anymore."

"I just wanted to let you know that we'll be heading out tomorrow," Sam Didinato said.

"So you think you'll find my old friend, Dawn Redeagle?"

"I'd like to think so. You did say he had horses, too, didn't you?"

"That I did. He had a stud and a mare. I don't know if he ever got them to breed. What is your plan?"

"We'd like to see if we can trade him for a few horses, and a few of the buffalo. If he's agreeable to that, we'll bring them back here and start up a herd."

"Pretty high aspirations," Tim remarked with a raised eyebrow, sipping his beer and peering at the pair over the lip of the bottle.

"You could say that. Hell, I'd like to try."

"I like your spirit, Didinato. This isn't the Army anymore, you've got free will, but if it's my blessing you're after, you have it, anything to help out," Tim said. He didn't know the other guy; he must be one of the few that came over on the Aussie ship. "Do you have a notepad and something to write with?" Tim asked, and the second man pulled out a pad of paper and a pencil. Tim gave them a list of things to look out for, things they'd need in the future, and the man dutifully wrote down every word Tim said.

"And the next thing, and this is very, very important," Tim said gravely.

"You got it, Sar' Major."

"Toilet paper. Bring as much asswipe back as you can, okay?" Tim added and then all three laughed heartily. "One last thing, give me a minute," Tim said, and went into the house. He was gone for a few minutes, and the two men looked at each other silently, wondering what Tim was doing. Tim exited the house then, carrying something that was very familiar two both of the soldiers.

It was the M16A1 that he'd liberated from his brigade's arms room so many years ago, right after the Event. He handed it over to the Specialist, along with four bandoliers of 5.56mm ammunition and a few 30 round magazines.

"If you find Dawn Redeagle, you give these to him, and tell them they're from me."

"Sure thing, Sar' Major," Didinato said, taking the offered weapon. "Anything else?"

"Yeah, tell him I said 'Gary Owen'. He'll know what I mean."

"Check," Didinato said with a nod.

"Oh, and Didinato, you did real well back on Volivoli. I was happy to have you with us."

"Thanks, Sar' Major! That means a lot!" he beamed.

As they two men were preparing to, Holly came out onto the porch, dressed in Wrangler jeans, one of Tim's t-shirts, her hair still wet from the shower. Tim made the introductions, telling them this lovely creature was the one who'd flown them there. They hadn't seen her dressed as a civilian before, and she was definitely a pleasing sight for the eyes.

"You gentlemen be very careful," she said.

"We will, Ma'am," Sam said, holding up the rifle. When he turned to leave, a breathless Ian came running around the side of the house, his face red as a beet. He put one foot up on the step, and tried to catch his breath.

"What's wrong, Ian?" Tim asked in alarm.

"It's April. We can't find her anywhere!" he replied, gasping for breath, almost in a panic. "She's never, ever strays too far, ever!"

"When was the last time you saw her?" "Right after brekky. Soon after you left, Tim, and then I saw her playing in the meadow. It's been hours!" Ian said balefully.

Robyn and Jimenez pulled up, and seeing the commotion, hopped out and ran towards the porch.

"What's going on, Dad?" Robyn asked

"Trouble! Grab your shit, ruck up, and follow me," Tim said, retrieving his carbine from inside the door and heading out towards Ian's house, leaving everyone standing there on the porch. He stopped and yelled out, "That was not a fucking suggestion. Grab your shit and follow me, goddamn it, right-fucking-now!"

CHAPTER 6:
ANCHORS AWEIGH!

Displacing 44,474 tons, with a length a squeak past 441 feet, a beam of just under 57 feet and a draft of 47 feet, the *SS Jeremiah O'Brian* wasn't a sleek vessel by any stretch of the imagination. It was made for utility, not to win any beauty contests, and its present condition left it looking all the more forlorn and neglected.

The once dark gray hull was now streaked with rust, and every surface, including its superstructure, with its tall single funnel directly amidships, was covered in over five years' worth of white bird droppings. But it was afloat and not listing, and had only taken on a small amount of water, which Mr. Nakamura had complete control of with the use of the bilge pumps now purring away below decks.

The early morning fog was burning off, and the sun's rays did little to improve the sight that Ensign Johnson took in from the starboard wing bridge, where he stood looking out over the harbor. His sipped his coffee and wondered if it was at all possible to actually get this hulk ready to go to sea. His enthusiasm for the project had disappeared over night.

The sound of the hatch from the wheelhouse opening was a relief to his troubled thoughts, and he turned to see Petty Officer Suplee step out with his own mug of coffee.

"Good morning, Mr. Johnson!" he said. "It's just another wonderful day in the Navy!"

"Morning, Harry," Suplee nodded, his blank expression remaining. "I just came up from the engine room. Mr. Nakamura has all the pumps running, and he says he's going to try to light off the boilers later on today."

"How are the bunkers?"

"They're about half full, sir. We'll need to top them off at some point."

"I figured that," Johnson said.

"Sure isn't the *Hughes*, eh, Mr. Johnson?"

"That it isn't. We'll have to top off the bunkers from somewhere. I hadn't planned on the city being in this condition," Johnson said, taking a sip of his coffee and looking out over the harbor again. The fog was thinned enough now that he could see the Bay Bridge, and he looked out past it.

"It was just the law of averages. What do you have in mind?"

"I had a look at the charts yesterday. I'm thinking of heading south, maybe San Diego."

"That would be a good idea, sir. We'd be able to get a lot of provisions there, and I can scrounge around and maybe get working radar set up on this tub."

"We'll find some pressure washers and get this goddamn bird shit cleaned off."

"And some paint. It'll take forever with just the three of us," Suplee added, "I would be nice if we had more hands."

"I don't think that will happen anytime soon, Harry," Johnson said, still looking out over the water. "When does Mr. Nakamura think we can sail?"

"Tomorrow maybe, if he can get all the boilers fired up. He sounded pretty optimistic."

"I'm glad one of us is."

"Bill," Suplee said, still finding it hard to call this officer by his first name, old habits died hard, "I think if we can get down to San Diego, to a decent port, we can get her ship-shape. It's just going to take a while."

"It's going to be a lot of work, Harry."

"You know something? I'm actually looking forward to it," Suplee said with an optimist's grin, which made Johnson smile.

"It's going to be a lot different than our last voyage," Johnson said.

"Anything would be better than that fucking nightmare."

"True. Now let's get below. I think Mary was tinkering about down in the galley trying to fix up some breakfast for us," Johnson said, tossing the remainder of his coffee overboard. The two men entered the wheelhouse, and traveled through the ship's passageways down two decks to the galley where they found Mary, who had two skillets on the burners and the aroma of hot food permeating the space. When they entered, she looked up at them and smiled.

"I hope you boys don't mind powdered eggs and fried spam," she said. "It's about as good as we're going to get for a while."

"It's a feast for kings, my dear!" Johnson said, grabbing a plate. Mary dished out platefuls for both men, and one for herself, and all three walked forward to the officer's wardroom mess, where they found young Billy sipping what looked like a glass of Tang and thumbing through a comic book. Both men had a sudden fear that he'd found Nakamura's nasty Hentai comics, but were relieved to see it was Bat Man. The boy looked up and smiled.

"Daddy, is this going to be our home from now on?" the boy asked, and Johnson ruffled the boy's unruly hair and smiled.

"It sure is. We'll sail the Seven Seas in search of adventure!"

"Cool!" the boy beamed and went back to his comic.

Johnson poured them all a fresh cup of coffee, and sat down to eat. A few minutes later, Nakamura entered. Mary told him there was still plenty of food in the galley, and to help himself. He bowed and left, returning a few minutes later with a heaping plate of spam and eggs, poured a cup of coffee and sat down at the table with them. It was beginning to get warm in the room from the rising sun's rays, now unhindered by the fog, beating down on the steel ship.

"It's going to get really hot in here later," Johnson said.

"I was thinking about that. I guess they didn't put air conditioning in when they built this tub," Suplee commented.

"It was probably low on the priority list back in '43 when the keel was laid."

"When we get to San Diego, I'll scare up some aircon units and rig them up in the living quarters," Suplee said, shoveling in another forkful of powdered eggs.

"That would be a good idea," Johnson agreed.

"When are we going to San Diego?" Mary asked.

"As soon as we can, there's not much here that we can use, and there will be more available at the big base there," Johnson told her, and then turned to Nakamura. "When do you reckon we'll be able to get under way?"

"I think maybe tomorrow, Johnson-San. The engine seems to be okay. I will know better when I have boilers running."

"That soon?" Mary asked in astonishment.

"Yes. It should be very possible. It look like ship was very well cared for. It just sit for long time now. Everything should work okay, and we sail fine!" Nakamura assured her.

"Do you think we'll have enough oil in the bunkers to sail for thirty-six to forty-eight hours?" Johnson asked the Japanese man.

"Hai. We have plenty for such a journey. Not much more than that though. We must fill up soon after."

"Forty-eight hours? That long to get to San Diego?" Suplee asked.

"It's not the *Hughes*, Harry. We won't be tearing around the ocean at over thirty knots. This ship was only designed for about eleven or twelve knots, so yeah, I'm figuring around forty-eight hours to get to San Diego."

Suplee let out a whistle as he let that information sink in. "Why so slow, Skipper?"

"Back in 1942, when the concept was first thought out, most of the current ships of the day only made that kind of headway. They had the technology to make engines that would propel a ship faster, but they thought it better to make the ships only go as fast as the current ones afloat."

"I'm still not following you. If they had the technology, why not build a faster boat?"

"They sailed in convoys, for protection. In order to keep the convoy in one cohesive unit, they could only sail as fast as the slowest ship in the convoy. No sense putting in a turbine that could make twenty knots or so, when the ship sailing next to them could only make nine or ten."

"I get you now," Suplee said, getting up to refill his coffee mug.

The young boy Billy, who had been sitting quietly the entire time, piped in with a question; "What's a 'knot', Daddy?" which made his father smile. He was thoroughly enjoying being a father.

"It's a measure of speed, Billy. One knot would be one nautical mile an hour. So a ship that is sailing at ten knots is going ten nautical miles an hour."

"That's how far you go in an hour, Daddy?"

"Exactly!" Johnson said, looking over at Mary, seeing her smile broadly. She stood and started to gather the plates. "C'mon, little man, help Mommy with the dishes, and later you can help Daddy with the sailing, okay?"

"Okay, Mom!" he said, picking up a few pieces of flatware and following Mary out of the wardroom.

When she was gone, Johnson looked at both of them men and sighed. "So tell me, what have you both figured out?"

"I think all will be in order," Nakamura said. "I will start the boilers and we will see, but have not found any problems with them or the engines. We can sail tomorrow if you wish, Captain-San."

Johnson nodded in satisfaction. "Do that now, if you'd like, Mr. Nakamura, the sooner we find out, the better."

"I will attend to that right away," Nakamura replied, getting up and leaving the two men alone.

Johnson turned to Suplee and asked, "Anything else?"

"Yes, sir. I can get a few simple household air conditioners, the window units would work best I think. I'll just use a torch to cut holes in the bulkheads and mount them in the cabins and wheelhouse. It should be a straightforward job. The auxiliary power unit and generators put out more than enough juice for the job."

"We'll do that when we get to San Diego then."

"It shouldn't be too hard. I'll run into town and pinch a bunch from an appliance store. The electricity to the cabins is 110 volts, too. Cutting the holes and fabricating the mounts will be the hardest part. The plumbing is in order. The heads and showers are working fine, and there's plenty of water in the freshwater tanks."

"Good, there's nothing worse than a clogged head on a ship." Johnson said, his unease and trepidation diminishing. He just wished he had more hands to do the grunt work.

"That's true, Skipper. Have you thought about navigation?"

"I have. I know this ship isn't as modern as we both are used to, but I can assure you, I do know how to use a sextant and I'll get you up to speed on celestial navigation. Sergeant Major Flannery also gave me an IVIS tablet, and that has a GPS receiver built in. If the charts we use aren't completely wrong, we shouldn't run aground anywhere."

"He's a great guy, for an Army type."

"That he is. He didn't have to let us come with him at all."

"I know, Skipper. We owe him a lot. He could have left us on that atoll," Suplee said, an involuntary shudder running through him.

"Have you tried to get hold of him on the radio?"

"I have," Suplee nodded. "I tried last night right before lights out, and again this morning. I got nothing. I was hoping to find out if Lieutenant MacFarland got back okay, but I did get hold of Sergeant Williams on Oahu. Everything is going well there."

"He's probably busy with getting things set up in Arizona. He's got a nice compound out there."

"That he does. I hope everything is okay."

"I'm sure it is, Harry. Oh, and another thing. We'll have to take on a shitload of seawater ballast before we sail, or we'll all be seasick before we reach the ocean."

"I'll get right on that now, Skipper. I hadn't thought of that."

"We'll worry about the paint and bird shit later. Let's just get this ship ready to sail, and once we're in San Diego, we'll worry about esthetics," Johnson said, knowing it wasn't esthetics at all. The bird droppings were caustic, and would act like acid to the paint and steel of the ship. It definitely had to be dealt with, however, it could wait for a few more days.

"I'll get right on the ballast, Skipper," Suplee said.

He departed into the ship, leaving Ensign Johnson alone where he sat with his thoughts for a few minutes, finished his coffee, and went up the two decks to his stateroom. It was spacious by naval standards, though the single bunk was a bit cramped for him and Mary, but the closeness was nice after their long separation. He undressed and took a hot shower, then dressed in clean work clothes. He'd always been a hands-on officer, never afraid to roll up his sleeves and get dirty, this was going to be a monumental job, and every pair of hands would be needed.

He went down to the boiler room, and after a short time, he and Nakamura got the boilers fired up, and the pressure rose and held. They decided to let them run overnight, to make sure that all was in order before setting sail. He walked through the ship, taking hours to do so. He wanted to know every inch of the ship, inside and out, from the bilges and cargo holds, to the crew's berths, to the pantry. After he made his tour, and finding nothing remarkable, he went back up to the wardroom and ate supper with the rest of his new crew.

After everyone retired for the evening, Nakamura and Suplee to their staterooms one deck below the captain's quarters and the wheelhouse, Johnson got his son to bed into what he now called his 'cabin', the bunk in the radio operator's shack on the opposite side of the superstructure from his stateroom. The boy thought it was just splendid.

Once the boy was settled, he walked out onto the starboard wing bridge and looked up at the night sky. The sun had set a few hours ago, and now the sky was painted with billions of stars, unhampered, most probably for a long time to come, by light pollution. He looked north, found Ursa Major and Polaris, and smiled inwardly. He recalled another time, on that horrible ship, looking up at a completely alien night sky, the Southern Cross replacing this familiar sight, and wondering if he'd ever see them again.

He took this clear sky as a good omen, for sailors are a superstitious lot, and made his way to his stateroom, where he found Mary already asleep. He shut the cabin door quietly, undressed, and curled up beside her in the narrow bunk, letting her long, dark hair caress against his chest. He was asleep in an instant.

The next morning, after a brief powwow of sorts, they got busy preparing the ship to set sail. The fog was again as thick as pea soup. The ship was not equipped with operational radar; the newer one of the two installed previously to make it Coast Guard certified had been fried in the Event; the second, original radar set from World War Two was in need of a few vacuum tubes, so it was decided to wait out the mist. It wasn't until mid-morning that they could release the moorings from Pier 45, where the ship had been tied all these years.

That in itself, would have been comical to watch, had it not been so deadly serious. With only three of them to do all the work, Suplee volunteered to go dockside and slip all the ropes off their cleats, rushing to each one the whole length of the ship, and then rushing up the gangway before the ship drifted too far from the dock, leaving him stranded ashore. He made it on board with only a minute to spare, and he breathlessly winched the gangway to its stowed position before collapsing on the deck, exhausted.

When he regained his strength, he made his way up to the wheelhouse, where he found Johnson, and a petrified Mary at the wheel. Suplee took over the helm. Johnson gave orders to Suplee, who operated the telegraph, to let Nakamura know when to increase power or reverse the engines.

No automation on this ship, Suplee remembered.

When Nakamura answered the telegraph from the engine room, they all felt a slight shudder through the deck, the single funnel belched a thick cloud of black smoke, and for the first time in over six years, the 18-foot diameter, four-bladed, manganese-bronze screw started to turn, frothing up the water in the harbor in a burst of raw power.

The ocean was still miles to the west, and Ensign Johnson did his best dead-reckoning by looking at the IVIS, the chart on the chartroom table, and looking out the wing bridge. He felt like a one-armed man hanging wallpaper, and they all breathed a sigh of relief when they sailed under the Bay Bridge, past the Presidio, and out into deep water. The headed directly west for a half hour, then turned to port, heading directly south, and they didn't completely relax until Half Moon Bay was well north of them.

The sun shone brightly, and the ocean was filled with gentle rolls, making the ship bob in spite of the ballast they'd taken on the previous day. A few seagulls flitted about, squawking noisily, and Mary went out to the wing bridge and let the cool sea breeze hit her face, trailing her long black hair out like a pennant behind her.

"What now, Skipper? You want to stay on this heading?" Suplee asked, and Johnson, who had been standing at the windscreen looking out ahead of them with binoculars, dropped them and turned.

"Yeah, this will do for now, Harry."

"Good," he said, and took two bungee cords he'd fashioned the night before, lashing the wheel in place, stepping aside for a moment. "Autopilot is set, Skipper!" he announced, making Johnson laugh for the first time that day.

"That's a good idea, Harry!"

"I thought of it last night. I'm glad I did; the helm on this tub is a pig. After conning from the *Hughes*, it's like getting out of a Ferrari and climbing into a garbage truck."

"By the time we get there, we're going to be exhausted," Johnson said with a frown.

"You said it, sir. Mr. Nakamura set up a cot down in the engine room. He said he'd take naps, but he'd be right there to answer bells for the whole trip."

"That will leave just us two to con the ship all the way, Harry."

"It's going to be a long forty-eight hours," he grimaced.

"We'll do six hours on, six hours off. The hard part will be getting into San Diego," Johnson said.

"We'll be fine, I think. We can pull into the harbor and drop anchor, then use the whaleboat to go ashore. That would save a lot of heartbreak, not trying to come alongside a dock when we're wasted."

"That sounds like a good idea, Harry."

"A good enough idea that it could have come from an officer, maybe?" Suplee asked jovially.

"Harry," Johnson said seriously, "as far as I'm concerned, you're a better officer than most, and you are my XO on this ship. That makes you an officer by default."

"I already have my own cabin, so I guess that makes it official, then, eh Skipper?"

Johnson laughed. "That it does. I'll sign the chit to give to you the pay raise this afternoon!"

"I don't know what I'm going to do with all that money, sir," Suplee quipped.

"Blow it on booze and hookers!" Johnson said between guffaws.

"San Diego is a wild town…" Suplee said, and then his face darkened. A frown creased his face as he remembered his probably long dead, pregnant wife he'd left in that town so many years ago.

Johnson saw his reaction and immediately felt bad. "I'm sorry, Harry. I didn't mean to dredge up bad memories."

"It's alright, Skipper. It's long in the past now. That's a distant memory for me," Suplee said, not too convincingly.

"Are you going to be okay?"

"Yeah, I'll be fine, Bill. I might want to go find my apartment, though, just to see, okay?"

"I think it's more than okay, Harry. In fact, I insist you do it. As soon as we're there and rested, we'll go ashore and you do what you need to do."

"Aye aye, Skipper," Suplee said. "I'll do that."

"It'll ease your mind, Harry. Do it," Johnson said.

Much to Suplee's relief, Mary came in from the wing bridge, interrupting their conversation.

"Would you men like some lunch?" she asked. "I baked bread this morning with some flour and yeast Holly gave us. I could make tuna sandwiches."

"That would be great, honey. With everything going on this morning, food was the last thing on my mind," Johnson said, and Mary came over and kissed him, then went below to the galley. Johnson felt a little embarrassed and the display of affection, and it showed.

"Don't worry about it, Skipper. Really, I'll be okay."

"Are you sure?"

"Yeah. I was a little jealous at first, when we got back to Pearl."

"Everything has been so screwed up, Harry. I do understand I've been extremely lucky. I mean, the chances of both of us, Mary and I, actually surviving were a long shot at best."

"But you did, and I'm happy for you. I do miss my wife sometimes, though I do understand. Maybe someday I'll meet some exotic beauty in some port we sail into. For now, I'm extremely grateful to be off that goddamn hell ship, and to be sailing happily with you," Suplee said. He walked back over to the helm and checked the compass.

"Are we still on course?"

"Aye, still on course, Bill. This thing works well, if I don't say so myself."

"We're going to be on our toes for the entire voyage. With no radar, we won't know what's out there after dark."

"That's going to be the hardest part. Even after all these years, there still might be some hulk floating around out there."

"True. And we won't have the firepower like we did on the *Hughes* to deal with any we see."

"Too bad these deck guns are just for show," Suplee lamented, pointing to the 4-inch deck gun mounted on the forecastle. The *O'Brian* had two, one forward and one aft. It was an armed merchantman, and the deck guns were there to fire back at any attacking U-Boats. This was a museum now, and those guns, along with several 40mm and 20 mm antiaircraft guns mounted in armored recesses on the superstructure, where most probably 'demilitarized' and were only for show now. Suplee made a mental note to check them all out later once they got to San Diego. Maybe he might be able to get them firing, though he strongly doubted it.

"I know what you mean," Johnson said. He sat down in the captain's chair and looked over at his friend, who was still standing by the helm looking out to sea. "Why don't you go below and get a nap in?" he suggested. "It's thirteen hundred now; I'll come down and get you at eighteen hundred, okay?"

"Sure thing, Skipper. I've been up since well before sunup. I'll pop down to the galley first and grab a sandwich from Mary, and then I'll turn in," Suplee said, and departed the wheelhouse, leaving Johnson alone with his thoughts. He stood, took the binoculars, and walked out the port wing bridge. Standing at the railing, he brought them to his eyes and scanned the horizon in front of the ship, and seeing nothing but miles of gently rolling waves, sighed and let them drop.

He looked up at the smokestack, and saw the black smoke that had billowed out earlier was gone, replaced by a barely discernible stream of white smoke. He figured the burners had finally cleared themselves of the accumulated crud, and were most probably burning at their optimum performance. He imagined how that dark smoke would have made the skipper of this ship anxious indeed, back during World War Two. It would have been like a giant neon arrow to any U-Boat commander with a watchful eye in a periscope.

He then noticed, for the first time, that Suplee must have found a brand new American flag and hoisted it up on the mast sometime this morning, and that made him very happy indeed. There would be no Jolly Roger flying on this ship, he decided. And if it did, it would be over his dead body. Johnson saluted the banner, then entered the wheelhouse again, walking up to the helmsman's station and checked the compass. It was still holding course, give or take a few degrees, and that was good enough for him. He sat back down in the chair, suddenly feeling very alone. He felt bad for Harry, and hoped someday he'd meet a nice woman. They'd become so much more than shipmates over the last few years, and he felt he was more like family to him than anything else.

His thoughts were broken by young Billy, who came bounding into the wheelhouse with excitement that only a child could exude. He was followed by Mary, who was carrying a plate with a tuna sandwich in one hand and a mug of coffee in the other. Johnson took the offered meal, setting the plate down on the arm of his chair.

"Thanks, honey. I sent Harry down to get some sleep."

"I know, he stopped into the kitchen and told me before he took a few sandwiches with him."

"It's a galley, babe," Johnson corrected.

"I know, silly. I almost fell coming up the stairs, too. I'm not used to this," she replied, poking him in the arm.

He winked at her. "Don't have your sea legs, eh?"

"I don't know how you get used to this," she said as Billy launched himself onto his father's lap. Johnson let out an 'oomph' and ruffled the boy's hair.

"Is my little sailor man enjoying the voyage so far?"

"I am! This is neat!" Billy exclaimed, and then pointed at the wheel, "Who's driving the boat, Daddy?"

"I've got it on autopilot!"

He hopped off Johnson's lap and ran out of the door to the wing bridge, and alarm flashed over Mary's face as the fearless boy fearless started to climb on the railing.

"Get down off there this instant, young man!" she scolded, and the boy, looking dejected, instantly complied. She turned to Johnson. "I swear he's going to give me a heart attack!"

Johnson laughed. "He's just being a kid and exploring."

"William Johnson! Do you realize how far down that is?"

"Okay, okay!" he said, then looked at his son, "Billy, please don't climb on the railings. Your mom is right, it's dangerous."

"Alright, Daddy," the boy said, looking down dejectedly at the deck and reentering the wheelhouse. He immediately walked over the front windscreen and stepped up onto the cast-iron radiators, hoisting himself up so he could see out.

Mary stood next to Johnson at the captain's chair and put her arm around him. He reached up and took her hand, looking into her eyes warmly.

"Thanks for the food, it's great," he said, after swallowing few bites of his sandwich.

"Can I do anything? I'd like to help more, if I can," Mary offered.

"It's going to be a long forty-eight hours. If you could keep the sandwiches coming, and keep the coffee urn filled, that would be fantastic."

"So I'm the delegated kitchen wench now, am I?" she asked with a wry look.

"No, not at all," he laughed. "If you want, I can start teaching you things here on the bridge, if you'd like."

"I'd like to help any way I can."

"Let's start off with your first lesson," he said. He told her about the helm, which she had a few terrifying moments on early that day, then the compass, the heading they were on, then the telegraph that sent signals to Mr. Nakamura in the engine room. It was a lot for her to take in, and she let him know.

"That's alright. As long as you can steer the ship and keep her on course it's a good start," he assured her. "I don't expect anyone to learn all this at once."

He looked at the compass, and saw that they were now a few more degrees off course, so he unhooked the bungee cords and made the corrections, explaining everything while he did so. It took a few moments for the ship to come back to the right heading, and he had to agree with Harry, this thing was a pig to con, coming from the *USS Hughes*. Once back on course, he re-lashed the cords, and then checked the IVIS and the charts, then made a notation with a grease pencil, marking the time and position on it.

"Everything is going smoothly," he said finally, tossing the grease pencil onto the chart table.

"Dad, Mom! *Look!*" Billy screamed.

Johnson turned to see what the boy was pointing to, and to his glee, saw a humpback whale break surface with a blast of white mist from its blowhole. It was only a hundred or so yards off the port beam, between the ship and the coast, several miles to the east.

"That is amazing, isn't it?" he commented, and the boy just looked at his father and smiled in childlike wonder. All three watched the whale for a while, and then Mary took the boy by the hand, kissed Johnson, and departed below, leaving the man alone once again. He thought about the whale, and wondered how well they were actually coming back with no people to hunt them. He hoped that one day the ocean would again be filled with these magnificent creatures.

He finished off his sandwich and picked up the growler phone to call Nakamura in the engine room. The man answered right away, told Johnson that everything was running perfectly, and praised the former crew for taking such good care of the ship. Johnson let him know what the watch plans would be, and for him to get as much rest as he could, while keeping an ear out for the telegraph and growler phone at all times.

He hung the phone back into its cradle, settling into the high-backed captain's chair. When he was in OCS he'd dreamed of his own command at sea, but this wasn't even close to the ship he'd envisioned, and that made him laugh. *Well*, he thought, *any command is better than no command. Still this isn't any aircraft carrier or frigate, and never will be.*

The next few hours went by uneventfully, and he only had to make minor adjustments from time to time to keep the lumbering ship on course. The weather held, and as the sun was low off the starboard side, he was relieved by Suplee. He gave a quick brief, noting everything he'd marked on the chart, their progress, where they were, and went below back to the rear of the bridge to his cabin where he kicked off his shoes, fell into the bunk and was immediately asleep.

The next twenty-four hours went by just the same, with the weather tuning nasty twelve hours out of San Diego. It wasn't a particularly bad storm, but the fact that they had no working radar and were nearing the coast made everyone very nervous indeed. Both Suplee and Johnson stayed on the bridge, sailing the ship by the seat of their pants, and by the time they headed east, and then turned north into the channel with Cabrillo National Monument and Fort Rosecrans on the port side, North Island Naval Air Station on the starboard, they were all extremely tense. They had to round the air station, sail through a narrow channel that ran southeast between the North Island and the City of San Diego for two more miles before reaching the US Naval Base on the east shoreline.

They were only making enough speed to make headway as they slid close to the base, a hundred yards off the port side of the ship now, and Johnson gave the signal to Suplee, who was standing by at the anchor winch on the bow, ready to drop anchor. He gave the signal to Mary, who was standing at the telegraph to call Nakamura to stop the engines. This she did smartly, and as the vibrations from the engine through the deck stopped altogether the anchor splashed into the blue-green water of the harbor.

Suplee waved up to Johnson on the port wing bridge, and started to make his way aft along the deck, and Johnson let out an audible sigh of relief. He walked over to the telegraph, and rang Nakamura for reverse slow, and again the engine hummed to life, reversing ever so slowly, so the anchor would set on the mud of the harbor bottom. When he felt it grab, he again signaled 'all stop' and then called Nakamura on the growler phone to secure from operations. He gave the orders for the boilers to be shut down, but to keep the auxiliary units running for power in the ship.

That done, he cocked his soiled and faded cap back on his head, looked at Mary and smiled.

"Honey, we're home!" he said. She came up, wrapped her arms around him, and held him tightly.

"I knew you could do it!" she said, kissing him hard on the lips.

"I'm glad you were sure," he sighed, and hugged her close. "I just hope we did the right thing by coming here."

"I'm sure we'll be fine, Skipper," Mary said playfully.

Johnson took his binoculars and scanned the shoreline and the naval base for signs of life. He was tempted to let out a blast from the ship's whistle, but decided not to. Not seeing anything outwardly amiss, he let the glasses fall from his eyes and stretched. He didn't feel so bad now about the bird shit covering his new command, for every ship visible here in the port was in the same shape. Every muscle in his body screamed, and all he wanted now was twelve or more hours of uninterrupted sleep.

Suplee made his way back up to the wheelhouse at this time, and he smiled broadly at Johnson when he saw him.

"We did it, Skipper," he said, coming over and shaking his hand.

"For a few minutes, I didn't think we would. Coming out of that last starboard turn, she took forever to respond, and I thought for sure we were going to slam right into the municipal piers," he said.

"I had all the faith in the world in you, Skipper."

Johnson smiled again, and looked around at his tiny crew. Nakamura, looking tired, dirty, and disheveled, came into the wheelhouse then, showing off his perfect pearl-white teeth.

"Mistah Johnson! You did it!" he said, bowing slightly. Johnson took his hand and shook it.

"I know it's been a trying voyage, but if you could, Harry, help Mr. Nakamura secure the ship. I'm going to take a long shower and get some sleep. When you're done, break open the booze and throw yourselves a party or sleep, or drink until you pass out. I'm going to go and slip into a coma."

"Aye, Skipper!" Suplee said, taking Nakamura by the arm and heading out into the ship.

Johnson looked at Mary and smiled tiredly.

"You look horrible," she said. "Go and get some sleep. I'll make some food for everyone, and look in on you later."

"As long as I look as bad as I feel, I must be still alive," he said, trying, and failing to make a joke. He looked out at the setting sun, now sinking below the horizon, silhouetting the Naval Amphibious Warfare base. He plodded to his cabin, kicked off his shoes, and fell face first onto the tiny bunk, where he fell fast asleep.

True to his word, exactly twelve hours later, Johnson woke with a start. He was slightly disoriented, then remembered where he was. He took a towel and walked off to the head, where he relieved himself, then stripped and took a luxurious, long, hot shower. After finally turning the water off, he stepped out of the tiny shower stall, dried off, and donned a pair of running shorts, then headed below to scare up some coffee.

He could feel the hum of the generator humming below decks, the slight vibration reassuring him that everything was in order. He stepped into the galley and over to the coffee urn that Mary had dutifully kept full during their short but intense voyage. Pouring himself a mug, he took a sip, wondering where everyone was.

It was like a ghost ship, and it was beginning to give him the creeps. He walked aft through the deserted crew's mess, and out onto the aft cargo deck into the bright morning sunlight. He saw that it was going to be another beautiful southern California day, like the ones he'd remembered so many years ago when he first was stationed here.

Again, seeing no one, he went back into the ship, and walked forward, back through the mess and onto the forward outside main deck. That was where he found everyone. They had their backs to him, and Mary, Billy, Suplee and Nakamura were all lined along the railing, looking out over the water at something he couldn't see. In front of them lay the sprawling Navy base and several ships could be seen in front of them.

He cleared his throat. "Hey guys, are we sinking or something?"

At the sound of Johnson's voice, Suplee almost jumped out of his skin, quickly turned, and looked at him with ashen skin, mouth agape. When he regained his composure, he let out a long breath that he must have been holding.

"Skipper, you scared the shit out of me!" Suplee said, his voice a few octaves higher.

"What's going on?" Johnson asked in concern.

"You'd better come and see for yourself." Suplee stepped aside to give Johnson some room on the rail. They were all looking down at the waterline, and Johnson let his gaze drop when he reached the rail. It was then his turn for his jaw to drop.

Some twenty feet below, right at the waterline, was a canoe, with three equally amazed faces staring right back at them. Johnson quickly regained his composure and called out to them.

"Ahoy! Who goes there?"

A man sitting at the stern of the canoe, paddle in hand, screamed, "Jesus Christ on a crutch! They are real, Steve!" and looked up at the ship's crew above them. "Ahoy!" he shouted. "Are we ever glad to see you guys!"

CHAPTER 7: PROBABLE CAUSE

It was dusk when the tired search party returned to Tim's house, and they all gathered around him as he walked up the few steps to the front porch and sat down on the top step. He gazed into everyone's eyes individually. "Okay, people. Go home and get some rest. We'll head out again in the morning. There's still a shitload of ground to cover," he said, too tired to stand up. No one spoke, but everyone left silently, Paula all but collapsing onto Ian's shoulder as they plodded away towards their house. Robyn sat down next to Tim on the porch, putting her head on his shoulder.

"We'll find her, Dad," she said quietly.

He put his arm around her shoulder, leaned over, and kissed the top of her head. He looked out over the meadow in the twilight. He knew from his years in the police department that the first twenty-four hours were the most important. If they didn't find the person they were looking for by then, the chances of finding them alive dwindled exponentially.

There were black bears, coyotes, mountain lions, and the occasional wolf all over this part of the country, and anything could have happened. Everyone was pulling together to find April, even that Colin guy. He was one of the first to volunteer to go out and search for April, which secretly surprised Tim. He still didn't trust him, and deep down he felt that somehow he was responsible for April's disappearance, though he couldn't prove it.

The front door opened, and Holly stepped out, followed by Izzy.

"I take it there was no luck?"

"None at all, and not a trace of her anywhere. It's almost as if she's vanished off the face of the Earth. I can't even find any tracks," Tim sighed.

"Would you like something to eat?" Izzy asked.

"No, I think I'm going to get a shower and hit the fartsack. I've got a feeling tomorrow will be another long day," Tim replied. He kissed Holly and entered the house without another word.

"It's really hitting him hard," Robyn said.

"I know, he's taking this rather personally," Holly said, coming over to Robyn and hugging her tightly.

"He shouldn't. He wasn't even here when she went missing," Izzy said.

Jimenez came around the side of the house, shucking a backpack he was carrying and tossing it on the porch. He walked over to Robyn and gave her a kiss.

"Any luck?" he asked.

"No, nothing," Robyn said with a shake of her head.

"No luck here, either," he said. Robyn took his hand and led him inside, followed by Izzy and Holly. They all went into the spacious kitchen, and Robyn got out two bottles of beer, handing one to Jimenez.

"Thanks," he said with a tired smile, twisting off the cap and taking a pull. "I think Tim wants to get an early start again tomorrow, Juan," Izzy said.

"He doesn't still think she's alive, does he?" Jimenez asked.

"Taco!" Robyn gasped, "Of course he does! We all do!" she exclaimed, looking into everyone's eyes, taken aback when she did not see the response she was hoping for.

"Soon we're going to have to face facts," Jimenez said, taking her hand.

"No! I won't give up hope!"

"Robyn, he's right," Holly said with a tone that hit Robyn like a brick wall.

Her eyes welled up with tears, her lower lip trembled. "No! She's alive and we will find her, you'll see!"

"Robyn, please think about it for a minute," Holly said.

"No, I won't!" she screamed, breaking the grip on Jimenez' hand, and bolting out of the room and up the stairs, where they heard her bedroom door slam.

"I'll go talk to her," Jimenez said, leaving Holly and Izzy standing in the middle of the room, speechless.

Izzy smiled warmly at Holly, in the fatherly way that always calmed her.

"I think you should go up to Tim and comfort him right now."

"Aye. I'll do that. What about you, Iz?"

"I'll be fine. I'll just go up and retire myself. I think everyone's lost their appetite anyway. We'll get up early and start again tomorrow. Nothing more we can do tonight."

"Are you sure, Iz?"

"Yes, I'm sure. Now run along and see to Tim. He won't admit it in a million years, but he needs you right now."

"I will, thank you, Iz," Holly said tiredly. She went upstairs, and when she heard Robyn's soft sobs, she thought to go and check on her, then thought better of it. Jimenez was with her, so she'd be alright. It was Tim she was worried about; she'd never seen him in such a state.

She went to the bedroom they shared and opened the door quietly. The lights were already off, but the light from the hallway behind her cast a beam of light ahead, sending her shadow across Tim's form, lying under the sheets. She shut the door behind her, stripped, and climbed under the sheets, sliding up behind Tim's form. She fluffed her pillow, and placed her arm around his waist, cuddled close, pressing her face into the center of his back.

"Are you awake?" she whispered.

"Yeah, I can't sleep."

"I figured as much. Do you want to talk about it?" she asked, squeezing him tighter.

"Not really."

"But—"

"But nothing, babe. In a few days, we're going to find a body."

"How can you be so sure?" she asked.

"Too many years as a cop is why I'm so sure. Even if nothing nefarious happened, she's been out in the woods for far too long. She'd be dead from exposure, if nothing else," Tim sighed quietly.

"If that happens, we deal with it. Until then, I think we should keep a positive outlook," Holly stated.

"You go ahead and do that. I'll be the realist."

"Why are you beating yourself up over this?" she asked, pleading.

"I'm responsible."

"No you are not, Timothy."

"Yes I am. People here look to me for protection, and I can't even do that. I couldn't even protect one young girl. How the fuck am I supposed to protect a whole goddamn community?"

"You can't. That's not what they're after."

"Then why did they come here?" he said, rolling onto his back.

"Tim, they didn't come for protection, they came for a sense of purpose."

"They all should have stayed on Oahu," Tim said angrily.

"They didn't. They came with us because they wanted to be a part of whatever we have here."

"Which is fast becoming a clusterfuck," he snapped.

Holly held him tightly for a moment, gathering her thoughts. "Tim, you're doing your best. We all are."

"My best isn't good enough," he said. "Ian and Paula trusted me to keep them and April safe, and I've failed."

"Tim, honey, the only thing you promised them, promised anyone, is that they could have a new start here. That's it," she said softly.

"I'm just so tired, babe," he said after a moment.

"Get some sleep. We'll try again tomorrow."

Tim lay there in the darkness, feeling Holly's warm skin next to his, and that gave him small comfort. Holly was soon fast asleep, but sleep eluded Tim for quite some time.

The next morning when they woke, Tim felt as if he hadn't gotten a minute's sleep. He kept to himself and didn't say anything, even when Robyn came down from her room, followed by Jimenez, who'd obviously spent the night with her.

There was very little in the way of conversation over coffee, except for plans being made on where they would continue their search for the missing girl. Everyone met up in front of Tim's house, and he went over the topographical map of the area with everyone, assigning a search area to each member of the search party. Robyn handed out fresh batteries for the Army issued handheld Motorola radios, and they all headed out.

It was decided that Holly and Izzy would stay at the house, sort of like a base-camp, and if they did find her, they would be in a central location, standing by with a radio of their own to come with a Hum-Vee and medical aid if needed.

After walking through the forest for several minutes, Tim stopped when he could no longer hear the sounds of the others. Adjusting the sling on his carbine, he pulled the folded map out of his pocket and opened it.

Everyone else was concentrating to the west and south, and he traced his finger over the lines marking an area a few miles away, to the north and east, a place that Colin had said he searched thoroughly the day before, and found no trace. He refolded the map, placing it back into his pocket and headed off in that direction.

He wasn't sure if it was his old cop instincts or old soldier instincts, but something was just not sitting right with that man's actions. Colin talked a good line of bullshit, and even made a good show of looking for April, but Tim had a very uneasy feeling. He made his way through the woods silently, skirting around the clearing that ran behind the house that Colin had taken over.

It was fast going, the carpet of pine needles made for a nearly silent journey. He didn't see any outward signs of anyone having been through the area, that was until he came across an overgrown fire trail cut through the trees by long-dead forest service employees. He didn't see it at first; there were many young tree saplings sprouting up all over the dirt road, but when he did spot the days old trail, he followed it easily.

The ground was dry and dusty, and since it hadn't rained in weeks and all of the snow had melted some time ago, he clearly saw the footprints that had to have been April's, alongside of a larger set, about three sizes bigger than his own. They were side by side, giving the impression that whoever had left them had walked together.

He followed the trail of the fire lane and back into the woods, and right before he was at the edge of another clearing, he was momentarily startled by several buzzards, who had been gathered around something lying on the ground, partially hidden by some fallen tree limbs and pine needles.

They flew off, squawking angrily at Tim's intrusion, and as he neared the shape on the ground, his heart fell to the pit of his stomach. She was lying supine, naked from the waist down, her legs splayed obscenely, and her dirty face staring up at him through the dark holes where her eyes had once been. He thought of the man, so many years ago in Bucks County, Pennsylvania who had hurt his friend Paul, that Tim had left to bleed to death. Had he suffered a similar fate?

He supposed so. But that animal deserved it. Not this girl. She didn't deserve this at all. His blood boiled as he stepped away from the horrid scene, pulled out his radio, and called Holly.

She answered immediately. "Holly, go to Quebec," he said, indicating she should go to a pre-arranged radio channel that they'd come up with between themselves, that no one else knew about. When she acknowledged, he changed his radio to that frequency and waited for her to call him.

"Tim, are you there?"

"Yeah," he said, pulling out his map and double checking his location. "I want you and Izzy to come to my location, grid number seven three five niner zero niner three, as soon as you can."

There was a short pause, then Holly replied, "That's nowhere near where everyone else is looking. That's been searched already."

"Just get here, and not a word to anyone else, okay?"

"Tim, have you found her?" she asked excitedly.

"Yeah," he said disgustedly.

"Izzy wants to know if he should bring his medical bag," she asked with hope in her voice.

"That won't be necessary. You two get here, okay?" he replied, irritated. "Get here now, goddamn it! I'll wait out on a fire trail." Tim took a breath, calmed himself, then said flatly, his voice now devoid of all emotion, "You should be able to pick it up just about a mile north of our house, off of the blacktop."

It was a tone that Holly knew all too well. She'd heard it before from him, before she even knew who he was. She'd been flying a Royal Air Force Lynx helicopter in Iraq at the time, and Tim's voice was the same emotionless monotone then, when he threatened to shoot her down himself if she didn't land her aircraft. A chill went through her when she heard it, and just as she had done in Iraq so many years ago, she obeyed without another word.

Tim walked back through the trees, and found a shady spot to sit with his carbine across his lap. He fished out his pipe and sat there puffing away; waiting for them to show, and his anger simmered. He should have done something. What though?

His thoughts were broken by the sound of the approaching Hum-Vee, and he stood. The four wheel drive cut an easy path through the saplings, and Holly pulled up to a stop next to him. She and Izzy got out with worried looks and came over to Tim, who still hadn't said a word. Izzy stood to the side and Holly put her arms around Tim.

"Where is she?" she asked.

"Follow me," he said, and headed off back through the trees, followed closely by Holly and Izzy. He had to shoo away the buzzards again, and when Holly saw April's body, she gasped.

"What do you think happened, Tim?" Izzy asked.

"It's pretty goddamn obvious someone—and I've got a good idea who—lured her out here, raped, and then strangled her."

"Who do you think, Tim, that Aussie chap, Colin?" Holly asked.

"Yeah, it had to have been him," he said, and went on to tell them both about what he and Ian had witnessed the previous week.

"Just by that? That's thin evidence, don't you think?" Izzy asked, trying to play the Devil's advocate.

"Iz, I know it would never stand up in a court of law, and it's all we have to go on. It's not like we can get a crime scene crew out here, and collect DNA. You can see by just looking at her it wasn't natural causes, by any stretch of the imagination. And Colin was adamant that he'd searched this whole area yesterday, wasn't he?"

"That's true, Tim. But—"

"But what, Iz?" Tim all but shouted, his voice seething with anger. "Both Ian and I saw him lurking around, watching her. When she went missing, he was one of the first ones to volunteer to start looking, and conveniently, he picked *this* area to look in, comes back, and says there wasn't a trace."

"What do you plan on doing?" Izzy asked.

"I haven't decided yet," Tim said, his voice now icy and eerily calm.

"Oh, Tim, it's so horrible," Holly said tearfully, kneeling down and brushing the pine needles off April's face.

"Remember what you said before, Tim, about following the Constitution. If you want to stick by that decision, there are rules we need to follow. You know that better than anyone here," Izzy pointed out, looking down at the body.

Holly tried to give the girl a little dignity by covering her up with a light jacket she was wearing.

"I know that, Iz. I'm all out of judges, prosecutors, defense attorneys and prisons," Tim said. Again, his mind was drawn back to those first few months after the Event, back in Bucks County, where he invoked what he'd called then 'Tim's Law', where he made himself judge, jury, and executioner. Could he return to that mentality again? He wasn't sure, but he knew he'd better do something.

"All this talk isn't going to get anything accomplished. Let's get her back to home, and we'll decide then. Someone is going to have to tell Ian and Paula," he added with a grimace, knowing full well it would be him telling them about April.

Tim took Izzy by the arm and walked back to the Hum-Vee. He opened the back tailgate and pulled out a green canvas tarp, then turned to Izzy.

"I don't know what to do, Iz," he said, tears coming to his eyes. "I want to go back to the compound, find that piece of shit, and put a bullet in his melon."

"It angers me too. But if we do that, we're no better than he is."

"You're right. What do we do? Throw him in a cage? For how long?"

"I don't know, Tim. Let's just get April back home, tell her parents, and then we'll take him into custody, and let everyone decide what we should do."

"Oh, a democratic form of a lynching?" Tim spat.

"I wouldn't go that far," Izzy said.

"Why not? Because that's what I think everyone will want to do with him once we tell them what happened! They will drag him out of his house without due process, and string him up from a tree!"

"Why do you think that?"

"Because it's what I want to do with the fucker, okay?" replied, fire in his eyes.

"But you won't, will you?" Izzy asked.

"No, I won't. Sorry, Iz, I let my emotions get the better of me," Tim sighed and let out a breath.

"Let's get April back home," Izzy urged, heading back into the trees, and Tim followed him.

They walked back down to the clearing where Holly was standing, tear-faced, over April's body. Tim couldn't remember just how many dead bodies he'd had to place into body bags in his lifetime, but he went about the task like an automaton, no emotion showing at all, like he was picking up the Sunday newspaper.

They went about their task gently and with as much respect as they could, and carried the bundle back through the woods to the waiting bed of the Hum-Vee. Tim got behind the wheel, started the engine, and they made their way back to Tim's house.

In spite of not letting on to what was happening, most everyone was standing there waiting for them to return, and Tim scowled when he saw them.

"Great," Tim spat, pulling up to a stop in front of the house.

"They must have heard me and Izzy leave in a hurry," Holly said.

Tim shut the engine off and got out. Everyone must have read the look on his face, as their looks of anticipation turned to horror. Paula, who was standing next to Ian, collapsed into his arms, sobbing uncontrollably.

"What happened?" Ian demanded angrily, trying to hold onto Paula and keep her from collapsing in a heap at his feet.

"We're not sure exactly, Ian," Izzy said, coming over to comfort the distraught woman. Tim looked into everyone's faces, and could almost feel their thoughts. He knew at that instant they blamed him, and it shamed him to the core. There was nothing he could do about it now.

A last few stragglers were coming out of the woods on the other side of the meadow, and the big Australian man who towered over them was bringing up the rear. Tim didn't hesitate. He straightened up, and marched over to the gaggle of people, ignoring their questions, brushing by them, until he was face to face with his number one suspect.

"G'day, mate! Any luck?" the man said, and in a blink of an eye, too fast for the man to defend himself, Tim lashed out with a balled fist, punching him as hard as he could right in the throat.

Colin's eyes went wide with disbelief and stunned and gagging, he fell to his knees at Tim's feet. Tim spat on the man, who was now curled up in a fetal position, clutching at his throat and gasping for air.

Tim made a move to plant a boot into the side of his head, but at the last minute, stopped himself. He looked down at the gagging man for a moment more, then Sam Didinato came up beside him.

"Sorry I delayed your trek," Tim said.

"No problem, Sar' Major. I was in no rush. What about him?" he asked, pointing at the heap on the ground.

"He raped and killed April. Get this piece of shit out of my sight before I beat him to death," Tim whispered to Sam, low enough that no one else heard him. The look in Tim's eyes told Sam everything else he wanted to know.

"You got it," Sam said, reaching down and grabbing the man by the collar. "Okay asshole, you're coming with me."

He dragged the stunned man to his feet, and then pulled a revolver out of a jacket pocket, cocked the hammer, and placed the muzzle at Colin's head.

"One wrong move, cocksucker, and your brains will be all over this clearing," he said.

The man, still stunned, asked in a raspy voice, "What's this about?"

Sam tapped the pistol on the man's head none too gently. "And shut the fuck up, alright? Open your dick-holster one more fucking time, I'll make you eat a fucking bullet." The color drained from the prisoner's face when he saw the look in Sam's eyes. "That's right, asshole. I don't even want to hear your sweat dripping, capisch? To me, you're no better than all them Hajjis I sent to see Allah."

Jimenez came running up with a roll of duct tape and promptly tore off a piece and unceremoniously slapped it over Colin's mouth. With that done, he took the man's arms, pulled them behind his back, and taped his wrists together, using far more tape than necessary. When he was done, he walked around and faced the now frightened man, and smiled.

"You don't even want to know what we do to child killers back in the barrio, bro," he said, taking a guess at what had happened, and winked at the man, then looked over at Tim, who was just now getting his boiling anger under control. "What now, Sar' Major?"

"There's a Sheriff's Office substation in town. There's bound to be a few holding cells over there."

"You got it, Sar' Major," he nodded, and then turned back to the prisoner. "Come on, cumstain."

Sam and Jimenez walked the man over to another Hum-Vee and shoved him roughly into the back, where he fell on his side. He was truly terrified, now, and was whimpering like a wounded dog through the tape over his mouth. The two men piled into the vehicle, started it, and pulled away, heading into town.

Tim stood there with his hands on his hips until they were out of sight. He turned then, and saw everyone looking at him silently. Holly was with Ian and Paula, trying to comfort the distraught woman. He walked over to the threesome, placed his hand on Ian's shoulder and squeezed. Ian looked at him, and through tear-stained eyes, nodded weakly.

Tim didn't say anything, there were no words to be found. He left everyone and plodded up the steps to his porch and entered through the screen door, letting it slam loudly behind him while the crowd watched the dust settle where the Hum-Vee had disappeared into the trees.

Sam drove with disregard to his passenger in the back. He pressed his foot down on the accelerator and hit every pothole, crack, and bump in the deteriorating road all the way into town.

By the time he and Jimenez had made it the few miles into the center of the town, Colin had been beat up just as if Tim himself had not been able to control his anger back at the compound. They pulled up in front of a one-story tufa stone block building that looked as if it had been built around the turn of the 20th Century, and there were a few dusty, disused Crown Victoria patrol cars parked out front.

By the door, was a flagpole with a tattered American flag still flying forlornly in the slight breeze next to a now faded wooden sign that read **Coconino County Sheriff's Office**. Jimenez got out of the passenger's side, taking a M4 Carbine off the rack.

"Give me a few minutes. I'm going to go and have a look-see," he told Sam, who nodded and walked over to the tailgate.

Jimenez was about to smash a pane of glass in the door with the butt of his carbine to open the door, but he reached out and grasped the doorknob first, and found the building was unlocked. He smiled, shook his head, and disappeared inside, leaving Sam alone with their prisoner.

Sam dropped the tailgate and inspected his cargo, and saw that he was still taped up pretty well, and he now had a fairly good sized gash on the side of his head that was bleeding a little.

"Okay, princess, time for you to take a walk," he said, hitting Colin on the foot with his pistol. Colin's eyes flew open, and he stared at Sam in sheer terror. He sat up with some difficulty, and by the time Sam got him to a sitting position on the rear of the Hum-Vee, Jimenez came back out of the door holding a large key ring and smiling broadly.

"What happened to him?" he asked Sam.

"I think he might have cut himself shaving," Sam said. He grasped Colin's arm. "Let's go, sweetheart."

They got the man to stand, and on uneasy legs, got him moving towards the building.

"Are there cells?" Sam asked.

"Oh yeah," Jimenez said, his grin widening. "And he's just going to love what we've done to the place!"

They walked through the doors into a dimly lit room, where a desk was set up, sort of like a reception area, a mummified man, still dressed in a tan Deputy's uniform, sat at it, deep, dark holes where the eyes once were staring out at them, lips dried and pulled back, exposing yellowed teeth in an obscene grin.

Colin stopped dead in his tracks, not wanting to move any further. Sam shoved him forward. "Don't worry about him, he's on lunch break, choad-smoker," he said to Colin, and then looked at Jimenez. "Where's the cells, Taco?"

"Over this way, I've got one all ready for him, special like. I think he's going to love it."

They went through another door, Jimenez in front, Sam shoving Colin none too gently forward down a short corridor to a line of gray-painted steel bar doors. He went halfway down the line and stopped in front of one that he must have opened in preparation, and waved their prisoner in.

Having resigned himself to his fate, Colin started to walk in the door, but stopped dead at the threshold. He moaned loudly through the duct tape covering his mouth, shaking his head in denial.

The cell was six foot wide by about eight foot deep, concrete walled, and had the obligatory stainless steel toilet and sink in one corner, and a set of narrow bunk beds along one wall. It was then that Sam saw what made Colin stop dead.

In the lower bunk there was another mummy dressed in a faded orange jumpsuit, one claw-like hand extended like a talon, mouth agape and the same dead eye sockets as the deputy in the foyer.

The three men cast a shadow into the cell from the dim sunlight coming through a barred, dusty window to corridor. Sam let out a laugh and rabbit punched Colin in the kidney, making him fall forward into the cell, landing face first on the floor, his head only a few inches away from his new roommate. When Jimenez saw that his feet were clear of the track for the door, he slammed it closed, and with the large, flat key, locked the door with a menacing clank that echoed in the empty stone building.

Colin scampered to the far wall, crying now. He placed his back on the wall and shimmed himself to a standing position, looking out in fear at his now smiling captors.

"What about his hands?" Sam asked.

"Oh yeah," Jimenez said. "Guess he's not going anywhere now. C'mere, asshole," he beckoned. "Back up to the bars so I can cut the tape."

Colin did as he was told, his body now shaking uncontrollably, and Jimenez took out a folding pocket knife and cut the tape binding the man's hands. He immediately spun around, and clawed at the tape covering his mouth, and when he was able to, he shouted, "For fuck sake, mate, you can't leave me in here with *that*!" glancing back over his shoulder at the long dead prisoner. Fear oozed out of every pore, like a malignant disease.

"I can, and I am, asshole," Jimenez said, devoid now of all emotion.

"We can work this out, mate!" Colin pled, his face turning a deep purple, veins in his forehead throbbing wildly.

"I'm in no position to work anything out, and I'm not your fucking mate," Sam said flatly, backing up to the far wall to escape Colin's outstretched hands.

"Ah shit! C'mon! You blokes were Army, right?"

"Yeah," Jimenez said, not wanting to elaborate the difference between the Marines and the Army. He was a Marine; Sam was the dogface.

"I almost joined the Army too, right after year ten in school!"

"Well fuck me running, Taco. Did you hear that? He *almost* joined the fucking Army!" Sam said, followed by a loud laugh that echoed eerily through the cells.

"Yeah, no shit, Sam. That makes us *almost* bros," Jimenez cracked.

"Australia and America are allies!" Colin said pleadingly.

"You haven't a fucking clue, do you, you worthless piece of shit?" Sam said, shaking his head in disgust. "We are not fucking bros, allies, or anything to you."

"Don't I have rights?"

"Oh here we go, Taco. His fucking rights," Sam said, rolling his eyes.

Jimenez stepped forward, grabbed the man's left hand that was sticking through the gray steel bars, took hold of his thumb, and in one twist, folded back his thumb to the point of it breaking, making Colin drop to his knees in agony. Tears were now streaming down his face as he looked up in submission at his two tormentors.

"Lesson number one, fuckstick. The only right I know of that you have is the right to remain silent, so how about exercising that right, and shut the fuck up. The Sar' Major is in charge here. This isn't TV, this is real life, no shit. He'll follow the Constitution, that I'm sure of," Jimenez said. That gave Colin a ray of hope, and that showed on his face, which wasn't lost on the two men. Sam made the decision then to extinguish the dim light at the end of the tunnel.

"Laws here are a lot different than Australia, dickhead. The Sar' Major made it perfectly clear that he will follow *all* of the laws, not just US laws. You committed this crime in Arizona, and for your information, Arizona has the death penalty," Sam said, grinning.

"They sure do, Sam," Jimenez said. "We've got the gas chamber, down in Florence. I'm pretty sure the Sar' Major isn't going to want to drive all the way down there to gas this fucker. It'll be a waste of diesel. He'll find some rope, most likely, and you'll be hung from a cottonwood tree here in town," Jimenez said, and then spat on the ground.

"No! You can't let him do that!" Colin screamed, now completely terrified.

"You should have thought about that before you went out and killed that girl, asshole," Sam said, turning to leave. He'd had enough talk with this piece of shit, and he showed his contempt by walking out without another word.

Jimenez looked down on Colin, and for a brief moment felt sorry for him. It quickly passed. He reached into his pocket and withdrew a deck of cards he'd found on the desk outside. He tossed them through the bars at the now bawling man.

"There. Maybe you can talk your cellmate into a game of Spades," he said, then followed Sam out of the building to the waiting Hum-Vee.

Sam was standing on the far side of the Hum-Vee urinating when Jimenez came out of the Sheriff's building. He finished his business, zipped up his Wranglers, and got behind the wheel.

Jimenez climbed in the passenger's side, placing the carbine back into the rack. "You know," he said, glancing at Sam, "in the Marine Corps, they teach us to wash our hands after taking a piss."

"Taco, in the Army, they teach us not to piss all over our hands," Sam replied.

They could hear Colin screaming his lungs out, even from outside the building and over the running diesel engine of the Hum-Vee. Sam was tired of listening to it already, and put the vehicle in gear and sped away, spraying loose gravel from the parking lot which pelted the building and parked cars like shrapnel, and back towards the compound.

"So, Taco, were all the cells full?" Sam asked as he made the left turn onto the road back home.

"Nah, just that one, the rest were empty," Jimenez said and Sam almost choked with laughter.

When he regained his composure, he said. "Oh fuck, Taco. That's classic!"

"Serves the *maricón* right. I say we just leave him there to rot."

"Hey, I'm all for that, but you know the Sar' Major better than almost anyone. I figure he's got plans for him," Sam said, shaking his head.

"Yeah, he's one hombre you don't want to cross, I'll tell you that," Jimenez agreed.

"Yep. Oh, and it's 'hanged'," Sam said with a sideways glance.

"What is hanged?" Jimenez asked.

"Typical Jarhead, you gotta retrain em' after every meal break," Sam said, shaking his head. "You told him he'd be 'hung' from a cottonwood tree. The corrected term is 'hanged' from a cottonwood tree."

"Well I'll be dipped in dogshit. A dogface *and* a fucking grammar Nazi," Jimenez said, and they both laughed loud and hard.

CHAPTER 8: PIECES OF THE PUZZLE

The general had been sitting on a stiff-backed wooden chair in the hallway outside the Oval Office for what felt like hours waiting to be seen. The hallway was dimly lit, and the only light was coming through a window at the far end of it.

Even the president doesn't have power now, he thought. *Well, at least winter is over.*

He fingered the manila folder that was lying on his lap for the hundredth time, wondering again if it was the right thing to do, to give this man in the office the information it contained.

He looked at his watch, and saw that he'd been kept waiting for over an hour. His anger started to build, but he suppressed it. As that thought passed, the door opened, and an attractive black woman came out and smiled at him. She straightened out her clothes, which were in some disarray, and said, "The president will see you now, General."

He stood with a smile that was as phony as a three dollar bill, and followed her through the open door. The president was seated behind the massive desk, his jacket off and tie askew. He made a show of rearranging some papers on the desktop, and looked up.

"Good morning, General. Please come in."

"Good morning, Mr. President, I came over as soon as you called for me," he said. He stopped a few feet in front of the desk, but the man seated behind it neither stood, nor offered him a seat, so he just stood there.

"That will be all, Alicia. Please close the door behind you," the president said, and the woman dutifully turned and departed the room. He then turned his attention back to the general, finally motioning for him to take a seat. The officer sat on the more comfortable chair, and thumbed the folder yet again, trying to form words in his head, which had been lost as soon as he entered the room.

"So, General, tell me. Have you found out anything more?"

"Yes we have, sir," he said, feeling sick.

"Get on with your brief."

"We've been able to decipher most of the Ham Radio transmissions and the pieces of the puzzle are falling into place. Because they're using the Ham bands, it's hard to tell exactly where they are, but things that were said point to at least three locations now."

"How so?"

"None of it is voice traffic, it's all Morse code, and a few of their operators are pretty goddamn quick on the key, especially the one in Arizona," the general said.

"Arizona? I thought you just said you couldn't tell where they were?"

"We can't, not with a hundred percent certainty. However, it certainly fits. We have three distinct transmitters, one we believe is on Oahu, one that's mobile, somewhere on the West Coast, and another station in northern Arizona."

"What are they saying?"

"Not a whole lot, at the moment. There are several other stations they talk to all along the Pacific Rim, but the main traffic is between Hawaii and Arizona."

"Do you know who has the codes?" the president asked, sitting up in his chair and leaning forward.

"Sir, the station in Hawaii referred to the station in Arizona as the '*National Command Authority*' and '*The President*' on several occasions," the general said, bracing himself for the coming explosion, and he wasn't disappointed.

"National Command Authority? The National GODDAMN Command Authority?! *I'm* the goddamn National Command Authority!" the president exploded, pounding both fists onto the desktop, spittle flying from the corners of his mouth. "Do you know who this person is?"

"We think we do, sir."

"Then who the fuck is he?" the man demanded, rage building up, his eyes of fire.

"Mr. President, you must realize we don't have the resources we once had. We're going on a lot of assumptions and conjecture at the moment."

"As you keep telling me, General. Please, tell me what it is you do know!"

"Sir, we can't be one hundred percent certain... it seems like one man has taken it upon himself to take over as president, and has been calling himself that in communications. You remember me telling you about John Thompson, sir? He was an analyst with the CIA before the Situation. He broke the code they were using, did some research, and was able to come up with one probable candidate."

"How did he find out who this imposter is?" the president demanded.

"Most of the computer systems were fried when the calamity hit, because we had started using off-the-shelf civilian computers that weren't hardened for EMPs. Some of the DoD networks are still up, but barely. A simple check though USAPERS, and we think— again we're not sure, but we *think*— it's a soldier from the 28th Infantry Division, the Pennsylvania National Guard."

"USAPERS?"

"It's an acronym sir. It stands for US Army Personnel Records, sir, a database," the general stated.

"Who the fuck is he then? Does he have a name?" the president demanded.

"Sergeant Major Timothy Flannery," the general said, then held his breath.

"A sergeant-fucking-major? You have got to be joking, General! How does a fucking enlisted man get hold of the codes for our nuclear arsenal?"

"We don't know sir," he sighed.

"Was he the one involved in that battle you told me about before?"

"We believe so, Mr. President," the general said, his nerves so tight now he was ready to jump out of his skin. They'd still not told the president of the missile launch, and wouldn't, for as long as possible.

"Give me everything you've got."

"From what we gathered as of this morning: after the battle, they made their way back to Hawaii, by ship, we believe. Who, we don't know. They stayed there for a time, and right after I told you they'd taken satellite photos of the airport in Arizona, a group, including the sergeant major, made their way there to set up another settlement."

"And are you saying they flew there?" the president asked in disbelief.

"It's the only way they could have gotten there so fast, so yes, that fact, and the Keyhole photos of the airport they tasked, point to them having a working aircraft."

"You're telling me some fucking asshole enlisted man has got not one, but *two* fucking communities set up, he's got a working aircraft, he's got my fucking codes, and to top that all off, he's calling himself the *president?*"

"That's pretty much it, sir," the general said, his heart pounding in his chest, threatening to burst out of his ribcage. He was finding it increasingly difficult to catch his breath, so he took a few deep breaths, but the calm he'd hoped for eluded him.

The man who once was the Secretary of Housing and Urban Development leaned back in the high-backed leather chair and stared at the general for some time, a blank look painted on his face. The silence was deafening, and the general sat in his seat in quiet desperation, sweat now pouring down his face. He wanted to scream, jump up and run, but pure fear kept him riveted on the chair, folder in his lap all but forgotten in his sweaty hands.

The time dragged on as the two men stared at each other, and the general almost jumped out of his skin when the president finally spoke.

"I'll say this once, and only once," he said in a voice so deadly calm it would have turned even the most hardened criminal into a cowering imbecile. "You go and find that dimwit major, have him mount up an operation. You tell him to go out to Arizona and find this piece of shit."

"Yes sir!"

"When he does, he's to secure those codes and bring them back to me."

"Is that all, sir?" the general asked.

"No, that is not all. I want this bastard imposter brought back to me, and I want him to secure whatever aircraft they have, *and* the pilot, and bring them back with him also."

"Yes sir, right away!" the general said, standing, hoping to make it out of the Oval Office in one piece.

"Just a moment, General," the career politician said, waving him to sit back down. "Arizona is a big state. Do you have a place for them to head to?"

"Yes sir. It's a small town just south of the Grand Canyon. The airport they took photos of, and the town itself, is called Tusayan."

"I never heard of it."

"I'm guessing they're either in that town or close by. Nothing much else around there." "Get it done, General. Don't just sit there and gape at me!" the president spewed. "Yes sir!" the general said. He did a correct about-face and strode as fast as he could towards the door. He found his way out of the now crumbling building and to his Hum-Vee parked outside of the west entrance.

He drove himself the short few blocks over the National Guard Armory on Capitol Street that sat within sight of RFK Stadium, Kingman Lake, and the Potomac River, where he parked and entered the building. Seeing a man dressed in Army ACU utilities, he asked where the major was.

"He's in his office... sir," the man said, saying the word 'sir' almost as if an afterthought. The general ignored the slight and walked down a long, dimly lit corridor to an office at the end.

The door was slightly ajar, and the general walked in without knocking. A short, balding man in a brown Army t-shirt looked up from a paperback novel he was reading, and seeing who had entered, started to get up.

"Please, stay seated, Major," the general said, sitting down on a chair across from the desk.

"What brings the pleasure, General?" the major asked, putting away his pulp fiction novel.

"How was the last foraging expedition, Major?"

"It was as good as to be expected, sir. We've gone as far as Richmond to the west this time, and we think we have enough canned food for about a year now. There was a huge Wal-Mart distribution center there."

"So you found the mother lode, eh, Major?"

"Not quite. A lot of the cereals and other foodstuffs were long gone and spoiled, but there were a lot of canned goods. We had to make five trips, but there's enough food for the foreseeable future, at least twelve months' worth."

"That's good news," the general said. "How soon can you mount up another mission?"

"Mission, sir?"

"The president wants you to make another mission, a big one."

"How big, sir?" the major asked excitedly, sitting up a little straighter.

"He wants you to head out west again, to Arizona."

"Why Arizona?"

"We think the codes, the ones you went searching for last year, are located there."

"Is that so? We didn't find a trace of them at the wreckage in Iowa."

"We've gotten some new intelligence in the last few days, and he wants it acted upon immediately."

This information piqued the major's interest, and he leaned forward, placing his elbows on the desk.

"What can you tell me?" the major asked.

"It seems that an enlisted man, a sergeant major from the 28th Division, has the codes, and he's set up a settlement in northern Arizona."

"So this is a military operation?"

"I'd say so, Major. The president wants you to take as many men as you think necessary, head out there, find this man, place him under arrest, secure the codes, and bring them both back here to Washington."

"Anything else?"

"We believe they also have a working aircraft. You're to secure the pilot of that aircraft, and bring them back also."

"Do you have any idea how many people he has with him out there?"

"That we don't know. It can't be very many; it's not a very big town where we think they're located at."

"That's not a whole lot to go on, sir. With all due respect, that's a long way to go on just a few suppositions," the major said.

"I'm afraid that's all we have right now, Major," the general said, knowing the major was correct.

"I understand, sir."

"How soon can you get an expedition ready?"

"A few days. I've got to put together the logistics. It's going to be a long one. It took weeks and weeks to get as far as Iowa last time. The roads and highways aren't in the best condition anymore."

"I just need it done, the sooner, the better."

"Yes sir. I understand. We'll have the whole summer. If we get out there too late in the year, we stand the chance of getting caught in another blizzard like we did the last time," the major said, shuddering involuntarily at the memory of that cold winter a few years ago. He didn't want to repeat that.

"I suggest you get a move on then. The president is making this a high-priority."

"Yes sir. I'll start on it right away. I'll go myself, and take a company of men with me."

"Do you think that will be enough?" the general asked.

"I think so, it'll leave us a little light on defense of the city, but I think we can do it."

"Get it done, Major."

"Yes sir, I'll get right on it. We should be ready to go in a day or two; I've just got to work out the logistics."

"Let me know, Major. And here is some information you may find useful," the general said, standing, and then remembering the sweat-stained folder in his hands that he'd meant to give to the president, tossing it onto the major's desk.

"Thank you, sir. I won't let you down," the major said eagerly, fingering the folder greedily.

"It's not me you should be worried about letting down, Major," the general said gravely.

"Eh, yes sir, I copy you loud and clear, General."

The general exited the office, leaving the major to his thoughts. He walked out of the building silently, got back into the Hum-Vee, and made his way over to the Pentagon, where he found John Thompson in the conference room in front of an ancient Ham radio rig he'd set up at the far end of the table. A coaxial cable ran from the back of the radio and up through the acoustic ceiling tiles, probably to the roof, the general thought.

When John saw him, he looked up from the dials and removed a set of headphones. "So, what did the president say?"

"He wasn't happy at all, John," the general said, sighing and plopping down in a chair near the far end. He looked around the room with a frown. The place was filthy. Soot from kerosene lanterns covered mostly everything with a thin black film, and he could smell the mold that must be growing in the walls, leaving him wondering what kind of upper respiratory condition he'd get from the constant exposure.

"I didn't think he would be. But we couldn't hide it from him forever."

"No, that we couldn't do. I'm afraid we might have kicked up a hornet's nest with this though."

"What gives you that idea?" John asked.

"I don't know, a gut feeling."

"He *is* the president, like it or not. He wants those codes, and the major will get them for him."

"I know that John, but something, deep down, is telling me we should just leave this sergeant major out in Arizona alone."

"General, you're getting paranoid. What are one man and a handful of people out in some hole in the wall place going to do?"

"Are you forgetting that this one man, only a few months ago, launched a thermonuclear weapon at an atoll in the middle of the Pacific?"

"True," John conceded.

"And the major, well, you know as well as I, that he can be a little rash in his decisions."

"What were his orders?"

"Quote: The major is to mount up an expedition, head out there to Arizona, secure the codes, and the aircraft, bringing our good sergeant major, the codes and the pilot back to Washington unquote," the general said.

"I agree, the major can get a little excited, but everything should be fine if he takes enough men with him."

"Have you read this man's 201 file?" the general asked.

"I have. He's no legendary 'Rambo', General."

"No, he's not. But he's had an impressive career, John. Airborne, Ranger, Combat Infantryman's Badge, Bronze Star and Purple Heart in Grenada, and the youngest instructor ever at the Jungle Warfare School in Panama. The First Gulf War, then Iraq for several tours, then again in Afghanistan for several more. Not to mention whole pages of things completely redacted in the early 1980's, which you should know well enough shouts 'CIA' from the rooftops. And on top of that a civilian police officer in Philadelphia for a lot of years. That's one man who is not to be fucked with, that I will say."

"I also recall reading he flunked out of the Special Forces selection course, General. He's not a super soldier," John said.

"John, I'm not trying to argue with you. No, he's no Rambo, but I think we should handle this a little differently. Have you tried contacting them directly?"

"Actually, I have. Just now, in fact," John said, pointing at the radio. "They basically told me to go fuck myself."

"Oh come on, really?" the general asked after a laugh.

"Yes, really," John said, picking up a notepad and began to read; "Quote: To whoever this is, I don't care if you're the Queen of England, we have a president, so go fuck yourself, unquote," he said, tossing the notepad on the table unceremoniously.

"Are you sure?"

"I know my Boy Scout Morse Code is a little rusty, but yeah, I'm sure."

"And then what?"

"They sent that message and then dropped off the air. Well, not right off the air. Right after they sent that reply to me, they boosted their power, and then ripped off a five-digit number sequence, three times over, then everything dropped off. I think it was some kind of warning or something."

"Do you know what the numbers were?"

"I don't think they meant anything, except for a warning," John said, rubbing the bridge of his nose. "They set up a code, sometime way in the past most probably. It might have just been a word, like 'monkey' or 'taxicab', something easy to remember, and easy for a man on the Morse key to rattle off. When everyone hears it, they drop off the air, radio silence. I wouldn't be surprised if they have a prearranged radio frequency they all went to, or some other alternative means of communication we're unaware of. Simple field craft from a security and intelligence standpoint."

"Just like that?" the general asked, snapping his fingers in the air.

"Yes, General, just like that," John said, wondering how this man got that star on his shoulder. "They most probably have use of the military satellite communications network. I know they've been using the IVIS, and logic dictates that if they are using that, they probably have control of the former, also."

"Can't we access that also?"

"We could, for a time. It's how we knew about the Keyhole tasking. Right after the last photo flyby, we were locked out of the system. Whoever is in charge out there locked the system and secured it. We're effectively deaf and dumb from this point onwards."

"Didn't you just say, only a few moments ago, that this man wasn't some super soldier, no Rambo, and we shouldn't be too worried about him?"

"From the amount of intelligence I've gathered, he is rather insignificant, considering the military might we can bring to bear on him."

"Military might? What military might? He's the one with the codes for the nuclear arsenal, and has proven he will use them."

"Would he really launch a missile at himself?" John asked, not knowing the full story of what had actually happened on the tiny atoll of Volivoli. If he had known that story in its entirety, he'd change his way of thinking. "I mean, come on, General, think about it. If he's faced with our good major and a hundred or so soldiers right on his doorstep, do you think he'd nuke himself?"

"You do have a point, John," the general conceded. "How do we stay in contact with the major?"

"I'll have to scare up another Ham setup, a portable one like this, and I also think I can get a few Sat-Radios working for ourselves, though I'm not going to promise anything at this point," John said, making a motion with his thumb towards the radio. "If I can get a few Sat-Radios working, I'll never in a million years able to listen in on their transmissions."

"Why not?"

"They're scrambled. We'd have to know the exact algorithm, and they're a million or so of them they could be using, along with the frequency that they're using. It'd be a million-to-one shot to figure it out now."

"You can set us up one that we can use, though, right?"

"Yes, I can do that."

"Then do it, John. The president doesn't want any delays with this."

"I'm going to take this set home. I'll work from there. I'll do what I can to see if they're on another frequency," John said. "I'll let you know what, if anything, I find out."

"Good. Please do that. Figure out a way to keep in touch with the major, also. I think that will be very important."

"That it will be, General," he agreed, adding, "I'll be able to pass on any information I can gather to him, also."

"Tell me, John. How did you find out his name?"

"It was just a guess. I never broke their code completely. I just got a name at first, and then they were calling him 'Sergeant Major', so I searched the database for that rank and name, and came up with him," he said, shrugging his shoulders. "It was pretty straightforward. The Army didn't have a lot of sergeant majors. The pool of names gets smaller as you climb up the food chain."

"Then you're not a hundred percent sure it's him?"

"No, not a hundred percent, but all the facts are there."

The general sighed. "With everything as tenuous as it is here, I don't think it's wise at this point to go off on this errand."

"I know, and I agree, but that's what the president wants, so that's what the president will get," John said.

"We need to concentrate on things here. If we have another winter like we did this past year, things will get ugly. The power needs to be restored. We need to get food for the people, and not just canned pork and beans."

"And clean water and medicine. Did you know we had several cases of Bubonic Plague last month?" John said.

"The president doesn't want to hear about it," the general said angrily.

"It's only going to get worse."

"This is why I need you to get a radio to the major, and keep in contact with him every step of the way. I don't want him to get out there and go stomping around like the Gestapo. They are Americans out there, remember, so we need to keep him on a very short leash," the general said.

"I'm just a worker-bee, a drone. The president tells you to find something out, and then you come to me, and I dig up the information and give it to you. It's up to you and the president to act on the intelligence I provide."

"I know that, John."

"It's always been that way. I can only give my recommendations. I know we need all this other stuff, food, medicine, electricity and running water. If we don't get those things, and soon, the shit will definitely hit the fan."

"To tell you the truth, John, I do not want to be anywhere near the epicenter when the shit begins to fly," the general agreed.

"Nor do I, General."

"So tell me, what do you think?"

"Do you really want to know?" John asked.

"Yes, I do."

"Off the record?" John asked the general, a little smile crossing his lips.

"Spill it, John. I'm getting too old and tired to be pussyfooting around."

"From all the information I've gathered, they've got it good out west and in Hawaii. They've got plenty of food, electricity, running water. This sergeant major has got all of his proverbial shit in one sack. Things are well on their way to being as normal as they can be, unlike here, where we're hanging on by our fingernails. It's a miracle that things haven't imploded by now. It actually sickens me, what's going on here in DC. This place was a cesspool before, now it's even worse."

"I'm just following orders," the general stated flatly.

"That's what they all said in Nuremburg," John remarked wryly.

"That's unfair, John!" the general shot back.

"Be that as it may, but it's already a police state here, and we've all been taken over by a siege mentality."

"What are you suggesting?"

"I'd say leave these folks out west alone. It seems like all they're trying to do out there is get settled and survive. We should put all of our energy here into doing what they've managed to do out there. Get the power on, and get food for the people, not go off and try to rule the world."

"The president will never go for it, as long as he doesn't have the codes, or access to the satellites."

"When he does get them, do you think he's going to just sit back and start farming communities? No, he's going to 'project his power' all over the goddamn place," John said, getting angry himself.

"John, you'd better be careful where you say these things," the general warned.

"You asked me what I thought. I'm telling you. I haven't said anything to anyone else about how I feel," he lied, knowing he talked at length about this almost every night with his partner. "I'm not suicidal. I don't say anything to anyone about how I really feel."

"I'm frustrated with everything, just like you."

"Have you tried to reason with him?"

"I'd have better luck getting a camel through the eye of a needle," the general sighed.

"So we just sit and wait, and see what happens."

The general nodded. "Pretty much."

"So, we're just going to sit and wait, watch the good major head out west, and most probably destroy the last vestiges of civilization?"

"It's all we can do."

"Is it, General?"

"Yes, it is. We swore an oath, both of us, to obey the orders from the man sitting over at 1600 Pennsylvania Avenue, and that's exactly what we'll do."

"Yes, that's what we'll do, General," John said sadly. He made up his mind right then that he'd do something. He didn't know what, but he knew he'd do *something*. There were several thousand people here in the city that didn't need any more hollow promises, and he knew now that the general was a lost cause. "I think it's time we ended this conversation, John. Do what you need to do to get a radio to the major, and have it over to the Armory as soon as you can."

"Yes sir, General. Did he say when he'd be ready to leave?"

"He said he'd need to work out the logistics, maybe a few days."

"I'll get right on it and have something over to him tomorrow afternoon, probably."

"Good, I'll leave you to it then," the general said, getting up to leave. "Keep me updated."

"Will do."

"I'm going to take a walk. I need some fresh air," the general said, now deflated.

"You do that. I'll work on getting a radio to the major, and then I'm going to take this rig to my house and set it up there."

"Okay, John, and again, not a word of our conversation to anyone."

The general left the conference room and headed outside. He was short of breath and felt as though the walls were closing in on him.

He hadn't decided where he was going, and once outside of the building, made his way across the west parking lot, crossed the highway, and into Arlington National Cemetery.

He wandered around the now overgrown lawns, through acres of white headstones of his fallen brothers and sisters. Once the home of another Army General, Robert E. Lee, the site was taken over to inter the dead Union soldiers during the Civil War, some thought to insult the Confederate General.

The general walked for hours, weaving his way this way and that until, in the twilight of that spring day in Washington, he sat on the marble steps that led up to the Tomb of the Unknown Soldier.

His mind cleared somewhat by his long walk, he looked out over the vista and wept silently. He wasn't sure exactly why he was crying, but it poured out of him for some time.

He thought about what John had said, and knew in his heart of hearts that the man was right. However, he had sworn an oath, and he did have his honor. Then he thought of all those who had died defending what was once a great nation, many of those surrounding him at this very moment. He wept for everything that was lost, how every last one, if this last little piece of America was lost, would have died in vain.

That thought angered him to the core. He'd had over thirty years' service to this country, fought and bled, led men in battle, and survived it all. One cold November night six years ago, in the blink of an eye, humanity was all but erased from the face of the Earth.

He had wandered around for days, much like the way he'd done this day, until he started to meet up with other survivors, then the new president emerged, and for a while, he thought everything was going to be alright.

Had it all been a dream? Was humanity gone for good? Was what this new president had made for them what they needed, or would it all crumble like a house of cards with the slightest puff of breeze he knew for sure was just over the horizon?

He looked out over the marble monuments, saddened by the lack of care they'd received in the last few years. Weeds and debris were sprouting from every crack and fissure in the stonework, and soon, nature would most assuredly take back what was rightfully hers.

That last thought weighing heavily on his mind, he stood, brushing off some soil that was on his trousers, hung his head sadly and plodded back towards the Pentagon where he'd left his Hum-Vee.

Duty, Honor, Country. That's what had been ingrained upon him from the very onset of plebe year at the US Military Academy at West Point.

Duty, Honor, Country.

When he passed through the front gate in the last light of day, he saw the flag flying, torn and tattered, on a flagpole. It may be torn and tattered, a shadow of what once was great, but it was still his flag, by God. As he passed, he rendered a smart, proper salute, and with new-found steel in his spine, he marched a little straighter, his footfalls echoing in the silent, darkened city.

He knew then, without a shadow of a doubt, what he must do. Did he have the mettle, the intestinal fortitude to do it?

Only time would tell.

CHAPTER 9:
A LONG SUMMER

Tim sat on the bleachers along the first base line of a now overgrown Little League baseball diamond on the outskirts of town. The outfield grass was tall, and several ponderosa pine saplings we reaching for the sky by the second base line.

He looked out over the field, and through clouds of puffy white fluff from a cottonwood tree, his mind traveling back to a time long ago, and to a different baseball diamond.

It was the summer of his sixteenth year. He was stepping into the batter's box from the on-deck circle and the pressure was on. It was the deciding game in the City All-Stars. The score was five-six, and it was the bottom of the ninth inning. There were two outs, and bases were loaded. His team needed two runs to win this game and take the trophy home, and that reality hit home as soon as he stood in the box and looked down at the pitcher, who stood there eyeing him devoid of all emotion.

He wiped the sweat off his brow with his sleeve, and stood in his batting stance. He wasn't the best hitter on the team, and he could almost hear the moans of his teammates in the dugout. He was the worst batter on the team...

The pitcher wound up and threw the ball, and he swung with all his might, only to be rewarded by the 'whap' of the ball, landing into the catcher's mitt, and the umpire yelling, "Strike one!"

Undeterred, he stood at the ready again, and thrice more the pitcher threw his best fastball, but this time he kept his eye on the ball, didn't swing, and was rewarded by the umpire calling them balls.

He rolled his head to loosen the kink in his neck, and then the pitcher wound up again, throwing a fast breaking ball that Tim swung and missed. The count was now three and one, and the whole field got very quiet. It was almost as if someone had muted the crowd in the bleachers.

He crouched yet again, and stood at the ready. The pitcher looked at him for what seemed like an eternity, wound up, and peppered a fastball that was like a blur. Tim swung again, and missed, hearing yet again, that sickening sound of the ball landing home in the catcher's mitt.

The count was now three - two, bases loaded, winning run on second base. He stepped out of the batter's box for a second time, swung the bat a few times, and stepped back to the plate.

As he crouched in his batter's stance, time slowed down to half speed and the pitcher wound up. The ball screamed in, and Tim, not taking his eye off the blur, swung with all his might at the speeding projectile.

And then the sound.

Not just any sound, *the* Sound. The sound of Kentucky ash hitting speeding stitched leather in that sweet spot, the sound that every person in the stands heard and knew what it was...

Crack!

He felt it flow from his hands, up his arms, through his body and down to his toes, that *feel*...

The bat made a full arc around him, and he let it drop from his grip, and tore down the first base line with all the power he could muster. Halfway to first base, he chanced a look to see where the ball was, and when he saw it arcing up, further and further, deeper into centerfield, he slowed a little. When he saw it clear the outfield fence not by inches but by yards, a satisfied grin swept over his face, and he slowed his sprint to a leisurely jog.

He saw the centerfielder, who had been in a mad dash to catch the ball, stop, drop his shoulders in defeat and slam his baseball cap onto the ground in anger. The crowd erupted with cheers, and by the time Tim had rounded third base, his whole team was standing at home plate, hands extended, to high-five him when he touched home.

His teammates surrounded him, and as one, picked him up and started to carry him around the infield in an impromptu victory parade, and in his revelry, he looked out over the stands, searching, searching for the one face he so desperately wanted, *needed* to see...

That face wasn't there.

Why couldn't you have been there on that day, Dad?

"Penny for your thoughts?" came a familiar, pleasantly lilting voice, and he looked down at the bottom of the bleachers to see Holly climbing up. When she made it up to where Tim was sitting, she sat down next to him. "Izzy said you'd probably be here."

"Is that so?"

"Aye, he said he's seen you sitting up here a time or two the last few days," Holly said, taking hold of his arm. "What are you thinking about?"

"A time long gone," he said, staring out over the field.

"Did you used to play?" "Yeah, back in high school."

"A game I never understood. I prefer cricket. Were you any good?"

"Not really," he said sadly. "I was just thinking about my dad, actually."

"You've never talked about your past, Tim. Good thoughts, I hope?"

"Good and bad. He did provide for us growing up, but there were a lot of times he wasn't there. He'd promise he'd be there, then he wouldn't show up."

"Was it work?"

"Yeah, he worked a lot."

"A copper, like you?"

"No, he worked for the Department of Defense. He was important, always being called away for something or another."

"I'm sorry, Tim," she said, resting her head on his shoulder. "Are you worried you won't be there for our child?"

"The thought has crossed my mind."

"I have all the faith in the world in you, Sergeant Major."

"I'm glad you do. It seems like the older I get, the more I'm turning into him."

"He raised you rather well, I think."

"Oh, don't get me wrong. He was, in a lot of ways, a great dad. We never wanted for anything; we always had food on the table and a roof over our heads. But there were a lot of broken promises over the years."

"And you're afraid you'll make more promises you can't keep?" Holly asked softly.

"I've already failed, Holly. I couldn't protect April. Now we've got some piece of shit sitting over in a jail cell that I've got no clue what the fuck I'm going to do with."

"You and Izzy will work something out. There's got to be some good traits you've gotten from your dad."

"Well, there's one," he said.

Holly slapped him on his arm. "You are so naughty!" she scolded him.

"I come by it naturally," he replied, then laughed. "From the very beginning, all I wanted was to be left alone, and that is one thing I think I have in common with my dad."

"Was he a loner?"

"No, not really."

"I don't understand then."

"When we were kids, my maternal grandparents had a house on the south Jersey shore, in Wildwood. A few times a year, Thanksgiving, Christmas, Easter, we'd all pile into the car for the two hour drive down from Philly. When we'd get there, my mom and grandmom would sit in the parlor drinking tea and gabbing. Me and my brother would head down to the beach, while my dad would immediately head to the spare bedroom upstairs and 'nap' for the whole afternoon, only to come down at dinner, eat, and head back up for another nap, until it was time to go. We never stayed overnight."

"So you're saying your dad would go hide and nap, so he didn't have to listen to your Mum and Gran yammering all day?" Holly chuckled.

"Pretty much."

"Are you saying I yammer, Timothy Flannery?" she asked, crossing her arms.

Tim laughed loud and hard, and put his arm around her. "No, babe, I am not saying you yammer, but I can identify. I just want us to be left alone here, that's all. I want us, all of us, to have the lifelong equivalent of my dad's down the shore naps."

"I'm sure you'll have that."

"Are you? I'm not. There's so much out there beyond our settlement that we have no idea of. We do have it rather good. We've got plenty of food, electricity, hell, we even have a few working televisions and a huge library of DVDs. With the exception of millions of corpses lying around, it is just as if nothing has ever happened. My biggest fear is that at some point in the near future word will get out about this place and survivors will start flooding here."

"Would that be so bad?"

"It's a double-edged sword. On one hand, the more people we have, the more we'll be able to do. On the other, the old problems will come back. We saw it on Oahu, and here again, with that Colin killing April."

"That wasn't your fault, Tim."

"Deep down I know that, but I can't stop thinking I'm partially responsible."

"So what do we do, Tim? Do we run away and hide somewhere else? This is our home, Timothy. If we do that, we'll be running away from the unknown for the rest of our lives, and I know it's not in your nature to run away from anything," she said, fire now brewing in her eyes.

"I won't run, no. I do think that maybe we should have stayed on Oahu."

"Be that as it may, we're here now, and this is our home. Give it a chance to work, Tim. Not only for you, but for me and Robyn, the baby, and everyone else."

"Sometimes I think it's all a little too much."

"Tim, it's been almost two years since Izzy and I first met you."

"I know. Seems like I've known you both my whole life," he said, putting his arm around her shoulder, pulling her close. "And for that I'm eternally grateful."

"Just promise me one thing?"

"And that would be what?" he asked, kissing her on top of her head, and then playfully tugging on her long, thick ponytail.

"Give it a year. Let's stay here a year and see what happens. If it doesn't work, I'll be the first one to help you pack for the trip back to Hawaii."

"I'm sure Jerry would be glad to see us." "Aye, he would."

"I'll think about it."

"It's all I can ask."

"Sam Didinato and John Meadows left yesterday. We're down to only ten people here now," he said.

"They'll be back. When they return, they'll have the buffalo with them, and maybe a few horses."

"That other guy, the railroad guy, will be back at some point too. Robyn hasn't heard from him in a week or so. He was in Nevada somewhere the last time he checked in."

"It will be fine," Holly stated.

Tim had yet to tell her about the emergency warning Robyn had picked up on the Ham radio from Jerry Williams the other day. He'd told her to keep quiet about it for now, until he decided what to do about it. Though there was nothing at all he could do about it, it did worry him.

When Robyn had come running into the kitchen and told him of the warning, he went to the secure military satellite radio that they rarely used and called Jerry on a scrambled frequency he knew was secure. Jerry had told him that someone saying they were in Washington, DC and representing the US government had contacted them and demanded they state who they were. Jerry, not trusting anyone at this point, had issued the emergency warning and everyone went offline until they could figure out another frequency to use. Tim understood the ramifications, and concurred with Jerry. They'd have to find something else now that their communications were compromised. There weren't enough of the satellite radios to go around to every station, and no realistic way to get them to everyone even if there had been.

He felt extremely vulnerable right now, but he didn't dare let on to Holly, or anyone else at this point. That transmission might have been nothing, just some lone nut case with a Ham radio. The chances of there being a viable government anywhere in the world, let alone Washington, DC, after all of this time were astronomical, but he'd better know for sure before he said anything to anyone.

What if there *was* a government in DC? Was he then now doing the wrong thing by not trying to contact them? Wasn't he breaking the law by saying, no matter how well-intentioned he was, that he was the president? He let that thought slide from his mind for now and turned his attention back to Holly.

"Okay, babe. It will be fine."

"Stop worrying over things you have no control over. Isn't that what you always say?" she poked at him.

"Touché," he said, taking her hand. "Let's head back; my ass is getting sore sitting here."

They made their way down the wooden bleachers and through the tall grass out onto the road leading back into town. Tim held her hand tightly, and still, after all this time, felt like a teenager with her. Every time he was with her, his heart was light.

"I can't believe you walked all the way out here," he said.

"Izzy says I need to keep active and get plenty of exercise. Besides, you walked out here yourself."

"That I did," he agreed, "but I'm not five months pregnant."

"I'm not an invalid, Timothy." "It's only a mile to where I left my Hum-Vee. You didn't walk all the way from home did you?" he asked.

"I had Izzy drop me off. He was going to the doctor's office he's setting up as a clinic, so I hitched a ride into town."

"I left my ride by the jail. I checked in on our prisoner earlier."

"How was he?"

"Definitely cowed. Taco was coming in to give him lunch. Maybe he's still there."

They walked silently down the middle of the road, and looked forlornly at the darkened shops along Main Street, debris and dust covering everything. It still saddened him to the core, every time he was in town, but he brushed the thought aside. There was no use mourning the past.

They made their way down the road, and when they came into sight of the Sheriff's Office, they saw another Hum-Vee parked near Tim's in the lot among the dusty and disused patrol vehicles.

"Taco must still be there," he said, and picked up his pace a little.

When they set foot into the tiny, weed-strewn gravel lot, the side door burst open, and Jimenez came staggering out, blood covering his face.

Holly and Tim raced to the reeling man, who looked like he was about to fall over. They caught him just in time, and helped him to sit down on the concrete steps.

"What happened, Taco?" Tim demanded.

"Ah shit, Sar' Major. He clocked me good," Jimenez gasped, holding his head.

Tim looked at the man's head, and not seeing anything but a good gash and a swelling knot, stood and left him with Holly. He pulled his .45 automatic from a hip holster and bolted inside.

Holly sat down next to him, dabbing the blood on his face with a handkerchief she'd taken from her pocket. "Sorry," she said when he winced.

"It's okay, Ma'am. Nothing is hurt except my pride," he replied, trying to smile weakly.

Tim came out of the building, face red with anger. He placed the pistol back into the holster and looked up and down the street.

"I'm sorry, Sar' Maj—"

"Don't worry about that right now, Taco. Are you okay?"

"Yeah, I was just telling Holly that nothing hurt except my pride."

"What happened?"

"I came into town to give the asshole some lunch. I opened the cell door, and told him to stand at the far wall, just like you told me to do. He was on me in a flash. Hit me with something, I don't know. Everything went black for a while."

"Well fuck me running," Tim said in frustration.

"Did he get your piece?"

"I didn't have a handgun, but my carbine was in the Hum-Vee," Jimenez said.

Tim walked over and peered inside it, and was rewarded with the sight of the M4 still secured in the rack. He then went to his vehicle and saw that his was still safe, then checked each of the parked police cruisers, to again be rewarded by the sight of each shotgun firmly locked into its rack. "Well, thank fuck for small wonders," Tim said when he joined Holly and Jimenez. "He's not armed, as far as I can tell."

"I'm really sorry," the young man said again.

"Taco, forget about it. The only thing that's important is you're okay. He only hit you on the head, so no damage was done," Tim quipped, hoping to ease some of the man's hurt pride.

Now what the fuck are we going to do? he thought.

"Tim, we need to get him over to Izzy and have him checked out. He might have gotten a concussion," Holly said, helping Jimenez to his feet.

"You take him over to see Iz. I'll start looking around."

"Come on, Juan. Izzy's clinic is on the next block, do you think you can walk?"

"Yes, ma'am," Jimenez said, standing a little unsteadily.

Holly led him away. Before they were out of sight, Tim called out, "Taco, how long, do you think?"

"I dunno, Sar' Major, a half hour, maybe?"

Tim nodded his head and waved them to go, "You two get over to Izzy's. I'm going to start looking around."

Tim hopped into his Hum-Vee. He drove all over town, several times, and then up onto Interstate 40 and drove for several miles in both directions, finally giving up after a few hours. It would be like finding a needle in a haystack. He had no idea where Colin might have gone, or in what direction, he'd need a whole company of searchers with a helicopter and infrared cameras to find him at this point.

He cursed and punched the steering wheel, then started back into town. He pulled up in front of the clinic that Izzy had opened, shut the engine off, got out tiredly and entered the building. The reception area was empty, but he knew there wouldn't be a receptionist.

Tim walked through a door to the side, and hearing voices, followed the sound to an examining room, where he found Izzy, Holly, and Jimenez, the latter seated on the examining table, a gauze pad taped to his head. They all turned when Tim walked in.

"Any luck?" Jimenez asked.

"No, I didn't think I'd find him. He could be anywhere by now," Tim sighed, plopping down on a chair by the door. "How's your patient, doctor?"

"He'll have a headache tomorrow morning, but he should survive," Izzy said.

"Yeah, I figured that. Mexicans and Irishmen have hard heads."

"Tim, what are you going to do?" Holly asked.

"You two get Taco back to the house, and I'll go and break the news to Ian and Paula. They're not going to be excited about this."

Jimenez hung his head. "Ah shit, Sar' Major. I'm really sorry—"

"Stop it, Taco. It's partly my fault. I should have never let anyone with him alone like that. Stop worrying."

"If you say so, Sar' Major," he replied dejectedly.

"I'll come with you, Tim," Izzy said. "I was about done here today anyway."

"Okay, Juan, let's get you home," Holly said, helping him to his feet.

Tim got into his Hum-Vee, and Izzy rode with him, while Holly helped Jimenez into the passenger side of his vehicle, then followed Tim back towards their compound.

She caught up with him as he was turning into the dirt road the led up the house and pulled up next to him. She got out, and as she was helping Jimenez out, Robyn came out of the front door smiling, but the look faded when she saw the bandage on Jimenez' head.

"Oh, Taco, what happened?" she asked, running up to him.

"I beat up a fist with my head," he said with a weak grin, letting Holly and Robyn help him into the house.

"You wait here, Tim. I'll be right back," Izzy said, and entered the house, leaving Tim to sit on the steps of the porch. He reached into his pocket for his pipe, and then remembered he'd left it in the kitchen that morning.

Izzy came back out holding two bottles of beer. The old doctor handed one to Tim, and sat down beside him, twisting the top off of his own beer.

"I think I might need this today. I've still got to go and tell Ian and Paula," Tim said, taking a long pull from the bottle.

"I thought you might."

"Ah, fuck, Iz. What am I going to do?"

"Are you going to go out to look for him again?"

"No, I think it would be a waste of time."

"Why?" Izzy asked.

"He could be miles away by now. I'll go and check his house after I talk to Ian, but I'm not expecting him to have gone back there."

"True. He would truly be more stupid than I thought to have done that," Izzy agreed. "So then what?"

"Nothing more to do really. Arizona is a big state, but he's not familiar with the area or terrain outside of here. He's most probably headed east from here, maybe to Flagstaff. From there, he could find a vehicle maybe, and be gone for good. That's what I'm hoping."

"Is that what you're going to tell everyone?" Izzy asked.

"Yes. It's the truth. I'm not going to sugar-coat it."

"So he's gone then, as far as you're concerned. Will be no justice for April?" Izzy asked.

"Now wait a goddamn minute, Iz," Tim snapped. "If you think for a second that I'm happy about this, you're wrong. It would be a complete waste of time and effort to go looking for him; you know that, I know that. We've just got to take our lumps and get on with the day to day shit."

"I'm just playing the Devil's advocate for a minute, Tim. The others will want to know your reasoning."

"I know, Iz. I'm sorry for jumping down your throat like that. I'm just so frustrated," he said, and then it was time to drop the other bombshell he'd been keeping. He told Izzy about the warning and the message from Jerry on Oahu, and when he was finished, Izzy let out a whistle.

"What do you think that means?"

"I don't know, Iz, but I'm more than just a little worried about it."

"Should you be?"

"I'm not sure. Part of me wants to believe that even if there was a new government back in DC, they don't have the manpower or the resources to come out here, or even know where we are."

"And the other part?"

"The other part is telling me to pack up everything and get the fuck out of here."

"Even if they could, they have no idea where we are, do they?" Izzy asked, with real concern.

"No, they're probably in the same boat as us, technology wise. Right before we left to come back here, I locked out the whole system. No one can access the satellites now except me, and Jerry back on Oahu. I gave him the codes for them right before we left."

"So now we've got a fugitive running around out there somewhere who already raped and killed one of us, and now you're telling me something's brewing back east. That's not good, Tim. Not good at all," Izzy said, taking another long pull off the bottle.

"You don't need to remind me. I already promised Holly I'd try to make a go of it here, at least give it a year. Now I'm not so sure."

"We are fairly well hidden here, Tim. And now, thanks to Robyn, everyone is up to speed in the use of the weapons," Izzy said.

"Yeah. Like a little drill sergeant she is. She had everyone out on the range we set up every morning for over a week before she said she was satisfied. Came in one day after she was done, cursing like a trooper, saying if one more person called the rifle's magazine a 'Clipazine', her head would explode," Tim said, laughing.

"Chip off the old block, eh?" "That she is. I'm going to tell everyone this afternoon not to go anywhere alone, and never to go unarmed."

"Good idea," Izzy agreed.

"Ah shit, Iz. I didn't want to turn this into an armed camp."

"Living with a siege mentality is never good for one's soul. I know that's how Holly and I were, for a long time back in Colorado."

"It was the same with me and Robyn until we found this place. Everything's changing now. Summer will be here soon enough. It was really dry the last two, and we've got to trim back some of the trees by all the houses in case of a forest fire. That's a big priority. Food won't be a problem, but we've got to get wood cut and dried for next winter, a lot of it."

"We've got to do all of those things, I agree. Getting back to our fugitive, are you absolutely sure you want to leave him out there?"

"I'm not sure at all, goddamn it! What choice do we have? We could spend weeks out looking for him, and even if we do, we're still back to the problem of what we're going to do with his sorry ass."

"It must be a difficult decision to make, and I don't envy you."

Tim let out a sigh and drained his beer, then looked at the bottle longingly.

"Do you want another?" Izzy asked.

"Maybe later, I need to keep my mind clear right now. Maybe I'll get drunk after supper," Tim said with a rueful laugh.

"Good idea."

"Iz, I want you to reconsider moving into town. I know you want to, but I think the safe bet right now is for you to stay here."

"Under different circumstances, I'd argue with you on that. You're right, though. We've got safety in numbers here."

"It's only for a short time. I know you want to set up your clinic in town, but since everyone is here, you'd be better off setting it up in the compound. Maybe take over one of the other houses?"

The sun, which had been burning hot all morning, was suddenly blotted out by a dark shadow, and it made both men look up. A cumulus cloud was building to the south, its bottom black and bloated. There was no sound yet, though by the looks of it, a fairly good thunderstorm would be borne soon.

"It's an early one," Izzy said, gazing up at the gathering clouds.

"Yeah, it's about a month early. It just reinforces my thoughts about getting the trees trimmed back. It just takes one lightning strike to start a forest fire, and I don't want that to happen." Tim shuddered, remembering all too vividly the raging firestorm that swept through Philadelphia so many years ago.

"I hope this isn't a bad omen."

"Same here, Iz."

"I'll agree to set up here. Actually, it's more practical. Everyone *is* here, so if they need medical attention, they won't have to go far."

"I was thinking the same thing when you first brought it up, but I know you can be stubborn when you set your mind on something."

Izzy guffawed. "That's the pot calling the kettle black, now isn't it?"

"Me, stubborn? What on Earth ever gave you that idea, my good doctor?" Tim asked theatrically, and they had a good laugh for a minute, and then Tim grew serious again. "We go about things here as usual, getting the trees cut back from the houses, getting firewood ready for next winter, do a little hunting. Mundane, everyday stuff, and I'll spread the word today about keeping together, no going out alone, and staying armed at all times. We won't tell them about the other stuff. Only you, Robyn, Holly, and I know about the warning from Jerry. I don't want everyone getting paranoid. I'll tell everyone to keep their doors locked at night too."

"Yes, that would be a prudent warning. I might go up and take over Colin's house for my clinic since he won't be using it anymore."

"You might as well."

"What are you going to tell them to do if they see him?" Izzy asked.

Tim stood up, put his hands on his hips and looked around the clearing. The clouds were stacking up rather quickly, and there was a gathering breeze that was coming with it. Both men could smell the rain now, which was surely coming their way. Tim looked down, frowned. "I'm going to tell them if they see him, put a bullet into him."

"Just like that?"

"Just like that, Iz. No fucking around with him this time. I should have done it the day we found April's body," Tim said with a grim, determined nod.

"What about all the things you said about following the laws, and the Constitution? Are you just going to throw that idea out the window?"

"Iz, I meant that, and I want to do that. But we're a little thin to be thinking that far ahead at this point. I was foolish enough to even consider it when we placed him in that jail cell."

"Fair enough, I guess. It's not like we have a judge and a few lawyers about to have a trial. It was pretty cut and dried what had happened," Izzy agreed grimly.

"It doesn't make it any easier on my conscience."

"I wonder if the same thoughts occurred in the minds of the first European settlers here, so many years ago," Izzy mused aloud.

"That thought has crossed my mind a couple of times also. It's just about the same. They were here, alone, with no direct contact with the rest of the world, pretty much on their own in the wilderness. They could have been on the moon for all that mattered," Tim said.

"And they did okay, didn't they?"

"That they did. And so shall we. But, Iz, let's make sure we don't have any witch hunts like in Salem, alright?

Izzy gave a little laugh at that one. "I agree. What else do you plan on doing?"

"As soon as you say Taco is okay, I think he and I will take another trip over to Camp Navajo to see what kinds of goodies we can scare up, stuff we can use for defense."

"No siege mentality?"

"I can't rule that out for now, Iz. It's a whole new world, one we're still learning to deal with."

"I'm sure you'll be able to work out a good defense for us."

"It's something I'm not used to, Iz. I'm more of an offensive thinker."

"As most good soldiers are," Izzy said sagely. He stood and made a move to head inside. "I think I'll go check in on my patient."

"Wow, a doctor who makes house calls."

Izzy grinned and entered the house.

Tim heard the distant rumble of thunder. He walked over to his Hum-Vee and retrieved his carbine, slinging it over his shoulder, then went up the dirt road that led up to the other houses in the compound.

"Let's get this over with," he said to the trees, and headed up the road towards Ian and Paula's house.

It was going to be a long summer.

CHAPTER 10: FAIR WINDS AND FOLLOWING SEAS

The sounds of the Andrews Sisters, complete with the pops and crackles of the old vinyl 73 rpm record, one of hundreds Suplee had found in the radio shack of the ship, came out of the speakers in the officer's wardroom of the freighter. Suplee had thought it would be a nice idea to have it piped throughout the ship during the day.

Everyone sat at the long table enjoying a breakfast that Mary had made that morning. In between bites, their three visitors told them their individual stories of survival.

The oldest one, a man in his late thirties, bald as a cue ball and tattooed in full sleeves, set down his coffee cup and sighed. "So there you have it. After everyone died, we sort of found each other, and made a go of it here on the base over the last few years. We thought we were the only ones left, then the other day we saw this ship sail in, and we were in shock."

"I'll bet," Ensign Johnson commented.

"You said that you were going to be sailing this ship over to Hawaii. I talked it over with Steve and Beth last night, and if you'll have us, we'd like to come with you. Help you crew the ship."

"I can't say that we don't need the help, Chief," Johnson said. "I know you were a Navy man, a chief petty officer, and I could use your expertise. Harry here was a Petty Officer on our last ship. We've been through a lot together, been through hell, actually. He's now my First Officer on this ship. I know you outrank him in the old life, but things are different now. You won't have any problems with that, will you?"

"No, sir, none at all. We all understand completely. We just want the opportunity to do more than just survive. We all thought that we were the only ones left, for a long, long time. Now you say that there's a settlement in Pearl, and another one in Arizona? Hell, I'm just happy to see you all!"

"Alright then. I know I need the help." Johnson turned to his other visitors. "Do you agree with him?"

"I don't know a thing about ships, I was a manager at a diner, Steve said. "I'd like to learn, and be of use." He was in his early thirties, bespectacled, and had long, mousy brown hair, and a pleasant enough disposition.

"A diner, eh? Maybe we can utilize you here, and you can help Mary in the galley," Johnson said.

The only other visitor, a slight waif of a girl in her early twenties that had short, severely cropped blonde hair that still had the remaining streaks of pink from a bad dye job still visible smiled broadly, and added, "I was a student at U-Cal. Liberal Arts. I don't know how useful I'd be, but like my friends said, I'd like to be helpful."

"I'm sure we can find a place for all of you," Johnson said. "Like I said, though, this is a ship, not a democracy. What me, Mr. Suplee or Mr. Nakamura say, goes."

"Anything you say, Mr. Johnson," the Chief said. "And I guess you can call me Ken."

"Welcome to the *SS Jeremiah O'Brian*. I guess you'd like to move in as soon as possible, and there are plenty of cabins to choose from below, so take your pick."

"Thank you, sir, we'll do that right away. What's the first order of business?" Ken asked.

"First thing is, I'd like to get her alongside the docks, and then fill up her bunkers with oil. Then we've got to get some pressure washers on deck and get all this bird shit cleaned up, and get the rust painted. It's going to be a big job, and you'll be happy to know I'm one of those officers who doesn't mind getting dirty."

"Sir, I'm glad you said that. She is a sight. If you want, we can get started on that this morning," Ken said eagerly.

"Alright then, that's settled. Mr. Nakamura?" Johnson said, turning to the Japanese man. "If you could, fire up the boilers after you're done eating."

"I start right away, Johnson-San," Nakamura said, picking up his cleared plate and standing with a respectful bow, and then leaving.

"I'll clean up here," Mary said, leaving the rest still at the table.

Johnson looked over his now doubled crew. "It'd be nice to have a few tugs to help us alongside the pier," he said. "But I think we should do okay without tearing too much up."

"Agreed, Mr. Johnson," Ken said.

"Sir, once we're alongside, I'd like to do that thing we discussed before," Suplee said.

"Absolutely, get that out of the way, Harry. I think it'll clear your mind."

"Yes sir. I'll get right on making preparations to get underway, Skipper," Suplee said, standing and leaving the wardroom.

Steve and young Billy started to clear off the table of the dirty dishes, leaving Ensign Johnson and Beth alone. The woman looked at the officer with a puzzled look after watching Suplee leave.

"Anything wrong?" he asked her.

"No, I was wondering what you meant by 'do that thing' is all," she said, unabashed, and that made him raise his eyebrows. The girl was rather outspoken, he'd noticed, saying whatever popped into her head without thinking it rude or nosey. Johnson decided that no harm would come of telling her.

"Mr. Suplee had a wife who was expecting, here in San Diego before everything happened. This was our home port, and he had an apartment not far from here. He just wants to go over, and, well…" he trailed off, becoming uncomfortable all of a sudden.

"He wants to be sure she's dead. I understand. I'll go with him, if you don't mind, I've got a car. It's rigged to run on propane. Ken did it."

"You'd better ask Harry first. It is kind of a personal mission," he said.

"I understand. I'll ask him," Beth said, and then left him alone in the wardroom, leaving him with his thoughts.

He still hadn't told anyone else about the warning from Jerry on Oahu; only he and Suplee knew about it. He decided to let it rest for the time being. There was nothing they could do about it, and getting the ship seaworthy was his number one priority.

Johnson left the wardroom, heading down to the engine room to help Nakamura with the boilers. It took several hours to get the steam up to pressure, and with a mad dash from the wheelhouse to the wing bridge, and frantic signals on the ship's telegraph, they finally brought the lumbering ship alongside the main fueling pier of San Diego Naval Base.

After another mad dash to get her tied up securely before drifting back out into the channel, they got a diesel generator out to the fuel oil pumps, ran the hoses up the ship's bunker fill ports, and soon they were transferring thousands of gallons of oil from the holding tanks on shore to the ship.

Johnson was on the bridge, staring out at the naval base, while Billy was playing with the ship's wheel and making motor noises without a care in the world. Johnson looked at his son and smiled, hoping the boy could hold onto his innocence as long as he could. Movement in the corner of his eye drew his attention, and he looked over to see Suplee entering the bridge. He walked over to the boy and ruffled his hair.

, "Skipper," Suplee said to the boy, "you sure did a great job getting the ship to the dock!"

"Aye, aye, Mr. Suplee!" the boy beamed and saluted. Suplee returned the boy's salute and walked out to the wing bridge where Johnson was still standing.

"I told Mr. Nakamura to secure the boilers for now, that we'd probably be here for a few weeks while we get the ship ready, Skipper. Smoking lamp is out, and we're taking on oil at a good rate. Ken is supervising the fueling, and we should be topped off in a few hours."

"Very good, Harry, is there anything else?"

"Not really. Ken also says he knows where a few pressure cleaners are, so we'll get on that tomorrow, and then get some paint on the rust. I'll head over to the ship's stores tomorrow to see what we can stock up in the way of food. He says there's still shitloads of non-perishable stuff over there, it's what they've been living on these last few years. We should be well set, I think."

"Harry, do you think you'll have a problem with him?"

"You mean the rank thing?" Suplee asked. When Johnson nodded, he said, "Not at all. We had a good talk earlier when we were setting up the fuel oil pumps. I told him everything we went through on the *Hughes*. He understands completely. He'll be a team player. I think they're all just as happy as pigs in shit to be with us."

"As long as you're okay with it. I want to know of the first inkling of any problems though, got it?"

"Aye, Skipper."

"We've been through too much to let some ego bullshit get in the way."

"No problem, Bill."

"I mean it, Harry. The first feeling of shit you get, I want to know about it," Johnson insisted.

"Skipper, I'll let you know, I promise. Now, that other thing..." Suplee said, looking out over the basin.

"Yeah, you head out and take care of that," Johnson said with a nod of encouragement. "Go and get the girl, Beth. She said she had a car, and that she could drive you around for any errands you need to run."

"We've already talked," Suplee said with an odd look on his face, sort of a cross between bewilderment and a smile.

"Get on to it. Daylight is wasting away."

"I'm going to see if I can scare up some air-con units too."

"Make that a priority. It'll be like an oven below decks soon, and then we'll all be sleeping out on the forecastle."

"Okay, Skipper. I'm off."

"Harry," Johnson said before he walked away. "Take a rifle with you."

"What for, sir?"

"That wasn't a suggestion, Harry. These new people may not have seen anyone else, but it never hurts to be safe."

"Aye, Skipper. I'll grab one of those M4s that the sergeant major gave us."

"Be careful out there."

"I will, Dad," Suplee quipped, leaving the bridge and making his way down to his cabin where he retrieved a carbine from his locker. After loading a 30-round magazine in the weapon, he shouldered it and headed down the three decks to the gangplank, which led onto the pier. He did a quick inspection of the fuel lines running up to the ship, and seeing everything was in order, he looked around for Beth.

He found her sitting Indian style smoking a cigarette on the hood of a beat up and rusted Yugo. She smiled when she saw him, flicked the butt aside, and hopped down.

"This is your car?" Suplee asked, wide eyed.

"I know it's not much, but it gets us around town," Beth said, heading to the driver's side door, which squealed loudly when she opened it, its hinges sorely in need of lubrication.

"A Yugo," he said with a snort, and got in the passenger's side, sitting down on the dusty and cracked seat. The sun was high and bright, and the day warm, so he rolled down the window as they drove through the base, letting some cool air into the overheated interior.

"Thanks for driving," he said amiably. "Hey, it's been a while. Could I bum a smoke off of you?"

"It's been a while for what, Harry?" she asked with a coy, sideways smile. She handed him an open pack of Marlboros with one hand without taking her eyes of the road. Suplee took one out, and lit it with a butane lighter she held out, blowing the smoke out the window.

"A little stale, but beggars can't be choosers," Suplee said, savoring the smoke.

"There's a bucket load at the PX on base. A lot of everything," she said, giving him a sideways glance as she headed out of the main gate.

"Head up Division Street, my place is over in Valencia Park," he directed, and Beth turned the wheel and headed east.

"The complex on the corner of Valencia Parkway?" she asked.

"Yeah, that's the one."

"I know right where it is."

The drove along in silence, and Suplee looked out at the passing buildings. Everything looked rundown, weeds growing everywhere. Dust and dirt coated everything, and years of paper and trash had accumulated in every nook and cranny. It looked like it hadn't been occupied for a thousand years. He didn't see any bodies, but it had be over six years since that terrible day, and all would have been consumed by buzzards and coyotes a long time ago. He was glad of that, but the thought of that still made him shudder.

Beth turned into the parking lot that was lined with tall, dead palm trees. In fact, Suplee realized, *all* of the trees around were dead, and he wondered why. Then it hit him, most of Southern California was really a desert, and the vegetation had only thrived in this city because of irrigation. With no people or power to run the pumps, the water ran dry, so the trees died.

She pulled up in front of the building that Suplee had indicated and shut the engine off. She looked over at him questioningly. Suplee looked at the façade of the two-story building and sighed, making a move to open the door.

"Do you want me to come with you?" she asked.

He thought about it for a moment, then shook his head. "No, you stay here."

Suplee got out, retrieved his carbine, and headed into the courtyard. He walked through a gate and passed a swimming pool that all of the apartments faced. Once filled with sparkling clear water and surrounded by children's laughter, it was now dead, only half-filled with dirty water, an ugly dark green from an algae bloom. It was now nothing more than a mosquito farm. He made his way along the path that led to his front door.

He stared at it for several moments, thinking about what to do. He'd lost his keys years ago. He took the carbine and racked a round into the chamber, taking the safety selector and placing it on three-round burst.

Taking aim at the doorknob, he squeezed the trigger once, and a short blast erupted from the rifle with a deafening roar in the enclosed area. The door splintered some, but the lock held fast. He laughed at himself.

"I guess that only works in the movies," he cracked out loud.

He slung the carbine back over his shoulder, kicked out with his booted foot just to the right of the doorknob, and was rewarded by the sounds of cracking and splintering wood as the door flew inwards.

He stood there another moment, looking into the darkened portal, and then went through the door. He scanned the sparsely furnished living room. Everything was covered in a thick layer of dust, but other than that, looked pretty much as when he last saw it.

He wandered around the apartment, looking at this and that, and then went down the short hall towards the bedroom. A sickly-sweet smell permeated this part of the flat, and as he neared the closed door to the sole bedroom, he reached for the doorknob with a shaking hand.

His heart was beating so loud he thought that it might beat out of his chest, and in the dim light coming through the bedroom window, he saw a form, blackened and mummified, lying half covered on the bed. The same mousey blonde hair he remembered from so long ago was spread about the form's head like a sick halo.

He looked over to a crib that had been erected next to the bed, saw a small form wrapped in a dusty pink blanket and he began to shake. Bile rose in his throat, and he turned to leave, not before his breakfast came up, spraying the wall in the tiny hallway. He rushed to get outside, but made it as far as the living room again, where he dropped to his knees and vomited the rest of his stomach's contents on the pale gray carpet that he'd always hated.

He vomited until he was dry-heaving, and when he was truly finished, he braced himself on the cheap IKEA coffee table and stood on shaking legs. He looked up, and through tear stained and blurry eyes, saw a figure standing in the doorway framed by the bright afternoon sun.

He pushed by the figure and out into the courtyard where he collapsed into a dirty lounge chair by the filthy swimming pool. He set the carbine down on the seat next to him, and placing his face in his palms, wept loudly, sobbing uncontrollably. He felt a hand on his shoulder, then an arm circled around him, pulling his head down into a warm, inviting bosom.

He felt Beth's hand in his hair, and she cooed comfortingly while he cried. After a while, the sobs slow down, and he looked up at her.

"I heard the shots, and I figured I'd come to see if you needed help," she said softly, running her fingers through his hair.

"I shouldn't have come. I knew what I'd find," he said, sniffling up some snot that had leaked from his dripping nose.

"You had to," she said.

"I shouldn't have come… I just had to find out."

"Now you know. I'll probably never know what happened to my family for sure," she told him, taking out a tissue and handing it to him. "Here, blow your nose."

He took the offered tissue and blew loudly several times, clearing his sinuses. He smiled at her weakly. "Thanks."

"C'mon, cutie!" she said with a grin, standing and taking his hand. "Let's get out of here."

"Where to?" he asked, following her back to the car. She didn't say a word until they were both back into the battered Yugo and headed west on Division Street.

"I'm taking you someplace nice. Somewhere I haven't been in a while.

She lit a cigarette, handing him the pack. He lit a smoke too, and was pleasantly surprised when she took his hand.

They drove through dead, empty streets through town and she took the route 75 Causeway across to Coronado, and followed that down where it headed south again, turning into Orange Avenue then Silver Strand Boulevard, passing the US Marine Corps Amphibious Warfare Center until finally stopping along the side of the road that edged up to a strip of deserted beach that kissed the Pacific Ocean.

Stopping the car, she hopped out, grabbed a blanket from the cramped back seat, then walked onto the beach. Suplee was still sitting in the car, looking out at her.

"Don't just sit there, c'mon!" she yelled, and ran down towards the water. Suplee reluctantly exited the vehicle, leaving the carbine behind, and followed her down to where she'd spread the blanket on the sandy white beach.

He sat down on the blanket and looked up at her standing only feet away. With a sly smile, Beth crossed her arms and grabbed the bottom of her tank top, and with one yank, pulled it over her head, exposing firm breasts with nipples pointed to the sky.

"I'm going for a swim!" she exclaimed, kicked off her sandals and cut off shorts, spun, and ran naked into the surf. She swam out a few yards. "Come on in!" she yelled at him.

"Harry, you'd better do what the lady says," he said to himself, stood and stripped. He ran out through the surf, swimming up to where Beth was treading water. She closed in on him, wrapping her arms around his neck, and kissed him deeply and passionately.

They broke the kiss and looked into each other's eyes for a moment, and then Suplee grabbed her hand and led her out of the surf, up the beach to the blanket she had laid out. He plopped down, and pulled her down on top of him, kissed her deeply again, more urgently this time.

He rolled her onto her back, and climbing on top of her, entered her easily. The made love frantically, madly, and when it was over, Suplee fell by her side on his back, breathless. The sun's rays warmed their bare skin, and she laid her head on his chest, hair still wet from their dip in the sea.

"That was incredible," Suplee said, running his fingers down her spine.

"Yes, it was," she replied, moving up to kiss him again. When their lips parted, she said, "It's been a really long time."

"It has, hasn't it?"

"Far too long."

"Didn't you and Steve or Ken…you know?"

"Steve, Ken, and I have one thing in common, Harry. All three of us like boys," she snickered. She sat up, located her tank top, and pulled it on, much to Suplee's dismay. He was enjoying looking at her naked body, and he reached up and caressed her breast through the thin cotton.

"You're telling me they're both gay?"

"Yes, unfortunately for me the last few years," she said. She stood and pulled on her shorts. "You'd better get dressed, or you'll get sunburn places you shouldn't be!"

Suplee pulled on his blue jeans, and after Beth picked up her sandals and the blanket, he followed her to the car. She tossed the blanket in the back unceremoniously, and they both got in. He looked at her for a moment before speaking,

"So you've been alone with two gay guys the whole time?"

"Talk about irony," she said wryly, started the car and drove off. "I thought it was me at first. Then one night, it was shortly after we all met, we got a little drunk and I put the moves on Ken, and well…"

"He let you know he had eyes for Steve," he finished for her. He lit a cigarette, and blew the smoke out of the window. The breeze felt good coming through the open windows of the ancient Yugo as they sped back towards the base.

"I resigned myself to a life of celibacy," Beth said. "I thought us three were the only ones left."

"And then we showed up."

"I know, right? We saw that ship of yours come steaming up the channel, and I thought to myself, *please, if there really is a god, let there be one heterosexual man on board!*"

"Lucky for you."

"Yes, lucky for me. I just didn't know that one as cute as you would be on it when my ship finally came in!" Beth reached over and took his hand, and he looked at her in amazement, turning red at the compliment.

"It's been a long, long time, Beth," he said. He took another drag of the cigarette and looked out over the causeway. He could see their ship tied up at the pier, and wondered if it might actually work.

"Are you going to be okay, Harry?"

"I think so. I just had to know, you know?"

"I bet you think I'm some kind of heartless bitch, coming on to you like that, right after …"

"Under normal circumstances, maybe. However, this is far from being anywhere near normal. It hasn't been normal for me, for any of us, in a long, long time. I knew she was dead. I knew my kid was dead. I resigned myself to it a long time ago, back when me and Johnson were still on the *Hughes*. I just needed to see for myself, is all. What we did, well, it was fantastic, and I don't think either of us should feel guilty about it," he said, flicking the butt out of the window.

Beth pulled the car up along the curb next to an overgrown park, which looked more like a dried out meadow than an inner city park. She shut the car off, and got out, grabbing the blanket. She walked through some dead brown grass up to a picnic table, and Suplee followed her, wondering what she was up to.

She spread the blanket out on the tabletop, and in the shade of the dead trees, stripped off her top again. She tossed it aside and put her hands on her hips, tilting her head to one side. "We won't get sunburned here."

Suplee stripped and took her in his arms. They made love a second time, slower this time, less urgent. When they were finished, they lay together on top of the table looking up through dead branches and the sky. The sun had crept west, and daylight was waning.

"We'd better get back to the ship," Suplee said sadly. He didn't want to lose the moment.

"Yeah, they'll wonder what happened to us," Beth agreed, standing reluctantly, and began to dress. They walked hand in hand back to the car and with Suplee at the wheel this time, headed off towards the base.

Halfway back, Suplee snapped his fingers. "Damn, almost forgot!"

"Forgot what?"

"Forgot about the air-con units. You are quite the distraction," he said with a wicked grin.

"I'll take that as a positive thing, Harry."

He turned into a huge appliance store parking lot a few blocks from the main gate to the base. When he and Beth went up to the glass doors and Suplee tried to pull them opened, he found them locked securely. He took the carbine out of the back seat, flicked off the safety and fired one round into the middle of the glass pane.

A neat, round hole appeared in the center, and being safety glass like that in automobile windows, it cracked and splintered into thousands of pieces but stayed intact.

He used the butt of the rifle to beat out the glass until all of the shards were piled on the dusty tiled floor of the showroom like millions of diamonds. He took Beth's hand and carefully walked through the opening into the darkened store.

They walked through the aisles of refrigerators, washing machines, and stoves towards the rear of the store until they found the rows of window unit air conditioners.

"Here's what we need," he said, tapping on the dusty shell of a General Electric 2,500 BTU window unit.

"Just this one will cool the whole ship?" she asked.

"Oh no, we need about twenty or thirty of the bastards."

"We won't fit them in my car, silly!"

"I just wanted to see if they have enough. I'll check the back to see if they do, and we'll come back tomorrow with a bigger vehicle."

Beth followed him deeper into the dim building. He walked through a set of double doors that had a sign on it that read 'EMPLOYEES ONLY' and cursed himself for not thinking to bring a flashlight.

The storeroom was dark, but there was enough light coming through the skylights in the roof to let them see, and as their eyes grew accustomed to the dimness, Suplee found what they were looking for. Satisfied, he took her hand and turned to leave when he heard a noise in the rear.

A chill rose up his back and he grabbed the carbine slung across his back reflexively, shouldering it and aiming into the darkness.

"What is it?" Beth whispered, clutching his arm in a death grip.

"I don't know, probably nothing. Let's get out of here," he said in a normal voice, which sounded like a scream that echoed through the darkened room. They made their way back out through the store and into the parking lot without further incident, where they got back into the Yugo and headed for the base.

"That place gave me the creeps," Beth said.

"Actually, the whole city gives me the creeps. I never thought I'd hear myself say this, but I can't wait to get back to sea."

"It's the same for me, Harry, every day for the last several years. I can't wait to get out of this place and sail the seven seas with you!"

"It's not all fun and games, Beth. It's a lot of hard work. That ship of ours is over eighty years old, and was designed to be manned by over thirty men," Suplee said.

"Living here has been so hard. Not so much with lack of food, mind you. It's just the fact that we're surrounded by millions of corpses. Every time I drive out, I just think of the millions of dead everywhere. It gets to you after a while."

"It's a necropolis," he said flatly.

"Yeah, that's a good word for it, a City of the Dead. I for one want to keep on living."

Suplee pulled up to the dock next to the ship and shut the car off. The both got out and made their way up the gangplank onto the ship, where they were met at the top by Johnson.

"How'd it go?" Johnson asked.

"About as much as I expected, Skipper," Suplee replied.

"That bad, eh?"

"We made a few other discoveries, Captain," Beth said with a wide smile.

"Oh?" Johnson asked. "Did you find the air con units?"

"Yeah, we found those, too," Beth said and Suplee turned beet-red. Johnson looked at Suplee with a quizzical look.

"There's an appliance store not far from here. We'll have to go back tomorrow with a bigger vehicle, but there's more than enough to fit every cabin in the ship."

"Good. If you think it can wait a few days, I think the priority should be getting all this shit cleaned off, paint the rust, and slap some Brasso on the bright work," Johnson said.

Suplee and Beth made their way to the upper decks, where they excused themselves and entered Suplee's cabin, leaving Johnson standing in the passageway wearing a grin.

"Well, well, Harry. Seems like you got yourself lucky with this shore leave," he said, and headed towards the galley.

It took them several weeks, but with everyone's help, they were able to get the years' worth of accumulated bird droppings off of every surface on the ship, and not one, but two coats of fresh gray paint on all the rusted surfaces. Suplee's plan to outfit each of the cabins with air conditioners worked like a charm, and even the galley and mess decks were now cool. He'd done the job so well, in fact, they looked like they'd always been installed.

The fuel oil bunkers were again topped off, and the galley's stores were loaded with as much food as they could stow. They had found several intact containers of flour at the ship's store on the naval base. Mary was busy in the galley baking several fresh loaves of bread that Johnson and Suplee could smell up on the bridge, and the pleasant aroma made their stomachs rumble in anticipation.

Black smoke poured out of the lone funnel and trailed behind the ship as they passed Cabrillo National Monument and left Coronado in their wake far to the east. They were in blue water now, steaming for Pearl Harbor.

Johnson was out on the port wing bridge looking down onto the cargo deck where Steve and Beth were busy stowing the mooring lines just the way that Suplee and Ken had shown them. Ken was in the engine room with Nakamura, and he heard the reassuring throb of the powerful steam engine through the decks. Like Suplee had told Beth a few weeks prior, Johnson too was very happy to get to sea and get out of the dead city.

He took a great breath of sea air into his lungs and smiled. He then entered the bridge, where he found Suplee standing at the helm and looking at the binnacle and ship's compass, ensuring they were on the course set forth by the captain.

"How's it going, Harry?" Johnson asked when he walked into the bridge. It took a minute for his eyes to adjust to the dimness and he saw that Suplee was smiling broadly.

"Right on course, Skipper, doing about nine knots. I spoke with Mr. Nakamura this morning, and he figures we might be able to squeeze about two more knots out of her if we can get all the years' worth of accumulated barnacles off the hull."

"I figured as much. Maybe we can get some help in Pearl with Sergeant William's men to get her into a dry-dock."

"It'd be nice if the hull was a tad sleeker, eh?"

"Like the *Hughes*?" Johnson asked wryly.

"Well, yeah. Twenty-five to thirty knots is a lot better than nine any day."

"True. This is just right for my liking though. Those tin cans will always give me nightmares from now on."

"Sorry I brought it up," Suplee said in an unusually tiny voice.

"Don't sweat it, Harry. I know she's a tub, but she's all ours. So what if it's going to take us two weeks to get to Pearl?"

"The ship's complement is a whole lot nicer too, Skipper," Suplee said cheerfully.

"I'll bet."

"I've been meaning to talk to you about that. I know you probably think I'm some kind of shit for doing that, and I'm sorry."

"Sorry for what?"

"You must think I'm some kind of asshole for hooking up with Beth the same day I go and find my dead wife and child. I didn't even bury them for Christ sake."

"I think nothing of the sort, Harry. It's a completely different world now, and the rules have changed. You're a great guy, and a fantastic shipmate and sailor. You deserve to be happy."

"That might be right, but some rules are still the same. The law of the sea, civilization ends at the waterline. Beyond that, we all enter the food chain, and not always right at the top," Suplee deadpanned, and that made Johnson laugh heartily.

"I never took you as a Hunter S. Thompson fan."

"I read a lot, Skipper," Suplee said. "So you're cool with it?"

"Yes, Harry, I'm cool with it. I'm glad you're happy."

"I am. I just kept up a false hope, I think. I saw you with Mary when we first got to Pearl, and I had high hopes that I'd find my wife alive too. I knew better. It's just that seeing them both lying there in my apartment took all the wind out of my sails."

"It's a far different world now. As far as I am concerned, everyone on this ship is now family as well as crew," Johnson stated.

"Thanks, Skipper."

"We also have to keep this tub afloat and get her to Pearl, so that gives us all added incentive to do a good job."

"And incentive to stay on top of the food chain!" Suplee added with a grin.

"That too," Johnson agreed.

"I do have to say this, Bill. I've got this odd feeling it's not going to be boring at all sailing with you!"

"I hope not, just as long as it's not as exciting as our last voyage."

Steve and Beth entered the bridge then. "All of the lines are stowed," Steve informed them. "Anything else you need us to do?"

"I need to you spell Harry on the helm for a while, Steve. I need him to be rested to con the ship over the mid watch," he said. "Harry, you go and get yourself some rest. I'll show Steve what to do here on the bridge. It's a clear afternoon, we've got fair winds and following seas, and we're in deep water now. I don't foresee any problems."

"Aye, Skipper," Suplee said, stepping back from the wheel. "Mr. Johnson has the con, Steve has the helm!" he announced, and walked over to Beth and took her hand. As they both went to leave, Johnson called out, "And I mean rest, Mr. Suplee!"

Suplee smiled broadly and disappeared into the passageway with Beth in tow.

Johnson took a few moments to go over a few things with Steve, who listened and nodded, taking it all in. After he was settled in his new job, Johnson took a moment to scan the ocean in front of the ship. Satisfied all was in order, he hung his binoculars on the binnacle and sat down in the captain's chair with a sigh.

"This is all exciting," Steve said.

"Well, Steve, let's hope it doesn't get *too* exciting. A nice, quiet, and easy voyage is what I'm looking for."

"Eh, yeah, I mean it's all new to me. I've never been out of California, let alone on a ship in the ocean."

"Fair winds and following seas, Steve." Johnson then got up and walked out onto the starboard wing bridge, letting the sea air hit his face. His thoughts went back to what Suplee had said, how he thought that sailing with him would be exciting.

Well, he thought, *let's not get too exciting.*

He had a bad feeling creep over him. He looked out over the sea again, and a few seagulls squawked and circled the ship. He looked down to the wake, where two dolphins were playing and racing with the ship as she plowed on westward. It was a beautiful day, and indeed a perfect day for sailing. He hoped there were no storm clouds brewing beyond the horizon. He was now a seasoned sailor, and he knew better. Things in the future were going to get very exciting indeed, and there wasn't a thing he could do to change it.

They were nowhere near the point of no return yet, and California was still visible and a brown smudge on the eastern horizon. No, he couldn't turn back. He walked back into the bridge, and seated once again on the captain's chair, tried to relax as best he could. He thought about the long chain of bizarre events that had led him to this place and time and shook his head in disbelief.

If someone had pulled him aside six years ago, right before he sailed out of Pearl Harbor on the *USS Hughes,* and told him that one day in the near future over six billion people would die in the blink of an eye, and that he and Suplee would be on a nightmare voyage with an insane captain fighting for their very lives, he would have laughed in their face.

It wasn't so funny now.

His mind again turned back to what Suplee had said about the food chain, and he had to agree. Untold thousands of ships over the centuries had sailed off over the horizon, never to be seen again, their fate unknown to all but those who sailed with them.

A nearly imperceptible shudder when through his body at the thought. Only time would tell how things played out. He let the ship's engines' vibrations relax him as he settled his mind for the long voyage ahead.

CHAPTER 11:
AN EMPTY VESSEL

It was an unusually hot mid-June afternoon at Camp Navajo, and Jimenez was stripped to the waist, glistening with sweat as he hefted the last of what seemed like thousands of cases of MREs to Tim, who was standing in the bed of the deuce-and-a-half truck parked outside of one of the myriad bunkers they had gained access to.

Tim and Jimenez had broken into the Army post's headquarters building and found the keys to all of them, along with a ledger in the quartermaster's office, listing what each bunker contained and how much. Like the bunkers on Volivoli atoll, it was a virtual laundry list of military equipment, ammunition, and rations.

Tim tossed the case into place with the rest, dropped down onto the dusty, overgrown access road, and handed Jimenez a warm bottle of Gatorade. The younger man downed it in three huge gulps. He wiped his mouth with the back of his hand, and tossed the empty bottle into the dark recess of the building, where it bounced loudly off the poured concrete floor out of sight of the two men.

"That was the last of it, Sar' Major," Jimenez said, wiping the sweat from his brow. "I don't understand why you wanted all the MREs."

"One can never have enough ammo, food, or dry socks, Taco."

"The ammo I can understand, and with this place, we've got enough to fight off a whole division. But we've got enough food at home, why the MREs?"

"These will be back up, just in case. I want every house to have enough of them to feed everyone for a few weeks. I know what the winters can be like up here, and we could all get snowed in for a few weeks at a time. Until we've grown enough fresh vegetables and fruits, and figured out ways to store them over the winter, this is an insurance policy," Tim said, sitting down by the rear wheels of the truck in the shade.

"Okay, I'm with you now."

"Better to err on the side of safety, Taco."

"When those squids get their shit together, and that railroad guy figures how to get the trains running, maybe we'll have fresh pineapples and shit from Hawaii."

"Until then—"

"Until then we get by with what we've got and fall back on the best and surest way to block up one's colon the US Government ever devised," Jimenez cut in, which made Tim laugh.

"Taco, you've obviously never had C-Rations. Why they even put toilet paper in them is beyond me," he said with a shake of his head.

"It won't be long now, eh?" Jimenez said.

"The baby you mean?" Tim asked, and Jimenez nodded. "Izzy says that it could be any day now."

"Pretty exciting, eh?"

"You could say that."

"There might be more babies soon," Jimenez said, which made Tim snap his head up and glare at Jimenez, who paled noticeably.

"Taco, if you're trying to tell me you've knocked up Robyn I—"

"Oh shit, Sar' Major, not that I know of!"

"Not that you know of?" Tim asked incredulously.

"No, sir! I was just thinking about what I heard Ian telling Izzy the other day, that him and Paula are trying to have one!"

"Is that so?"

"Sar' Major. You know how Robyn and I feel about each other. I'd never hurt a hair on her head. But that *will* probably happen too… at some point," he finished, the last coming out as a whisper.

"I know that, Taco. I'm not sure I'm ready to be a father yet, let alone a grandpa," Tim said with a sigh.

"You already are a father, Tim," Taco said, testing the waters. It was the first time he'd called him by his first name.

"It's a little different with a baby, Taco."

"So we'll learn together. I'm looking forward to being an uncle, Tío Juan. It's got a nice ring to it!"

"Uncle Taco," Tim laughed. "It sounds like a burrito cart I got food poisoning from once in Balboa, Panama back in the eighties."

"Every family needs one beaner," Jimenez cracked. He stood and brushed the dirt from the seat of his pants, held his hand out to Tim, and helped the older man to his feet.

"You know, Taco, you're okay for a jarhead," Tim said. "Let's get this show on the road."

"Okay, Sar' Major," Jimenez said, not wishing to push his luck any further with the first name.

"One more thing, Taco. You call me 'Tim' one more time I will rape your soul," he said. "We are not bestest friends, we will not be holding hands and singing Kumbaya and playing grab-ass in the showers, got that?"

Jimenez nodded, not sure if Tim was joking or not. They'd started off towards the cab of the truck, when they heard the approaching sound of a speeding Hum-Vee, then saw the vehicle bouncing towards them being trailed by a huge plume of dust from the road, headlights flashing, and now the horn was beeping.

It slid to a stop feet from their parked truck, blanketing the pair in a cloud of fine, choking dust. They heard, but didn't see the door to the Hum-Vee open, then Robyn's voice in a loud shout: "Dad, come quick!"

As the dust settled they saw Robyn, half out of the vehicle, waving frantically for Tim to come to her. "What is it?"

"Izzy says it's time, and for you to come back now!"

"The baby?"

"Yeah, it's coming now!"

"Taco, you take the truck and drive it back to the compound. I'll go with Robyn!"

"You got it, Sar' Major!" Jimenez ran back to the truck while Tim ran to the passenger side of the Hum-Vee, hopped in. Robyn climbed back behind the wheel, spun out in a wide turn to head back to Williams, leaving Jimenez in another cloud of dust.

As they bounced back down the service road towards the entrance to the camp, Tim asked, "Is everything okay?

"Yes, Dad. Everything is alright. Holly's water broke about an hour ago, and Izzy sent me to get you."

Tim relaxed some, holding on as Robyn sped down the dirt track and onto the overgrown road leading out to I-40. "Slow down, I want to get there in one piece!"

"Dad, you're the one who taught me to drive, remember?"

"Yeah, yeah. I know. So, is everything fine?"

"Yes. Izzy said Holly is doing fine, and so is the baby, so cool your jets."

"Good."

"It's all really exciting!"

"Just don't you and Taco get any ideas," he said.

"Dad, don't worry. Juan and I have talked about it, but we want to wait a little while."

"Good idea. Maybe when you're about thirty or so."

"Dad, I know you think I'm still your little girl, and in a lot of ways I am," Robyn said, turning onto the onramp of I-40 and heading west, "and I love that. But I'm not a little girl anymore. Taco and I love each other."

"I know, Robyn. It doesn't stop me from caring about you." Tim sighed. "He is almost ten years older that you."

"Dad, don't even go there," Robyn snapped, holding up her index finger. "Taco and I have the same age difference as you and Holly. And you said it yourself, you'd like to see a new community sprout up, to have civilization come back, and to make that happen, there's going to have to be babies, lots of them."

"Alright, alright already," he said in resignation. "Let's get through this one first."

"Dad, it's going to happen at some point, so prepare yourself," Robyn laughed, and Tim groaned. His little girl was grown up. "I read once somewhere that you'd need at least a hundred and sixty people in a settlement so as not to have kids with extra fingers and toes or webbed feet sprouting up in a few generations, and we only have a fraction of that now," Tim said.

"A fairly deep gene pool?"

"Yeah, with a little chlorine added from time to time." Tim smirked. "I'll have to talk to Izzy about that."

"There's something else I need to talk to you about, Dad. I know your mind is on the baby right now, but this can't wait."

"What is it?"

"I know you said to not use the HAM radio because of the strange messages that you and Sergeant Williams got, but I was playing around with my stuff this morning after you and Taco headed over to Camp Navajo. I got this weird message. I didn't reply, but it wasn't from any station that's familiar to us," she said, driving around the bigger of the bumps in the cracked and deteriorating asphalt of the highway like she was in a slalom track.

"What did it say?"

"It was weird. Whoever is behind the key was slow, sounded like he was really rusty, with a lot of misspellings. It was a warning to us."

"To us?" Tim asked, perplexed.

"Specifically to you, they knew your name," she said, popping a piece of chewing gum in her mouth. "The message was, quote: urgent, inform soonest Sergeant Major T Flannery that an armed force has departed Washington, DC three weeks prior, headed to Arizona to arrest you, secure the codes, and transport you, any operational aircraft, and its pilot back to Washington, unquote."

Tim let out a long, loud whistle and shook his head. "Aren't you the little ray of sunshine."

"Don't shoot the messenger, Dad."

"I'm not, Baby. It's just something I've been afraid of since we got back, I just didn't think it'd be so soon."

"What are you going to do?" "I haven't a fucking clue. I'll have to talk this over with Izzy and Taco. We'll have to do something."

"Can they arrest you?"

"Again, I haven't a clue. Maybe there really is someone who's president, and somehow they found out I have the codes, and want them back."

"But you don't have them! They were vaporized on Volivoli!"

"I know," Tim lied, knowing full well he still had them squirreled away in the basement of the house.

"How did they know your name?"

"There's been enough communication between here and Oahu over the last few months, and my name has been in enough of them. The airwaves are open, and whoever has been listening broke our code, I guess." "They couldn't possibly know exactly where we are. We never, ever said the name of the town, only that we were in Arizona."

"I'll have to have a meeting with Izzy and Taco, and I'll get hold of Jerry on the Satcom radio and see what he has to say. The message said that a 'armed force' left Washington a few weeks ago. They're probably only using vehicles, and with the condition of the roads, it will probably take them weeks to come this far west. We have no idea what the bridges over the Mississippi are like," Tim said, his mind now going a million miles an hour.

"So it could be weeks if not months before they get here," Robyn said.

"Yeah, and we know they're not flying. Why else would they want our aircraft and pilot?"

"I agree," Robyn said. She onto the red dirt road that led up to the compound, pulled up in front of their house, and shut the engine off. "So what do we do?"

"I don't know yet. Don't say a word to anyone else about this until I talk with Izzy and Taco. Right now I've got more important things to worry about," Tim said, hopping out of the vehicle and sprinting up the stairs to the front door.

He ran inside and called out for Holly, only to be rewarded by the sound of a baby's loud wails coming from upstairs.

"Shit!" he exclaimed, and bounded up the stairs, following the sound. He made his way down the short hall to his bedroom, where he saw Izzy standing by the bed, smiling warmly. Holly was holding a wrapped little bundle. The sound of the baby's crying had stopped, and he saw that Holly had exposed one of her breasts and the baby's mouth was locked onto the nipple, sucking away happily.

Holly looked over at him and smiled tiredly. "There you are. Come and meet your son!"

"Tim sat on the edge of the bed, a huge grin splitting his face. He looked down at the small wonder feeding happily, and looked up into Holly's eyes. "He's beautiful."

Holly sighed. "Aye, he is."

"Fastest delivery I've ever seen," Izzy said. "Mother and baby are doing splendidly!" The baby took its mouth away from the nipple and yawned widely. Holly covered back up and looked at Tim. "Would you like to hold him, Dad?" she asked.

Tim took the bundle from her gingerly. "So tiny...," he remarked, looking over the newborn in his arms. He had Holly's deep green eyes and Tim's shock of dark hair.

"Have you two thought of a name?" Izzy asked.

"No, not really," Holly said.

"Walter," Tim said.

"Your father?" Holly asked, and Tim nodded.

Tears were welling up in his eyes and he was finding it difficult to speak. He gingerly handed the infant back to Holly, and wiped the tears from his eyes.

"That's a nice testament. I'm sure he'd have been proud," Holly said.

"I'm sorry I was late," Tim said. "I wanted to be here."

"It's okay, Tim. He came out pretty fast."

"I know, still..."

"You'll be here by my side for the next one," she told him with a twinkle in her eyes.

"Next one?" Tim gaped.

"Aye. I think we'll have a few more," she teased.

"We'll talk about that later, babe," he replied, leaned over, and kissed her tenderly. He brushed a few wayward strands of hair away from her eyes and caressed her cheek. "I think mother and son need to take a little nap now," Izzy said, hanging his stethoscope around his neck. "Just give me a minute, alright?" Tim asked, and Izzy nodded and left, closing the door behind him. Holly reached up and caressed his cheek tenderly. "Timothy, don't worry not being here. He came awfully fast. Robyn got to you as fast as she could."

"This changes everything," Tim said.

"What do you mean?"

"I have even more reason to protect you and him. The stakes just got a little higher."

"We'll both protect him. What are you worried about?"

"Nothing, just that now we have him, and it means that life will go on."

"That it will, Tim. He'll have us to protect him, and to teach him everything we know," she said, leaning back into the pillows and yawning.

"I'll let you two have a little nap, okay?"

"Aye, I am tired," she whispered, her eyes droopy.

Tim leaned in and kissed her forehead gently and whispered, "I love you, babe."

"I love you too, Tim. Now go on and go talk with Izzy. I know how much you and he love to kibitz."

"Let me know if you need anything."

"I will. I love you, now go on and get out of here and leave a tired mother to sleep!"

Tim kissed Holly again, then kissed little Walter on the head. "We'll be right downstairs, babe. Call if you need anything."

Tim headed down the stairs to the kitchen, where Robyn was making a pot of coffee. Izzy was standing by the counter with his hands in his pockets.

"I've got a little brother!" Robyn said excitedly, hugging Tim tightly. "Can I see him?"

"Not right now, Robyn. Holly and Walter are taking a nap," Izzy said.

"Walter?" she asked.

"Yeah, it's my father's name," Tim said. "I thought it would be a good name for him."

Robyn poured cups of steaming coffee for all of them, then sat down across the counter from Tim.

Tim took a sip of his coffee, set the cup in front of him and sighed. "This is all a little much for me to grasp. So much has happened these last few years."

"I know, Dad. You raised me up okay, you'll do a great job."

"Robyn is right. You will do a fantastic job," Izzy agreed, sipping his own coffee. "You've got everyone here to help out, too."

"Yeah, Dad, you're not alone now," Robyn said, taking his hand.

"All the more reason to be worried," Tim said, gripping his mug tightly.

"Why would you be worried?" Izzy asked.

Tim dropped the bombshell. He told Izzy what Robyn had told him on their way back to the house, along with his fears, and when he was finished, it was Izzy's turn to let out a whistle.

"Do you have any ideas?"

"No, Iz, I don't. I want to wait until Taco gets back from Camp Navajo, and maybe get Ian over here. He was in the Army reserve in Australia a while back, so he's the only other one here with military experience. We'll have a brainstorming session, and maybe come up with a plan. Right now, I don't want to say anything to anyone, especially Holly. No sense getting everyone worked up."

"Good idea," Izzy said. "What does that tell us?"

"It tells us that there might be a president back in DC, and he's probably pissed that I've been running around saying I'm him."

"That could very well be the case. It also tells me that first, they don't know exactly where we are, and secondly, that they don't have a working airplane or anyone to fly it. That could work to our advantage," the old doctor asserted.

They hear Jimenez' truck pull up in front of the house and Robyn went outside and greet him, leaving Tim and Izzy alone in the kitchen with their thoughts.

Tim let out a long breath. "I told Holly just a few minutes ago that Walter raised the stakes, and he did, by a thousand. And you know what? The more I think about it, the angrier I become."

"What do you mean?" Izzy asked

"When everything first happened, the Event, I mean, I thought I was completely alone. For a while I was okay with that. No more responsibilities except to keep my own sorry ass fed and warm. Then I came across Robyn."

"And that made you change your perspective," Izzy commented knowingly.

"I knew I had to protect her, no matter what. Turned out we wound up taking care of each other. Then we meet Dawn Redeagle, who told us of this place. We were comfortable here for quite a while, then you and Holly came along, and the stakes were raised again."

Izzy nodded and returned to his coffee, which was cold when he went to take a sip. He poured himself another cup, topped off Tim's cup with the pot, and sat back down.

"It's hard to explain," Tim said, picking up his thoughts. "There was no country left, no laws. We had to make it up as we went along. I did try to make sure we did the right thing every step of the way."

"How does this explain your anger?"

"I'm getting to that. We found the Football, the codes for the missiles... I never thought I'd use them, but our backs were against the wall on Volivoli. Shit, Iz. I've called in artillery on the enemy, even an air strike or two in the past. But order a launch for an intercontinental ballistic missile? Fuck. That was some serious shit."

"So I've been told. You did it to give the rest a chance to escape, because you knew that crazy captain would have never stopped after he got the codes. You launched that missile with full knowledge that you would be vaporized along with that ship. You were going to sacrifice yourself to save the ones you love. Tim, if that isn't an expression of true love, I don't know what is. You have no idea the respect I have for you for doing that."

Tim said nothing, so Izzy continued with a question, "So now what is getting you so angry?"

Tim let out a breath as if he'd been punched in the gut. "Iz, it's like this. All any of us ever wanted was to be left alone, to build back civilization if you will, the way we saw fit for ourselves. Now here comes someone again, who doesn't know us at all, and wants to take something away from us. What that is I don't know, but like that crazy captain, someone else just won't leave us the fuck alone!"

"I see," Izzy stated flatly.

"Do you? I mean every step of the goddamn way there's been someone that wants to take away what we've got. The first few months after the Event, I met up with the first person I'd seen since it happened. A guy named Paul. Before I could get him moved to my place, a group of fucking animals killed him. Before they did, they tortured and sodomized him for hours. Then right before we found the Football, two other assholes kidnapped Robyn. I had to do things, terrible things, just to get her back in one piece."

"You've told me. Holly and I had gone into hiding a few times when we were still in Colorado because of people like that."

"Then there was that captain, terrorizing the whole Pacific Ocean for fuck sake. Where does it all end, Iz?"

"I see your frustration, Tim, and I agree. The question I have for you now is, what do you plan to do?"

"I'm not sure. I'm beginning to regret coming back here to Arizona. We should have just stayed in Hawaii. There we'd have a whole ocean around us," he replied.

"We're here now, and this is our home."

"I know, goddamn it! We've all been through so much, and it infuriates me that again, some fucking asshole is going to try to take it away from us!" Tim said hotly, face turning red. "I knew nothing good would happen by us bandying around that I was president. Now there's probably a real president back east, and I'm guilty of violating all kinds of laws, and the fucking Constitution of all things. Something I had always swore to 'uphold and defend'."

"So what if there is? I think the time for all of that has passed," Izzy said. "If there is someone back east who says they're president, I say to hell with them! Listen to me now. I'll make this perfectly clear. I too took that oath myself so many years ago. Six years ago, in the blink of an eye, all of that went up in smoke. Yes, we want to follow that same constitution, and that's a splendid idea. But to what end? Washington had become a cesspool of corruption years before the Event, and if there is someone back there who is a successor to our last president, what makes you think he or she will be any different? With you as our leader, things will be honest. You here and Jerry back on Oahu. You two have what we used to call in the Navy 'all of your shit in one sack', so to speak," he said, and sat back on the stool, crossed his arms across his chest, letting what he just said sink in.

Tim knew deep down what Izzy had said was true, but he'd never thought in his wildest dreams he would ever be put in this position. He looked up into Izzy's eyes. "So, you're saying I just say 'fuck them', and commit treason?"

"In a nutshell, yes, that's exactly what I'm saying. The old laws are gone. It's up to us to decide what's right for us, not some politician back in DC."

"Do you know that Robyn and Taco are thinking about starting a family?" Tim asked.

"Yes. They've talked to me about it," Izzy said. "You've got your son, Holly, Robyn, and Juan to protect, along with the rest of us. It's a big decision to make."

"I know. I feel the weight of the world is resting on my shoulders."

"In some ways it is, Tim. I don't envy you."

"Now that that decision has been made," Tim said with a resigned sigh, "how do a handful of us fight off an 'armed force'?"

"Sergeant Major, have you forgotten all of your lessons from your time in the Army?"

"No," Tim stated.

"We learned a long time ago how a small, irregular force can defeat a large regular army, Tim. And I'm not talking about the Revolutionary War. I'm talking about the Viet Cong."

"Okay, I'm following you now," Tim said, and Izzy could almost see the wheels spinning behind Tim's eyes.

"There's the old Tim we all know and love coming back," he said, a grin splitting his face. "We have the advantage of knowing our territory. It's our home field advantage. You and Robyn have lived here for over five years. You know every contour on the map by memory for miles around. I know this old salt was a sailor, but I do know some tactics."

"Can we beat them?"

"We don't need to beat them, we've just got to stop them. Make it too expensive for them to keep coming back."

"We can try. It would help if we knew more," he said, warming to the idea.

"That's true. Like how many are in this force, how they're armed, and where they're coming from," Izzy listed.

"We know they're coming from the east."

"There's only a few ways in and out of here, and from what I'm told of your adventure on Volivoli, you know how to set up one hell of an ambush."

"Are you sure you're a doctor? You sound like a soldier now, Iz," Tim told the man.

"At times like this, in my mind, I'm back on my PBR on the Mekong River. I only know from what I've been told, but I've heard you and Jerry did pretty much the same thing on Volivoli."

"Yeah, but we had two squads of soldiers to do it, not a handful of civilians."

"Hopefully time will be on our side. Let's get together tonight after dinner and we'll come up with a plan."

Tim agreed as Jimenez and Robyn came into the kitchen. Tim turned to Jimenez. "Taco, I've got a job for you."

"Shoot, Sar' Major."

"I want you to divvy up the MREs to everyone evenly. While you're doing that, I want you to tell Ian to come down here, say, around 1900 hours."

"Sure thing, Sar' Major, any reason?"

"OPSEC, Taco. Robyn, you go with him and give him a hand, and you can give debrief him on what you told me earlier."

"Okay, Dad. You haven't told Holly, have you?"

"No, and don't tell anyone else here. I'm going to need you to get on the secure SATCOM when you get back and message Jerry. He can't do anything from where he is, but I'd like his opinion, and maybe some ideas."

"I'll do it as soon as we get back from the rounds, Dad."

"What's going on?" Jimenez asked.

"Robyn will let you know, Taco. And we'll talk about it at length tonight after supper."

"You don't want me to tell Ian?" Robyn asked.

"No, just tell him I need to talk to him tonight. I'll let him know when he gets here." "Let's go, Taco. I want to get this done fast, so I can come back and see my new baby brother!" she exclaimed, taking Jimenez by the arm and steering him out of the house.

"Kids," Tim said, shrugging his shoulders.

"Do you think she understands the gravity of it?" Izzy asked.

"Yeah, she's just excited about the baby is all. She'll have her war face on tonight at the meeting."

"Speaking of the baby, when are you going to tell Holly?"

"I haven't decided yet, though I can't keep it from her long." Tim said, looking at his coffee cup. "I hate keeping things from her, but I don't want her worried right now."

Izzy looked at his watch. "I'll go up and check on her and the baby." "Thanks for setting me straight, Iz."

"You didn't need me to do that. You knew all along. I just helped you find your thoughts." Izzy got up, placed his coffee cup in the sink, and left Tim alone in the kitchen.

Tim sat there for another minute or two, and then stood, placing his cup in the sink along with Izzy's, and went to the basement door. He plodded down the steps and made his way to what he called his 'arms room', a cinderblock-walled room with a heavy, solid steel door on well-oiled hinges, secured with a padlock.

It was originally designed to be a fallout/storm shelter by the contractors who built the place, but now it was where he kept all of his military hardware, ammunition, weapons, and emergency supplies, and where he'd squirreled away that notebook he had copied over all the launch codes into so many years ago.

Taking his key ring off of his belt, he found the one that fit the padlock, unlocked it, and opened the hasp. Reaching inside, he found the light switch, and walked into the now brightly lit room. He stood in the center, hands on his hips, and surveyed what he'd amassed, nodding in satisfaction.

A metal shelf unit covered the whole far wall, containing cases and cases of MREs, medical supplies, and other incidentals. He reached in between two boxes of gauze bandages, and pulled out the dog-eared notebook, staring at it for a long time. He flipped through the pages, seeing his neat, block letter printing on each page, and satisfied it was all still there, he put it back silently.

"I'm of the mind to take that up and toss it into the fireplace tonight," he said aloud to the empty room. However, he knew he wouldn't. He sighed and retraced his steps, pocketing his pipe and tobacco pouch that he'd left there earlier and headed back through the steel door, securing the padlock, and headed back up to the kitchen.

Once there, he glanced at his watch, and seeing that it was almost dinner time, decided to start throwing something together. He got a few cans of chicken soup together to heat on the stovetop, and made some ham sandwiches with the homemade bread he had perfected baking over trial and error over the last few years. When he had finished, and had the table set, everyone appeared as if by magic. Even Holly came down, along with the baby. She placed him in a tiny bassinet that Robyn had secured from somewhere, and they all sat around, ate, and made small talk until their appetites were sated.

Tim carried Walter back upstairs with Holly, and placed him in a crib next to the bed, then helped Holly get under the covers.

"Thanks, love. I don't know what I'd do without you," she said, pulling the blanket up to her chin.

"And I don't know what I'd do without you, babe," he replied, sitting down on the edge of the bed, taking her hand and then looking over at the wrapped bundle a few inches away. "He's sleeping soundly."

"Aye, for now. If he's anything like the way he was when he was still inside me, he'll be a restless little bugger."

"He's beautiful," Tim said.

"That he is, so innocent."

"We've got a monumental job ahead of us," Tim said, almost in a whisper. "He's an empty vessel, and you and I have the job of filling it up."

"And we have to make sure what we fill him will all the right things," Holly said, taking his hand and holding it tightly. Tim kissed her lips gently. "I love you, Holly."

"I love you too, Timothy."

"I'm going to head down now; I'll be up in a while."

"Please don't be long, honey. I need to hold you tonight."

"I won't, babe. I promise," he said. "Get some sleep, I'll be up in a while."

He turned the bedside lamp off, and walked out of the room, closing the door silently. He went out onto the porch, where Robyn, Jimenez, and Izzy were waiting for him.

"How is she?" Izzy asked.

"She's lying down. She's still plenty tired," Tim said, pulling out his pipe and sitting down on the porch steps. The sun was low in the trees to the west, and it would soon be twilight. He filled the bowl of his pipe, lighting it with a wooden match, and puffing a few times until it was lit.

"Did you tell Ian?" he asked Robyn.

"Yeah, Dad, he said he'd be here."

Just then Ian, carrying a case of beer, rounded the corner of the house. He walked up and presented the carton to Tim. "Congratulations, mate!" he said with a toothy grin.

"Thanks, Ian. The baby isn't why I asked you over tonight though," Tim said, puffing away on his pipe. "You might want to sit down."

Tim then told everyone all he knew up to that point, and when he was done, Ian let out a long whistle, reached for the case of beer, and pulled out a cold bottle of Miller. He twisted the top and downed a huge gulp, wiping his mouth.

"Fair dinkum?" he asked, and Tim nodded. Jimenez, feeling a little cheeky, reached into the case and pulled out two more bottles, handing one to Robyn. Tim got one for himself.

"Yeah, Ian, as far as we know, it's fair dinkum."

"Fuck me dead," Ian said, sitting down on the steps, took another pull of his beer. "That's why I called you all together," Tim said. "Robyn, were you able to get hold of Jerry?"

"Yeah, he said to put together a plan, and then float it by him and he'll go over it to see if there's any holes in it."

"I should have a rough plan together, with all of your help, tonight. Taco, do you still have a list of everything at Camp Navajo?"

"Yes, Sar' Major," he said, tapping his forehead. "I've got most of it right up here."

"What about explosives?"

"There's shitloads of it. TNT, C-4, det-cord, not to mention a shitpot of artillery rounds, 105mm, 155mm, and the 8-inch shells. There's even a bunch of mortar rounds. 40mm, 81mm, and 4.2 inch shit, along with about a trillion rounds of small arms ammo."

"Ah, the mortar. That's what I trained on in the reserves," Ian said.

"Is that so?" Tim asked. "I've got something to show you, then. So there's plenty of stuff that goes boom?" he asked Jimenez.

"There's shitloads of it," Jimenez confirmed, finishing his beer, and grabbing another.

Tim had to smile; this was the first time he'd had a battle planning session over a case of beer. If they had that much explosives, they could... His grin widened, and then he quieted everyone down. When he had everyone's attention, he told them of his plan.

When he was finished, they all agreed it was a sound plan, and they chimed in with ideas, improving on Tim's original idea, going over it time and time again. Tim asked Jimenez one last question, after he finished his fifth beer of the evening.

"Taco, is there any commo stuff, field phones and shit?" "Yeah, but not in the bunkers, it's over in the building next to the motor pool. There's plenty of it, field phones, pack radios, all kinds of shit like that."

"I'm going to make out a grocery list tomorrow morning, and then you and I are going on a little shopping trip."

"Sounds like a plan, Sar' Major!"

"Goddamn right it's a plan, Taco. Now I'll leave all of you and I need to go cuddle with a sexy Scot," Tim said, standing a little uneasily. It'd been a while since he'd been this drunk, and it showed.

"You were going to show me something?" Ian asked in the darkness.

"Oh yeah, I almost forgot. Come with me," he replied, waving Ian to follow him. Tim went around to the back of the house to a large barn. He fumbled a little with his keys, then got the door open and lights on.

Tim and Ian stepped into the barn, lit by a few fluorescent lights in the rafters. Inside was a Hum-Vee with a .50 M2 Browning machine gun mounted on a ring mount, and behind it, an olive green Army tarp covering something.

Tim walked over to the tarp and grabbed one edge of it, pulling it off with a flourish. Seeing what Tim had exposed, Ian laughed a little.

"I'm not going to ask where you got it. I guess a lot of this stuff is just lying around now, eh?"

"That's right. Ian, I give you the M252 81mm mortar," Tim said, gesturing like a showgirl, on a game show showing off one of the fabulous prizes Ian had just won.

"It's been a while, but I still remember the basics."

"That's all I need you to remember. I've got about a hundred rounds of HE, and about twenty-five of smoke right here. From what Taco said, we can get shitloads more. If we set it up and I give you a fire mission, do you think you can drop the rounds where I want them?" Tim asked, serious now.

Ian nodded. "Yeah, mate, I can do that. It'd be a piece of piss."

"That's all I'll ask of you."

"I just wish that Colin bastard would be on the receiving end," Ian spat.

"This is not the time for that, Ian."

"You're right. Sorry. I'll drop those rounds right where you want them, Tim."

"Let's get out of here and get some sleep. We've got a busy few days ahead of us," Tim said, leading Ian back out of the barn. Tim turned the lights off, locked the door and the two men parted.

Ian back to his house and Tim into his. Only one of the pair was sure of themselves that night...

CHAPTER 12: WHERE THE BUFFALO ROAM

Sam Didinato roused groggily in his sleeping bag in the early morning hours. The cooking fire he and John Meadows lit last night had burned out hours ago, but in this early July morning on the plains of Kansas, it wasn't needed for warmth.

The sun was only a few degrees up from the northern horizon, and already he could tell it would be another hot day today. He sat up, seeing his travelling companion still asleep in his own bedroll, worn leather saddle at his head being used as a pillow.

The four horses they'd acquired, along with the ten buffalo calves, were still tethered to two cottonwood trees only a few yards behind their camp. All of the animals were undisturbed, munching happily away at the high grass by the trees.

After following Tim Flannery's directions, and with a great deal of luck, they actually had found the old Native American, Dawn Redeagle, several miles northwest of Lincoln, Nebraska. With a great deal of bartering, the two men were able to secure three mares and a stud horse, all broken and trained by Redeagle, along with ten yearling bison calves, and it only cost them their propane powered Chevy 4X4, several cases of MREs and the M16A1 rifle that Flannery had given them as a gift to the wise man.

Now, two weeks into their return trip back to Williams, Arizona, they were camped just north of an overgrown four-lane concrete paved highway once was known as Interstate 70, about ten miles west of Salina, Kansas.

Didinato unzipped his bag. He put on a fresh pair of socks, then his boots, knocking the heels of each in turn to dislodge any wayward critters who may have found their way inside overnight. He scratched at his face, feeling a five day growth of stubble, and decided to shave this morning.

He nudged Meadows, and the man stirred from his slumber with a groan.

"Tonight let's find a place where there might be a bed or two, eh, mate?" John said.

"I thought you Aussies were supposed to be tough. Convict stock and all that?" Sam kidded.

"You can get fucked, mate. Give me a nice, comfortable bed any day!" John said, rubbing the sleep from his eyes. "I need a cuppa'."

"Give me a minute and I'll get the fire going. I just want to brush my teeth," Sam said. He rummaged through his saddlebags for his toothbrush and a crumpled tube of toothpaste.

"I'll get the fire going," John offered.

Sam put a good dollop of paste on his brush and began scrubbing his choppers. As he brushed away, he mindlessly strolled around, making his way to the top of a small rise a few yards away from camp. From the top, he could look down onto the highway, only a few hundred yards south of their camp. What he saw there, making its way west on the road, made him stop and drop to the ground instinctively.

"John, whatever you do, don't light that fucking fire right now!" he called back.

"What is it?"

"Come up here and take a look, and bring my binoculars," he said in a muffled voice, toothbrush still sticking out of his mouth. "Keep low!"

A few moments later, John was lying on the ground next to him, holding out his binoculars, which Sam brought up to his eyes, scanning the scene before him.

"Who are they?" John asked.

"I don't know, but I doubt they're the local Kiwanis club on an outing," Sam said.

Parked along the shoulder of the highway before them were several Hum-Vees and military trucks, and several men, all armed, milling around by the vehicles and road.

He reached into a cargo pocket of his pants and retrieved a notepad and pencil, writing down everything he could see, remembering his lessons in scouting he learned in the Army.

"What do you think they're doing?" John asked.

"I think they just stopped for a piss break."

"They don't know we're here?"

"I doubt it. If they did they'd already be up here," Sam said.

"Maybe we should go down and talk to them," John suggested. "Maybe they're friendly."

"I seriously doubt that. Just look at them." Sam dropped his binoculars on the ground in front of him. "If they were friendly, why go that well-armed?"

"I see what you mean."

"If they were just traveling, they'd have a few people armed for protection, not everyone. This is a military convoy of some sort," Sam said.

"Where do you think they're heading?"

"West, judging by the direction their vehicles are facing. Beyond that, I don't know," Sam said.

A man by the lead Hum-Vee shouted something they couldn't hear, and waved his arm in a circle over his head. The men milling around started to move, climbing back into the trucks and Hum-Vees, and all the engines fired up. When all the men were in the vehicles, the lead Hum-Vee started off, followed by the rest.

The two men on the hill watched the convoy head out of sight westward, and when there was no doubt that they could no longer be seen by anyone looking out of the rear vehicle, Sam sat up, making another notation in his notepad. "I think we ought to let the Sar' Major know about this."

"Fucking oath, mate," John agreed.

"After all that's happened, there's only one reason to go around the country like that, and it's not good," Sam said, standing up. "I mean, shit. Anyone who's left is just trying to survive at this point. This tells me there's a big group of people somewhere, enough to mount up a military operation like that."

"We've been all over half the country out here, and the only other person we've seen was that Redeagle bloke," John said.

"They're going somewhere, for a purpose. No reason to waste fuel like that either. Whatever reason that is, it can't be good," Sam told John.

He retrieved the Satcom radio from his saddlebag and turned it on.

When it didn't fire up, he swore to himself. "Shit. The battery is dead. I probably left it on by mistake the last time we checked in."

"Is there a way to charge it?"

"Yeah, I've got a little solar panel set up that Robyn made for me but it'll take a few hours. You might as well get that fire going so we can make some coffee," Sam said, pulling out the charging unit and setting it up in the sun away from the trees.

They busied themselves with the morning chores, checking on the horses and their livestock, and when the coffee on the fire was boiling, they enjoyed the drink with some canned pork and beans.

After their morning meal, Sam loaded his carbine and took a walk down to where the odd convoy had been parked. He walked up and down the track looking at odd bits and pieces lying on the ground. Satisfied that they hadn't left anything useful, he made his way back to the camp.

"Did you find anything?" John asked.

"No, but I did learn a little bit."

"What?"

"For one, they're not all that well disciplined for a military operation. They left all kinds of garbage lying around," he said. "When you're in a military operation, you never leave any trace that you've been in a place. There were empty MRE packets, toilet paper, cigarette butts, soda cans and shit lying around down there. Just by me taking a five-minute walk around, I could tell that there was a company-strength unit there, and which way they went. Total shit OPSEC."

"OPSEC?"

"Operational Security, simple shit every soldier learns in basic training. They even pulled off to the side of the road, leaving tire marks. If they were smart, they'd have just stopped in the middle of the road, as not to leave any marks. It's not like they had to worry about traffic."

"I always wondered why you even buried the traces of our campfires. It makes sense now that you say it."

"And just a bit more intelligence I can relay back to the Sar' Major."

"Any ideas on who they were?"

"None at all, but I know they're not real soldiers. Some of them might have been, but they're not well trained or led. Hell, even the group me and Sergeant Williams put together on Oahu had their shit together better than this bunch," Sam said, pouring himself another cup of coffee from the battered and blackened old pot.

"You've got to have some idea what they're doing, Sam. They're certainly not out on a holiday trip."

"I couldn't say for certain what they're up to. Worse-case scenario is they are some land-based version of that crazy ship captain we dealt with on Volivoli."

"This wouldn't be good."

"No, that would definitely be un-good."

"Do you think they'll find our place back in Arizona?" John asked with a worried look.

Sam shook his head. "Not unless they are specifically looking for it. Just like Australia, out here in the west it's big, and there's a lot of places to hide. Our place is off the beaten path. Even if they stumbled into the town of Williams, they'd have to look through several thousand acres of forest just to find the compound. Besides, they're on I-70, three states away. Williams is on I-40, well to the south of here. This road will take them into Utah, where it ends, and then they can go south into Nevada or north into Idaho."

"What if they did find us?"

"Then they're fucked," Sam said. "There are only a handful of our people left out there, and they'd be sitting ducks. I don't think they'll ever find them, but to be on the safe side, I have to let them know."

He headed over the where he'd set up the solar charger. He turned on the radio and was rewarded by a beep. It synced with the geosynchronous military communications satellite. The battery level was only at 50%, but it was sufficient for the call he needed to make. He unplugged it from the charger, and walked back over to his seat on a log by the campfire.

After first ensuring he was on the right frequency, Sam depressed the push-to-talk button. "Diamondback Six, this is Prairie Dog One, over."

He had to repeat the action three more times before he got a reply.

"Prairie Dog One, this is Diamondback Six, over," Robyn's cheery voice came back, deceptively clear over the Satcom radio, as if she was standing a few feet from him.

"Diamondback Six, I need to speak with the Sar' Major ASAP, over."

"Sure thing, Sam. Hey, Holly had the baby, and it's a boy! Dad named him Walter."

"That's fantastic, Robyn. I really need to talk with Tim though."

"Okay, I'll get him. Were you able to find Mr. Redeagle?"

Sam pressed the button again, and with more than a little frustration, replied, "Yes, Robyn. That's not what I'm calling to report. If you could go and get the Sar' Major, I'd really appreciate it!" he said into the radio, scratching the back of his head.

After what seemed like hours to Sam, Tim's voice finally crackled through the radio. "Prairie Dog One, this is Diamondback Six actual, over."

"Diamondback Six Actual, standby to copy SITREP, over."

"Roger, wait one, over," came the reply. After a minute, the radio came to life again, "Go ahead with SITREP, over."

Sam pulled out his notepad, flipped it open to the page where he'd made his notes earlier, depressed the button and began to speak. "About two hours ago, I witnessed a company-strength unit, seven vehicles. Three Hum-Vees and four mike niner three niner, travelling west on Interstate seven zero, approximately one zero miles west of Salina, Kansas, over," he reported, indicating four M939 five-ton 6X6 military tucks, a larger version of the 2 ½ ton M35 'deuce and a half'.

There was a short pause, then Tim came back, "How were they armed?"

"Small arms, rifles and a few SAW's, far as I could see. They did have two Ma' Deuces on two of the Hum-Vees, but nothing I could see that was any heavier," he said, meaning the M2 Browning .50 caliber machine guns. "They stopped right on our front door for a fifteen minute piss break, then left, heading west."

"Anything else you can report?"

"They were sloppy, they left all kinds of garbage when they stopped. It doesn't look like they're all that well disciplined. Other than that, nothing else to report."

"Uniforms?"

"A mix and match hodgepodge, Sar' Major. ACUs with some civilian clothing thrown in."

"Are you in a position to shadow them?"

"We could try, Sar' Major, but we're on horseback at the moment, and have some livestock with us too," Sam reported.

"Horseback? I take it you found Redeagle?" Tim said, slight amazement showing in his voice.

"That's affirmative. We've got a few horses and some young buffalo. It cost us our vehicle. Redeagle was a hard bargainer."

"I'll bet. Are you on your way back?"

"Affirmative. We can try to bird-dog them, but it'll be slow going."

"Do what you can, Sam. Everyone here will appreciate it. I was hoping for information like this."

"You were expecting them?"

"Yes, Sam. I was," Tim replied. "I'll give you a rundown later. I've been expecting them, and it's important that you do all you can to follow them, and report back what you can."

"You've got it, Sar' Major. We'll do what we can."

"Check back again, this time tomorrow."

"WILCO, Diamondback Six. Prairie Dog One, out," Sam said into the radio with a slight sigh, and then let out a long whistle, looking over at John, who had gone pale.

"Diamondback Six Actual, out," Tim's disembodied voice came back over the radio. Sam turned off the radio and plugged it back into the solar charger to give it time to fully charge.

"We're to birddog them," Sam said, walking back over to the cooking fire and pouring himself another coffee.

"How will we do that on horses? We'll never keep up with them, and we've got the bison with us too."

"I think it's going to be a lot easier than you think," Sam said.

"How the fuck is it going to be easier?"

"As sloppy as they were a few hours ago, it'll be easy enough. They'll be leaving a trail of breadcrumbs for us to follow."

"I see. We won't even have to get close to them, let alone catch up to them!"

"Exactly. I love it when the enemy has shitty OPSEC."

"Is that what they are?" John asked, taking another sip of coffee. "The enemy?"

"The Sar' Major gave that impression, so we'll treat them as such from now on."

"I thought all that shit was over and done with," John sighed.

"So did I," Sam concurred.

The two men finished their coffee in silence, then made preparations to head out for another day of riding, this time with more due care and diligence.

They broke camp silently, and as they headed over the rise that had concealed them so well earlier, the only thing that they left was some buffalo droppings and horse manure.

They led their herd down the hill to the shoulder of the highway, and once on the tall grass of the median between the east and westbound lanes, turned west, following far behind the military convoy.

The pair made good time, and at the end of the day they decided to stop for the night at a truck stop a few hundred yards off the interstate in a place called Russell, Kansas.

There was a weed strewn parking lot with several rusting semis parked in rows, a covered area with several fuel and gasoline pumps, and a convenience store and diner attached.

To the rear of the diner was a fenced in area that looked like it had once been a dog park for travelers to use, so Sam and John herded their livestock into the enclosure. After placing all of the animals inside and making sure all had plenty of water, they shut the rusted gate securely behind them.

They took their saddles, rucksacks, and saddlebags with them over to the diner, where they figured that even if there were no beds, they'd at least be able to sleep inside for the night. The day had been clear, but in the gathering twilight of the day, clouds built up to the north and the sky was threatening to storm.

There was the sickly-sweet smell of decay throughout the room, and in the dim light, they could see several forms that had once been live people here and there, now almost completely decayed to the point of just being skeletons, time, rats and mice having done their very best to eradicate what was left.

"All this time, I should be used to seeing those," John said, pointing to a body along the far wall.

"I don't think I'll ever get used to it. We can sleep outside by the pumps if you want," Sam suggested.

"Nah, mate. She'll be alright. We can't escape it, we just have to live with it now."

"It doesn't bother me, and if it's alright with you, we'll just stay here," Sam stated. He picked up his carbine. "I'm going to take a look around. I won't be long."

"Alright, Mate. I'll put the Billy on for tea," he said with a smile in the growing darkness.

Sam walked out into the darkness, while John busied himself lighting a kerosene lantern, then extracting a sterno stove from his saddlebag and setting it up on one of the diner's tables.

He took the battered and blackened coffee pot and prepared what Sam had called 'cowboy coffee', which was a liberal handful of coffee grounds tossed into the water to boil.

After that was done, he produced a can of beef stew, poured the contents into a saucepan, and set it next to the stove. A flash of lightning lit up the dusty interior of the diner, followed shortly after by the rumble of thunder.

"Yeah, mate," he mumbled, "it looks like a good night to be indoors, dead bodies or not."

The sound of rain reverberated off of the roof of the building, and when it really started to come down loudly, he moved the now brewed coffee off of the single burner and placed the saucepan in its place on the stove.

He heard a door opening, startling him, and breathed a sigh of relief when he saw Sam come back into the room carrying something he couldn't make out in his hand. It wasn't that he was frightened exactly, just the fact of being alone in the room with all the bodies, seen and unseen, unnerved him a little, and he was happy to see his companion return.

Sam walked up to the table, and smiling, placed a six pack of beer on the table.

"It's warm, but beer is beer," he said, sitting down opposite John. "What's for tea?" he asked, feeling a little strange for calling supper 'tea'.

"Beef stew, and I've got coffee ready."

"Sounds good. I scrounged around in the convenience store side, but it looks like they've been through here already. The shelves were picked clean of everything. I found the beer hidden behind the counter," Sam told his partner, reaching for his saddleback and pulling out two metal bowls.

Another clap of thunder sounded loudly, and John asked "Do you think this storm will make any cyclones?"

"Do you mean tornadoes? Possibly, it *is* summer, and we're in Kansas."

"Should we be worried?" John asked.

"If the wind picks up, then dies suddenly, and it starts hailing, we'll go look for a walk-in freezer or something. I don't think this will be anything more than an evening thunderstorm though."

"If you say so," John replied uncertainly.

When the stew was hot, they poured themselves heaping bowls full and ate in silence, and when they were done eating, Sam pulled off a can of Coors and handed it to John.

"Here ya' go. One Colorado Kool-Aid for your after dinner aperitif!"

"You beauty! Cheers!" John said, popped the top of the can and took a sip, Sam following suit with his own can.

"So you said it looked like they were through here, too?" John asked.

"Yeah, they cleaned out the place of anything that could be of use, and made a complete fucking mess too. One of the dipshits took a dump in the corner. They're definitely not real soldiers, or if they are, they are so far gone from the reservation they're a lost cause."

"Is that a good or a bad thing?"

"It can cut both ways," Sam said. "With a professional soldier, I'd know what to expect. These guys are an unknown variable. Loose cannons. They could either run away at the first sign of trouble, or go off half-cocked and filled with testosterone because they've got the guns, and shoot up anything that moves. Hajji was sort of like that in the 'Ghan. On the other hand, them being this sloppy will make it so easy to follow them from a long ways' away. We won't ever have to get close to them to get a fairly good idea on where they're going."

"So we just head back, follow them, and see which way they go?"

"And report back to the Sar' Major. Simple stuff, and we're heading back that way anyhow, so we'll just take a different route than the one I was thinking. No biggie."

"You're the expert," John said, popping the top of a second beer.

"I'm just a grunt."

"You know more than me. I was a chartered accountant before the world went to shit."

"An *accountant?*" Sam chuckled. "You ride pretty well for an accountant."

"I was raised on a cattle station," John said. "I know a few things about horses. It's why I wanted to come with you in the first place."

"You guys have some really big ones down there. They make even our largest ranches look tiny," Sam said, sipping his own beer, and then leaned back in his chair.

"Not everything is bigger in Texas," John joked.

"Let's finish our nice adult beverages, get ourselves some sleep, and do it all again tomorrow."

John downed his beer and got another. The two men made small talk for a while longer, listening to the storm pass and fade into the distance. After they were done, they unrolled their sleeping bags, extinguished the lantern, and retired for the night.

And so it went, for the next four days. They followed Interstate 70 westward, making good time, travelling thirty or so miles a day. They never once saw the convoy during this time, though their trail was unmistakable.

Shortly after they crossed over the Colorado state line near the town of Burlington, the two men came to the top of a rise in the highway, and Sam saw something that made him yank back hard on the reins and shout, "Whoa!"

He spun on his mount to face John, who was trailing the herd about fifty yards to the rear, and motioned for him to stop. Sam rode his horse down, herding the buffalo back behind the rise.

"What is it?" John asked after riding his own mount up to Sam.

"They're right over that hill, about a click west."

Sam looked around for a moment, and spied a farmhouse off to the south. "Over there. We'll backtrack a bit, and then circle around to the south to avoid being seen. We'll use the house for cover and check them out."

"Hopefully, there will be a pen or something to put the animals into."

Sam spurred on his horse, herding the bewildered animals back the way they had just come.

It took over an hour, but they did exactly what Sam had wanted, coming up behind the farmhouse. There was a paddock by a barn, and they made quick work getting the animals secured. They unsaddled their mounts, and took all of their personal gear and rifles to the rear porch where Sam broke in easily.

On the second story of the house, Sam found a bedroom at the front that faced the highway about five hundred yards to the north of them. There were two single beds in the room, and by the looks of the decorations, it once was a young girl's bedroom. Photos of horses, teddy bears, and teen idols that Sam didn't know the names of were pinned up everywhere.

He dumped his saddlebag and rucksack onto the bed to his right, and looked out the dirty window. He could barely see out, so he muscled it open, and it screeched on dried and splintered runners. It was so loud that he froze in place, looking out at the stalled convoy, wondering if they'd been heard.

After a few seconds, his heart stopped trying to beat out of his chest, and he sat down on the bed, taking his carbine and leaning it against the wall next to it.

"What are they doing?" John asked when he was seated on the bed opposite.

"I'm not sure," Sam replied, reaching into his saddlebag for his binoculars. He scanned the length of the parked vehicles a few times, and then dropped them to his lap, leaning back on the bed. "It looks like one of the Hum-Vees broke down and they're trying to fix it," he said, handing the binoculars to his companion.

While John took a look, Sam said, "The lead one has its hood up, and it looks like someone is fucking around under it."

"I see it now. Everyone else is just milling around," John said. "So we just sit here and watch them?"

"That's about the long and short of it, buddy."

"Sounds boring," John said with a wry smile.

"Ninety nine percent of soldiering is sheer boredom," Sam said.

"What about the other one percent?"

"That's pure and utter abstract terror," Sam said with no emotion, picking up the binoculars again.

"That's the part I'm worried about."

"As long as we do our job here the right way, they will never know we're here. I suggest you just sit back, relax, and enjoy that bed. It's only noon, and this is going to give the horses a decent rest."

"Us too," John said and stretched out on the bed. The moment the man's head hit the pillow, he was sound asleep.

After about two hours, Sam's eyes began to grow heavy, so he woke John up. "My turn for a nap."

John sat up and rubbed the sleep out of his eyes. He took the binoculars from Sam's outstretched hand, and like John had done earlier, Sam was instantly sound asleep.

They did this every two hours, and after the sun fell below the Rocky Mountains far off to the west, they kept up the vigil in the darkness. Sam wouldn't allow the lantern or a fire lest they be spotted, so they sat in the darkness, eating cold MREs and taking turns watching with increasing boredom at the convoy splayed out on the shoulder of the highway before them.

"It'd be nice if we had some more beer, eh mate?" John opined into the darkness.

"Yeah, but I want to keep a clear head tonight. It looks like they've decided to stay the night. They've just lit two fires. That's stupid. If I were in charge of that fucking unit, I'd have light and noise discipline, fifty percent alert, and have a few LPs set up a few hundred meters out. They're treating this down there like a goddamn Boy Scout jamboree."

"Thankfully you're not in charge down there. It's making our job that much easier," John quipped.

They could hear the men below them now, laughing and carrying on, becoming louder as the night progressed. Cheers went up, then a few angry yells, and then it sounded like a fight had broken out. More yells and taunts in the darkness, and then the sound of the .50 caliber machine gun rattling off several rounds into the night, red tracers slashing the darkness like hot coals.

A few more shouts, these sounding more demanding, then the sharp crack of a 9mm pistol firing two rounds, and everything got quiet below for a few moments, then a few more shouts that, even though the two men couldn't make out the words, sounded to Sam like an officer of NCO barking out orders.

The two men hidden in the house looked at each other in the darkness, and Sam shrugged. After the shouts below, the men in the convoy settled down, and from the looks of it, most had finally gone to sleep.

The fires were burning down to a faint red glow, and now Sam could see the glow of a few cigarettes or cigars. Sam shook his head in disgust, while also thanking their lack of discipline.

When everything seemed to have calmed down along the highway, Sam decided that it was safe enough for them to both get some sleep, and well past midnight, both men fell asleep in the abandoned farmhouse.

It was early morning when they were both awakened by the sounds of diesel engines starting. Through the open window, they saw the men climbing into the trucks and Hum-Vees, and one by one, each vehicle headed out, continuing west towards Denver.

"It looks like they gave up on that Hum-Vee," Sam remarked. John looked closer, and indeed, the lone Hum-Vee was there, hood up, alone except for a few still-smoldering fires along the shoulder of the road.

"Want to go down for a look?" John asked.

"We'll give it a while to give them time to clear the area. Let's get some coffee brewing, and then we'll take a look-see."

They went about their morning chores, and when the coffee was brewed, they sat in the bedroom and had their breakfast. When they were done, John said "I'm going to take a look around here in the house; there might be some stuff we can use."

"I'll pack up this shit. Just don't take forever."

Sam went about packing up their scant belongings, carrying everything out to the paddock, taking a few trips, piling everything by the gate. When he was finished, he saw his companion exit the house, carrying a cardboard box.

"The lady of the house must have been really into canning. Half the basement is filled with this stuff," he said, setting down the box, pulling out two quart mason jars filled with what looked like apples.

Sam took one of the offered jars. "I guess," he said. "Which lends to another question. Where are the people who lived here?"

"I wondered that myself. There's no bodies, no car in the drive either. Maybe they were away on holiday when the world turned pear shaped."

"Could be," Sam said. "We'll find some way of transporting as much of this stuff back with us as we can. First thing's first, let's go down to the highway and see what we shall see."

The two men took their carbines and started down the hill, walking through waist high grass, over the guard rail, and onto the weedy shoulder.

The first thing they noticed was more garbage, then several empty beer bottles and hard liquor bottles strewn around. That explained the rowdiness they'd heard last night. There were three campfires, just smoldering embers now, and down the opposite direction both men spotted a large form lying by one. Their curiosity piqued, they walked that way, but they weren't even halfway to the form when Sam recognized it for what it was, the shape of a human body, splayed out and shirtless by the fire.

It was a white male, covered in tattoos and a thick beard. It looked as if everything of value had been stripped off his body, leaving only a soiled and torn pair of ACU trousers covering his lower body.

There was a dried pool of blood spread out, halo-like from the dead man's head. Sam pointed out to John two neat bullet holes in the man's body, one exactly mid-chest, between his nipples, the second over his right eye on his forehead, about a centimeter above his bushy eyebrow.

"That answers any questions about the two pistol shots we heard last night," Sam said. "Either one would have been fatal."

They walked back down the road towards the broken down vehicle, where Sam checked under the hood, while John took a look inside the apparently stripped interior.

"They have a cracked block. This isn't going anywhere," he said loud enough for his companion inside the vehicle to hear. "Did you find anything in there, John?"

"I found this under the seat in front," John said, handing a thick brown folder over to Sam.

He leaned back on the bumper and cocked his patrol cap back on his head, opening it up. He recognized it straightaway as a US Army 201, or personnel file. "This is odd, finding something like this," he said, and then paged through haphazardly, not really reading what was inside, not until a name jumped out and grabbed him by the throat.

He paled noticeably. "Fuck me running!"

"What is it?" John asked.

Sam held out a piece of paper from inside the folder to John's face. "It's a personnel file from the Army. Read the name on the top," he instructed.

John squinted in the early morning sunlight, and read: FLANNERY, TIMOTHY X PANG SMG 169 89 0238

"Holy shit is right!"

CHAPTER 13:
A RUMOR OF WAR

"So just when were you going to tell me?" Holly asked angrily, face as red as her hair, fire in her eyes.

"Babe, listen. I was—"

"No *you* listen, Sergeant Major! Unless you've completely forgotten, I'm part of this group too, and I am an officer in the military. I think I bloody well have a right to know!"

She was standing at the open screen door to the porch, holding Walter in her arms. Tim, Jimenez, Izzy, and Robyn were all sitting on the porch discussing the report from Sam Didinato, and it was obvious to Tim that she had overheard most of what was being discussed.

Now it was time for some damage control. "Robyn, why don't you take care of Walter for a few minutes? Holly and I have a few things to talk about," he said, standing up and motioning for Holly to come with him.

"Sure, Dad," Robyn said, gingerly taking the sleeping child from Holly. The other two men looked away as Holly walked over to Tim, who took her arm gently and led her off the porch and across the meadow towards the trees on the far end.

When they got to the tree line, Holly stopped and spun to face Tim in the darkness.

"Well?" she demanded, hands on her hips. "You think you're talking to some daft wee lassie here?"

"Babe, I was going to tell you tonight. We just got word from Sam this morning about the men on their way here."

"You knew for a few *weeks* they might be coming!"

"Yes, we did," Tim assented.

"Why didn't you tell me a few weeks ago then?"

"I didn't want you to be worried. You had just had the baby, and you needed the rest. I was going to tell you everything when I knew for sure."

"That doesn't make it right, Tim," she said, tears welling up in her eyes.

Tim put his arms around her in the darkness and held her tight. He felt like an ass right at this moment, but he still thought he did the right thing by not telling her right away.

She didn't say a word for several moments, just held onto him tightly, and sobbed into his chest. She sniffled once, and then said "So now what?"

"Now we make preparations for when they arrive."

"You're not thinking of fighting them, are you?"

"The thought did cross my mind."

"Tim, there's only a handful of us! How can we fight back against so many?"

"We did it before, on Volivoli. And this time you and Robyn will be far away from here, along with Walter."

"What do you mean?"

"What I mean is I want you and Robyn to take Walter and the other women here in the C130 and fly out of here. Down to Luke Air Force Base, and sit it out down there."

"Why?" she asked defiantly. "Don't you think us womenfolk can fight too? This isn't a wee fly wank in the toilet with the Kay's catalogue open at the underwear section!"

"It's not that, babe. From what we've been led to believe, they not only want me and the codes, they're coming for the plane and its pilot too. I just want you and the plane far from here if the shit hits the fan. They can't take something that isn't here," he said, hoping he was getting his point across. He'd never seen her so angry.

"I have a splendid idea, Tim. Why don't we *all* just fly out of here?"

"Because, this is our home."

"Tim, damn it, we've been through so much!"

"Exactly why I'm not going to run away from this now. We all have been through so much together and separately since the Event. At every step of the way, there has been some asshole trying to take what we've got away from us."

Her anger spent, she went to him, wrapping her arms around his torso, and then sighed and squeezed him tightly. "Let's go back to the house, and finish the plans we were discussing," Tim told her.

They walked hand in hand back to the house, where they found Jimenez and Izzy on the porch. "Where's Robyn?" he asked when he got to the top of the steps.

"She took Walter inside and was going to put him to bed," Izzy replied.

Tim sat back down on his favorite chair, Holly taking the seat next to him. When they were comfortable, Tim got Holly up to speed, filling in the blanks that she still didn't know.

When he was finished, she sat for a moment, and then said, "So you're telling me there is really a president back in Washington?"

"That's about the long and the short of it, ma'am," Jimenez asserted.

"And someone—you have no idea who he is— told you his plans?"

Tim nodded and started to fill his pipe.

"If that's the case, doesn't he have the legal right to those codes?" she said. "And I thought you didn't have them anymore." The anger was flashing back in her eyes again.

"I still have them. I copied them down into a notebook long before we ever met you and Izzy."

"Wouldn't you be breaking the law then?"

"Most definitely. To tell you the truth, I really don't give a shit. The world changed six years ago. The old laws don't mean a thing anymore," Tim said, striking a match to light his pipe. The light from the flame lit his face eerily, giving him an almost demonic look, accented by the cloud of smoke.

"Holly, Tim is right," Izzy said.

"Tim has been saying all along that we've got to follow the Constitution, that we've got to let it govern our lives so that we can build back civilization. By disregarding who we now believe is the president, isn't that going against everything he's said all along?"

"Since I first found out about this, I had a lot of time to think about it, a lot of soul-searching," Tim said. "You are absolutely correct. We've got to follow the Constitution. However, I've also believed, and have followed this one simple rule in my life, for as long as I can remember: if a law or order from a superior is unjust or immoral, isn't it my moral obligation as a human being to disobey those laws or orders?"

"We can't use the Nuremburg defense, Holly," Izzy said.

"But if he or she has the legal right to those codes, it's not an unjust or immoral order to return them!" Holly pointed out.

Tim sat there silently, and thought about what she'd just said. She was right, he knew, but the feelings he'd had welling up inside him finally came out.

"Here's what I have to say about that, and if it doesn't sound right, if you all think I've gone off the deep end, then we'll pack up and leave tomorrow," he said. "That crazy ship captain wanted those codes, and we know why. I wasn't about to give them up to him, or anyone else, not now, not ever."

"That was the right thing to do there, Tim. He wanted them for all the wrong reasons, but this, if it's true that the government is still intact, is a whole different thing!" Holly said in exasperation.

"Maybe that's true. But look around you. Six years ago the world went to shit, from what exactly I don't think we'll ever know for sure." He paused for a moment to gather his thoughts then went on. "The one thing that I do know for sure is, from the very beginning, I just wanted a quiet, safe place for me and Robyn. Then you guys came along, and I wanted the same thing for all of you. For my entire adult life, I've been fighting someone else's wars, for people and a government that forgot a long time ago what they really stood for."

"Because you're a good man, Tim," Holly said.

"A good man? Honey, if you knew half of what I've done in my life, you wouldn't say that at all," Tim spat, standing and walking over to the porch railing. He placed his hands on the wooden rail, his back towards them, and hung his head. "Have you ever heard the term 'False Flag'?"

"I've heard the term," Izzy replied.

"A false flag operation is basically a dirty trick, writ large. You do something really nasty, and make it look like the other guys did it."

"Like burning the Reichstag," the old doctor said.

"I don't understand you, Tim," Holly said.

Tim kept his gaze out over the dark meadow. He took in a deep breath, held it for a moment, and then let it out in a rush of air.

"What I'm about to tell all of you I've never told anyone about, ever. It fills my nightmares, and I don't think I'll ever get the image out of my head, and it'll stay there until I'm dead."

He was quiet for a few moments, inhaled again, and with a trembling voice, began. "Back in 1986, I had just made sergeant. I was regular Army then, stationed in Panama. On paper, I was cadre at the Jungle Warfare School at Fort Sherman. Most of the time I was, shall we say, 'loaned out' to several agencies— the FBI, the DEA, the CIA— for …special jobs."

"That's some serious Secret Squirrel shit, Sar' Major," Jimenez said.

"Yeah," Tim said, nodding. "Squirrelly is a good word for it. To make a long story short, the Sandinistas were the bad guys; allegedly, the Contras were the good guys."

Tim turned to face his audience, folded his arms across his chest and leaned against the railing. "One night a whole platoon of us, carrying nothing that identified us with the US government, dressed in Czech uniforms, toting AK47's, bee-bopped into a friendly Contra village, roused everyone out of their beds, then dragged all of them, every man, woman and child out to a field…"

"Oh…" Holly gasped, bringing her hand up to her face in shock.

"Yeah. Do I really need to go on?"

"No, you don't have to go on," Izzy said.

"I was twenty-one, Iz. Almost thirty years ago now, and I still see it when I close my eyes like it just happened."

"That was a long time ago, Tim. You're a different man now," Holly said, rubbing her arms as if a chill had crossed over her.

"Exactly."

"Please explain," Holly said.

"It's like this, and it seems so simple to me, but correct me if I'm wrong. I knew when Robyn and I found the codes in the field around the wreckage of Air Force One that I'd have to protect them from anyone who wouldn't respect their power."

"You did. You kept them from that crazy captain," Holly said.

"Be that as it may, you have no idea the weight that was on my shoulders when I keyed those codes into the computer back on Volivoli. I've been through a lot in my life, and never have been as scared as I was that afternoon."

"I can imagine," Izzy said.

"Izzy, no disrespect, but no you can't. You honestly have no concept. I knew at that moment, the moment I hit the 'enter' key, what that bombardier in the Enola Gay had felt. Not the ones who history says dropped the bomb. Not Paul Tibbetts, the pilot, not Harry Truman. It was the bombardier who dropped that bomb and killed all those people."

"That shortened the war by months, and saved thousands of lives," Jimenez said.

"Did it, Taco?" he asked, not waiting for a reply. "So there I was, launching a nuclear weapon, the first one to do so in anger since World War Two, and that scared the living shit out of me."

"I'm still not following you, Tim," Holly said softly, her heart breaking because she could feel the pain in Tim's voice.

"The world ended six years ago. We moved on, tried to live a good life, be good people. But in every step we took, there was some asshole trying to take it away."

"Yes, that's true," Izzy said.

"Now we've supposedly done away with the last tyrant. We have a little community set up here, Jerry is out on Oahu doing the same thing, and we have our intrepid sailors out sailing the Seven Seas. All my life I've fought for what is right, and seeing what the government was capable of doing, of endorsing, and for the most part, I was totally helpless. I was just tool to do their bidding, knowing they were corrupt, unable to do anything about it. Now I can." He let what he'd just said settle with everyone, let them digest it.

"Tim, if there is a president, he has the legal authority to have the codes," Holly said.

"That's true. Let me ask everyone this… the world as we knew it has ceased. What have we been doing since? What is Jerry trying to do out in Hawaii?"

"Rebuilding civilization?" Jimenez said, like a question.

Tim snapped his fingers and pointed at him. "Exactly, we're trying to rebuild society, civilization. We're not trying to *rule the fucking world!* None of us has any grand illusions on our own self-importance. We haven't commandeered some ship, and gone tear-assing all over the Pacific Ocean terrorizing who's left. We're not threatening anyone. We just want to be left alone to live our lives as we see fit. We don't want, or need, someone who doesn't know us tell us how to live our lives. That had gone on for far too long in the old world. So long, in fact, that most of us forgot what it's like to be really free."

"But, Tim," Holly started to say.

"No buts, Holly," Tim said gently. "Yes, I want to live under the rules of the Constitution, but I want to go back to 1775 when those smart men wrote it, back to the basics. Not live under the thinly veiled lies that we were spoon fed. I was sick and tired of others telling me how to live my life, what I could and couldn't do, all because they, the anointed ones, knew what was best for me, as if I was too stupid to figure it out on my own."

"I'm all for it, Sar' Major. I know exactly what you mean," Jimenez chimed in.

"None of us wanted to be in this position. I know that. And if you want to leave, I won't stop you."

"I'm staying, Tim. I'm not going anywhere without you," Holly said, steel in her voice. "But I don't get what you mean about the president. You haven't come right out and said it, but you only have one transmission of warning, then the report from Sam yesterday telling you about the troops. What makes you think anyone means us harm?"

"I haven't come right out and said it, it's only a feeling in my gut. And again, I could be wrong, very wrong. I'll put it to you as a question. If this guy, or woman, saying they're president is so benevolent, why would someone in his camp risk sending me a message to warn me? Why send a whole company of troops to quote 'retrieve the codes, arrest me, bring me, the codes, the aircraft, and pilot back to Washington DC' unquote?"

"Now I'm following you, Timothy, and now I'm in one hundred percent agreement," Izzy said. The sound of the screen door opening distracted everyone for a moment, and they all looked to see Robyn coming outside, lantern in one hand, six pack of beer in the other.

"I figured we all needed a drink," she said, handing out cans, popping one for herself and sitting on Jimenez' lap. She looked at Holly. "Walt is sound asleep. I'll go and check on him again in a few."

"Thank you, Robyn," Holly said, then turned to Izzy. "Getting back to what you just said, Iz, you understand? I sure don't."

"Like Tim said, if this president of ours is so benevolent, why is someone in his camp, a Benedict Arnold so-to-speak, warning us, and why is he sending out an army to arrest Tim and yourself, and bring you all back to DC?"

"If he was so concerned about the country, the last thing on his mind would be sending troops out to arrest someone," Tim said. "He should be making sure the power is on, the people are fed, the home fires burning, all that."

"Yeah, he'd be sending out, what do you call them, diplomats or something, right, Sar' Major?" Jimenez asked.

"That's right, Taco. He'd be sending out envoys all over the country. He'd be trying to get communications working again, bringing people together, and not trying to get his hands on the nuclear codes. If I was in his position, that's exactly what I'd be doing, and those codes would be way down on the bottom of my list, just below contracting gonorrhea."

"Is that really enough, Tim?" Holly asked.

"It's enough for me to know I want nothing to do with him, or her, and more than enough to know I don't want to give up the codes. If I could, I'd find each and every silo in the country and fill every goddamn last one up with concrete. I don't want the power, and I sure as shit don't want some other nutcase to have the power," Tim asserted.

"Aye, I guess you're right," Holly said after a moment's reflection.

"Let's finish up the plans were making," Tim said, coming back over to the group, pulling up his chair. He pulled pulling out a topographical map of northern Yavapai and southern Coconino counties.

He motioned Robyn to hand him the lantern and set it next to the map that he'd spread out on the wooden cable spool that he'd been using as an outside table. He set his pipe down next to the lantern and studied the faces in his group. When he was sure that he had everyone's attention, he cleared his throat and began.

"Alright, we've already discussed that I want Holly to take the C130 down to Luke AFB, along with Walter, Robyn, and the other three women, and stay there until everything here is clear."

"When do you want us to leave?" Holly asked.

"I don't know just yet. Didinato says they've just entered Colorado on I-70, and he and John will be bird-dogging them as best they can, but they might have problems keeping up."

"Why?" Jimenez asked.

"He's on horseback, and has several head of buffalo with him," Tim told the young Marine.

"Horseback? No shit?"

"Yeah, Taco. Seems he found our friend, Dawn Redeagle and traded his ride for the horses and the buffalo. He'll be a while getting back. There is good news. He reported the conditions of the roads are getting bad, and the convoy is not travelling much faster than them. I kind of figured the roads would start to go downhill after a while. There's a big span over Hell Canyon just north of Drake on Route 89. When I was out there a few weeks ago looking for more junipers to cut, I saw that it had collapsed into the canyon. The bridge piers were probably undermined by a flood at some point, and just fell in on itself."

"So you figure the roads all over the country are starting to deteriorate?" Izzy asked.

"Everything is, really, when you look around. Nature is taking back what man has tried to make his. I knew it'd only be a matter of time."

"So they might take as much as a few weeks more to get here?" Robyn asked.

"Yep, that's what I figure. That will work for us. That, and the conditions of the roads. Sam said they were here," he said, pointing to another, larger map of the western half of the United States. "Just a few clicks west of Burlington, Colorado. Now they can take two routes. They could stay on I-70 and continue through Denver, over the Rockies, into Utah, where they can pick up I-15 and head south into Arizona via Nevada, coming through Las Vegas, and picking up I-40 to the west of us in Needles, backtracking from the west."

"Are you sure they'll come that way?" Holly asked.

"No, they could also come down from Utah the way Robyn and I did, on Alternate Route 89 at Colorado City, across the North Rim of the Grand Canyon, and come down through Flagstaff. I'm not convinced they'll come that way, though, through the Rockies. No telling what kind of shit through the passes could be blocking them. It was clear when Robyn and I came through a few years ago, but that was then. Several years, and most probably several heavy snowfalls have most probably done all kinds of damage in the passes. Landslides, avalanches, ground heaves." Tim pointed at the map again. "If I were them, I'd come through Denver, pick up I-25, and head south from there into New Mexico, pick up I-40 in Albuquerque and head into Arizona that way."

"That does make sense," Izzy said.

"What do we do, Dad?" Robyn asked.

"Taco, how much TNT did you say there was at Camp Navajo?"

"Literally tons of it. Five point six tons, to be exact," Jimenez told Tim.

"Good, because we're going to drop a bunch of highway bridges, and a few railroad ones too, just to be on the safe side. Our wayward Aussie railway man will probably not like it, but that's too bad."

"Which ones?" Jimenez asked, leaning into the map that Tim had moved into view of the two counties.

"The bridges over this gorge here, a few miles east on I-40," he pointed. "Both spans, east and westbound traffic, and the railroad bridge about five hundred meters to the south. And these two spans here, just a little east of Ash Fork, along with the railroad bridge to the north."

"We shouldn't have to worry about them coming from the south, and that bridge is already down on Route 89."

"Yeppers. The only worry I have from that direction is that they could find the dirt road from Drake, and come up through that way. I can lay a few antitank mines there if we want."

"What about them finding Camp Navajo?" Holly asked. "If they find that, won't they be able to raid our supplies there and turn them against us?"

"Babe, you're good at history, and you're British. What was the first thing the UK did when the threat of a German invasion was imminent in 1940?"

"Aye, I remember. They took down all the road signs," she said, then added indignantly, "and I'm Scottish, ya' Mick bastard!"

Ignoring the slight to his heritage, Tim replied, "Right, they took down the road signs. That's what we'll do. You can't see it from the highway, in fact, the only thing you can see from the highway there is a Harley Davidson dealership. If there's no signage, there's no Army depot."

Izzy chuckled. "What else have you got up your sleeve, Tim?"

"I'm going to have Ian on the 81mm mortar here, about three thousand meters away from the east side of the span we'll drop here, well within its maximum range. They won't be expecting a rain of high explosive rounds falling on them."

"What if they come this way?" Jimenez asked, pointing to the road coming south from Tusayan.

Tim nodded somberly. "You're turning into an infantryman, Taco. That's where I'm worried too. It's sort of an Achilles heel. They could come up from Flagstaff, up Route 180 into Valle, and then take Route 68 south, right into the middle of town. There's absolutely nothing to block them that way, no bridges to blow. That's why I want the mortar here, so if needed, Ian can shift fire over to this junction north of town at Elk Ridge. That's about it for now. I'll figure out a few firing positions once I can look over the area a little better when we blow the bridges. I meant what I said before, I want all the women and kids gone out of here, the sooner the better."

"Anything else you'd like, Tim?" Izzy asked.

"Yeah, a battery of 105mm howitzers and the whole 1st Battalion of the 75th Ranger Regiment."

"We'll beat 'em, Sar' Major," Jimenez said gleefully.

"Tim, you can't really think you can beat them, not with what little we have?" Holly asked, fear in her eyes.

"No, I don't think we can beat them. I don't plan on it either."

"Then why, for God's sake?"

"Holly, I said I didn't plan on beating them. I *do* plan on stopping them in their tracks."

"How, Tim?" she gasped. "There's so few of us, and from what you've said, there's over a hundred of them!"

"I'll make them pay dearly for every meter of ground they want to take. That's about it," he said, folding up his maps.

"We don't plan on taking them on in a head to head fight, Holly," Izzy said, trying to reassure her. "This is going to be guerilla warfare at its finest. Tim and the rest of us will fight from hiding, just like the Viet Cong did so many years ago."

"Are you going to fight too, Izzy?"

"I fought in a war a long time ago, and I have no qualms about fighting again, if the cause is just. And this, I think, is a just fight. I don't like it at all, but I know we have to, for our very survival."

"Aye, I agree it is, but you all have to promise me one thing," Holly said. "Promise me you'll stop if it looks like you're going to be killed, okay? Give me that, please. If it looks bad, please just give up so you can live another day."

Tears were welling up in her eyes again, and before she could get an answer, she spun on her heels and bolted inside the house.

"Dad, do want me to go and talk to her?" Robyn asked.

"No, leave her be. I'll go up in a few minutes, check on Walt and I'll talk to her."

"If that's it, then, Taco and I want to get to bed," she told him, and Tim winced.

He knew it was happening, but it didn't mean he had to like it. In his mind, Robyn was still that disheveled waif he'd come across in southern West Virginia so many years ago. She would always be his little girl.

Robyn took Jimenez by the hand and led him into the house, leaving Tim and Izzy alone on the porch.

Tim walked over to the railing again and looked out over the moonlit meadow. There were several dozen elk that had come down from the tree line unnoticed by them as they sat on the porch, and Tim watched them silently grazing over the tall grass. Somewhere off in the distance, he heard a few coyotes yelping.

"Izzy, tell me I'm doing the right thing," he said.

"I don't think we have a choice, Timothy. We could run away, but I know that running is not in your nature, and never will be. Besides, they'd find us no matter where we went anyway. Like you said, this is our home."

"You're right, I won't run, and this is our home. Why can't everyone just leave us alone?" "I don't know, Tim. I don't know," he said, then handed Tim another beer.

"Thanks. I think I'll have one more then call it a night."

"Me too. Strange world, eh?" Izzy said, twisting off the top of the now tepid beer and sitting back down in a chair next to the table. Tim sat down opposite and held up his bottle in salute.

"To a strange world," he said, and took a swig. "You know something, Iz, right before the Event, I was going to pull the plug. I had made up my mind on the way home from Afghanistan. I was going to put my retirement papers in to both the Army and the Police Department. I thought I had it all planned out. I was going to retire, sell the house, and Connie and I were going to move down to Florida, to the Keys. I was going to do nothing but fish and drink beer."

"Sounds like a good plan."

"I thought so. I got home to Philly, and found my house was in foreclosure, and Connie had split to points unknown with some cowboy from Montana."

"It happens a lot in wartime, I saw it a few times when I was still in the Navy."

"I saw it with my men a few times too, but it's one of those things you never think would happen to you."

"Yes, it always happens to the other guy. We're always shocked when it happens to us, and we shouldn't be."

"I'm getting too old for this shit, Iz," Tim told his friend.

"We all are. Another thing I've been meaning to ask you... I've noticed your gait has changed a little. How are your knees?"

"Always the doc, eh?" Tim smiled. "My knees are fucked, Iz. They sound like Rice Krispies. I know it's arthritis, but there's not a lot I can do about it."

"You're correct. It's not like you can go down to the VA hospital, put in a claim and get knee replacements. I want you to start taking glucosamine. It'll help rebuild the cartilage in your knees. You can get it at the drug store in town, in the vitamin section."

"If it'll help, I'll do it," Tim said, and downed the last of his beer. "And with that, sir, I will say goodnight."

"Goodnight, Tim. I think I'm going to sit out here and watch the elk graze and listen to the coyotes yelp for a while."

"I'll leave you to it," Tim said, stood, and made his way into the house. All the lights were off, but there was enough moonlight coming through the windows to light the way through the living room and up the stairs to the bedroom. He opened the door as quietly as he could, and when he entered, he could see Holly lying on her side.

He tiptoed across and around to the crib, where Walter was clutching a tiny blue blanket, sleeping soundly. Tim knew it wouldn't last long; he was waking every few hours, crying for his mother's milk.

He went to his side of the bed and undressed, pulled back the sheets, and climbed into bed. When he was getting settled, he felt Holly stir.

"Sorry, babe. I didn't want to wake you," he whispered.

"That's okay, love. I wasn't asleep," she replied in her soft voice, her lilting accent singing in his ears. She rolled over and put her arm over his chest, laying her head in the crook of his arm.

"I'm sorry I kept anything from you."

"It's okay now, but please, don't ever keep anything like that from me again." He lay there holding her, looking up at the ceiling for a time, wishing it all could go back to the time before they left and went to that island. But no, they wouldn't have Walter now, and that little life over in the crib was the main reason, the *only* reason he was taking a stand now.

"Do you think you can stop them?" she finally asked.

"Yes, I do."

"How? It just seems so impossible."

"Have you ever heard of Carlos Hathcock?"

"No?"

"I guess you wouldn't have gotten too much Vietnam War history in Scotland," he said, still whispering as to not to wake the baby. "He was a Marine sniper, the best of the best, ballsy fucker. Anyway, one day he and his spotter, also a Scout-sniper, were in the jungle staking out a long ditch next to a rice paddy. Not another friendly around for a long ways. They're set up inside the tree line, not making a sound. Along comes this whole company of North Vietnamese soldiers. Not Viet Cong guerillas, these were trained soldiers. They weren't two hundred yards away from them."

"What did they do?" she asked, and Tim knew he'd set the hook. It was time to reel his catch in.

"They began to snipe at them, him from one end of the formation, his spotter from the other, and for over twenty-four hours, had that whole entire company, over a hundred and thirty men, pinned down in a ditch. By the time they bugged out a day later, they had killed over a hundred of the bastards, and had the rest running for their lives."

"You made that up!"

"No, it's the truth. I have the book downstairs on the bookshelf. The whole story was independently verified by another Marine unit that came through after they radioed in the location."

"So that's what you plan on doing?"

"In a way. I'll have a mortar for support, they didn't have one of those," he said, only telling a half-truth. Carlos actually had a few batteries of howitzers at his beck and call on the other end of a radio, and had used illumination rounds fired by those batteries all night to light up the whole area, and also to lob in some HE rounds once in a while to keep them pinned, but he wasn't about to tell Holly that.

"And you promise me you'll leave like they did when it gets to a point you can't do any more?"

"Yes, as long as you stay down in Phoenix until I say it's alright to come back," he said. "Besides, I have even more reason now to stay alive. And all the more reason to do what's right. I just want Walter to be able to grow up in a world that he doesn't have to be afraid of anything, babe."

"Aye, that's why I love you so much," she said, leaning up to kiss him. She lingered on his lips, and then the kiss grew more urgent. The broke the kiss for some air, and she smiled at him in the darkness.

"Would you care to fraternize with me in an unlawful manner, Sergeant Major?"

"I would love to, Leftenant, but isn't it too soon after the baby?"

"Not at all, Sergeant Major. The doctor informed me today I was able to return to my wifely duties in the bedroom."

"Oh did he now? That is good news, considering you're not my wife!"

"Be that as it may, I would still like to fool around with you," she said, leaning down to his chest and biting his nipple lightly.

Tim rolled his head back and moaned, running his hands through her long, thick hair. She reached down with her hand, found what she was searching for, and discovered he was more than ready. She rolled on top of him and guided him into her, and sat up, hands on his chest.

She began to move him inside of her, and then she came back down, keeping the rhythm, and kissed him passionately.

Just before she came, Walter let out a loud wail, breaking the moment.

Holly rolled off of Tim and sighed, and then they both laughed.

"Someone's hungry," she said.

Tim turned on the bedside lamp and propped himself up on an elbow, his head resting in his hand watching Holly pick up his son lovingly, bring him up to her breast where he immediately found the extended nipple with his mouth and began to suck greedily.

"That's a lucky kid," Tim said playfully.

It was an image he wanted to keep in his mind forever, this beautiful woman, holding an equally beautiful baby, breastfeeding, and not a care in the world.

It would be one of the last happy images Tim would have, for a long, long time.

CHAPTER 14:
CHARLIE MIKE

The convoy stopped for the evening by the on ramp to E470 off of I-70 outside of Aurora, Colorado, and the city of Denver could be seen just a little further west.

The sun had crept below the distant Rocky Mountains, but there was still enough light to see a lone soldier walking from the rear of the line of parked vehicles on the side of the road.

The man, who had ridden in the trail vehicle, was checking with the driver of each vehicle, and from time to time spoke with the men dismounting and stretching sore muscles from the cramped, uncomfortable, and long journey.

When he made his way up the formation to the lead vehicle, a dirty and well-worn Hum-Vee, he stopped at the front of it. The driver, a young black kid, had his head on the steering wheel and was snoring loudly. He could see another form seated on the front bumper, a cloud of putrid cigar smoke wafting around his head.

He cleared his throat to get the other man's attention. "All set, sir, nothing to report."

"That's good, Sergeant. Are the men preparing to bivouac?"

"Yes, Major. They're breaking for chow and some are scrounging for firewood."

"Alright then, we'll set out again first thing in the morning," the major said, cigar clenched between his teeth.

"Sir…" the sergeant said tentatively.

"What is it, man?"

"Sir, we've been at it for several weeks. I was thinking we could stay here for a few days, maybe scrounge around over in Denver for some better supplies. We're completely out of the MREs we brought with us from DC, and we've been subsisting on what we find in these truck stops and convenience stores. Not only that, sir, the vehicles are in need of some maintenance. Losing the Hum-Vee the other day set us back yet again. The men are really cramped now."

"I'll take that under advisement, Sergeant," the major said with a curt nod.

"Sir, the men need the rest. The roads are in a lot worse shape than we expected, and it didn't help us any having almost all of the major bridges over the Mississippi impassable," the sergeant said, pleading.

They had come across I-40, but when they reached the Mississippi River in Memphis, found that bridge had collapsed into the river, and was a twisted heap of metal and concrete surrounded by several wrecks of barges and ships that had been washed downstream, half submerged in the muddy brown water. Not only had that, the several years' worth of heavy rains and spring thaw snowmelt had apparently sent the mighty Mississippi over its flood levels several times, washing away whole towns and roads in its wake on both banks, to the point the entire river basin was completely unrecognizable, and impassable in most places. Nature had surely taken that area back with a vengeance.

They had had to travel north, all the way into Wisconsin, before they found a usable bridge, where they crossed into Minnesota at Minneapolis. That little detour had cost them several weeks' travelling, taking them hundreds of miles out of their way.

"Well, Sergeant, I'll make out a Disposition Form to complain to the Department of Transportation."

The sergeant sighed at the sarcasm. He'd known several 'high-speed, low drag' majors like this in the past. Before the Event, the sergeant had been in the Maryland National Guard, and was also a State Trooper from there also. But he had to watch himself; he was one of the truly rare lucky ones, both he and his wife had survived that horrible night, and if he wanted to keep the nice house he'd been allowed to live in, he had to toe the line.

George Orwell was right, he remembered. Some pigs are more equal than the others and he wanted to stay 'more equal', so he bit his tongue, which was a wise thing to do. The major had the power to take it away, and he didn't want to be thrown in with all the rest of the population of Washington, scraping and begging for food, living in hovels. He didn't reply, just stood there at parade rest, and waited for the major to speak again. "Sergeant, I think you know how important our mission is, don't you?"

"Yes, sir, I'm well away of the importance of the mission. I'm just suggesting two days to rest, and take care of the vehicles and the men."

The major produced a bottle of Jack Daniels from one of his pockets, un-capped it, and took a healthy pull, right from the bottle. He handed the bottle to the sergeant.

"Take a drink and relax, Sergeant."

"I'll take a pass, sir," he replied, looking back down the line of trucks parked along the guardrail. He could already see the lights from several fires lighting up the sides of the vehicles, and he inwardly cringed.

Nothing like light and sound discipline, he thought angrily. Right now they could be spotted for miles away, and then the men just wouldn't be quiet either, so they could also be heard for miles away also. Any enemy that might want to could surely target them without much trouble.

But there wasn't an enemy out there in the darkness, was there? No, there couldn't be, he remembered, but then that odd nagging feeling he started to get a few days ago returned. When they were still in Kansas, he was almost convinced several times that they were being watched, but he kept shrugging it off as paranoia.

Thankfully, the rowdy, drunken fights had stopped. The major had ended that once and for all with the help of his Beretta M9 and two 9mm rounds to the offending person. Crude, but effective.

The major still wouldn't put a stop to the nightly campfires, and that angered him. He added it to the increasing list of things the major did that he didn't like, but couldn't change. He just hoped the major would listen to him and let them do some maintenance on the vehicles and forage for some better supplies.

"Sergeant, let's get some chow, shall we?" the major said, walking to the rear of the Hum-Vee, where he rummaged around the cluttered mess of gear and produced a one burner camp stove. He set that up on the tailgate, opened a can of beef stew, and poured the contents into a pot.

"Have you found the dossier sir?" the sergeant asked.

"I'm sure I must have left it in the Hum-Vee we left in Kansas. No great loss, I have all the information I need about our target," the major said, stirring the stew with a spoon.

"What if someone finds it, sir?"

"I wouldn't worry yourself over that, Sergeant. It's just the personnel file of a middle-aged soldier of no great importance."

"It's intelligence, sir. It'd be useful to someone," the sergeant persisted, leaning against the tailgate. "I think he had a good record, Major. He had an exemplary Army career in Iraq and Afghanistan, and even before that."

"I disagree. He's a nobody, and a rogue. We're tasked with bringing him to justice."

"I remember some stories about him. I didn't know him personally, we were never in the same unit, but there were stories about him in Iraq. Even if they're only half true, he's still a ballsy bastard."

"Ah, the old war stories. I wouldn't believe them too much. He may be a legend in the Army, but he's still just a man, and one man can be beaten."

Undeterred, the sergeant went on. "I heard one story; it went through the whole country like wildfire. He had been ambushed on the initial drive into Baghdad. An RPG took out his gunner and driver in his Bradley. He radioed a chopper that was flying by to pick up his wounded, and when the pilot refused to land, he got right on the radio and threatened to shoot the bastard down if he didn't land. That shows me he's a man of principle, and willing to go out on a limb for his men."

"I don't believe it. Even if it was a true story, it doesn't tell me that at all. It shows me a picture of a man who has no respect for authority, a soldier who had no business being a private, let alone a sergeant major. He should have been court martialed, not promoted." The major lifted lifting the pot to his face and breathed in the aroma. He offered some to the sergeant, who held out a canteen cup. While the major was pouring the stew into the cup, he continued, "All the more reason we need to go out there and bring him back. The world has gone mad, and we're left to rebuild it, Sergeant. This new world of ours needs order and discipline. Something the president knows about. We were sworn to obey those orders, not to set up camp out in the desert somewhere and proclaim yourself as king of the world."

The sergeant took a plastic spoon out of a pocket in his ACUs and spooned a mouthful of the steaming food. When he swallowed, he said, "I agree, sir. But the point I'm trying to make is that we shouldn't underestimate him at all. I think that's why the general gave us his 201 file to begin with, to let us know what we're up against."

"One man, Sergeant?" the major asked between spoonfuls. "What exactly can one man do against a whole company?"

"He's well trained, Major, unlike most of our men," the sergeant informed them. "I've just now got them to stop firing their weapons all over the place. Most of the men now only have half of the ammo we issued to them in DC. That's not good. It's another reason I think we should head over to Denver tomorrow; we can find a few gun shops and replenish our 5.56mm ammo."

"You do have a point there, Sergeant," the major relented. "We'll send out a patrol into the city to find more ammunition."

"And some food?"

"Yes, we'll send them to get food also. Is that's all that's bothering you?"

The sergeant hesitated for a moment, then, looking down at his canteen cup, said, "Sir, I know this might sound crazy, but I've felt like we've been being watched these last few days."

The major guffawed. "You think we're being watched? By whom? There's no one left!"

"Like I said, sir, it sounds nutty, but I feel it. It's creepy. I've felt it before, in the Ghan and Iraq," the sergeant said. He almost added 'you wouldn't know about it,' but he kept his thoughts in check. He knew the major had never once been overseas; the lack of the combat patch on his right shoulder told him as much, along with the nutty decisions he'd made in the past that would have surely never have been decided on by someone with combat experience.

Yeah, the major was a Pog, for sure, and most probably a Blue Falcon, a 'buddy fucker,' someone who'd throw his friend under the bus in a second to gain some advantage.

"Sergeant, I can assure you we're not being watched," the major said, smiling in the darkness.

"Sir, have you seen any horses?"

"Horses? You know there are no horses, Sergeant. They were all killed that night in The Cull."

He hated when the major used that term. The first time he'd heard it, he thought the major was joking. He called it 'The Great Cull,' as if what had happened was God's cull of all that was bad with humanity, leaving only the righteous to lead, and the rest, sheep to follow. It sickened him, but again, he kept his mouth shut out of self-preservation.

"Major, I know that, but the last few days, along with my feeling, I swear a few times I could smell horse manure when the wind was just right."

"Sergeant," the major said with a condescending laugh, "we just came through Kansas. The entire state is filled with horse and cow shit."

The sergeant decided not to risk saying anything further. He'd at least gotten the major to allow a patrol to find some food and ammo for the men, and considered that a small victory.

"Sergeant, go wake up my driver, there's a little of this stew left, see if he wants it," the major ordered, setting down the pot on the tailgate, and pulling out another one of his nasty cigars.

"Yes sir," the sergeant replied. It made his blood boil, knowing that he was no leader. *Definitely a Blue Falcon*, he thought. Any leader worth his weight would have made sure his men were fed before they had a single morsel to eat. Then he felt a little ashamed at himself, also, because he had imbibed in the food himself, knowing full well the young kid was right there, snoring away. He should have offered to feed the man first.

Was he turning into a carbon copy of the major now? He reached into the open window and gently tapped on the kid's shoulder. "Hey, Nuggets. Wake up. Food's on if you want."

The man stirred and looked over at the man waking him. "Yeah, Sarge, I am kinda' hungry, y'know?"

"Grab your canteen cup. The major's got some stew on the burner."

"Thanks, Sarge. I was dreamin'a some nice peach cobbler my ma useta make," the younger man said, getting out of the Hum-Vee stiffly. "I can smell somthin' Sarge."

"The major had some beef stew in the back."

"Thanks," the boy said.

"I've been meaning to ask, Nuggets. Why do they call you that?" the sergeant asked, truly curious.

"Ma' real name be Jamal, but when I was a baby, the only thing my ma could get me to eat was chicken nuggets from Mickey-D's. So everybody just started to call me 'Nuggets' an it jeskinda' stuck, y'know?"

"It's not the fine cuisine of MacDonald's, but it'll fill your belly, Nug," the sergeant said, patting the young ersatz soldier on the back. When they reached the tailgate again, the sergeant said, "Sir, I'm going to head back to the rear of the convoy and make sure everyone's settled. I'll see you in the morning."

"Okay, Sergeant. Me and the private here will settle in for the night, wake me if you need anything," the major said in a tone that said 'don't you dare wake me up.'

The sergeant started to make his way back towards the rear of the line of vehicles, and halfway back, he stopped and looked out over the darkness. Everything was black, no lights or signs of anyone watching them from a distance, the only smells were of campfires, tobacco, and another substance burning, that in earlier times he would have exploded in a rage. However, those days were long past, and the major didn't seem to care, so why should he?

It was one thing to have them all liquored up; to have them smoking dope was another thing altogether. But there was nothing he could do about it since the major didn't care. When he got back to his vehicle, he saw a man standing by the guardrail relieving himself. It was his driver, another what he called 'real soldier,' a Specialist 4 who had once served as an infantryman in the 101st Airmobile division. When he heard the sergeant approach, he zipped up his fly and turned to face him.

"Hey, Sarge, any news?"

"No, just the same old shit."

"Just a different day, eh?"

"That's about the long and the short of it. I did convince him to let us put together a patrol tomorrow to run into Denver to scare up some ammo and food."

"Thank fuck for small favors," the specialist said, rummaging around in his Alice pack. "I squirreled away some MREs, do you want one?"

"I ate some stew with the major, but yeah, I could eat some more."

"I've got Mediterranean Chicken, or Spicy Penne Pasta. Take your pick," he told the sergeant, holding up two of the brown plastic packages.

"Pasta," the sergeant said, and the Specialist tossed him the package. He caught it deftly, and sat down in the open door of the Hum-Vee. He cut open the bag, and pulled out the contents, pocketing the toaster pastry, the wheat snack bread, pudding, and peanut butter, saving them for later. Slicing open the main meal packet, he eschewed the heater and decided to eat it cold, using up the entire bottle of Tabasco sauce. The two soldiers talked while they ate, mostly small talk, about life before, but not too much of that, it was too painful for them.

The specialist had finished his main meal, and was slathering cheese spread on his vegetable crackers when he stopped suddenly, looked at the sergeant. "What do you really think of all of this?"

The sergeant chose his words carefully before replying. He picked his teeth absently, looked out the windshield at a growing thunderhead far off in the south, lit up like a Chinese lantern by lightning, too far away to hear any thunder yet.

"To be honest?"

"Yeah, give it to me, warts and all."

"I think it's a waste of time and effort, not to mention resources, we could use back in DC."

"Yeah, I was thinking the same thing, Sarge."

"Just don't go around talking like this in front of the troops, okay?" the sergeant said, looking at the specialist gravely.

"Shit, I mean, so what if this guy is out here saying he's president? I sure as shit don't give a fuck. It's a big goddamn country, and we got a slice of it back east. I say let's turn this dog and pony show around, head back home, and leave this guy to his cactus and shit."

"Because we have orders, that's why. I don't want to be here anymore than you do. Let's just go out there, arrest this guy like the president wants, and bring him back. Then we can go about our lives again."

"That's what's bugging me, Sarge. You were the cop in Civvie Street. Can we really do that?"

"Arrest him, you mean?" the sergeant asked.

"Yeah. I mean, isn't there some such shit like the Posse Comitatus rule somewhere?"

"The Posse Comitatus Act was set up during the Reconstruction after the Civil War. It's to limit the US government's use of the active military to enforce state laws. It doesn't count the National Guard. It doesn't concern us, because we're acting under the authority of the president to arrest a member of the US Army for violation of the UCMJ," he told the specialist, "the Uniform Code of Military Justice, which governs the US Military, basically the Army's own Criminal Code."

"I understand," the specialist replied, not understanding at all. "So we're not locking up some civilian, he's still in the Army, and we're going to toss him in the stockade."

"Basically."

"Alright, I think I'm going to hit the fartsack, Sarge. That is unless you have anything for me to do?"

"Nah, I think I'm going to turn in myself," he said, ditching his garbage from the MRE.

The specialist grabbed his sleeping bag and tossed it on the roof of the Hum-Vee, took his M4 and set it up on the roof next to his bed for the night, climbed up, curled up into a fetal position, and was sound asleep in seconds.

The sergeant shook his head and laughed a little, never ceasing to be amazed at how fast soldiers could fall asleep in the field. He grabbed his own sleeping bag and his rifle, walked over to a tree a few yards off the weedy highway on-ramp and spread out the bag, pulled off his ACU top, and rolled it into a ball to use as a pillow. He then shucked his boots, and crawled into the lightweight bag. He lay there for quite a while, listening to the hoots and hollers from the men in the convoy, but they weren't getting too rowdy now, not after the lesson in discipline they were taught from the muzzle of a M9 pistol a few days ago.

His mind wandered back to the thunderstorm off in the distance, and he thought, a little too late, that he might get wet sleeping uncovered like this. He studied the clouds, lit up intermittently from the inside by flashes of lightning, and after several moments, determined that it was travelling west, so he relaxed again.

He thought about what the specialist had asked him earlier, and he told himself that orders were orders, especially if they came directly from the White House. He'd do what he needed to do. He'd follow his orders faithfully, and get back to his wife in DC. With that thought, he fell into a deep sleep, his last vision that of the distant thunderhead lighting up the night sky.

The next morning, the major, true to his word, allowed the sergeant to send out a patrol into Denver to scavenge for more ammunition and food.

He chose five men, all hand-picked real soldiers, ones who weren't conscripted after the fact and had actually been in the military in some form before the world went to crap.

He had also gotten several of the men remaining to do maintenance on the vehicles, and by the time the patrol returned in the afternoon, most of the vehicles were ready to continue rolling.

The patrol brought back several hundred rounds of civilian .223 ammo, the same as military 5.56mm, and that was issued out to the men as evenly as possible. They had also found a National Guard armory, and were able to procure several cases of MREs, along with cases of canned soups, potted meats, spam, and canned corned beef and vegetables.

Along with all of that, they must have raided a liquor store, because they had brought back, against all suggestions to the contrary, over a hundred bottles of whiskey, rum, and gin.

The major, deciding it was too late to travel, decided to spend an extra night in bivouac along the highway. One intrepid soldier, halfway through the day, suggested that they all head over to the Best Western hotel by the toll-road's exit, and maybe they could spend a night in a real bed.

The major thought it was a capital idea, and sent the man and two others over to investigate, but was disappointed at their report upon returning. They had found that half of the hotel's roof had collapsed over the last few years, probably from a heavy snowfall, and was totally uninhabitable, and the rooms that were still weather tight, were filled with the mummified corpses of their previous overnight tenants, who were never checking out.

They camped again along the side of the deteriorating highway, but were forced to sleep in the vehicles, because sometime after sundown, several bands of thunderstorms came through, soaking the entire area.

Rested and fed, they started off mid-morning the following day, heading south now on E470, where they found the exit ramp for I-15 near Centennial, Colorado and headed south again.

Because of the continuing decline in the conditions of the roads they travelled, and having to navigate around several ancient truck and car pileups, they only made seventy-five miles that day, and stopped for the night just south of Pueblo.

The conditions of the roads were only one of their hurdles; several times through their journey now, they'd had to stop because of severe thunderstorms, with hail and rain so heavy it brought the visibility down to zero, so it took them a full two more days to reach the New Mexico border, near the tiny town of Raton.

They made camp for the night at a rest area that had covered picnic tables, and the men had a barbeque of a sort, and again, the next day they headed out late, due to refusals of some of the men to rise at sunrise.

The unrest in the group was beginning to unsettle the sergeant, and he was having a difficult time keeping his words in check to some of them, for they were a truly undisciplined mob, and they had him outnumbered. At times, it seemed to him that they were listening only to humor him.

He brought this fact up to the major the next evening after they had set up camp in a truck stop in Santa Fe, not far from Albuquerque.

"Really, Sergeant?" the major asked incredulously.

"Yes, sir, it's starting to be a strain. The men have no outlet for their frustrations, and they see no end to this. The ones that do see us reaching our objective soon only realize they have the return trek to deal with once we've completed the mission."

"And how do you feel, Sergeant?" the major implored.

"Sir, I'll follow my orders."

"How pleasant to hear, Sergeant. I know you'll follow your orders, because if you don't, you can kiss goodbye that nice house you and your wife live in."

"I know that, sir, but that's not why I'll follow orders. I took an oath to do so, and I take that oath very seriously," he replied, hating the fact that that had to be thrown in his face, to be threatened like that. He was a better man than that.

"That's very nice to hear, Sergeant. Now let us go and have a motivational meeting with the troops, shall we?"

"Anything you say, sir."

He followed the major over to where most of the troops had gathered, some shirtless in the afternoon summer sun, drinking warm beer and smoking stale cigarettes.

When they were close enough, the sergeant yelled out, "At ease! Listen up, people. The major has something to tell you!"

It took a few moments, and the major stood in the center, puffing away at his stinking cigar. When they were all assembled and settled down to the extent he could talk to them, he said, "I understand there's been some dissention in the ranks. I'm here to let you all know again how important our mission is to the country, and to the president."

There were a few grumbles from the crowd, but no one spoke up.

"Gentlemen, we were tasked by the president of the United States himself to set out on this journey. Somewhere out there, west of us, is a man who is detrimental to our country. Some might say seditious, I say the word traitor. He has been claiming he is the president, when we all know he's not, we know the real president is safe, back in Washingto—"

"I bet he's not eating spam or MREs!" a voice came from near the back of the group of men.

The major chose to ignore it, and continued. "Men, I know it's been difficult, long journey, and it's not over yet. Once we get to Arizona, we will find this man, and bring him back with us. He's violated the law, and the president demands justice. We, gentlemen, are that justice!" he said, raising his voice loudly in mock anger. The show worked, and a wave of hoots, shouts, and catcalls came forth from the men.

Seeing his showmanship was working, he plugged on. "We didn't know how bad the roads would be, or that the bridges over the Mississippi would be washed away, or damaged beyond repair. But like the soldiers that we are, we continued the mission. Charlie Mike. That is all I want to hear from you now, when asked anything, I want the reply to be 'Charlie Mike!' loud and clear, got that?"

"Charlie Mike!" was shouted by several of the men, but not all. This didn't satisfy the major. "What was it? I can't hear you!"

"Charlie Mike!" was yelled louder, by several more men, still not all, but it was enough for the major for now.

"Like you've known from the beginning, there's a rogue soldier out there west of us, just over those mountains," he said, pointing at the distant Rocky Mountains for emphasis, "and we're going to bring him to justice. But that's not all!"

That last statement got everyone's attention, and he smiled inwardly.

"That's right. You heard me. That's not all. There are a few details that up until now you haven't been told," he said, and that brought some renewed grumbling from the men.

"Settle down and let me finish. My orders were to bring back this man, the aircraft he has at his disposal, and the pilot of said aircraft."

You could have heard a pin drop when he finished that last statement, and he looked at all of their faces with delight. He had their full and undivided attention now. He grinned broadly.

"That means, gentlemen, that we will be flying home. What has taken us almost two months to accomplish, on our return will be hours, not days and weeks!"

When he was finished, he let the last words truly sink in, folded his arms across his chest smugly in satisfaction as a loud roar and cheer went through the crowd.

The sergeant looked over at the major in shock. He leaned in to his commanding officer and whispered in his ear, "Do you think that was wise, telling them that?"

"I don't see why not, Sergeant. It's the truth. He's got a plane out there, and we're to ferry it back. No sense us all riding back in vehicles."

"Sir, I need to talk to you about this," the sergeant hissed in a whisper.

"Alright, give me a minute," he said, then turned back to his men. "That's all I have for now, get some rest, we have another long day ahead of us tomorrow!"

The men broke up into gaggles of four and five men, scattered with great cheer and glee, and when they were finally gone, the major beckoned the sergeant to follow him back to his Hum-Vee.

As they walked, the major asked his companion, "So, why do you think it was a bad idea to tell the men about the aircraft?"

"What if we get out there, the aircraft is only a Piper Cub, or other puddle jumper?"

"Sergeant, we'll cross that bridge when we get to it. I don't see a problem with telling the men a little something to boost their morale, do you?"

"No, not at all, but what happens then when we get out there and it is some little plane? Yeah, we can take it back, have the pilot fly some of us back, but can you imagine the reaction if that's the case?"

"I think you're overreacting, Sergeant," the major said in his saccharine-sweet voice of condescension that annoyed the shit out of the sergeant.

"No, sir, I am not overreacting. What will we tell the men? Oh, too bad, we've got another two month truck ride back home?"

The two men stopped at the major's Hum-Vee, to find Nuggets sound asleep at the wheel, which seemed like his natural position. The major stopped to relight his cigar, and when he had it fully going again, looked at the sergeant.

"Sergeant, I don't think that will be the case. This rogue madman had satellite capabilities. He's been able to call up spy satellites, so I'm thinking he's got at least a C17 at his disposal. We'll all be able to fly home," the major said, pointing at the sergeant's chest.

The soldier just looked at his superior in disbelief for a moment, and then whistled. "Are you telling me he's got control of the military satellites?"

"That's what I'm telling you, Sergeant."

"Holy shit, sir, maybe he's watching us right now for Christ sake!" he said loudly, looking up into the night sky involuntarily, as if he could spot the orbiting satellite. "We might have thought this one out just a little longer. I mean, fuck. We should have brought more men. Who knows what the fuck we're up against, Major?"

"You know what I think, *Sergeant?*" the major said, emphasizing the word as though to let the man know who was really in charge. "What I think is some crazy old grizzled soldier with far too much time in rank, and suffering from PTSD, finally snapped when the Cull happened, and like that Colonel Kurtz in the movie *Apocalypse Now*, has gone off the reservation and is gone completely insane. That's what I think, Sergeant!"

"Maybe that's the case, but if he has that kind of control, that kind of power, don't you think we ought to step back and rethink just going off half-cocked, sir?"

"What could he possibly have that can stop us from bringing him back, Sergeant?" the major asked, in the voice of a school teacher talking to a particularly dense student.

"He could, Major. Have you thought about that?"

"He's not Rambo. I've read his file, so have you. There's nothing in there that's overtly threatening."

The sergeant was starting to feel the creep of a migraine coming on, and he wondered what he ever did in his life to deserve this. He took a breath. "No sir, he's not Rambo. But shit, he's got more combat experience than most people I knew. Grenada, Panama, the First Gulf War, Kosovo, Somalia, Iraq for three tours, Afghanistan for five tours, two Bronze Stars, a Silver Star, Distinguished Service

Cross, Purple Heart, Combat Infantry Badge, HALO, Master Parachutist, Air Assault, Pathfinder, Ranger Qualified. Besides a shitload of stuff that's been redacted starting in the mid 1980's, and that screams of Secret Squirrel CIA shit. Fuck sir, shall I go on?"

"He failed the Special Forces 'Q' course, Sergeant," the major replied smugly.

"Sir, how can you be so cavalier about this? So, he failed the 'Q' course. Haven't you ever failed anything?" he spat angrily.

"I most certainly did not fail at anything, Sergeant. I was top of my class at VMI also, I'll have you know!"

Oh great, the sergeant thought. *Now he's bringing up college.* It was no use arguing with the man, so he just sighed and said nothing.

"Is that all, Sergeant? If so, I think it's time we turned in and had a night's sleep. We've got another long day ahead of us tomorrow."

"No, I've said my piece. I'll do whatever you say, sir."

"Good. I'm tired. Go get yourself some sleep, and you'll look at it from a different perspective in the morning." He placed his hand on the sergeant's shoulder in a fatherly way, which had the opposite effect of its intentions. It only further infuriated the sergeant. He walked away, back towards his Hum-Vee, leaving the major to his delusions of grandeur.

The next morning, they started out earlier than what had become normal, as most men in the unit had higher expectations and were all buoyed by the thoughts of flying home in a plane, something that none of the men had seen for several years.

The sergeant had to give the major one thing, as his pep talk the night before did serve one purpose, and that was to lift the sinking morale, and there was less discontent in the ranks.

They made their way south from Santa Fe into Albuquerque, and despite several rusted hulks of what used to be semi-trucks and cars along the way, found the ramp onto I-40 westbound by mid-afternoon.

Several miles west of Albuquerque, they stopped at a truck stop to refuel and rest, and the sergeant made his way through the convoy on foot, making sure that all was going to plan and the refueling was done quickly and efficiently.

It was slow going, as always. They still had to siphon the diesel for the trucks and the Hum-Vees from parked semis, and it took a while. Those not helping with the refueling were busily tearing into the new MREs they'd gotten in Denver, and every time the sergeant stopped to chat with his men, he could feel a renewed sense of purpose running through them.

I guess the major did know what he was talking about, he thought. Still, he worried about the chances of the plane being some Cessna or Piper. When he made it to the front of the convoy, he found the major's Hum-Vee parked under the portico covering the fuel pumps of the truck stop. Nuggets was found as usual, sound asleep, head on the steering wheel, and he wondered how anyone could sleep so much.

"Ah, Sergeant. How is the refueling going?" the major asked.

"Going along nicely, sir, we should be done in about a half hour."

"Good, good, anything new?"

"No sir, all is about the same. Morale seems to be up quite a bit," he conceded.

"See, Sergeant? I know what I'm doing. Have you felt like we're being watched again, Sergeant?"

"No, not today, not for several days, if fact. I think it just might have been nerves."

"I see," the major said, nodding. Then he got a weird look on his face, and his jaw dropped. The sergeant turned to see what the major was gaping at, then it was his turn to look dumbfounded.

Coming out of the storefront of the truck stop, a large, disheveled, barrel-chested man with long scraggly hair on the back of his head and a shaggy beard on his face was walking wide-eyed towards them.

The sergeant instinctively reached for his M4, then realized too late he'd left it in his Hum-Vee at the back of the convoy. He mentally kicked himself for being so sloppy. They stood stock still as the man approached, and when he was within feet of them said, "Fuck me, mate! Am I ever glad to see you blokes!"

The accent was familiar to the sergeant, so he was the first to speak. "Are you Australian?"

"Fucking oath, mate! The name's Colin. Colin Milford," he said, holding out his hand to shake the sergeant's.

"Where did you come from, besides Australia?" the major asked, shaking the man's hand.

"Arizona," he replied, smiling.

CHAPTER 15:
REINFORCEMENTS

The 5,500 BTU air conditioner that Suplee had installed in the captain's office on the *SS Jeremiah O'Brien* hummed quietly.

Johnson sat at his desk, finishing up the entry in the ship's log; he never failed to make the daily notations. After an uneventful two-week journey from San Diego, the ship was tied up at the famous '1010' dock at Pearl Harbor Naval Base, called that because it was exactly one thousand ten feet long. Several men from the island were now busily chipping away the rust and flaking paint on the hull and superstructure in preparations for a fresh coat of Navy Gray.

Johnson closed the ledger and set his pen down when someone knocked on the door. "Come," he said.

The door to the office opened, and Jerry William appeared, a quizzical expression on his face.

"Excuse me, Mr. Johnson, do you have a minute?"

"Sure, Jerry, come on in. And belay the 'Mr. Johnson' stuff, call me Bill," Johnson replied, sitting back in his swivel chair.

Jerry entered the tiny office and closed the door behind him. He pointed at another chair that was against the bulkhead. "May I?"

"Sure, pull up a seat. What can I do for you?"

Jerry sat down and rubbed the back of his neck. "Sir, I was wondering about these cranes on the ship. How much weight can they lift?"

"That I'm not sure about. I guess we need to ask Harry or Ken about that. Why do you ask?"

"I remember seeing old newsreels of them loading Sherman tanks into these Liberty Ships during the war. I figure they must be strong enough to lift thirty-three tons."

"A couple of them might be capable of that."

"An M3 Sherman from World War Two weighed around thirty-three tons, and a Bradley weighs a little less than that, around thirty tons, right?"

"I wouldn't know, Jerry. I'm a sailor, not a soldier," Johnson said. "Why the interest in loading armored vehicles?"

"You know about the messages that Tim and I have gotten, right?"

Johnson nodded. "Yes, you let me know about them when we sailed into port."

"I just got off the radio with Tim a little while ago. It's a fact now, there's a group, probably a company-strength unit, moving from Kansas on its way to Arizona to take Tim into 'custody.' They need help back there."

"What do you have planned?"

"I don't have a plan yet, just an idea. I wanted to float it by you first, and if you said it was feasible, I'd start drawing up a better plan."

"What's your idea?"

"Tim is a smart soldier, one of the best I've ever had the pleasure of working with. But he's outnumbered back there. He's only got about eight people left from the twenty that went back with him. He wants to fight them, but he's going to lose if he doesn't get some help."

"So your idea is to load up the hold with tanks and men, and head back to the mainland to help him?"

"In a nutshell, yes," Jerry said. "Look, Bill, I'm just a platoon sergeant. I've never planned anything like this before. Thirty soldiers are the most I've ever commanded before the world ended. I think we can do it, but I need some more ideas."

Johnson sat back again in his chair, looking intently at Jerry for a few moments. His elbows were propped on the armrests, fingers together, contemplative look across his face for several moments.

"Jerry, I'd like to help any way I can. I owe a lot to Tim. I've got a lot of things going on here, and I appreciate the help of your men," he said. "There's still a lot of work to be done on the ship yet, but I'll get Harry and Ken up here, and I'll ask them what they think. In the meantime, you go home and come up with a plan. We'll come over to your place later this afternoon to discuss it."

Jerry nodded. "Do you want me to plan it out as if it's doable?"

"Yeah, think it out that way. Once I talk to Harry and Ken, I'll know better, but we'll assume at this point that we can move the equipment."

"And if we can't?" Jerry asked.

"If we can't, we can't. We do have to try," Johnson said, standing. Jerry stood also, and held out his hand, and Johnson took it in a firm grip. "I promise we'll do our best to help."

Jerry left the office, leaving Johnson alone with his thoughts. His eyes drifted over to the far bulkhead, ideas and images tumbling across his mind.

He reached across his desk, picked up the growler phone, and called down to the boiler room. Nakamura answered immediately.

"Mr. Nakamura, is Suplee there by any chance?"

"Ah no, Skipper, he not here all morning," Nakamura said cheerfully.

"If he shows up, let him know I'd like to talk with him," Johnson said into the handset. He replaced the receiver and stood, donning a ball cap and heading out to the bridge, only to find that deserted also.

He walked out to the sunlit wing bridge, and looked down at the work party on the forecastle, busily sanding, chipping, and painting the exposed metal with primer. He spied Ken, stripped down to his waist, carrying two five gallon pails of primer.

He thought of using the loudhailer, but decided that would be lazy, and something Old Lead Bottom on the USS Hughes would have done. He made his way down the three decks to the cargo deck, out a hatch that had been propped open, and forward past the closed cargo hatches to the bow of the ship.

Ken saw him and came over to him. "Good morning, Skipper. Have you come down to inspect our work?"

"No, Ken, I trust you'll have everything shipshape. I was actually looking for Mr. Suplee."

"Suplee said he was heading over to the base ship's store about an hour ago. I'm not sure when he'll be back. Is there anything I can do for you?"

"Actually there is, Ken," Johnson said. "What can you tell me about these cranes?"

"Not much. They're pretty rudimentary, not hydraulic, steel braided cable, and powered by electric motors."

"Do they work?"

"I think so. For as old as she is, everything else works on her. I can check them out if you'd like."

"Yes, please do that," Johnson said. "Find out about their capacities, how much they can hoist aboard at one time."

"Aye, aye, Skipper. Is there anything I should know about?" Ken asked, curiosity piqued.

"Not right now. I'll explain later when you find out if they'll work or not. When Harry comes back, report up to me in my office."

"Sure thing, Skipper!" Ken said, then turned to another man who was bent over painting an area of bare metal with the copper colored primer. "Hey, Jim, take over for me here, the Skipper has got me on a special mission."

"I'll leave you to it, then," Johnson said, leaving the men and heading back to his office. He made it to the open hatch leading into the superstructure, then decided to do a walkthrough of the ship, something he hadn't done in since they had tied up to the pier a few weeks ago.

He checked his watch, saw that it was only 10 AM, and set forth aft to begin his inspection. It took him a few hours, and he was satisfied that all was going according to schedule with the painting and preventative maintenance throughout the ship.

He stopped in to speak with Steve, who was happily preparing fresh roast pork for supper in the galley. The aroma teased Johnson's senses, and made his mouth water. He left the man to his work, and climbed the steps, called ladders on a ship, to the bridge deck.

Once on the bridge, he prepared a pot of coffee on the drip coffee maker Suplee had set up on the aft bulkhead. While that was brewing, he walked out onto the wing bridge again, in time to see a camouflaged 6x6 truck pull up to the gangplank, and Suplee exiting the cab.

Several men began unloading the truck at Suplee's directions. Johnson waved down to his second in command, which Suplee returned with an exaggerated salute.

Johnson stepped away from the railing, heading back into the bridge, where he found the coffee had finished brewing. He poured himself a cup and headed aft to his office.

He busied himself going over records of overhauls in the past, double checking to see if there were any hidden recurring problems with the ship. Finding none, he sat back, finished his coffee and waited for Suplee to arrive.

He heard a knock, and then Suplee's face peered around the edge of the door.

"Come in, Harry. Did you speak to Ken?"

"Yes sir," Suplee replied. "He's right behind me." Suplee planted his butt on the edge of Johnson's desk and motioned for Ken to take the only other chair.

"I know you're wondering why I've gathered you here tonight," Johnson said ominously in a comic voice once they were all seated, and the other two men laughed at Johnson's theatrics.

Suplee said, "Ken told me you gave him a special job today, and you wanted to talk to both of us."

"I had a visit this morning from Sergeant Williams. He was wondering about the ship's cranes, and if we might be able to load up some tanks in the hold."

Ken laughed, then asked, "What's he plan on doing, invading someplace?"

"You're not too far off the mark, Ken," Johnson said, then gave a brief rundown of Jerry's idea.

When he was done, Suplee said, "I'm all for it, Skipper, if it's possible."

"What's so special about this guy back in Arizona?" Ken asked.

"Ken," Johnson said, "Harry and I owe our lives to that guy back in Arizona. In fact, if you want to get down to brass tacks, everyone throughout the whole Pacific Rim who's survived the Event owe their lives to him."

"Yeah, Bill's right. You remember our story, where we got saved on that atoll?" Suplee said to Ken. "This guy is the one that saved us."

"I get it," Ken said. "So you want to load some tanks? I know that Abrams weighs something like sixty tons. The two cranes closest, fore and aft, to the superstructure are only rated at fifty tons, so I wouldn't chance it."

"I think he was talking about the Bradley fighting vehicles. He said they only weigh thirty tons," Johnson said.

"Okay then. The fore and aft inboard are rated for fifty tons, the outer cranes are only rated at ten tons. So yeah, in theory, we can load up a few Bradleys," Ken informed Johnson.

"We'd have to figure out how many he wants, to see if we can fit them all in the holds, then we have to figure out fuel storage for them, and bunks for the crews, and whatever other incidentals he wants to bring aboard," Suplee said.

"Then we can do it?"

"I don't see why not, Skipper. The number one hold is already set up in troopship configuration. I think the museum staff who maintained her did it for display purposes," Ken said.

"Great. Then I can let Jerry know we can do it. Now all we have to find out from him is when he wants to sail, and where to," Johnson said.

"I don't think Arizona has a deep water port, skipper," Ken said, "unless California finally did fall into the ocean."

"Hey, Bill, wasn't one of those Aussie guys some kinda' railroad guy? Said he was going to get the trains running?" Suplee asked.

"That was the idea, for us to have a direct link to Tim in Arizona and Jerry out here on Oahu."

"I hadn't heard any news about that, maybe they got the trains running."

"I hope so, Harry, or it'll be a long drive from Cali to Arizona," Johnson said. "And that, my friend, will be Jerry's issue. We'll just get him there."

"Are you thinking back to San Diego?" Ken asked.

"That would probably be the best port. I told Jerry I'd come over this afternoon to his place when I found out about the cranes. I'll discuss it with him then."

"Is that all, sir?" Ken asked.

"Yeah, that's it for now. I'll let you know more when I talk to Jerry."

"I'll head back deck side to finish up the detail then, if you don't mind, sir."

"You go ahead, Ken. We'll talk after chow tonight. I think Steve is roasting a whole pig."

"I can smell it now!" Ken said, getting up to leave.

"I don't have to add that this is to be kept quiet for now, do I?" Johnson said.

"Mum's the word, sir. Loose lips sink ships, and all that shit. I'll keep it to myself."

When Ken had left, Suplee asked, "Skipper, if your dream was to become the commodore of an amphibious task force, it's about to come true."

Johnson laughed. "Well, a one ship task force is better than a no-ship task force. Not exactly what I had in mind when I took command of this ship."

"Do you think Jerry can pull it off?"

"Now that I know the cranes can lift the Bradleys, I know we can get him there. The rest of it will be up to him. It's a long drive to Arizona from San Diego," Johnson said, standing. "I need to go and tell Mary I'm heading over to Jerry's."

"Mary went with Beth earlier to Honolulu. She took Billy with them, some sort of shopping trip," Suplee said. "Want some company?"

"Good thing I hid the credit cards," Johnson said, and Suplee laughed. "Unless you've got anything better to do, sure, come along."

The men proceeded through the ship, down the gangplank, and got into the cab of the 6x6. Suplee fired up the diesel engine, lit a cigarette, put the truck in gear, and headed out.

They made it the twenty miles to the western side of the island, to the hamlet of Mákaha. After a few turns, they found Jerry's modest bungalow at the end of a tiny road that ended at the beach.

They walked together up a footpath covered in crushed seashells to the lanai, where they found Jerry sitting at a table, notebook open in front of him.

He smiled as the men stepped up on the porch. "I heard you pull up. I was just making some calculations. Have a seat."

Johnson and Suplee both sat at the table and Johnson said, "I talked it over with Ken and Harry here, and they say we can lift the Bradleys with the cranes."

"Great! I just spoke with Tim about an hour ago. He says he could really use the help."

"I'll say. How many did he say he was up against?"

"He's not a hundred percent sure, he thinks it's around a company-strength unit coming at him. Not a lot from a purely military point of view, but he reckons he'll only have about four people left to fight them after he sends Holly and Robyn off with the plane."

Suplee whistled. "Shit, only four people? If I was him, I'd just pack up and leave while he can!"

"I agree, and I told him as much just a while ago," Jerry said somberly.

"He won't, though, will he?" Johnson asked.

"No. He's dead set against running. Says he's got a few surprises for them, and I don't doubt it, but the odds are stacked way against him."

"What's your idea?"

"This is what I've got so far," Jerry said, looking down at his notes. "Over at Schofield, there's a whole company's worth of Bradleys and Abrams that just came back from the Ghan a few months prior to the Event. I figure I can get about four of them operating. I've got some men working on that right now. Between those four, and about a hundred or so men from here, we can put together a formidable force to deal with anything that's up against our people in Arizona."

"How long before you're ready?" Johnson asked.

"I figure about a week. How long do you reckon it will take to sail to San Diego?"

"About two weeks," Johnson said. "How long does Tim figure he has before they get to him?"

"He's not sure. He said the unit was last seen somewhere near Denver, that was several days ago. At this point, he's fairly certain they have no idea exactly where he is, so that might buy us some time."

"You mean they might spend a month or more tearing around Arizona looking for him?" Suplee asked.

"Yeah, though we can't know for sure."

"How did he find out all of this?" Johnson asked.

"Remember that guy from my group from Volivoli that went over with him?" Jerry asked.

"Yeah, Sam something or other," Johnson said. "He was going to find some old Indian and get some buffalo or something."

"Apparently he was successful. He was on his way back from Nebraska with a few of them, and just by chance, he stumbled upon the convoy, Tim tells me. He's been shadowing their movement since."

"Jerry, I want to help. I'm thinking it might be too late though."

"I agree," Suplee said. "By the time you guys get out there, it might be all over. I figure three weeks, then another week or so to get to where they're at overland. That's a whole month."

"Did you find out if that railroad guy was ever able to get a train running?" Johnson asked.

"No," Jerry said, shaking his head. "Tim hasn't heard from him in several weeks. I don't expect any help from that quarter. The Bradleys use up shitloads of go-juice, and an overland trek with them will play havoc on their tracks. They were never designed to travel hundreds of miles in one shot. They are usually trucked in close on lowboys or by rail to where the action is, and then offloaded. A hundred miles or so in one shot is all they can handle before shit starts to break on them."

"So, basically, you're telling me that even with all the effort we might undertake to get you there, it's essentially futile," Johnson said.

"Maybe so, maybe not. I do know that from the time Tim and I first got the warning from whoever it was back in Washington to the time Sam first saw the soldiers heading that way, it was over two months. Something slowed their progress west, something we don't know about," Jerry said.

"It was probably the roads," Suplee said. "You should have seen the roads back in Cali. And 'Frisco was a complete mess."

"That's what I figured myself," Jerry said.

"That could hamper your travel also," Johnson said.

"That's a chance I'm willing to take, Bill. I've got to do something."

Johnson sat there for a few moments in deep contemplation. He let out a deep sigh. "I can get you to San Diego. We can load up as much fuel and ammo you need to take, and the men."

"Great, Bill! Thanks!" Jerry beamed.

"Hell, it's the least I can do. I've got the ship, and we weren't planning on anything like a couples cruise."

"I wasn't looking forward to the entertainment," Jerry cracked.

"Good, because our band sucks," Suplee said. "They only know two songs."

"And the all-you-can-eat buffet leaves a lot to be desired," Johnson added.

"I understand. Look, I just wanted to ask you what you thought. I may be setting out on a fool's errand, but if I sit back and do nothing, I'd never be able to live with myself," Jerry said, almost as if he was trying to convince himself.

"Then it's settled," Johnson said.

"Oh, something I should have asked right off the bat— how's the ship coming along?" Jerry asked. "No sense even planning this if it's not ready."

"Don't worry about that, Jerry. She's ready now. Except for a few minor painting jobs, the bunkers are full and everything is ship-shape," Johnson said cheerfully.

"The only thing that needs to be done is the bottom, below the waterline needs to be scraped and repainted. There's a lot of fouling and barnacles that takes a few knots off our blisteringly fast top speed of eleven knots," Suplee said. "She needs to go into dry-dock, but I guess one more trip to 'Diego and back won't hurt."

"I can plan on everything being ready a week from today?" Jerry asked hopefully.

"That would be a safe bet, Sergeant," Johnson said. "If that's all you need from us, we'll head back to the ship."

"I think so. If I think of anything else, I'll be sure to let you know," the lean black man said, looking at his watch. "Jan will be home soon, and I promised I'd have dinner ready."

"Jan?" Johnson asked with a wry smile on his lips.

"Yeah, you remember her. She was the pretty little blonde dentist who fixed your broken tooth," Jerry said.

"Oh, I remember her," Suplee said appreciatively. "Lucky guy!"

"Everyone needs someone!" Jerry stood, closing his notebook. The other two men stood also, and shook his hand. "I see you have found someone too, Harry."

"Yeah, I call her my mermaid. She came paddling up to me one day out of nowhere singing her siren song."

"I think we all need a little domestication," Johnson said. "It cleans up our rough edges."

"That it does, and gives us a little adult supervision," Jerry said, leading them back down the path to their vehicle.

The two sailors climbed back into the truck, and Suplee started it up. Johnson leaned out the passenger window and called out to Jerry over the sound of the diesel engine, "Keep us informed. We'll make the ship ready for whatever you decide."

"Wilco, Captain!" Jerry exclaimed, and waved as they away.

Suplee turned onto the highway leading back to Pearl. "So, Skipper, what do you think?"

"What I think is that we have a job to do. Frankly, whether we think it's a fool's errand or not, we owe it to him and Tim to help. Besides, we're not the ones who will be fighting, we're just driving the bus."

"Crazy world, eh?"

"Insane," Johnson said, looking out at the passing countryside.

"I can't help but think of all the crazy shit that we've been through, Bill, all those years on that fucked up ship."

"And us launching those Tomahawks at Pearl. I still feel so guilty about that."

"You took a big chance when you retargeted those missiles. You do realize what would have happened to you if Ol' Lead Bottom had found out, don't you?"

"Yeah, I do. It doesn't stop me from feeling guilty about launching them. Hell, about *all* the shit we've done. If by helping Jerry move some men and tanks from here to the mainland helps assuage my guilt a little bit, I'm going to do it."

"I'm one hundred percent behind you, Skipper," Suplee said. "It'll be a quick hop to 'Diego and back, like shit off a shiny shovel."

"Like what? I've never heard that one before!" Johnson chuckled.

"I heard one of those Aussie guys say it once, and I thought it was funny."

"One of the ones who went over with Tim to Arizona?"

"Yeah, the big guy, balding, kind of a know-it-all," Suplee said. "I know who you're talking about. Seemed like a bullshit artist to me."

"Yeah, he seemed like he was full of shit to me too. I wonder if the sergeant major feels the same?" Suplee said, deftly steering the truck towards the pier where the Liberty Ship was moored.

"I'll ask him next time I see him," Johnson replied, looking out over the base. He took note of how, even here in paradise, nature was rapidly taking back what was hers. Weeds grew out of every crack of pavement, grass was tall and un-mowed, and vines were creeping up the sides of every building.

They passed the docks where other ships were moored, ships that were built to go into harm's way, Man O'Wars, now silent sentinels covered in bird droppings like a bronze monument to a long forgotten war in some town park.

As they pulled up alongside the ship and parked, Suplee took note of Beth's Yugo parked near the gangway. They had brought it with them, lowered into the hold next to several World War Two vintage Jeeps and trucks that were put there by the now long dead museum staff who lovingly kept the old girl afloat and steaming.

"Looks like the girls are back from spending all of our sea pay, Skipper."

"I see that," Johnson said, alighting from the passenger side. "Maybe they found my credit cards after all."

"Hell, you're an officer, you make the big bucks."

"I try not to spend it all in one place like a drunken sailor on a Cinderella Liberty like you do, Mr. Suplee."

"Don't laugh, Skipper. I did that in Hong Kong on my first cruise."

Johnson chuckled. He let Suplee go first up the gangway, slapping him playfully on the back as he passed.

When they reached the top of the gangway, Suplee said, "Bill, I'm going to find Beth. I'll see you in the wardroom later?"

"Sure thing, Harry, I'll be in my quarters if you need me," Johnson replied, entering the hatch and disappearing.

Suplee saw Beth up on the forecastle, in the armored ring that held the now demilitarized 5" gun. She was leaning on the edge of the armor plating, back towards him, gazing out at something unseen by him. He made his way across the weather deck and passed the closed cargo hold hatches, then up a short ladder to the gun emplacement, minding the 'WET PAINT' signs placed thoughtfully by Ken's paint detail earlier.

Beth's back was still towards him, and she still hadn't heard his approach. She was silently looking out over the inner harbor, towards Ford Island Naval Air Station and Battleship Row, where the USS Arizona monument stood, brand new American flag flying over it, no doubt placed there by one of Jerry's men.

The USS Missouri was across the water also, looking forlorn, and her entire superstructure was covered in white bird droppings, rust streaks running down her once proud sleek gray hull to the waterline. The sight saddened him.

He tiptoed up behind Beth, playfully covering her eyes from behind, leaned in and whispered, "Guess who?"

She giggled and grabbed his wrists, spun, and wrapped her arms around his neck, kissing him gently on the lips. "I missed you today. Where did you and the captain get off to?"

"We went over to see Jerry. We'll be sailing in about a week," Suplee told her, hugging her close.

"Why so soon?"

"He wants us to take some equipment and men back over to the mainland. It'll be just a quick hop there and back."

"A quick hop, huh?" she laughed, poking him playfully.

"Two weeks there, two weeks back."

"That's a whole month. What am I going to do?" she asked, pouting.

"Honey, you are coming with us," he said.

"Really?"

"Babe, I made a promise to myself right after we met that I'd never, ever go to sea again and leave someone I love behind. You're part of the crew now, and you can steer the ship just fine." Suplee kissed her, and then placed his forehead against hers.

Beth gently caressed his cheek, looking deeply into his eyes. She saw the pain that was still there, although he'd never admit it.

"It still bothers you, eh?"

"It'll haunt me for the rest of my life."

"I won't leave you. If you were going to leave me, I was just going to stow away!" she teased, sticking out her tongue. Her face darkened. "I still can't imagine the things you said happened on that ship."

"Bill and I kept ourselves sane by having each other to talk to. If it wasn't for him, I'd have gone completely crazy."

"So tell me," she said, changing the subject that she knew was painful for her lover to talk about, "what's the soldier want to take over to the mainland?"

"Oh, nothing much, just a few tanks and a hundred men or so," he replied as nonchalantly as he could.

"Tanks? Men? Please don't tell me you're going off to war?"

Suplee took Beth into his arms and held her tightly, kissing the top of her head. "No, babe. If there's any fighting to be done, it's going to be in Arizona. We're just taking him and his equipment to San Diego."

"Good. You'd think that after everything that's happened, so many people dead, and after what you went through, people would stop fighting."

"Yeah, you'd think so."

"Why is he going over there?"

Suplee gave her a brief rundown on Tim, his settlement in Arizona, rehashed what he did on Volivoli, and how everyone here on the island felt about him.

Beth walked back over to the edge of the gun emplacement and looked out over the harbor again. She sighed deeply. "I guess that some things are still worth fighting for. I don't have to like it though."

"I'm not asking you to like it. But I think it's important."

"It is, Harry. Look out there," she said, pointing out to where the *USS Missouri* was moored, and toward Battleship Row. "Every time I look out there, I can still see those old black and white newsreels, the ships exploding, the bodies in the water. A chill crosses over me. I haven't told you. My great grandfather was here that morning. I only met him a few times, and I was still young when he died. I remember a photo of him in his Navy uniform my grandmother kept on her mantel. He looked so young. He was just a boy then, and it frightens me that unless we stop fighting and learn to get along, even more boys will die."

"I want that too. Maybe this will be the last time," Suplee said, knowing in his heart it wouldn't. Something he heard Tim say once came to mind: *'There will always be someone who wants to rule the world'*, and Suplee knew he was right.

"Maybe, maybe not. I had a brother killed in Afghanistan right before everyone died. My mom cried for days and days, and I just kept asking myself what was it all for?"

"That's a question I can't answer, babe. I wish I could."

"Maybe you can talk him into coming back here. You said we're safe here. We've got thousands of miles of ocean surrounding us here."

"That, I think, is no longer an option."

A whiff of something wonderful briefly wafted by their noses, and all thoughts of death and war drifted away from their minds. Suplee's stomach rumbled, and reminded him he hadn't eaten since morning chow.

"That smells wonderful!"

"Steve is such a great cook. He could whip up dog food and make it into fine dining."

"Let's go get some chow before it's all gone," Suplee said, taking Beth by the hand and leading her away.

"Oh, all you sailors are all alike. Try to win us over with your fancy talk and great food."

"I'll bring some chocolate and nylons next time!"

CHAPTER 16:
SPIES LIKE US

John Thompson sat hunched over a notepad in the dim light from the lantern, his finger poised over the Morse key, his other hand holding the earpiece for the headphones tightly to his left ear, sweat pouring off him in the oppressive heat. Washington, DC, he was reminded every summer, was actually built on top of a swamp, and in the summer the heat, combined with the humidity, was almost unbearable without the luxury of air conditioning.

When the beeping of the dots and dashes finished, he picked up a pencil, wrote down a few words, and tapped out a reply. He took off the headset and turned off the radio, looking at the words he'd written. He leaned back in his chair and sighed. The headaches that came and went were now becoming more frequent, and the pounding only accentuated his fear of being discovered.

He had set up the ancient Heathkit Ham radio in an unused back bedroom of his Georgetown brownstone, the thick coaxial antenna cable snaked out the window up to the roof, were a homemade dipole antenna stretched between two wooden masts that he hoped would stay unseen by any curious and inquisitive passersby.

He pulled open a drawer on the battered wood desk, and saw the old Webley .445 pistol. He kept that, among other things, hidden from Barbra. She didn't like guns and he didn't want her overly worried.

Satisfied it was still there, he quietly shut the drawer, and was startled by a voice. "John, are you coming to bed?"

He nearly jumped out of his skin, and spun to see her standing in the half open door, old and frayed housecoat wrapped tightly around her, despite the sweltering heat. Her shoulder length chestnut hair was neatly brushed out, but her brilliant blue eyes were tired, face drawn with exhaustion.

"Just coming now, babe," he said hoping she didn't see everything in the room. He kept it locked when he wasn't there so she didn't look in; he didn't want her to worry. However, the proverbial cat was out of the bag now. His heart beat loudly in his chest as her eyes left him and scanned the room for the first time.

"What is all this stuff, John?" Barbra asked, walking over to a map of the world that was taped to a bare wall, colored pushpins placed in various locations, post-it notes with scrawled notations placed by more than a few of them.

"It's work stuff, babe. Nothing to worry about," he said unconvincingly.

"John, for a spy, you can't hide things very well," she replied, turning away from the map. "Tell me, please. I'm worried about you."

"It's nothing," he said. "I'm not a spy. I was just an analyst on the European desk before all this."

"Maybe so, John, but you've been acting like a spy for a few months now. And you're having nightmares. Please, please talk to me!"

He reached out and took one of her hands, squeezing it gently.

"Alright. I figure I owe you as much. Let's go downstairs. I'll fix us both a drink and I'll tell you."

"Everything?"

"Yes, babe," he sighed. "I'll tell you everything."

He picked up the lantern and led her out of the room, locking it behind him. They walked down the narrow corridor and down the stairs to the first floor, lit only by the yellow light from the flame. He wished the solar panels he had set up on the roof would power more than the refrigerator, but he was pushing his luck as it was with the radio every night; there was barely enough juice to power those two, let alone lights and an air conditioner. The house felt like an oven even with all the windows open, and he couldn't even imagine what it was like in the other hovels that people were living in all over the decaying city.

He went to the kitchen instead of the living room. It was towards the rear of the house, and it would be less likely anyone would overhear what he was about to say through the open windows.

He led Barbra to a chair at the table where they shared now infrequent meals, setting the lantern in the center. He silently retrieved two rocks glasses, then a bottle of Jack Daniels from the cupboard.

John opened the freezer door, and for a second stood there and let the cold air hit his face. He grabbed a handful of ice cubes from the tray and plopped a few into each glass, pouring a healthy double shot of the potent brown liquid into each. He then pulled out a two liter bottle of flat Coca-Cola, and topped off the glasses.

He sat down across from Barbra, sliding her drink across the tabletop, quiet for a few moments, trying to figure out where to start.

Barbra took a sip of her drink, set the glass down and asked, "Who were you talking to? The men they sent out west?"

"No, I was talking to the envoy that we sent to Europe several months ago," he said, taking a sip of his own drink, feeling it burn on the way down.

"I thought you had said no one heard anything from them since right after they got to England?"

"That's only what I told the general and the president. I've been in contact with them for months."

"Why?"

"Because things are coming to a head here, it's getting dangerous. I warned them not to come back, and to let everyone on that side of the ocean to stay away."

"Stay *away*! John, we need all the help we can get!" she almost screamed.

"Keep it down!" he hissed, reflexively looking behind him at the open kitchen window.

"John, I see the suffering daily. We're almost out of the most basic medical supplies, food is running out, and people are starting to die! If we don't get some help soon, it's going to get worse. I know it sounds crazy, that things could be even worse than they are now, but believe me, it will."

"I have my reasons," he stated.

"Honey, you promised to tell me everything!"

He looked at her in the lantern light and sighed. She was right, he did promise. He inhaled deeply and held it for a few moments, then let it out in an audible whoosh. He looked down onto the bare tabletop. "I think the president has lost the plot."

"Ya think?" she said, words dripping with sarcasm. "John, he promised all these people a whole lot, and has failed us in every way. I don't have to tell you there's no food left, there's no power, no running water, and no sewage. Dysentery is endemic, we've had several cases of malaria, and just today the doctor thinks we've had our first case of cholera. It's goddamn medieval!"

"Not to mention the cases of pneumonic plague," he said. "All the more reason I'm doing what I've been doing."

"Please explain, because it's not making any sense to me at all..." Barbra trailed off, taking a gulp of her drink.

"The president is slipping. The men we sent out west for instance; they're not going out there to find medical supplies, or food, or solar panels or wind turbines. He's sent them out there to get one man; who has what he thinks he needs, and he'll stop at nothing at this point to get it."

"That's insane! What could one man possibly have that he'd want?"

"You're going to shit yourself, I'll tell you that," he said. Before he continued, he stood, went over to the open window, and stuck his head out. He looked around, and not seeing anything or anyone in the darkness, came back to the table and sat down. "He wants the codes for the nukes," John said, looking Barbra right in the eyes.

"He wants the codes for *nuclear missiles*?"

"That's what I said, babe."

"This is all a little too much. I don't understand," she said, brushing a wayward strand of hair away from her face. "Why the hell would he want those when there are more important things he needs to be having done? Can't the general do something?"

"The general is firmly in his camp, so are Tom and the major. I'm all alone with this. I'm not a hundred percent certain, but I think the man found the codes in the wreckage of Air Force One several years ago. He was a sergeant major with the PA National Guard," he said, downing the rest of his drink. He stood and got the bottle, and then the Coke from the fridge, setting it down on the table.

He fixed himself a fresh drink, topping her glass in the process.

"How do you know he has the codes?" Barbra asked.

"He's used them," John said flatly.

"*What?*" she gasped and her jaw fell open.

"You head me. He's used them to launch one missile we know of."

"If that's the case, he's just as crazy as our president for Christ sake!" she said incredulously.

"Maybe, maybe not," he said, then went on to tell her what he did know, some conjecture woven in, about the rogue ship's captain terrorizing the entire Pacific Ocean, and how he'd found out that there was a very successful settlement now on Oahu and several of the outer islands in the Hawaiian chain, how this sergeant major had made his way back from Hawaii, and now had an equally successful settlement in Arizona.

When John was finished, he took a swallow of his forgotten drink, dropping the empty glass on the tabletop as if to put an exclamation point at the end.

"You found out all of this by listening to the Ham radio and breaking their codes?"

John nodded.

"And the president knows all of it?"

"No, not all of it. I've only told them a tiny fraction of what I've found out. The president would come unglued if he knew about the launch. In hindsight, I wish I'd never told them anything."

"Why?"

"Because I think they're doing a great job out west, and frankly, I think they should be left alone."

"The thing that keeps nagging my mind is this; why not just get things back together here? Why the quest for the codes? What could he possibly do with them now?"

"Rule the world. I said he's lost the plot, on an epic scale."

"John, we need help here. Maybe this sergeant general or whoever can help us here, help us get the lights back on, get the water running?"

"It's sergeant major and you're right. We should be sending out an olive branch to him, but we're not. That nutty major is going out there, and most probably he'll destroy everything this guy has set up, loot everything else, and bring this guy back in chains so the president can hoist him up on a petard in a public display to show everybody here who's the boss."

"So what are you doing?" she said, getting animated, her fear turning into anger.

"The first thing I did was warn our good sergeant major and his compatriots on Oahu, though I don't know what good it'll do," he said, pouring another drink. He was starting to feel looser, and the words were flowing easier now. "I think it won't do any good except to let them know the good major is on the way and not let him be blindsided. In the end, he'll either be killed or captured."

"What about the envoy?" she asked.

"Not a lot to tell there. For all the president knows, he's missing in action since shortly after he landed in the United Kingdom."

"What has he told you?"

"Not a whole hell of a lot at first. When I finally convinced him I wasn't on the president's side, he was a bit more forthcoming. He's contacted two settlements, one in London, and another one in Hastings, of all places. They're a lot better off there than we are, and they don't want anything to do with our fantastic *leader*." The last word was spat out like it was poison.

"John, do you remember when we first met?" Barbra asked after pondering all this for a moment.

"I do," he said.

"We thought the world had ended, and we were the only ones left. It was just you and I."

"We got along, and survived."

"That first horrible winter we worked as a team, stayed warm. We were terrified, but we had food. When we started to meet others, and we came here and found even more people, and that there was a president, we were elated. He promised so much."

"Yeah, and we thought that everything was going to be alright then."

"That was when there were still plenty of things laying around that we could use. No one thought that all that stuff would someday run out. No one had the forethought to plan for that eventuality."

"We were just as guilty, babe. We thought all of it would still be there for years."

"We did. Everyone just took it for granted that out leader would take care of our every need."

"Yeah, just like before the Situation. People were accustomed to having the government take care of them. No one was self-reliant anymore."

"It's the same now, John. What we need here is someone who'll get everyone together, to work to get things back on track. Get the power on, get the water running, get farms producing food. Not someone gathering canned spam and beans from ever farther out of the city, only to have what little is brought back be rationed out piecemeal, the best of it going to that asshole in the White house, the crumbs to us unwashed masses."

"Did you know that there was another riot yesterday?" John asked, and Barbra nodded.

"Yes, we got some of the injured in the clinic."

"Do you know what it was about?"

"No, I never did find out," she said.

"It was over toilet paper. Fucking toilet paper!" he almost screamed. "I used to read about the long lines for bread, tiny allotments of fatty meat, and toilet paper, of all things, in the old Soviet Union. People were starving, but the fat cats in the Kremlin were eating caviar off gold plated dishes," John said, taking another drink. He was feeling quite good. The liquid had lubricated his tongue, and what he really felt was starting to come out.

"Those Russians were spending billions on nuclear weapons, while the citizens were starving. It's no different than here and now, only on a much smaller scale," she said sadly. "The president doesn't give two licks about us. Maybe he didn't come right out and say it, but his actions speak volumes. He only cares about his power, not us in the slightest. Now you tell me some other guy has those codes, and has launched a nuclear bomb somewhere. Maybe killed hundreds or thousands of people, and you think *he's* a good guy?"

"I'm not sure of his intentions when he launched the missile, but from all that I gathered, it was a last resort kind of thing. He didn't, and still has yet to lay claim to ruling anyone. You said it yourself a few moments ago, actions speak louder than words. This sergeant major out west has shown me he just wants to be left alone, him and his other settlement in Hawaii. He does have the power on, he is feeding his people, and they're all working together. Nuclear weapons or not, he seems to have his shit together, unlike the former Secretary of Urban Renewal," John said, pouring himself yet another drink.

"A last resort? John, have are you listening to yourself? Maybe he might think that a last resort is to launch another missile here on Washington because of that wingnut over on Pennsylvania Avenue. We could *all* be killed, damn it!"

"Do you think I haven't thought of that?"

With a fearful expression, she reached out and took hold of his hand. "John, we've got to get out of here. We have to leave right now!"

"We can't."

"Why can't we?" she gasped. "We can pack up a few things right now, and be far away by morning!"

"He's ordered all the guards at the checkpoints around the city to not let anyone leave, 'for our own safety' he says," John told her, downing his drink in one gulp, ice long gone.

The color drained from Barbra's face. "Oh my God. You mean to tell me we're all *prisoners* now?"

"That's about the long and short of it." He topped off their drinks and sat in silence, letting the alcohol flow through his blood.

"What are we going to do?"

"I'm not sure exactly, babe. I do know I just can't leave all these people to suffer and die. They've all been through the same nightmare as us, and we deserve better."

"We can't stay here. We're completely out of antibiotics. We have been for a while. What can you do?"

John swatted a mosquito that had landed on his neck, and thought for the first time about Yellow Fever, something he'd never dreamed of in a major city in the States before, and he shuddered. "I know we can't stay here, but I just can't let everyone here suffer much longer. We need someone who is a leader. Someone who will get everyone together again, not just scrounging around for scraps. I warned the sergeant major because I think he's the one that I think can pull us all together again."

"How in the world can one man, a man that's thousands of miles away in Arizona, help us now? Especially since they've gone out there to arrest or possibly kill him to get what they want?"

"That I couldn't tell you, but I'm going to help him anyway I can."

"What about us?" she asked.

"When I've done all that I can, you and I will get out of here. Go to Florida like you suggested a few months ago."

"You've already said they've blocked all the exits. How are we going to do that now?"

"Leave that to me. We can't leave now, but it's a big city, and there's bound to be holes somewhere. They haven't erected a Berlin Wall," he said.

"Yet," Barbra remarked flatly, arms now crossed over her chest.

"Not yet, no. I need to find a hole. There are not enough people to watch every egress route. In the meantime, I'm going to do everything I can to help this guy out west."

"How will you do that?"

"By doing exactly what I have been doing, babe, giving him as much intelligence as I can get to him. Which, to be honest, isn't a whole hell of a lot."

Barbra took another sip of her drink, took the bottle, and poured herself another shot, eschewing the Coke altogether.

"This sergeant major has the right idea, I think. From everything I've gathered he's rebuilding their society using the Constitution as a guide. That in itself is a good indication of his intentions. If we could just start a dialogue with him, pick his brain for more ideas, we'll all be better off. The one thing I can do— and I should have done it a long time ago—is give the sergeant major the radio frequency that the major is using, so he can listen in to what they're talking about."

"I've been meaning to ask you, how is it that the radios are still working when all the other electric stuff isn't? None of the medical equipment we need works, and we could really use some of that stuff."

"Whatever killed everyone a few years ago came with what I think was an EMP."

"Electromagnetic Pulse, I remember, you told me about it before. It fried all the circuit boards and stuff. That doesn't explain the radios."

"All of the older stuff that doesn't have micro circuitry wasn't affected. Like my vacuum tube Ham radio upstairs. It's what the sergeant major is using. Those and all the military electronics, like the satellite radios and things like that were all hardened and shielded to protect against EMP. The major would have the same sort of radios also. I'll just radio him with the frequencies and he'll be able to listen in. Eavesdrop, so to speak."

"Everything you've been doing is so damn dangerous! What happens to us if you get caught?"

"It can't be helped." John took her hand across the table. "Let me asked you a question; why did you become a nurse?"

"That's easy, I wanted to help people and ease the suffering."

"Exactly," John said, his eyes drawn to a moth that had found the flame in the lantern and was fluttering around the yellowed globe, casting wild shadows around the dimly lit kitchen. "I'm only a second-generation American. My grandfather is Dutch. He was in Holland during the Second World War and at the young age of sixteen, was in the Dutch Underground, fighting the Germans. He told me the stories when I was a child, how he and his friends would run messages to radio operators from the various resistance groups and help the allies. He had to escape after his parents were arrested and executed by the Nazis. He fled to England, then after the war immigrated to the US. He never let me forget how important freedom was, and how special our country was.   When I graduated high school and went on to college, I decided right then and there I'd do all I could for my country. I failed the enlistment physical for the Army," he chuckled, "I got flat feet. Then I saw an advertisement for the Central Intelligence Agency. I thought of how brave my grandfather was, even as a kid, and I made up my mind to get a job with the CIA."

"So you became a spy," Barbra stated, her eyes twinkling playfully in the lantern light.

"Not quite. They didn't make me into some James Bond, but I did have a degree in European relations, so they put me to work as an analyst, which suited me. I never, ever forgot my grandfather's words about how important our way of life was, and promised myself I'd do anything I could, no matter how insignificant it might seem, to protect it."

"And?" she prodded.

"And now I *am* a spy. This is not the shining light on the hill that Ronald Reagan spoke of anymore. If I can do anything at all to get some of that light back, I'll do it to. The United States might have died six years ago with everyone else, and it may never come back, but if this one sergeant major can bring back something similar, I'll do anything in my power to help that along. I have to."

"You're right. America died, and it certainly isn't here," Barbra agreed. She too was lightheaded and, added to her sheer exhaustion from working fourteen hour days in the clinic, was getting drunk herself.

"It's more than a town, or a city, or even borders on a map. It's an idea, one that I won't let die. I hope you understand."

"So you're willing to throw everything we have together away for an idea?"

"It's not just an idea anymore. It's an *ideal*. We have to strive for it, because if we don't, we'll be reduced to nothing more than slaves, and that, babe, is something worth fighting for. Yes, if it comes down to it, we die for it. I can't let what is left of humanity slip into another Dark Ages."

"And once you can't do any more, if it gets too dangerous?" she asked, gripping his hand tightly.

"Then I promise you we'll leave. I'll find a way out. First I'd need to finish here."

"We'll go away? Someplace far, far away from here?"

"Yes, I promise. Soon," he reassured her. "I'll start to gather what we need tomorrow, but I've got to keep up appearances. And heading into the Pentagon every day I can find out more."

"Just be careful," she said, tears welling up in her eyes. "I lost one whole family six years ago, and I'm not willing to lose you too. I couldn't..." she put her face in her hands and began sobbing.

John's heart sank. He stood on unsteady legs, circled the table, and pulled her into his arms.

"I won't do anything stupid, I promise, and if it gets too dangerous, we'll get out of here and go anywhere you want to go."

She sniffled a few times and he pulled her face to him and looked down to her.

"I need to ask you to do something for me. For us I mean."

"What is it?" she asked.

"I know you're short on medical supplies, but if we need to bug out, we need some stuff for us also. Can you get some things?"

"Like what?"

Anything you can think of. Not a lot, just stuff that we might need, things that we can take in a few backpacks. We'll be travelling light if we do leave," he told her.

"*If?* We *are* going to leave. I couldn't stand another winter in this godforsaken place!"

"Okay, okay. *When* we leave," he corrected himself.

"I'll try. We're so low on everything."

"Just try, babe. We only need enough to tide us over until we get far enough south we can forage for ourselves. Mostly every place within a hundred miles or so has been stripped bare, so we'll need some things until we get to where they haven't looted yet."

"When do you think we'll be going?"

"I don't know, maybe in a couple of weeks. Things are going to come to a head soon out west, and after that, I don't know what's going to happen. We got to be able to leave quickly if things go sour."

He kissed the top of her head, and looked down at the lantern. The moth that had been flitting around the flame had been joined by another, and now they were sharing a kind of macabre dance, their shadows eerily large on the ceiling and walls.

Barbra slipped from John's embrace sat back down at the table, and with a slightly shaking hand, picked up her tumbler and took another sip. John returned to his own seat and poured himself another straight double shot of the whiskey.

"Might as well have another drink," he said, smiling at her. She returned his smile weakly, and held out her glass for a refill.

"I haven't been this drunk since my first year in nursing school," she giggled.

"You sheem to be holding your liquor quite well," John slurred. "After tonight, I need to get drunk!"

"Do you have to go to the clinic in the morning?" he asked.

"No, the doctor gave me the day off. He wanted me to rest."

"You have been working a lot, I was getting worried." John sipped on his drink, the bottle of Coke completely forgotten.

"Sixteen straight days, I'm exhausted," she said. "John, do you think you can do any good?"

"I'm going to try."

"Ever since we first met, I could tell you were a man of principle."

"Like the old song says, 'you've got to stand for something or you'll fall for anything'. I've got to take a stand now."

"And you've drawn me into your web of cloak and dagger, Mr. Bond!" she said, holding up her glass in a toast. "To spies like us!"

He raised his own glass. "Spies like us!"

"I know it wasn't a martini, shaken, not stirred, but would you like to take me to bed, Mr. Bond?" Barbra asked, a mischievous twinkle in her eyes.

"Yesh, I would, Moneypenny!" John said in a really horrible Sean Connery imitation.

She cracked up laughing. "Bond never bedded Moneypenny!"

"I just rewrote the screenplay, my dear," John replied. He took Barbra by the hand, leaving the two moths to their nocturnal waltz.

CHAPTER 17: SI VIS PACEM, PARA BELLUM

Tim sat with his back against a tree inside a copse of trees on a hill overlooking Interstate 40 a mile east of Williams. It was a hot day for northern Arizona, and Tim looked out over the area with a pair of Zeiss binoculars. He dropped them to his side, pulled out a plastic one-quart canteen and took a few swallows of water.

He had his M3 grease gun lying in his lap, an ancient AN/PRC-77 radio propped up next to him. He was dressed in full Army ACU camouflage and patrol cap, as was Jimenez, who was seated similarly, a few feet to his right.

Tim replaced the cap to his canteen, and put in on the ground next to him, looked over at Jimenez. "Did you ever see this before?"

"No, Sat' Major, I just fixed planes."

"I'm going to make an infantryman out of you yet. I can't have my kid running around with a Pog," he told the younger man, smiling. "Taco, you are about to see what one man can do with a radio. Hand me the map," he said, holding out his hand, and Jimenez passed over a topographical map.

Tim unfolded it, and checked the grid references for his intended 'target' for the exercise. "Taco, way back in 1985, I was still a corporal. I got sent to Fort Sill, Oklahoma to take the thirteen foxtrot course, Artillery Forward Observer. It was by no means the hardest, but it wasn't an easy course. I needed a secondary MOS for promotion to E-5," he said. MOS meant 'Military Occupational Specialty', in civilian terms, his 'job' in the Army. "Anyway, during the course I learned firsthand the power a nineteen year-old can have with one of these," he said, holding up the telephone-like handset to the radio.

"I'll bet," Jimenez said.

"Watch and learn, Taco," Tim said, bringing the handset up to his mouth. He pressed the push-to-talk button. "Wombat One, this is Lizard Six Actual, over."

He released the button and waited for a response. A few seconds later the radio crackled, and Robyn's disembodied voice came back over the speaker. "Lizard Six Actual, this is Wombat One, over."

"Wombat One, adjust fire, over."

"Lizard Six Actual, send it, over."

"Wombat One, grid alpha tango seven three three zero five niner eight four, two one zero zero mils, troops in the open and soft-bodied trucks, over."

"Roger, I copy grid alpha tango seven three three zero five niner eight four, two one zero zero mils, troops in the open and soft-bodied trucks. Break, one tube, eight one mike mike, two rounds, HE, two five seconds, out."

"I copy one tube, eight one mike mike, two rounds, HE, two five seconds, out," Tim repeated into the handset.

A few seconds later, Robyn's voice came back over the radio, "Shot, over."

A moment after that, Tim and Jimenez could hear the distant 'crump' of the mortar firing two thousand meters to the west, and Tim replied, "Shot, out," over the radio handset.

Robyn again came back on the radio. "Splash, over."

Tim replied, "Splash, out," and brought his binoculars back up to his eyes. The two men could now hear the loud whistle of two 81mm mortar rounds shrieking overhead, then the first round impacted in the center of the highway's median and the base of a young pine, and detonated with a loud 'wham!' followed by the second round five seconds later, a few meters to the left on the cracked, weed strewn asphalt, with the same results.

While the thick black smoke and dust barely settled, Tim again held the handset to his mouth. "Add five zero, left one hundred."

"Roger, add five zero, left one hundred, shot, over," came Robyn's reply.

"Shot, out!" Tim said into the radio, and the whole process was repeated. This time the two rounds landed right on and near the fading double-yellow line in the center of the westbound lanes of the deteriorating interstate.

Jimenez let out a long whistle, and as the dust and smoke dissipated, looked over at Tim in awe. "Holy shit, that was intense!"

"Told you," Tim said winking at him. He picked up the radio handset. "Wombat One, this is Lizard Six Actual. Beautiful job! Mark down your numbers and secure for a while. I'll have another fire mission for you in a while, Lizard Six Actual, out."

"Roger, Wombat One, out!" came Robyn's cheery reply.

Tim turned off the radio to conserve the battery, and stood, slinging his M3 over his shoulder and hanging the binoculars around his neck. "Taco, if you think a few 81mm mortar rounds was intense, you should see a Time-On-Target mission with a few batteries of 155mm howitzers. That shit is in-fucking-tense. Just imagine two, three, maybe even four howitzer batteries, all firing from different locations, all perfectly timed, so that every goddamn single round hits the target at the exact moment."

"Fuck me! That's got to be a sight!"

"You'd cream your jeans," Tim assented. "Let's head over to our secondary position and do the same thing on Route 64."

"Sounds good," Jimenez replied, slinging his M16, and picking up the radio. The two men walked a short distance to where they had parked their Hum-Vee, tossed their gear in the back, and headed back west towards the interchange of Route 64.

"It looks like Ian remembered what he was taught a while ago," Tim said as he drove the pair over the deteriorating road.

"I'll say. When are we going to start setting the charges on the bridges?"

"We'll start on that tomorrow. I wanted Ian to get the mortar bore-sighted first. I didn't want a short round dropping and setting off the charges prematurely."

"That makes sense," Jimenez said. "Do you think we can pull it off?"

"I'm old-school. 'Rules of engagement' don't sit well with me; they never have, especially when the other side doesn't follow the rules. When I first enlisted, most of my senior NCO's were Vietnam vets. I learned from them to fight dirty, and fight to win. That's exactly what I plan to do now."

"You are absolute badass, Sar Major."

Tim laughed a little at that. "You think I'm badass? I'll tell you something. My uncle, my dad's older brother, enlisted in the Marine Corps in 1935. He spent a few years in China, and when World War Two broke out, he spent the entire war hopping from island to island in the South Pacific."

"He could have been on Volivoli at some point."

"Yeah, maybe, he went from Guadalcanal to Tarawa, Tinian, and then Iwo Jima. After that, he was a drill instructor at Parris Island."

"I never went to the Island. I did my boot camp in San Diego," Jimenez said.

"I figured that. Hollywood Marine," Tim cracked, knowing that anyone who enlisted in the Marine Corps west of the Mississippi River went to San Diego; hence they were called 'Hollywood Marines'.

"I'm still a Marine!"

"Yeah, you are a Jarhead," Tim conceded. "Anyway, after his stint at the Island, my uncle went to Korea. He was one of the Frozen Chosen. I can't imagine what it was like to fight in that cold fucking winter on the Chosin Reservoir, fighting back wave after wave of Chinese."

"Ballsy fucks," Jimenez agreed.

"Yeah, and then some, but his story gets even better," Tim continued. "He survives that, fights on until the end, and comes back Stateside for several years. He retired in 1955. So he's home in Philly, driving a truck for a living, bored out of his fucking mind, and he tried to reenlist into the Corps, but they think he's too old and give him a pass."

"Tough bastard, eh?" Jimenez asked.

"Yeah, he was," Tim said. "Right next to the Marine Corps recruiting station there was an Army Recruiter. He walked in, showed them his discharge, and they signed him up right away."

"No shit? He joined the Army after twenty years in the Crotch?"

"Yep, he went on to do twenty more years in the Army, nine tours in Vietnam, and retired finally in 1975. He retired as a command sergeant major, and the one thing I remember was him standing in his Class 'A' uniform with more shit on his chest, more medals than I'd ever seen on one person. I was amazed that he could stand up for all the goddamn medals. It was impressive to a ten year old."

Jimenez looked out the windshield at the passing forest and whistled appreciatively.

"I couldn't begin to list all the medals he was awarded over those forty years, but I don't even come close to standing in the shadow of that epitome of badass, Taco."

"He must have been proud of you, eh? When you enlisted I mean."

"He died when I was still in school. He lived down in Georgia, and we never got to see him often."

"I think you're a lot like him," Jimenez said as Tim pulled over to the side of the road near the off ramp to Route 64.

"I'm not even close. I try, but I'll never be that man. It was a different time, a whole different world."

"I think we'll make that world again someday. With Walter, and everyone else here," Jimenez said, exiting the vehicle, grabbing his rifle and radio.

"I'd like to think so, Taco. Bring back the principle."

"I'm willing to do everything I can to help with that, Sar' Major. And I hope someday I'm half the man you are."

Tim looked at Jimenez. He didn't know how to respond to that, so he just left it hang in the air like a balloon on a summer's day.

They went about repeating exactly what they had done a while ago on I-40, calling in a few mortar rounds on a spot that Tim had determined would be the best spot for an ambush. When they were done, they watched the dust settle and the smoke dissipate, then packed up their gear yet again and made their way back to home.

"Do you think we're ready?" Jimenez asked.

"As soon as we get the explosives set on those bridges east of us, we will be."

"What about Izzy?"

"He may be pushing eighty, but I'm not getting any fucking younger either. He fought in 'Nam, and he's got the testicular fortitude. That mortar is supposed to be crewed by six men, and it'll just be him and Ian lobbing explosives. He'll be fine."

"It's been a long time, and he's a doctor now, not a soldier. Isn't he supposed to have taken an oath or something against fighting?"

"Sometimes you have to fight, no matter what your convictions are to the contrary. This is where the rubber meets the road. I don't think he'd be able to live with himself if he left with the women."

"Speaking of that, Robyn's not all that happy that you're making her leave too."

Tim pulled the Hum-Vee up in front of his house, shut the engine off and turned to look at Jimenez. "Well, Taco," he said, "she's not staying, end of fucking story."

"I was just saying. I agree with you."

"Alright, let's get this shit squared away," Tim said gruffly, the old sergeant major coming back out in him.

As they were carrying their gear in from the Hum-Vee, a second one appeared from around the back, driving up the dusty road from the other direction. It parked next to Tim's, and Robyn, Izzy, and Ian got out, all smiling broadly.

Tim set his pack and weapon down on the steps, and walked over to the three, who were now collecting their own gear from the back.

"Good job," Tim said, walking up to them, hand extended. Ian took his hand and smiled.

"Shit, mate, that brought back some memories!" Ian beamed.

"It was a great job. You put those rounds exactly where I wanted them. I'm sure you'll be able to repeat it if the shit hits the fan."

"No worries, mate. I've got the numbers all written down, and I've got the ground marked so all I have to do is move the tube to the new markings if you need me to change fire. It's all dialed in."

"So it's secured?" Tim asked.

"Yeah, I've got the tube still set up, but I've covered it with a tarpaulin, along with the ammo. All we have to do is go out, uncover it, and start dropping rounds."

"Good. Again, great job," Tim said.

"Now it's beer thirty?" Ian asked with a smile.

"You took the words out of my mouth," Tim replied.

"Dad, that was fun. I wish I could be around when we start to drop rounds for real!" Robyn said gleefully, and Tim's face darkened.

"You, Holly, the baby, and the rest of the women will be down in Phoenix when that happens."

"But, Dad—"

"No buts, goddamn it! End of fucking story," Tim snapped, pointing his finger at her like a pistol.

Dejected, Robyn raised her hands in mock surrender.

Tim turned to Izzy. "How are you doing?"

"Never better, Tim. I feel like I'm twenty-five again!"

"Are you going to be okay with this, dropping high explosives on people?"

"It's not like I haven't done it before. Yes, it's been a long time, and I do have my Hippocratic Oath to think about, but then there's the greater good to think about also. I'll be fine, don't worry about me," the old doctor said in his best bedside manner.

"I'll go and get the amber nectar, won't be but a few ticks!" Ian said, and headed off on foot to his house a few yards up the road.

"We ought to start thinking about some homebrew beer," Tim said, watching Ian disappear around the side of his house.

"Yes, or maybe even a still," Izzy agreed. "The beer is starting to get stale."

"Vodka!" Jimenez chimed in.

"That's a great idea there, Taco. Cheap vodka is good, really good vodka is, well, almost better than sex… almost," Tim told the young Marine in a scholarly tone, quickly regretting his comment when he glanced at a blushing Robyn.

While they waited for Ian to return with the beer, they unloaded their gear and stacked everything together just inside Tim's front door. Robyn and Jimenez went off towards the kitchen, and Izzy excused himself to find the bathroom, leaving Tim alone in the living room.

He climbed the stairs and walked down the short hall toward his and Holly's bedroom, where he found mother and child asleep on the bed, little Walter held gently in Holly's arms.

He smiled at the sight, and stepped back into the hall, closing the door quietly behind him. He then made his way back downstairs and out to the front porch, where Ian was waiting with a Coleman cooler, a cold beer already in his hand. When he saw Tim e he opened up the lid, fished around in some ice and pulled out a can of beer, which he tossed to Tim.

Tim caught the can deftly and popped the tab. He sat down on the step and held the can up in salute. "Thanks. Nice and cold."

"Yeah, Paula was nice enough to have a slab on ice in the esky for when we got back," Ian said.

"Nice of her," Tim remarked. The door opened, and Jimenez stepped out, followed by Izzy. Ian fished out another beer, tossing it to the young Marine. He caught it and sat down next to Tim on the step.

"Where's Robyn?" Tim asked.

"She's up in our room. She said it was almost time to check in on the satellite radio with Sergeant Williams, she'll be down soon."

Tim winced inwardly at the term 'our room'. He knew it was a fact that his little girl was now sleeping with this man, and he really did like the man, which was why he continually broke his balls.

"So we're all set then?" Ian asked.

"Just about," Tim said, "Me and Taco will set the charges on the bridges east of here tomorrow, and then we're as ready as we'll ever be." He set the can down on the step next to him. "We'll go over it again. Taco and I will be in the first position, about two hundred meters from the bridge. When we see them approach, I'll give the warning order."

"And Ian and I will get the mortar ready," Izzy chimed in.

"Yes. I'll let a few of them across the span before I drop it, and as soon as I trip the charges, I'll give you the order to fire," Tim said.

"How many rounds do you want us to fire?" Ian asked.

"Twenty or so. I'll give you a cease fire before that if need be."

"Are you sure you don't want any Willie Pete?" Ian asked, meaning white phosphorous rounds.

Tim shook his head, "No, I thought about that. It would be effective, but it's too dry out in the forest now, the danger of a forest fire is way too great as it is with the high explosive rounds, but I'm willing to take that chance. No sense ensuring half the area burns up and destroys what we're trying to protect. HE will be fine."

"Okay," Ian acknowledged.

"Then we'll stand by to fire more rounds, or shift fire at your direction," Izzy picked up.

"Good," Tim said. "Taco, what's our job?"

"Our job is to lay suppressive fire with rifles, single fire only, no rock and roll. Choose targets individually, one round per target, closest targets first. We don't let them see where we are, and move around from position to position to let them think there's a shitload more of us than there really is," Jimenez finished.

"Like we planned earlier, Holly will take the Herc to Phoenix with the rest, preferably long before they get close enough. I'd prefer a few days prior, though without reliable intelligence we won't know for certain when they'll arrive, if at all."

"Have you heard any more news from Sam?" Ian asked, finishing his beer and belching loudly.

"No. They lost them a few days ago outside of Denver. It was too built up to get near enough to them without being seen, so Sam did the smart thing and held back, skirting around them to the southeast. He's hoping to pick them up south of there on the New Mexico border."

"I hope they do," Jimenez said.

"Yeah, so do I," Tim agreed. "I just wish we had more time."

"And a few more men," Ian said.

"That might be a possibility," Tim said, taking a huge gulp of his beer. He felt like getting drunk today for some reason, and if it was going to take a case of beer to do it, he'd do it.

"How?" Izzy asked, raising his eyebrow.

"I think Jerry has something planned. He told me a few days ago. I didn't say anything before, because I saw the improbability of it. However, it seems our intrepid sailors did get their boat to Pearl. Jerry talked to them a week or so ago, and thinks they might be able to scrape together about a hundred men to come back here for reinforcements, along with a few Bradley fighting vehicles."

"That's great news!" Ian exclaimed.

"Don't get your hopes up, Iz. They have to sail from Pearl to San Diego, which will take at best two weeks, and they haven't left yet. Once they get to the mainland, they've got to travel overland several hundred miles from California to here, and knowing the Bradley like I do, that will take a few more weeks."

"Oh, I see what you mean," Izzy said in a sad voice.

"Yeah, they'll be too late. I don't think we have four weeks, I suspect we have about two at the most."

"Too bad our railway man hasn't found a way," Ian remarked.

"I thought that myself, Ian," Tim said. "We haven't heard a peep from him in over two months. He's on the MIA list for now."

"So we're fucked?" Jimenez asked.

"I don't hear a fat lady even warming up for the last song yet, Taco. What we're going to do is bloody their fucking nose."

"I don't want to sound like a downer, Sar' Major, but how? There are a lot more of them than us."

"From everything that Sam has reported back to us so far, they're far from being a well-disciplined, well-trained, or well-led military unit. They sound like a bunch of dickweed-dumbasses, and that, my friends, is a huge advantage to us. A well-disciplined body of troops would react a lot differently than a group of unorganized men with no experience. Sure, there's most probably some of them that have seen combat in Iraq or Afghanistan, but I'm betting the majority will be a bunch of civilians with guns. When Ian and Izzy start dropping high explosives on their collective grapes, it will be a clusterfuck."

"So they might just run?"

"Possibly," Tim said. "We don't know for certain, but there's a very good chance they will do just that."

"That makes sense."

"How many Claymores did you get from Camp Navajo?"

"Thirty."

"And we've got a shitload of det-cord. It's going to be one pisser of an ambush, I'll tell you that much," Tim said confidently.

"Like we did on Volivoli?"

"Bigger. When that bridge blows, all hell will break loose."

"That's settled then," Izzy said, taking another beer out of the cooler. "We can all sleep well tonight."

"Maybe you can, Iz, but I haven't slept well since our first hint of this."

"I don't think any of us has, Tim," Ian said somberly.

The front screen door opened with a bang, and Robyn exploded out the entrance.

"Dad, can I talk to you?" she almost screamed.

"What is it?" he asked loudly.

Robyn bounded out and breezed by him, down the stairs and up to the cooler at Ian's feet.

She reached in, fished through the ice and brought out a can, popping the top. She swigged at the beer, and when she was finished, wiped her mouth with the back of her hand.

"That's my demure little girl," Tim said with a wry smile, then asked, "What is it?"

"I talked to Jerry on the Sat-radio. Everything is going according to plan there; they've got four Bradleys loaded up, and a hundred men, along with a few Hum-Vees with TOW missile launchers. They'll be ready to sail tomorrow."

"That's great news!" Ian said.

"That's not all!" Robyn exclaimed, eyes wide. "After I got off the radio with Jerry, I fired up the Ham radio and—"

"Damn it! I told you not to—" Tim cut in.

"Dad, shut up a minute and just listen!" Robyn said. "Like I was saying," she continued, sticking out her tongue at Tim playfully, making a face, "I fired up the Ham just to listen in for any other news. While I was going through the bands, I picked up that guy in Washington again, Dad. He knew your name! He gave me this," she said, fishing out a scrap of paper and handing it to Tim. "He said he wished he could do more, and he told me to tell you 'good luck'."

Tim took the paper, and looked at it, a grin spreading across his face.

"What is it, Tim?" Izzy asked.

"I'll be dipped in dogshit," Tim said in astonishment. "Robyn, did this guy tell you his name?"

"He just said to call him 'Deep Throat', whatever that means."

"That means, Robyn, we have a benefactor back east," Izzy said, then turned to Tim again. "Well, what did our deep throat give us?"

"He gave us the satellite radio frequency that our adversaries are using."

"Madre de Dios!" Jimenez whispered.

"That's a boon, mate!" Ian said, taking out another beer and popping the top. "This calls for a celebration!"

"I wouldn't celebrate too hard, gentlemen. We'll see. This might be a red-herring," Tim said, waving the scrap of paper in front of his face.

"I'd listen in, Tim, just in case it isn't," Izzy advised.

"I will, Iz," Tim said, pocketing the piece of paper. "Every little bit helps."

"Why would someone do that though?" Ian asked curiously.

"I was wondering the same thing, Ian," Tim said. "I'm guessing whoever it is, is either acting as a disseminator of false information, or really doesn't dig what's going on back east."

"False information?" Ian asked.

"Yeah, like a double agent, sort of. He's acting as if he's on our side, giving us this information, but in reality, he's actually working for the other side, giving us bullshit so we'll act a certain way."

"To our detriment," Izzy added in understanding.

"How would that work?" Robyn asked, as she walked over and planted herself next to Jimenez on the steps.

"It's like this, Robyn; during World War Two, in the months preceding the Normandy invasion, the allies set up the First U.S. Army group, supposedly located in southeastern Britain under the command of General Patton. It was created to give the Germans the idea that the allies would invade in a completely different area than where they were actually going to have the landings by the use of double agents and fake radio traffic. It was all bullshit."

"So on the morning on June 6th, the Germans had sent most of their reserves miles away, so when the allies landed, they weren't in a position to counter attack," Izzy added with a scholarly tone.

"Exactly," Tim said. "There were plenty of other deceptive plans used throughout the war, but that one sticks in my mind. The Krauts figured if Patton was commanding this Army group, it had to be real."

"Don't forget another slightly macabre operation, Mincemeat, I believe it was called," Izzy said.

"Oh, yeah. That was a good one!" Tim snickered.

"What was that one, Dad?"

"It was ingenious. The British took a dead guy from the morgue in London. He'd died of pneumonia, but it would look to anyone that found him like he'd drowned. They dressed him up in a British Army officer's uniform, handcuffed a briefcase to his wrist filled with all kinds of top secret papers—which were all false— then one night they took the body by submarine and set it adrift off the coast of Spain, where it would wash up."

"Wasn't Spain neutral?" Ian asked.

"It was," Izzy said. "But the Germans being Germans, were quite cozy with the Spanish, and the British knew that the Spanish authorities would let the Germans have a gander at the contents of the briefcase before they turned everything over to the British consulate."

"They even gave the guy a burial with full military honors," Tim said.

"That's fucked up," Jimenez said with a laugh of his own.

"I see," Ian said. "So you think this bloke is feeding us false information?"

"I'm not sure," Tim said. "It could be, then again, this guy might be acting out of completely altruistic principles. We just don't know."

"Why would he warn us to begin with?" Robyn asked.

"Yeah, it wouldn't make sense if it was false information. Why tell us at all?" Jimenez said.

"That thought has crossed my mind. If they were going to blindside us, why tell us at all? They could have easily left us alone, unawares, until one day we wake up to find ourselves surrounded."

"That would be a good point to take into account," Izzy said.

"Fucking oath, mate, he could have just not told us at all," Ian said.

"I'm just going to play it by ear for right now," Tim said. "Robyn, have you heard any more from Didinato?"

"Not since yesterday," she replied. "He said he was still trying to catch up with them, and he said he'd get back to us tonight sometime."

"Alright, you've got radio watch again tonight."

"How is Sam coping?" Izzy asked.

"I'm not sure. It must be a pain in the ass with the buffalo and the horses. But he's a good soldier and knows his business."

"Following a line of trucks and Hum-Vees must be difficult," Izzy said.

"That's true, but from what he's been reporting to us, they're leaving a trail so obvious a blind man could follow it. I don't think he's gotten within a mile of them since they first stumbled across them in Nebraska," Tim told the man, reaching out for another beer that was offered by Ian.

"Which leads us back to the original question," Izzy said. "If this person was feeding us false information, why tell us anything about the soldiers coming. Tim, they may know about you, and our settlement here, but they had no idea about Didinato or his trip to the prairie. If it was a ruse, they'd have to have known about him, to let him see them on the move."

"Like they meant for us to see them coming?" Tim asked incredulously. "That in itself, if true, would be a monumental gamble with time and materiel."

"That's why I think we should take into account what this man, or woman," Izzy added in deference to Robyn, "in all likelihood is telling us the truth."

Tim nodded slowly. "I agree. We should trust, but verify."

"Quoting Ronald Reagan now, eh, Timothy?" Izzy grinned.

As he was still laughing, Paula came around the side of Tim's house and walked up to Ian. She bent down and fetched a can of beer for herself out of the melting ice, and popped the tab. "Oi, I should have known you'd be down here getting on the piss."

"Ah, it is 'She who must be obeyed'!" Ian said, putting his arm around the diminutive woman. "We were just going over some plans."

"You lot couldn't organize a piss-up in a brewery," she said, poking him in the side.

"I dunno, ma'am. We're doing a good job of it right now," Jimenez said, draining his can.

"Oh, I almost forgot. I was going to give something to you this morning," Tim said to Ian. "Robyn, go run in and get that thing I was saving for him."

She nodded and went back into the house.

"For me?" Ian asked.

"It's just a little something I found a week ago when I was scrounging around in that town south of here, Chino Valley," Tim said. "I think you'll like it."

Robyn came back out of the house then carrying a rifle, and when he saw it, Ian's eyes lit up. She walked over to him, and racked open the bolt, checked to see if the chamber was empty before handing it over to Ian. Tim smiled, as she did exactly what he'd taught her so many years ago: never hand over a weapon without checking to see if it was loaded, and never hand someone a loaded firearm.

Ian took it from her. "I haven't seen one of these in years!"

"What is it?" Jimenez asked.

"It's an L1A1, standard issue rifle for the Australian Army. Or at least it was up until the early 1980's," Tim told Jimenez.

"Shit, mate, thanks heaps!" Ian said, looking over the rifle. Paula looked at the weapon with distain, and then noticed something on the butt stock.

"What's that?" she asked.

"It's an inscription that the previous owner had carved there. It reads; 'Si Vis Pacem, Para Bellum'," Tim replied.

"What's it mean?" Robyn asked.

"If my Catholic school Latin is correct, it means 'if you want peace, prepare for war' or something similar."

"You are correct, Tim," Izzy said.

"That's what we're doing," Jimenez said, and as if to add emphasis, the sound of distant thunder from a yet unseen storm rumbled through the valley.

CHAPTER 18:
HAMMER & ANVIL

The convoy was parked along the shoulder of the westbound lanes of Interstate 40 by a string of souvenir shops, which had once hawked 'authentic' Navajo crafts made in the People's Republic of China.

The map that the major had unfolded and spread out on the hood of the Hum-Vee said it was the town of Lupton, Arizona, a few hundred yards west of the New Mexico border. However, a brief scan of the area told the major and the sergeant that there wasn't much to the place, save for the tourist traps and a few bare, red-rock mesas. It was early morning, the sun had just peeked over the hills to the east, and the clear, cloudless sky hinted at another long, hot day.

The major looked at the handful of men standing around his Hum-Vee, and then ran his finger over the blue line that marked I-40. "Gentlemen, it's about another one hundred and sixty miles to Flagstaff. I'd like to make it to there before sundown."

"Sir, the roads seem to be in a lot better shape out here, so I don't see a problem with that. We are a little low on fuel, though I think we've got enough to get to Holbrook," the sergeant replied, tapping a dot on the map. "It looks to be a lot bigger than this 'town', so we should be able to scare up some more fuel there."

"Agreed, Sergeant," the major said. "It looks to be around seventy miles or so, about halfway."

"Yes sir," the sergeant replied, not wanting to correct the major's math, wondering where the extra thirty or so miles went. "If that's it, Major, I'd like to get the men ready to travel."

"In a moment, Sergeant. I want to go over a plan I've come up with," the major said through teeth that were clenched around an unlit stump of cigar.

The sergeant sighed heavily, set his M4 on the hood next to the map and nodded. "Okay Major."

"I'm glad I have your approval, Sergeant," the major said, voice oozing sarcasm. He pointed again to a point on the map. "We're here. We'll head westward, then, when we reach Flagstaff, we'll split up. It will be a perfect hammer and anvil maneuver. I want you to handpick a group of men to head north here," he said, pointing to another point on the map. "I want them to take Route 89 here, travel north, then pick up Route 64 south of Cameron, where it will continue west before turning south again at the Grand Canyon north of the airport in Tusayan."

"Sir, that's the long way around. It looks like it would be easier and faster to get to the airport if we send them up Route 180, where they can pick up 64 in Valle, south of the strip. It'll cut off several miles of travel."

The major shook his head and said in a condescending tone, "That would be the case if we were on a sightseeing trip, Sergeant. Our new friend Colin has given us the information we need. They'll never expect anyone to come from that direction, so that's the way I want them to go."

"Are you sure his information is correct?"

"I am. Send a few men up to secure the aircraft in Tusayan, while the remainder of us continue west on 40 to Williams. Once we've obtained our objective in Williams, we'll bring the rogue sergeant and the pilot up to the airport, where we'll fly back to Washington."

The sergeant looked down on the map in the early morning sun and frowned. He dared not tell the major it wasn't a hammer and anvil maneuver, but let it go to humor him. "If you say so, sir."

"I do say so, Sergeant. Our friend Colin, or should I say 'mate'," he said with a smile, "has given us all the information we need. We no longer have to go searching for our quarry; we know right where he is. Not only that, we know how few men he has. It should be an easy task to secure what we need!"

"I'm still a little uneasy about this whole thing, Major. What if this sergeant major has gotten some reinforcements? Colin hasn't been there for a few months, and his whole story about being run out of town after a misunderstanding is a little suspect, if you don't mind me saying, sir."

"I do mind you saying, Sergeant. I've found or Australian friend rather engaging. His story fits in with what I was told back in DC. Our good sergeant major gone rogue has set up himself a little enclave, like Gary Cooper in *High Noon*. He'll not expect us, and we should take him completely by surprise."

"Gary Cooper was a good guy in *High Noon*, sir," the sergeant pointed out.

"I don't like smartasses, Sergeant," the major said, folding the map up in a huff. "That's the plan, just carry it out. Go and get the men ready to travel."

"Yes, sir, right away. I'll tell everyone to plan on a short stop for fuel in Holbrook."

"You do that, Sergeant, and when we get to Flagstaff, hopefully this afternoon sometime, you'll have the men picked for the hammer."

"I'm on it, sir." The sergeant picked up his carbine and headed off, followed by the other men, leaving the major at his Hum-Vee. He walked around the Hum-Vee, opened the passenger side door and climbed in. He reached over and shook his driver awake. The young man roused slowly, and through squinted eyes, looked over at the major.

"Are we ready yet?"

"No, the sergeant is getting everyone together now; it'll be a few more minutes."

"Are we going to get that guy and his plane today?"

"No, most likely it will be tomorrow, Nuggets."

"It gonna be a lot of action, mebbe?" Nuggets asked hopefully.

"No. It will probably be just a quick in and out. He won't know what hit him," the major said, grinning widely.

"Aw, man! I wanted to see some real action like all them guys in Afgranistan!" the boy moaned.

"I'm sorry, Nuggets, but I think he'll just see all of us, wet his pants and give up," the Major reassured his young driver, not bothering to correct his pronunciation of Afghanistan. The boy's English was horrible, and was filled with ghetto slang.

"But we's gonna fly home though, right?"

"Yes, we will," the major said.

"Good, cuz' I getting' a sore butt sitting in this Hum-Vee all da' time!" he replied, reaching around and rubbing his backside theatrically. "It be's a big plane?"

"Our good friend from Australia tells us it's a big cargo plane, a Hercules, though we won't be able to take everyone all at once."

"Dang!"

"Don't you worry, Nuggets, I'll make sure you and I get on the first flight. Rank has its privileges, you know," the major told the boy.

"I never been on no plane before."

"You haven't?"

"Nope, I's ain't never been outta Baltimore befo' everybody up and died."

"It's a big country," the major said, waving his hand out to the barren vista through the windshield.

"Too big fo' me. I jes wanna get back to DC is all. Not much at all out here anyways," the boy said, shaking his head, and the major laughed a little.

"Yes, there isn't much out here at all," the major agreed.

"So they won't be no big battle?"

"No, Nuggets. This crazy sergeant out west of here will probably take one look at us, piss his pants, and give up without a whimper. Trust me," the major reassured the dejected driver, and then fished out a Zippo lighter and lit the stub of his cigar, filling the cab of the Hum-Vee with noxious blue smoke.

After several minutes, the major's radio crackled to life. He picked up the handset and brought it to his ear. After a brief transmission, he replied curtly and motioned for his driver to start the engine. He set the handset down, and reached out the open window with his right arm, making a circular motion, and then, like a large snake, the convoy moved out westward along the barren highway.

Throughout the morning they continued westward, through the Petrified Forest National Park, and reached Holbrook by midmorning, where they found a truck stop just west of town.

The convoy of Hum-Vees and trucks lined up along the outside of the building, where the sergeant, who was riding in the trail Hum-Vee, dismounted and walked the line of trucks, gathering a work party to scavenge for diesel fuel.

The sun was already high in the cloudless sky, the temperature had already reached the 80 degree mark, and all those who weren't siphoning fuel from the trucks parked around the complex had escaped the stifling confines of the backs of the canvas covered military vehicles and were seeking shade anywhere they could find in the still, hot air.

The sergeant found his own spot of shade underneath the portico of the convenience store/diner, but he wasn't alone for long. As he sat down on the concrete pavement with his back to a brick wall, pulled out his canteen and took a drink of tepid water, he spied a large, smiling man walking up to him. It was the barrel-chested Aussie, Colin. He strode up to the sergeant, and without asking, sat down next to him with a plop.

"G'day, mate! Hot day, eh?"

"Yeah, it's a hot one," the sergeant said, putting his canteen away and looking at his new companion with a sideways glance.

"Riding is a lot better than walking," Colin said.

"That it is. Tell me, you walked all the way from Williams?"

"Yeah, it was a long hot walk too. Not much out here in the way of food and water."

"You're lucky to be alive," the sergeant said with a slow nod, his gaze out towards the other men fueling the vehicles.

"S'truth, mate! I figured my chances were a lot better than back there. They were going to kill me!"

"So you've said. Tell me again how you escaped?" the sergeant asked skeptically.

Colin started off with a grin, relishing his story, never tiring of relating his exploits. "They had me locked up in a cage, and the morning they were going to hang me up from a tree, I overpowered the guard they had and I ran off into the bush."

"How'd you overpower him?"

"Well, mate," Colin said, glint in his eye, "he was a little brown bastard. Mexican I think. I don't know about all you blokes here. Anyways, he was a skinny little shit. I came up behind him and snapped his neck like a twig!" he beamed, holding out his dirty hands proudly.

"I'm impressed," the sergeant said dubiously.

"Yeah, I've been in a few brawls in my life. I could've been a boxer."

"Sounds like it," the sergeant replied. He'd already come to the conclusion that this asshole was a 'coulda'. I coulda' done this, I coulda' done that. He'd known people like that his whole life, and they were basically full of shit.

"Why were they going to string you up?"

"Ah, shit! That's easy! That bloke out there in charge, he's got this pretty little Sheila, and she was sweet on me," he said gleefully. "Long blonde hair, blue eyes, about nineteen I think. Well one night that Tim bloke caught us rooting, and that's when he chucked a dummy spit and tossed me in the cage."

The sergeant looked at the big, unkempt man, and asked, "Was it his wife?"

"Nah, his daughter. She couldn't keep her hands off of me, I tell ya. I get that from a lot of women."

"I'll bet," the sergeant replied, inwardly shuddering at the thought of any woman finding him even remotely attractive. Personal hygiene was way down on this guy's list of priorities.

"Yeah, the guy is stone jealous, even his own woman, the pilot lady. She's a right Pommy bitch. She was giving me the eye too and he was seeing red."

"Pommy?"

"Yeah, a Brit. Stuck up bitch she was on the outside, but I could tell she was after me too! She had long ginger hair, tight little bum. She wanted me."

"So this sergeant major flipped out and locked you up?"

"That's about it, mate. He couldn't stand this rooster running around with his chooks," Colin said smugly, thumbing his chest proudly.

"I'll make sure to not let you near my wife then," the sergeant said in mock fear, but inside it was the truth. He felt dirty just sitting this close to him, and mused inwardly that if this man ever came close to his wife back in DC, he'd slice his heart out with a rusty bayonet and feed it to him.

"Better not, mate!" Colin said. "Women can't resist me!"

"What else can you tell me about him?"

"He's got his own little kingdom out there, rules it like he's king of the world. Has all kinds of food hoarded, but won't give any out, keeps the best for himself."

"I see. How many men does he have?"

"Not a lot, the Mexican bloke, some old doctor, and few other Aussies that came over from Hawaii with us and their Sheilas. That's about it."

"No weapons?"

"Yeah, he's got a few, the guns you blokes are carrying, a few pistols."

"So just some M4 carbines and a few handguns?"

"Is that what they are? Yeah, I guess. I'm not familiar with them too much. I prefer fighting with me hands!"

The sergeant looked out over the sunbaked, weed strewn asphalt shimmering with a hint of mirage in the dry air. *So, they only have a few carbines and pistols, and only a handful of men,* he thought. Maybe he should relax a little.

The stockpiles of food also piqued his interest. That would definitely be an added plus, to bring back a stockpile of food with them.

"They've got a stockpile of food?"

"Yeah, got plenty for a lot more people than they've got, enough I reckon for a few years."

"We'll have to bring it all back with us, whatever we can carry," the sergeant said, more to himself than to Colin.

"Yeah, well, they've got a few of those trucks, like these ones," Colin replied, waving his hand towards the convoy.

"And the Hercules. That'll carry a bunch back. I'm sure the president will be quite happy with it."

"Do you think I'll have a place in Washington?" Colin asked hopefully.

"Yeah, I'm sure the president will be happy with all the help you've given us."

"Good. I want to help!" Colin said.

The Specialist trotted over to the pair. "Hey, Sarge, the men are just about finished," he reported once he stopped at the men's feet.

The sergeant looked up, relieved that he was finally going to get away from this unsavory fellow. "Good, let's get everyone loaded back up and we'll head out."

"Check, Sergeant!" the Specialist replied, spinning on his heels and heading back towards the parked vehicles. The sergeant stood, shouldered his carbine, and looked down on the still seated Colin.

"Thanks again for all your help. You'd better head back to your ride, or we'll leave you here," he told the man, only half joking.

"Yes sir!" Colin said, standing.

By the time he made it back to his Hum-Vee at the tail of the formation, the major's Hum-Vee was already heading out on the highway, speeding west. He opened the passenger side door and tossed his rifle in unceremoniously, climbed in, and motioned for the Specialist to head out. They fell in behind the last 6X6 truck. The Specialist fished into his pocket, and pulled out a can of snuff, and handed it over.

"Dip?" he asked the sergeant, who took the offered tin. Packing it, he opened the can and took a pinch of the finely cut Copenhagen and placed it under his lip.

"Thanks," he said, handing the tin back. It was a nasty habit, he knew, and his wife hated it, especially the spitting, but she was a few thousand miles behind them to the east, and she'd never know of his small indulgence.

"So," the specialist said, spitting out of the window, "I see you and that Aussie guy were getting all chummy."

"Yeah, I was letting him know he's so much of a Bro now, he can come over to my house and fuck my sister."

The Specialist snorted. "Ah come on. He's helped us."

"Maybe so, but I don't trust him. He's got an axe to grind with the sergeant major we're after, and he's not telling the whole story."

"Yeah, I got the impression he was a bullshitter from the git-go. Think he's a Blue Falcon?"

"Gold plated," the sergeant commented. "Something he's telling us just doesn't sit well with me."

"He's a 'coulda', I'll say that much."

"Yeah, he's definitely one of those. It's just some of his story doesn't ring true with me."

"I know, like him fucking that guy's daughter. If it's true, it sure wasn't voluntary," the Specialist said with a grimace.

"I've read the guy's 201 file. He doesn't seem like a guy who would string someone up just for knocking off a piece, even if it was his own kid. I can tell when someone is spoon-feeding me horseshit, and that Aussie is oozing it."

"So everything he said is garbage?"

"No, I didn't say that. It's just from my years of being a cop, I can tell that some of his story is crap. The rest is probably true, like how many men he's got the weapons he has, that sort of shit. The whole story about his escape, him breaking the guy's neck," he shook his head, "I'm not buying it. This sergeant major doesn't seem like he'd surround himself with a bunch of pussies."

"True. I'd never let the fucker get that close to me if I was guarding him."

"Exactly," he replied.

"So this plan of the major's," the Specialist ventured. "What do you think about it?"

"I think it's stupid, that we shouldn't split up, but he's in charge."

"It does seem harebrained. Who are you going to send?"

"I'll send you with a few guys in a Hum-Vee. I know you won't let anything fuck up with the plane."

"You'll stay with the major?"

"I'll keep up the rear, since he wants to go charging in like the Seventh Cavalry. I should be up front though, in case shit turns sour."

"Ah shit, we've got him just by sheer numbers, Sarge."

"Maybe, but unlike the major, I've got this niggling little feeling that this sergeant major isn't going to fold like a bad hand in Vegas."

"What's he have out there, five, six men, and a bunch of women?"

"Something like that," the sergeant replied. "Our friend couldn't give us an exact number."

"We've got the firepower and the numbers on our side. It'll be a cakewalk," the specialist said dismissively.

"Don't be too sure. You were in the Ghan, weren't you?"

"Three tours with the Third ID," the Specialist replied, meaning the Third Infantry Division.

"How many of the Hajji just gave up right away, even when they were outnumbered five to one?"

"Not many, but they were better armed than this mob we're after."

"Yes, if you believe everything is gospel according to Colin," the sergeant said.

"Sarge, all I'm saying is we've got over a company of men. He's got what, five or six, with some rifles? We don't even need fucking air support even if we had it," the Specialist said, waving his hand dismissively.

"I'm not saying it won't be easy, I'm just saying we shouldn't go stomping in like gangbusters."

"I think you're prejudiced. You just don't trust that Colin guy is all."

"He's not the only one I don't trust," the sergeant said warily.

"You trust me, don't you?"

"Yes, I trust you. That's why I'm sending you to secure the C-130. I don't trust the major, and I especially don't trust the sergeant major."

"That goes without saying about the good major, and I agree, the sergeant major is an unknown. Besides Colin's bullshit story about him being the biggest cocksman since John Holmes, well, what's the old saying? The enemy of my enemy is—"

"Our ally," the sergeant finished for him. "Yes, I'm familiar with the saying. You were a grunt, right?"

"Yes."

"When you were in the Ghan, did you ever once just go be-bopping into a village where you knew Hajji was?"

"No," the Specialist conceded.

"Even if you had ironclad, solid intel that there was only a handful of goatfuckers with AK's?"

"No."

"No, you didn't. You set up a defensive perimeter outside of town, formed a rally point, and then sent in heavily armed patrols to probe for ambushes. You never, ever rolled into anyplace like you were the lead float in the Rose Bowl Parade."

"That was different," the Specialist replied.

"How is this any different than the Ghan?"

"First, this fucker out here has no clue we're coming, or that anyone even knows he out here, unlike Hajji, who always expected us to come knocking."

"Alright, I'll give you that. But tactically, is it smart to go traipsing into anyplace?"

"No, but I doubt this guy has any clue we're coming. He's probably sitting out there all fat, dumb, and happy."

"The last thing in the world this guy is dumb. I've read his 201. He didn't get to be sergeant major from being stupid."

"Our major is pretty stupid, and he's got himself promoted," the specialist said.

"That's true, but he's one of those high-speed, low-drag majors, who if the world hadn't gone to shit a few years ago, would never have seen light colonel, let alone a general's star. He's gotten as far as he has by ticket punching and blowing smoke up his Commander's ass. He's a completely different breed of soldier than our sergeant major, who I believe wouldn't have had any time at all for our fearless leader back in the old Army."

"True," the driver said.

"I'll say this much," the sergeant went on. "This Flannery guy is a fucking legend. He was in combat in Grenada back when I was still in grade school and you were still a glimmer in your daddy's eye. He spent two years in the Ranger Regiment, and then youngest instructor ever, at the Jungle Warfare School in Panama. Whole sections of his file are redacted, which tells me CIA shit. He then went on to the first Gulf War, Somalia…"

"Blackhawk Down kinda' shit?"

"Yeah, Blackhawk Down kinda' shit. Then on to Iraq, and then the Ghan several times. And, just for shits and giggles, he was a civilian cop in Philadelphia for a shitpot of time. He even threatened to shoot down an Allied helicopter in Iraq over an open radio net, where everyone and their grandmother heard it, and he walked away with a shit-eating grin on his face. No, I do not think this is going to be a pushover at all."

"What do we do?"

"For starters, I'm going to try to talk our major into letting me send out a few patrols in advance once we stop for the night in Flagstaff."

"That's another thing, Sarge. I don't think we should stop for the night. We should set up outside of that town and go in there tonight. Catch them asleep or fucking and shit."

"I agree. But our leader doesn't like doing that. I think he's afraid of the dark," he said, and his driver let out a little laugh.

"I've been meaning to ask, what did the major do before all of this?"

"I think he was in APERS," the sergeant laughed, meaning Army Personnel.

"Isn't that just peachy? He's a fucking Pog."

"We've got orders, and we'll follow them."

"Check, Sergeant. I just hope he doesn't go all full-hooah on us."

"You and me both," the sergeant said.

"You think he'll let you send out patrols?"

"I doubt it. He hasn't listened to me a whole lot in the past," the sergeant replied with a deep sigh.

"Fuck, Sarge. Aren't you the shining glow of positive reinforcement this morning?"

"I'm glad I can be of service," the sergeant said with a wink at his driver.

They passed through Winslow and saw the green sign with white lettering that read: FLAGSTAFF 55.

CHAPTER 19:
STAND TO

Tim climbed up and over the guardrail along the edge of the highway overpass of Interstate 40, and holding the end of a thick black cable, flopped down on the shoulder with his back to the rail. He took the edge of his t-shirt and mopped his brow to clear his face of the sweat that was pouring off of him.

He pulled out a canteen and gulped down the warm water, then poured the remainder over his head, running his fingers through his short-cropped graying hair vigorously. He rolled his head to get the kinks out of his neck, and saw Jimenez coming through some brush that had overgrown the median that separated the east and westbound lanes, holding a spool of wire, paying it out behind him.

When the younger man saw him, he continued over to where Tim was seated, sitting down next to Tim when he reached the rail.

"That's about it," he said. "I've got the eastbound span and the railroad trestle all wired up."

Tim took the lead of the wire from Jimenez' spool, spliced his wires together with the others, and then wrapped it tightly with friction tape.

"This bastard is going to be fucking loud when it goes," Jimenez said, standing.

Tim followed, and they walked westward, Tim paying out the wire behind them, toward one of several hidden positions they'd prepared two hundred yards in the distance overlooking the highway and set just inside the tree line.

"Will it be enough, Sar Major?"

"Taco, I'm a grunt, not a combat engineer, but I'm thinking the amount of TNT we've just placed will probably take out the Empire State Building."

"I figured that. Why so much?"

"I haven't a clue how much, or where to place the explosives, so I'm using the old 'overkill' rule."

"Why use ten pounds when a hundred will work just as well?" Jimenez asked with a sideways grin.

"A competent engineer would only need a few charges, placed at the right places, to drop the spans. I don't know what the fuck I'm doing beyond wiring the goddamn shit, so I've decided to use enough to make sure the fucker goes down, no matter where or how I placed it."

"I like your style, Sar' Major!"

"It's one thing Rangers can do really well. We can fuck shit up and break shit. And I intend to break the fuck out of it," he said with grim determination as they neared the tailgate of the Deuce and a half they'd parked along the side of the highway.

"Oh, I've got a surprise for you," Jimenez said. He climbed into the darkened bed and into the shadows.

Tim leaned on the tailgate, setting down the spool and peering in to see what his companion was doing. He could see Jimenez bending down, then picking something up and walking back towards him holding a large tube. When he could see what it was, Tim grinned widely. It was an AT-4, a man-portable antitank weapon, the great grandson of the old World War Two bazooka.

He took hold of the offered green fiber tube and looked up at Jimenez. "Where'd you find this?"

"I figured we'd need a little help, so I looked through the records over at Camp Navajo when I was searching for the demo blocks. I picked up ten of them."

"Outstanding!" Tim said, hefting the weapon.

"You'll have to show me how to use it."

"It's easy. Hop down and I'll give you a rundown."

Tim gave him a brief tutorial on the finer attributes of the rocket launcher, and when he was finished, handed it back to his partner.

"Just check your back-blast area before firing the thing."

"Gotcha!"

"Is everything else set?" Tim asked, leaning on the side of the truck in the shade.

"I have the M-240B set up over there," Jimenez said, pointing to a place inside the tree line about a hundred yards off the shoulder of the road. "The claymores are set up in a daisy-chain just like you had them set up on Volivoli. I can trip the claymores from that position."

"And the blasting machines?"

"They're over there, in or primary position, along with our M14's and the Prick-77," he reported, using the slang for the PRC-77 radio.

"Good. Take five of the AT4s over to where you've got the 240B, and I'll take the other five over to the main position. Meet me back there once you've finished."

Jimenez took five of the rocket launchers, slung them over his shoulder and jogged off down the road. Tim grabbed the remaining five, picked up the spool of wire, and started off to their prepared position inside the tree line overlooking the highway.

He made his way up the hill, and into the trees, where their hastily dug two-man foxhole was prepared. He dropped into the hole, feeling the coolness of the shade and the moist earth. Seeing all was exactly as Jimenez reported, he set the spool down and laid his M3 Grease gun on the berm.

Looking around to the front of their position, he double checked that the camouflage was in place, and his fields of fire were clear. Satisfied, and with nothing else to do, he leaned back on the rear wall of the hole, fumbled in a pocket for his pipe, pulled it out and filled the bowl.

He watched a pair of tiny chipmunks scurry around the base of a ponderosa pine a few feet away, blissfully unaware of him, and of the impending maelstrom that would soon engulf the entire area.

As he watched the two creatures, a wave of darkness overcame him, and he suddenly felt very tired. Was he doing the right thing? he wondered. Was he throwing everything away? Was it only his pride that he was defending?

He felt like going back to the house, walking up the stairs to his bedroom, crawling into his bed and going to sleep, to hell with what was left of the world. He puffed on his pipe, clouds of sweet-smelling tobacco smoke surrounding his head, and his mind drifted, back to that very first night so very long ago, when Holly first came to him in the darkness. It seemed like a million years ago now.

He wanted that time back so badly, a time when he didn't have a care in the world, where the weight of a thousand freight trains wasn't resting on his shoulders. Why didn't everyone just leave him alone! He wanted to scream to the heavens. He knew it wouldn't do any good, so he smoked his pipe and waited for Jimenez to return.

He soon spotted the young man, and when Jimenez got to the rim of the pit, he said, "All set," then dropped down next to Tim.

When he was settled, Tim pointed to the front of their emplacement.

"Okay, Taco. I'll go over it again." Jimenez grinned. "I'm going to let the lead vehicle, maybe two, get across the span, then I'm going to trip the charges."

"Check. I'll be over at the emplacement with the 240B, and when they start to dismount, I'll trip the daisy-chain and let loose on the machine gun," Jimenez recited.

"Once you've gone through one belt of ammo, fall back to the secondary position, and start picking them off with your M14," Tim continued.

"Once I start doing that, you'll call Izzy and Ian on the radio, and they'll start dropping the rounds on their melons."

"Correct. And Taco?"

"Yeah, Sar' Major?"

"I know you're no grunt, but just think of it like you're back at the rifle range. One round, one target," Tim instructed. "Once we've expended all of our ammo we've got cached at the emplacements, we'll fall back together to the other position overlooking Route 64."

"What if they can regroup here?"

"I'm hoping they don't. Between the blast from the bridges blowing, the claymores, mortar rounds dropping on them and our sniping, whatever command and control they have will completely dissolve."

"Do you think they'll come down 64 also?"

"Maybe, so we've got to head back that way fast. I'll park a Hum-Vee back to our rear about a hundred yards, so we can make a mad dash back."

"You got it, Sar' Major."

"The whole point, Taco, is not to let them get anywhere near the houses at Colman Lake."

"Can we do it?" Jimenez asked.

Tim looked back towards the bridges. He pointed out to the spans. "From that bridge westward, we will make them pay, and pay dearly, for every inch of real estate they want. This whole fucking valley will be sopping wet with blood."

Jimenez nodded slowly, his face cold and blank, dark eyes smoldering.

"What is it, Taco?"

"Aren't you scared?"

"I'm scared shitless."

"You don't show it," Jimenez replied.

"From the moment I reported to basic training, from my very first day of Ranger School, that day in Grenada, Iraq, Afghanistan, hell, even when I was a cop, I was scared shitless every fucking day," he said firmly, letting it sink in.

"You've always seemed so brave," Taco said. "Even when we first met, you know, when I had drawn down on you all in Phoenix? I was the one scared, and you just walked up to me like I was holding a banana, not an M16."

"Inside my head, I was shitting my pants."

"You sure do hide it well."

"It's not the fear itself; it's the ability to overcome that fear and ranger up and soldier on, in *spite* of it."

"I don't think I'll ever be able to do that like you do," Jimenez said, leaning back on the far wall, and pulling out a bottle of Gatorade. He uncapped it, took a long pull, and then handed the bottle to Tim.

After he took a swig, Tim handed it back. "Only a fool or a crazy person says they're not afraid, Taco. You've just have to conquer it. It's all one big mind-fuck, and once you've realized that, you'll have it beat. You did fine on Volivoli, I know you'll do fine here."

"So you're afraid of dying?" Jimenez asked.

Tim let out a loud laugh. "Taco, that is the one thing I'm not afraid of. It's the only inevitable thing in life. We all are going to die at some point."

"What about everything else?" "Everything else, Taco? The whole deep question which has kept far smarter men than I awake nights for centuries?"

"Well, yeah. I mean, I know you don't believe in God. I don't either at this point. I think that's a consensus with everyone these days, but it's got to mean something!" Jimenez exclaimed.

"I'll tell you what I think," Tim said, refilling his pipe with fresh tobacco. "As long as you've tried to live a good life, fought for what you believe is right and just, and left a lasting legacy, the memories of yourself after you go, then that's all it means."

"You want to keep on living, don't you?"

"Taco, I'm not getting any younger. My knees are shot, my vision is going, and my hearing is fucked. We're not built to last," Tim said with a sad smile. "If I can leave a good world for Robyn, Walter, Holly and yourself, I did goddamn good, and I can die happy. And if I can't, I'm going to take as many of the motherfuckers with me as I possibly can. I came into this world kicking and screaming, covered in someone else's blood, I'm not afraid to go out that way either. That's the one thing I'm not afraid of," Tim finished, then leaned forward on the berm of the foxhole, looking out over the still and empty highway.

"You told me that once before, on Volivoli. You know what?" Jimenez said, coming over and leaning forward on the berm also.

"What's that, Taco? I'm batshit crazy?"

"No, that's not what I was going to say at all."

"Then what were you going to say?"

Jimenez laughed a little. "I grew up in the Barrio in South Phoenix. My padre, my dad, he was a gangbanger. He got killed when I was still a kid. Shitloads of drugs and gang shit. The only way out was the Marines."

"I understand."

"Tim," he said, daring to use his first name, "I never had a dad. You're the closest thing I ever had to one."

Tim was dumbstruck. He knew a lot of young soldiers over his career had looked up to him, but this was the first time anyone had ever just come right out and said it.

"And you, Taco, are the wetback beaner son I've never had."

"All's I'm saying… shit, I don't know what to say," Jimenez uttered, tears welling up in his dark eyes.

"All joking aside, Juan, you are like a son to me too. I break your balls all the time because I like you. I may not be around for too much longer, and it'll be up to you and Robyn to take care of Holly and Walter, and whatever half-breed little yard apes you guys decide to start popping out, okay?"

"That's the first time you've ever called me Juan," Jimenez said with a smile.

"Don't get used to it, Taco," Tim replied. "And remember, it's up to you to keep the dream alive, got it?"

"Got it, Dad!"

"Don't call me Dad or I'll tear off your head and shit down your neck."

A gentle breeze blew up through the trees, they watched the chipmunks play in the carpet of needles. They looked out on the serene vista before them, lost in their own thoughts for the moment, when Tim's face grew dark again. He drew in a deep breath, held it, and then let it out in a whoosh of air. He fumbled with his pipe, which had gone out, then turned to face Jimenez.

"There's one more thing I need you to do," Tim said quietly.

"What is it, Sar' Major?"

"It's very important. I need you to do this, no, you *have* to do this. No ifs, ands or buts. It's got to be done."

"Anything you want."

"In the basement of the house, down where I keep the extra guns and ammo next to the food storage area is a metal shelf. On that shelf is a spare IVIS tablet, and under that is a notebook. If things turn to shit, Taco, I want you to get as far away from here as possible, try to get down to Luke with Ian and Izzy and meet up with the rest of them and the C-130."

"Okay," Jimenez nodded, perplexed.

"I want you to take the IVIS tablet and that notebook down there to Phoenix, and when you get down there open that notebook up and follow the directions on the first page."

"I don't…" Jimenez started to say, then stopped, his mouth dropping open and the color draining from his face. He stared at Tim for a moment, then said in astonishment, "Fuck me running! You aren't serious, are you?"

"I am, and close your mouth or you'll start collecting flies."

"I thought… I thought you said the codes were vaporized along with everything else on Volivoli?"

"They were," Tim said flatly.

"You copied them, didn't you?"

"I did."

"Why?"

"I really couldn't tell you. Something inside me told me to do it, for insurance, I guess."

Jimenez leaned against the side of the pit and let out a sigh. He shook his head in disbelief. "I don't know. Shit."

"Taco, I need you to do that for me. Do it if I'm killed or captured, okay?"

"But where?"

"You know where," Tim told him.

"Here? You want me to nuke here?"

"No, not here, Washington."

"You've got to be shitting me, right?"

"No, I'm not shitting you. Just do it, Okay?"

"Ah shit."

"Look, you're learning to have a lot of responsibility now. A lot more than you or I ever wanted or asked for. Whoever is pulling the strings back in DC doesn't have everyone's best interest at heart, that's a given. You and I want a good life for ourselves and our children. If we let whoever is back there continue, it'll only get worse, not better. You do that, and then get yourself and the rest back to Oahu."

"If that's the case, why don't you just launch one right fucking now?" Jimenez demanded.

"Taco, get ahold of yourself," Tim said sharply, "I won't launch one now because that still wouldn't stop those men coming west. Besides, it might not come to that, alright?"

"But why—"

"Listen to me, okay? I'm telling you this for a worst case scenario. Fuck, I'm not even sure any more of them will fly. Back on Volivoli I took a monumental leap of faith that they would, but the next time someone keys in those launch codes, they might not. We've got to keep them out of the hands of that person back east, at all costs, that I'm sure of."

Jimenez sat down on the floor of the foxhole, his hands shaking uncontrollably. Tim looked down at the younger man, and softened his voice considerably. "Taco, it's nowhere near certain. I hope to fuck you don't have to, but if things turn bad here, take the codes and the IVIS, get down to the plane and do it, then make your way to Oahu. Build it back up, like we all wanted, like we've talked about so many times in the past. A few minutes ago you asked about fear, and I told you that you'd have to learn to conquer those fears. This is the time, right now, where the rubber meets the road."

"Okay, Sar' Major," he replied, standing up. "I hope the fuck it doesn't come down to that. Nobody else knows?"

"No, only you and I."

"Okay. okay, I'll do it."

"Once the mortar rounds start falling on their grapes, they might run away. We just don't know."

"We'll make em' bleed, eh?" Jimenez asked, fire back in his voice now.

"Abso-fucking-lutely!" Tim reassured placed his hand on the man's shoulder to comfort him. "Are you okay now?"

"Yeah, I'm good to go, Sar' Major."

"Let's get our shit secured here and get back to the house."

"Sure thing," Jimenez said, climbing out of the hole, and picking up his rifle.

As Tim was climbing out, the two men heard an approaching Hum-Vee and they spun towards the direction of the noise.

The Hum-Vee skidded loudly to a stop, and Robyn rushed out, carrying an M4 carbine.

"Dad! Taco!" she shouted. "Dad!" she gasped. "I've got news!"

"What is it?" he asked when she got close enough they didn't have to shout.

"I just heard over the sat-radio on the frequency that guy gave us that they're in Flagstaff!"

"Taco," Tim said, "you take the deuce back to the house, and I'll go with Robyn."

"Got it!" he replied, and bounded down the hill past Robyn without saying a word.

Tim picked up his M3 and led the way back towards the Hum-Vee. "Anything else?"

"Not much. I think they're going to camp out for the night there, then come at us in the morning."

He hopped into the still-running vehicle. Jimenez blew past them in a cloud of black diesel exhaust, and Robyn fell in behind him on the cracked and rotting asphalt.

Tim sat in the passenger seat, silent, a million things running through his mind. When they turned onto the off-ramp to Williams, he asked, "Anything more you can tell me?"

"Whelp," she replied, "I didn't get any names. Their radio procedure is shit, the main guy in charge is a major, and there's another fuckwit the major is calling 'sergeant'."

"Any ideas where they're going?"

"Yeah," she said angrily. "They know exactly where the fuck we're at. They mentioned Colman Lake, the C-130, Tusayan, everything!"

"Un-good," was all he uttered.

"Yeah, un-good. It sounds like they're going to split up, come in from the north over Route 89 and here to the east on 40," she said, speeding through town.

"Do you have your bug-out bag packed?"

"I packed up a few things this morning when you and Taco were playing with the explosives."

"What about Holly?" he asked. When he didn't get a reply right away, he looked over at the girl, and repeated himself. "What about Holly?"

"She says she's not going," Robyn replied sheepishly.

"What?" Tim exploded. "When the fuck did she tell you that?"

"Right before I came out to get you. She said she's sending Walt with me in the plane, that I'm competent enough to get it to Luke, but she's staying with you."

"The fuck she is!"

"Dad, don't shoot the messenger!"

"Goddamn it! All this, and now I've got to deal with this bullshit!" he shouted.

Robyn pulled the Hum-Vee up to the front of the house and Tim leapt out of the vehicle without waiting for it to stop. He bounded the steps onto the porch, threw open the screen door, and entered the house, calling out for Holly. He heard noises up in the direction of the bedrooms, so he took the stairs two at a time, marching down the short hall to the bedroom that he and Holly shared.

Bursting in, he found Holly seated on the edge of the bed, Walter in her arms, breast exposed. His son was suckling on the nipple greedily, not a care in the world, totally oblivious to what was coming.

Holly looked up at him with tears in her eyes as he stood angrily in the middle of the room, hands balled into fists at his side. He looked at them both for a moment, and then finally said, "What's this bullshit Robyn told me, that you're not going?"

"Tim, Robyn can fly the plane down to Luke. I'm staying with you."

"Goddamn it! I want you and Walt safe!"

"Now you listen here!" she said loudly, still comforting the child in her arms. "I left you once, and that was a big mistake. I'm not going to do it again!"

Tim reached over to her and gently took his son in his arms, holding him close to his chest. He looked down on the tiny, innocent life in his hands and smiled sadly.

"Babe, I understand that. Really I do. But the time for all of that is over. You need to leave right now, you and the rest. They're already in Flagstaff, and will probably be here by mid-morning tomorrow. I don't want any arguments, please."

"I need to be with you."

"Walter needs his mom. If you stay here, there's a very real possibility that he'll lose both his parents tomorrow. Don't you see that?"

"He'll have Robyn," she said in a tiny voice.

"He should have you."

"Tim," she said, standing and coming up to him. "I thought I lost you once, on Volivoli. I can't bear the thought of losing you again."

"It can't be helped. You need to get out of here right fucking now!"

She rubbed his unshaven cheek. "Babe, I can't leave you."

"You're going to have to," he said, handing his son back to her. She took the infant, and held it close, kissing the top of his head.

"It's all so quick," she said after a few moments, "Tim, do you remember the first night I came to you?"

"Yes, I do," he said, the memory coming back to him for a second time that day.

"If I have to go, Tim, if I've got to leave you, and possibly never see you again, I want one more night like that," she said, choking back tears.

He sighed, knowing his resolve was crumbling. He hated to see Holly cry, and it tore his heart out. However, he knew they were both toying with disaster if she stayed.

He fell silent, and taking them both in his arms, held them tight, little Walter safely sandwiched between mother and father. He ran his fingers through her long red hair and kissed her forehead.

They stood like that for a few moments, when Walter started to coo and giggle a little. Tim loved the sound of the boy's laughter, he had just started to do it recently, and Tim never tired of hearing it.

He wondered if that laugh would continue, if there would be anything left after tomorrow to laugh about, and his heart sank. Holly stepped away from Tim and strode over to the crib that Walter slept in next to their own bed. Placing the child down, she turned to Tim, and plead, "Please, Tim. Give me that. Just let me have one more night with you?"

Tim sighed again, and looking up towards the ceiling, slowly nodded his head. It was going against his whole grain of reasoning, but he knew his woman wouldn't, shouldn't, be denied this one last request.

"You've got to promise me you will be on that plane first thing in the morning. You *will* be leaving here tomorrow, and that is the end of that discussion."

"I love you so much, Timothy."

"I love you too, that's why I want you safe," Tim said, taking her into his arms again.

"I'll go. Now you go and get a shower, mister! You stink!"

He peeled off his t-shirt with an evil grin and walked towards her.

CHAPTER 20:
CONTACT

The interior of the C-130 was dark and hot, despite the early morning hours. Holly was in the pilot's seat, Robyn to her right, and Walter was snug in a car seat, strapped securely in the flight engineer's seat between and behind the pair of women.

As Holly and Robyn went through their pre-flight checklist, Paula was standing behind them, watching with curiosity. Holly flipped the main battery switch, and frowned deeply when the main power light didn't glow.

"Shit," she spat, sweat building across her brow.

"What is it?" Robyn asked, looking over at the pilot.

"The bloody battery is flat!" she said, and started to unbuckle her harness. Robyn reached over the throttles and grabbed her arm.

"You stay here, what do you need to be done?"

Holly looked out the side cockpit window and scanned the apron. "Over there, by the front of the terminal. There's a white cart, a mobile APU. You need to take the Hum-Vee and bring it over to the nose. You'll probably have to jump-start it with the Hum-Vee, and then plug the slave-cable into the receptacle."

"What's an APU?" Robyn asked.

"It's an Auxiliary Power Unit. It'll give us enough juice to start the bloody engines."

"I'm on it!" Robyn said, unbuckling her harness and climbing out of the seat. Holly grabbed her arm to stop her. "Robyn, make it quick. I only need to get one engine turning. As soon as you get it started and over here, plug the bastard in. I'll get the number four engine turning, and when I do, unplug the damn thing and get back in here."

Robyn headed back to the cargo hold. When she got halfway there, she stopped, and returned. Holly looked at her with a questioning gaze. Robyn picked up her M4 Carbine and smiled. "American Express, don't leave home without it!"

She spun on her heels and retraced her footsteps to the still-open side door of the fuselage. Leaping out, she landed flatfooted onto the tarmac and ran to the parked Hum-Vee.

She drove over to the APU unit and found the ignition switch. She hit it, but its battery was also dead.

Going back to her vehicle, she retrieved the jumper cables, hooking them up to the Hum-Vee's battery, then looked for the APU's battery. She found it after a few moments searching, and attached the clamps to the battery terminals.

She glanced back at the waiting Hercules and saw Holly's head sticking out of the open cockpit window, a wisp of red hair fluttering like a pennant in the early morning breeze. She smiled and waved, then gave a thumb's up gesture and hit the start switch on the APU.

It started to crank over, and turned and turned, but refused to fire up. She waited a moment, then hit the button again, and this time it turned a few times, and she was then rewarded by the diesel engine firing up in a cloud of black smoke.

She let it idle for a few more moments, then unhooked the jumper cables, tossing them to the ground in a heap. She then drove the Hum-Vee around so she could hitch the cart to the pintle hook, and when she had it secured, drove the rig over to the nose of the aircraft.

She revved the APU up to speed, and over the screaming diesel, shouted out to Holly, whose head was still out the window several feet above her.

"Where do I plug it in?" she yelled.

Holly stuck her arm out, pointing down. "Right there, there should be a little door. Open it and there's a receptacle to plug the slave cable into!"

After a second of searching, Robyn located door and opened it, then uncoiled the slave cable from its rack on the cart, and dragged it over to the nose where she deftly plugged it in. When it was secured, she stepped back into Holly's line of sight, and gave another thumb up.

Holly disappeared into the cockpit, and even over the scream of the APU, Robyn could hear the sound of the Hercules' engine turning over. As soon as Holly had it up to speed, her head emerged from the window again, and made a gesture to Robyn to unplug the APU.

This she did smartly, and got back into the Hum-Vee, driving it clear of the aircraft. She got out, and switched off both, and then started to walk back towards the aircraft. Now Holly had two of the aircraft's turboprops turning, and the third's propeller was beginning to turn, so she didn't hear, but saw, out of her peripheral vision, movement coming around the terminal building. She turned to look, and what she saw made her knees go weak.

It was a Hum-Vee, but not one of theirs. It was painted Desert Tan, unlike the forest green ones they had, and there was a man behind a .50 M2 machinegun on a mount atop of it.

She broke out into a dead run and launched herself into the open side door of the aircraft. When she was inside, she made a mad dash into the cockpit. Breathlessly, she screamed at Holly, "We've got company!"

"What?" Holly asked, her eyes wide.

"There's a Hum-Vee coming through the apron! We've got to go!"

Holly throttled up all now turning engines, and the Hercules began to taxi away from the main building, towards the end of the runway. Robyn patted Holly on the shoulder, and when the pilot turned, screamed in her ear over the sound of the engine, "I'll try to slow them down, just get us off the ground as fast as you can!"

Holly nodded and went back to controlling the taxiing aircraft. Little Walter was beginning to cry, as the deafening roar of the four turboprops hurt his delicate ears. Holly glanced down at her son with a sad frown, unable to comfort him as she steered the careening cargo plane down the taxiway. *Why, oh why didn't I listen to Tim yesterday!* her mind screamed in accusation at her, and her heart sank. Clutching her carbine, Robyn ran through the empty cargo hold and stopped next to the controls to the rear ramp. She hit the 'down' button, and the hydraulic rams began to whine, lowering the wide ramp. When it reached a position level to the deck, she stopped its downward travel, and then racked a round into the chamber of her carbine.

Going down onto her knees, she slid into a perfect prone-position, exactly the way Tim had shown her to do so many years ago. Using her thumb, she flicked the safety from safe to semi-auto and sighted in on the now stopped Hum-Vee.

The bouncing plane made it difficult to acquire a steady sight picture, but she was able to put the sights on the tan vehicle on the apron. She inhaled, exhaled calmly, and squeezed the trigger.

The crack of the rifle was drowned out by the sound of the now screaming engines, but she was rewarded by the feel of the rifle's butt recoiling into her shoulder. She fired off five more times at the diminishing vehicle, waited a beat, and fired five more times, expended shell casings rolling around on the cold steel deck of the hold.

***

"Holy shit, they're shooting at us!" the man manning the heavy machinegun screamed as he racked the charging handle, gripped the twin 'spade' grips and depressed the butterfly triggers.

"No, wait!" the specialist shouted, exiting the Hum-Vee. His words were cut short when he fell to the ground clutching his throat, great jets of arterial blood fountaining out in spurts. A bullet from Robyn's carbine had hit him just behind the Adam's apple when he stepped out, and he died almost immediately from loss of blood, gurgling his last breaths in a red foamy mess on the ground next to the Hum-Vee.

The specialist's death sealed the fate of the Hercules, which was now at the far end of the runway, engines at full power as Holly released the brakes. The specialist had known the stakes and the importance of saving the aircraft, but with his death, the panicked men that had accompanied him now saw blood in their eyes.

The man on the roof mount fired the big machinegun at the aircraft, which was rapidly gaining speed back down the runway. The other two men exited the Hum-Vee and fired their M16s wildly at the speeding plane.

When it reached a point where it was almost beside them out on the runway, the nose lifted, and they could see a figure on the ramp that was still lowered, flashes of red pointing out at them from it.

The big .50 caliber machinegun chugged away at the rising craft, and suddenly a puff of smoke came out of the inboard nacelle and, as the landing gear left the runway, started streaming black smoke.

***

Robyn was still in the prone position with her rifle, and when the plane reached a point where she could re-engage her target, she began to fire again until the bolt locked back on an empty magazine.

She rolled to her side to retrieve a fresh magazine, letting the expended magazine fall, and when she brought the fresh one up to slam it home, she felt the Hercules leap into the air, tilting the deck upwards at almost a forty-five degree angle, the rear ramp facing the concrete runway now ten feet below, where gravity began to take over.

Robyn hadn't secured herself, and now found herself sliding unchecked towards the opening, the runway a blur below her.

She clawed at the steel decking in panic, tearing out a few fingernails and letting her carbine slip from her grasp. She screamed when she exited involuntarily from the speeding aircraft, falling to the ground where she hit, bouncing obscenely several times before coming to a stop in a crumpled heap on the runway, shattered carbine laying several yards behind her, useless. The Hercules' engine was now on fire, belching black smoke.

**

The three men fired on the retreating aircraft until all of their weapons were empty. When the bolt finally locked back on the .50, the man at the trigger watched the departing plane trailing smoke, a blank expression on his face.

He looked down at the body of the dead specialist and shook his head. He looked at his other companions, who were looking back at him with stunned expressions, and said, "I think we just fucked up."

"Is he dead?" the other man on the ground asked.

"Yeah, he is."

"Oh fuck. The Sarge is gonna kill us!"

The man at the machinegun said, "I think something fell out of the plane when it took off. Over there, let's go!" he shouted to them, and they all piled back into the Hum-Vee and headed off to where the machine gunner had pointed.

They sped down the runway, and when they neared the crumpled mass on the concrete, the driver stopped the vehicle. The three men got out and walked over to the still form.

Seeing the blonde hair spilled out, arms and legs twisted in an unnatural position and oozing blood from various spots, the tallest of the three gasped, "Shit, it's a girl!"

"Oh fuck. What are we going to do?" another of the trio asked.

"Sarge and the major will fucking kill us!" the first man said fearfully.

An almost imperceptible moan escaped the form lying at their feet, and all three men recoiled.

"Shit! She's alive!"

"Quick, get her into the Hummer! The plane is coming back!" the first one shouted. He looked south and saw the Hercules making a wide turn, heading back towards the airport, engine trailing smoke.

They grabbed fistfuls of Robyn's clothes and lifted her up, a loud scream escaping her lips. They tossed the girl into the back of the Hum-Vee unceremoniously, piled in behind her, and sped off in the direction that they'd come.

**

Holly fought with the controls, trying to gain altitude. She turned around and looked at a pale-faced Paula and screamed, "Where's Robyn?"

"She fell out!"

"What do you mean she fell out?"

"I think she was at the back, shooting at those people, and when the plane took off, she rolled out the door!" Paula screamed over the noise of the engines.

Holly manhandled the yoke and with great effort, turned the aircraft around, heading back north towards the airport. It was losing hydraulic fluid she knew, for with every movement she made on the controls, they got heavier and heavier. The hydraulics must have been hit, and coupled with the engine fire, it was only a matter of time now before the plane would fall from the sky, but she had to see if Robyn was alright.

With grim determination, Holly got the plane level again, if only a few hundred feet off the ground, and pointed the nose back towards the runway.

Even at that speed, she could see as they passed back over the airfield that Robyn was nowhere to be seen, but she saw the tan Hum-Vee racing away, the man on the mount with the large machinegun spinning to face her.

As she passed overhead, she could see the red tracers arc up in a wild spray towards the Hercules, and then heard several metallic sounding pops of the bullets hitting the fuselage.

Holly heard a tortured scream, and whipped her head around to see Paula lying on the deck, blood streaming out of a gaping hole in her stomach. She looked down at Walter, who was also wailing loudly, face red and streaming tears. Her heart sank to the pit of her stomach.

She muscled the yoke and pedals, and again turned the plane south with all of her might. She was streaming sweat from every pore in her body, hands slick on the controls.

Looking out the left side window of the cockpit, she now could see the red licks of flame coming out of the nacelle that had been hit, hit the fuel cut off switch to shut the engine down, and then hit the fire extinguisher, but nothing happened.

"Shit, shit, shit!" she screamed, and hit the fire extinguisher control a second time, again with no discernible effect.

She fought to gain altitude, the plane fighting to gain space between the ground and itself as they sped southward towards Williams, then Phoenix, which seemed to her to be a million miles away now.

"I've got to get to Luke," she whispered. "I just have to!"

***

Tim stood in his hidden position overlooking the highway, an M14 rifle propped up on the berm, blasting machine next to it. Both he and Jimenez had gotten to their pre-set positions well before sunrise, and he'd taken the time to double check the wiring for the explosives and then, when he was satisfied all was in order, connected the leads to the 10-cap blasting machine and set the twist-handle in its receptacle.

He couldn't see Jimenez from his position, so he picked up the handset of the PRC-77 radio and depressed the talk button. Eschewing proper radio procedure, he asked, "Taco, are you ready?"

"I'm ready," he got in reply. He then asked, on the same frequency, if Izzy and Ian were ready, and got two clicks of squelch in reply, letting him know that the two men back at the mortar were at the ready also.

He could hear the approach of the convoy, and he steeled himself for the upcoming events. The rising sun was in his eyes, making it difficult to see to the east, but that couldn't be helped. You couldn't exactly tell your enemy what time of day to attack.

Squinting through the glare, he saw the lead Hum-Vee, trailed close behind by several 6X6 trucks, and several more Hum-Vees behind them. He picked up the blasting machine and placed his hand on the handle.

The lead Hum-Vee was now crossing the span, traveling at about forty miles an hour, and he let that one cross, getting closer to his position. When the first truck was mid-span, he dropped to the bottom of his foxhole, whispered, "Here it goes!" and twisted the grip.

He knew it would be loud, but he wasn't prepared for what came next. There was a deafening, ear-shattering **boom**, and then Tim was slammed to the far wall of the foxhole by an invisible fist, the wind knocked out of him. The sky turned black, the whole world exploded, the earth physically moving all around him, and he was choked by thick, cloying dust that filled the foxhole.

There was a continuous roar of noise, and he shook off the initial shock of the blast, slowly standing. He could barely see through the thick wall of smoke, dust, and debris that had completely engulfed the entire area, chunks of twisted steel and concrete raining down over the entire area, thrown skyward for hundreds of yards in every direction. He peered out over the mass of destruction before him and started to laugh.

"Jesus jumping Christ almighty!"

It would be the last time that day he would laugh. In fact, it would be a long time before Tim Flannery ever laughed again.

It took a few minutes for the dust and debris to finally settle enough to see what lay before him, and the destruction, while not total, was more than what he'd hoped for. The lead Hum-Vee was on its roof, wheels still spinning. The truck that had been on the span when he'd set the charges off was nowhere to be seen, completely vaporized, no doubt.

The follow on vehicles were in disarray, the truck that had been several yards to the east of the bridge was laying on its side, burning fiercely, plume of black smoke reaching up into the morning sky. There were several bodies strewn about the area around it, some slowly starting to move, but most lay still, pools of blood here and there around the twisted, burning truck.

He picked up his M14, took aim, and scanned the area for targets. Nothing moved at all, save for the few crawling injured, then he heard what sounded like pops through his still-ringing ears, and saw the flash of what must have been Jimenez triggering the claymore mines, then he heard the rattle of the M240B machinegun, and realized that his companion must have acquired some fresh targets.

He caught movement to his front, several forms running towards him, away from Jimenez' rapid fire, in hopes of escaping the certain death of the machinegun. They were running right into Tim's sights. Tim took careful aim at the lead man on the far side of the chasm created when the bridge disintegrated in the blast, and squeezed the trigger.

He hit his target in the chest from a hundred and fifty yards away. The lead man fell face first onto the rubble-strewn highway. His following companions stopped in shock, giving Tim time to fire a round at each of them. One man's head exploded, covering his friends with his brains and bits of skull, and the ones still alive turned and ran back the other way in panic, and Tim continued to fire the rifle at their retreating forms, hitting them in the back, one by one.

The ringing in his ears wouldn't go away, and he could barely hear anything, but now could make out the pops of other weapons firing, then the louder crack of Jimenez' M14 barking away in a steady, methodical fire.

"Just like on the rifle range, Taco," he whispered, fired one more round, and changed magazines. He picked up the radio's handset again. "Fire for effect!"

He threw down the handset, brought the rifle back up, and scanned his front, but found no targets. He never got a reply on the radio, though he did hear the high-pitched whistle of the first mortar round scream overhead, and he smiled.

***

Even at the tail end of the convoy where the damage was minimal, the shock was complete. The sergeant, a combat vet, was addled and his ears were ringing. He sat dumbfounded in the passenger seat of his Hum-Vee for a moment, and looked at the destruction in front of him.

His driver stared ahead, seat wet from where he'd urinated on himself, looking through the cracked and splintered windshield, mouth agape. Grabbing his carbine, the sergeant carefully opened the door, and stood outside, looking around warily. He could hear firing to the front, but couldn't see who was firing, or where it was coming from.

He stuck his head back into the vehicle at his driver and shouted, "Grab your piece and follow me!"

The man stayed put, soaking in his own urine. Disgustedly, the sergeant made his way forward to the first truck and yelled at the men to get out. Reluctantly, they started to comply, and when he had them all out, he got the men to follow him towards the front of the convoy.

He could now hear the screaming of the wounded, and using the stopped vehicles for cover, continued forward. He found two of the other trucks crashed together, where apparently the drivers in their fear had tried to turn around and smashed into each other. The two were now hopelessly locked together by the twisted metal of their bumpers.

He gathered those men also, and when he had a group of about twenty-five, he moved forward again.

The group he was leading made it a few yards ahead when he saw a man in the roof mount of a Hum-Vee, bravely, though not all that smartly, returning fire with the mounted M240B. His rounds were spraying wildly into the forest at nothing that the sergeant could see.

He went to shout at the soldier, then heard a distinctive pop a whoosh. A thin stream of white smoke trailed out from the tree line several yards to the northwest. Reaching out like a finger, the AT4 rocket hit the Hum-Vee. It exploded, a gout of red flame and black smoke leaping out, killing the man on top, and everyone else still inside, silencing the machine gun.

He grabbed the man next to him and shouted, "It looks like the fire is coming from over there, to the northwest! Get everyone behind cover to the left of the convoy. We'll move up under cover of the trucks!"

The man, his face streaked with dirt and sweat, fear in his eyes, complied, and was able to rally everyone to cover to the south.

"Sarge, what the fuck are we going to do?" one man screamed at him.

"We're going to move ahead, find out where that fire is coming from, and kill them!"

"It's like they knew we were coming!" another shouted, voice high pitched and panicked.

The sergeant didn't reply to that, but he knew the man was right. It was a carefully set out ambush, that much was true, and there was only one way that could have happened.

He saw the big Aussie cowering under one of the trucks. He looked at him in disgust, spat out some dirt, and yelled at the man to get over to where he was.

Colin, face white with fear, looked at the sergeant like he was crazy, then finally got up the nerve to scamper out from under the truck where he'd been cowering since the first blast.

When he reached the sergeant, he shouted, "What the fuck happened?"

"That's exactly what I want to ask you, *mate*," he said, 'mate' coming out of his mouth dripping with sarcasm.

Colin saw the look in the sergeant's eyes, and replied, "Look, mate, if you think I had anything to do with this, you're dead-set wrong!"

"We'll talk about it later!" the sergeant yelled. "You grab a rifle from one of the dead and come with me!"

Someone handed Colin an M16 from behind. He took the offered weapon, clutching it in a death grip.

"What the fuck else can go wrong today?" the sergeant asked no one in particular, and when his last word escaped his lips, he got his answer in the sound of the first mortar rounds whistling in. His bowels turned fluid when he heard it, knowing exactly the kind of death that was about to fall on their heads. "Incoming!" he screamed. "Take cover!"

***

As the first mortar rounds landed and exploded around the destroyed convoy, Tim got on the radio and called Jimenez.

"How are you doing?" he asked, in a deceptively calm voice.

"Like shooting fish in a barrel, Sar' Major. Like you said, a day on the range, and it's a target rich environment."

"Good. I'm moving to another position. Are you able to redirect fire until I get to my secondary?"

"No problem, Sar' Major, I got you covered," Jimenez replied.

Satisfied that Jimenez could handle things for the moment, Tim grabbed his rifle, the radio, and his rucksack, and crawled out of his hole.

He stood and looked around, surveying the destruction he'd caused. He looked down on the upended Hum-Vee, and saw a lone man crawling away from the destroyed vehicle.

Taking one more look around, he started to jog towards the crawling form. As the mortar rounds sailed overhead and exploded to his front, satisfied that his attackers were pinned down by the fire, he made his way over to the prone form.

When his shadow fell over the crawling man, the man spun around in fear, looking up into Tim's face.

"Don't hurt me!" the man begged. "Please don't hurt me!"

Seeing the man's gold oak leaf, Tim smiled wryly, crouched down and said, "You must be Major Malfunction."

"Please don't hurt me!" the man screamed.

Tim looked at the man with utter disdain, and then grabbed him by the collar and dragged him, kicking and screaming, begging for mercy, back behind the shattered vehicle.

"Hurt you? I ought to cut your fucking heart out, you piece of shit," Tim spat back at the man.

A mortar round fell a little short, and landed behind the Hum-Vee on the close side of the gorge, raining down chunks of shattered concrete on the pair. Tim never flinched, but the major curled up in fear, shaking uncontrollably.

Jimenez must have corrected fire at that point, because the sounds of the rounds hitting changed slightly, and were farther away from them now. Tim looked back down at his quarry, wondering just what the hell he was doing; he should be in his secondary position by now.

"What the fuck did you think you were doing, eh?" Tim asked, his voice icy.

"I was following orders! I order you to surrender now!"

"You know what, asshole? I stopped taking orders from pieces of shit like you six fucking years ago. You have no authority over me."

"It's you!" the major gasped. "You're the sergeant major!"

"Very perceptive, Major."

Tim heard moaning from inside the overturned vehicle. "Don't you go anywhere, Major. I'm not done with you."

"You can't…" the major stopped when Tim pulled out a .45 automatic from a holster.

"Just so you don't go running away," Tim told the man, brought the pistol up, and fired one round into the man's kneecap, and the major let out a girlish scream of agony. Tim left him and skirted around to where he could look inside of the wrecked Hum-Vee.

Peering inside, he saw a young black man, face covered in blood, moaning. He was heaped up in a ball, one arm twisted beneath him at what looked like a painful angle. The boy looked up at Tim, and through tears, said loudly, "Mamma, I can't feel mah laigs!"

Tim placed his pistol at the boy's temple, and whispered, "Go to sleep now, okay?"

"Go to sleep?"

"Yeah, close your eyes and it'll all be gone, okay?"

"Okay," the boy said. "It hurts so bad."

"I know. It'll be gone soon," Tim said, in a reassuring voice. The boy closed his eyes, and Tim pulled the trigger. The pistol's report was muffled by the enclosed space, and when he did the deed, Tim sighed sadly.

Scooting back to where the major was still lying, screaming in agony, Tim brought his face close to the screaming man and said, "Now, what am I going to do with you?"

***

Holly was still fighting the controls. Inexplicably, her vision was starting to blur. She wiped her face to get the sweat out of her eyes, and for the first time, felt a warm wetness on her left leg. Looking down, she saw that a round from whoever had been shooting at them had pierced the fuselage and tore a hole in her thigh. Because of the adrenaline flooding her bloodstream, she'd never felt it at all.

Walter was still screaming, and she looked down at him, feeling completely helpless to calm her son. She looked further back, and saw the still form of Paula, lying silent and unmoving in an expanding pool of blood.

She turned her attention back to the controls, and fighting the yoke, tried vainly to keep the aircraft in the air. The pedals wouldn't move and the yoke was like lead. Warning lights and alarms were now sounding throughout the cockpit, and she could smell smoke coming from somewhere behind her.

Looking out ahead, she saw the thick black plume of smoke outside of Williams, and tried with the last remaining ounces of energy she had to turn the Hercules in that direction.

"I'm so sorry, Walter. I'm so sorry Tim…" she said, tears filling her eyes.

***

The mortar rounds fell all around the shattered convoy, and the screams of the wounded and dying could be heard over the shrieks of the incoming rounds.

For Tim, time seemed to stretch out, seconds seemed like minutes, minutes like hours. He could still hear the crack of Jimenez' M14, so he knew at least he was still in the fight.

Tim turned his attention back to the bleeding, screaming major. "Please!" he begged.

"It looks like you're having a bad day, Major," Tim said, and then was startled by a huge shadow blotting out the sun. It was followed a second later by the scream of the C-130's engines at full-throttle, and both men looked up to see the gray fuselage pass overhead in a blur at top speed, the one engine closest to the fuselage on fire, spewing a thick stream of black smoke like a kite's streamer behind it.

It was so low, Tim could see the individual rivets, count the streaked stains from hydraulic fluid down its wings, as it flashed by in a blur. He followed the aircraft southward, then it slammed head on into the side of Bill Williams Mountain, exploding in a fireball. All sound stopped, except for the moans of the wounded; even the mortar had stopped firing, for everyone must have seen the spectacular sight of the Hercules auguring into the side of the mountain.

Time stopped at that instant, and Tim gazed at the burning wreckage for what seemed like hours. He then heard a blood-curdling scream, then the rapid fire of a M240 firing off a long sustained burst.

Tim's gaze dropped to the shirking man at his feet. His blood had turned to ice. He let his look bore holes in the man's soul, and then nodded ever so slowly. He whispered in a very calm and deadly voice, "Yes, you are about to have a very bad day indeed…"

The major screamed.

CHAPTER 21:
FOLLOW ME!

The sergeant had rallied a handful of his soldiers, and now they were taking cover in the overgrown median that separated the east and westbound lanes of the interstate.

The initial shock of the Hercules slamming into the mountain had worn off, and he'd gotten control, now he needed to figure out what to do next. There had been several more AT4 rockets fired at the convoy, and every last one of their vehicles that hadn't been destroyed in the initial blast were now heaps of twisted, burning steel, totally destroyed, each burning hotly, thick black smoke billowing out of each.

The mountainside was also ablaze, and the smell of burning flesh, jet fuel, and melting plastic now enveloped the entire area. The sergeant had heard, along with the rest of his men, the blood-curdling screams of some poor bastard well to the front, and the sounds made their blood run cold.

The machinegun that had fired a few moments ago had silenced, now the only thing heard was sporadic rifle fire, a methodic pop here and there, and the sounds of the wounded, moaning and screaming. *At least the goddamn mortar has stopped firing,* he thought thankfully.

He took a chance, and popped his head over a slight rise, surveying the scene in front of him. The only thing he could see from his vantage point through the thick smoke of the burning vehicles were the bodies of the dead and dying.

He was unable to see where the fire directed at them had come from, or determine how many he faced, but the one thing he knew for certain was the destruction of his unit was almost utterly complete. He knew was the fire was coming from somewhere to the west and north, on the far side of the gorge that was now inaccessible because the bridges had been blown in the most devastating way imaginable.

He pointed to one of the men. "You go out to the south, onto the eastbound lanes. You'll have cover if you stay on that side. The trees will hide your movements. Go up there and see if you can find a way across."

"If you say so, Sarge," the man replied reluctantly.

"Do it now, goddamn it! If we stay here we're going to get killed. We've got to get around them somehow. Now move your ass!"

The man took off, disappearing through the bushes, and the sergeant sat with his back against a tree, letting out a frustrated sigh.

"What now, Sarge?" another man asked.

"We wait for him to come back. If he finds a way across that gorge, then we'll go and find whoever is shooting at us and kill them."

"What about the major?" the man then asked.

He hadn't heard from the major since before the initial blast, and told himself that he'd been on the far side of the bridge when it blew, and was most probably dead by now. It was up to him now, to continue the mission, if he could.

"I don't know. He's probably dead," he told the man. He pulled out his radio, and tried to contact the major anyway.

***

Tim's mind was in a rage now, as he walked away from the bloody body of the major. He looked east, and through the smoke of the burning vehicles, he could see bodies strewn everywhere. Somewhere, off in the distance, Jimenez was now firing round after round into anything that still moved in the kill zone, and into bodies that were most assuredly very dead now.

He wiped the blood from the blade of his Ka-Bar knife on his pant leg, and taking one last look southward towards Bill Williams Mountain and the burning wreckage, his blood boiled. The fire from the crash had set the forest ablaze, and now the air was thick with the smoke of that fire too.

He sheathed his knife and, not turning back to look at his handiwork at the up-ended Hum-Vee, picked up his rucksack. With rifle in hand, he was about to head off towards Jimenez' position, when he heard an unfamiliar voice crackle over a radio.

He spun back towards the Hum-Vee, and listening as best he could through still-ringing ears, followed the sound to the cab of the vehicle. Crouching down and looking past the dead driver, he spotted a satellite radio laying in the jumbled mess of the contents of the interior.

"Major, can you hear me? Please give me a SITREP, over."

Knowing he'd better get out of there quickly, Tim went against his better judgment and brought the radio up to his mouth, depressing the push-to-talk button. "The major is dead, asshole."

"Who is this?" came the reply.

"I think you know exactly who I am. Your major is dead," Tim said, voice robotic and devoid of all emotion. He looked around at the carnage. "It looks like most of your men are dead too, or soon will be."

"You murdered them!" the radio crackled.

"You want to talk about murder? That Hercules that slammed into the mountain was piloted by my woman; my daughter was in it, along with my four month old son. Don't talk to me about murder, asshole. The plane just didn't self-destruct, it had a little help. Your people killed my family, now I'm going to fucking kill every last one of you."

"That had to have been a mistake! My men were supposed to secure it, not shoot it down!" came the panicked reply.

Tim took a look up into the sky, and through the clouds of smoke, could see buzzards already starting to circle the carnage before him, drawn, perhaps, by the stench of burning flesh. He keyed the radio again. "Be that as it may, asshole, soon you are going to be a tasty brunch for the buzzards, along with the rest of your men. You killed my family, and for that, you're going to pay."

Without waiting for a reply, he turned off the radio, and pocketing it, hefted his rucksack, picked up his rifle, and ran in a crouch to the wood line, in the direction of Jimenez.

***

The sergeant sat, face drawn, looking at the radio. The handful of men around him had heard the conversation, and now they stirred uneasily. He looked over at Colin, who was cowering behind a tree. He motioned for the big man. "You, come over here!"

Colin slunk over to the sergeant, and when he was close, sat down.

"Are you sure they only have only a few men?" the sergeant asked.

"Yeah, I swear. It's him, and a couple of other blokes. That's all."

"You'd better be telling me the truth."

"I am! Fucking oath! That's all they've got!"

The man that the sergeant had sent out to scout came scurrying back, crouching down in front of him. "There's a railroad bridge just to the south, about twenty yards into the woods. It crosses the gorge there," the man reported breathlessly.

"It's still standing?"

"It looked like it was wired, but for some reason it didn't blow."

"Or maybe it's another ambush, and they want us to start across it before they blow it," the sergeant said.

"I don't think so. The wires look like they've been cut," the man told him, "It looks like they were all wired together, but the wires were cut before it could all blow."

The sergeant came to a decision. "Follow me!" He led the way towards where his scout had come, the men following reluctantly.

***

Tim had made his way through the woods, following the sound of Jimenez' methodic rifle fire. It did indeed sound like a man on a rifle range, and when Tim came through the brush behind him, he saw that Jimenez was in the prone position, just outside of the foxhole they had dug, calmly firing round after round at the dead, along with the dying.

As not to startle him, Tim slowly approached from behind, and squatted down beside Jimenez.

"Taco," he said. "Cease fire."

Jimenez squeezed off another round at a man two hundred yards to his front who was crawling out from underneath one of the burning trucks, where apparently he'd taken cover earlier in the ambush.

It was a perfect shot, and Tim was impressed by the marksmanship, and he thought to let him know later, but now wasn't the time. He had to get this man under control, and now. He was finding it hard to keep himself under control as it was, and he still needed the young Marine.

The bolt on the M14 that Jimenez was firing locked back on an empty magazine, and he calmly thumbed the magazine catch, releasing the empty, inserted a fresh magazine into the rifle's magazine well, and released the bolt.

As he took aim at another unseen target, Tim placed his hand on Jimenez' shoulder and squeezed gently. "Taco. Cease fire. They're all dead out in front."

Tim could feel the man's muscles tense, and they felt like steel cables stretched to the breaking point. Jimenez sagged a little, and rolling to his side, looked up at Tim through red rimmed, tear-streaked eyes.

"They fucking killed them, Sar' Major! Robyn, Holly, Walter! All of them!"

"I know, Taco. Now is not the time. We've still got a job to do."

"How the fuck can you be so fucking calm!?" he screamed back at him.

Tim lowered his face to inches from Jimenez' face. "Taco, I am not fucking calm," he hissed angrily, "not by a long shot! And if you don't keep your fucking voice down, I will skull-fuck you!"

Jimenez snapped out of the funk he was in, wiped his eyes, and sniffled the snot that was dripping from his nose.

Tim grabbed the handset to the PRC-77. "Get your shit together, Taco, and get ready to move out." He pressed the push to talk button on the handset. "Izzy, you and Ian okay?"

The radio crackled to life, "Yes, Tim. We're okay. And yes, we saw," Izzy replied sadly.

"Stand by for another fire mission. Taco and I are getting ready to move to the secondary. Prepare to shift fire."

"Roger. Good luck."

"You too, Iz," Tim replied, standing and picking up the radio. He turned back to Jimenez, who was looking back at him with a deep hatred burning in his eyes.

"Let's get to Hum-Vee," Tim said.

"As long as I can kill a few more of the fuckers, I'm with you," Jimenez replied, and they headed out into the forest to the place they'd left their vehicle, leaving the burning carnage behind them.

***

The sergeant led the way across the double-tracked railroad bridge and took cover on the west side of the span, waving the rest across. He looked down under the structure in shock. The amount of TNT blocks placed there would have taken out a skyscraper. No wonder the other bridge had blown so spectacularly. He grabbed the first few men across, and had them stay with him while the rest ran past and into the woods beyond.

When they were all across, he turned to the three he had stopped, and pointed down underneath the trestle. "I want you three to go down there and start pulling wires. I don't want this bastard to go off and leave us stranded on this side. Got that?"

The three men looked down at all the explosive charges placed all over the bridge and didn't reply right away, making the sergeant angry.

"It wasn't a fucking suggestion. Do it, now!" he shouted, leaving them at the bridge and making his way a few yards into the brush. The rest of his men were standing around as if they were waiting on a bus to arrive. No over watch, no security, nothing. His head was pounding from a tension headache that threatened to tear the top of his skull off, and he wanted to scream at them, but then realized they weren't real soldiers at all, just a bunch of scared men with machine guns, and that was a very dangerous combination.

He had to get around to the rear of his quarry, try to find out what the hell had happened up at the airport, and why the specialist hadn't reported back yet. He motioned for everyone to gather around.

He was about to formulate a plan for a counterattack when a sound drew his attention away. It was a metallic clink, and then the sounds of a wooden crate being opened. It was coming from several hundred yards to the southwest, the opposite direction that he had planned on heading. There was the sound of a radio's squelch being broken, then another metallic clink.

He smiled for the first time that day, and looked around at the faces of his men.

"Come with me."

***

Tim pulled the Hum-Vee up and parked it where it was hidden from view, within walking distance to their positions overlooking the intersection on I-40 and Route 64.

Route 64 wound its way south from the Grand Canyon, passing under Interstate 40, where it curved westward, turning into the main street of the town of Williams a few miles further on. Tim had selected a spot on the overpass, looking down on Route 64 and northward.

The two men lugged their gear up the embankment towards the highway and made it to the top before they could hear the chatter of automatic weapons fire. They looked at each other, mouths agape. They could hear the high-pitched crack of M16s and M4s firing three rounds bursts, and then heard the reply of a deeper *crack, crack, crack* of what could only be Ian's L1A1, then the staccato chug of Tim's M3 Grease gun that he'd given to Izzy.

"Ah shit!" Jimenez said, climbing over the guardrail to the shoulder of the highway. "We've got to go back and help them!"

"We can't, Taco. By the time we get back to where they are it will all be over. We can't fucking help them, alright?"

Tim climbed over the rail and started off towards the westbound lanes and the shoulder overlooking Route 64. Jimenez followed him, and when he was set up, pulled a pair of binoculars out and scanned the horizon to the north. Seeing nothing yet, he lowered them, and then checked his watch.

He was surprised to see it was only 9 AM. Only forty-five minutes had passed since he'd tripped the ambush. He wiped his brow, and then sighed. "Three weeks, Taco. We needed three weeks. Jerry could have been here and things would be a lot different."

"Let's just kill em' all, and then let God sort them out," Jimenez said.

"I thought you and I were of the agreement there was no god?"

"I'm starting to reconsider."

"How? For fuck's sake, look around you! Would a loving god let all this shit happen to us?"

"I don't know, Sar' Major."

"Or is it that you might just hope to see Robyn on the other side? Is that it?" he asked incredulously. "Taco, she is fucking dead, okay? She's not coming back, she's not in heaven or hell, she is fucking dead, along with Holly, Walter, and Paula, end of fucking story!"

"Maybe I just want some poor, sorry-assed motherfucker to sort out all the sorry fucks I'm going to kill today," he stated flatly.

"We'll deal with that later," Tim said.

"Look!" Jimenez shouted, pointing over Tim's shoulder to the road heading north. Tim spun, and in the distance, could see a lone Hum-Vee speeding southward towards them.

"Get ready!" Tim ordered, and Jimenez grabbed an AT4 and prepared it to launch at the approaching vehicle.

Both men readied weapons. "Steady, Taco. Don't fire until I tell you to."

The vehicle drew nearer, reaching about four hundred yards, when Tim said, "Hold on a minute, Taco. Cover me!"

Tim leapt over the guardrail and bounded down the berm towards the road below.

Jimenez watched in amazement as Tim made it to the road, and casually strode out to the middle, straddled the faded double yellow line and faced the speeding Hum-Vee.

Though the vehicle made no indication it was going to stop, Tim never flinched as it came closer and closer, and then, when it looked like he was about to be run down, it skidded to a halt a few feet from where he was standing.

A man clambered up awkwardly through the top machinegun mount and manned the big .50 caliber weapon and trained it on him. "Who the fuck are you?" the man shouted.

Tim slowly walked toward the Hum-Vee, hands raised over his head, and made it all the way to the driver's side door. "Hi there!" he said with a grin. "I'm with the local Volunteer Fire Department, and I was wondering if you gentlemen had any spare change to donate. It's a good cause!"

"Stay away!" the driver said.

Tim ignored him, placing his left hand on the roof and leaning in. The man on the roof mounted machinegun couldn't see him anymore, and he was too close now to depress the barrel of the big gun down at Tim, effectively placing him completely out of the equation.

Tim looked into the interior. He saw two more men, the driver and a passenger, and then saw Robyn in the back seat, unconscious, battered and bruised, bleeding from a gash on her head. With his right hand, he slowly reached behind him, the men distracted by his boldness.

"Actually, I'm from the local Rotary Club," he said, as his hand felt the butt of his .45 automatic in his waistband.

"You're him!" the driver shouted, and made a move to gun the gas when Tim, in one fluid motion, pulled the pistol out, pointed it at the face of the driver and squeezed off a single round, blowing his face off in a blast of smoke, bone, and blood.

The pistol recoiled in his hand, and even before the slide had slammed home on a fresh round in the chamber, he pointed it at the passenger and shot that man in the face also.

Slow to react, the man on the .50 caliber machinegun tried to grab his own pistol, but a single crack from Jimenez' M14 resounded, and a 7.62mm bullet hit the man in the chest, blowing a gaping hole out his back. Eyes wide with disbelief, he died, slumped over the gun.

"Get down here, Taco!" Tim shouted, and then walked hurriedly around to the passenger side, opening the door and leaning in over Robyn's crumpled body. He brushed some hair away from her once beautiful face, which was now battered and swollen, turning an angry purple.

"Baby, it's Daddy. Can you hear me?" Tim whispered. The girl stirred, face contorted with pain, then her eyes fluttered open.

"Daddy, I tried to stop them, but I couldn't. I'm so sorry."

"Don't you worry about that now, baby," Tim said softly.

Jimenez arrived at this time and looked into the vehicle in shock. "Robyn, you're alive! Oh fuck, I thought you were dead!"

"Daddy, it hurts so bad!" Robyn cried, tears welling up in her swollen eyes. She was sobbing now, and then coughed a few times, wincing in pain, and spat out a gob of blood.

"It's okay, baby, Daddy and Taco are here to take care of you now. It's going to be alright." He turned to face Jimenez. "Get those bodies out of the Hum-Vee. We'll take her to the house."

Jimenez manhandled the bodies free, and dragged them to the side of the road. He then climbed atop the still running vehicle, and with some effort, was able to dump the man's body that he shot over the side, where it hit the asphalt with a sickening thump.

They piled in, ignoring the blood and brains all over the interior, and Jimenez headed out. When they were under the overpass and heading in the direction of town, Jimenez asked, "Do you really want to go to the house?"

"Yes," Tim said, suddenly feeling bone tired.

"We've got to get Izzy," Jimenez said, speeding through town, Robyn wincing with every bump he hit.

***

"Cease fire, cease fire goddamn it!" the sergeant shouted over the din of the rifle fire, and while not as fast as he'd have liked, the men finally stopped firing their weapons.

He came out from behind the tree he'd been using for cover and looked ahead to where the mortar was positioned. The cordite smoke was still thick in the air.

One of the placement's occupants was slumped over, quite dead, a long semi-auto rifle the sergeant had never seen before clutched in his hands. Movement to his left drew his attention, and he brought his M4 up to the ready.

He saw the figure of another man, white shock of hair on his head, crawling slowly away, dragging a leg covered in blood. He approached the figure, and when he got to him, he kicked the weapon in his hand away.

"Don't you move, or I'll spread your brains all over the ground!" the sergeant commanded, and the man rolled over onto his back, facing his tormentor.

"Can you stand?" the sergeant asked.

"I doubt it, you've shot my knee off," Izzy replied, wincing in pain, defiant all the same.

Another of the sergeant's men came up to the pair, and the sergeant spat, "Get that Aussie fucker up here!"

The man retreated, and the sergeant returned his gaze to the supine man. "Do you have anything you want to tell me?"

"Not really. If it's all the same to you, you might as well put a bullet in my head now," Izzy replied, jutting his chin out, anger in his eyes.

"Sorry to say, old man, but I need you right now."

Colin came up to the pair at this time, and when he saw who was lying on the ground, his face split into a wide, toothy grin. "Well, well, well! If it isn't my old mate the good doctor!" he said, looking down with glee. "Sergeant, he's one of the cunts who was going to string me up!"

"Oh, really?" the sergeant asked.

"That we were," Izzy said. "I don't know what he's told you lot, but this man is a rapist and a murderer."

"You're full of shit, mate! He's lying, Sergeant."

"Oh, no I'm not. He lured a poor retarded girl off into the forest, where he viciously raped, tortured, and then killed her," Izzy said, trying to sit up.

"I ought to shoot you right now!" Colin shouted, bringing his rifle up. The sergeant slapped the muzzle away from his prisoner.

"I'll have none of that shit, okay, asshole?" he told the big Aussie, who backed away. Seeing the M3 lying on the ground, Colin walked over and picked it up.

"I'll just take this as a souvenir," he beamed. "I always saw it with that bastard major sergeant, now it's mine."

"You do that. Now go and get a couple of men to carry him," the sergeant told him.

"Carry him? Carry him where?" Colin said in shock. "You should kill the cunt here and now."

"Just fucking do what I told you to do!" the sergeant spat. Colin walked away, giving Izzy an evil glare, and then returned with two men. The sergeant told them to pick Izzy up, which they did none too gently, completely ignoring Izzy's shouts of pain.

"Now where is this compound they have?" the sergeant asked Colin.

"It's not too far, just over that way."

"Lead the way," the sergeant said, waving him forward.

***

Jimenez drove through town, and made the left hand turn onto the road towards Colman Lake, trying to avoid the cracks, bumps, and potholes in the deteriorating road the best he could. Robyn shouted in agony every time the tires hit another, and he hated to see her like this.

"Hang on, baby, we're almost home. We'll get Izzy to fix you up good as new," he said loud enough for her to hear.

She only moaned again when he hit a pothole, making the Hum-Vee bounce violently.

They made their way along the road, and then reached the side road leading up to the settlement that they called home. When they cleared the first set of trees and came out onto the meadow that fronted Tim's house, Jimenez slammed on the brakes, making Robyn scream in pain.

His heart fell when he heard her. "Sorry, baby."

Out in front of them, on the porch of Tim's house stood several men, rifles at the ready.

"What now?" he asked Tim.

"What now, Taco, is drive up to the house," he replied, matter-of-factly.

"That prick Colin is with him! That motherfucker sold us out!" he spat. "Izzy is with them too. He looks hurt."

"I see them both. Drive up to the house, and do exactly what I say, okay?"

Sighing, Jimenez took his foot off the brake pedal and casually drove up to the house, where he parked and shut the engine off.

Tim looked out at the men standing before him, and did something he'd never imagined himself ever doing.

He surrendered.

Getting out of the Hum-Vee, he raised his hands, and then slowly reached into his waistband and pulled his .45 out. He held it in front of his face, finger well away from the trigger. He looked in the face of the soldier standing in front of him, who he assumed was the sergeant. He was the only one who looked remotely military.

He thumbed the magazine release, letting the magazine fall out of the grip, landing on the dirt at his feet. He then tossed the pistol onto the sloped hood of the Hum-Vee, turned and went to the rear passenger door. He reached in and picked up Robyn as gently as he could. Cradling her in his arms, she felt so tiny, tinier that she'd been when he'd first found her in West Virginia so many years ago.

Looking at the men blocking his way, he strode defiantly towards them, carrying his precious cargo, breezing by them as if they weren't there. They stepped aside, unsure of what to do, making room for Tim to walk up the stairs, across the porch and through the front door to his house.

As he disappeared into the house, all the men stood around looking at each other, none of them knowing what to do.

"Stay here," the Sergeant said, and followed Tim inside the house, letting the door slam loudly behind him.

CHAPTER 22:
SURRENDER TERMS

Tim laid Robyn gently on her bed and sat down on the edge, taking her hand. Her eyes fluttered open, gazing at him sadly.

"Daddy, it hurts so bad," she told him in a soft, childlike voice.

"I know, baby. You just lay here and rest, and I'll get Izzy up here to have a look at you," he said, brushing a few wisps of her hair from her bruised and swollen face.

Propped up on a shelf over the headboard, he saw an old and familiar friend. He reached up and took hold of the old, tattered, and threadbare stuffed animal, and placed it in her arms.

"Here you go, baby. Bad Bear will keep you safe for now, okay?"

"Thank you, Daddy," she said weakly.

"I know you hurt right now, but can you tell me what happened?"

"I fell out of the plane, Daddy. They were shooting at us and I was firing back. I guess Holly didn't know I was laying on the back ramp when she took off, and I just sort of fell out."

"I'm just happy you're alive."

"Am I going to be alright?" she asked.

"It looks like you hit your head on the runway, so we might have to fix that, the runway that is, but I'll get Izzy up here to look you over just in case," he said jokingly, trying to cheer her up.

"I guess Holly and Walter are safe now?" she asked, her eyes boring into him. His heart fell, and he wanted to scream. He patted the top of her head. "Holly and Walter are someplace where they can't be hurt anymore, baby."

"Good. I was worried for a moment."

"Don't you worry now," he said. "I'm going downstairs now. I'll get Izzy to come up to take a look at you."

When he was halfway to the door, she asked, "Daddy, did we win?"

"Baby, you're safe, and that's all that matters now, okay? Get some rest," he said, turning away so she didn't see the tears in his eyes.

"Daddy, I love you."

"I love you too, baby. Get some rest. I'll be back later." He walked out into the hallway, shutting the door behind him.

He stood there for a moment to gather himself and wiped his eyes. He took a deep breath and walked down the flight of steps into his living room, where he found the sergeant, standing with his back towards him, looking over the rack of hundreds of DVDs.

When the sergeant heard him, he spun around and looked at Tim. He thumbed behind him at the rack of DVDs, and asked, "Can you actually watch them, on that TV?"

Tim stared at him for a moment, and then said, "We're not here to discuss my flat screen TV or my collection of *Hogan's Heroes* reruns."

"No, I guess we're not," the sergeant replied.

Just then, two of the sergeant's men came into the house, laughing. Tim looked at them and blew his top. "Get them the fuck out of my goddamn house!" he screamed.

The two men looked to the sergeant for direction, who just looked at them and nodded. As they went to retreat back outside, Tim called after them, "And you can get my other two men in here. One's a doctor."

They again looked at the sergeant, who said, "Do it."

After they walked out, Tim walked undeterred into the kitchen, followed by the sergeant. He pulled out two bottles of beer from the refrigerator and the sergeant's eyes lit up. Tim walked over to the round table, pulled out a chair and sat.

He motioned for the sergeant to sit opposite, and handed him the cold bottle. Dumbfounded, the sergeant took the offered drink, pulled out a chair and sat down.

Tim twisted off the cap from the bottle, and then took a long pull from the drink. He looked at it, and then took another long swig, putting the bottle down in front of him. Still no words were said, and Tim let the silence hang between the two men like a dark cloud, his eyes boring holes into the sergeant's head.

Over the sergeant's shoulder, Tim saw the front door open, and Jimenez came in helping Izzy, his arm around the man's waist. Tim pointed to the stairs. "She's up in her room. Are you okay, Iz?"

"I've had better days," Izzy said. "I'll fix myself up after I look at Robyn."

"Are you still bleeding?"

"No, I was able to stop it. It hurts, but I think I'll survive."

"Let me know if you need anything," Tim replied, and Izzy and Jimenez disappeared to the second floor of the house. Tim gave the sergeant his best sergeant major glare.

"You're forgetting who is in charge now, Flannery," the sergeant said, attempting to regain control of the situation.

"It's Sergeant Major, to you, dickweed," Tim spat. "And we're not here to discuss who is in charge."

"Then what are we here for?" the sergeant said, sipping on his beer, secretly enjoying the ice cold beverage.

"We're here to discuss the terms of my surrender," Tim said flatly.

"Terms? There won't be any terms. You're my prisoner."

"I know why you're here, and if you want what you came for, there will be terms."

"Oh, you do, do you? And just how do you know that, and how did you know we were coming?" the sergeant asked.

"I know a lot of shit I'm not going to tell you, asshole."

"Was it that Colin guy?"

"That asshole?" Tim asked, laughing a little, "No, it wasn't him. I'll tell you what, though. Don't let him anywhere near me."

"Or what?"

"Or, I'll fucking cut his heart out with a rusty bayonet," Tim said, leaning forward at the table.

That piqued the sergeant's interest; he did want to know why there was so much bad blood between those two. Maybe what the old man had told him was the truth, that Colin had actually raped and killed a girl. He let it go for now. "Sergeant Major, you killed over a hundred of my men this morning. What makes you think I'm in any mood to discuss terms with you?"

"I don't give a fuck about your men, or your mood. That plane your people shot down, the one that's smeared all over the side of that mountain? Well, that plane had my woman and my four month old son in it."

"I'm sorry. That wasn't supposed to happen."

"I'm not in a mood to forgive anything right now. I know exactly why you're here, and if you want to go back to Washington with at least part of your mission complete, you'll goddamn well listen to my terms."

"Alright, Sergeant Major. I'm all ears," the sergeant said, motioning with his hand for Tim to continue.

"First thing is, you'll leave my daughter and those other two men here when you take me back. Because that is what you're supposed to do, right? Take me back to DC?"

The sergeant nodded.

"You'll leave this place intact, no looting. You'll take only supplies you and your men, what's left of them anyway, will need for the trip."

"Now wait a damn min—"

"No *you* wait a minute. You want the codes, don't you?"

"Yes," came the grim reply from the sergeant.

"If you want the goddamn codes, you'll agree to my terms, end of fucking story."

The sergeant thought for a moment before speaking. "What if I just took everything anyway?"

"Then you'll never get the codes," Tim stated gravely.

"Oh, you think so? I could tear this house apart. I'll find them!"

"Have you ever seen codes for the nuclear arsenal? No, I didn't think so. I'd never seen them either. So you don't know what you're looking for, do you?"

"I could just beat it out of you," the sergeant said.

"I know that you've read my 201 File. Do you think that will work? You might as well just put a bullet in me, Sergeant."

The sergeant was silent, sensing he'd lost control, and had no clue how to get it back. It frustrated him that his prisoner had gained the upper hand, and he did need the man's help if he wanted to get back to Washington with the mission complete.

Tim pushed the chair he was sitting on away from the table and stood, walking purposefully over to the mantelpiece over the fireplace. The sergeant followed him with his eyes, wary that Tim might try some trick. Tim saw his actions, and saw the sergeant place his hand of the M9 pistol at his hip.

"Don't worry," Tim said. "No tricks."

The sergeant didn't reply, and didn't take his hand from his pistol either. He watched Tim lift up what looked to him to be an original Remington sculpture of a cowboy on a bucking bronco. Tim picked up a notepad, similar to the ones he used while he was still a cop in Maryland. He set the sculpture back down, and walked to the table, sitting down across from The sergeant again.

Tim thumbed through the notepad, and then tossed it over to the sergeant. "Here, now you have the codes for the bomb."

The sergeant paged through the notebook. "These are just a bunch of numbers and letters!"

"I know," Tim said. "That's why you need me to decode them."

"There should be a big binder, with plastic laminated pages," the sergeant protested.

"There was a big binder. It's gone now."

"Gone where?"

"They didn't tell you? I thought they knew," Tim said, slightly perplexed. Maybe the major had never told this sergeant the whole story after all. That was probably the case, he reckoned, he'd had plenty of officers in the past that only gave him part of the picture.

"Tell me what?"

"Really, I thought you knew," Tim said, now toying with the man.

"You'd better stop fucking around, Sergeant Major!"

"Or what? You'll torture me to get what you want? I know you know all about me. Do you think you'll ever get any information out of me that way?" When he didn't get a response, he continued. "Here's what you need to know. The original codebook was vaporized on a tiny atoll in the middle of the south Pacific last year. That's a handwritten copy that I've encoded, with my own code that I thought up all by myself. It's the only copy in existence," Tim lied.

"I see," the sergeant replied, tossing the notebook down on the tabletop, "And I need you to decode it."

"Pretty much," Tim replied, downing his beer.

"And how exactly was this original codebook vaporized?" the sergeant continued, and Tim gave him an evil grin.

"It sort of goes like this," Tim said. "There was another man, a sailor. He wanted those codes."

"I take it you didn't give them to him?"

"Of course I didn't. He was on this atoll, and had us cornered."

"And?"

"Sergeant, you were in the Ghan, right?"

"Yeah, what about it?" the sergeant glared.

"Have you ever heard of someone calling in artillery onto their own position when it was untenable?"

"Of course I have. Read about it, I mean. I've never..." he trailed off, all color draining out of his face. "Are you telling me you launched a nuclear missile at yourself?"

"That I did."

"You're crazy!"

"You may be absolutely correct, Sergeant. Now, knowing that little tidbit of information let me ask you another question. If I'm crazy enough to do that, what makes you so certain that when I was upstairs with my daughter, I didn't do it again?"

"You wouldn't have!" the sergeant shouted, his hands beginning to shake.

"I mean shit, what have I got to lose at this point?" he replied, looking at his watch nonchalantly. "It's been what, about ten minutes since I've been up there? We could all be about five minutes from being reduced down to the molecular level."

"You *are* crazy!" the sergeant screamed, and stood on weak knees.

"Sit the fuck down, Sergeant," Tim commanded. "I didn't. I could have though, so keep in mind what I'm capable of, shall we?"

The sergeant plopped back down heavily onto the chair, and stared at Tim for several moments, letting what he'd said sink in.

"So," Tim said, "shall we revisit my terms of surrender?"

"Alright," the sergeant replied, still pale.

"I go back with you to decode the book. You take what you need, no looting. And lastly, you leave the three people here, my daughter, her man and the good doctor. You have two Hum-Vees, the one out front, and one parked out by the highway. There's also a deuce and a half parked behind the house here. You can have those, nothing else."

"Alright," the sergeant agreed reluctantly after a long pause. What choice did he have? He couldn't torture the book out of the sergeant major, he'd never talk. He then asked Tim, "So what assurances do I have that you'll give up the codes once we get to DC?"

"None, just my word. Take it or leave it, Sergeant, because that's the only way I'm coming back with you."

"I could shoot you where you sit right now."

"You could, but you won't, will you?"

"No."

"I thought not. One last thing, and I meant it. You keep that Colin fucker away from me, or I'll do to him what I did to your good major."

"What *did* you do to him?" the sergeant asked, curious.

"Do you hunt, Sergeant? I mean, have you ever gone hunting?"

"Like as in deer hunting? Yeah, I used to all the time in upstate Pennsylvania with my dad and brother, why?"

"So did I. Potter County," Tim said, reaching down, unsheathing his Ka-Bar and holding it up. The sergeant could now see the dried blood on the hilt, and encrusted under Tim's fingernails. "So you've seen a deer gutted before."

The color that had started to come back to the sergeant's face drained again, and he nodded in silence.

"That's what I did to your good major, and I fed him his still beating heart."

"You're crazy."

"After all that's happened, I'm certain I'd give a good shrink a great paper to write. Just keep that fucker away from me, alright?"

"Agreed," the sergeant said, nodding grimly.

Jimenez came down the stairs and over to Tim, completely ignoring the sergeant.

"Sar' Major, Izzy gave her some morphine and she's asleep now."

"How is she?"

"He's not sure, but he is sure her arm and one of her legs are broken. He's trying to set them now, but he needs plaster cast stuff from the clinic in town."

"Alright," Tim said, then turned to the sergeant. "Can the Lance Corporal go to the clinic to get what he needs?"

"I don't see why not, at this point. If you don't mind, I'll send one of my men with him?" he asked sarcastically.

"Not at all, Sergeant," Tim replied.

Jimenez saw the notebook then. "Sar' Major, isn't that the cod—"

"That it is, Taco," Tim said, shooting him an icy glare.

"That's the—"

"Don't you fucking worry about those codes now, Taco. Go and get what you need for Robyn!" he shouted, hoping the man would keep his mouth shut.

"Roger, Sar' Major!" Jimenez said with a perplexed expression on his face.

The sergeant led Jimenez outside, and Tim took the time to get up and get himself another beer, not bothering to get his captor one, and sat back down at the table. He heard a Hum-Vee start, and then pull away. The sergeant came back in and looked at Tim. "I sent your man with one of mine, just in case, you know."

"I do. Now if you don't mind, I'd like to go check on my daughter."

"Go right ahead. I don't need to remind you not to try anything funny, do I?"

"I'm sure you've already got guards around the house. I won't try anything. I'm good at my word, Sergeant."

"I hope so, for your sake."

Tim started towards the stairs, then turned back to the sergeant. "If your men would like to take a hot shower, any one of the homes up this dirt road will have working water heaters and running water," he told him, giving him an olive branch of a sort.

"Thank you, I think we all would, actually," the sergeant replied with a genuine smile. "Just don't have them smash their way in, have them show a little respect. Most of the houses should be unlocked. If they aren't, keys to them will be under a mat on the porch." Tim plodded tiredly up the stairs, watched with curiosity by the sergeant until he was out of sight.

Tim made his way towards his bedroom. When he opened the door, the first thing he saw was the crib that Walter had slept in. He reached down and picked up the tiny blue blanket he'd slept with and brought it to his face. He could smell both Holly's and the baby's scent. He breathed them in, and the floodgates opened. He started to weep uncontrollably for the first time in a long, long time, and all the fears, crushed dreams and hopes, everything he'd kept welled up inside of him came spilling out.

Deep sobs escaped his lips and he staggered backwards, falling on the bed. He cried for a long time, until there were no more tears to shed. Holding the tiny blanket close to his face, he dried his eyes with it.

"I'm so sorry!" he wailed. "I failed you so miserably!"

He lay on the bed, staring at the ceiling for what felt like hours. His sorrow was soon replaced by rage, then that was swept away, replaced by determination.

Getting his senses back under control, Tim stood and went to the top of the dresser, where he'd kept a wooden box he'd gotten years ago in Germany. It was hand carved, and had ivory edelweiss inlaid on the lid. Inside, he kept a few precious keepsakes from before the Event.

He dug through it, and finding what he was looking for, pocketed it and headed down the hall towards Robyn's bedroom. Slowly opening the door, he stuck his head in and saw her sleeping silently, Izzy by her side.

Izzy heard him and turned.

"How is she?" Tim asked, coming over to the bed.

"She's a very lucky girl. Her leg is broken in two places, her left arm too. That, and several broken ribs, bruises, and contusions, but I think she'll be okay. I gave her something for the pain."

"That's a relief. How are you?"

"I've seen better days, Tim. My patella is shattered."

"That's got to hurt like a bastard," Tim said. "I sent Taco with one of the sergeant's men to get what you need."

"Good. The sooner I get a cast on her arm and leg, the better."

"Let me see what I can do for you, Iz. Come over here and sit down on the chair."

The old doctor complied with Tim's help. Tim took out his knife and cut open Izzy's trouser leg, removing the dirty, blood-soaked makeshift bandage that Izzy had put on himself earlier, exposing the nasty wound. He dragged over Izzy's doctor's bag and made short work of cleaning up the wound the best he could, putting a pressure bandage over it, then wrapping it neatly with gauze, finally taping it with medical tape.

"There, good as new," Tim said when he was finished.

"I'm impressed," Izzy replied.

"I did get my Boy Scout merit badge for first aid," he said. "Can I give you something for the pain?"

"No thanks, Tim. I gave myself a half dose of morphine when I gave Robyn a shot. Can I do something for you?"

"No, Iz. I'm okay."

"Are you sure?" he prodded.

"Iz, I'm as good as I can be. I'm not going to be singing any cheerful show tunes, if that's what you want to hear."

"Damn, and I was looking forward to a baritone version of 'Singin' in the Rain'."

Ignoring Izzy's weak attempt to cheer him up, Tim said, "Iz, I need to tell you this while I've got you alone. I'm not sure how many more times I'll be able to talk to you before I have to go."

"Go?"

"I'm going to be heading back to DC with these men."

"What? But why—"

"Izzy, listen. They think I've given them the codes for the missiles," he whispered.

"You didn't, did you?"

"No, I gave them the book with the codes we used on the Ham radio. There's nothing to them, but this sergeant doesn't know that."

"Why?" "The goal is still the same, Iz. The whole idea was for them not to get the codes, and I meant that. It'll take at least a month for us to get back to DC, maybe even longer."

"So you've convinced them that those notations are the codes?"

"I have. And I have to go back to 'decode' them for this president of theirs. It was the only way I could get them to leave you all here when I go. That way, you'll have enough time to get out of here, make your way to San Diego and get on that ship back to Oahu."

"I see," Izzy said crossly.

"Do you, Iz?"

"Timothy, you do know what will happen when they find they've been duped?"

"I know exactly what will happen to me, and I'm prepared for that eventuality. My fate is unimportant. Holly and Walter are dead, I can't change that. The important thing now is to get you, Robyn, and Taco to safety before things get ugly for me, and more importantly, keep the codes away from anyone who wants them."

"I see what you're doing, but I don't have to like it," Izzy snapped.

"I didn't want to have an argument with you over it. One more thing I need you to do," Tim said, still whispering.

"What will that be?"

"Taco saw me give the notepad to the sergeant. He almost let the cat out of the bag, but I stopped him before he could say anything more. I'm not sure if they'll let me talk with him in private, and I doubt they will let you and I talk like this again once their shock wears off."

"I agree."

"When Taco gets back here with the casts and shit, let him know what I'm doing."

"I will, Tim."

"Good, that's settled. I was afraid I wouldn't be able to come up and talk to you."

"I'm amazed that they let you, considering the pounding we gave them. I'd have thought they would be a lot less hospitable."

"I think the sergeant and his men would like nothing better than to drag us out and shoot us, to be honest, but he does have his orders, and those orders are to bring the codes back."

"Now he needs you for the codes," Izzy finished for him.

"And if he wants me, he's got to leave the rest of you alone."

"You should have been an officer, Sergeant Major," Izzy said.

"I could never be an officer and gentleman like you, Iz."

Izzy snorted. "Only by act of Congress, Tim!"

"Can I get anything for you?" Tim asked, standing on stiff legs, reaching down to help Izzy stand.

"Help me to my bed. I'd like to have a lie-down."

Tim put his arm around him and helped him out the door, and they hobbled their way down to Izzy's bedroom. Tim helped him over to the bed, where he sat with a wince.

Izzy shucked off his shirt and with Tim's help, took his boots, then his ruined trousers off, and swung his legs into bed, lying on top of the covers.

"Is there anything else you'd like?"

"No Tim, I'm going to have a rest now. Come and get me when Juan comes back so I can set Robyn's casts. I'm going to need help with that too, it won't be pleasant when I reset the bones."

"I'll come and get you," Tim said, but Izzy had already fallen asleep, so he retreated out of the room, shutting the door behind him. He made his way back towards Robyn's bedroom, and found her still sound asleep.

He went over to the bed, sat down, took her hand, and looked at her. His heart broke when he saw the bruises and cuts. Her whole face was puffed, swollen, and turning an ugly purple color.

With her good arm, she clung to Bad Bear tightly. That bear had been through a lot, he remembered. Coming all the way from West Virginia, to here, then to Hawaii, stowing away in her rucksack, lounged on the beach on Volivoli, then back here, always there to comfort her. He remembered when they'd first met, and when he'd asked why she named him 'Bad Bear', and how hard he'd laughed when she told him she'd blame the bear for anything bad she'd done in the hopes her mom would punish the bear.

Now she lay here in front of him, a grown woman, no longer a little girl. A brave woman at that.

She stirred, and her eyes fluttered and opened, eyelids heavy from the morphine. He squeezed her hand gently.

"Hey, Pumpkin. How're you feeling now?"

"I still hurt some, Daddy."

"Izzy will fix you up, good as new, baby. Taco went to get some things in town, and when he gets back, we need to cast up your arm and leg."

"I done broke em' eh?" she said weakly, her West Virginia accent returning a little.

"Izzy will fix them up for you, don't you worry."

"I forgot my PLF," she said, meaning 'Parachute Landing Fall', something Tim had shown her years ago when she asked how to land with a parachute.

"It's okay. Here, I got something for you." He reached into his pocket, bringing out what he'd retrieved from the wooden box earlier. He held it up in front of her eyes so she could see it.

When she saw what Tim held up, she broke out into a wide smile, "Daddy! Are those your jump wings?"

"Yep. The very first ones I got when I graduated Jump School," he told her. "You earned them today."

"Oh, Daddy, really?" "Yes," he said, nodding. He took the two clasps off of the back and pinned them to her dirty and bloodied flight suit. "There you go, Trooper. You are no longer a leg!"

"Thanks, Sar' Major! Holly will be proud of me!" she said happily, and when she did, a dark cloud crossed over Tim's face that she didn't miss.

"What's wrong?"

"Honey, there's no easy way to tell you…" he said, tears coming to his eyes.

"Holly and Walter are okay, aren't they?"

"No, honey, they're not. The plane crashed."

"They can't be dead! No, Daddy! No!" she wailed, and then winced in pain. Tim leaned down and held her as tightly as he dared, not wanting to hurt her.

They cried for some time, holding each other. And then, almost as if she turned off a switch, she stopped crying and pulled away from Tim. He looked into her eyes, now ablaze.

"Daddy, you've got to kill them."

"I know, baby," he replied, slowly nodding. "I know."

CHAPTER 23: VOYAGE
OF THE RESOLUTE

The old Liberty Ship bobbed like a cork in the gently rolling waves of the Pacific. Only a few puffy cumulus clouds scudded across the deep blue sky, and the new day promised to be another pleasant one for their crossing.

Ensign Johnson had just relieved Harry Suplee from the con, which had just finished another uneventful overnight watch on the bridge. One of Sergeant Williams' men had the helm, and Johnson was happy to have the extra hands to help sail the ship.

They were a week out of Pearl Harbor, only a day out of San Diego, and all of the gear and equipment loaded was still secure in the ship's holds. Williams, assisted by Ken and Suplee, had loaded four M3 Bradleys and several armored Hum-Vees into the holds, along with food, medical supplies, and ammunition. Johnson had just checked his GPS along with the navigational charts, and seeing all was in order, sat back comfortably in the captain's chair, legs crossed, cup of fresh coffee in his hand, when he saw Sergeant Williams enter the bridge, his own steaming mug at his lips.

"Good morning, Sergeant," Johnson said with a smile.

"Good morning! Is everything in order?" Williams replied, coming up to the captain's chair.

"Yes, all is in order. I hope you're enjoying your pleasure cruise!"

"I am. Some of my men are still a little seasick. A few were chumming over the rail again this morning."

"Some people never get used to it. To tell you the truth, on my first cruise, I was a little green around the gills for a few weeks, but now I'm used to the rolling, and feel at home at sea."

"A sailor's first love, eh?"

"That's true. We should be in Diego tomorrow afternoon."

"Good. Smooth sailing all the way."

"We've been lucky so far as far as weather is concerned," Johnson agreed. "You still think you'll be able to get to their place in Arizona in time?"

"No," Jerry said with a frown. "I think we'll be too late. I talked to Tim a few days ago, and he thinks they'll get hit soon."

"That's not good. You think it's a fool's errand at this point, I guess," Johnson said. "Have you told the men yet?"

"No, they're still pretty motivated. I'd like to keep it that way for a bit longer."

"I see. I hope everything is alright out there." Johnson looked out of the bridge windscreen at the vast, empty sea.

"So do I. Tim has his shit well secured, and if anything, he'll send them packing with their tails between their legs. I just wish we could have been able to get out there sooner," Williams said, and as the last words left his lips, one of his men, who had taken over the radio duties, came in, his face grave.

"Sarge, I just got off the horn with Arizona," he said.

"And?" Williams asked. The man shook his head and handed him a piece of paper.

"I wrote it down, so I didn't screw up the message. It's from that Marine, Jimenez." Jerry took the offered paper, read it, then looked back at the man. "Are you sure it was him?"

"Yeah, it was over the sat-radio. I recognized his voice. He was pretty upset."

"I'll bet," Jerry said. "Goddamn it!" he shouted, walking out the wing bridge and leaning over the rail, staring out at the wake of the ship, foaming white, in deep contrast to the blue of the ocean below.

Johnson got up from the chair and asked the radioman, "What was it?"

"Not good, sir, a lot of people are dead out there in Arizona," the man replied, slowly shaking his head.

Johnson walked out to the wing bridge and came up alongside Jerry. "So, let's have it."

"They got hit yesterday," Jerry said, handing the message over to Johnson, who read it rapidly. "Now, I think, we just ought to turn this boat around and head back to Pearl," Jerry said angrily.

Johnson read through the handwritten message again. "He says they took him, and they're heading to Washington."

"Yeah, it's a big kick in the nuts. I can't believe Holly and the baby are dead."

"He didn't say how it happened," Johnson said, tossing what was left of his coffee overboard and crumpling the message up into a tight ball with one hand before tossing it into the ship's wake.

"He didn't have to. He said the plane is total write-off, so that tells me they either were shot down or it crashed. Let's turn this dog and pony show around and head back home."

"Jerry, what if we got you and your men to Washington?"

"Now I think you're the crazy one," Jerry replied with a sad laugh.

"I'm serious. I know you can't drive your Bradleys across the whole country. What if we got you close enough to DC?"

"And rescue Tim? That's about the craziest thing I've heard since all this shit began," Jerry said, shaking his head. "What will you do, go through the Panama Canal?"

"No, that would be completely blocked with derelict ships."

"Then how for Christ's sake?"

"We go the long way!" Johnson said, and then retreated to the bridge, Jerry following, a bewildered expression plastered across his dark face. Johnson breezed past the helmsman, going over to the chart table. He rummaged around for a minute, and then pulled out a large chart that he unrolled on top of the table. "We've got enough fuel in the bunkers right now to get us as far as Lima, Peru. We can stop there, refuel and re-provision, and then keep on heading south, into the South Pacific." He traced a line with his finger on the map. "Around Cape Horn and then into the South Atlantic."

"How long do you think that will take?" Jerry asked.

"A month, maybe two, and it'll be a rough passage. This time of year, the waters around the Cape will be treacherous," Johnson said, looking into Jerry's eyes to gauge his thoughts.

Jerry turned away from the chart table and walked over to the hatch leading out to the wing bridge. He leaned on the sill, his back to Johnson. He was silent for a few moments, and then, without turning around, said, "Won't we be too late again?"

"We already know from the other messages from Tim that it took almost that long for that little army to get to where he was. Shouldn't it take at least that long to get back?"

"Maybe. The roads must be pretty overgrown, especially back east," Jerry said. He returned to the table. "It'd be a long shot."

"A million to one odds, I agree," Johnson told the big sergeant.

"You're right, though. We've come too far to let Tim's dream go up in smoke like that."

"We can't. We're all that's left of what could be good in this shitty world of ours," Johnson agreed, folding his arms across his chest.

"What exactly do you think we can do once we get there?" Jerry asked.

"That, my good friend, I will leave up to you. I just know I can't turn this ship around and give up. I'd never be able to live with myself if there was a possibility, however remote, that we could have done something, and we crawled into a hole and hid."

"What a way to start a day," Jerry sighed. "Okay. I'll have to put it to the men first. It's too big of a decision to make on my own. I'll see what they think, and I'll get back to you."

"That's a given. It's got to be one hundred percent agreement on this."

"I'll do it now," Jerry said, walking over to the bulkhead where the growler phone was located. He picked the handset out of its cradle, switched it to public address, pressed the push to talk button. "Now hear this! All hands, meet in the cargo hold with the vehicles in fifteen minutes. This is not a request." He replaced the handset. "I'll let you get back to running the ship, Bill. I've got to sell this idea to the men."

"Alright then," Johnson nodded. "I'll plot out a course for Lima right now while you do that, but I won't make any course changes until I hear back from you."

With a curt nod, Jerry left through a hatch into the interior of the ship. Johnson went to the coffee pot and poured himself another cup. He sat in the captain's chair and looked out the front windscreens contemplatively.

A few minutes later, Suplee came onto the bridge, poured himself a cup of coffee and came up to Johnson.

"What's the story?"

"Harry, why aren't you asleep?"

"I was about to turn in when I heard Jerry's announcement. What gives?"

Johnson gave him a brief rundown on what had transpired in Arizona, and Suplee let out a long whistle.

"Now we are going to sail to Washington, DC," Johnson told him.

"Who came up with that bright idea?" Suplee asked incredulously.

"Me. We have to do something, don't we?"

"That'll take a month or more!"

"I know, but it might take them that long to get Tim back to DC also. Jerry's going to down to talk to the men and see if they all agree. If it's not unanimous, we'll turn around and head back to Pearl."

Suplee caught the helmsman's eye. The man had heard all of the conversation between Johnson and Jerry and now this one with Suplee. He shrugged at the old-fashioned ship's wheel. "If you don't mind me saying so, I'm all for it. That Sergeant Major guy saved us in Pearl, and I think we owe him."

"I agree," Johnson said. "And I don't have to remind you what he did for us back on Volivoli. He could have just as easily left us there."

Suplee stared at Johnson for a few moments, and then a smile split his face. "Okay, I agree, San Diego or Washington, DC, what's the difference?"

"Several thousand nautical miles," Johnson said.

"Eh, in for a penny, in for a pound my mom always said. It's not like we have to be anywhere else."

"I guess. Now go back to your cabin and get some sleep," Johnson told his first officer.

"I'll let Beth know our honeymoon cruise has been extended," Suplee grinned. "So, Skipper, do you think we can do it?"

"I don't see why not. The lady may be old, but she's built well, and she's just as seaworthy now as she was in 1943. Besides, I have the best First Officer a man could ask for, and a great crew. Yes, we can do it."

"I guess that's settled. It doesn't matter, I'd sail anywhere with you," Suplee told his friend.

"I appreciate that, Harry. The feeling is mutual. But we won't know until Jerry talks to the troops."

"Let me know, will you? I'm going to turn in. It was a boring mid-watch and I'm bone tired."

"And, Harry? Get some sleep, okay? I know how you and your blushing bride like to make up for all the dry years."

Suplee winked at Johnson and disappeared through the rear hatch. Johnson looked at the new chart on the table, scratching his chin, deep in thought.

Below decks, Jerry burst into the dimly lit hold and climbed up on top of one of the Bradleys that were securely chained to the deck. Standing on the 30mm chain gun's turret, hands on his hips, he looked around at the mass of faces looking back at him. Clearing his throat, he asked in a booming voice, "Is this everyone?"

A voice from the back called out, "Some are still asleep; they were working overnight in the engine room."

"When I said everybody, I fucking meant everybody, goddamn it! Go and get them up! I've got something important to say!"

The man who had shouted out scurried away, back into the next hold where the bunks were set up. Feeling very tired all of a sudden, Jerry sat down on the turret, the long barrel of the chain gun sticking out lewdly from between his legs.

He scratched his head and the back of his neck, and when he looked up, the man he'd sent to get the others came back into the hold followed by several men who were yawning and rubbing the sleep from their eyes.

"I'm glad you ladies could join us. I'm sorry that I disturbed your beauty sleep, but I've got something to tell you all!" he shouted, standing on the turret again. He looked around with a scowl, then softened and let out a sigh. "I'm sorry. I know you're all volunteers, and you didn't have to be here. I keep forgetting this isn't the army anymore."

When he thought he had everyone's attention he started. "Like I said, we're all volunteers. You know what we're on this ship for, and why it's so important. I've just received bad news from Arizona. Really, really bad news," he said, then went on to tell them of the deaths of Holly and the baby, and how most of the people who had departed Oahu were lost. He also told them of Tim's capture, and his being transported back to Washington, DC. He let it sink in, before he spoke again.

"Are there any questions?"

A man who was standing in the front of the formation, stepped forward and shouted, "So when are we going to go to DC to kick some ass?" and when the last words left his mouth, the crowd erupted with cheers, applause, and shouts of approval.

Jerry raised his hands. "Okay, okay. I like the enthusiasm! Now settle down! At ease!"

When there were all quiet enough for him to continue, he did. "That being said, it's not going to be easy. I know for some of you this short crossing hasn't been a pleasure cruise," and there was laughter and joking around, and some good natured teasing of the few who were still seasick.

"So here it is. I'm going to lay it all out for you, and I won't sugar-coat it or feed you a load of bullshit. We can't drive all the way cross-country with the Bradleys. We can't use the Panama Canal, because it's most probably choked with derelict ships, and it would take an army of men a few years to clean up any mess that we'd face. So the next question is this, are you all prepared for an extended sea voyage?"

There were several replies in the affirmative, and more shouts of approval. When the men had settled down yet again, he went on. "I'm telling you right now it's going to be at least a month, or even longer. We'll have to sail all the way around South America, and the seas will be at times rough. It's going to be a long, messy trip, with only a few stops for fuel and food, if we can find it."

He didn't get any replies and there was silence through the hold. "Okay, so here it is. You're all volunteers, and I can arbitrarily say that we are now going. I need you all to be one hundred percent with me on this, if we have any dissent at all, we turn the ship around and head back to Pearl. Now who is with me?"

A shout went up so loud from the mass of men it echoed, in a roar, which startled a fruit bat that had somehow stowed away in the hold and was sleeping, hidden in the upper beams in the darkness. The bat screeched noisily at being disturbed, and flitted about high above everyone's head, making swooping circles, trying desperately to escape the light and the noise.

They all laughed at this, and Jerry shook his head and muttered to himself, "That's right, I must be batshit crazy!" Alright. Now that we have a consensus, you can all go back to what you were doing, and I'll go and let the good captain know we're going to DC!"

Another round of cheers, whistles, and catcalls erupted in the confines of the cargo hold. Jerry hopped down from the top of the armored fighting vehicle, and as the crowd of men dispersed, he walked over to one of the men he'd appointed as NCO. "Jimmy, I need you to keep up with the schedule of training."

The man nodded. "No problem. I'm on it."

"I mean it. I want to keep the men busy. It's going to be a long trip, and we need to keep everyone occupied. If you see anyone just sitting around, find something for them to do, okay?"

"I've got a new roster posted, and those not assigned to help with the daily operation of the ship I've got cleaning weapons and running the Bradleys for a half hour every day so the batteries don't take a shit."

"Good. And another thing, check with Mary and Steve up in the galley and see how much food we actually have. We may need to start rationing."

"Okay. I'm also going to check how much fresh water we have. We might have to start rationing that too."

"Bill said something about salt-water soap. I think he loaded a bunch of it before we left Pearl. If that's the case, we'd be better off using seawater for showers."

"Jerry," Jimmy asked, "do you think we can pull it off?"

"Pull what off?" Jerry asked. "The trip around South America or taking care of unfinished business once we get to DC?"

"Both." "Only time will tell, Jimmy. Only time will tell." He slapped the man on the back. Without another word, Jimmy departed into the ship. The bat had disappeared somewhere, and now Jerry stood alone with his thoughts.

Yeah, he thought they could do it. No problems there. But would they be able to make it in time? He fervently hoped so, for everyone's sake. He took one last look around and stalked off, making his way back to the bridge to let Johnson know they were prepared for the journey.

As he made his way through the ship, he saw several people busily working away at various mundane chores, painting rust spots, coiling ropes, mopping the floors… *decks* he corrected himself; it was a deck, and sailors swabbed the deck not mopped the floor. He smiled, and thought he'd never get used to this life at sea, he'd much prefer to be on dry land.

He made his way up to the weather deck and walked along the rail, looking out to sea. It was a pretty nice day. He saw a few seagulls approach and circle the ship, realizing they must be close to San Diego. His mind went back to his history lessons, and though of those first brave sailors who had sailed westward from Europe hundreds of years ago. They had still thought the Earth was flat then, and were sailing into the dark unknown. After months at sea, surviving raging storms and other perils, how elated they must have been when they saw the first sea birds in a long, long time, knowing they must be close to land.

He let that thought slip back into his mind and entered the superstructure, winding his way further upwards. When he passed the galley, he could smell something wonderful cooking, and his stomach rumbled when the aroma passed his olfactory senses.

He let that slip away as well; his first order of business was to let the captain know that his plan to navigate around South America and into the Atlantic Ocean was a go.

He finally made his way to the bridge, finding Johnson sitting comfortably in the captain's chair, sipping on what seemed to be a never-ending cup of coffee. *He probably bleeds coffee,* Jerry thought as he approached the chair.

Seeing Jerry come into the bridge, Johnson asked, "What's the verdict?"

"I'm surprised you didn't hear the cheering all the way up here," Jerry replied. "It's a go."

"They're all for it?"

"To a man, Bill." "Alright then," Johnson replied, then told the helmsman to steer a new course that he'd already plotted.

Jerry walked up to the windscreen and looked out over the forecastle and bow and let out a little laugh. "I love the irony."

"How's that?"

"When I was growing up, I'd hear tales from my granddad. He was a World War Two vet. He hated the water, and couldn't swim. He didn't want anything to do with the Navy, so he enlisted in the Army. I'm about the same. Swimming isn't my forte, you know," Jerry said, turning away from the window. "It's why I joined the Army myself. Anyway, he enlisted in the Army, and was trained as a tread-head in the all-black unit, 761st Tank Battalion. He had gotten shitloads of medals in France and Germany before the war was over."

"You must have been proud of him."

"I was. Pop never did like the water all that much. Myself, I think he was afraid of it. But he wanted to do his part for the war effort, and even though things were a lot different back then, as far a race goes, he went willingly," Jerry told the skipper.

Johnson enjoyed these stories, so he motioned Jerry to continue. "So how does the irony fit in?"

"I'm not sure what his thought processes were, or how he thought he'd get to Europe to fight the Krauts, but boy was he pissed when he saw that they were loading them all up on a troop ship!"

The ship was heeling to starboard, turning south, and the sun's rays changed direction, casting shadows behind Jerry as he stood, and Johnson, along with the helmsman, who had been listening silently to the story also, let out a laugh.

"I'll bet," Johnson said. "That's a good story."

"Well, like I said, I love the irony. Here I am, like him, hating the water, heading off to war in a goddamn troop ship," Jerry said, pearly-white teeth showing in deep contrast to his dark complexion.

"I'll make sure your cruise is a pleasant one, Sergeant," Johnson told him.

"You'd better. The food is good, but the nighttime entertainment leaves a lot to be desired," Jerry pointed out in mock seriousness.

"It'll be like the Love Boat."

"At least it's not a dry cruise, Skipper," Jerry replied.

"But of course. I'll always ensure the men get their daily ration of grog. And the floggings will continue until morale improves," Johnson joked.

"So here I am, going off to war in a troop ship, just like my granddad did. Hell, he might have even sailed on this tub," Jerry remarked.

"He might have at that, Jerry."

"I never thought I'd be going to war with my own goddamn country is all," he said. "I just hope we can do what's right, Bill."

"I know what you mean. It's our whole future at stake now."

"I've always thought it all wasn't about what world we live in right now, it's the world we leave for our kids," Jerry said.

"Exactly," Johnson said.

"After that terrible night, the night everyone died, I had all but given up hope," Jerry said.

"I think a lot of us had. Surviving was our only hope at all, and even then it was pretty grim."

"There was no hope, none at all. Most of us had given up hope of a god, because what all loving and omnipotent being would let that happen? I mean what the fuck had we done to deserve that?"

"Not a damn thing," Johnson replied.

"Your captain on that destroyer made life a living hell for everyone along the Pacific Rim."

"I'm sorry about that, Jerry," Johnson said, saddened by his actions on that ship.

"That's not your fault, Bill. You were caught with no escape, so don't even think about that," Jerry said. "Then, along comes Tim. He had a plan to make everything better. Maybe not the way things were, because we wouldn't want to go back to that, would we?   He wants to live in peace, build society back up, with a firm grasp of what's right and wrong. Go back to the basics of what our country was founded on. He, like the rest of us who've served in uniform, was sick to death of all the fighting. Fighting for something we'd lost sight of years ago. We didn't want to fight, but we were still willing and able to do so if the cause was right."

"And just," Johnson agreed.

"And just," Jerry said, nodding his head. "Sure as shit, once we got rid of your nutty captain and had things well together, along comes some other asshole who wants to rule the world."

"Just like that Tears for Fears song from the '80s," Johnson said and Jerry laughed.

"I haven't heard that one in years," Jerry said. "So now we're faced with a fight for our very survival, it's our freedom or enslavement. I don't take too kindly to the thought of being a slave. Too many of my ancestors had to deal with that."

"I agree with you. This is our second American Revolution, I'd guess you'd say."

"Bill, did you know that only three percent of the colonists were on the side of Washington?"

"No, I never knew that."

"It's true. I've got almost two hundred men here with me to fight. That's a full twenty percent of the population of Oahu. The percentages don't lie. This is, I think, bigger than that first War of Independence."

"And our leader, Washington, Jefferson, Paine, Adams, and Ben Franklin all rolled into one, is in trouble."

"You know," Jerry said, "he actually hates being put in the same category. He blushes and gets angry."

"Go figure, a brigade sergeant major who's humble," Johnson laughed.

"Here we are, our little one-ship task force, sailing off to make history," Jerry said.

"Task Force Resolute," Johnson said, picking up his binoculars and scanning the horizon.

"Resolute...that's a good name for it," Jerry said and walked out to the wing bridge, letting the warm breeze hit his face.

CHAPTER 24: 750
GRAINS OF DIPLOMACY

Tim sat with his back against a tree, just outside the ring of light given off by the campfire along the side of Interstate 80, halfway between Lincoln and Omaha, Nebraska.

The trip had taken them eight long days, and they had stopped for the evening. He tried to block out Colin's incessant, beer-fueled bragging, and the nightly stories got taller each night, enough so to make Tim want to beat the man unconscious. The sight of him, every day, strutting around so cockily with Tim's M3 Grease gun, infuriated him.

He held himself back, because he knew if he did that, he'd surely be killed. The men the sergeant still had were wary of him, even though he'd come along peacefully, almost docilely. He promised them he'd be no trouble, had come along without a fight, without thoughts of escape, and they had left him to his own devices for the most part.

He sat puffing on his now battered pipe, lost in his own depression, thankful that they'd let him have his one simple pleasure. Waves of emotion washed over him, the thoughts of his infant son, of Holly gone now, of Robyn, lying in her bed bruised, battered, and crying as he left, knowing he'd probably never see her again. He knew it was depression, and his appetite had suffered considerably, but he couldn't shake it.

They'd departed the very next day after the ambush and his subsequent surrender and good to his word, the sergeant had complied with his terms, leaving Jimenez, Robyn, and Izzy back in Williams, not looting, taking only what they'd need, leaving the three survivors enough to get by at least one winter by themselves. Besides, there was only so much you could cram into one deuce and a half.

With each mile covered, his depression grew darker, and his mind went over, time and time again, things he'd should have done differently. If he could turn back time, somehow he could make it all better for his now destroyed dreams.

His mood and gloominess waned slightly when they had entered Nebraska, and every mile travelled eastward across the empty, deteriorating highway he looked out, hoping to get a glimpse of Dawn Redeagle, his huge teepee, and what now must be his vast herd of bison grazing lazily over the plains. With every day that passed, the scenery staying the same, never seeing his old friend or even a sign of his passing, Tim's mood sunk lower and lower again, and now it was threatening to completely consume him.

He'd not felt this low since the first weeks back in Philadelphia so many years ago, and the big Australian's crowing over the campfire did nothing to alleviate the feelings. Tim sat alone in the darkness, his eyes burning holes into the bragging man's back, who stood by the fire, casting shadows across the desolate rest area, and his audience sat rapt, eating up every word.

Tim caught movement out of the corner of his eye, and turned to see the sergeant approaching, holding two canteen cups. The man came up to him, squatted down, and handed him one of the steaming cups. "Here's some coffee, Sar' Major." Tim took the offered cup, brought it up to his lips and sipped the bitter black drink. They had no sugar, and he grimaced slightly. He nodded his thanks to the sergeant.

The sergeant sat down next to Tim. "I want to thank you for not trying anything."

"What choice do I have?"

"You could try to escape."

Tim chuckled morosely. "Where would I escape to?" he asked, waving his free hand out into the darkness. "There's nothing and nowhere to escape to."

"You do have to eat something, you know. You haven't eaten anything all day."

"Fattening the calf before the slaughter?" Tim replied ruefully.

"No, not at all. You're my prison—"

"Don't remind me," Tim cut in.

"And as my prisoner, you're my responsibility."

"Your hospitality overwhelms me, Sergeant."

"Look, Flannery, I'm just following orders."

"I vas just followink orders, Mien Herr," Tim muttered in a bad German accent.

"That's uncalled for. You of all people should know about following orders."

"Legal, moral orders, yes," Tim said.

"We have a real president, and the Constitution, and everything back in DC. Civilization is coming back, and so will the country."

"Ah, yes, the president. Wasn't he the secretary for Urban Development before everyone died?" Tim asked, eyebrow raised.

"That doesn't matter. He was the legal successor. Now he's in charge, and he's issued me orders."

"The one who holds the conch," Tim said, nodding slowly.

"The what?"

"The conch. Have you ever had a chance to read the novel *Lord of the Flies?*"

"No, I never read it."

"It's about a group of schoolboys who got marooned on an island, and started to govern themselves," Tim said, staring out into the night.

"What's that got to do with anything?"

"These boys find this conch shell. Whoever holds it has the say. They start out okay at first, but the whole thing deteriorates into chaos, and they turn into savages."

"Are you saying we're like that?"

"Not exactly, but I know all about your little dystopian paradise your president has got set up. Sounds like a real garden spot, I tell you."

"It hasn't been easy," the sergeant admitted, wondering where Flannery had gotten that information. "If you want to make an omelet, you have to break some eggs."

"Swell," Tim snorted. ":You're quoting Lenin now. His ideas of a Utopia kind of took a shit, too."

"But—"

"But nothing. All we wanted was to be left alone. We had everything we needed and weren't bothering anyone. Every step of the way, around every fucking corner, was some asshole trying to take what we had away. You're not the first."

"We all want it to be back the way it was before," the sergeant replied.

"Well, it's *not* the way it was before. It'll never get back to that," Tim spat. "Now you've got your little pocket of what you call civilization, ruled by the one holding the conch, and you're taking me back. You'll hoist my body up on a petard as an offering to the beast. I know how it works, Sergeant."

"Where do you get the idea it's so bad back there?"

"Sergeant, I know all about the food shortages, the riots, the summary executions, the lack of electricity, running water, the sickness and disease, and frankly, I didn't want any part of it. Yeah, a real dystopian paradise," Tim said, setting down the canteen cup, and refilling his pipe. He struck a match, puffed a few times to get the bowl lit, and looked at the sergeant through the smoke with hot, burning eyes.

"How do you know so much?"

"A little bird told me."

"Look. I've got my orders, and my orders were to go out, arrest you, and bring you back."

"Arrest me? Is that what I am, under arrest?" Tim asked.

"Yes, that's exactly what you are."

"I'm not even going to ask what the charges are, Sergeant. You said you have a president and the Constitution, is that right?"

The sergeant remained silent, but nodded his head.

"Alright, so you have that. And the rule of law, correct?"

"Yes, damn it!" the sergeant said a little too loudly, making some of his men glance over from the campfire. He called out that everything was alright, and returned his attention to Tim.

"I guess the president threw out the Posse Comitatus rule then?" Tim said.

"What do you mean?" the sergeant asked, knowing damn right well what Tim was talking about.

"Oh come on now, Sergeant. You were a cop, and an MP. You should know good and well what the Posse Comitatus rule is. The Federal government cannot use the Army for police powers inside of the fifty United States. You, as an active duty NCO should know this, by rote. You have no arrest powers over me, and by doing so, have broken the law yourself."

The look on his captor's face told the tale, and Tim knew he'd gotten control again. But how to put it to use?

"Look, Flannery," the sergeant said in exasperation, "I've got a wife back in DC. I have other things I have to think about too."

"You're all equal back there, but some of you are far more equal than the others. I bet you even have a really nice house you and your woman call home, don't you?" Tim said. "I had a wife and a child back in Arizona myself, but they're both spread across a mountainside now, aren't they? All because the one holding the conch wanted something I had. He was more worried about a set of codes than getting the lights on, or getting the water running, or setting up farms to grow food for you all."

"That wasn't supposed to happen."

"No, I guess it wasn't. Same as billions of people dropping dead in one fell swoop wasn't supposed to happen. But it did. Your president had the golden opportunity to make everything right, but he got a taste of power and it lured him in. Now everyone that survived has got to suffer because he wants to rule the world."

"It'll happen. It's just going to take time, is all," the sergeant said, but his voice betrayed his feelings. He still wondered how Flannery knew about the riots and the food shortages, though he'd save those questions for later. "Look, Flannery, these decisions were made—"

"Far above your pay-grade, I know. I've used it far too many times myself when I actually didn't make the decisions. I stopped taking orders from those people the moment the world took a shit."

The sergeant looked away, not wanting to look into Tim's eyes, for fear of him seeing into his soul. The handful of men sitting around the fire burst out into laughter, at one of Colin's stories, no doubt. What was it this time, he wondered? How many women he'd fucked? How he scored the winning goal in a football game? Flannery was right on one account, that Colin asshole was full of shit.

Tim changed the subject then, not wanting to push the sergeant over the edge. He'd said what he meant to say, getting exactly the reaction he had hoped for, to place some doubt into his mind about what he was actually doing. "So, Sergeant, how long exactly did it take you to get out to Arizona?"

"It took a week short of two months."

Tim did a little mental arithmetic. "Hmm. I figure a little less time getting back, now that you've scouted a way. That'll still put us back after winter hits."

"Yeah, I know," he assented, taking another sip of his cooling coffee. "I was hoping we could get back sooner."

"I didn't think the roads would be as bad so quickly myself," Tim said.

"Most of the bridges across the Mississippi are down or impassable. We had to go as far north as Minnesota to cross. The whole greater Mississippi Valley has been flooded several times from the looks of it. Not much left."

"Only seven years. The Earth has a way of taking back what's hers, eh?" Tim asked, for the first time in a genuinely friendly tone.

"Yeah, it has, hasn't it?"

"The nights are getting longer, and colder. I hope we can get to DC before the snows hit. I don't look forward to riding out a winter with his sorry ass," Tim said, pointing a thumb at Colin, who had the men around the campfire roaring with laughter again.

"If that happens, you'll have to fight me for the chance to kill him, Flannery," the sergeant said, smiling wryly.

"Don't worry, I will," Tim said.

"Kill him or fight me?"

"Both," Tim said. "Now, if you don't mind, I'd like to get some sleep."

"Are you going to sleep out here?" the sergeant asked, standing up and tossing out the remainder of his coffee.

"Yeah, I've got my fartsack right here. Don't worry, I'll still be here in the morning," Tim said, pulling up his rucksack and taking out his sleeping bag.

"Just remember, no funny shit, okay?"

"I promise, Sergeant. You were good at your word back in Williams; I'll be good at mine."

"I'll leave you be then. See you in the morning, Sergeant Major."

"I'll have a nine AM wakeup," Tim called back to the man, who didn't bother to answer him, just shrugged and walked away. Tim smiled, knowing he'd gotten under his captor's skin this time. He'd probably lay awake all night thinking of what Tim had said to him.

He shucked his boots, unrolled his sleeping back, and rolled up his field jacket for a pillow. Climbing in, he shut out the noise of the men still at the fire, curled up, and with new thoughts running through his mind he fell asleep right away, and slept soundly for the first time in over a week.

The next morning, after everyone was roused from sleep, the sergeant made short work of rallying the men together and getting all their gear repacked and ready for travel.

Tim was in the rear seat of the sergeant's Hum-Vee, sitting behind the driver on the left hand side. The sergeant was in the 'shotgun' seat in the front. The rest of the men were dispersed in two other Hum-Vees and Tim's deuce and a half, and the little convoy was now nearing the outskirts of Omaha.

Tim had the window rolled down, letting the breeze hit his face. It was a pleasant morning, not too hot, not too cold, a few puffy clouds in the deep blue sky. It would have been a perfect day had it not been for the circumstances in which he found himself. He had felt fine the previous evening, though now, in the harsh light of day, his depression returned with a vengeance. His mind drifted back to the US Army's Code of Conduct, a list of six articles that he'd sworn to abide by. He'd never even thought of violating them before, now that he'd broken the second rule: *Article II: I will never surrender of my own free will. If in command, I will never surrender the members of my command while they still have the means to resist.* His heart sank.

He'd done what he had to do, not so much for his sake, but for the sake of Robyn, Izzy, and Jimenez. He thought about what he'd told the sergeant the previous night, that he'd not try to escape, and then though of Article III: *If I am captured I will continue to resist by all means available. I will make every effort to escape and to aid others to escape. I will accept neither parole nor special favors from the enemy,* and he knew in his heart of hearts that he'd have to try.

He didn't have long to wait. Just after they had passed the road sign stating they'd entered the city of Omaha, there was a loud thump, like they'd hit something in the road, and Tim felt it through his seat in the rear of the Hum-Vee.

The engine chugged a few times, and then seized in a cloud of steam and white smoke, stopping it dead in its tracks.

"What the fuck was that?" the sergeant demanded.

"I dunno, Sarge," the driver said.

There was another thump, and this time the driver's side windshield exploded, a neat round hole appearing, cracks spreading out in the tempered glass like a spider's web. A millisecond later, the driver's head disappeared in a crimson mist, spraying the inside of the vehicle with blood, brain matter, and bits of bone.

Instinctively, Tim opened the door to the Hum-Vee, hitting the asphalt hard, and rolling away onto the shoulder of the road, seeking cover. He shimmied underneath the guardrail and into a drainage ditch, trying hard to get as low as possible.

He heard other men in the vehicles shouting, and dared to lift his head high enough to see what was going on. There was a whoosh over his head, and he saw a man who had jumped out of the rear of the truck fall backwards onto the ground, a loud audible slap as if a hand had hit him in the chest. Seconds later, Tim heard the distant crack of a large caliber rifle. Someone was shooting at them, but who?

The whoosh and then the crack followed several more times, and each round fired damaged another of the small convoy's vehicles. Whoever was shooting at them was doing a damn good job of disabling all of the vehicles and spreading terror in the unit.

With the exception of the driver of the Hum-Vee and the man who had rashly decided to stand out in the open, no other people had been hit, and now they were all taking cover on the opposite side of the road from where Tim had sought refuge.

He could hear the sergeant yelling out to the men, trying to gain some sort of order in the chaos, Tim all but forgotten in the confusion. Tim chanced another look, and saw that all of the vehicles were now completely disabled from the gunfire. Whoever was shooting at them had to be using a big .50 caliber rifle to do this amount of damage and still not be seen, and the shots were being fired from quite a distance.

He decided to use this opportunity to escape now, not caring who was shooting at them. He started to slowly back away from the top of the ditch, thinking of getting as much real estate as he could between him and the sergeant's men, when he felt a weight on his back, and then a rough, strong hand pressed against his mouth, clamping tight.

His thoughts of escape now dashed, he deflated and went limp. He felt the hot breath of whoever was laying on his back by his ear, and then heard a man whisper, "Don't move, and don't make a sound!"

His mind raced, wondering if he should fight or just give in, then something in his head told him not to resist, that this voice was familiar and he should heed the words.

"Gary Owen!" came another whisper, and the hand slowly moved away from his mouth. Tim turned, and was face to face with his old friend, Dawn Redeagle, his long, dark hair tied back, a red headband tied around his brow. Tim's eyes lit up.

"I'll explain later. Follow me!" Dawn said, and set off down the drainage ditch in a crouched run. Tim lay there for a moment, stunned, and then set out behind the man, crouching, hoping they hadn't been seen.

Tim needn't have worried; the still unseen gunman had the rest of the party pinned down, and every few moments, another whoosh, then the following crack came, and somewhere, now behind the fleeing pair, softball-sized divots of asphalt were exploding in front of the cowering soldiers, effectively keeping their heads down.

The two men ran along the length of the ditch for several yards before Redeagle took a left and headed through some tall grass going north, where there were several dilapidated houses standing.

Redeagle rounded the side of the closest house, followed closely by Tim. When they got to the side of the house completely hidden from the highway, Tim saw the old Chevy Suburban parked, engine idling. Redeagle jumped in behind the steering wheel, tossing his M16 onto the dashboard.

Tim got in on the passenger side, Redeagle put the vehicle in gear, and laying a goodly amount of rubber on the weed-overgrown suburban street, tore off away from the pinned down men on the highway.

"Well that was rather exciting!" Redeagle said, a grin splitting his face.

"I'll say," Tim replied, breathless from the sprint, looking back over the seat to see if anyone was following. "How did you know?"

"I don't think anyone will be following, Tim," Redeagle replied, turning the wheel and coming to an abrupt stop in front of a six-story office building where he shut . off the engine. "Good intel, Tim. And it's really good to see you!"

"Shit, it's good to see you too. It's been a long time."

"That it has. Come on, there a few people that will be just as glad to see you also," Redeagle said, hopping out of the Suburban, taking his M16. Tim trailed him into the building through a shattered glass door, their booted feet crunching on the glass-strewn, tile-floored lobby.

Tim glanced over to the receptionist's desk, seeing the mummified body of what appeared to be a night watchman, his thermos covered with dust on the counter. The sight gave him a chill.

Redeagle headed over a door marked 'Fire Escape' and then saw the look on Tim's face at the sight behind the desk. "I don't think I'll ever get used to that myself."

"Some things I guess we'll never get used to." "I think it'll be up to our grandchildren to finish cleaning up the mess," Redeagle said, pushing open the door, exposing the darkened interior to a set of concrete stairs that led up into the building. He pulled out a flashlight and lit up a narrow part of the stairwell. He started up the stairs, Tim following closely behind.

"I normally try to stay away from built-up parts of the country," Redeagle said, "but sometimes there's no alternative. It's getting dangerous. Things are starting to fall apart. Just last year, I was over in Lincoln and the whole façade of a building collapsed right in front of me."

"Every time I go into a town, I see more and more houses and buildings falling apart. I knew it would happen, I just never thought it would happen so fast," Tim said in the darkness, their footfalls echoing in the narrow confines of the fire escape and they made their way farther up.

"This building is fairly new, and of mostly steel construction. I figure it has another ten or twenty years before it really starts to fall apart. It's the older, unreinforced brick structures which are falling to pieces."

"I guess the water is getting into the mortar, and the freeze/thaw cycles are doing the rest."

"The weeds and plants taking root, also. The roots get into the tiny crevasses, and act like little hydraulic jacks, gradually pushing apart the buildings when the plants and trees grow bigger. Soon, most of the older buildings will be piles of rubble, I'm afraid."

They reached the landing at the top of the stairs, standing in front of a gray metal door marked 'roof'. Redeagle placed his hand on the doorknob, and smiled at Tim in the darkness. He opened the door and Tim squinted in the sunlight. As his eyes readjusted, he followed Dawn out onto the sun-bleached tar paper roof where industrial sized air conditioning units sat silent, like the gravestones of the building's former occupants.

The pair walked out onto the roof, and Tim immediately saw two other men by the parapet, two lawn chairs set up, and a big, Barrett M82 semi-automatic .50 BMG sniper rifle, bipod still extended, set up on the edge overlooking the highway almost a thousand yards away.

Standing by the bizarre setup, was Sam Didinato and John Meadows. Both were smiling broadly, and Tim came up to them, grinning. Sam hugged Tim tightly.

"Tim, I'm so glad to see you!"

"I'm glad to see you two, myself," Tim said, hugging him and slapping him on the back. "There's nothing like 750 grains of diplomacy, eh? So how the hell did you know?"

"We had been following the fuckers, like you know, but we lost them outside of Albuquerque, then Taco go hold of us and let us know what had happened," he said sadly. "I'm sorry about Holly and your kid, Tim."

"It's too late to do anything about that."

"Anyway," Sam went on, "me and John decided to release the buffalo and ride as fast as we could back to Redeagle."

"We had to help in some way, mate," John added. "We figured they'd come back east the same way they came."

"You decided to rescue me," Tim stated grimly. "I'll have you know that second shot came within a red cunthair of taking my head off. I heard the fucker whiz by my goddamn ear!"

"Sorry," Sam said with a sheepish grin. "Here's a rag, you've got a little brains and shit on you." He handed Tim a rag he produced from his back pocket. Tim took the offered rag and wiped the blood and brains from his face. "Hell, Tim, it was easy. Just like shooting Hajji in the Ghan."

Tim looked over the parapet, southward towards the highway where he could see the vehicles, now all disabled by the rifle fire. Several of the sergeant's men were milling around, now feeling safe enough to venture out in the open.

"Are you going to let them go?" Tim asked.

"I don't see a reason to waste any more ammo. They're not going anywhere anytime soon unless they want to walk. I put a round into each engine block. They're hoofing it now," Sam said. "We've got a camp set up on the other side of the Missouri River in Council Bluffs," Redeagle said. "It overlooks the interchange between I-80 and I-29. We can drive there and see which way they're going if you want a little retribution."

"Let's get some distance between us and them, and we'll decide what to do then. Thanks again," Tim said.

The men packed up all of their gear and headed down to the lobby, all four of them doing their best to ignore the dead watchman, and piled into the Suburban.

With Redeagle at the wheel, they sped through the deserted and decaying city at breakneck speed, reaching the camouflaged camp in less than a half hour. There were two tents set up under an Army cammo net about two hundred yards off the highway between two vine covered buildings sitting atop a rise. Tim also saw that two horses were tied up farther behind the camp, happily grazing on the tall grass.

Sam took the big rifle and set it back up in a place he'd already prepared as an observation post. Tim had immediately stripped down to his waist, and Redeagle put a pot of water on a camp stove to boil.

While Tim was washing up, John broke out a few MRE packs and handed them out. When Tim was finished, he sat down in one of the folding camp chairs, set the MRE packet down on the ground next to him, and retrieved his pipe from his pocket. While he filled the bowl up and the other men dug into their meals, his mind went through the various options that lay before him.

He could head back to Arizona to be with Robyn, Jimenez, and Izzy, but it would only be a matter of time before this asshole president sent out more people to bring him back.

He lit his pipe, puffing away. "So Taco got hold of you?"

"Yeah. He told me they're alright, or as alright as they can be. He's scared though. I could hear it in his voice," Sam said.

"Tell me what you know."

"Taco let us know everything that happened. I think he got hold of Jerry too."

"Jerry was on his way from Oahu. Not sure how much good that will do now."

"Me and John made up our minds to leave the buffalo and ride as fast as we could back to where Dawn was." "Fucking oath, my arse is still sore!" John said.

"I'll bet," Tim grinned. "Go on."

"We rode until we Dawn."

"When they told me what happened, Tim, I couldn't sit there and let it happen. It was my idea to try to free you, if we could," Redeagle said.

"We figured we had a day or two to get ahead of them, so we hopped into the Suburban and found that building overlooking 80," Sam explained. "I decided to create enough confusion that you might have a chance to slip away."

"You sure did do that. I still say that second round was just a teensy bit too close," Tim said.

"I had no idea you were in that lead Hum-Vee, Sar' Major, or I wouldn't have taken out the driver like that," Sam said defensively.

"Do you have any idea what you'd like to do, Tim?" Redeagle asked.

"Sort of. I found out some intelligence while I was with them. Apparently almost all of the bridges spanning the Mississippi are down or impassable. They had to go all the way into Minnesota to find a crossing."

"Then we know which way they'll go," Sam replied.

"I was thinking that since we have the vehicle, I can try to stay a couple of steps ahead of them all the way, and harass the fuck out of them all the way back to DC. If you'll let me use it, that is."

"Hell, Sar' Major, we'll all go!" Sam told him emphatically.

"No, I won't hear of it. I'm going alone."

"No, Sar' Major, we're going with you," Sam stated.

Tim looked into all of their faces for a moment, and then nodded, "Okay. But, Dawn, you've done enough."

"I don't mind helping," Redeagle replied.

"You've done enough. I know that you've got your own settlement, and a family to worry about. I'm not going to hear of it. I thank you so much for what you've done, and you took a huge risk this morning for me. Now time for you to head back and get on with what you've got."

The old Native American sat silent for a few moments, and let the words Tim had just said sink in. "Alright, Tim. At least let me help you a little today, and then I'll head out in the morning."

"Thank you," Tim said. "There's been too much heartbreak already. I'd hate to think of your woman and child without you. Sam, any ideas?"

"I figure it'll be a couple of days before they get their wits about them. They'll either be walking, or have another vehicle, though I think they'll be on foot for a while."

"Agreed," Tim said, puffing on his pipe, feeling a little more like his old self with each passing minute.

"With that in mind," Sam said, "I figure you and John head east tomorrow along I-80, and I'll hang back a bit. I'll keep an eye on them, and ride my horse forward, reporting their movements to you by the sat-radio."

"Sounds like a plan," Tim said. "And then we can fuck with them along the way."

"We'll take it to them," Sam said. He handed over his M4. "I think you'll need this. I've got another one."

Tim took the carbine, placing it on the ground next to the forgotten MRE. "I'll take the Barrett, too."

"Sure thing. I found it in a gun shop in Lincoln. I've got about two hundred rounds for it too."

"I'm sure I'll put it to good use," Tim said, grinning evilly.

"Oh, another thing, Taco told me that Colin fucker was with them. Is that true?" Sam asked.

"Yeah," Tim said, fire in his eyes. "I've got a special treat for him too if I can get my hands on the bastard."

"Sar' Major, you may have to stand in line," Sam said.

Tim let that statement hang in the air, and with nothing more to be said at the moment, they went about tidying the camp in preparation for nightfall.

When the sun had slipped below the Rocky Mountains well off to the west, Tim sat alone, his back to a tree, looking out over the deserted highway below the hidden camp. He sensed, more than heard, movement to his rear, and turned to see Dawn Redeagle approaching almost silently in the waning daylight.

He sat next to Tim, looking out at the same sight.

"It never ceases to sadden me," Redeagle said, "looking out at the empty highways like this."

"It does the same thing to me, Dawn. All the people gone..."

"We have to try to make a better world for our children, Tim."

"I fucking tried, Dawn. They wouldn't let me," Tim spat bitterly.

"Now you want retribution, and I sympathize. Do me a favor?"

"What's that?" Tim asked, looking into his friend's eyes in the approaching darkness.

"Please stay on the moral high ground. Don't debase yourself and let yourself be dragged down to their level."

"Dawn, all I can say is I will try. I can't promise anything else."

Redeagle nodded, leaving it at that. He'd said what he wanted to say. It would be up to Tim now to either heed his words or not.

"Any ideas on what you'll do if you're successful enough to make it all the way back to Washington?"

"I guess I'll cross that bridge once I get to it," Tim replied.

"Another word of advice," the old Arapaho man said. "Don't go and burn that bridge once you've crossed it."

"Again, I can't promise anything. I've made too many promises to people I couldn't follow through on. Now I just want a pound of flesh."

"Just make sure that pound of flesh isn't rotten and maggot-infested."

"I understand," Tim told his friend, remembering the words that Robyn had said, through tear-filled eyes: *Daddy, you've got to kill all of them.* Those words were burned into his soul, and it was one promise he told himself, he would keep, even if it took him getting killed to do it.

"It's the world we'll leave for future generations, if we're to survive as a people. Let's not leave them a world filled with hate, okay?"

"Hate is all I've got left now."

"Don't let it burn you alive," Redeagle said, patting him on the knee, and slipping away back towards the camp, leaving Tim alone to watch the last of the sun's rays slip behind the mountains to the west.

CHAPTER 25:
HIT AND RUN

Tim lay prone on a cold, windswept hill overlooking Interstate 70, halfway in between Hagerstown and Frederick, Maryland, the big .50 caliber rifle in front of him. John Meadows was lying next to him, shivering in the mid-December morning, temperature only in the teens with no indication of warming.

The sun was blotted out by a heavy gray blanket of clouds, which threatened snow, while the two men waited for the radio to come to life. The three men had played cat and mouse with the sergeant's party all the way from Iowa, and now, eight weeks later, were only a day's journey away from Washington, DC.

From Iowa, Tim had let his quarry start out eastward for a few days, letting them get their guard down before making the first strike. It wasn't a big strike as far as combat was concerned, just a single shot fired, killing one of the sergeant's men from a distance of over 900 yards. The big Barrett rifle was good at that. The soldiers on the road never even heard the shot until the unlucky man was lying dead in the center of the road, gaping hole in his chest, a pool of blood spreading out from his lifeless body.

And so it went.

Over the preceding weeks, Tim and John raced ahead in the battered old Chevy Suburban fueled by propane, Sam Didinato on his horse staying well off in the distance, radioing ahead to Tim the location of and direction in which the sergeant's party was travelling.

The road leading back towards Iowa was marked with the bodies of the sergeant's men, strewn out over the countryside like breadcrumbs. Sometimes Tim would let them go on for days without taking a shot, then hit them, never taking more than one shot in a day. The psychological impact of his actions was devastating to the travelers, and exactly what Tim had planned on doing.

What was left of the sergeant's unit was now a shattered shell of what it once had been. The men were jumpy and shot at anything that appeared even slightly to be a threat to them. He knew that none of them slept anymore, especially after what Tim at the time though was a foolhardy and unnecessary chance.

One evening, three weeks prior, Didinato decided on his own to really screw with them. Using all of his years of field craft, he sneaked right into their enemy's camp and made off with their only radio, leaving them alone and directionless.

Scared, paranoid, cold, and hungry, they were now nearing where Tim and John had set up their sniper's nest again. Tim listened for the sound of the approaching old and rusted Buick Skylark that he had allowed his prey to get running a few weeks prior.

It was the third vehicle the sergeant's beleaguered party had obtained on the harrowing journey back east, and Tim had let them travel, once even let them get a whole week, before putting a.50 caliber bullet through the engine block.

He had several chances to disable the vehicle, and with the.50, it would have been just as easy to deny them transportation. He'd reckoned he'd give them one last straw of hope to grasp onto, no matter how tenuous and fleeting that hope would be, because this would be the finale, right here this very morning, Tim had decided the evening before.

"Shit, mate! How do did you Yanks ever learn to live in this fucking cold!" John said, his breath coming out in wisps of steam that dissipated rapidly in the cold, bitter wind.

"You never get used to it. I know I never did," Tim said, bringing his binoculars up to his eyes and scanning the empty road before him. He dropped the glasses onto the ground inches from his face and scratched at the three weeks' worth of beard he'd let grow. The itching was beginning to annoy him.

"I used to think three or four degrees Celsius was cold. This is just fucked," John said, shuddering. "I can't feel me fucking feet."

"Be thankful it hasn't started snowing yet," Tim said, gazing up into the slate gray sky. "We've been lucky so far, though I think that's about to run out."

"I wish it would warm up a bit."

"So do I, but we'll have to wait until April now," Tim said.

The radio crackled to life. Tim picked it up and heard Sam's voice, clear, steady and calm, come over the tiny speaker.

"Tim, this is Sam, do you read me, over?"

"I copy you, Lima Charlie, over."

"They've just started out. They should be at your position in about two zero minutes, over."

"Thanks. Start making your way here. The fun is about to start. Out," Tim said, stowing the radio into his ACU pants pocket. "John, get ready."

John readied his carbine while Tim tucked the butt of the rifle into his shoulder and peered through the Bushnell 10X40mm rifle scope out at the road before them.

The cold wind was coming from directly behind them, making Tim happy that he'd not have to adjust for windage. It still chilled the two men lying in wait, but it shouldn't affect the flight of the bullets.

They heard the approaching car a few minutes before they saw it. Looking through the scope, Tim saw the old, rusted Buick appear around a bend in the road five hundred yards west of them, thumbed off the safety, and centered the scope's crosshairs on the left front tire. Taking in a deep breath, he pulled the butt stock tight into his shoulder, placed his right index finger on the cold metal trigger, exhaled, and squeezed. When the trigger broke five pounds, the gun barked loudly, and the recoil Tim felt was satisfying. The bolt travelled rearward violently, ejecting the spent round, and started forward again, stripping off another fresh round out of the magazine, chambering it, slamming it home, ready for another shot. All this happened in a millisecond, just as designed.

When he recovered his sight picture that was momentarily knocked askew from the rifle's recoil, Tim took another look through the riflescope. The tire was already flat, a big chunk of rubber missing and flopping around the wheel well as the car came to a stop. Satisfied that his shot was right where he wanted it, Tim waited, keeping the crosshairs on his target.

To the vehicle's occupants, it would appear at first to be just a blowout, for they wouldn't have heard the shot at all from inside the old car. It rolled to a stop along the overgrown shoulder and the driver exited, squatting down in front of the ruined tire to inspect it.

Tim placed the crosshairs directly between the man's shoulder blades, and when the man stood suddenly and shouted something unheard to the vehicle's occupants, Tim squeezed the trigger, the round striking his target right where he wanted.

A gout of blood erupted from the man's chest, spraying in a fan over the car's windshield, and he dropped lifeless in a crumpled mass by the left fender of the car.

"Good shooting," John whispered.

Tim stood, picking up his M4 carbine. "Follow me."

**

Jimenez climbed the wooden staircase to the second floor of the house wearily, having just finished a rather unpleasant task that took him most of the morning. He peeled off his t-shirt, which was soaked with sweat in spite of the cool autumn morning.

Using it as a rag, he wiped his brow and chest and plodded off down the hallway to the bedroom that he and Robyn shared. He slowly opened the door, and peering inside, saw Robyn lying quietly, eyes closed. Her left arm and right leg were covered in stark-white plaster, and her complexion matched, for she was growing paler every day, and getting more and more lethargic, to Jimenez' horror.

He sat on the edge of the bed. Her eyes fluttered open weakly, and he brushed a loose strand of hair away from her eyes. "Hey, baby," he said, bending down and kissing her on the forehead.

"Hey, Taco," she replied, "is it done?"

"Yeah," he replied sadly. "I got him out over by that tree he liked to sit under."

"I wish I could have helped you, babe," she said.

"It's alright. I handled it."

"Izzy was my friend, too, Taco," she said, starting to cry.

"I understand. The only thing I want you to do is get better."

"I'm trying, honey, but I feel worse," she said.

Jimenez put his hand on her forehead, and felt how hot she was. He took a rag that was soaking in a bowl of water on the nightstand, wrung it out and put in on her head, not knowing what else to do.

"I'm racking my brain for anything that will help you feel better," he told her, and wondered if she didn't have some sort of internal injuries that Izzy hadn't found. Her lower abdomen was swollen, hard to the touch, and each day she grew paler, and wasn't able to hold down any food.

If she didn't eat soon, she'd waste away to nothing. He was scared, very scared. Over the last few weeks, he'd seen the wound that Izzy had received in his knee fester, in spite of the hefty doses of antibiotics he was taking, until the leg turned gangrenous, and finally, unable to do anything more, the blood poisoning had run rampant in his old, tired body.

Izzy had finally succumbed to it the previous evening, and that was what Jimenez had spent the entire morning doing, burying his friend at the edge of the forest. In the late morning sunlight coming through the bedroom window, he was witnessing Robyn slowly get sicker, and it tore him apart.

He hadn't felt this alone, this hopeless, since the very start, when everyone died, and he was rapidly losing control of his emotions. Try as he might, he couldn't hold it in any longer, and started to cry unabashedly. He knew he needed to stay strong for her, he just couldn't hold it in any longer.

He rested his head on her chest and wept, and Robyn took her good arm and held him as tightly as she could.

"Babe, I'm so scared," he said in between sobs.

"I know, Taco. I'll be alright. Daddy always said I was too ornery to die," she said, which instead of reassuring him, elicited another bout of sobbing from Jimenez.

"I don't know what else to do!"

"You need to Ranger up, goddamn it! Get some intestinal fortitude!" she said.

"I'm trying, I really am."

"I'll get better. I just have a bug is all. Daddy will get back soon, and everything will be okay," she said to him, her voice tired but reassuring.

He thought about Tim, whom he hadn't heard from in over a month. He thought about the promise he'd made to Tim, and also of the promise he'd made to Izzy in his last gasps of air, making him promise he'd take care of Robyn. He was so full of doubt.

He lifted his head from her bosom, and through tear-streaked eyes, tried to smile weakly. Robyn wiped the tears from his eyes. She took hold of his hand and looked at his fingernails.

"You're filthy. Why don't you go get a shower, and then come back and cuddle me? You haven't done that in a while."

"What haven't I done in a while, babe?" he asked. "Cuddle you, or take a shower?"

"Both. Your personal hygiene has been lacking considerably, Lance Corporal."

"Babe, I love you so, so much," Jimenez said.

"I love you too, Taco. Now go, I'll be here when you get back."

He stood and gazed down at her, frowning. She was already asleep again, eyes closed, holding onto Bad Bear tightly.

He trod silently out of the room, closing the door gently. He made his way down the narrow corridor to the bathroom, where he stripped out of his dirty clothes, turned on the hot water in the shower and let the steam fill the room. The hot water gradually eased the aches and pains of his muscles, and when he started to feel better he lathered up and scrubbed the dirt from his body, digging the encrusted red Arizona soil from under his fingernails.

Rinsing off, he let his mind wander, bringing back memories of the past, of his growing up in the Barrio of South Phoenix, all the horrible things he'd witnessed in his young life, and how, when it seemed like his life had no purpose left after everyone had died, Tim and Robyn had come along, changing things forever.

He'd joined the Marine Corps, hoping to get away from the squalor, and had thought that had made him into a man. He had been sadly mistaken. It took the end of the world and that grizzled old sergeant major to make him into a man, and Robyn, the love of his life, to teach him of responsibility.

Yet again, his life had been turned upside down. Tim was gone, and no matter how much Robyn wished and hoped, he probably wasn't coming back. He was alone again, and even Izzy, a grandfatherly figure he was always able to talk to even when Tim wasn't available, was now dead and buried. Jimenez felt completely alone and was swiftly sinking into a pit of despair.

Not bothering to get dressed, he padded back towards the bedroom naked thinking of Robyn again, and how sick she was becoming. She was lying on the bed angel-like, the late morning sun coming through the window bathing her in golden light.

He drew the curtains closed, darkening the room considerably, tiptoed back to the bed, and carefully crawled in beside Robyn. He put his arm around her, and in her slumber, she moved closer to him, nestling up to his naked body.

He sighed again, kissed her head, and whispered, "Baby, I don't know what I'm going to do if you leave me."

***

Tim circled around a dilapidated shed near the road, and when he got within a few yards of the disabled Buick, he could hear the voices of the sergeant and Colin. He squatted down in the cold morning air, using thick blackberry bushes as cover. John Meadows came up behind him silently, and Tim raised his index finger to his lips.

Tim peered around the corner of the wooden building, and could see the sergeant standing on the far side of the road, the disabled car between him and Tim, and Colin, standing near the body of the driver, hands on the M3 machinegun. The third passenger was at the rear of the vehicle, trunk open. He was rummaging around for the jack and the spare tire, it appeared.

Tim knew that the weeks of minor attacks , one or two shots here and there, had made his quarry lax, thinking this time was like all the rest. They felt comfortable, thinking that those two shots would be the only ones, and felt at ease standing in the open the way they were doing now.

Thumbing the safety off his M4 carbine to three-round burst, he motioned to John to go around the other side of the shed. "Wait for my signal," he whispered.

"What's the bloody signal?"

"You'll know," Tim responded. "Take out the fucker at the trunk."

John disappeared around the side of the shack as Tim eased his way forward. He was bringing his carbine up to his shoulder as he rounded the corner. The sergeant caught sight of him and shouted out a warning, and then dropped out of sight behind the car.

Tim swore to himself, and drew a bead on the only target he had, Colin. Colin was turning in alarm towards Tim, trying to bring the old submachine gun up to bear, but Tim beat him to the draw and let loose two rapid bursts, sending six rounds out as fast as Tim tapped the trigger.

Colin spun on his heels, screaming in pain and dropping to his knees. Tim dropped into a prone position, still holding his sights on the screaming Aussie, who finally fell into a fetal position next to the dead body in the middle of the road.

Tim heard more screaming from behind the car, and knew it must be the sergeant. He heard the sounds of another M4 firing to his right and behind him, and he saw out of his peripheral vision the man who had been by the trunk drop to the ground, the old style bumper jack clanking loudly on the asphalt, the spare tire that the man had been wrestling out of the trunk rolling away like an oversized donut.

Two down, one to go, Tim thought, straining to see where the sergeant had gone. He saw movement from underneath the car, and could then make out the sergeant's booted feet, exposed from mid-shin down.

Tim squeezed the M4's trigger, letting loose another three-round burst, skipping his shots off the pavement and underneath the car, striking the sergeant once in the ankle. The man screamed in pain, dropping his own weapon, and fell to the ground behind the car.

Tim stood cautiously, keeping the muzzle of his carbine pointed at his closest threat, the screaming Colin, writhing on the road. Never taking the rifle from his target, Tim walked over and kicked the machine gun way from his hand. John rounded the shed at this point, holding his carbine at the ready, and approached the rear of the car.

"Are you good, mate?" John called out from behind the car. "This bloke's dead."

"I'm good. Too bad this piece of shit isn't," Tim said, looking coldly into Colin's eyes. With satisfaction, he could see the terror there, and smiled when he saw a dark stain on his crotch. "Pissing yourself, already? The fun hasn't even started yet," Tim said cruelly.

John came over hurriedly, and nodded to Tim, pointing his rifle at the center of Colin's chest.

Taking another look around, Tim readied his carbine and rounded the front clip of the car, to find the sergeant seated, back to the door, grimacing and holding his ankle. Tim kept his weapon trained on the sergeant as he approached.

"Don't move a fucking muscle," Tim hissed.

"I don't plan on doing anything, Flannery," the sergeant said.

Tim reached down, taking the sergeant's M4. He fingered the magazine release, dropping the magazine out of the well onto the ground, and then racked the charging handle to eject the round in the chamber. Once the rifle was cleared, Tim tossed in onto the Buick's roof and looked down on the sergeant.

The whole time, Colin was screaming and moaning in pain loudly. Tim looked over at John, who was at the trunk, checking the gas bottles. "Shut him the fuck up, okay?" he instructed.

Walking over to the writhing man, John kicked him hard in the side of the head, silencing him, and almost as an afterthought, spat on the unconscious Aussie.

"It's always the biggest, toughest assholes who scream the loudest for their mommy, eh?" Tim said to the sergeant amiably.

They heard the clip-clop sound of a horse approaching, and Sam Didinato rode in a fast trot up to the scene. When he reached his comrades he dismounted, letting the horse wander off. Taking his own M4, he walked over to Tim, and looked down at the wounded sergeant.

"Now what?" Sam asked.

"I haven't thought that far ahead, Sam," Tim responded, squatting down and frisking his prisoner, taking the man's M9 pistol and pocketing it before he stood again. He reached into his parka's pocket, and pulled out a set of handcuffs, tossing them to Sam. "Put these on this asshole and look at his foot. Give him a Band-Aid and an aspirin."

While Sam was doing that, Tim went back around the car to where John and Colin were. A dark red splotch of blood was creeping across Colin's lower abdomen.

Kneeling down on the cold asphalt, Tim said to John, "Help me get his clothes off."

"You aren't seriously thinking of helping him now, are you, mate?"

"Fuck no. I just want to help him truly experience a wonderful winter in rural Maryland," Tim said, winking at John and unlacing Colin's boots, pulling each one off and tossing them as far as he could into the overgrown shoulder of the road.

When the two men finished stripping Colin, Tim took note of his wound. He was a little disgusted that he'd only hit him once, in the lower abdomen. It was a nasty wound, though, and there was no telling what damage the little 5.56mm bullet had done.

Tim retrieved another set of handcuffs, and tossing them to John, said, "Drag him over to that guardrail, and cuff him to it."

Tim walked back over to where Sam was tending to the sergeant's ankle. "What's the prognosis, doctor?"

"He's out of contention for the Boston Marathon this year, but he'll live," Sam quipped, wrapping the man's shattered ankle with a battle dressing. "Let's head to that farmhouse over there," Tim said. "We'll spend the night there, and then in the morning, he and I will go have a little chat with the president."

"Shit, you aren't serious, are you?"

"I am. This shit has got to end, one way or another."

"It's suicide," Sam said in alarm.

"Your man is right, Flannery. You go there now, you know what will happen," the sergeant said.

"My mind is made up, Sam. Go and get the Suburban, will you? I left it over that way about five hundred meters. It's parked behind a barn."

Dejectedly, Sam left the two men and walked off through the underbrush in the direction Tim had pointed out. Tim took in the denuded trees and shivered involuntarily. It felt like it was getting even colder, and he wanted to get into some kind of shelter soon.

He peered down the road at Colin, naked and unconscious, cuffed to the guardrail. It was a shame it was winter now. He'd liked to have tried something he'd heard of long ago. The Native Americans sometimes would take a prisoner, strip him down, and stake him to the ground over an anthill. He liked that idea for this piece of shit, but even the bears would be in hibernation by this time, and the only predators about would be a few coyotes, maybe a few wolves. The ravens and buzzards would have a feast once the big man bled out.

Tim hoped it would be a while, maybe a few days. He also hoped that he woke from his daze, so he would be awake during his suffering. Yeah. That would be fitting.

He stopped himself in mid thought, and wondered if he was turning into some kind of animal. He'd never been this sadistic before; why was he reveling in another's suffering so much?

As quickly as that thought entered his mind, he erased it, not caring about it anymore. The image of April's dead body was burned in his mind, and she needed justice, even if it meant lowering himself down to a primeval level to achieve it.

Devoid of all emotion, Tim looked down on the sergeant with icy, unblinking eyes. The sound of the approaching Suburban drew their attention, and a single crow cawed somewhere off in the distance.

***

Jimenez lay with Robyn for a long time, shadows lengthening on the far wall, sleep eluding him. Robyn was still asleep on the bed, her faced pained and her breath ragged in the darkening evening.

He was lying close to her, his arms around her tightly. He nestled into her, and kissed her neck. "Baby, please get better," he whispered. "I love you so much."

It was late, and he was mentally and physically drained from burying Izzy. He closed his tear filled eyes, finally drifting off to sleep, wishing for some kind of miracle he knew would never happen.

***

Tim, Sam, and John were in the living room of the old, rundown nineteenth century farmhouse, the sergeant lying on the floor by the fireplace, asleep. They had built a fire, warming the room considerably. They were eating an evening meal of MREs that were well past their use-by date.

Tim chewed the last bite of his chicken tetrazzini. "My word is final, guys. Tomorrow morning, you two take the Suburban and the horse, and head back to Arizona or Nebraska. Either way, I'm heading out from here alone."

"If you're not going to let us come with you, I'm going back to Arizona. I think Taco is going to need us," Sam said emphatically. "I wish you'd change your mind."

"I'm all for coming with you too," John said, sipping on a canteen cup of coffee.

"I'm not going to sit here and fucking argue with you two. I'm going with the sergeant here, you two are going back west, end of fucking story." Tim tossed the empty packet into the fire. "Sam is right about one thing, Taco is going to need you both to help with Robyn and Izzy."

"Are you sure they're alright?" John asked.

"We haven't heard from them in a few weeks, but that doesn't mean anything. We haven't heard from the sailors coming from the Pacific in a while either, so I can't say for certain either way. At this point I am choosing to think that no news is good news."

The wind had picked up, and they could no longer hear Colin's screams from where he remained cuffed to the guardrail. Tim thought that he'd probably already died in the cold. It was well below freezing now, and no one could have survived in that with no clothes on.

He wondered why Jimenez had not contacted them in the last few weeks. He had a deep, sinking feeling wash over him all of a sudden, and frowned.

"What is it, Tim?" Sam asked.

"I'm used up, Sam. I'm done," he said, "I want you guys to get the fuck away from here, head back west."

"What about you?" John asked.

"I said I was done. I meant it. Don't worry about me anymore. Once you get back there, try to finish what we started, alright?"

Neither of the other men responded, just looked at his face in the firelight. Tim stared back at the men, a cold wave of despair washing over him. Try as he might, he couldn't shake it. He didn't know why, but he felt his life was nearing an end, getting to Washington was the last thing he needed to do. Everything else he'd ever cared about and loved was now gone forever.

He had nothing left to live for now. Deeply saddened, he sensed that something terrible had happened back in Arizona.

He just had one more task to do before it was truly over…

***

Jimenez woke with a start in the darkness, bathed in sweat. He didn't know how long he'd slept or what time it was. The only thought in his mind right now was the horrible dream from which he'd awakened.

Over and over again, he saw the image of the big C-130, smoke trailing from its engines, slamming into the mountainside in a plume of red flame and black smoke.

He felt out for Robyn in the darkness. He touched her arm, and felt an icy bolt through his hand that ran all the way to his heart. He gripped her wrist and leaned over to her, placing his ear to her chest.

"Robyn! Are you okay?"

"Taco, I was asleep," she said, in a barely audible whisper.

"Oh shit, baby. Robyn, I thought you were dead!"

"I dreamed I was Taco. I'm back now."

"Back?"

"I was back in West Virginia for a while. I was running through a meadow, chasing after Geoffrey. Now I'm back," she told him in the darkness.

"Who's Geoffrey?"

"Someone from a long, long time ago, Taco. Daddy was there in the meadow too."

"Yeah, baby?" Juan asked, snuggling back up to her. "What did the Sar' Major do in your dream?"

"He told me to tell you not to dick around anymore, and do that chore he asked you to do."

Jimenez had another icy chill run down his spine and shivered involuntarily. His mind raced, and he remembered what Tim had told him about fear and how to overcome it.

"He told you to tell me that?"

"Yeah, he said to stop dicking around, and just do it. Hold me Taco, I'm so cold."

"Alright, baby."

"In the morning do what Daddy told you to do."

"Alright."

"Promise me, Taco. Promise me you'll do it."

"I promise, Robyn."

"Good. I love you, Taco," she said, sounding more like her old self.

"I love you too, Robyn," he said softly, hearing her breathing rhythmically, already fast asleep. He lay there for quite a long time, hoping it wouldn't have come down to this.

He knew it was over. He just had to do what Tim had asked.

CHAPTER 26:
THE END OF THE LINE

It had been a long, harrowing journey around Cape Horn and Tierra del Fuego into the South Atlantic Ocean. The *SS Jeremiah O'Brian*, had sailed northward through pounding seas between the Falkland Islands and the Georgia Islands, slowly but surely making her way towards their final destination.

Eight weeks later, they were only a hundred and fifty nautical miles south-southeast of the mouth of the Chesapeake Bay. Seagulls were circling the ship and it sailed westward, the sky a dark gray that threatened more snow squalls.

The wind was picking up, the seas were swelling six to eight feet, and the bow of the ancient Liberty Ship rose and fell drunkenly. All hands on board were still motivated, though morale was dwindling, as the long trek had started to take its toll. Johnson, who was now at the con, was glad they were nearing their destination. Everyone needed a rest, and soon.

He sat back in the captain's chair looking out of the forward windscreen of the bridge over the ugly gray of the Atlantic. The helmsman was fighting to keep the ship on course, and Johnson could hear his muttering curses under his breath. Johnson had a splitting headache, and the two Tylenol he'd taken hadn't eased the pain.

Suplee, who'd had the con over the midnight shift, had decided to stay up and stick around on the bridge to help Bill as they neared port, and had just come in from the wing bridge, shutting the hatch behind him with a loud bang. He removed his oilskin overcoat and hung the wet coat on a peg on the rear bulkhead.

"We're almost there, Skipper," he said.

"That we are, Harry. We should be picking up Cape Charles on the radar in about an hour," Johnson said, checking his wristwatch.

Suplee pulled out a pack of Marlboros and lit a stale cigarette with a Zippo lighter, exhaling a cloud of smoke in the overheated bridge. "You still want to bypass Norfolk and Portsmouth?"

Johnson answered, "Yes. Jerry wants us to try to get him as close to DC as possible, so I'm going to try to get as far north into the Chesapeake as possible. Annapolis will do us nicely."

"We can always sail back south to refuel and provision at Norfolk." The cigarette hanging from his lips, Suplee walked over to the windscreen and frowned, his back to Johnson. "You still having those bad feelings?"

"For a few days now. It's like something is trying to tell us this was a very bad idea. That and I've got a bear of a headache."

"I've got one too. Had it since last night," Suplee said. "I think we'll be alright. We'll tie up at Canoe U, unload Jerry's equipment and men, and get the fuck outta Dodge," Suplee stated, taking another drag off his smoke. "What do you think of the strange message we got the other day on the Ham?"

"Beats me. I did do what the guy asked, and forwarded the message to Tim. He seemed to know who the guy was, but was really, really surprised to hear from him. It was almost as if he'd heard from a ghost," Johnson said, shifting in his seat as the ship took another powerful hit from a large wave.

"It did seem kinda' odd. '*Dan Kruger from Korotonga sends him best wishes.*' Did you ever find out what he meant?"

"I asked Tim, but he never elaborated. He knew the name, that's for sure."

"What's 'Korotonga?"

"I had to look it up on the charts. It's an island in the South Pacific, Northwest of Fiji." Suplee turned on the wipers on the front windscreen as the ship entered another snow squall, the bow almost disappearing in a white cloud. He took another drag. "And the other news… that's pretty bad. I can't believe they're all dead out in Arizona."

"I know," Johnson said with a sad nod. "Tim let us know yesterday."

"Those fuckers in DC have a lot to answer for," Suplee spat angrily.

"We'll let Jerry take care of that from here on out. We've done our job."

"I guess some things never change. A royal fucking by the fuckers in DC, yet again," Suplee said. "When will it ever end?"

"I'm hoping soon, Harry."

"Did Tim say anything more?"

"No," Johnson answered. "Only that he reckons he'll be in DC today sometime."

"You'd think after everything that's happened, people would at least try to be nice to each other," Suplee said, walking over to the old vacuum-tube radar set and peering into the hooded eyepiece.

"I don't think that'll ever happen, Harry. Not in our lifetime. Maybe our kids will finally learn about how to—"

"Holy shit!" Suplee shouted.

"What is it?" Johnson asked, spinning in his seat.

"I've got something on the radar. It's big!"

"It's too soon for us to pick up Cape Charles," Johnson said, walking over to the radar.

"It's not Cape Charles. It's the wrong direction. It's big, and moving, and to the northeast," Suplee said, his voice excited.

"It's only about a thousand yards off starboard!" Johnson said. He and Suplee grabbed their binoculars and went out onto the exposed starboard wing bridge. Through the tapering snowfall, they saw the shape of a huge, gray-sided warship emerge, its bow slicing through the swells, sending out sprays of white foam. 'D97' was painted in black on the hull amidships, the way the British Navy did—unlike the white numbers, closer to the bow, as the US Navy had done— the White British naval ensign flying proudly from the mast to the rear of the main superstructure.

As the warship approached, the two sailors saw an aldis lamp start to flash from its bridge. Suplee, the faster of the two with Morse code, read the message aloud: "Ahoy *SS O'Brian*. This is the *HMS Edinburgh* of the Royal Navy, prepared to heave to."

Letting his binoculars hang from his neck from the strap, Johnson said, "Isn't this just wonderful."

***

Tim drove the battered and rusting old Buick down Wisconsin Avenue, through Chevy Chase, Maryland, and slowed when he approached the intersection of Wisconsin, Western Avenue and Military Road. He was having a difficult time keeping his thoughts in order because of a terrible headache he'd had since right after he'd gotten word from Jimenez about Izzy. Try as he might, he couldn't shake it, along with his building feelings that this was about to come to an end.

He wept inwardly about Robyn and Juan, alone out there in Arizona, but he knew there was nothing he could do now for them. He'd failed both of them so terribly. He shook off that feeling, but the pounding in his head remained.

To his right, there was a shopping mall, its parking lot now completely overgrown with weeds and short trees, cars parked forever in the asphalt lot, gradually being swallowed by the returning forest of weeds and trees.

He had reached the border between the State of Maryland and Washington, DC proper, and knew for certain he'd reached the end of the line. A pair of dirty Metro buses had been pushed together, forming a roadblock, and several Hum-Vees and military trucks were in the area, well-armed men milling around in the cold.

Tim stopped the car a few yards from the roadblock, and saw that several men had their rifles trained at his vehicle. Tim turned to the sergeant, who had said nothing all morning. He was turning a pasty gray and didn't look well at all. Tim figured his shattered ankle didn't tickle one bit.

"So, this roadblock?" Tim asked, pointing at the buses. "Is it here to keep people out, or to keep people in?"

"What do you think, Flannery?"

"Oh, you don't want to know what I'm thinking," Tim replied. He faced forward, keeping both his hands on the wheel as not to spook the armed guards approaching his car. He reached over with his left hand and rolled down the window, letting in a blast of frigid air. A man holding an M16 came to the window, pointing the muzzle right in his face.

"Who the fuck are you?" the man demanded.

"I think the proper question should be 'halt, who goes there?'," Tim said.

"I think you're a smartass," the sentry said, and thumbed off the safety.

"It's better to be a smartass than a dumbass," Tim said, smiling in spite of his splitting headache.

"Outta the car now!"

Tim moved to comply, but the other guard, who had come up to the passenger side, shouted, "Hey, it's the sergeant!"

"Yeah, it's me. Let us through, will ya?" the sergeant said.

"What happened to the major and the rest of your guys?" the guard by Tim's window asked, leaning in.

The sergeant looked over at the man and replied coolly, "He killed them," pointing at Tim.

"How did he do that?" the man asked, wide eyed.

"I used my secret magic powers, asshole. Now let us through, the president wants to see me," Tim said.

"It's *you!*" the man gasped. "You're the one!"

"I see my reputation has preceded me," Tim replied.

"Listen, soldier," the sergeant said, "I'm not fucking around, okay? Let us in. The president wants to talk with this man."

The sentry stared at the sergeant for a few seconds, blank look on his face, and then spun on his heels and made a motion for the man to open the roadblock. Several men manhandled the buses out of the way, making room for the old Buick.

A Hum-Vee with a man standing at the .50 caliber machine gun mounted on the roof started up and drove through the opening. Tim put the still running car into drive and followed, ignoring the silent stares of the sentries at the roadblock.

They entered the deteriorating city, and Tim looked around at the dilapidated buildings, unchecked weeds growing, garbage everyplace, and shook his head with disgust. Further and further they drove onward, and he began to see how bad it really was. Whole city blocks of buildings had been burned, and now stood gutted, trees growing out of cracks in the sidewalks, branches sticking out of shattered windows.

It was simply a shell of the past, and nothing anyone could do now would ever bring back its former grandeur. It saddened him to the core, only helping to accentuate his pounding headache that now threatened to tear his head off.

Word must have spread quickly, Tim thought. As they made their way deeper into the dying city, people were appearing, first in ones and twos, then more and more came out of hiding, lining their route.

They were scarecrows; skinny shells of once proud Americans now brought down to their basic level by malnutrition and hopelessness. Clothes hung loosely on skin and bones, and hollow, gaunt eyes stared back at them.

These were once people who had survived what they thought was the worst, and had come to this city in the hopes of a better life, only to have those dreams shattered by reality.

It could have all been solved had not one man, the man Tim was about to see, thought of his people first, and not himself. But that was the way of all politicians, wasn't it? Caring only of themselves and of their own luxury and wellbeing, not once thinking about their constituents, forgetting who they actually worked for.

He drove further on, following the Hum-Vee escorting them as they turned onto Pennsylvania Avenue and towards the White House. Tim tried to think of others ever since that terrible night everyone died, but it had gotten him nowhere and he was about to see exactly where it all ended in a few more minutes.

The Hum-Vee drove right into the White House grounds, past an empty guardhouse, and up to the West Wing portico, stopping under the cover. Tim pulled up behind the vehicle and shut off the engine, getting out. Two guards appeared from inside, came up to him and roughly frisked him for weapons.

They only found a Beretta M9 pistol in his waistband, tossing it onto the Buick's roof. They spun him around and shoved him towards the doors.

"You better take your sergeant to a doctor. He's got a bum ankle," Tim remarked.

The two guards ignored him and pushed him through the doors into the West Wing lobby, and then to the left down a dimly lit corridor. Reaching the end, they made another left hand turn; walking past the Cabinet Room until finally they reached the door leading into the Oval Office.

THOMAS J. WOLFENDEN

The door was guarded by another man, who opened the door and the two other sentries pushed Tim through, shutting the door loudly behind him.

Tim stood for a moment, taking it all in. He was actually standing there, in the Oval Office. He'd never in a million years thought he'd be standing there, and in spite of his raging headache, was awed.

He saw a balding, fat man, tie hanging loosely around his corpulent neck, eyeglasses propped up on his head, seated behind a massive wooden desk.

That must be the president, Tim thought correctly. He sure wasn't missing any meals, unlike his people starving in the streets. Another man, who Tim hadn't seen when he first entered, stood. He was a tall man, dressing in a threadbare US Army officer's uniform that had seen better days. The silver general's stars on his epaulets were polished though, and Tim had to laugh a little at the comic sight of these two characters.

The fat man stood, and motioned Tim forward. "Sergeant Major Flannery, I presume? Just the man I wanted to talk to."

"Yeah, that be me," Tim said.

"You should stand at attention, Sergeant Major," the general spat. "This is the Commander in Chief."

"Now, now, General. He's my guest. Show him a little respect, won't you?" the president said amiably. "Come now, Mr. Flannery. Have a seat."

Tim walked forward a few steps until he was a few feet from the desk. "I think I'll just stand, if it's all the same to you."

"Suit yourself," the president said, and Tim thought again of the message from Jimenez the day before. Through his clouded thoughts, he thought again of the bizarre message from Jerry also, and of the name of a man he thought was long dead and gone. The pounding in his head was worse now, and he thought of its significance.

Dan Kruger. Thirty years ago, in a little hamlet in El Salvador. He could still smell the cordite, smell the death... see all the bodies stacked like cordwood. They called it 'False Flag'; Tim called it slaughter. Slaughter for no reason, that was, except for someone else's political gain. And why after all these years was this CIA operative from a time long past contacting him now? He certainly wasn't a friend of Tim's, and Kruger contacting him right at this time was more than a little bizarre.

That operation so many years ago, early in Tim's Army career, an operation so black, so covert, that in the old days Tim wasn't even permitted to think about it, let alone speak of it. It was supposed to have been fast, quiet, in and out, never to be mentioned by anyone. But how was he ever supposed to erase the memories that were seared into his head, into his soul?

And now, this man from the past had crept back into his thoughts at a time when he needed all his wits about him. It nagged at him, and he couldn't make sense of it.

What did it mean? Tim didn't know, so he withdrew that thought from his mind, knowing it was far too late for him anyway. He only hoped that Jerry would be able to finish it off. He knew that Jerry and his men were too late to save him, but maybe not too late to save everything else from a far greater catastrophe for the future: this obese man standing before him.

No words were spoken by anyone for a few moments, and everyone turned at the sound of the door opening again. A very attractive black woman entered, carrying a silver tray with a cut lead crystal tumbler filled with water.

She came right up to the president and with a smile, held out the tray to the fat man that suddenly reminded Tim of Boss Hogg from the old *Dukes of Hazzard* TV show of his youth.

"Aspirin for your headache, sir," she said sweetly.

"Thank you, Alicia," the fat man replied, taking the pills from the tray, along with the glass. As quickly as she came, the woman departed silently.

Headache, Tim thought. *Him too, eh?* It seemed to be going around this morning.

***

The man and the woman had been walking for weeks, their car finally giving up the ghost in North Carolina. The roads were increasingly bad the further south they went, most long ago overgrown with kudzu, making driving impossible anyway.

It was late in the morning, and they had stopped along the side of Georgia Highway 77 to rest in the cool, pleasant morning. They had crossed into Georgia from South Carolina earlier, and were now in what had once been Elbert County.

The man took a long drink of water from a canteen, then handed it to the woman. After taking a drink, she smiled at the man and said, "John, what's that?"

He turned to look where she was pointing, and saw a rock structure, obviously manmade, sitting just off the road on a hill. He shrugged. "I don't know. It's kind of odd, though, sitting out here in the middle of nowhere."

"Maybe it's some Civil War monument," she said.

"I don't think so; I don't recall any battle fought out this way."

"Let's go take a look," Barbra said, bounding off.

He had to smile at her enthusiasm. Since they'd escaped from the hell of Washington, DC a few weeks ago, the further south the pair had gotten the better they both felt.

Except for this morning, the headache that had been creeping up all morning reminded him with a vengeance. Even so, he reveled in her glee, and chased after her in the tall grass. He caught up with her near the big stone structure where she was looking at something in the ground. He came up behind her, putting his arms around her waist, nuzzling her neck.

"It says it's the Georgia Guidestones Center cluster, erected March 22, 1980," she read aloud.

He looked over her shoulder and saw the same, and engraved in the stone, just below that sentence, it read, *'Let these be guidestones to an Age of Reason.'*

"I remember hearing something about these when I was still in college. Some unknown group had them erected back in the 1980's as a guide for a future culture after an apocalypse," he told her.

They walked hand in hand over to the larger structure. It was three stones standing together, like a smaller Stonehenge. There were ten guidelines listed in several different languages. The circled the stones, and when they found the one that had the inscriptions in English, they began to read aloud.

"'Number one, maintain humanity under 500,000,000 in perpetual balance with nature.'"

Barbra read the second line: "'Guide reproduction wisely — improving fitness and diversity.'"

"'Unite humanity with a living new language,'" John read.

Starting to choke up, Barbra read, "'Rule passion — faith — tradition — and all things with tempered reason.'"

John felt overwhelmed. He pulled her close, continuing, "'Protect people and nations with fair laws and just courts.'"

"'Let all nations rule internally resolving external disputes in a world court,'" Barbra said through trembling lips.

"'Avoid petty laws and useless officials,'" John read, then chuckled.

"'Balance personal rights with social duties,'" Barbra read aloud.

"'Prize truth — beauty — love — seeking harmony with the infinite,'" John said, teary-eyed himself now.

Barbra read the final line: "'Be not a cancer on the Earth — Leave room for nature — Leave room for nature.' John, honey?"

"Yeah?" he said, holding her tightly.

"Do you think it'll ever happen?"

"I don't know, baby. I do know they could have saved some money carving this thing," he told her, running his hands through her hair.

"How?"

"All they had to do was engrave 'don't be dicks' on it. That should have been enough to get their message across."

Barbra giggled through her tears. "Well, mister CIA, let's not dick around, and get our asses to the Keys."

"Sure thing, honey," John said. He took her hand and they walked off together towards the highway, never looking back.

***

"So," said the president, looking at Tim. "You didn't come all this way empty-handed. You have the codes?"

"I believe the sergeant had them, sir," the general said. "I've sent someone to bring them up."

The fat man nodded, sat back down in the high-backed leather chair, and bore holes into Tim with cold, empty eyes. Tim returned the cold stare with one of his own. The headache he'd had all morning was pounding in his skull, making it difficult to think straight.

His mind went back, to the vision of the Hercules slamming into the mountain; of Jimenez coldly picking off each of the soldiers who were sent by this man; of the vision of Robyn lying, bleeding and battered in the back of the Hum-Vee; and he wanted to lunge out at this prig, wrap his fingers around his fat neck, and squeeze until the man's head popped.

As quickly as that thought arose, it faded. He thought again of that odd message earlier... *Dan Kruger from Korotonga sends his best wishes.'* Had he really survived too? What was Korotonga?

The sound of the door opening again drew his attention, and the attractive woman breezed in. She walked up silently to the president and handed over a battered and dog-eared spiral-bound notepad that was very familiar to Tim.

The president took the book from her hands and paged through the notepad. He frowned, paging paged deeper into the book, then with a disgusted sigh, tossed the book to the general.

"I can't make anything out in this."

The general opened the notebook and started to page through it, frowning as well. "I don't know what this is, Mr. President, but it's not the codes for the nukes."

"What?" the president shouted, standing up and circling the desk, almost tripping over himself in the process. He snatched the book from the general's hands, and looked through it again. Beads of sweat were forming on the man's forehead and his face was turning a deep shade of purple.

It looked to Tim that he was about to have a stroke, and he smiled in grim satisfaction.

"What the fuck is this?" the fat man shouted at Tim. "Where are my codes?"

"Oh, *those* codes," Tim said. "Those codes were vaporized when I nuked Volivoli."

"You— you nuked… you nuked *where?"* he sputtered, inching nearer to Tim menacingly.

"Uh, sir, we uh, w-we neglected to tell you," the general stuttered.

"Tell me what?" he asked in a shout, never taking his eyes off of Tim.

"The sergeant major ordered a nuclear strike on an atoll in the South Pacific, sometime last year."

"He *what?"* the fat man shrieked.

"We thought it was best that you didn't know, sir," the general said meekly.

"*We?* Who the fuck is *'we'?*, Not that bastard John from the CIA, was it?"

"It was all of us. We thought it would've been counterproductive."

"I'll tell you what is 'counterproductive, general," the fat man responded, his voice low and dangerous. "What's counterproductive is this man standing here in front of us, barring and blocking my absolute power!"

The president spun towards Tim, and in a flash that belied his bulk, lunged at him. He hit Tim with the full force of his weight, knocking them both to the carpeted floor.

"Where are my codes?!" he screamed, spittle flying from his mouth, fat sausage-like fingers trying to gain a grip around Tim's neck.

Tim, slightly winded by the attack, looked up into the screaming man's face and smiled. "They're on the corner of buy a map and go fuck yourself."

He then balled up his fist, and in a short rabbit punch, jabbed the president in the solar-plexus, knocking the big man off of him. The fat man let out an *'oof'*, but Tim, his reflexes faster, rolled on top of the floundering fat man and began punching him in the face.

"Help me! Shoot him, goddamn you!" the president squealed, and the general pulled out a Beretta M9 from under his tunic. He thumbed off the safety and aimed the pistol at the two figures rolling around at his feet.

Tim saw this out of the corner of his eyes, and spun away just as the general pulled the trigger. The sound of the pistol firing in the office was deafening, and the president gasped in pain, looking immediately at the neat round hole directly in the center of his chest, his pure white Brooks Brothers shirt turning crimson in an ever widening splotch of blood.

Tim looked up at the general, who was staring in shock at what he'd just done, and leapt at him, trying to wrestle the gun away in one final act of self-preservation. Tim seized the man's wrist and twisted, but the general backed away out of reflex, and in the process pointed the muzzle right at Tim's chest.

There was another deafening bang, and Tim felt a burning sensation in his chest, and as if someone had cut the strings controlling him, he dropped to the floor, the weight of a thousand freight trains sitting on his chest.

Gasping for breath, he lay there, bleeding, looking right into the dying eyes of the man who had up until a few minutes ago been president.

***

Jimenez sat on the ground near a pile of loose soil where Izzy was buried. He'd left Robyn fast asleep. Whatever fever she'd had had broken after her bizarre dream and message from Tim, and now he sat totally alone in the world. The sky was completely overcast, and the temperature was well below freezing, not unheard of in the higher elevations on Northern Arizona.

He thought about everything that had happened, and thought it ironic that the end of the world had brought him the most happiness, however fleeting. He remembered, also, what Tim had asked him to do, wishing he had the strength to actually do it. Robyn had told him that Tim had come to her in a dream and instructed him to do it, so now he'd have to man-up. He would do it, but he didn't have to like it.

"Taco," Tim had instructed. *"In the basement, there's a notebook and an IVIS tablet. If things turn to shit, I need you to take them and do this one last little thing for me..."*

Flipping open the IVIS tablet, Jimenez turned it on, waiting for it to boot up. He looked up at the sky, tears flowing again. He'd never cried so much in his life.

He wiped his eyes, sniffled a few times, and adjusted the satellite antenna he'd set up earlier. The program he'd opened synchronized with the geosynchronous orbiting satellite somewhere in low-Earth orbit high above him.

"I'm sorry, Robyn, I'm so sorry," he whispered, knowing full well that Tim was right now, at this very moment, in Washington, DC. Using one finger, he typed: "DESPERADO"

Tears filled his eyes completely, and he didn't see the single snowflake fall and land on the screen, only to melt away just as rapidly.

***

Johnson stood on the wing bridge shouting minor corrections out to the helmsman from time to time. They were now deep inside the Chesapeake Bay, following the wake of the British Destroyer that was leading the way.

A British officer stood next to him, face placid. The sub-lieutenant had come over to the *Jeremiah O'Brian* on a motor launch through turbulent seas after Johnson had ordered the ship to heave-to.

"You're telling me, that our apparent president sent out an envoy over a year ago, and instead of the envoy telling everyone how great this guy is, they told everybody he was crazy?" Johnson asked, looking sideways at the officer.

"That's about the long and the short of it, Captain. He told us that this man had gone crazy and things were fast going to ruin here. London decided to do something about it," the British officer said with a curt nod.

"I don't know how you knew about us," Johnson replied, still not a hundred percent certain he could trust this man, but he needed to, he knew. The destroyer had enough firepower to send the old Liberty Ship to the bottom of the bay in a few minutes if the lieutenant so wished.

"We didn't. It was blind luck on our part that we met up with you out here."

"Sergeant Williams is sure happy to see you guys," Johnson said.

"How's the head, Skipper?" Suplee asked, coming over and standing beside him.

"It's getting worse, actually," Johnson replied, rubbing his temples.

"Mine too," Suplee said. "Nice to have a little naval support," he added, meaning the leading warship.

"Yeah, funny, eh?" Johnson said. The two men could now see the Seven Mile Bridge directly ahead, and Annapolis to the west between the snow squalls passing from the west over the ever-narrowing Chesapeake Bay.

"I have a bad headache myself," the sub-lieutenant agreed.

"Seems to be going around this morning, Lieutenant," Johnson said.

"Do you think it's too late?" Suplee asked.

"Yeah," Johnson said, "I do."

Everything started to grow paler and paler all of a sudden, until in one bright flash, their whole world turned a brilliant white, erasing everything.

***

Tim lay on the carpet. He knew he was dying. He tried to raise his arms, but they were like dead weight, and nothing moved when he told it to. He lay on the carpet in the Oval Office, staring at the face of the dead man lying on the floor a few feet away, dead eyes staring back in mute accusation.

"Oh my God, what have I done?" he heard the general say from somewhere off a thousand miles away. Tim tried to turn his head, but all his energy was completely gone. He heard a few more sobs, then he heard the click of a hammer being cocked, followed by the general saying, "I'm so, so sorry..."

Another deafening bang came next, and then the sound of a body hitting the floor.

Tim's vision was narrowing, things paling considerably, though his hearing was still acute. He heard the door open, then a woman gasped in horror at the grisly sight before her. His sight continued to fail, washing out as if some unseen hand was brushing whitewash over his eyes. He could hear his last breaths, gurgling and strained. He coughed, and could taste the coppery taint of blood.

Everything was turning whiter and whiter until finally his vision went white; a white so brilliantly bright as if to outshine all the suns in all the galaxies in the entire universe...

His last conscious thought was of Robyn and Holly, and of little Walter. His heart ached, but soon, all too soon, those fleeting memories were pushed aside. The white light engulfed him, his pain too. Along with his memories, it was all washed away, like a sand castle in the rising tide.

EPILOGUE

Jerry Williams stood under the West Wing portico, hands in the pockets of his parka and back to the icy wind blowing across what was now an overgrown meadow in front of the White House. An M3 Bradley fighting Vehicle sat on the driveway, engine idling, its 30mm chain gun in the turret facing outward a few yards behind him.

Two of Jerry's men had several of the White House guards on their knees, hands on their heads outside of the French doors, holding their carbines at the ready for one sly move. To the right of them, three supine forms lay under a hastily laid tarp that threatened to blow off with the next good gust.

"So, is that the president and your sergeant major?" queried the British naval sub lieutenant who was standing next to Jerry in the shadow of the portico.

"Yeah. And an Army general. I don't know his name, but his wound is definitely self-inflicted."

"I'll take your word for it, Sergeant."

The sound of a Hum-Vee pulling up beside the Bradley made both men turn. A figure got out, pulled up the collar of a Navy pea coat, and hurried over to the two men.

"Jerry, I just got off the horn with Jimenez out in Arizona," the man said. "He's about to fall to pieces with regret."

"I'll bet. I'm just happy that Minuteman III he launched decided to malfunction so spectacularly. How far up in the atmosphere do you reckon it detonated?" Jerry asked.

"I don't have a clue, Jerry, but I'm thinking several thousand feet above what was programmed," Ensign Johnson shrugged. "But man, were we lucky it did."

"You ain't shitting, Bill."

"Jimenez is about to come unglued. I think the sooner you get on the radio with him and calm him down, the better off he'll be. He's totally alone out there for now. Well, he's got Tim's daughter with him, but apparently she's been badly hurt and is still not able to do much. Apparently, Tim told him to launch a missile if things went totally to shit, and he did. He had no idea we were out here, and he's devastated that he almost vaporized us," Johnson said.

"What do we do?" the sub lieutenant asked.

"I think Jerry is the one to ask," Johnson said. "I've just got a ship to run now."

"Me?"

"Yeah, you, Jerry. It's all in your hands now. I think it's what Tim would have wanted."

"I don't know about that, Bill, I—"

"Hey!" shouted one of the men guarding the prisoners. "One of these dead guys just moaned! I don't think they're all dead!"

THE END?

ABOUT THE AUTHOR

Thomas Wolfenden was born and raised in Philadelphia, Pennsylvania, and is an honorably discharged veteran of the US Army. He's worked in several different jobs throughout his life, spending fifteen years in law enforcement and the private security field. He's been an automotive detailer, ambulance driver, nuclear medicine delivery courier, dairy barn cleaner, and most recently he has worked as a ballast regulator operator, a switchman, conductor and a locomotive engineer on the railroad. He's travelled extensively through the United States and abroad, and lived in several states, Pennsylvania, Arizona, West Virginia, Kentucky, Idaho, and Florida being a few. He has written several Op-Ed pieces for various local newspapers, and up until recently kept a political humor blog. He's a Life/Endowment member of the National Rifle Association and a strong supporter of the 2nd Amendment. He now spends his time between the United States and Australia with his life partner, Catherine.

KING ARTHUR AND THE KNIGHTS OF THE ROUND TABLE HAVE BEEN REBORN TO SAVE THE WORLD FROM THE CLUTCHES OF MORGANA WHILE SHE PROPELS OUR MODERN WORLD INTO THE MIDDLE AGES.

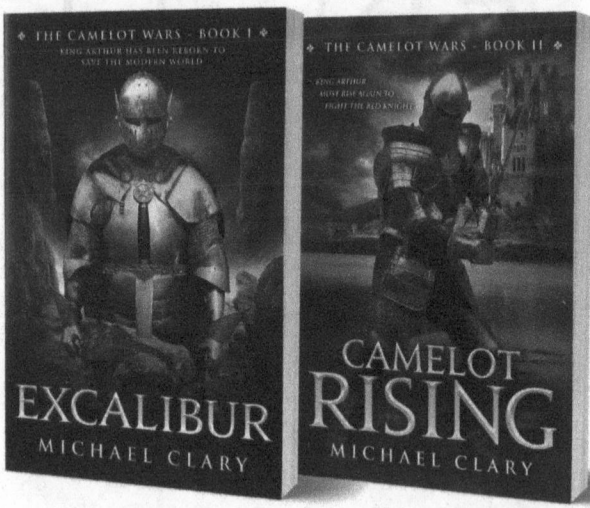

EAN 9781618685018 $15.99   EAN 9781682611562 $15.99

Morgana's first attack came in a red fog that wiped out all modern technology. The entire planet was pushed back into the middle ages. The world descended into chaos.

But hope is not yet lost— King Arthur, Merlin, and the Knights of the Round Table have been reborn.

THE ULTIMATE PREPPER'S ADVENTURE.
THE JOURNEY BEGINS HERE!

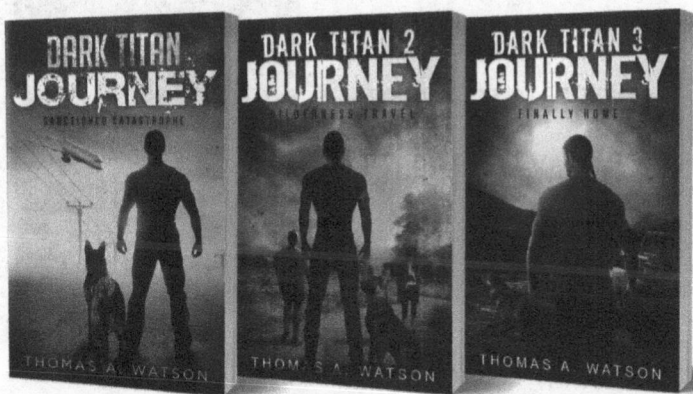

EAN 9781682611654 $9.99   EAN 9781618687371 $9.99   EAN 9781618687395 $9.99

The long-predicted Coronal Mass Ejection has finally hit the Earth, virtually destroying civilization. Nathan Owens has been prepping for a disaster like this for years, but now he's a thousand miles away from his family and his refuge. He'll have to employ all his hard-won survivalist skills to save his current community, before he begins his long journey through doomsday to get back home.

THE MORNINGSTAR STRAIN HAS BEEN LET LOOSE—IS THERE ANY WAY TO STOP IT?

An industrial accident unleashes some of the Morningstar Strain. The

EAN 9781618686497 $16.00

doctor who discovered the strain and her assistant will have to fight their way through Sprinters and Shamblers to save themselves, the vaccine, and the base. Then they discover that it wasn't an accident at all—somebody inside the facility did it on purpose. The war with the RSA and the infected is far from over.

This is the fourth book in Z.A. Recht's The Morningstar Strain series, written by Brad Munson.

PERMUTED
PRESS

WE CAN'T GUARANTEE THIS GUIDE WILL SAVE YOUR LIFE. BUT WE CAN GUARANTEE IT WILL KEEP YOU SMILING WHILE THE LIVING DEAD ARE CHOWING DOWN ON YOU.

EAN 9781618686695 $9.99

This is the only tool you need to survive the zombie apocalypse.

OK, that's not really true. But when the SHTF, you're going to want a survival guide that's not just geared toward day-to-day survival. You'll need one that addresses the essential skills for true nourishment of the human spirit. Living through the end of the world isn't worth a damn unless you can enjoy yourself in any way you want. (Except, of course, for anything having to do with abuse. We could never condone such things. At least the publisher's lawyers say we can't.)

PERMUTED
PRESS